Praise

"Karen Michalson's first fiction release since her Enemy Glory trilogy is a genre-blending narrative that combines rock n' roll and mythology with magic realism and crime fiction to create a highly palatable story with a distinctly unique flavor. . . . Readers who enjoyed Michalson's Enemy Glory trilogy will find this novel a much deeper, richer—and more intimate—story. Blurring the lines between reality and fantasy, the author delivers a strange and beautiful narrative tapestry woven with threads of music, myth, and magic. . . . Adventurous fantasy fans—particularly deep readers—will find this genre-hybridized novel addictive." – *BlueInk Review* (Starred Review)

"*The Maenad's God* is the latest book by Karen Michalson. The author tackles several heavy themes masterfully. It's a tale that will keep you on your toes, guessing what's real and imaginary and what to expect next. Michalson takes the reader in one direction when the expectation is the opposite, making it a thrilling read. The author artfully deals with Peter's evolving sexuality brilliantly and in a way that is both challenging and not too explicit. . . . I cannot praise *The Maenad's God* by Karen Michalson highly enough. It is a mind-bending masterpiece." – *Literary Titan* (5/5)

"Michalson's prose, as narrated by the loquacious Pete, is by turns wisecracking and obsessive. . . . Even so, Pete's quest takes him in unexpected occult directions, opening up an intricate world of ecstasy and paranoia. . . . the novel's angst and atmosphere—both authentically '90s—make for a strangely alluring reading experience. An engaging, snaking, and spirit-tinged murder tale about obsession and control." – *Kirkus Reviews*

"Mystical, lyrical, and inhabited by gods, *The Maenad's God* is a surprisingly supernatural love story. . . . The book's exponential eccentricity is captivating: it moves between mystery elements, those of magical realism, and a dark moodiness." – Aimee Jodoin, *Foreword Clarion Reviews*

"An engaging metafictional romp through an improbable New England." – Tucker Lieberman, *Independent Book Review*

Other Books by Karen Michalson

Nonfiction

Victorian Fantasy Literature: Literary Battles with Church and Empire

Novels

The *Enemy Glory* trilogy:
Enemy Glory
Hecate's Glory
The King's Glory

The Maenad's God

Karen Michalson

2/23/2023
Annmarie -
Congratulations on winning the Kirkus Giveaway.
Enjoy the read!
Karen Michalson

ARULA BOOKS

Worcester/Gondal/nowhere

THE MAENAD'S GOD

Edited by Donald Weise

ARULA BOOKS

First mass market edition: December 2022

The ISBN of this book is 978-0-9853522-6-4

Printed in the United States of America

For Bill

these things always are

The universe was not made by god or mortal. It always was, is, and will be a relentless fire. By measures it ignites itself and by measures it dies.

Heraclitus
On Nature

Stave One

Consider this a kind of prayer to the heartless void, for I am now in joyless communion with a dead god.

Peter C. Morrow, former Special Agent
Boston Field Office of the Federal Bureau of Investigation
Date: Eternity

Stave Two

Monday morning, August 17, 1992.

I, Special Agent Peter C. Morrow, am sitting with my feet on my dinted metal desk, leaning back luxuriously in my dangerously unstable swivel chair, and contemplating all the loveliness of my pale green cinder block office. I am sort of amusing myself by seeing how slowly I can breathe without passing out. It's a much more interesting exercise than filling out reports. It's also healthier than remaining completely conscious, as each precious breath of lousy air is delicately seasoned with asbestos dust. The dust has been spreading like so many cancer cells out of my office's cracked ceiling for the past six months. The union people will plaster up the crack sometime this year or next, but I must wait on their good graces to reduce my risk of dying of cancer before I die of this job. You see, when the dust began, I sealed up the crack with masking tape and immediately earned my whole department a write-up for union rules violation. So my boss made me take it down. Reason? Seems my humble effort to extend my life expectancy could cost some stooge who is incapable of honest work a job, and given the choice, the government considers my life of lesser worth than the stooge's, because the stooge's union boss's brother-in-law pays protection money to our esteemed senator.

And my boss, of course, who is terribly brave in the face of the attempted murder of one of his agents, but is also desperately seeking promotion to some cushy, well-paid do-nothing post in Washington, finds it greatly in his interest to have the same list of priorities as the government. So I had to listen to him fume about how I should know better than to tangle with the union and get us all in trouble and how it doesn't look good if government employees can't all respect each other and work together on friendly terms in the present anti-government climate.

Which is all very well for him to say, as government-ordained incompetence isn't killing him.

Item. I am to fearlessly risk my life to pursue and capture fellow government workers who go berserk and shoot other government workers, but I am to fear the power of the almighty union to level rules violation fees under threat of things "not looking good" should anybody ever care to investigate who fixed my lousy cracked ceiling.

I plastered it myself a few days ago and so earned another write-up. And a day of annoyance while the union people, who can't be bothered to fix the damn thing but have all the time in the world to notice if somebody else does, took four hours to chip away the plaster before cheerfully announcing that they'd be back "sometime" to fix it. And they left all my impeccably typed reports coated in white cocaine-like powder, which I turned in anyway, to my boss's dismay, as they were reports on a recent drug bust and his name was on top. And despite my warranted outrage at the union's intrusion, my boss went nutso at me, waving his hands around and shouting for all the building to hear that I had no business telling the union Gestapo officer who wrote me up that a) he *was* a Gestapo officer and b) I'd send him a box of inflamed lung if the union didn't fix the damage and c) dropping a Nazi armband in his lunch box that some Klan guy I arrested for arson once flipped at me.

And then when I whipped out my pocket-sized government-issued copy of the US Constitution that I have dutifully sworn to uphold and protect and pleaded first amendment rights he ordered *me* to calm down and stop being so goddamned intellectual about everything.

Which is why I am making a half-hearted show of mindlessly staring at the walls. My door is wide open, and I want the boss to wander by and ask me what I am doing so I can act stupid and ask him to order me to start being intellectual again. I have a nasty habit of making absurd points and throwing them over other people's heads.

But then again, I am an English major. Or was, at one point in ancient history before I decided I needed a job and the FBI took up my offer for their own mysterious reasons. Never figured that one out. Thirteen years ago I got drunk and screwed around with an application someone handed me at my college's pathetic job fair just to see how far it would go. Wrote this horribly funny, horribly juvenile parodic essay that I whimsically entitled in big, black, boldface letters, "Why I Want to be a COP." And I really got into the whole writing experience, describing in detail how I creamed my jeans for the flag when I was eight years old and didn't know what it meant except that it felt good until my father, a WW II veteran who killed and ate forty-three Germans while starving on a besieged mountaintop in Austria with nothing but a Boy Scout buck knife and a rubber band to his name because the Italians had already killed him (twice) for breaking out of a POW camp in Vietnam with his bare hands explained it all to me on a hunting trip in the Adirondacks, where we killed deer and good fine trout like Hemingway and I decided we ought to put everyone in jail and clean up America now for God and gumbo before the blue laws got rescinded by socialist liberals and the family falls apart and we all turn into communist drug addicts—

And they fuckin' hired me.

Interviewer said it was the best essay he'd ever read. I was, of course, intrigued. But since my *summa cum laude* in English had earned me a good job pumping gas for my uncle's convenience store in Pittsfield, I felt I needed a few seconds to consider the consequences of this career change. The interviewer said he "understood" and praised my family loyalty.

Me, I try not to understand anything. Makes my job easier.

Take my office decor. Please. I survey the idiotic government anti-drug posters which lend such *éclat* to my homey little workplace. Black and red geometric lines that probably took some government graphics wizard three months and a ruler to think up, with god-awful yellow lettering unctuously announcing to any drug lords who happen to wander into a fed's office looking for the answer to life's problems that "Drugs are for dopes and dopes are for drugs." Hmmm. Certainly makes me think about life, love, and the universe to see that piece of cleverness staring me in the face every morning as I guzzle my thermos of extra-caffeinated Jolt. And they made me take down a color print of Botticelli's *La Primavera* as "inappropriate to our work environment" because some dullard might complain about being able to see through the Three Graces' robes.

But I woke up too late this morning to make myself any drugs—I mean coffee. So even though I am trying to look as if an interesting thought never battered against my solidly closed mind, I am really taking my sweet time deciding whether or not to go down the hall for some joe. It is not a trivial decision. I have not eaten since last night. If I get myself some brew, I will feel less miserable physically, and if I feel less miserable physically, I will be less likely to tell my boss to go to hell when he walks past my door, and if I do not tell my boss to go to hell, I will be less likely to get another reprimand for insubordination. Three of those in one month and they make you take a vacation. Which isn't a bad deal, as you still get paid and everything, but I wanted to save it up until Columbus Day so I could use the time to go camping and horseback riding in the New Mexico desert during the off-season. Right now it is late August, which means the sun owns the desert and so New Mexico camping is right out. Figure I might as well be working.

However, as to decisions. My boss usually leaves his door open so as to feel important and play guard with the coffee machine to make sure we all leave a quarter so the secretary doesn't get shortchanged, even if we do all get hit up for a coffee fee every month. And lately old Fearless has been saving up all the inane cases for yours truly. You see, because of my extensive formal training in "critical thinking" and all that, I usually get the nut cases. My first boss once reasoned, fairly accurately, that since I was capable of thinking logically and poetically at the same time, I was probably gifted with the ability to understand the kind of screwball violent behavior that my less "humanistically inclined" colleagues found incomprehensible. And since I've had a lot of success on those cases, they're usually mine to keep. That, and the Mob (talk about government that works), because I once took another agent's place investigating an illegal interstate trucking operation when some secret committee of government accountants decided that the IRS was short on cash. Mob work can be a lot of fun, as you get to meet and drink espresso with more unbelievable characters than you get in a typical day in Congress, but it isn't steady, as it tends to depend on who is paying off which important office holder that month. It's really the lone crazies who pay the rent.

But for a while last spring, for reasons of his own, Fearless was saddling me with a lot of missing persons cases, which weren't too bad except when I began to sympathize with the missing person rather than with the missing person's "concerned" relatives and started doing what I could to slow things down. You talk to some of the parents of missing children and you understand instantly why the kid ran away. Had one guy whose teenage daughter refused to cut her hair. So he cut it for her, and cut up her face as well. Her delightful mother righteously buried herself in a television program "to avoid a fight" while her husband made a hole through the kid's left cheek with a paper punch. But that one, thanks to my quiet non-effort, managed to escape.

But then there was Melanie Ann Miller, whom you might have heard of. I still have a newspaper picture of Al Kanesh, another agent here at the field office, proudly returning the frightened girl to her parents weeks after I discovered her whereabouts and decently chose to play dumb about it. What the paper didn't say was that the poor girl was a few days shy of her eighteenth birthday, was supporting herself waitressing under the table up in Nashua, and ran away in the first place because her stepfather liked to raise welts across her back with a horsewhip. And in five more days the kid would have been eighteen and free and clear of torture, so it was no skin off my ass to keep my mouth shut about her whereabouts. And she was a sweet kid who brought me free sandwiches because I was the only person she'd ever known who asked if she needed anything, and so she decided I was "nice." She liked to make top of the line sandwiches special with all the works, her own creations, for "nice people" she liked. "Nice people" seemed to mean me and an elderly man who got to feel important when he gave her twenty-dollar tips. The restaurant was run by an older couple who had recently immigrated from Greece and didn't know any better than to be happy with a good employee's good work and so they never checked her working papers. And they all seemed to get along, as far as I could tell. Mellie lived with them upstairs and there were no horsewhips and no problems and she made terrific sandwiches and was learning Greek and quickly growing into a terrific smile.

But Kanesh got into my "extra-secure" computer file "by accident" with the boss's help and figured out where Mellie was. Which put me in the position of having to hand the poor girl back to her wonderful family because the goddamn Department of Social Services types have some bizarre article of faith that says if you're unlucky enough to have a psychopath for a father you're better off getting abused by him than taking your chances elsewhere where you could end up in a gang or a cult or even worse, quietly supporting yourself like an honest citizen.

How else can I explain what happened to Mellie? I know I did my moral duty. That is, I passively refused to "get her" by dicking around for a day, so Kanesh drove up and got her and brought her home like a big hero and got his face all over the papers.

And I got a tearful hysterical phone call from Mellie the next day, but there wasn't a hell of a lot I could do to defend the citizenry against aggression at that point because it was now the DSS's sole affair. And guess what? At the big family reunion dear old dad took out his Marlin .22, killed his wife, poor little Mellie who made sandwiches for nice people, and killed himself. One of his sons found his brains in the salad bowl. It was Father's Day. Nice touch, huh? He was upset at the dog for interrupting a Red Sox game.

But pledge my heart and hope to die, DSS "couldn't have known" this would happen because the goddamn handbook says differently, and they can't be expected to predict things like that, "human nature being what it is," even though I told them the first time I met the guy that he was about as normal as a Tufts School of Social Work graduate. My boss said he wouldn't have put it quite that way, and I told him I was only doing my best to frame things in a way the DSS might be able to relate to, comradeship between us government types being good PR and all.

Anyway, when one of the whiny, supercilious social workers who helped Kanesh return the girl home politely suggested, with all the righteous sensitivity of his psycho-babbling breed, that Mellie's death was my fault because, as a federal agent, I set an example of violence to society by carrying a gun, I decided to set him a personal example of violence by popping him one on the jaw. Which earned me a six-week paid vacation in the Rockies.

Under other circumstances, there would have been an extended investigation leading to a quiet transfer or dismissal, but the *Boston Herald* and the radio talk shows made a *cause célèbre* out of the case, cashing in on the anti-government, anti-DSS feeling so healthfully rampant right now, and put the governor and the social service people through the media-wringer, so I became something of a popular hero in my absence.

But when I returned from my summer camping trip two weeks ago, Fearless took me off missing persons because the controversy was still sort of raging in the circles he cared about and gave me report and clean-up work to do. Report work means ghost writing for colleagues who can't put a coherent sentence together and pretending that I'm not really embarrassing anyone with my knowledge of English. Clean-up work sometimes means knocking on strangers' doors and telling them in my professionally concerned voice that someone found their favorite child's decomposed body in an industrial waste site and would they like to come have a look so I can finish my flawlessly written, asbestos-sugared report? And I haven't taken to these assignments too well, not because I find it sad to sit across a kitchen table from a grieving family that insists on showing me photographs of a smiling kid in a cheerleader uniform, but because once I hit my thirties, things like that suddenly ceased to be sad. Maybe thirteen years ago I believed the line that everyone is special and worthwhile and precious and all that, but that's because I didn't really know anyone then. Now I know everyone and the line doesn't wash.

Let me explain. Sometime in my late twenties, and certainly by my early thirties, I dimly and reluctantly started to realize that there's nothing charming to do in life. There are six billion people on the planet. Except for cultural and language differences, which aren't all that great after the first five minutes of contact, "human nature being what it is," about 5.999 billion of them are fairly interchangeable. Everyone says the same things on the same occasions and struggles like hell to make sure those same occasions become a daily event. Everyone slogs out of bed in the morning. Everyone then has a rousing family fight. Everyone sacrifices the better part of every day to some useless, senseless job. Everyone sacrifices the better part of every evening to that same job, fights again with the family to kill an hour, or mumbles through practical non-conversations about bills and groceries. Some people stare through a few idiotic TV commercials to break things up, and then come morning it all starts again. Life is such fun. And the fun keeps going for decades, *for decades*, one miserable water-torture day at a time, right down into generations of perfectly matched graves.

Wait, I forgot. There's more. Some people look forward to going out to dinner on a Friday night when they might get to eat a few dead shrimp on a stick and I suppose that bit of trivia gets them through the endless weeks. Some look forward to "doing something someday," but as the years roll by "someday" never comes, or when it does come their bodies are too old to get up and meet it, and whatever remains of their hearts is too derelict to care.

Really, why live? I'm not asking an idle question.

While I was camping in the mountains, I looked into the stars and gave them names and thought about the distances I was seeing into and knew that for every Mellie who gets shot there are millions who don't. The best, most original part of her life was sneaking sandwiches to people she liked—that part was *really* her, if you know what I mean, even if it did take living around the law to bring it out. But time would remove that specialness too. No one likes to say it, but people get redundant.

And if she had lived to die at twenty-five or eighty-three, how many people out of a world population of six billion would even notice? I know I wouldn't. In a month or two I probably wouldn't even have noticed her on the street, and I'm a "nice person," someone she really believed gave a damn.

And if my boss died, would *anyone* care? Sure, there'd be an office collection for flowers for the widow because that's the way things are done and no one wants to look callous. We'd all chip in an honest dollar and move on. And there'd be another jackass bucking for promotion to Washington to take his place. And another jackass to take his place *ad infinitum*.

Anyway, the last time I went for coffee, my easily replaceable boss decided to get me killed. And I've reached a point where I'm not all that angry about it. This was just before all the sordid business with Mellie last June. Put me on that god-awful nut case. The suspect, who wasn't even a real nut as far as real nuts go, was just a pathetic old man who had lost his candy business to the recession and decided to spend his golden years writing badly spelled death threats to everyone in Congress. I sort of felt sorry for the guy, because really he had lost everything he'd spent his life working for, but I nevertheless did my duty and busted him. The reason I nearly got killed is because my partner for that nothing case, Sidney Crensch, wrote the book and the movie on incompetence. His father is a congressman, which probably helped some with the research. And that is all anybody seems to know about Crensch's background, except that he's crazy. First time we got introduced, he broke the ice by bragging about carrying an Uzi into a MacDonald's back in his Idaho hometown to "get a reaction from the locals."

"Did it work?"

"I'm here, aren't I?"

Wonderful. Then he popped old Fearless's belt buckle by boasting that his congressman father had been an OSS man but that nobody is supposed to know this. He himself had undergone six or seven or thirteen or seventy-six (the number kept changing) secret initiations into the "Brotherhood," a self-styled secret-secret group of aging CIA special operations people whose only link with real intelligence gathering appeared to be a shared delusion of being James Bond. He had also been trained by Mossad and MI5 and the French Service of External Documentation and Counterespionage and by the Boy Scouts and Captain Marvel's Militia and the SPCA and who knows what else. Told old Fearless he had an uncle in the KGB.

"That's almost as impressive as having a father in Congress," I ventured to remark, in the interest of friendly collegiality. Fearless sent me off to copy a report.

Asked Crensch once, with all of his grand I-Spy-on-Your-Grandmother's Dirty-Underpants credentials, what he was doing in the FBI. I mean, wasn't interviewing serial killers and nut case parents of runaway kids kind of tame stuff for a guy like him?

"Domestic surveillance," he winked. "But I'm working incognito, so don't tell anybody who I really am." He waited for me to say something.

I kept him waiting until Fearless came into earshot. "All right, who are you?" I asked in my urgent "I understand your reluctance to speak, but I can help you with your problem" whisper that I usually reserve for reluctant stool pigeons who have seen too many cop movies.

"I am," he looked around, "the FBI." He actually said this seriously, so I nodded with exaggerated solemnity. Then he laughed. "Get it? It's a joke." Then he looked fierce. "The FBI is a fuckin' joke." He raised his hand palm outwards. "No offense." Then my boss laughed, because after all he wants a promotion, and Crensch's father could be a help, and Crensch laughed again, and I sent myself back to my reports. Who knows? Crensch probably thought he really was doing surveillance, although as near as I could figure Fearless was just giving him nickels and sending him out to sip *café au lait* at the French consulate to keep him out of everyone's hair.

Anyway, the truth was that Crensch was ours because he liked to play cop as much as anyone else in the field office and Dad liked to keep him a continent away from his Idaho constituency and Fearless needed to suck up to Dad. And on the Candy Man case he was mine, Uzi and all.

It was in the middle of Roxbury, with the suspect sitting quietly in the back seat, and the car lawfully stopped at a red light, that Crensch decided to confide his "secret plan" of the day. "Gonna give the Boston cops a treat," he whispered for no comprehensible reason. "Watch and learn." He rolled his window part way down and waved his weapon around to "get a reaction" from the drug dealers on the corner. "Hey—hey you," he called to a knot of young men who didn't look like they valued their lives any more than I did, "take a toke on this," and he opened fire on a second-story window of an abandoned building, sending glass flying into the street, the gang flying into some poor bastard's place of business, and a brick flying through our car's back window and smacking poor Candy Man in the back of the head. I immediately pushed the gas pedal against the floor, lurched the car into the intersection, and gave the Boston cops a real treat by getting us hit sideways by a squad car. Crensch laughed his ass off like it was the best joke he'd ever heard in his life and immediately got reassigned to the consulate and bragging about his prowess as a G-man. I got the paperwork. And Candy Man got a lesson in government at work.

Decisions. The coffee machine was on the other side of my boss's always open door. So, when my story begins, I was in the absurd position of deciding whether my life was potentially worth a cup of bad coffee. I glanced at the fortress of reports I still had to fill out and decided that it was.

Item. Most of the time you might as well be dead. It's only going to get worse.

"Hey, Morrow," yelled Fearless from down the hall. I did not answer. "Hey, Morrow, get in here." I did not move from my comfortable chair, but I squeaked it to let him know I was deliberately forcing him to come to me. He took the bait and heaved himself into my doorway. I looked up at him with my wide-eyed "dumb southern boy" expression that I picked up hiking with a mountain man in Alabama a few years ago who reminded me of Walt Whitman. He looked at all the reports he had assigned me to do. "You busy?" His tone was unusual, the sort of thing meant to pass for polite solicitation.

"No." I said this with a straight face.

He nodded and choked on the asbestos. "Come into my office, then. Need your expertise on this one."

On the way to his office, I ostentatiously filled my dirty mug with coffee but I did not leave a quarter. Ordinarily I would, but by "stealing" the same coffee that my fee has already allegedly paid for, I was making one of my famous statements. Fearless hesitated, dug into his pocket, and tossed in a quarter for me. Since he was treating, I knew that something I really ought to say no to was up.

"Come in." He closed the door part way. I settled into a brown plastic padded chair and made "serious" eye contact with him across the desk. "Gotta case for you, but I'd prefer it if you didn't hot dog it on this one too much. Keep it cool, stay low, no problems, no publicity." He was gently alluding to the social worker I'd decked, not the police car fiasco Crensch brought on, which pretty much got hushed up to everyone's satisfaction except mine. "For now you're on it alone. Think it's mob related."

"Good. I like dealing with the Mob. That's where I cultivated my remarkable sense of style."

He ignored my brilliant touch of humor. "Know anything about Ithaca?"

"Only Homer's."

"Whose?"

Really my boss was so remarkably informed. "Homer. Eighth century B.C. Name refers to one or a group of poets who created the *Iliad* and the *Odyssey*. Ithaca is where faithful Penelope waits for Odysseus, her adventurer husband, to return home after twenty years of wandering through an interesting life of murder and mayhem—"

"Yeah, right. Cut the smart crap. Not Ithaca. I meant Rome."

"Rome. No, never heard of it," I drawled, slightly comforted by the fact that Fearless could, after all, with some effort, read. Although I could see where he might confuse Ithaca for Rome, the names being so similar and everything. "So. Is Rome like a town?"

"Now, listen. Rome, New York. There's an army base nearby, and there's a young private, one Claude F. Hopner, showing more money than he ought, probably dealing, so the commander wants us there to put on a show."

"Why not send in the guys from Albany or New York?"

"New York's usually busy for crime."

"Really?"

"Hey, ask a stupid question, Morrow." I had to admit, it was a stupid question. New York never had anyone to spare. "And you've got more mob experience than anyone in Albany."

"Right. All of my work experience is mob related." Fearless looked blank so I chose not to pursue the analogy.

"Anyway," he glanced fiercely at the woman at the coffee machine until the reassuring plop of a quarter freed him for less important matters, "there's reason to believe that Hopner's supplier is a member of a new Utica branch of the Nunzio family, and you dealt effectively with some of those guys here in town a few years back. So I'm suggesting you leave your name around. They'll remember you. If it's known that you personally are making the trip to ask questions, it might send a message up the line to the right people to lay off the base, which is all the commander cares about to keep his general happy, and all we need to do to keep the commander happy. Short and easy assignment."

"Why do we need to keep the commander happy? Is his brother running for office?"

Fearless looked sheepish. "His cousin—look he's an important fundraiser, a lot of people owe him favors, could pass a favor along—"

"Never mind. For the commander's honorable cousin, I shall forgo the considerable pleasures of my current assignment and reluctantly take a day trip to Rome."

"You mean you'll go?"

"Do I get a dinner allowance?"

"You get to eat in the officers' club. Six-hour drive." He glanced at his watch. "Ten now. You could get there by five o'clock. Stay the night on the base." It was a dismissal so I didn't move. "Well?"

"How do you know it's the Nunzio family?"

"They're one of the few old families that's not squeamish about drug dealing. And they have a history of "taking in" their more troubled brethren without the typical gangland stuff, which usually makes the papers and gets everybody upset. The Utica Mob is suffering from the recession like anyone else. They've historically confined their activities to skimming off the arcade business and extorting protection money from local establishments. But they're beginning to understand that you can't extort what isn't there, and there's always money in drugs, and the Nunzio people are going shares in the drug business in exchange—uh, look Morrow, you've got to go and none of this is that relevant to what you need to do."

"In exchange for?" I followed up. "I was an English major, boss. I love irrelevancies."

He shuffled in his chair. "The Nunzios aren't a bad family, as far as mob families go. Run a lot of legitimate stuff—construction, fish markets, entertainment, wholesale food industry, liquor distribution, sanitation services—"

"Unions."

He ignored the remark. "Hey, some of the older guys even donate bucks to the Church. And the Church slides a portion over to some of our friends on Beacon Hill who campaign for some of our friends in Washington—"

I remained mildly stone-faced. "Hmmm. Really? I never would have guessed. How utterly fascinating—"

"All right, Morrow, cut the sarcasm. I ain't sayin' it's right—but it *is*, it happens and since it isn't illegal for people to make campaign donations there's nothing we can do about it. Look here's the dope—"

"Here's the what, sir?"

He sighed. "It's just an expression. The Nunzios are cleaning up Utica. Street gangs are getting less visible, fewer drug arrests are making the paper, the citizens are thinking the drugs are disappearing and families are taking their children out for Sunday afternoon walks. And since a good strong mafia presence tends to dampen random drug violence"—I laughed appreciatively and he laughed like my laughter suddenly made him comfortable—"well, it's true. The point is, the mayor is happy, because he gets points with the President's Council for declaring Utica a 'drug-free zone,' and some impressive endorsements for his upcoming run for Congress—"

"Gotcha. But if we really interfere with the mafioso drug trade, and the gangs take over and the city goes nasty just before elections, the mayor gets to blame you, and there's no telling where his career might take him—"

"Look, just warn them off the goddamn base and come back, got it?"

"Yes, sir. Uh, sir?" I said in my best fresh-out-of-training green recruit's voice.

"What is it?"

"Sir, do you think, that since my mere presence in a strategically important place like Rome, New York is enough to scare the Mob off one of our crucial defense bases, that if I were to say, suddenly leap out of the broom closet and make faces at a union brother, that I could scare him and his cohorts into fixing my ceiling?"

"You know something, Morrow, you're a damn good fed but you've got one hell of a prize attitude."

"I know." I started to leave, paused in the doorway, and turned around looking terribly confused. "So how do *you* pass the time on a slow day?" Then I tossed him a quarter and flashed him a smile. And to his credit and to my surprise, he actually chuckled a little as he caught it.

Stave Three

Monday evening, August 17, 1992.

I brought my attitude with me all the way to Rome.

The fact that it took me six hours to get there and two hours to find the base didn't improve my demeanor much. Turns out there's an air force base in Rome, and I wasted all kinds of time there first because my map was wrong. The army base was one of those pseudo-secret affairs that guys like Crensch get off on. Meaning it wasn't really a full-fledged base for a full-fledged army unit but a series of rusty barracks with open access and some training fields and a desultory looking guest house for whatever commander happened to be killing time there. I couldn't really figure the place out. It wasn't functional, it wasn't abandoned, it wasn't anything that clear. I later learned it was being "phased out." The army had been "phasing it out" for about ten years.

I bumped out of the woods and saw a field in need of mowing with a few sad-looking metal targets reflecting the setting sun. I drove past a rusty guard booth with nobody in it, brought the car to a grateful stop in a circular gravelly area, and unrolled the window to freshen the stale day-old breath of the car's air conditioner. The wind ruffled a marigold patch near one of the barracks; the flurry of color contrasted with what felt like a temporary lull in whatever it was that happened here.

Then I noticed a couple of aggressively attenuated recruits with marginal expressions of dutiful interest gathering up painting supplies near a line of freshly whitewashed fence. The smell of paint was attracting bursts of mosquitoes, so I hesitated leaving the car in my short-sleeved summer-issue fed shirt and I reluctantly rolled the window back up. No one questioned or greeted me. No one seemed terribly excited by my presence so I took out my clipboard and scribbled down some meaningless impressions and tried to waste time by looking official until the base commander, Colonel Rinkowski, might come out and meet me. But after fifteen minutes of "creating a presence," during which I might as well have been back in Boston for all the attention I drew, I began to understand that I'd never get back to Massachusetts if I didn't make myself known to somebody.

So I was about to open my car door, exit, and slam it closed with an air of efficiency and confidence in case the colonel was watching, when a young lieutenant approached, saluted for some unknown reason, and introduced the base commander to me through the window I was quickly rolling down again to catch his words. Apparently there was some protocol thing going on so I saluted back, which seemed to please Rinkowski. Then the lieutenant nodded and took off into a large building beyond the barracks.

I got out of the car and Rinkowski immediately dispensed with all niceties of greeting, brusquely explaining to me as I extended my free hand that the "base" was originally an army wilderness camp and was still being used for certain wilderness exercises, like survival camping. I don't think he knew this for a fact. He sounded like he was defensively spewing bullet items from a cheat sheet he hadn't bothered to read, and that his stimulating explanation was supposed to account for any deficiencies or irregularities I might notice.

"I do survival camping for fun," I offered in my friendly, "feds are human too" voice, which sometimes eases conversation by fooling people into thinking that guys like me do anything for fun. My collegial attempt to establish common ground immediately set him off.

"Not so necessary anymore in the new army," he barked, lest I get the uppity idea that a mere federal agent like myself could perform highly challenging military exercises like freezing my ass off in a snow fort for my own amusement. "Closing the place down. Moving most of it to White Plains." He was yelling at me in an impersonal way that suggested yelling had become his only means of expression. Which I suppose I can respect.

"Well, I suppose New York's a good place for wilderness training," I joked. "You could turn your unit loose in the subway for extra points."

He stiffly smiled and his face cracked. Literally cracked. I know there's an old joke about that, but when Commander Rinkowski smiled, his face filled with funny wrinkles like it didn't really want to smile but since it was smiling, the skin had to do something about it. "Yeah, time to retire," he said incomprehensibly. I've never known a military type yet who could follow the thread of a conversation for more than ten seconds.

I tried to get down to business. "So what should I know about Private Claude F. Hopner?"

"Hopner?" I couldn't tell whether he was surprised that I knew the name, or trying to pretend that he didn't know it all that well. He stepped back and stared at the whitewashed fence as if he was personally affronted by the change in scenery. I hate these assignments. Officers are never sure what they're "allowed" to know so they all have to act like they don't know anything and by the time they get to be fifty or so the act usually catches up with them. And to reassure the colonel that it was "OK" to talk to me, I had to explain to him while he waved away mosquitoes why he called my boss in the first place.

"Ah, yes. Right. I think Hopner's AWOL by now. No one can find him."

Eight freakin' hours in the car for this. "You're sure he's gone?" I asked with mild enthusiasm.

"You want to come into the club and ask around?" he spurted harshly, as though the idea of my "asking around" had just struck him as potentially brilliant and useful, but being an idea, he had to get rid of it before it grew into a way of life and became a liability for promotion.

"Why? If he's gone your problem's gone," I said reasonably.

"Yeah, I guess so." Rinkowski spoke through tight lips, like he might be giving away an important feature of the national defense. Then, in one of those incomprehensible shifts of awareness military officers tend to displace meaningful conversation for, he offered defensively, "It's a decent club."

There was a certain childish bid for approval in his tone, an expansively needy sharpness that seems to be native to old military officers who have spent the last thirty to forty years living to please a superior. My first question had inadvertently suggested disbelief and so Rinkowski wanted me to come see for myself that all was right with his world and to absolve him of any alleged transgressions against military order. Some officers get so addicted to affirmation and approval that they make comically desperate bids for it whenever their psyches need a fix, and always when you have much better things to do than become a substitute den mother. Rinkowski sounded like he suddenly needed to "prove" to me Hopner really wasn't there anymore, so I could in turn "approve" of him and his newly "cleaned" base and maybe say nice things about him in my soon to be irrelevant report. Not that old-style military officers of his type generally read reports, that's what most of them use their secretaries for, but they all have an instinctive fear of being mentioned unfavorably in them.

"Could you point out any of Hopner's acquaintances to me?" It was the least I could ask in the line of duty because it was always possible that in Hopner's absence someone else might be dealing.

But the colonel was finished with Hopner. Either Hopner's friends belonged to some new realm of proprietary information he wasn't sure he was supposed to know about, or else he simply didn't hear me because the fence had once again attracted his interest. "It's a good club," he repeated with painfully subdued severity.

The way he said this told me Rinkowski really needed me to step in and admire his club. But there was also a subtle defensiveness to Rinkowski's voice and demeanor suggesting that the club would more than compensate for the semi-indigent feel of the rest of the place, that he himself was used to commanding better things, and that my "asking around" wasn't so much a priority as an excuse for seeing the best he had to offer. He wanted a good write-up. So I made a show of seriously considering his five-star invitation, but the only thing I was really considering was how to get through this assignment in the fastest way possible and get home. Damned decent of Hopner to take off like that and leave me an opening for retreat. Damned inconsiderate of the colonel not to do likewise.

Then I remembered I had best make a show of doing something, so I would have something to write a report about tomorrow. "I suppose I could use something to eat. I guess I could just go in and leave my calling card around and skedaddle." I wasn't too keen on spending the night here. And since I live considerably west of Boston, in a cozy wooded area south of Worcester, I figured I might make it home by midnight if I left right away and wasn't too religious about keeping to the speed limits.

Suddenly, he was the jovial, show-offy host. My polite interest had put him at ease. "Good. Let's go. Chicken stew tonight."

Unbelievably, there actually was a club in this place, occupying the same large building that the lieutenant had entered, but it resembled more of a fancy cafeteria-style mess hall than a proper officers' hang-out. And it wasn't limited to officers, because once we settled into a corner, I noticed very few officer uniforms among a fair number of enlisted men and women. Rinkowski saw me looking around. "Everyone eats here," my host explained as if he was defending something he didn't like to defend. "Part of phase-out." But a second glance told me there were differently marked sections for officers and the "other ranks." Our table was bigger than the others and occupied its own corner section. A little plastic sign spelled out "Base Commander" lest anyone doubt who was supposed to sit here.

As soon as I sat down, I tried to get some fill for my report by brandishing my clipboard and bringing up Hopner one last time via that standard annoying question, "Why don't you tell me the whole story you told my boss?"

But Rinkowski wasn't in a chatty mood. He had gotten me into his hang-out and that was that. The commander immediately stood up and glanced at his watch. "I'm sorry. I've got some things to do." He said this gruffly, although he probably was sorry. He didn't seem like the sort who was keen to do too much besides play uniformed figurehead until retirement. He motioned to a couple of middle-aged women in white uniforms and hair nets working behind a long food counter. "You can go up and give them your order." He said this helpfully and eagerly, as if his base sported the only cafeteria in the world and I, wretched civilian that I was, might not know what to do or how to behave in such an excruciatingly demanding social situation and so might be grateful for his guidance.

What the hell, I only had a light lunch at one of those miserable thruway stops, and I was getting hungry, so I played along. "Really?" I asked like I was quietly in awe.

"Oh, yeah," he said enthusiastically, apparently pleased by my tone. "I'll go up with you and they'll know you can have as much as you want. It's good stew." The line began near the door so Rinkowski followed me on his way out. "Give them your choice," he prompted.

"Uh, chicken stew," I said brightly as one of the women ladled some thick yellow-gray slop on a finely cracked thick white plate and tossed in a couple pieces of toast and wilted broccoli.

"Good choice," he complimented me. "Remember, you can have seconds if you want." He nodded formally at the women and left.

"Who's he?" one of the women asked the other.

"New commander, been here two weeks," said the first, smiling at me to move it along with my slop. "Probably be gone soon, when the exercises end." I was heading towards the cashier. "Oh, you're with the commander. You don't have to pay," she called out.

"Thanks." I brought my tray back to the corner table and thought about what to do next. I supposed it would be rather unprofessional of me to simply stand up and announce my name and business to my fellow diners, although under the circumstances it was the most efficient way I could think of to get this increasingly pointless job done. Or I could make the rounds table by table and throw my business cards around and ask all and sundry to share their thoughts on Hopner, which might send the required message if he had cohorts here or he decided to come back and heard about my friendly interest. At any rate, it would certainly fill up space in my report and make me sound terribly busy and dedicated to the pursuit of justice and all that, and I might get some good stories out of it to make it worth my time. Or I could just eat and go home and say that I created a presence for all the difference to real law enforcement it would make.

I glanced at my watch. Seven-thirty. Vote for the latter. Commander seemed "happy" enough, in his way. Hopner was probably out of the picture for good. I started to shovel the cafeteria-style slop in my mouth that I had driven eight hours to enjoy, and anticipated the night journey home, and considered whether I could get away with not showing up at the field office tomorrow since Fearless was expecting me to stay the night here anyway. Then I got busy noticing that I was actually so hungry that the stew didn't taste as bad it looked, and I was marveling over life's little mercies when I felt someone approach my table and a shadow fell across my plate and I was suddenly eating bread and darkness.

"You the guy we're supposed to talk to? About money?" said an eagerly enthusiastic voice. The voice belonged to a young man who was looking at the "Base Commander" sign. He was definitely not army. He had striking shoulder-length blond hair pleated in tight dreadlocks which were held in place by brilliant multicolored plastic bands, and that had to have taken hours to do. I envied him his free time. And excess bucks, for it looked like a professional job. He was wearing an ancient-looking black T-shirt that bore the faded picture of a skull grinning over a nude woman with a whip, and over the picture were the words "The Dead." His belt buckle had little diamond chips that may or may not have been real diamonds, and his jeans were faded to near white with a hole wearing through one knee. But his boots looked like real leather. Hand tooled and expensive. Type you really shouldn't wear places if you liked to use your feet without blisters.

He extended his hand like he thought I was expecting to meet him, and I noticed that the back of his wrist was tattooed with a dagger and a rose. He was wearing a couple of rings that could pass for expensive if not for tasteful. "I'm Elb."

"I'm a fed." I don't know why I said this. I extended my hand and shook his warmly with a cheerful glad-to-meet-you smile.

"Cool."

Well, the guy didn't seem put off or anything. In fact, he sat down next to me and made himself at home. "Elb," I said with long, slow consideration, for lack of a better conversational opener as I once again took in his costume. He had to possess a hell of a lot more insecurity than I ever did to dress like that. "Unusual name," I remarked with friendly wonder.

"Elb P. McCrae," he said as if to remind me.

"What's the P. stand for?" I asked for the hell of it, and because it kind of amused me that someone with his taste in evening wear would insist on sporting a middle initial.

"Penny. It's my mother's name." His self-consciously understated tone suggested that this was "kind of a supercool private thing a guy like me couldn't possibly appreciate," so I decided he was probably right and changed the subject to something that would get me home faster.

"Know anything about Claude Hopner?" I didn't expect an answer, of course. I only asked so I could honestly tell Fearless that I had asked someone. And I figured since Elb clearly wasn't military and so had no connection to this grand "case" I was wasting a day of my life on that asking him would do the least amount of harm and get me home faster while keeping me sort of honest.

"No. Is he the guy we're supposed to see?" he asked eagerly, as if he'd suddenly been waiting all his life to meet him. I noticed three or four slightly scruffier but similarly attired guys, minus the dreadlocks and expensive accouterments, coming through a side door that opened onto a platform and setting up musical equipment. I supposed the "club" was having some sort of entertainment tonight.

"You with the band?" I asked dryly.

"Hey, yeah, how'd you know?"

"Just a guess." I smiled my "gotcha" fed smile. "What do you call yourselves?"

"Black Dog. After the ghost dog from British folklore. We're really great. We're from Toronto. You'll love us."

"Yeah? What do you play?"

The question seemed to throw him for a few seconds. "Uh, good stuff. Rock and roll, heavy metal, some blues."

"Noooooo," I said with slow surprise, as if I never would have guessed from their appearance that they were a rock band. "I mean, what instrument do you play?"

He looked a little put out. "I don't play any instruments. Just hang out and get gigs—bass player's my cousin. We met a few weeks ago. He's great."

I was curious about how it worked out that he only met his cousin a few weeks ago but I didn't really feel like pursuing the issue. And I was about to get up and leave for home when one of the band members, a tall, lanky twentysomething with an open face and shaggy, dark peach-blond hair, came bounding over to Elb and said urgently, "Gotta have some cash. The dragoons back there," he seemed to mean the cafeteria workers, "just told Jade nobody gets to eat without money or a voucher." He turned to me as an afterthought. "Hi."

"Hi," I said, beginning to leave.

"This is Xander," said Elb as I was standing up. "Mean guitarist." He seemed to be saying this more for Xander's benefit than mine.

Xander looked like something boyish in him wanted to smile at the compliment but that he had also recently become too "professional" to show any reaction to such trivia as praise. "Is this Claude Hopner?" he asked anxiously to keep himself from smiling. "Are we going to get paid?" I sat back down. Sometimes investigators get lucky without even trying. Elb quietly kicked his "mean guitarist" with his expensive boot.

"Uh, no, my name's Morrow. Pete Morrow." I winced as soon as I said it that way, because the construction really does sound dopey when you're carrying a clipboard and trying to wipe chicken stew off your face with a paper napkin. I handed him a card. He didn't look at it. "How do you know Claude?" I asked casually, as if Claude and I were very good friends.

"I don't. Elb knows him." Xander turned to Elb as if for confirmation. So did I.

"Cool," I said.

"Well, I don't *know* him," Elb said easily. "Talked to someone on the phone about setting up the gig. Might have been him. Who knows? Said to talk to the commander." He looked at me. "*You* know who he is?"

"I know he's AWOL," I said with my best practiced air of implying an intimate knowledge of all sorts of juicy mysteries, while passively watching for Elb's reaction.

Xander blew it for me. "Oh, wow, you mean the commander's AWOL?" The question gave Elb the perfect excuse for shading out with soft laughter any natural reaction that I might have noted in him.

"No, Xandie, but our contact person might be. Here." He took a large roll of bills out of his wallet and gave Xander two Canadian twenties. "See if they'll take these for grub. And tell Marty and Jade not to spend them all in one place."

"You want anything?"

"Yeah, a receipt. They should reimburse us dinner cost for playing." Xander took off.

"You carry a lot of cash," I said.

"Yeah." He didn't seem too fazed by the comment. "Birthday present from my sister. What's for dinner, anyway?" He looked at my plate.

"Chicken stew."

"Cool. Guess I'll grab some later." The band members were up in the line and Xander seemed to be tasking his mental faculties to the breaking point as well as those of the rest of the band by trying to work out the rate of exchange with the cashier. "Meantime better find the colonel. Know where he is?"

"You might try the guest house."

"Yeah, I might. Thanks." He said this like a heavy compliment, as if I'd just given him a thousand bucks and the gratitude of his tone was supposed to be a payment in kind. Then he left.

Item. Rinkowski calls in the feds to put a little heat on a private who appears to be dealing for the Utica Mob so he can do his bit for the general to keep his base on the right side of respectable. Fed arrives and same Rinkowski is not terribly enthusiastic about the matter anymore. Did the local Mafia or their new bosses, the Nunzios, get to him? Guy arrives from Canada flashing money around and lies to a fed about not knowing same private. And even though his traveling companions are clearly famished, as evidenced by the way they're all quickly eating without talking, this same guy puts off eating to go talk to Rinkowski alone. Which suggests that whatever his business was with the colonel was more pressing than food. Something was up between Rinkowski, Hopner, and this Canadian impresario. Something international, and bigger than the Utica Mob's local drug business, that possibly implicated the Nunzios. I was hooked.

So I immediately decided it might be of interest after all to hang around for the rest of the show. I watched the band members finish their portions, go up for seconds, and commence to rapidly eating again. And then I resolved it might be highly educational to chat with them collectively in Elb's absence, so I bussed my tray and made my way over to their table. "Hey, Xander," I greeted him like we were old buddies as I sat down uninvited amongst the band.

"Hey." He sounded like he was pleasantly surprised to see me again after a long absence. Then, "Hey—" as he tried to remember my name. He covered his memory lapse by introducing his bandmates. "Jade, Marty, and Les." He indicated each one in turn.

"Pete Morrow," I introduced myself to the table. "FBI."

The one named Marty immediately choked on his stew. He was wearing a khaki muscle shirt, dog tags, and had hair closely cropped enough to be army. From his reaction I idly wondered if *he* were AWOL, but said nothing. I repeated his name with deliberate friendliness to increase his nervousness while he wiped his face and coughed. "Marty."

"We're legal," he franticly assured me. "We're from Canada."

"Marty's a drummer," said Xander, breezily explaining one non sequitur with another.

Marty nodded and spoke again. "Les does keyboards." From his tone I presumed this was Marty's subtle way of implicating Les in whatever it was he thought I might have on him.

So I turned smiling to Les, whose bespectacled, intellectual-looking face and studiously morose expression contrasted well with his Spuds McKenzie T-shirt, but Les would have none of the spotlight. "Well, I *play* the keyboards, but Jade here gets credit for most of the arrangements." He said this rather dolefully, I thought.

"Jade uses Les's gear to compose on." Xander breathlessly trounced in with a strange proud defensiveness, as if it was his own personal accomplishment that Les didn't compose and Jade did. "But Les spent a year at Juilliard."

"Was Juilliard a fun place?" I asked.

"No," Les said flatly. "That's how I met Marty." It was deadpan humor and apparently referred to a well-established in-joke because everyone, including Marty, laughed.

"Except I wasn't there," Marty added anxiously, despite his laughter. I couldn't tell if he was always this high strung or just reacting to my presence.

"He's never there," explained Les. "That's why we let him hang out."

"I was staying in New York with a friend—a friend who was studying the *law*," Marty hastened to assure me.

"And what were *you* doing?" I teased the drummer. "Avoiding the law?" The question got more laughter.

"No, that's Jade's job now," said Xander helpfully.

So I glanced over at Jade, Elb's newly-discovered cousin, to show my great interest in his musical accomplishments. He met my gaze and smiled a little but said nothing. It was a coolly polite, "We've got business to attend to so why are you bothering us?" kind of smile, but I also got the impression that his silence wasn't so much meant to rudely put me off as to cut the conversation short and hurry along his friends, for I saw him glance quickly around the table and then at the partially set up musical equipment on the little platform. He quickly finished his stew and pointedly brought up his tray. The others took the hint and did likewise. Despite Xander's chatty, almost cheerleaderish manner, Black Dog was clearly Jade's band.

I remained at their table because it was front center the playing area and watched them prepare to play. Marty seemed to be having some problems with his drum kit and Les went over to help him. I watched Jade connect his bass to a black box that he placed on top of an amplifier. He kept striking the strings and adjusting the tuning knobs as he studied the red and green lights flashing on the box. As I sat there trying to formulate a way to interview Elb's quiet cousin, who was currently making a job of "avoiding the law," Elb himself returned and lightly sat down next to me, showing no reaction to my having switched tables. "Find the colonel?" I asked.

"Sure. Found each other. Hell of a chatty guy. Swapped war stories. Split a Japanese beer. He's all right. Gave me a voucher to send back for pay so the gig's on." He took out a piece of paper and a hand-held calculator and deftly converted the amount to Canadian currency. "You got any requests?" he asked me with all the excessively polite solicitousness of a dealer in illegal goods. "They can play anything. Check out my cousin. He's the best bass player in Canada. In the world, probably." But before I could answer he called up to the platform, "We're on." Jade nodded and glanced around to see if his fellow musicians were ready yet. They weren't. Marty seemed to have gotten his thumb stuck in one of the metal rods propping up one of his cymbals and Les went back over to help him untangle himself.

"How about 'Puff, the Magic Dragon'?" I asked for the hell of it.

"Cool," said Elb. "I'm sure they probably know it." The way he said this I wasn't sure *he* did. "They know everything. Who did that? The Velvet Underground?"

"I don't know," I said gravely, suppressing a smirk. "Think it might have been the Stones."

"Yeah, right," said Elb, as if he knew this all along, "the Stones. Hey guys, turn on some 'Puff, the Magic Dragon' for Peter here." Les looked up over Marty's drums to see if Elb was joking. I smiled and nodded in his direction to assure him he wasn't. Never hurts to appear vaguely unpredictable when commencing an investigation.

Jade glanced over at Xander and shrugged. "And now," said Elb cheerfully, "I've got to get myself some gruel. Didn't get to eat on the road."

"Better hurry. Looks like the kitchen's closing."

"No, caf chow disagrees with me. I was going to take the van out and find something decent, though I hate driving it again through that gravel pit they've got here." He probably meant the road through the woods. "Righteous stones from hell kick up and ruin the paint job."

"Maybe the colonel will let you use a staff car," I said in mock obeisance to his refined tastes.

He grinned a little. "Nah, still too bumpy. Know any good restaurants locally?"

"No, locally you'll have to settle for roadkill," I joshed him.

"Yeah, I can get that at home." He said this like a cool put down to my friendly attempt at humor, or like another subtly understated boast, as if he needed to let me know that he was long bored with refined dietary habits that someone like me wouldn't know how to dream of appreciating.

"Yeah"—I repeated his languishing tone, and then continued with a sympathetic air of world-weariness, like I too was bored with roadkill and was also rather proud of recently breaking beyond that now déclassé area of fine dining—"for real food you'll probably have to go into Utica or Rome."

The quick stiffening of his mouth told me that he did not care for my implied familiarity with his household cuisine. "Right then, to Rome," he announced a little more sharply and a little less grandly. "Tell the guys I'll be back, if they ask." Then he shoved himself off into a quick exit.

I briefly considered following him, but under the circumstances there was no way Elb would miss the fact of being followed, so there was no way I would discover anything useful. Better to let him run his course without interference and pick up information later, if I was still to have anything to do with this whole Hopner business later. Then I considered going off to query Rinkowski about Elb, to see if I could glean anything remotely useful from the old man, but since I was now planning to stay the night here I decided there would be ample time for that excruciating interview later. That is, if Rinkowski decided it was "OK" to remember who the hell Elb was by later. Or who I was. It made more sense to stay put and watch the band and look for an opportunity to interview Jade.

So I leaned back in my seat and watched "the best bass player in Canada, or in the world, probably" as he strode forward to the mic and introduced the other band members. Sitting at the table and making myself cozy with his friends had not given me leisure to really study him. But sitting through an hour set without breaks gave me ample opportunity to observe. And the first thing I noticed was that his appearance was more striking and unusual than his cousin's. Elb clearly invested tortuous amounts of cash into his dreadlocks and boots and jewelry to get you to notice him so he could make you feel like his inferior once you did. And that seemed to be the real payoff for Elb. But Jade you simply noticed, because he had one of those faces that simply would get noticed, on stage or off, while his bandmates all had the scruffy redundancy of known types.

Catalogue. Xander, as he played, was jogging along a thousand late August beaches or pumping a thousand weights or playing a thousand tennis games in a thousand gymnasiums. He probably lived off salad and fruit juice without really thinking about it or making his diet an "issue" the way a lot of physical types do. He was the guy everyone had a passing acquaintance with and sort of knew had once been on a track team. I filed him as athletic without quite being an athlete.

And Marty looked so extravagantly normal that I knew him as everybody's neighbor's nice enough young adult son from down the road who *would* be serious about his music even though his parents' circle all agreed that it was past time for him to grow up and get a real job. All of his anxious excitability seemed to surge out of his personality and open out forcefully into his drumming, and I suddenly realized that Marty was also the latecomer to every summer clique from Maine to California. The guy somebody else always knows and brings in, who dresses so "straight" and keeps his hair so well-trimmed and short that everyone assumes at first blush he has to be a "narc" or a "fed" until he opens his mouth a few times and tamely reveals that he is merely a madman. He really "wasn't there." I found myself rather liking this quality, in a shallow sort of way, because I hadn't happened to come across it in a while.

And when the music moved the gloomy looking Les to slip a rare smile over to one of his bandmates, I knew him too. He was strolling through life reading science fiction novels, Robert Heinlein especially, and wearing that T-shirt with the formula for LSD printed on the back—you know, the one that allegedly has a mistake in the formula somewhere that all the nerds feel honor bound to point out to you. But Les didn't strike me as being insecure enough to be a proper nerd. He looked like all the guys I used to know in school who could quote Monty Python movies front to back and bullshit intelligently on the latest fashionable eccentricity in quantum physics but couldn't discipline themselves to "settle down" into anything resembling a college major, which may have explained his leaving the conservatory. The kind of guy who managed to be too intellectual for both real life and school.

Body, emotion, and mind. Intensely human. Intensely common.

But Jade was different. Classic features. Aquiline, as the hack writers used to say in old novels when they needed a short-hand way of designating nobility. Long, dark, abundant hair framed his face like a river of night frames pale dreams, and the pale dream of his face reminded me of a character out of a fantasy novel or a medieval romance, or something equally otherworldly. I kept looking at him and thinking that he really wasn't supposed to be here, that he ought to be strolling through an ancient myth, a wandering bard solemnly conjuring beauty for a war-weary king.

Mellie probably would have liked him, I thought with unexplainable sadness.

Then I rudely broke myself from reverie and asked myself what the hell was I thinking about. It was his job to charm and entertain, and he did it surprisingly well, but it was now my job to psyche him out, and I was suddenly being remiss to lose myself in literary images. I made another effort to study him, and I noted that he had far too great a range of expression and far too much intelligence and generosity in his laughter to be the front man of a heavy metal band, and yet the contrast made him an excellent choice for the role. You kept watching him because he came across like an extended feeling of surprise.

Jade led the band through a few old standards like "Red River Valley" and "Greensleeves," which sounded captivatingly bizarre and good-naturedly humorous in their flat electrical arrangements, because the choices contrasted with all expectation. And because Jade's voice conveyed an unexpectedly respectful intensity that the novel musical arrangement delightfully juxtaposed. Then "Greensleeves" segued imperceptibly into Led Zeppelin's "Stairway to Heaven," which I thought was a rather pretty idea, and the band played it faithfully to the original except for the addition of some softly haunting chords on the keyboards. Then the rocking end of "Stairway to Heaven" became a high energy version of the slow intro to Lynyrd Skynyrd's "Free Bird" and the end of "Free Bird" segued into a prolonged medley of several more seventies rock standards during which Jade retreated to the background and played near Marty. There were no vocals. Instead, Xander took front center and did a lot of guitar solos where the vocals should have been. Xander's playing impressed me, because I sensed a capacity for subdued emotion there that wasn't terribly obvious in him when we spoke. And then, unbelievably, Jade stepped back to the mic and the band played "Puff, the Magic Dragon," which he actually had the graciousness to sing to me from the little stage, since it was my request, and so of course I set myself to look pleased while feeling a little chagrined that everyone in the club was now thinking it was really "my song." Then the set went into another old standard, "Lavender's Blue," that segued into "O Canada" and ended with "The Star-Spangled Banner."

The latter caused everyone present to put their hands on their hearts and stand up in case their superiors were watching. So I stood up too, thinking that Black Dog knew how to get a standing ovation. Then Jade courteously thanked the audience and set down his bass, as the other members of Black Dog began to quickly break down their equipment. And it was only as they all disrobed, so to speak, that it became clear from their rushed demeanors that army base clubs were really not their sort of thing. My impression from their lack of chatter was that they knew they had done their jobs rather well, thank you, but that this was all an odd business for them and they were now impatient to get on with things elsewhere.

Marty was having trouble with his kit so Jade was now crouched down helping him. Elb had not yet returned from his repast so here was my opportunity to interview his mysterious cousin alone.

I settled on the direct approach, and strode over towards nervous old Marty, who was now literally buried in his drums. "Hey, Jade," I called in the same friendly tone I had previously used to address Xander.

Jade tilted his head back with a friendly but impersonal expression, as if to say "Yes, go ahead, I have a minute now." His eyes were as bright as they were brown and still warm from his playing. His openness unnerved me. I had absolutely no idea why it should, but I got the feeling that he still considered himself "at work" and that whatever I had to say to him had better be worth his time. So since flattery is worth most people's time, I tried flattery. "You sing about dragons like you mean it."

"Doesn't everybody?" he asked with simple good humor, but as he said this he was already dismissing me and speaking to Marty and helping him to move a bass drum, and so the question had the tone of a private joke between them.

"Where'd Elb go?" Marty asked Jade, ignoring my presence.

"Went to town for grub," I offered like I was already one of the gang.

Marty sighed. "It's going to take me a while to break this down. Why don't you go see if the van's back before I lug this stuff out the door?"

"Sure." Jade took himself off through the side door, still full of work and therefore completely oblivious to my presence. So I followed him.

Outside was all August crickets and warm spongy night. I hadn't felt the sun all day because I had been driving, and so the lingering heat heaved itself into me like a shabby reminder of discomfort, and the mushy air felt like a dirty secret as I felt my shirt sticking to my suddenly sweat-soaked skin. The crickets sounded unnerved, their chirps loud and angry protests, as if nature had just informed them that they were scheduled to die in a few weeks. *Nothing is clean here*, I thought.

Jade was a few paces ahead of me, strolling jauntily across a grassy stretch of the compound and presumably heading for the gravelly parking area. I called out to his back as I caught up to him. "Hey, Black Dog."

He turned and met my eyes with a quick expression that conveyed a mild "what now?" as if he couldn't imagine what I might possibly have to say to him. He was occupied with "band business" and didn't care to have me taking up his time, and he clearly considered it a bit odd or obtrusive of me to follow him outside. And I admit, it suddenly did feel rather awkward.

"Good show," I tried for openers.

"Thanks," he said quickly, as if he didn't mean to offend, but likewise didn't mean to get into a prolonged chat with me when there was work waiting for him indoors.

"No, I really mean it," I said, falling into step beside him, "You guys are going to be world famous someday."

Since we were now walking together, he probably thought it would be rude not to respond to my compliments. And the way I had just set things up, it probably would have been, because I made sure to act like I was waiting to be favored with a response and *would* feel hurt not to get one. "A lot of bands are 'world famous in Canada' and that sort of thing. We just play." He said this like he didn't really care to speak, but since we were walking together, and speaking wasn't costing him time, he might as well say something.

"I liked your arrangements."

He looked a little surprised. "They were all pretty much off the cuff." Then, as if he didn't mean to imply that my taste was naive, he explained, "Although tonight was a bit unusual for us. We usually play all original stuff, but Elb wanted us to hold back from our usual sort of performance and just play standards. He didn't think the audience would appreciate our usual style. Most of the covers you heard tonight we either just learned or one of us happened to know so the others caught up. We plundered a few things from lesson books to fill in the hour set. Black Dog isn't really a cover band."

"What is Black Dog—*really*, then?" I asked lightly, to disguise my curiosity concerning the band's apparent relationship to Claude Hopner.

"I like the way you ask that. Black Dog is *really* an idea—like anything else. You see, it's not like we never do covers because we'd never get gigs if we only played our own stuff. So we tell club owners we do songs by well-known bands, and then we learn one or two of the most obscure pieces done by the same well-known bands, the kind of stuff even a dedicated fan might not immediately recognize, and play those to keep sort of honest. Since, with any luck, no one will recognize the songs, our overall set creates an impression that we are entirely original, which puts us in a different class than a cover band."

"Sounds like the semi-honest way I deal with work," I laughed. "I'm sorry I missed an original Black Dog performance." Having warmed him up to talking, I swung the conversation round to Elb. "Elb says you're the greatest bass player in Canada."

"He would say that," Jade offered lightly in return. "He's never heard me play."

"He says you're cousins."

"I know his sister. She introduced us."

"Then you're not cousins?"

"Cara's sort of a kissing cousin." He smiled softly at the night.

"Then what's he?"

"Sort of a friend of the band. Sometimes gets us gigs. I don't know." He turned to smile at me and shrugged. "Never been one to explain relationships. You'd have to ask Elb what he is, if you really care to know. It keeps changing." He said this with an air of good-natured amusement over Elb's changeability.

"I understand Elb recently had a falling out with Claude Hopner," I ventured, to see what sort of reaction I might elicit.

"Really?" Jade stopped in his tracks and doubled over laughing, so I stood there smiling as if I shared in the joke while I waited for him to finish. "I'm sorry." He recovered himself and started walking. I kept pace with him. "I try not to understand anything. Makes my job easier."

Now it was my turn to stop and force myself to laugh a little to cover up my sudden disorientation. For it was disorienting to hear this stranger utter words that I thought were solely my own, words that I considered proprietary to my own cherished bad attitude. But I was too professional about matters to let my new acquaintance simply turn the subject out into night and heat like that. So I tried to get him to talk further on Elb and Hopner via an issue that was presumably closer to his own interest.

"Hope it doesn't affect the band."

"Affect the *band*," he laughed again like my comment was terribly naive. I suddenly realized that I had just inadvertently revealed that I really didn't know what I was talking about. But he wasn't so much laughing at me as just laughing at the idea of there being such a problem. One issue apparently had nothing to do with the other. "No one in the band even knows who the hell Meister Hopner is. He's one of Elb's deals." He was still chuckling. "Hopner has achieved the status of an in-joke among us. Les calls him Claude Godot."

"Why?"

"Because he never shows up. Like the character in the Beckett play."

I was once again nonplussed. I did not expect this rag tag rock band had even heard of Beckett. Jade's casual literary allusion made another intriguing sort of contrast with my expectations. "Yes, right. I know the play," I said conversationally, even though I hadn't read it in about ten years.

Jade studied me a minute like he never would have guessed I knew how to read, let alone read Beckett, and was pleasantly surprised by the revelation. "Cool." I couldn't tell if he suddenly considered us friends, but it felt for a second like we might be. Which was jolting. But he didn't seem put off by my questions, so I continued.

"How does Elb know him?"

"No one's sure Elb does know him. He talks about him a good deal."

"What does he say?"

"Anything he likes. He lies. He makes things up. He has fun with it. What does anyone say about anyone else?" We reached the parking area as he said this. My car was still there, but there was no sign of the van. There was a piece of paper attached to the windshield and I excused myself to get it. The whitewashed fence looked bright and other-worldly in the light of a lamp post, and the gravel looked all warm and still the way untraveled roads often look on summer nights. I read the paper as I went back to Jade. It was a goddamned parking ticket, informing me I had no right to leave my vehicle there without "clearance."

Jade had waited to listen for the van, and a wide lumbering kind of silence now settled uncomfortably between us. Courtesy seemed to demand that it be broken. "Do you like dragons?" he suddenly asked as if he was trying to entertain me with something he thought I might be interested in. I felt slightly embarrassed at the matter-of-fact way he seemed to consider dragons a subject of appropriate interest to me as I stood there with ticket in hand.

"Do I like dragons?" I asked absently as I contemplated the $50.00 parking violation fee and thought about how I might get the field office to pay.

"I mean, most seventies types usually ask for 'Free Bird.'" He sounded slightly amused, but in a damnably friendly way, as if we were a pair of old souls and he could tease me with impunity because he had always known me with impunity.

"Oh—" I waved my hand nonchalantly and stuffed the offending citation in my shirt pocket. "It was sort of a joke."

"Too bad," said Jade quietly. "I kind of like dragons myself." He looked out into the direction of the road coming in from the woods. "And seeing as you've just been burnt"—his smile gently acknowledged the citation—"I thought we might try to raise one out of the dark and see if he could help."

"Is that what you do when you violate the law? Raise dragons?" I teased.

"No. If it's only the law and not anything to bother myself about, I just ignore it. What do you do?" he asked me in return, as if it was the most natural thing in the world to ask a fed and he just wanted to swap information. "Do you feel guilty because of your job?"

"No, I don't feel guilty." I thought about it and found myself answering honestly, "When I break the law I just get an adrenaline rush." Then I bit my tongue, because I didn't mean the conversation to suddenly go off in this direction. I also didn't want to pursue dragons because I was afraid I might not come back. It was all too weirdly comfortable for comfort, if you know what I mean. Jade was laughing heartily and good-humoredly. Apparently, I amused him.

But I wasn't getting paid to amuse him and I tried to get our exchange back on a more useful track. "So, why does Elb lie to you?" I asked in my best "you-can-tell-me-anything-don't-you-want-to-come-clean-to-someone-who-can-help-you" voice. Adding a touch of concern, as if you know about some danger you can shield the interviewee from, often garners useful information. But not in this instance.

"Because it's fun, probably." Jade answered with a gentle enthusiasm and looked with a brief, gentle intensity through my eyes with his clear ones. His manner was oddly comfortable and familiar. Most people have one of two reactions around federal agents. They either voluntarily tell you everything and more than everything you need to know out of some pathetic need to earn approval from an authority figure by wasting an afternoon of his time, or they put on a nervous act like they're hiding something (even if they aren't) because they think they're supposed to or they're afraid you might figure out that they violated a leash law ten years ago or something. But Jade didn't treat me like I was an agent investigating a case. He spoke to me like we might as well be friends for a minute, seeing as there was nothing else to do to kill the time while waiting for the van. It had somehow gotten understood that there was no need to return to the club and help move things until the van was back. "You should try it sometime. When you're not working, I mean."

"What makes you think I don't?" I have no idea why I said this, or why I suddenly felt slightly defensive.

"I don't think. Here, Pete." He sat on a large painted boulder near the lamp post and made a mock theatrical gesture. My name sounded comfortable when he said it. "Pull up a piece of dandelion root and tell me a lie." He was suddenly strangely formal and intent and playful and I felt like he was teasing me or setting up some practical joke he could tell his friends about later. But he also seemed sincerely interested in what I would do, and for a second I felt like he was interviewing me.

"Tell me one of Elb's lies about Hopner," I insisted.

"And then you'll grace me with one of yours?" he lightly bargained.

"Sure. Deal." It was cheaper than cash and cleaner than plea bargaining.

"All right," said Jade in a seductive storyteller's voice that one might use to cajole a small child to sleep, "sometimes Claude Hopner is a club owner who owes Elb money and favors. And sometimes . . . he knows a club owner, who owes Elb money and favors. And sometimes . . . he used to be a club owner who owes Elb money and favors. But most times he is the guy we have to meet who is never there and whom Elb alone is privileged to know. And Elb knows all kinds of interesting things about him. That he is a singer, and a fortune teller, and a novelist, and busy leading a revolution in the bowels of Quebec, or practicing midwifery on cows, or making new discoveries as an 'independent researcher,' or dancing or riding balloon-shaped dragons through the sky. Hopner is a terribly Romantic chap who specializes in all those things you don't need any special qualifications for. Someday he'll make Prime Minister if he's not careful."

"So he's Canadian?" This was getting better all the time.

"Up until now he's been Canadian but this week he's a soldier in the U. S. Army."

"You don't think he's a really a private?" *I must check records on him*, I thought.

"I told you, I don't think." He descended from the boulder and stretched himself out on his side in the wretched heat-churned grass and blew dandelion seeds to the dark. "But to answer your question, I don't think he's really anything. I don't think he's real. That is, in the accepted sense of the word." He sat up and leaned against the boulder. "But what the hell? That shouldn't stop you from seeking him out. He might be a nice person anyway."

"So let me understand this—"

"Why?"

"Habit. You've never met Mr. Hopner yourself?"

"No."

"Haven't you ever wanted to?"

"Not really."

"Why not?"

"I don't want to meet anyone who knows how to live better than I do." The sound of a large vehicle moving with painful slowness along the stony woodland path ended the conversation. But we looked at each other for a minute through the summer dark before Jade spoke again. It had been a minute's friendship, but it had been a friendship, and for me minutes like that are hard to kill off, they come so rarely. I found myself wondering if it was my reluctance or his that held him there from completing his work. Jade's conversation really, well, entertained me, but I didn't fully realize this until our little chat was about to be over. "Well. Better go help Marty move stuff," he said rising without further hesitation. "But you still owe me a lie. And you government types are much better at it than we artists."

"All right," I chuckled, giving him a copy of my card. "Next time we meet I'll be prepared to lie to you through my teeth. Tell Elb I'd like to match wits with him in that department."

"Think you'd win?"

"I don't think," I shot back. He laughed appreciatively. "Nature of the job. And call me if you ever want to talk about Hopner." I didn't suppose he would, but I suppose it was a way of keeping the means of contact open. I had liked our conversation, in a mildly surprising way, and there really wasn't that much I liked anymore. As he walked away I felt an unexpected let down, and suddenly knew I had really been enjoying myself without meaning to. Dragons and stories in the dark. What a report. I waited in the darkness behind the boulder for the van to pull slowly into the parking area. From my vantage point I could see Elb without being seen in return unless I chose to make myself known. I could also see the Ontario license plate and I made a point of jotting it down on a little notebook in my pocket. The paint job was fairly distinctive and detailed, although I couldn't see most of it from my angle of vision. The front bore a giant dagger and a rose that matched Elb's tattoo and I could see part of a dragon guarding a little black dog holding a ruby on one side.

Elb did not get out of the van immediately. He stayed inside with lights and motor off for about ten minutes. I had no idea what he was doing. And it wasn't until the club door spilled light in the distance, and Les and Marty emerged with their arms full of drum kit, that Elb chose to swing open his van door and lightly jump down into the parking lot. Then I saw him kiss one of his rings and I heard him mutter something fairly weird like, "Thank the lady moon for a boon" as he ambled over to the rear of the vehicle and slid open the back doors. Then he magnanimously waited until the bandmates had lugged their stuff all the way to the van before he offered to help. "Better hurry, friends," he cajoled, "It's at least five hours to the border and it'll be dawn before I get you all safely home."

"Let Jade drive and we'll make it in four," said Les. Marty laughed a little.

"Yeah, I might," said Elb. "If I get tired enough. Good moon for a night drive, though."

I saw Jade and Xander emerge from the door, carrying their guitar cases and laughing and talking about something I couldn't catch, although I found myself straining to hear Jade's voice above Xander's, in case he was saying anything useful about our interview, and well, because he sort of amused me. Les and Marty were returning to bring out more equipment, and after they passed by Jade and Xander, it was clear that Xander was doing most of the talking, complaining about how boring it was to do covers for military types who wouldn't know good innovative music if they sat in it. By the time they approached the van Elb called out chidingly, "Xander, Xander. Humor me for once. You're all playing in Fendra's two weeks from Friday—all original, all yours. We got pay towards more equipment, and I need you all to keep positive and help me to get the word out—" and the rest of the sentence was lost as they went behind and shoved in the guitar cases. Jade and Xander quickly returned to the building, leaving Elb by himself. He leaned against the van, whistled, uttered more incomprehensible phrases to the moon, swatted mosquitoes that the light was attracting in his direction, and generally seemed to make himself useless as the four band members emerged with Les's portable keyboard, assorted amplifiers, and cable. And since they were weighed down, they were moving slowly and not speaking. It took them several minutes to cross the grassy area. Elb watched them impatiently and then condescended to help a little as they loaded the rest of the equipment into the van. "All set?" he asked.

"I think I might have dropped a drumstick," said Marty. Les sighed audibly.

"Well, why don't you go look for it," said Elb with sudden sweetness, as if to counteract Les's sigh. "Besides, someone ought to police the area before we leave."

"Marty ain't too handy with police," said Les. "And he'll take forever if he can."

"I'll go, then," volunteered Xander.

"Right," said Marty, as Xander started off. "Go. Uh, Elb. There was no one left in the club when we left it. Are we supposed to lock up or tell somebody we're leaving or something? Or just go?"

"Why don't we just go?" muttered Les.

"I suppose we can just go. But why don't you leave a note thanking the U. S. Army for its fine food and hospitality?" Elb said graciously, as if he were suddenly Mr. Manners himself. "Never hurts to leave a good impression." As Marty bounded away after Xander, the others clustered together and waited. The absence of chit chat bespoke a strong desire to hit the road.

It didn't take Marty long to return. He found two drumsticks in the grass and was now presuming dangerously on Elb's good nature by beating out a rhythm on the paint job. "Here comes Xander," said Elb to stop him. "Time to go."

"Hey, Elb," Xander called out. "There's an old guy sitting at the bar by himself wearing a uniform who might be the colonel. But he wouldn't talk to me. Just kept staring at me like he didn't know me or wasn't sure I was supposed to be there. Think he might be drunk. Tried to tell him we were leaving. You think you ought to go in?"

Had to be Rinkowski getting himself through the night. Wonderful. And if he were drunk he wouldn't "know" me either and I was hoping for a room in the guest house and a waver on the parking ticket. "Cool. Let's all go pay our respects to the commander," said Elb unexpectedly, as if it might be fun. And actually, I supposed it might be a bit of a lark to see a drunken Rinkowski, not to mention getting a fix on what the hell there was between Elb and the commander. It certainly might be diverting to bring up Hopner's name between them and see what happened.

So, as they all moved off to the club, I sauntered into the back of the crowd. "Pleasant moon," I remarked to Elb as if I'd just been on a lengthy stroll.

"Hey, Pete, where'd you go?" asked Jade, making me welcome into the group.

"Dragon riding," I said in an I've-got-a-secret voice like Crensch's.

"Is that my lie?" said Jade in mock-enthusiasm, spreading his hand over his heart like a pledge.

"No, it's true. I've been moon watching," I added significantly. "Hey, Elb, you missed a damn good show tonight. Thought at least a few people might even get up and dance."

"Not here," opined Les.

"Well, maybe just to be polite," I tossed out.

"Does anyone ever dance just to be polite?" asked Jade earnestly.

"I don't know. It's a fine night, though, don't you think, Elb? Did you roust up a good meal?"

Elb didn't answer because the club door provided him an excuse not to. We all went inside and there was Rinkowski, just as Xander had said, leaning up against the wall at a little bar and staring at us in the confused uncomprehending way military types have. So I saluted him, and Jade chuckled at my theatrics. He had clearly been drinking because there was an incredible stink of alcohol coming from his corner. But since he could only have arrived when the band made their last collective trip out, he had to have been drinking elsewhere before he made his trip over here. There was a glass of something yellow like Scotch sitting in front of him and I wondered if that were some of the highly praised Japanese beer.

"Hey, Commander," I approached. "Want to thank you and Mr. Hopner for tonight's excellent entertainment." As I got closer, I noticed that his crisp collar was soaked in red, and that a wide swathe of duct tape appeared to be circling his neck and holding his collar in place. An instant later the vibrations of our combined footsteps caused the colonel's severed head to fall off and knock over the drink, which sent up a noxious odor like the flesh of a rotting animal. Then, in horrible slow motion, the glass rolled across the bar and crashed to the floor and the rest of the body fell off the chair. The band members were all screaming, Marty the loudest, and I was doing my best to look professional but the odor from the glass made me want to vomit. And as the body fell I could see that the chest cavity had been neatly hollowed out, and that someone had placed an ice pack inside and a large black gruesome looking trout, frozen and curled like an ancient fossil. I forced myself to look closely. The trout had a handwritten slip of paper taped to its side. The note read: "Hopner's sardines. Easy to open. Easy to clean."

"Roadkill?" I said pointedly to Elb, who was pretending to be brave enough to look over my shoulder but had his eyes turned away from the gruesome sight.

Marty was still gasping. It sounded like he was saying, "I didn't do it, I didn't do it," but he was choking too much for the words to be clear.

"Guess old Claude's gone fishing," said Les from somewhere behind me.

"Don't worry, folks," said Elb lightly, straightening out and affecting not to be affected. "The law's here, and I'm sure the check's still good."

I turned and saw that the others were now just looking away in silent shock and disgust. Except Jade, who met my eyes and smiled a little. "Guess you've got yourself one hell of a gig there, Pete," he said. The way he said it I suppose it was something of a congratulations. Or a weirdly intimate compliment.

Bridge

Monday night, August 17, 1992 – Wednesday afternoon, August 19, 1992.

Much to speculate. After performing all the little duties dead bodies require of the government, and pretending to the Rome police that I had clearance for them to come up and bring the whole mess to a morgue for the requisite autopsy, and questioning everyone on the base worth questioning, and illegally reading and making myself personal copies of confidential files until near-dawn, and then harassing more of the same people with more of the same questions for another day, I had less idea than when I'd first arrived what this fascinating new deal was. And the deal was getting more fascinating by the minute. And the corpse was getting to be the least of it.

But taking things in order. I have certain personal rules that kick in under certain investigative circumstances.

Rule number 1. As to murder, everyone's a suspect until proven otherwise. And that includes the corpse, for I have seen some really original suicides in my time. The kind you almost want to congratulate the guy for thinking up and giving you a bit of a challenge over.

Rule number 2. Once proven otherwise, everyone's still a suspect. Ref. Rule number 2A.

Rule number 2A. There's no such thing as proof. Proof is reality's wishful thinking.

Rule number 3. Don't tell boss rule number 2 or you'll be writing up reports on why everyone is a suspect until the case goes dry and nobody is and you get blamed for it.

Rule number 4. Whenever possible, investigate properly (i.e. illegally) before one's trusty colleagues invite themselves in, screw up the evidence until it fits into all the "proper channels" and can be understood and appreciated by all, including the press, and generally ruin all the fun.

I was feeling pretty good compared to my normal mood because I'd never gotten as far as rule number 4 on a murder case before. The juiciest cases, meaning the really neat stuff that pops out of the edges of life and promises to challenge and entertain for months, never fall pure and unsullied into one's normal workday. When the nut cases hit my desk, they generally do so through the watchful medium of the Bureau's finely tuned bureaucracy and my first exposure to the evidence is via someone else's report, and that someone else is usually a committee of semi-literate police officers from different states who begin by hiding information from each other and end by censoring everything relevant from me lest I, as a rival member of the executive branch, happen to show any of them up by actually solving the case. Or I hear all about it on the news, including how "special federal investigators" have been called in, about three or four days before Fearless finally throws it my way.

You see, no one is allowed to be a lone-hero investigator anymore. Sherlock and Sam are an overweening threat to the viability and cleanly obscured intentions of the government, and so the real thought-work cases are closely monitored and closely contaminated by the powers-that-be so that no one gets too flashy and dangerous with his yellow legal pad and solitary powers of deduction. None of us are hired to think too hard lest it hurt those around us.

But I clearly had first dibs on this one, and as I intimated above, this one was getting to be a real doozie. And since I now had a line on making my life a little less boring for a while, I figured why blow it on protocol?

First pass.

To begin with, per rule number 2, I provisionally, but only provisionally, ruled out the band members for the simple reason that, except for very short periods of time, I was with them all evening.

Note. One. I was with Jade all evening except for that weird ten-minute stretch when the band was back in the club and Elb was sitting in his dark van, but ten minutes wasn't enough time to execute a human body like that. And move it. And set it up like the guest of honor at an Irish wake. And break down musical equipment. I've cleaned out enough deer on hunting trips to have some idea of what it takes to ransack a bony frame of its contents, and it takes a lot longer than ten minutes if you wish to be neat about it. And this murder was not a hack job, not even in the literal sense. Whoever carved up the corpse did it leisurely and artistically, and well – skillfully. They left a piece of polished wood to spread open the ribcage, and carefully painted two ribs a bright, day-glow pink. They had also nicely curtained the damage with Rinkowski's uniform so the hole wasn't obvious from a distance. And even though the other three band members were out of my sight while I was out night-walking with Jade, there were witnesses in the club who all affirmed that Xander and Les were busy bailing Marty out of his drum kit during that time. According to the witnesses, none of the three ever left the club.

Two. The witnesses were two privates who were on kitchen duty and were helping the two middle-aged women who had worked the food counter to wipe down tables and clean the place after the audience left. The women were civilians and had gone home, but I got the privates' names and extension numbers from a work roster that hung over the bar. So I called them in their barracks. Without mentioning the murder, I queried them and both gave the same account of seeing the three band members until Jade returned. Neither knew Hopner. I learned later that they were both seen returning to their respective barracks right after they'd finished work, and that they had left with the two women and seen them get in their cars and leave for home. So those witnesses were also, then, provisionally cleared.

Three. Marty and Les made their first trip out of the club when the workers left, and Jade and Xander hadn't been by themselves inside for more than three minutes before emerging with their guitar cases.

Four. All I could determine was that when Marty and Les then returned inside, they saw no one else in the club besides themselves, and I knew that they weren't out of my sight for more than a few minutes during that second trip either. And so in the four or five minutes after Marty and Les left the club on their second trip out and before Xander returned to police the area, someone just happened to show up to set up the body at the bar. And that someone walked boldly through either the main entrance or the side door to the club, in plain sight of most of the base, because those were the club's only points of entry. And clearly neither Elb nor the band members brought the body in, because I saw them all during those four to five minutes when the corpse would have made its entrance. And when Xander made his solo trip back inside, he didn't spend more than a few seconds in the club by himself, enough to see the old man staring at him and leave to tell his friends about it.

So the members of Black Dog were only of professional interest by association. Because if it weren't for Elb's vaguely understood association with Claude Hopner and the note bearing Hopner's name (which I gingerly removed and kept to myself for future reference before the police arrived), there was no inherent reason, and no known motive, for suspecting any of them of anything.

But Elb was gone for long enough stretches of time to make the top of my party list of folks I'd like to get to know more intimately. Especially because he had the unrivaled distinction of being both the only person I knew of who last saw the victim alive and the only person who was understood to have even a nodding acquaintance with Hopner's reality. And yet, save for rule number 2, I didn't think he was directly involved in the murder itself, for reasons both intangible and hard. When Marty announced that there was no one in the club, it was Elb's suggestion that he return for his drumsticks over Les's protestations that he wanted to leave. If he knew anything about the murder he surely could—and would—have taken up with Les's sentiments and urged everyone to head for the border. Fast. He would have, to quote Les, "let Jade drive." Certainly not prod everyone into paying respects to a corpse and then insist that they all hang around to be questioned. Because Elb did insist that they all talk to me, just to "keep things honest," as he said, a statement I found particularly droll coming from him. But besides such human intangibles, the hard evidence was that his clothes didn't look like he'd just butchered open a human body himself. And there had only been one pair of tracks leaving the gravelly area when I talked to Jade, so I knew the van didn't leave and return while the band was performing. The van left. It went somewhere. And Elb was willing enough to say where without my asking. Said he'd eaten at a Thai restaurant in Rome. And he showed me his credit card receipt, which indicated that he paid for his dinner at nine-forty p.m. And the time worked out in his favor. Left the club at eight-twenty. Half an hour to Rome, make it eight-fifty he enters restaurant. I saw him return to the base at ten after ten. But alibi notwithstanding, I was sure he knew lots of helpful stuff for the asking. And I had to ask.

While I was questioning Xander on what he had seen when he returned to the club alone, and eliciting no new information, Marty got so sick from the foul odor and so shuddery over the sight of the corpse that Jade and Les had to help him outside to vomit in the grass. Xander went to join them immediately after I finished talking to him, because the smell was also making him queasy. Which was fine, because sick as I felt, I wanted to query Elb alone. But Elb looked so sick and pale with the odor that he asked if we couldn't go out in the open air, too. Besides, "he was superstitious" and "dead people weren't quite his thing." I didn't want to leave the corpse because I didn't want anyone else discovering it, tampering with evidence, or spreading the word just yet, so I compromised by moving back to the platform and standing in the open side door as the others helped Marty off to lie down in the van. The night air brought a little vomit out of Elb as it contrasted, and therefore intensified, the horrible odor inside. I offered him a clean handkerchief after he let loose in the grass.

"So did you two have a falling out, or what?" I smiled like we were great pals as he gratefully wiped his face.

"Falling out?" He sounded crestfallen, as if my question's implied accusation was terribly rude of me after all the "help" and "cooperation" he had been willing to provide. He handed back the cloth like it was a dirty bribe he was suddenly sorry he'd taken from me. "I partied with him," he insisted with more than a touch of dismay, as though that made the murder almost as unfair as my question, or partying with the colonel made him one hell of a more democratic, tolerant kind of guy than I clearly was. I was supposed to admire the breadth and variety of his life experiences, and his superior willingness to drink with just about anybody.

"Must have been quite a party," I commented, as I glanced at the headless, hollowed out corpse.

"Look, he was in party mode, what can I say?" Elb's eyes were swimming with a thickly wet disgust and his face was still pinched and blanched. Much of his earlier "sophistication" had already vanished and my refusal to idolize his life's most recent piece of party exotica suddenly dissipated the rest. I realized I was now talking to someone who felt deep humiliation and resentment over being scared and was doing a poor job at hiding his fear.

So I relented in my attempts to shuffle his nerves into enlightenment. "Did he know who you were?" I asked in a more congenial, confiding tone of voice.

"Not at first. No, he didn't," said Elb in a come-to-think-of-it tone. It seemed hard for him to admit that the colonel didn't instantly recognize him or remember his business. "I had to explain myself, but once I set him straight it was cool. Gave me the voucher. Signed it without a problem." He offered the latter information like he was trying to excuse himself for something, but wasn't quite sure what he was excusing himself for.

"Can I see it?"

Elb anxiously reached into his jeans pocket and gave me a little folded set of carbons.

"I don't suppose I could copy this? For my records?"

"Sure, if you think it's useful," he said fervently, as if he were about save my soul or he thought I was about to save his. "In fact, here," he took the bundle back and tore off one of the sheets, "you can have a copy. The two white ones are for my records and I'm supposed to send the green one back. Guess that's how the military does things. But I don't need two copies for my records."

"Thanks." I stuffed it in my shirt. "So what did you two talk about?"

"His life. His accomplishments. War and peace. He asked me if I wanted to see pictures of his grandchildren. So I said 'sure' and he kept showing me photographs of people he killed in Vietnam. Carries them in his wallet. And gives them names."

"Gives them names?"

"Yeah, he really does. In fact, he named two of them Claude right before my eyes, come to think of it. Claude One and Claude Two. And the others were Hewey, Dewey, and Lewey. Yeah, it was righteous weird, now that I think about it. Called them his 'personal art collection' and his 'poor sick puppies' and his 'native high points' and his 'Tullamore Dew.'"

"Sounds like Rinkowski was quite a sport," I said amiably. "And so his photography collection was a friendly accompaniment to your Japanese beer?"

"It was like that. And he told me about the war, like I said."

"What did he tell you?"

"That he didn't miss the food, mostly."

"What did you think of the photographs?"

"I thought they were kind of sick. But what can I say? Not my idea of entertainment, but whatever you're into is cool, I guess." Elb was trying, with small success, to sound nonchalant. "He seemed pretty happy with his gig. Weird thing was, he kept singing advertising jingles and telling me if I ever wanted to take up his hobby, he'd show me how, bring me on board like the fine young man I was," Elb was calling attention to his non-military issue attire here, "and call me his son. I told him I wasn't the army type, you know, but it was nice of him to ask, in a way." Elb said the latter like he was trying to boast of himself being a damnably understanding guy, all told. He could appreciate a generous compliment, no matter where it came from.

"And how did he take your cold rejection?" I needled.

Elb looked vaguely alarmed by my word choice. "He was cool about it. Said he had some things in his back room I could practice on if I wanted to try. But I really wasn't into that scene, if you know what I mean."

"Things to practice on? Photography or killing?"

"I wasn't sure. That part was really weird. I wasn't too sure what he meant. The colonel was friendly about it and everything, and seemed so friendly through the whole thing I really didn't notice it too much, but"—Elb paused and made brief eye contact—"he really wasn't right." Then he tried to jerkily shrug it off. "Well, I guess some people get like that after a while."

"Get like what?" I prodded.

"Used up, if you know what I mean. More weirded out than just plain weird. Like the guy only had one bit of oddness for his life, and would play and play that bit forever. You got the feeling if he wasn't dead he'd be showing the same photographs for a hundred years. He was like flat with it. Friendly, but flat. You know?"

I didn't know, so I asked him about Hopner's fairy tale life, intimating that Jade had told me much more than he actually had.

"Yeah, he's into a lot of things," he agreed, suddenly seeming easier with the change of subject. "Uncle Claude's a busy guy."

"So he's your uncle? You've met?"

"No, I just call him that. But we might have met," he added hopefully. "I've talked to a few people on the phone who might be him."

"Don't you know?"

"Well, Claude's sort of a mystery man. He doesn't seem to like you to know."

"Know if it's him?"

"Know if he's your uncle or not."

"Hmm," I said noncommittally, "that's a different kind of hobby."

Elb hesitated, then affected a "super-mature" nonchalance. "So I figure who he is his business. I don't really care. His gigs pay so why push it, you know?" He sniffed a little. "I think he's French."

"His last name doesn't sound French."

"It doesn't have to with Claude. Besides, it's only his last name this week."

"What was his last name last week?"

"Didn't talk to him last week. Look, he usually doesn't have a last name. It's mostly just Claude. Or Cloud."

"Mr. Cloud sounds like a real prize. I'd like to know him. How do you get a hold of him?"

"You basically don't. He calls me through my mother."

"So your mother knows him?"

"I don't know. She might. It's hard to say with my mother." He looked visibly agitated, so I shifted the subject.

"Does anyone know him? Does he have a job? Like a real person?"

"Look, I don't know if he's ever like a real person." Elb was struggling with my horribly skewed perspective here. It was beyond his energy and ability to explain Claude to someone as dull as me.

"Is he real?" I pushed, "Or are you just having fun with it?"

"Well, you can have fun with it," said Elb uncertainly. "But not all that much. I don't know if I'm having fun. His money is real. If Claude calls through a gig, the check comes. That's all I care about."

"Who signs the check?"

"It depends. Sometimes it's a bank check. Sometimes the club owner. If there is one."

"If there is one?"

"Well, sometimes there might not be a club."

"But you still get paid?" I was understandably confused so I pushed him for an explanation but all I could get from him was that Claude, or Cloud, occasionally dropped a dime and said, "Play at such and such a place at such and such a time," and the band would go play and Elb would mention Claude's name of the week and the money would be there.

"Does he pay you a lot?"

"It depends on the gig." He hesitated and then lectured defensively, "Look, sometimes the gig can be at two a.m. on a Scarborough cliff overlooking Lake Ontario, or in a hay field near the city, or after hours near the lion pit of the Toronto Zoo. Then money shows up in the mail," his voice dropped off into a mumble, "or in my boot or under my pillow or something."

"Old Cloud there seems to be a regular tooth fairy."

"Yeah," said Elb, suddenly more animated, "that's a good way to put it. He's like the tooth fairy. When he's regular."

He's like the tooth fairy.

I tried to look serious and considerate while I imagined throwing that one down in my report. "So, Elb," I continued in a terribly friendly, paternal sounding voice, "your Uncle Claude gets you gigs and everything, but you tell me you've only been with the band a few weeks. How does that work?"

"Oh, I've been with the band longer. Met Les and Marty last winter in a club when they were with another band. Then Xander came in last March and the three of them hooked up. They've been around."

"So your cousin's new?"

"Yes and no. They needed a bass player and Jade knew my sister. But he also knew Xander. They used to play together a long time ago. They've all been around the scene."

"And Claude called you before Jade got involved?"

"Sure," he said doubtfully.

"When did he call in this one?"

"About two weeks ago."

"Well," I said, "since you have a voucher, perhaps you won't find the money in your boot this time."

He grinned sheepishly, "That part's really my mother. Sometimes the money comes addressed to her and she gets it in the mail and sticks it someplace where I'm sure to find it."

"You mean he calls you through your mom?" I asked this slowly, as if I still needed clarification on the matter, which of course I did.

"Not exactly. My mom might break open a bone and make the phone ring first, and then it might be him. Or it might be my sister Cara who just moved upstairs calling down to whine about something." I could tell he wasn't overly fond of his sister, despite her generous birthday gift.

"So your mom might break open a bone and make the phone ring," I remarked casually, as if I actually understood what the hell he was talking about.

"Sort of. You kind of have to be there."

Probably true, but I bravely pushed on for whatever use or fun it might be worth. "I seem to remember playing that trick when I was a kid," I softly reminisced. "But I used to make the phone ring by dialing the first six digits of my own number and hanging up while the seventh was in progress. Never thought to use a bone."

"Well, like a chicken bone—a wish bone or something." He held his shoulders stiffly and defensively. "I don't know what she does with the bone." He apparently thought I was criticizing his ignorance.

"So what does your mom do in general?"

"I don't know."

"You don't know?"

"She does whatever she can get away with. It's hard to explain my mother to people." He squirmed around as if he was on the point of breaking down here and suddenly wished he were off in the van with his friends.

"Why don't you try? I'm pretty good with explanations."

Elb made resentful eye contact. "My mom's sort of like a witch. OK?"

Sort of like a witch.

It was all quite a rap, and some of it was nearly as entertaining as Jade's colorful ramble, but the bottom line was that I had to let them go, because technically I had no legal grounds to detain them. And much as I would have enjoyed Elb's company and creative insights for a while longer, without a warrant and without having seen him do anything, I couldn't arrest him or stop him from returning to his native land. So I told him I wished him and the band luck, and he gave me his address and phone number in case I had any more questions. Then he promised to call me if he learned anything. Right. He left quickly through the darkness and I heard a van door open and slam close with a good deal of energy and the engine immediately start up and the vehicle tear out of the place at top speed, despite the precious paint job. And so they all left for Canada with the Constitution's blessings.

Next spot of weird tea. After Black Dog left and the police removed the body, I actually had a modestly inspiring bit of gab with Colonel Rinkowski himself, death apparently being no issue to a pair of newly bonded cronies like us. After sweet talking the lieutenant who originally introduced us into opening the commander's office and the personnel files to me at one a.m., which wasn't hard once I flashed I my badge and told him ambiguously that it was "regulation" to give me access, I learned that Rinkowski was the name of the colonel who had left the base two weeks ago and was now stationed at Fort Shafter, near Honolulu. I also learned there was no file on Hopner and no file on any new commander.

So I called Fort Shafter to offer my condolences, figuring that Rinkowski might be waiting for some official confirmation of his own death, and that if he lived on the base and I threw enough authority around, I might be able to catch him at home. It was one-fifteen a.m. here so it would only be seven-fifteen p.m. there. He was at home, and as I worked through channels to get him on the line, I felt the silence of the northern woods crowding around me and the oddness of the hour filling someone else's workspace felt like a foreign silence. And I suddenly found myself playing with the idea that I was "something like a witch." After all, I was literally speaking backwards through time, which I supposed was an approved method of ringing up the dead from the Isle of the Blessed halfway around the planet. And I was doing so on someone else's phone bill so I wouldn't have to make whatever information I gathered official if I didn't want to. Did I like dragons? I supposed Circe herself never had it this easy.

So when Rinkowski got on the line, I introduced myself and figured the least I could do was ask him how he was feeling. Fine, he told me. Was in the middle of a late dinner. Stuffed fish.

"Good choice," I said heartily. Then I told him there was a routine drug investigation going on and asked him if he knew Private Hopner. No, he didn't. Didn't even remember the name, but then he didn't make it his business to fraternize with the troops. Didn't know anything about his replacement either. They change leaders every six weeks or so in Rome. That was Rome, wasn't it? Up in the woods but close enough. People supervise exercises there for a few weeks and then move back to their original post. Not really a base anymore. Getting phased out soon.

"How's your cousin?" What cousin? "The fundraiser." None of his cousins were fundraisers for anybody, as far as he knew. And no, he didn't call the FBI from Hawaii to go to Rome. Was he supposed to? he asked anxiously. Did I have him confused with somebody else?

"Probably." I hung up and questioned the lieutenant. "Didn't you introduce the new commander to me as Rinkowski?"

"Yes, sir."

"Why?"

"Orders, sir. That's what he wanted to be called."

"What's his real name?"

"Nobody knows."

"What did he do here?"

The lieutenant hesitated. "He got killed here, sir."

"I mean, what kind of work was he involved in here?"

"Nobody knows."

"Why isn't there any personnel record on him?"

"I didn't know there wasn't. I never looked."

"What sort of exercises was he brought in to supervise?"

"The usual. Target shooting, hiking, wilderness survival. But he doesn't supervise. Troops don't spend a lot of time on the base. Usually out in the woods."

"So it was unusual for the troops to gather in the club tonight?"

"Yes. But not unusual between exercises. There is a long-standing order from a past commander that no one has countermanded. Every other week is mandatory recreation night from hiking and camping. Everyone has to be there."

Mandatory recreation. From hiking and camping. Only the military could come up with such an oxymoron. Twice over. "I see. So who supervises the exercises?"

"Captain Crillio. But he goes away for man-rec. He's visiting his family on Long Island today. But you could phone him. He is on twenty-four-hour call while he's gone."

"So, what does the commander do when everyone is off hiking?"

"Nobody knows. Someone said he thought he was moving things and refurnishing the guest house. I guess he's just supposed to be here."

"Doesn't that strike you as unusual?" I looked in his blank military-issue face before I realized the absurdity of my question.

"No, sir. Nobody does anything here. It's phase-out."

So I took advantage of Crillio being on twenty-four-hour call, looked up his file, and dialed his home number. I woke him up, naturally enough, and after his voice firmed into coherency and I heard his wife yell at him to take it in the other room, and he dutifully and clumsily changed phones, he told me he had no idea the commander had been replaced, because he'd been out on "camping maneuvers" for two weeks, but that wasn't unusual. Things were like that during phase-out. And he had no idea what the last commander or the one before that did, either. They all just came and went. It wasn't his job to know. But they did pass "some kind of" inspection last spring. Never heard of Hopner. Black Dog? Never heard of them, either, but they were always bringing in bands for mandatory recreation lately. He thought that was the commander's job and that I might ask him about it. Man-rec was really sort of a PR thing and they sometimes let the local civilians and kids come for free. Usually brought in military bands though. Or magicians. Or clowns.

Or clowns.

The only thing I kept getting was that no one knew Hopner and no one knew the now nameless corpse. And the corpse himself hadn't known why I was called onto the base either, because I remember having to explain it to him. So I wasn't even sure now who placed the call. But something was definitely "righteous weird" as Elb would have said.

When in doubt consider the Mob. At the moment, the Mob was a possibility for thought, not action, because I knew firsthand that when it came to killing, the Nunzio family, at least, didn't usually dick around with the fancy stuff. If they had to whack someone, they just blew the guy's head off and left the pieces where they fell. But the Nunzios weren't as trigger-happy as some other families, so many of the elders having gone semi-legit and everything. It may have been local Mob, which probably wasn't quite so couth. But I kept thinking that it had to take some time and thought to work up the body like that, and, when all's said and done, the new Mob is a fairly thoughtless crew; the underlings are kind of like us government workers in that they don't get paid to think much in the first place.

But I couldn't rule out a mob killing, because other than the phone invitation via Fearless and the art-school-student-on-a-bender style of the thing, it was a stealthy, efficient, professional looking affair. But if it was the Mob I had no fix on the point, if there was a point, which was getting more and more doubtful. Maybe the corpse's cousin was the fundraiser. Maybe the corpse was the fundraiser, and there was some kind of mafia-politico stuff going on that would be terribly exciting for the mayor's opponent to leak to the press and terribly awkward for Fearless to have me make an issue out of. Or maybe the corpse was Hopner, for all anybody seemed to really know. I had asked the morgue to send the autopsy report to me directly, and that, of course, would tell me more, but for now I could only guess with what little I had.

Lies, dreams, stories, surprises and someone dead at the bar without head or heart or anything else that used to live.

And forget motive. No one I talked to knew the new commander well enough to have a motive. Hell, no one knew him. And I couldn't figure out why a commander who wasn't a commander, who wasn't anybody anybody really knew, would call in the FBI to investigate a private that nobody except some wannabe manager of a rock and roll band seemed to know—and he didn't really "know" him. That is, if the corpse did make the call. Which I now doubted. Yet somebody clearly wanted the feds involved in this one.

Which was the only part that sort of made sense, because if there's absurdities to invest in, you can do worse than call in the government for broker advice. Me, I just like to think about absurdities until my mind bends into them and they begin to make sense, but the government pretty much buys stock in them. And hoards them up for years until they grow into task forces.

Maybe Jade was right. Maybe none of this was real. So far, no one with any definable claim to existence had been killed and no one who lived too close to reality had been implicated. It all promised to be a fine case. I couldn't wait to get cracking.

So I spent the night on the base, cradled in the odd wilderness north of Rome, the funny upstate New York farmy-woodland that still feels like 1976 and probably always will. I went into the guest house without asking permission, planning to nap a little for a few hours in the predawn in order to refresh myself for the coming day. And of course I took full advantage of this generously assumed hospitality by subtly ransacking the rooms, looking for the back room where Elb might have found things to photograph or kill, he wasn't sure which, and found that the place was pretty much empty. The only argument for furniture was an old couch that stank horribly of must and rain rot. There was a black and white TV running a test pattern on the living room floor. I turned it off. The ensuing silence had an odor of dwindled corruption. Maybe dust lived here, or old ceiling rats, for one or two rat corpses fell from a hole in the ceiling. They were plump and eerie looking and had shut up little faces like dried up babies and a silly thought occurred to me that maybe they had now been reborn as rat babies somewhere. I found two empty beer bottles on a shelf, a piece of rotten apple shimmering and pulsing with ants, and a super large, unopened container of Boraxo Powdered Soap—the Better Way To Remove (last word scratched out—"Dirt," probably). *Remove the word, remove the object?* I found myself idly thinking, and then idly wondering when I'd thought that before. Wasn't that magical thinking I once heard in a mythology class? My night ramble with Jade was really pulling up the old useless perfection of my early book learning. Well, magic or not, it didn't work here because the place was filthy. No phone. Small kitchen with cabinets stuffed with crumpled yellow newspapers. Sink covered with wire mesh. I raised the mesh and saw a large, black, coiled snake. I think it was dead, for it had that dry dead reptile smell about it. There was moldy cheese and a nest of dead rats in the refrigerator. The freezer had a dead sparrow in a baggie and half a green popsicle in paper stiff with frost.

Refurnishing the guest house. Did anyone even live here? The place had been phased out into something uninhabitable.

So I wasn't about to make myself at home. I went back to my car to nap a little and found another freakin' parking ticket on the windshield, swore at the moon because it was there to be sworn at, and crawled into my back seat to sleep a little.

And I slept, because I had a weird dream of old dragons like black snakes crying in undersea caves. And I kept walking by a tall painted boulder jutting out of the sea, because I wanted to get treasure by drowning myself in an underwater palace and somehow Jade was sitting on the boulder and wouldn't let me drown until he told me yet another story. And waves rough with fish kept coming and it was a smooth, rainy sort of dream that led seamlessly into waking with the early sun smearing warm rivers of bright-morning-in-a-strange-place across my eyelids like thick paint.

But the dream also led to me thinking about Jade all day, or intensified my memories of our conversation. Phrases from the previous night kept falling into my workday when I wasn't paying enough attention to keep them out. And even when I was paying attention, and acutely aware that several of my maneuvers were clearly illegal, and mulling over how best to fudge them in my eventual explanations so that what little evidence I had would still "count," I kept thinking about him asking me "how I felt" about breaking the law. And then I'd just catch myself—well, feeling more energetic than normal, walking faster into a barracks or talking more animatedly when questioning someone, before recalling that nothing fundamental had really changed in my life, and that the field office was still reality.

I didn't find myself liking him so much as liking the period of time that passed between us and wishing that I could carry that feeling with me, or wishing that I could have a sensible life passed in casual remarks about dragons and myth. Black Dog's bass player made me feel like something out of myth, after I had recognized him as such, and it was a novel, exciting feeling to be humanly recognized as someone beyond my usual self.

Did I like dragons? the refrain in my head kept going. *Of course. Knew all about them. Just ask the bass player. He'll tell you all about it.*

I had a fine breakfast of lumpy Farina in a makeshift dining area near the now cordoned-off club house, which they made me pay for. And things around the homestead seemed to go on as usual, *sans* commander. This was the second day "between exercises," when more fences got whitewashed and more housekeeping got done until Crillio returned, so I pretty much killed the day waiting for the autopsy report, going over the grounds, talking to more people about absolutely nothing relevant, going through the personnel files again, and generally collecting everything I could before reporting the business to Fearless and giving my colleagues an opportunity to play havoc with havoc. But I fell into another bit of weirdness while traipsing through the files.

I still had the silly notion of getting my parking tickets cleared, and talking to the MP who was wandering around loose last night leaving them had a lot of merit, in case he had noticed anything relevant to Rinkowski's final club appearance. So I picked up the phone and dialed the extension for the base guards. Learned there was one base guard. Period. But he came willingly to see me. Knew nothing about tickets. Didn't have enough cars during phase-out to issue tickets, parking was pretty much open. He was in the club for man-rec all evening and then in the barracks. And I knew the first part was true, for I remembered seeing him in the club, and I was later able to confirm the latter. So I showed him the tickets and asked what I should do with them. He didn't know. He didn't even recognize them.

After he left, I noticed I had taken out the carbon copy of the voucher Elb had given me along with the tickets and all three documents were lying in front of me. And this was all quite fascinating. Because the signature on the voucher was H. M. Rinkowski, Base Commander. He had also written in a description of services rendered—musical entertainment. The signature on the first ticket, issued at 9:08 p.m. when I was still in the club, was also H. M. Rinkowski, and the written description of my "violation" matched the writing on the voucher. So the living corpse had doled out parking tickets for fun and grins shortly before his death. Good deal, I thought, justice works. But there was more. The second ticket, which had been issued at three-thirty a.m., was also signed in the same handwriting, long after the ersatz commander was dead. And now he was using the name Hugh McCrae Rinkowski. McCrae as in Elb P.? Naah, no relation—just an easy coincidence. What the hell was going on?

I figured since I was clearly in charge anyway I could leak things to Fearless as I saw fit and the tickets and such were mine to keep mum about. I was really getting too hooked on the whole bizarre business to want to share.

So I hung around and finally, around six p.m., the autopsy report was hand delivered. And it was a beauty. The corpse had no I.D. In fact, the corpse had nothing but a wallet full of war pictures and a bent Canadian dime. In summary, I learned the following.

Cause of death: Obvious.

Subject rapidly decomposed on table. Subject had been chemically treated with a compound that no one could analyze but which rapidly decomposed body tissues. Same chemical found in nearby glass. Brain removed and replaced by a live mouse. Mouse had a pink ribbon around its neck and the ribbon was attached to one of those computerized greeting cards that play "Happy Birthday" when you open it. And inside the card was a pair of old ticket stubs to a Grateful Dead concert, dated September 17, 1978 at the Great Pyramid, "deep in the season of apricots." (Be there or be square, I suppose). There was a deep cut in the inside left thigh from which a quantity of fat had been removed and in which someone had placed an old-fashioned green Coke bottle still containing brown sludgy syrup and a note which read, "Coca Cola vintage 1929, drink of generations. Eternal youth and eternal fun." The trout had been poisoned in sugar water. Its stomach contained a cheap little child's ring with a red stone in a red and yellow plastic bubble, the kind you get out of a bubble gum machine, and inside the bubble was also a circular strip of paper which read, "eat well, fishie ☠ worms are free and don't you know that every act is an act of love" The last "e" in love was the first "e" eat and so on the phrase read into infinity. The bottom of the left foot was freshly tattooed with the title of a Rolling Stones song, "Dancing with Mr. D."

The guy who delivered the report asked me what I wanted to do.

Much to his credit, he didn't seem to expect an immediate answer. So I told him with great officiousness that I was in charge of the case and would make my report in Boston. In the meantime, I wanted to go back with him to get a first-hand look at the evidence. And so, paying my last respects to phase-out, I followed him down to Rome without anyone seeming to notice my departure.

All right, Rome. There's still more weirdness coming.

The morgue wasn't weird. They made me wait around for two hours for the sake of waiting around, but the morgue was a normal morgue, with nothing of the old phase-out about it, except that the "subject" was now all dust in a bag. The caretakers handed over the little sealed baggie of all the personal goodies, minus the mouse, and wished me luck.

Since it was getting on to nine p.m. and I hadn't eaten dinner and I could charge it up to the field office, I decided that I might as well dine at my pleasure. So I looked up the Thai restaurant Elb had eaten in on the previous night, thinking it might be a kick to see where he hung out.

And the restaurant was one of those deceptively classy places that look small and economical on the outside but are bristling with taste on the inside. White tablecloths and silver and fresh flowers proclaimed that the place was being defiantly upscale in this small upstate town. A "we'll class ourselves right out of business if we have to" kind of affair. The tables were yuppie "authentic" with bright eating mats on the floor and huge Thai statues peering into your plate and there was even a Buddhist altar in the back for a touch of the home country. I hoped the food was good.

But the place might have been closed, for there was absolutely no one to greet me or take my order, and so I walked around inspecting the artwork, and my attention was immediately arrested by a painting of a large Indian elephant. The elephant was covered with elaborately painted Thai figures in conical caps, and the hand printed sign below said they represented twenty-four minor divinities. The elephant's trunk curved into the body of an exotic snake, known as a *naga*. *Nagas* live by water, informed the sign, although I didn't see any water in the painting. I was struck by the heavy, baby fat, chunky stillness of the elephant, by the two dozen deities frozen and flattened to his sides and back like war trophies, and by the litheness of the snake his trunk was always imperceptibly becoming. And then I read with an involuntary clutch that the *naga* was a kind of dragon. Then I realized I was thinking of Jade again and suddenly thought it would be pleasant to hear one of his lies in a place like this. Something told me he'd make the snake *and* the elephant come to life. And then I realized I hadn't really come here for any good reason except that Elb had been here and Elb was maybe Jade's cousin, and it was like a last link to the band or something, and I began to feel a little silly. I had no business here, really, it wasn't my style of place. I clearly had a lonely life. One comfortable conversation, no doubt already forgotten by one of us, and I found myself so starved for companionship that I was feeding myself off the leavings of mass-produced Thai art.

Suddenly a waitress emerged out of the back kitchen and shyly asked me if I needed help. She was a teenager whose English wasn't wonderful, but after she told me I could sit anywhere I wanted and I ordered something called *talay tong*, which turned out to be a spicy seafood specialty, I managed to learn from her that she did remember Elb. The past two nights had been slow, and Elb's flamboyant appearance made him rather noticeable. "The man with the—" she ran her hand over her straight dark hair to indicate his bright blond dreadlocks. I nodded. "Yes, he was funny," she pointed out the table he sat at. "Is he friend of yours? Are you supposed to meet?" she asked.

"He's sort of like a friend."

She smiled. "He also order *talay tong*. And silver soup. Very religious. He was kneeling at altar and lighting all incense. We had to buy more today." She said this like she was trying to be polite concerning my friend but didn't want me to bust the incense budget like he did. I assured her that I wouldn't. "He was with NPA? You know him?"

"Sure," I lied. "What's the NPA?"

She glanced over at the bar and smiled merrily and inquisitively at a sullen bartender who wasn't there before, but was unmistakably there now, a huge, angry looking mass resentfully taking in our conversation with folded arms. "Neighborhood Protection Association," he yelled, like he didn't want her wasting time in chatter, even if there weren't any other customers in the place and I wasn't in any particular hurry to eat. "Tell him we already gave." He started shoving glasses around and she smiled nervously and returned to the kitchen, quickly re-emerging to sit near the door and smoke a cigarette.

"How much did you give?" I yelled back to the bartender. "Gotta keep the records straight."

He was still shoving glasses around. "We gave. Ask Nick. He was here."

"Hey, you mean Nick came in with my friend?" I asked the waitress.

"Yeah, he got his money," the bartender yelled. "Should be no problems."

"Yeah, but I gotta know how much," I insisted.

"Then ask Nick how much," the friendly guy went off to the kitchen. I called the waitress over.

"Why do you pay the NPA?"

"For protection. To make no problems. To get deliveries. To get parking lot plowed in winter." Just as I thought. Strictly Mob. Classically Mob. Obviously right down the line Mob. And old Elb there was dining in high style with one of their gophers when the murder happened. Better and better.

"Did you hear anything they talked about?"

"No, I don't remember what they talked. Nick the man left early and then your friend danced over and lit up all the incense." Of course she remembered the incense.

"He *danced* over?"

"Well," she smiled shyly, afraid she got the English wrong, "I mean he was very happy about something."

Like I said, the whole thing was a doozie. So I ate and paid and gave her my card, signing the back, "To Nick, best regards, Pete" and penciling in a little fire-breathing *naga* for fun and confusion.

All right, home. My thoughts kept driving me like a suicide out of hell, so I earned myself a speeding ticket near Pittsfield.

"Where you going?" The cop opened with the usual irrelevancy.

"FBI. Boston Field Office. Important matter." I flashed him a card and told him I was investigating a case. I know the protocol is to use the badge, but I had a few cards ready to hand in my shirt pocket and the damn seatbelt laws kind of squashed my enthusiasm for squirming around and digging out my wallet. I really wanted to get home and hit the sack. Wake up by afternoon and take a fresh angle on all the night's weirdness before going back to work.

It took him five minutes to read it. He paced around his car and pursed his lips and tried to make out the printing where he thought I wouldn't notice. Then he got on his radio for about ten more minutes. Then he made his way back. "You with the state?" he demanded.

"Only in the generic sense."

"What?"

"Yes."

"What's your name?"

"It's on the card." Why do I always get held up by the ones that make me think? I mean, it's not like a *majority* of Massachusetts cops can't read. You'd think the law of averages would dictate that I wouldn't always have to deal with the bottom twenty percent.

"Yeah, but what's your name? You have to tell me."

"Why?"

"You have to tell me your name," he repeated with all the warm conviction of a toll booth attendant demanding fifty cents.

"Uh, Sidney Crensch."

He scanned the card again. "Yeah, but your card here says Peter C. Morrow."

"So why'd you ask?"

He promptly returned to the safety of his radio. Thirty seconds later he was back. I was slightly surprised that he didn't get lost on the way. "OK. This isn't a license." He handed back the card like he had just caught me trying to pull a tricky maneuver on him.

"Really? Nooo. Are you putting me on?" I looked shocked and dumbfounded and embarrassed and chagrined all at once. Then I studied the card closely and made him wait as I slowly mouthed every word on it, including the field office's zip code, as if I were just a tad more literate than he was. Then I looked up and said with all the conviction of a religious revelation, "Huh. You're right. It's not a license." I tucked the card back in my shirt pocket. "Does that mean I can go, officer?" I asked sweetly.

He looked annoyed. Not at my slow reading, which he seemed to instinctively appreciate, but at my use of his title. "The station said there's no FBI office in this part of the state."

"The station is right."

"I need to see a license and registration. You been drinkin'?"

"Yes. Coffee." I handed him my papers. He didn't look at them. He was staring in amazement down the Mass Pike at a convoy of three tractor trailers hauling away at about seventy-five miles per hour. "Am I interrupting something?" I asked politely.

But he was already off to his radio. Never mind the blessed trucks. Ten minutes later a backup unit pulled up behind me with two more cops inside. And I sat there waiting while the three of them went through some arcane ritual in their separate cars before they approached me again en masse. "All right," said the first cop. "Get out. Slow. Hands on the car."

I suddenly, for a brief moment of insanity, wished I was Sidney Crensch, Uzi and all, but I followed orders like a good little citizen while one of the cops frisked me. "You got a gun," he breathed in amazement when he found my piece. "What's it for?"

"Shooting people," I said blandly, as the officer gingerly removed my 10mm semi-auto Smith & Wesson from its holster.

"Who'd ja shoot?" he asked with some excitement. I couldn't tell if he was happy or what.

"People who threaten cops." I said this slowly and thoughtfully, in a Clint Eastwood kind of voice, gazing into the distance for effect, like I was the great champion of law enforcement. My colleagues were absolutely thrown by the sentiment.

"You do that a lot?" one of them finally asked, somewhat awed.

"Only at work."

"What do you do for work?"

"I'm a cop." I had been waiting to wow them with this, of course. But I had miscalculated the effect. Now they were assiduously underwhelmed.

"Impersonating an officer?" one of the newcomers asked the first cop, just to be clear about things.

"He says he's been drinking," said the one who first pulled me over. "Name on license and registration don't match up."

"Car's registered to the field office," I tried to explain, but nobody wanted to get caught listening to a "suspect" in front of the others.

"Could be a stolen vehicle," the cop smoothly continued. "Computer's down to check. Caught him speeding."

"How fast was he going?"

"Don't know."

"Then how do you know I was speeding?" I asked reasonably, to no avail.

"Give him the breathalyzer." They clearly didn't know what else to do. When in doubt, Massachusetts cops generally haul out the old breathalyzer. As the first cop went to his car to get the thing, one of the others ordered me gruffly, "You got a license for this." He probably meant to use a rising inflection somewhere, but it didn't come out that way.

"Wallet's in my back pocket." The cop relieved me of my wallet and started flipping through my credit cards and stuff. "Hey, he's FBI. Boston. All right," he said with annoyance, "So you really are a cop. What are you doing here at one forty-five in the morning?"

I dropped my hands and turned around. "Slumming."

They handed back all my stuff and had a quick "how to save face" discussion while I was putting myself back together.

"Sixty-five sound fair?" one of them asked me as I was opening my car door to leave. I didn't understand the question, but it sounded like he was trying offer me some kind of deal.

"Fair for what?"

"Driving out of your jurisdiction at such a late hour and forcing us to waste our time." I didn't feel like explaining that the entire country was my "jurisdiction." I only wanted to get home. "We'll say you were only doing sixty-five."

For some reason I suddenly wished that I knew how to conjure dragons, because the image of three Keystone Cops running away from a fire breathing dragon amused me. But instead I got another ticket, which it took all three of them fifteen minutes of combined effort to fill out. And all the way home, in the midst of my other pressing concerns, and this part was really weird—I kept wishing that Jade had been there. He struck me as someone interesting to share this sort of experience with, someone who would have lightly appreciated the context of me breaking the law, or something.

When I finally pulled into my driveway, it was the dim side of a summer dawn. I thought briefly about going to work after all, because I knew I would be expected, but I let the thought pass without much effort. I was really too tired and caffeine poisoned to sleep or think about anything much. So I disconnected the phones to avoid Fearless's dutifully disruptive wake-up calls and stripped out of my clothes and lay uneasily on my bed and stared quaint images into the ceiling. Outside the birds were screaming to greet the morning in my woods while inside, deep inside, my thoughts went vague and high and distant and slowly began to cave under the caffeine. And then it was myself caving and I slept, finally, into a strange long dream.

And here be dragons, as the old maps used to say. For somehow I was wandering in the woods that protect most of my seven-acre property from my annual ambition to landscape, and forgetting that I wasn't really there. The air was turning murky and cold, so I wanted to wrap myself in a childhood blanket that I hadn't seen or thought of in twenty-five years, when my foot struck something hard and long like a dead log, and I fell onto a thick, black, reptilian tail mottled with bright yellow flecks. The tail rattled convulsively along my ankles and along the hard ground as I instinctively grabbed it to push myself up and a huge dragon rose out of the underbrush and shrieked and fluttered its wings like a scared grouse, suddenly carrying me into the panic of its flight. And as I lurched forward on the tail for balance, we were already clearing the tree line and I began to understand that I was dreaming because my surroundings felt heavy and stiff like a dream. But I also began to understand that I was now fully captured by this dream and that I couldn't control what was happening.

Unlike Icarus, my old friend from Greek myth, I did not sail too high and melt my homemade wings to sunny destruction. But I did ride on the dragon's tail, which was now a shiny, shimmering green and beautifully tacked up in bright Thai saddle cushions and fluttering Chinese ribbons like strips of dull cloudy rainbows. The flight was bouncy and uneven and the tail kept punching dark holes in the pale sky, and so we only got as far as a field of cows belonging to an old widow on a nearby hill. The field was square and tilted in our flight pattern, and the cows lay scattered on the ground like random benches inviting lonely trespassers to take their ease before the incoming August storm.

I could see the neighboring spires of Southbridge as echoes in the distant summer haze, and then the torrid gray around us exploded upwards into a thundercloud spewing rain like fire. And we were dropping hard and dizzy out of the thundercloud and spinning in wild helpless circles in all the rain, and a wind that killed with cold kept bearing us down as the dragon fought upwards against it to gain the warmth of the cloud. I was godawful airsick and clutched against his tail, which was now dull and wet and slippery and devoid of ornaments, and so I nearly spun off twice.

But the third slip was the real one, for then I did drop and the dragon flew elsewhere, leaving me grasping all the empty terror of being suddenly alone in the sky and falling fast with the desolate rain. There was now a hard green ocean rising to smack me but I missed the water and slammed instead into a clumsy mountain of sand.

And now lucidity becomes nightmare, for the mountain could not absorb my fall and so I kept falling through sand that buried my path for none to see. My falling kept making a horrifically secret tunnel to the base of the mountain where suffocation was certain while waves crashed somewhere in the heat of the startled earth below. Of course I was going to die. I was going to die breathless with mouth and eyes and ears and lungs of sand. And then I lay like a crumpled corpse, fetal positioned into a prehistoric cave burial down in the third stomach of the silent sand mountain, all red powder on my bones and soft clay impression with a wispy strand of seashells like a useless pacifier in my scarce fist. My neck and back wrenched painfully with an ugly, old sweat that the sand will forever refuse to absorb.

And to get out of the surprise of the trap, I need only stand up, stand out of the mountain, which was stifling me grain by grain by world-loads of grain, fall reeling out of bed, and answer the goddamned phone.

Which wasn't really ringing, because, as I said, I had disconnected it. It had only been ringing somewhere out of the whirling sand in my dream and somehow it woke me into standing out of the mountain without meaning to. But this did not prevent me from picking up the receiver and confusedly mumbling, "Hello" to the utter silence of disconnect before I was thoroughly aware of my life again. And then I just sat on my bed and stared at the corner of my dresser where the phone was and tried to gather in the dream. For I knew that the dream-dragon was my last shadow of a shadow's link with the spirit of that charming conversation of two nights ago, and I was loathe to leave it. Even if the dragon was now more my fancy than his creator's. And even if the conversation had been turned and prodded so much in my memory that my memory couldn't possibly be anything but a personal fantasy. No more substantial than Elb's expansive Uncle Claude.

But when I finally had to come awake and face the reality of the remaining work week and beyond that into the rest of my life, I felt an inexplicable depression, like there was a perpetual loss in my life that I'd always been draining through but never knew how to stop. Did I like dragons? Really? Jesus H. Christ, what a stupid, fucking pointless question. And here I was with nothing better to do than to sit stark naked on the edge of my bed at three-thirty on a Wednesday afternoon and stare at a dead telephone receiver and dredge out an answer. Grow up, Morrow, and get yourself a life that works.

I sat for a few terse minutes over the end of the feeling. The question closed, sailing down through foolishness and out into the safety of irrelevancy. Like a tortuous jaunt through a garden bedecked storybook world, a world so terrifyingly flimsy it deflowers in a horrifying burst of delicacy before your very thoughts. A never ever after.

I recovered. I let officious reality take the dragon business neatly out of sight and properly consign it to the flames that once shriveled my childhood wishes into old blisters of sanity. The dead flames. Of a dead mythology. Then I rose and showered away all the nonsense in my head and stoically prepared myself for work the next day. Put together a Mellie-type sandwich. Swiftly fell back into normal routine of hating my life.

Stave Four

Thursday, August 20, 1992.

The FBI occupies one of the ugliest buildings in Boston. The John F. Kennedy Building, which looks like a large white bone with windows and crumpled aluminum on the top, is, for my money, the most impressively designed monument to government waste this side of North Korea. Beyond impressive. I know I can't think of any suggestions for improvement, except maybe building three more. And then following the grand old tradition of giving them all away and buying them back again at three times the original cost of construction to make the loss positively spiritual. Because they really did a pretty good job with it, all told. They should really give out tours.

It's glorious, really. The low-rise is especially clever, and efficient in its own way, as it only takes about five minutes to bring on that eerie, back side of time sensation one normally has to wait six or eight hours for a delayed flight in an airport to achieve. And just like the Washington National Airport in late June, you can see a skeletal sun burning through the windows around four-thirty p.m. like a hole chattering ultraviolet nothings out of hell. It isn't a good sun. Sometimes it hisses at me as I escape for home.

The inside of the building is a bone, too, a governmental wonderland of hard-earned emptiness. It's mostly uninhabited. I know colleagues who get nervous traversing the place alone. Kanesh always rides the elevators with a safe little group. So does Fearless, although he likes to pretend he doesn't. Not that I hold it against them, since the building also shelters the IRS and the Immigration Disservice and the Being Human and Whatever people, and I tend to get nervous around those groups as well.

But as to going it alone in the elevators, I stopped giving a damn years ago and it probably shows so much in my general demeanor that the crazies who wander in from time to time think they recognize a brother and keep a respectful distance. And the ones who don't I just figure for an ex-congressman or an applicant or a local cop or something. And if I'm in plainclothes and in the right mood, I can usually have fun enticing some brave crime-fighting new hire who doesn't know me yet to nervously get off and wait for another ride.

We sit pretty up on the ninth floor in a thoughtfully inconvenient location behind a rather exotically arranged *Dragnet*-goes-yuppie-for-a-day type reception area. You walk through serious double glass doors, the kind that ought to introduce a badly written TV series and which decorously proclaim, "Federal Bureau of Investigation," in earnest letters on a dark logo. Very awe inspiring. Especially since the union had the logo stenciled in backwards for a few weeks until Marcie, our receptionist-secretary, made a comment about it to Fearless. Then they made us the Department of Energy for a day, because the stencil "had to be used up" and they had "somehow gotten ahold of one." Then they finally got the logo right and so everyone got something safe to fill their office chatter with and express a resoundingly empty approval for. Marcie bubbled about it for nearly a week.

Anyway, the reception area is supposed to make suspects and informants and drug lords feel homey and comfortable and all that so they believe they can drop in and talk to us like old friends, which many of them are. Tempt them over to our side by showing them a slice of the straight life in our fine decor. And so there was a silver tea service on one of the tables as a prop to pleasantries until somebody in the field office stole it. And the tables are all fake mahogany, like the kind of furniture one finds in one of the pretentiously better insurance offices, with soft subdued lamps that remind you of somebody's sick, rainy childhood out of the 1940s that somehow got thrown forward in time.

But the rest of the room doesn't throw me anywhere. There are also delicate vases and silk flowers decorating the tables, don't ask me why, and a large "Corinthian leather" couch dominating one wall. And the walls would put a mid-range hotel room to shame. Delicate blue paisley wallpaper with plush matching carpet and assembly-line crafted paintings too tastefully meaningless and abstract to offend or move anybody. All very chic. And then, square over the couch, stapled into the wallpaper, in the place of honor, are the most recent issue post office-style "ten most wanted" posters, just to cheerfully suggest a goal in life to some of our guests and to lend an air of professionalism to our work environment.

This week we have a special on gentlemen wanted for destruction of government property and on bank robbers. I have no idea why we just don't hire everybody and get it over with except efficiency isn't our strong suit. I mean what with guys like Crensch wrecking police cars and with traffic cops sticking me up for cash and social workers plotting the murder of innocent young girls and the union killing me with cancer and everybody's dollars getting robbed and squandered on great glaring structures of emptiness, what the hell? At least the criminals don't need special training for the work.

But anyway, I was rooting for the newcomer who'd been on the charts for about two weeks and was holding steady at number ten, a quixotic chap who dressed like an outlaw from the Old West and kept trying to rob empty freight trains with a Colt single action army. The kind of gun that was popular among outlaws before smokeless powder got invented and everybody threw theirs away. The guy's piece had to be worth anywhere between seven and ten grand. And he had to be reloading his own bullets with black powder to fire it, so he was putting a lot of work and energy into living his Jesse James fantasy. I wondered if he knew the trains were empty or if he was just making some kind of empty point. In either case, I silently wished him luck.

Marcie sits behind a little divider and mostly refuses to notice anybody. Unless she's flirting with one of the new guys or looking like a self-important duck as she waddles around behind Fearless with an "I'm privy to important secrets" set to her jaw. I used to think she was just as dull as everybody else in the field office, until I learned that Fearless got it straight from some handbook that most informants are more comfortable if they believe they are not being noticed or talked to. Which probably explains why so many of them want to bend your ear about their pathetic lives and personal problems for hours on end and seem to revel in the look of attention you give them. So he told her to look the other way when people enter and "make them feel alone." And she does. Better than one of those hokey one-way mirrors that pompous grocery store owners still think might fool people into stealing a strawberry and getting caught. The ten most wanted could easily open a referral service on our living room floor and Marcie would dutifully look the other way.

I whisked past the dutifully unobservant Marcie and turned into the hallway, toying with the idea of pretending I'd been in all day yesterday to see who I could fool. But the moment I went to work coughing down asbestos and composing a semi-believable report on my Roman adventure, Fearless darkened my office door and invited me down the hall to his place for a morning chat. So I grabbed my briefcase because things tend to disappear from the offices and for reasons that defy rationality, I was keeping my strange bag of lucky charms from the corpse with me. I stayed cheerful and buoyant. Fearless didn't even glance at the coffee machine and he closed his door all the way so I supposed there was more important stuff at hand than folks bumming their morning buzz and quarters. Then I noticed he had the *Boston Globe* spread out on his desk. "I'm not even going to ask, Morrow."

"All right," I said good naturedly enough, assuming he was making the requisite issue over yesterday's absence. "Then I won't have to bore you with an answer." I turned to go. "Is that all I need to know? Shall I leave the door open for you?"

He couldn't contain himself. "So aren't you going to tell me what the hell's going on?"

"Oh. Well. Since you are kind enough to *ask*, boss, I forgot to set my watch a day ahead and got the time screwed up. Happens when you cross the Atlantic. But I got a fearsome blessing from the Pope, so it should be all right—"

"What the hell is this?" He was waving the *Globe* at me.

"A newspaper?" I guessed.

Then he read. "Nameless man posing as a base commander found disemboweled at army wilderness camp near Rome. Body spontaneously decomposed at morgue." Then he catalogued all the bizarre objects found in the corpse, including the mouse. "'Objects now in the keeping of the FBI.' That you Morrow?"

"No, that's Crensch."

"Do you or don't you have the objects?"

"Well, not all of them. The mouse got away."

He continued reading. "Last commander, Gary R. Rinkowski, now stationed at Fort Shafter, Hawaii, has no comment except to say that he has already been questioned by a special federal investigator"—he broke from reading—"that you, Morrow?"

"I don't like to think of myself as special, boss, but yes, we talked."

"Camp in process of being phased out. Operations continuing as usual—"

"I can believe that. Nothing interferes with phase-out. It's the next best thing to God."

He threw down the paper, the effort of finishing the article apparently being too much for him. "I don't care for the wisecracks right now, Morrow. Where were you yesterday? Your phone was disconnected."

"I needed a sick day. The corpse was quite a sight, sir, as you can imagine."

"You saw the body then?" The question was a reprimand uttered in a tone of dismay.

"Found it. Look, boss, I was about to write up a full report for you." I really didn't want to reveal more than I had to, and writing would help me fix up the right kind of story to keep the right kind of people off my back.

"Think it was the Nunzios?" he asked slowly.

"Don't know yet. Could be. Anything's possible right now. Meant to ask you—the living Commander Rinkowski told me that none of his cousins are fundraisers. He also knew nothing about Private Claude Hopner and his drug deals and he told me he didn't make the call to us." Since Rinkowski's name was in the paper I saw no harm in revealing that much, as it would be easy to check and would serve to explain our telephone chat. "Do you have a name I can check out?"

"No." He shifted awkwardly. "The caller didn't give me his cousin's name. But he told me his cousin was well-connected in the political scene, and—" he looked like the subject or the ease with which he was swayed by politics and promotion embarrassed him, so I decided to help him out.

"Sure, and how could you know the guy wasn't who he said he was and why make enemies out of potential friends?" He looked less embarrassed. His foible was understood and forgiven. But the fact was, he thought he was sending me off on another do-nothing nonsense case and now I had a flashy bit of business to hot dog it on. And having been there first, he couldn't very well take me off the case. But now that there was press attention and all he was worried about attracting heat from the DSS groupies who tend to develop unhealthy obsessions about guys like me and write long letters of complaint to their representatives. Which, depending on the social trend of the season, could be a stumbling block to old Fearless's wish for advancement. "So." I tried to mollify and flatter him with a question, as if he were being included in my thoughts. "Do you think the caller was the imposter?"

"Could be." He flipped the back of his wrist in the air to indicate that he didn't really know. "But that doesn't really explain anything."

"No, it doesn't. But I was wondering if I could listen to the tape." The field office routinely records all incoming calls. "I spoke to the dead before he died, and I might be able to tell if it was him that placed the call."

"Morrow," he sighed, "I personally don't care what you listen to, and if you've got ideas I'd like to hear them. But I'd prefer it if you stayed officially off the case until further word. If it is Mob, the Nunzios are basically keeping Utica clean and the mayor won't be publicly blamed for a death on federal property outside the city. So let's not set a crime wave going to interfere with his run. And if it isn't Mob, we haven't been officially invited in to deal with a murder yet. Got a call from the Pentagon and the army ain't exactly overjoyed that we jumped on this business and the press got in it before they even knew what the hell was going on. General who oversees the camp thought it was all a practical joke when he first heard about it from a reporter and hung up on her. And now that the facts are coming out, he looks like a fool and the public is asking whether this is another military cover-up. It's an election year and issues like this become footballs and before you know it, we'll have Congress investigating this thing. And unless someone real asks us in, we've got no business with it." He leaned back nervously in his chair and sighed again. "Did you scare off the drug dealer?" It didn't occur to Fearless that if the colonel was a ruse the rest probably was too.

"I understand he's AWOL."

"Good. That part's done. Look, then we needn't bother to be too public with our investigation. Impersonating a commander is a military matter and the military is understandably embarrassed that a civilian could wander in and take a colonel's place with no one really noticing. But, again, that's not our problem. I learned yesterday that the real replacement never got his orders but that's taken care of now. Situation's normal in Rome."

"All right," I said, barely disguising my disappointment. "So what am I doing officially?"

Fearless dropped his eyes and sweated a little as if he wished to avoid my reaction. "I've got a missing pet scam for you," he mumbled.

"A what?"

"Some one's scouring the neighborhoods for posters advertising reward money for missing pets. Since most people include a photograph or description of the animal, it's pretty easy to claim to have found Rover or Felix, take the money, and run."

"Perhaps the local cops would like to get in on that one." The ambiguity of my statement went, as usual, right over Fearless's balding head.

"Well, the deal is a lot of the scam is a long-distance affair. Someone has his lackeys scout neighborhoods from Boston to Tampa collecting information. Then he calls from Texas or California claiming that he was in Boston yesterday and happened to find—fill in animal description of your choice. And of course he doesn't want a reward, but he can't afford to send Fido back on a plane, and the money would sure help pay for airfare. Please wire to—. And of course, Fido never shows. Or he finally shows up at a neighbor's but the money's already gone. It's interstate, it's phone lines, and it's ours."

I yawned. "Why not give it to Kanesh? He'd look great in a photograph with a stray dog and a recovered Social Security check."

"Because he's officially on drug duty."

"Drug duty," I said enthusiastically. "Sounds like a cool assignment." Fearless pretended to ignore me by dropping his eyes to the newspaper, which had a way of shifting the subject back to the murder.

"Of course, we can't really ignore this case," he said. "On the chance there's more developments. Or anyone should ask what we're doing."

"All right," I said, catching his drift. "So then *officially* who's on it? Just in case anybody asks."

"Crensch." Fearless spoke as if he didn't really want to say it.

"*Crensch?* Why?"

"Because you've got a rep. If you're on it, and it's Mob, the Nunzios will think we're out to nail them."

"Aren't we?" I forgot to remind him that, per instructions, if it was Mob, I had been passing my cards around the base enough to make my presence known anyway.

"You've got a history with the Nunzios, and if it's pure gangland nobody cares and why make problems for the mayor's run? Crensch is an unknown."

"I like the way you put that."

"He'll send a safe message. And he's spent enough time at the consulate to wear out his usefulness."

"And Crensch won't do much harm. And his father will keep Congress at a distance so no pol with shady connections need worry about discovery."

"Something like that. It's cosmetic, Morrow. I'm not ordering you off it, but understand you're not officially on it."

"Which means?"

"If you should *happen* to get ideas, fork them over." Fearless didn't care to elaborate. I was supposed to understand his message. I was not supposed to let on that I understood anything. But I happened to be in a more-than-usually understanding mood.

"Which means if I solve the case under the table, you won't stand in my way. And if it turns out to be politically expedient to solve the case, the arrest gets made and Crensch has to get the credit, because he's on it and Dad will be proud and able to make speeches about his family's fight against crime. And if there's a public outcry to do something, we can safely look like we're doing something without doing anything at all so no congressman need get embarrassed. And if I solve the case but it's not expedient to solve the case, we file the information for further reference and no one gets credit, except maybe the Mayor of Utica for lowering his city's crime rate. Gotcha," I said, as if I admired his perspicacity. "*Yes!*"

"Look, Morrow," he winced, "we all know you're a regular wizard when it comes to investigating the bizarre stuff, and you've gotten all the awards and recognition there is to get, but there's nothing wrong with sharing the glory for everybody's benefit. And besides, you might learn a few things from Crensch. He's sharp in his own way."

"Is he sharp enough to know I'm ghostwriting him?"

"No." Fearless smiled at my wit. "Look, I don't trust him to keep your involvement mum, and if it's Mob, it behooves us to keep your involvement mum. You and

I will know who really strikes gold and if there's gold to be struck, I've got faith you can do it. In the meantime, write up your report and *officially* I'll put you on . . ." Fearless chose his words carefully. "Drug law enforcement detail. But that's nominal. If anyone asks, you're really loaned out from drug duty to recovering cats and dogs."

"So no one in the field office has to know what the hell I'm really doing." That was the way I liked things, actually.

"That's the idea. Although you don't have to work too hard at making that one believable, if you know what I mean."

"Can I not work too hard at home?"

"You had enough vacation time this summer." He winced again. "Why don't you keep up a presence here for a while? A lot of the guys are beginning to envy your record for days off and looking for ways to compete. Which I don't need. Oh, and it would be a good idea if you turned over your stash for proper keeping. That is, if you're not busy with it. You'll still have access, of course."

So with a good deal of reluctance, I threw the goodie bag out of my briefcase, since the newspaper had accurately listed the contents anyway. I gravely wished him luck.

When I returned to the reception area, Marcie was talking about her date last weekend to one of the new hires, who seemed to be under the impression that politeness dictate he hang around and listen. Marcie never had much to say to the female agents, who understandably never had much to say to her either, but she always brightened up the guys' day by chattering about her dates and boyfriend problems. So I had to wait for her to finish boasting about how boring it was to date some loser from the Harvard Business School that just wanted to spend all his money on her to get laid before she could be bothered to interrupt herself for something as trivial as investigative work. I asked for the tape. "Sidney was listening to it yesterday," she told me in her officiously flirty way. "He'll probably want it back."

I closed the door of my fine office, coughed on the flying asbestos dust, and played it through the battery-operated tape recorder the government gives me to keep in my desk so it isn't too obvious and discomfiting when I take it out and plop it on the desktop to record conversations. The audio wasn't great, but I managed to transcribe the following.

"FBI," said Marcie's goody-two-shoes-aren't-I-cool-to-be-working-here phone voice, which irritated more the longer you worked with her.

A pause. Then, "Uh, yeah, right. This is Colonel Rinkowski, Rome Army Base. Like to speak to the supervisor."

"The supervisor is busy. What do you need to speak to him about?"

"I just witnessed a crime I need help with."

"You need help with a crime?" Marcie was utterly oblivious to the entrapment implications of this question. She had once been instructed to repeat what callers told her to ensure clarity on the tape, and she was merely carrying out orders. The caller didn't respond, so after a few seconds Marcie continued serviceably, "It will take a while to get somebody for that. OK?"

Apparently it wasn't "OK" because the caller immediately changed strategies. "I really need help with a highly secret matter of the utmost concern."

"Just a minute." The caller had seen enough movies to luck on to the right passwords.

Sound of clicking, then, "Fred Pallader, FBI," answered Fearless with marked irritation. So much for endowing informants with the blessings of comfortable solitude.

"Yes, Mr. Pallader. This is Colonel Rinkowski, Rome Army Base. You in charge?"

"Yes. What can I do for you, Colonel?" Fearless toadied, unsure who Rinkowski was, and so suddenly his voice was pleasant, a voice that had all the time in the world.

"I, uh, think there's a drug dealer on my base you ought to know about. Name's Private Claude Hopner. That's Hopner as in hops. Like to have you send some of the boys out to shake him down."

"How do know he's dealing, Colonel?"

"I've seen him."

"Why not have the MPs arrest him, then?"

"I mean I've seen him showing off wads of bills. And heard rumors. It's probably drugs."

"Think his supplier is off-base?"

"Yeah, I'm sure of it. But he's on base." The latter part of this statement was said with some urgency.

"Mob?"

Long pause. Very long pause. "Uh, probably not. I don't know. I don't think it's Mob. Just him. No need to chase after some mysterious mob connection. I just need a presence here, say tomorrow. Tomorrow night would be best. Can you send some people out?"

"Well, Commander, that isn't much to go on. I don't know what you expect my people to do."

"Uh, you know my cousin's a fundraiser for the, uh, New York Political Action Committee." (*What the hell was that?* I wondered.) "He's from Ithaca, and I know he could do you a favor in return sometime. I need the place, you know, just checked out to keep the general happy. You can even eat and spend the night if you want. Just come create a presence, talk to the private. Make it look like the place is being watched."

"All right, I'll have someone out tomorrow. Put in a good word to your cousin for me."

"Sure thing. You got it. Thanks, thanks a lot." The conversation clicked off into static.

I was absolutely nonplussed. The caller was Elb.

Neat! And he wanted us there to harass his imaginary friend, but he didn't want us messing with his mafioso buddies. Curiouser and curiouser. So, our outgoing lines being secure, I thought it might amuse me to dial up the number Elb had thoughtfully provided me with and ask him if he'd "learned anything yet" and if his friend Nick had gotten my greeting card.

"Wenbir's Hardware," said a warm and busy sounding woman's voice.

"Elb P. McCrae, please."

"McCrae. No such person here," she responded with that hospitable briskness that only Canadians can pull off without sounding rude. "You must have the wrong side of the world."

I read her the address he gave me. It was not the same as the store's. No doubt Elb's calling card was a lie too and he had hoped to lose me by jotting down a random address and phone number. So rather than get the stories tangled, I politely hung up. Then I did the obvious and dialed international directory assistance and promptly discovered what I should have known all along. That there was no listing in the Toronto phone directory for either Elb or for his mother, Penny McCrae. So I tried Cara, his sister's name. Nothing. And then, I asked for Jade McCrae, on the chance that sometimes cousins have the same last name. Nothing still. And then I remembered the name on the parking tickets and asked for Hugh McCrae.

"Quite a family," said the operator, slightly irritated with the number of my requests.

"I suppose so," I answered.

"Well, there's lots of McCrae's, but no Hughs." She spoke with momentous flatness meant to cover helpless irritation, "I'm not really supposed to spend all day with one person. That it?"

"No." I tried Claude Hopner for the hell of it. Nothing. But really, in his case what did I expect?

"Is that all?"

"Thanks. Last request. The name is Fendra's. I think it's a club in Toronto." She gave me a phone number and a business address, informed me that her time with me was up, and clicked off.

So I called Fendra's, not really expecting a bar to be open this early in the morning. It wasn't. But the answering machine listed upcoming events, and I learned that Black Dog was indeed scheduled to play there Friday, September 4 and Saturday, September 5, two weeks from tomorrow, which happened to be Labor Day weekend south of border. Ten-dollar cover.

As I hung up I wondered what it would be like to see them, to see Jade again, to experience a line-up of Black Dog originals in front of a hometown audience, no holding back. And I stared at my cinder block walls and wondered if I would be disappointed by renewing my fantasy-memory with reality. Then I put the thought away. Black Dog was not part of the investigation. Although if seeing the band was the only way to question Elb again, well, then I supposed I'd have to sit through the show. After all I was *unofficially* on the case, so it wasn't as if I would be traveling 500 plus miles to chase down something as silly as a feeling remembered out of a conversation. I had legitimate reasons for throwing some camping gear in my car and making the trip. Besides, my *unofficial* involvement meant crossing the border and questioning foreign citizens would be easier than it was supposed to be. Much fewer channels to clear and no CIA brethren to explain my life and evidence to if I took a vacation north like a private citizen and happened to take in the local culture and hang out with a few acquaintances. I could manage an *unofficial* vacation. I could leave early Friday morning from home and let everyone think I was doing dog duty somewhere in Boston so I wouldn't even have to count it as a vacation day. The more I thought about it, the more convinced I got. Besides, it was a weekend.

But I had one more piece of business to try. Got on my computer and tried to access Interpol to get a read out on Elb's license plate number. No go. No access. Which sometimes happens. Marcie rang my desk phone. "Peter," she said in an irksome tone that was meant to be safely flirty. She always called me "Peter" in an unwelcome way that mocked the formality of my full name, just as she always called Crensch "Sidney" and Kanesh "Alan" in a breathy tone of mock-exasperation that was meant to be cute. When she really wanted to show respect she used short forms, so Fearless was always "Fred" even though properly he was Mr. Pallader. Not that he ever complained beyond a brief scowl. "Do you want something?"

"Probably."

"Huh? You keep buzzing my computer. What are you trying to do?"

"Buzz your computer, Marcie. See if it works right."

"If you're trying to reach Interpol," she must have read the destination off her screen, "you can't anymore. It has to go through me. There's a special code."

"Why?"

"I don't know." She probably didn't know, but she loved having 'special codes' almost as much as Crensch did. "Supposed to be more efficient."

"What's the code?"

"I don't know. Let me look it up." Took ten minutes. So much for efficiency. "It's eleven."

I really didn't want Crensch or anyone else in the field office honing in on my information. If Crensch got Elb's real address and phone number, he would blow the whole case in about a minute.

Fact was, I didn't want Crensch to get much. So before I returned the tape to Marcie, I decided to accidentally ruin it for Crensch's benefit, because why expose him to my chief source's voice more than necessary? Our cheap tape recorders are notorious for eating tapes, and it enlarges their appetite if you stop the take-up reel with a pen knife and push the fast forward button. So I rewound the tape to the beginning and did exactly that. And it mangled beautifully. Just as if the machine acted on its own. And I delicately removed the mangled piece and rewound it with a pencil and replaced the tape and repeated the operation again and again until the length of the conversation was pretty much chewed. Then I brought the machine out for Marcie and anyone else hanging around the reception area to get a good look at and complained bitterly about government issued recorders from Japan and when Marcie said helplessly and predictably, "It's the best we can do, Peter," I curtly suggested that she get the damn tape free of the capstan to which it was now wrapped. And her nimble tugging broke the tape of course and made the whole thing beyond repair. Much more convincing than claiming to have erased the tape by hitting the wrong button, which is the way the political hacks generally manage those things. And no one could really implicate me in having a secret motive to tamper with evidence. After all, things happen, and Marcie had done the breaking.

"Better throw it in the shredder," I told Marcie forlornly as if the accident couldn't be helped and I was apologizing for my outburst. "It's nobody's fault."

"That happens a lot," she agreed, throwing it in the "safe box" that took and destroyed papers and tapes, so glad to be exonerated of blame she was jiggling a happy little duck-jiggle in her chair. "I'll fill out a report on it. Did you get to hear it?"

"Not all of it. Didn't sound like much," I said casually. "Hey, Marce, you going on break soon?" Which was kind of a stupid question, because Marcie was always going on break. She practically lived and worked on break, if you know what I mean.

"I was supposed to. Do you need anything, Peter?"

"Thanks," I gave her some change. "Pick me up today's *Globe* downstairs, would you? And could you go down the street and pick me up some take-out? Number Two lunch special. And some aspirin? I was sick yesterday." And I came up with an embarrassingly long list of personal items I really had no business asking the secretary to get for me, except Marcie had recently made it a point of pride to shop for agents' personal items since Crensch managed to convince her and the new hires that none of us should be seen near the field office in public. The new hires, of course, seemed to like the myth of mystery he was propagating, or the power of getting someone to run errands for them, or something. And Marcie really loved being away from her desk. So everyone was happy unless Fearless had something that needed typing. Broke variety into a fulsome day.

"Who'll answer the phone?"

"I will. I'd like to use your computer to finish a report anyway. Keys are sticking on mine." Which was true, because of the asbestos.

"OK." She flew out the door. Marcie would brave the elevators alone for a long break. Except it wasn't bravery so much as a mystical superstition that nothing bad could happen to her because she worked for us, and that every nut on the street would recognize her grand importance to the field office. I thought she lacked imagination.

The moment she was gone, I accessed Interpol. It took twenty minutes to connect and send my request, so my errand list was overkill, but I didn't want to risk a computer being down somewhere and having to wait for a connection. Made sure to change the email address to that of my own PC. Although I've never been much of a computer hacker, I figured that would be enough for the return to bypass Marcie's terminal. Not that I expected she would blab or even remember something as trivial as a license plate run, especially when she could chatter about some dweeb from Harvard, but Fearless would certainly notice the request and ask her about it, since his PC shared an email address with Marcie's and it was rare for any of us to bother chasing Canadians. And I just didn't feel like making up a story for him to ensure that my best leads weren't getting passed along to Crensch.

Then I worked up an opaque report that left out Elb and company and pretty much only revealed what was already in the *Globe* article. When Marcie returned, I got her to sign an itemized voucher without reading it, and attached my dinner receipt and speeding ticket to the back, so the field office would have to pay for my scofflaw driving. And it did, eventually. Which was nice.

But while I was trying to screw the taxpayers into paying for my speeding violation, Crensch wandered over and took a violent fancy to my itemized voucher, which Marcie, ever eager to please an agent, let him have.

He studied it as if he were doing me a favor. "Rome's an interesting place in late August," he said mysteriously, rubbing the side of his nose to indicate that he knew tons of "secret stuff" about the area, and that he could say much if he chose, but being one helluva discrete guy, wouldn't. "And I don't mean the Pope."

"How's the consulate, Sid? Is it still there?" He looked like he couldn't answer my question without jeopardizing something really big. "I mean, with all the hot gossip you must be privy to over there, think the place might burn down by now?"

"Too dangerous to burn."

"But I thought you liked to flirt with danger," Marcie piped up. Sometimes she came up with a good sally in spite of herself.

"I only *flirt* with danger."

I think Crensch thought he was making quite a good joke about himself here, but I wasn't sure. It was the sort of joke conceited asses like to make about their favorite personal traits when they feel like proving that they're not really stuck on themselves, merely phony.

"He only *flirts* with danger because it's safer than going all the way," I explained.

Crensch put his arm around my shoulders and walked me away from Marcie so he could whisper something like they do in the spy movies. "Trust me?" he asked furtively.

"No."

"Good." He looked around. "'Cause I'm your friend."

"Thanks for the warning." I started to leave.

"And you should never trust your friends," he lectured loudly. "But you know that." Then he approached me again and said even more earnestly, "So, I'll tell you. Watch the French."

"Watch the French do what?"

"If you watch 'em, you'll see." Couldn't argue with that. "And remember, I never told you." And then, stepping back, he crowed loudly, "Thai food's a little spicy for me. A little spicy. Gotta drink it out of an old Coke bottle. With a fish."

Rather than risk letting on that I had any further interest in the Rome business, I disappeared into my office and closed the door. It took three hours to get a return, but it was worth it. The van belonged to Elb P. McCrae of 13 Oak Street, in York. No phone number. No traffic violations. Clean record far as I could tell. Well, it was an address he hadn't given me, so it might be correct. I'd find it on a map and if he wasn't at Fendra's and the band wasn't helpful in turning me on to their manager's abode, I decided I could do worse than just show up at the door, offer him a beer, and reminisce about Nick.

So. Got some kicks spending two weeks confusing the be jeepers out of everyone as to what I was actually supposed to be doing. Occasionally spent an afternoon listening to an old lady talk volumes about her missing cat or wandered into an endless drug law enforcement meeting where the undercover crowd would all turn out in their best street costumes to impress everybody with how well they passed for aspiring young drug lords. Although, in my opinion, most of them carried the act pretty dismally. It's only law-abiding citizens that are pleased to be mistaken for outlaws. I've never known a real criminal who didn't do his level best to pass for an honest man. But my wily colleagues were all trying to appear to be more criminal than the criminals and it really didn't work. As their progress on various "projects" and "operations" made abundantly clear.

There was one meeting that really begged idiocy for sense. It was my first formal coming-out to the drug side of the house, meaning even though I'd seen everybody around the field office for years, we were finally getting introduced. We were getting bits and pieces of the "there are kids out there who you'll never know, whose lives you are all risking yours to save" business, which made me think of Mellie. Everyone was doing their best to look terribly good and decent by taking long breaths of deeply respectful American air while looking attentively at Fearless. Fearless, to his credit, didn't fall too far into the brainwashing but he always seemed quietly impressed with the crew who did. He also seemed a little shy under so many self-consciously earnest gazes.

I spoke up and said it was a damn shame that anyone had to risk his life for someone he didn't even know, and everyone missed the point and took my barb as a compliment to their stoic bravery. Fearless shut me up by introducing me as an "observer" just off some special secret-secret detail that related to some special secret-secret nut case "with military interest," so it would be fairly obvious to everyone in the field office that I had the nut case out of the *Globe*. But a lot of agents aren't too skillful with the obvious, so I was able to hope that the comment would pass unnoticed. Then he mentioned I was also working Petscam and I smiled my assent as one of my colleagues meowed like a cat to be funny. And someone else had to bark like a dog because he had to be funny too. And someone else grunted like a pig and pretty soon we had a whole barnyard chorus going until Fearless smiled broadly and spread his hands for silence.

Then we all got down to the business of being self-important. This was the "business" portion of the meeting, my colleagues having gotten their social civilities out of their system.

Anyway, Kanesh immediately bore away the bell for idiocy by suggesting we form our own street gang for PR reasons and invite the local "youths" to join our fight against drugs. "Kind of a Guardian Angel thing," he oozed in a used car salesman's voice. "We could make commercials for local cable and go visit high schools and get our pictures taken with the mayor and everything."

Or clowns.

Charlie Piekarski, who always fancied himself something of a "pro-family values" kind of guy since his wife divorced him for sleeping around, seconded Kanesh's bright idea because "the young people of our city need healthy role models like us. The churches might want to be in on it, too," he added. "A lot of churches sponsor anti-drug programs and ask law enforcement people in to speak."

"Isn't that like a first amendment violation? Separation of church and state?" I asked idly.

"Not if we don't get caught. I mean, technically it could be but who's going to complain?"

"Uh, here," said Fearless, trying to smooth away the potential for an intellectual discussion regarding the Bill of Rights by distributing sheets of paper for everyone to sign. And we all had to sign some phony baloney pledge that we were "drug free" and adhered to "family values" and voted for candidates "of our choice" that supported such values (meaning the current administration and its cronies) and were all such absolute social outcasts when we grew up in the seventies that none of us ever tried a lick of pot ourselves. All of which made us absolute experts on the dangers of drugs and the inner workings of human nature. So I signed off that I didn't smoke, drink, undermine the family (the pledge didn't specify whose family), wasn't a homosexual, didn't look at naked women, would not attempt or advocate the overthrow of the U. S. government by unconstitutional means, didn't take baths on Sunday, was pure of heart and said my prayers by night (isn't there a similar superstition about werewolves?) and who knows what else. It was supposed to be "good for our public image" if we all attested to having perfectly boring inner and outer lives.

"Ever use drugs, Morrow?" asked Piekarski.

"No." I grinned. "And look where it got me." Everyone was satisfied with my response. Piekarski was joshing me about my notoriety for solving "unsolvable" nut cases, us nut-case types having an undeserved rep for being flashier than the agents on other detail. Although to look around at the undercover crowd you'd never know it. I decorously turned in the pledge. "No, never touched them. Gotta stay clean and sober to think like a nut case." Which is actually true. Most of the really hard to crack serial killers are straight as an arrow. They've got such a worked up and worked over imagination that a good drug euphoria would only be something of a nuisance and get in the way of all the fun. Anyway, everyone nodded appreciatively. They liked having an "observer" because it made them feel like they were worth observing.

So we all signed statements that made us sound like prize bores and Kanesh popped off again to say that we should "organize fun events to show that you don't have to use drugs to have fun."

"What do you have to do to have fun?" I asked as a deadpan joke referring to the pledge. Kanesh amazed me by attempting to answer the question.

"Well, in Houston they held a pig roast."

Some statements are too funny to contain. "Yeah, let's have a pig roast," I said enthusiastically. "City or state?"

Everyone got a good-natured laugh, because everyone had a cherished bust-that-got-away-because-the-local-cops-screwed-up story. But Fearless frowned at my innocent attempt at levity. "Well, it doesn't have to be real fun," the boss offered quickly and helpfully.

"Good," I quipped piously. "Some of us are afraid of real fun."

Fearless smiled. "How about something that looks good during an election year? Alan, I'll put you in charge of starting a PR social-oriented kind of program."

And since most "major drug operations" (this phrase must be spoken in deep "ultra-concerned" newscaster's tones to get the proper feel) are 90% PR for some pol to claim how "tough on crime" he is and everyone to get their grimly professional faces on the news to prove to their wives and girlfriends what big important men they're privileged to go bed with, a PR program was a fairly spiffy assignment. Kanesh beamed. He loved the goddamn press. Then we got an earful of meaningless statistics about how drug busts were up nationwide and drug use down (which didn't make much sense to me, but then, I don't get paid for making sense). And then there was a lot of gossip about a Providence-Boston "drug ring" that everyone boasted to know everything about but no one actually had enough hard information on to bust anyone involved. Because I had Fearless's permission to "act mysterious" I got up and went home.

So for two weeks I basically hung out. And when I couldn't avoid it, listened to Crensch brag about his French sources turning him on to an incipient revolution in Quebec, which seemed to be his latest bailiwick. Went home. Hiked around in the local woods and looked forward with more relish than I cared to feel to Labor Day weekend. Studied a map of Toronto. Idly thought up some safely noncommittal lies to give to Jade, should we happen to speak.

Fifth Business

Friday, September 4, 1992. Toronto. Fendra's.

Paid my ten Canadian dollars for entrance. Someone who looked unused to working, whose face wore his boss's vested authority like an ad for lost virginity, took longer than necessary to stamp a four-leaf clover on my hand and I was in. Settled myself behind a small table of darkness. Leaned into an obscure corner. Slowly took in my destination. Even with a city map, Fendra's had been hard to find, and what with a long day of driving through the boredom of the New York State Thruway and crossing the border and driving the QEW into Toronto and spending an hour locating the club and then cruising the nearby city streets for forty-five minutes to find a parking space, I felt like I'd just spent my entire life looking for this particular table in this particular corner. And now that I was here, all I wanted to do was get up and leave.

I was sitting in a fairly crowded bar in a strange city, and feeling in an odd, below the surface kind of way that I was really "supposed" to be home. Nine o'clock on a Friday night usually found me out on my open back deck, immersed in my latest literary escape or cleaning my gun collection. Right now I was supposed to be looking up from my book to mark a sudden twist of moonlight. Tonight I should be camping in the clearing I once made in my seven acres of woods, idly watching whatever night the stars and planets were showing me, trying unsuccessfully to count up those few experiences worth saving between birth and death, and feeling yet another autumn start its pass through my life. At this time, I was supposed to be alone and familiar with myself.

And yet as I sat there watching the other patrons, I realized that I had grown too familiar with myself for comfort. Part of me had become so mechanically sympathetic to the sluggish week-by-year-by-decade uniformity of my life that I half-believed I wasn't really sitting here in Fendra's at all, and that with a thought and a wish and a click of the heels I could be reading in my own backyard's night. Or rather, I suddenly felt depressingly like an old sea mollusk might feel dying on an Iowa plain. All clumsy instinct opening for tides a thousand miles away. Then soft parts burning in a horrid sun. Then foreign ants and fossil.

But another part of me suddenly felt like a piece of unfamiliar territory I just happened to get lost in. Because even as my thoughts kept running to home, my body kept insisting on my presence here with unwelcome turbulence. For as I surveyed the club like the professional I am, I couldn't stop thinking about Black Dog's—and Jade's—invisible proximity, that they were already somewhere on the premises, no doubt in the limited access service lot behind the club, for there was a door in the backstage wall that looked like it led outside. So as I studied the stage setup, a helpless stiffness kept bearing down on my shoulders, fight it as I would, and my breathing got strangely tense and rapid. When I leaned back against the wall an annoying flutter along the surface of my gut bespoke a nervousness I hated having but couldn't really stop. Despite my two weeks' pleasant anticipation of this event, I kept feeling vaguely wrong and uncomfortable about being here, as if I'd taken up someone's half-meant invitation to a house party and discovered upon arrival that I didn't know any of the guests and that my host had been more polite than sincere in inviting me.

Fendra's was not my world and I was quite alone in it. For one thing, Black Dog's stage gear looked nothing like it did in Rome. Marty's drum kit was more extensive than I remembered it and Les had a triple-decker keyboard station set up on one side as opposed to the single board I'd seen him use last time. Both drums and keyboards were decorated with garlands of bright red carnations, which seemed odd for early September, and there were about three times as many amplifiers than they'd had last time as well as other electronic boxes and pedals whose uses I didn't recognize, and several stage lights mounted on poles and on the ceiling. Tacked up on the back wall of the stage was a large bright banner like a pseudo-medieval tapestry, and the banner bore an emblem that matched the painting on Elb's van of a large dragon guarding a black dog holding a ruby. The dog in the tapestry was positioned over a dagger and a rose that matched both Elb's tattoo and the painting on the van's front. There were no words on the banner, no legend bearing the band's name. I supposed the legend was to be tacitly understood.

Also, everyone else in the place occurred in a group, and a lot of the patrons seemed to know each other as regulars in the local club scene, which reinforced my sense of unbelonging. And in my camping jeans and plaid shirt I felt a tad too American and sloppily dressed to pass for a local. Urban Canadians are subtly neater about casual wear than we are, and although this was clearly a rock 'n' roll crowd wearing the requisite rock 'n' roll jeans and T-shirts, unlike their American counterparts, some of these kids actually ironed their jeans and most had carefully tucked in their newly washed T-shirts. There was a thin veneer of politeness here that I'd never been cursed with in even my most callow moments and which you never see among young people in the States.

But "thin" was the operative word, for as I watched the patrons at the tables in front of me drinking and dully shouting gossip, I realized that under their politeness their voices had the defensive harshness of dashed expectations. I gathered from the chatter that the crowd here was either unemployed and taking their weekly night out on their parents' generosity, or working as gas station attendants or store clerks or any other myriad of minimum wage type jobs. Most of their lives had peaked in high school and some of them had recently discovered that they were on the downward side of their life fifty years too soon. Many were at the age when the novelty of bar hopping has worn out but the habit hasn't, and so they carried a perpetual look of disappointment. Some would carry that look into bars for the rest of their lives. Lives that had to be as miserable as mine.

Then my chest suddenly tightened as I thought again about seeing Jade.

So I was trying to hide my inexplicable nervousness from nobody in particular and idiotically reminding myself that it was "all right" to be there, that the club was open to the public and that I had paid my cover like anybody else and even if I wasn't a rock 'n' roll enthusiast that I wasn't breaking any laws that I knew of, and what the hell, I was here on business, sort of, and my business had certainly taken me into places more deservedly discomforting than this, when a young woman quickly squeezed through the tables blocking me from the dance floor, swiftly approached me, and smilingly saved me from my internal silliness.

"Hi. My name's Beth. What can I get for you this evening? Would you like to drink a Storm in a Bottle?"

Beth's clothes did not designate her as a waitress. She was dressed like anybody else in the bar, but she carried a little pad for writing orders on and she had an excited air of being new to the job, or maybe new to any job, an air I only picked up on because I was sitting there new to "the scene." Something about us made us strangers here together, and so I suddenly felt more solidly and irrevocably present.

"What's a Storm in a Bottle?"

"It's black cherry ginger ale and lemon juice with a triple shot of Bacardi." She smiled with soft enthusiasm. "It comes served in a black bottle you can take home with you." She used her fingers to outline the shape of the bottle in the air as she spoke. "They're really good," she assured me.

The excessively sweet tone of her voice conveyed that she instinctively recognized me as different from the rest of the clientele, and behind the sweetness she sounded youthfully anxious that I would have a good time anyway. She seemed touchingly eager to make my evening enjoyable, in the way that only young girls just starting out in the world and still liable to be occasionally impressed by life can sound. She probably half-believed in fairy tales.

"Why do you call it a 'storm'?"

"I don't know. That's what they're called." Like waitresses everywhere, she couldn't tell you anything about her work that her boss hadn't made her memorize and she really didn't like being asked anything that was off the script. But unlike some, she rose bravely to the occasion. "I guess if you drink them they're supposed to feel like a storm passing through."

Three shots of Bacardi probably did make one feel a little stormy. It was a good guess so I didn't pursue the question. "I'll just have a bottle of Molson Red Ale."

"OK." She made a note and turned to go.

"How's the band?" I asked her before I realized I had asked, and immediately felt slightly surprised at my own casualness.

"Oh, I hear they're really good," was her considered opinion. "One of my friends saw them at another club and said they're really good." She managed to sound both careless of my question and anxious to please. Beth struck me as broadly sweet and deeply mindless.

"Hey, Beth, do you happen to know a man named Claude Hopner, might work here?" Figured I might as well give the old boy's name a whirl, seeing as both Elb and Jade had loosely associated him with club owners. If Beth knew him, I was sure to hear, for she struck me as too deeply mindless to be dishonest.

Beth didn't know him. "I can ask my boss, though, if you want." She offered this help eagerly. My presence as an outsider implied a subtle compliment to the subculture, as if I was a welcome audience to the audience, and so she liked spending time with me and she seemed to enjoy showing off to me how much a part of the club she was. Like most recent converts to adult life, she was all invisible to her own newness.

"Sure. Tell him I'm a friend of Claude's, wondered if he was around tonight." Figured that would pique the owner's curiosity to come talk to me if Claude was an issue in his life. It would certainly pique Elb's, if he showed up tonight and heard about the inquiry before I got to him, because he'd have no idea who asked. But mostly I wondered what kind of story Beth would elicit and how it would compare to mine. She nodded and crossed the dance floor and squeezed through more tables to reach the bar, which stretched along the opposite side of the club.

And then I noticed that Elb was already here. As I watched Beth make her way through the crowded tables, I saw that he was sitting behind a table near the bar and nearly opposite to mine, a table that was partially blocked from view by people sitting at tables in front of it. Elb's table bore a little banner with Black Dog's emblem and there was a pile of T-shirts, cassettes, and CDs near a large metal cash box. A handwritten sign overhead proclaimed the prices and Elb had his calculator ready to rake in the dough, but no one seemed to be buying. I saw he was talking with an older man who might have been the owner and had to be mob. Not that I make easy guesses, but after a few years in the business, you get a feel for who's who, and like a lot of middle-aged gangsters, the guy seemed to take his costume and acting cues from the *Godfather* movies.

Which is pretty funny when you think about it, but a now retired colleague once told me that the Boston Mob never used to talk and act like mobsters until the movies came out, and then all the criminals turned into stereotypes. Oscar Wilde was right when he said life imitates art far more often than art imitates life.

Anyway, Beth leaned over the bar to give the bartender my order, waited shyly for her boss to finish speaking, and then delivered my message once they happened to make eye contact. From what I could see through the crowd, neither he nor Elb reacted to her request as anything unusual. The boss said something, Elb shrugged his shoulders, Beth smiled a lot at both of them and pointed me out, at which point Elb's head went suddenly stiff under his smiling expression as he did his best to give his full respectful attention to the owner and pretend he didn't know me.

While this was happening, the backstage door burst loudly open and another young woman entered and swiftly descended the platform. She was strikingly pale, almost pallid, with a midnight turmoil of waist-length hair and an unmistakable hard confidence bundling up her features. She was clearly "with the band." She carried bright red carnations in her hand. Elb was trying to be so engrossed in conversation that he didn't notice her approach until she forced the issue by interrupting the owner to say something to Elb, who looked visibly annoyed at her unabashed rudeness. But he apparently answered to her satisfaction, for while he was still speaking, she cut him off to exchange a few words with Beth. Then Beth pointed me out to her and while Elb looked on agitatedly the woman wrote something on a card and handed it to Beth. Something in her manner told me she greatly enjoyed Elb's discomfort. Then she kissed Beth on the cheek, gave her a carnation, took some cash out of the box, and quickly strode back outside without so much as a glance or an introduction to Elb's companion.

The owner, who clearly had no idea that I was a problem, got so busy watching the dark-haired woman swaying out the door in her tight jeans that he failed to resume conversation. And then he smiled in my general direction at the size of the crowd, still clearly ignoring whatever Elb was now saying to him.

Beth got my beer and some other drinks from the bar and made her way back to me with a tray. "I asked. He's not here. The man at the table says he's out." She smiled and helplessly shrugged as if to add "What can I say? I tried." She put a black bottle next to a beer bottle on my table. "But the woman I was talking to says any friend of Claude's drinks on her. Do you know her? Her name's Cara." So that was Elb's sister and Jade's "kissing cousin."

"Anyway, here's a free Storm to chase down your Molson." She sounded like this was unusual and that she was sort of impressed that I actually appeared to know someone here. At that moment she reminded me a little, but just a little, of Mellie.

"I thought your boss might know him," I said to keep the discussion going.

"I don't think he does. He asked the man at the table when he was going to get to meet Mr. Hopner, but the man just shrugged." Of course. "But you still get a Storm. Is your friend like an actor or something?"

"He's a lot of things. Why?"

"Cara says she's President of the Claude Hopner Fan Club and that she knows him personally. I didn't know he had a fan club." Beth sounded politely enthusiastic. "Do you know her? Are you, like, a member?"

"Sure. I'm like his biggest fan."

"You know there's going to be a Claude Hopner party?" She took out the card Cara gave her. "September 17th. Six p.m. I think it's a Thursday. Thirteen Oak Street. York." Bingo. The date of the Grateful Dead tickets in the corpse. What the hell were they celebrating?

"Thanks, maybe I'll be there." Someone called Beth over to another table, so I sat in my corner considering my next move. I was going to pay a visit to 13 Oak Street anyway. Really wanted to see the place. And rather than compete with the distractions of the club, I suddenly decided it would be more fruitful to interview Elb tomorrow at home. Tell him to thank his sister for the party invitation for an added kick. Give him an even more graphic sense of having been "found out" than he now had. Not a bad idea to keep him living on his nerves, keep him wondering what I wanted for a night. And having decided this, I suddenly felt calmer, because deciding to put off my interview meant I needn't talk to Jade tonight either and something like an internal pressure-valve lifted, and then I knew without self-argument that I was really here to see the band and have another conversation with Jade and the whole thing of my being here felt intensely stupid, because really I could just leave and find a camp site now and show up at 13 Oak Street tomorrow. What was I really expecting anyway?

But once again, as thought settled through my new calmness, it occurred to me that something wasn't right. Elb had told me that Jade had only joined the band a few weeks ago, and yet Xander had been fairly insistent about Jade's energy driving the quartet, about Jade doing the composing and arranging. The time didn't work out. The other three could have been calling themselves Black Dog before Jade arrived, and I supposed since Jade and Xander went back some years together, Jade could have arrived with original compositions they both knew, but the others would have had to learn them and the whole set up felt like the four of them had been around a while. And hadn't Xander said that Jade composed on Les's equipment? And there had been time to build up some local reputation, because the waitress's "friend" had seen them at another club, and the ten-dollar cover was a bit steep for a completely unknown band.

And there was Elb selling CDs and cassettes and T-shirts, so clearly they'd been around longer than a few weeks to get a supply of materials together. And all those Hopner ordered rehearsals and gigs, if Jade was in them, had to push the formation of the band further back in history. I made a note to check this inconsistency, which meant I now had a business reason to talk to Jade and had justified to myself a practical reason to stay for the performance. Which after all, I had paid for.

Cara came back in with Marty, who had traded in his khaki muscle shirt for a black one with black pants and sneakers. He was carrying a metal rod with a tambourine on the end of it that he had probably forgotten to set up with the rest his gear, and he immediately buried himself in his drum kit as if he was making last minute adjustments. Then Cara crossed the dance floor, looked over at her brother to make sure he was watching, and plunked herself down at my table. Elb looked pissed.

Cara coolly lit a cigarette and blew smoke under a No Smoking sign on the wall. "So, you're a friend of Claude's?" she said in a voice of shallow sophistication, as if someone had recently convinced her that she was an expert on this difficult subject and she wanted to size up my credentials or impress me with hers.

"So, you're Cara McCrae?"

She quickly smiled and nodded like she was immensely wise and had an unusual capacity for enjoyment other people couldn't appreciate but she didn't ask how I knew. "'Cept I don't call myself McCrae—that's my brother's name. I'm just Cara."

"I'm just Pete."

"Glad to know ya, Pete, glad to know ya. You're good people. Have a flower." She gave me a carnation and made an issue of rising and shaking hands with me for Elb's benefit. In fact, all of her friendliness seemed directed at me for his benefit. "So where ya from?"

"Boston."

"Boston. Boston." She said in a half-put down teasy voice that sounded like she meant to be terribly friendly and democratic and was all my pal but was also very sophisticated if you ever came right down to it. As if she knew all there was to know about the city but was too cool to spend any time there. "Good band in their time, Boston. 'Don't Look Back' is a great song. Nothin' better than it bein' summer of 1979 with a flatbed pickup truck and a keg of beer and a free weekend and Boston cranked up to party. Anyway, that's what my dear mama always says." She sang a few lines from the old Boston song, in a weird profundity, the way a pretentious undergraduate might quote from some deeply insightful seventeenth-century philosopher. She puffed on her cigarette and glanced fiercely over at Elb like she was the heroine in some melodrama about to get caught as a spy but still bravely pushing on with the act anyway.

She had seen too many movies too, and had copied all the mannerisms of Grade B screen actresses. I decided there had to be a daily family fight over who was the biggest snob, Elb with his taste for money and class, or Cara with her coolness. I could see why she irritated Elb. She already irritated me. At least the Mob conveys a charming innocence in its bad imitations. Cara kept trying to draw a kind of mystery around herself she didn't really own, and a kind of respect from me concerning emotional displays she didn't really earn, and if it weren't for her potential usefulness to the case, I wouldn't have bothered to cultivate an acquaintance.

"Sooo." She glanced in her brother's direction, clearly trying to extend our chat to prolong Elb's increasing discomfort. "Do you like music?" She spoke in the same tone Jade had used when he asked me if I liked dragons, and for some reason the echo of his voice in hers startled me a little. I didn't answer, but she continued, blowing smoke and tapping the ashes out of her cigarette and onto the table. "Who do you like to listen to?" It was a very important question, a catechism almost, a test.

"Frank Sinatra," I said, trying to be funny while refusing to enter into her game. Besides, if her brother were dealing with the Mob it was the sort of red herring that would get reported back and keep him wondering.

I thought she would sneer but she surprised me by looking politely indulgent, almost respectful. "Cool. Frankie had quite a following in the forties. Girls used to scream their heads off and commit atrocious suicides for Ol' Blue Eyes. He was good-lookin' in his time, too. See you've got classic taste."

"I read a lot of classics. I like Black Dog."

She nodded approval. "Yeah, they're cool. I know them really well. The bass player—Jade—" she pronounced his name for my information, "and I go back. Way back," she boasted. "Now we're cousins. Yup." She nodded. "Jadie's another screwed-up musician needs a good woman to straighten the boy out. But he's good people."

"I met him once."

"Oh yeah?" She was as uneasy with my encroaching on her domain of coolness as her brother had been in Rome, but much better at hiding it under pretended interest than he was. "I slept with him." Then she casually blew smoke out of her mouth as if it was no big deal. And now that she had outcooled me and the hierarchy of "good people" had been properly established, she was friendly and comfortable again. "We're having a party for Claude on the 17th. All good people. You wanna come?" She wasn't really asking so much as showing off that she was having a party. She looked across the room at her brother again as she said this.

"What's special about the 17th?"

"That's when people die. That's when Keith Moon started to die."

"Should I bring my own drugs?"

She smiled a little. "You're all right, Pete. September 17th is a strange night. Keith started to pass over the same hour the moon went into total eclipse over the Sahara like a natural pun. The Grateful Dead were playing 'Dark Star' through the Who's equipment before the Great Sphinx. Right in the middle of what the Egyptians call the season of apricots." She must have mistook my silence for disbelief. "It's true. My mother was there. Check out Ken Kesey's article in *Rolling Stone*, if you don't believe me."

"Sure. Wouldn't miss it for the world. Beth already invited me."

"Yeah, Beth's good people." She nodded approvingly, as if they'd known each other a long time and it were her divinely ordained role in life to approve of who was "good people" and who wasn't. By this point I was getting sick of the phrase.

"Thought you two just met."

"Oh, we did. But I can tell she's good people." She finished her cigarette. "C'mon, Pete, let's sit up front where we can see better." *And be seen by Elb better*, I thought, but I wasn't about to decline Cara's invitation and lose the opportunity to gather whatever further information I might from her.

Since there weren't any free tables I wondered where we going to sit. But she strolled over to a table directly across from center stage that was occupied by three younger women and plunked herself down in an empty chair. I followed.

"Hi. Mind if we sit here?" The question was rhetorical. She didn't bother to ask until after we had made ourselves at home, and her body language made it clear that she wasn't about to leave if they did mind. "I'm Cara. This is my friend Pete." I nodded. Cara gave each of them a carnation, in a cold-friendly "now I've paid for the table" sort of way, but the women accepted the flowers with sweet gracious smiles and so we had front row seats without question. Then she leaned back and watched Marty tweaking on a drum pedal for a few minutes and shook her head in mild disapproval to imply to the other women that she knew him. Then she stood up and announced, "Gotta have a beer. Anyone want anything?" and went back to the bar without waiting to be served. I wondered what Jade really thought about her and what sorts of conversations they'd had. Were they really lovers?

It didn't take Cara long to get beer because she just went behind the bar and helped herself to a tray full of bottles. Then she went up on the stage and handed one to Marty, who appeared to tolerate rather than welcome her, and chatted to him to show everyone in the club that she was pals with the drummer. Then she brought the rest outdoors. All of which seemed designed to torment Elb, who had followed all her movements with his eyes like he expected one of the beers himself. But if he did want a beer, he clearly had to get his own.

I wondered if she ever did anything not calculated to irritate her brother, but I did find her antics rather useful because I didn't mind bothering him myself. Stay unpredictable. Keep him guessing as to what I wanted.

Anyway, the remaining bottles were a round for our table, which our three companions eagerly helped themselves to, and so I now had two beers and an untouched Storm.

"You're not drinkin'," reprimanded Cara, her words also calling attention to the fact that she was. Then she glanced at her brother again. "Still talkin' to Guido. Wish we'd fuckin' start."

I had to laugh. "You mean the owner's name is really Guido?"

"No, that's just what I call him. He's really George. You should meet him. Good friend of Claude's."

But before I could question this contradiction to Beth's story, Elb ascended the stage and tried to get the club to notice him. And since there was now nothing between me and him but the dance floor, he couldn't miss me, so I politely saluted with the black bottle, much to Cara's obvious edification, for she quietly chortled and then tried to look solemn and natural in Elb's direction. Marty, who now sat up ready behind his drums, was making an effort not to look at Cara.

Elb's hair was no longer in dreadlocks but hung straight and loose and blond under a dark wide-brimmed hat. A white silk shirt hung over his dark jeans, his waist girdled in an expensive looking belt. He wore a dark silk scarf that matched his hat loose around his neck and the same expensive boots he'd worn in Rome. He walked up to the microphone, making a grand effort to look like he was enjoying his role despite Cara, who lit another cigarette before asking if we minded if she smoked, shook her head again to indicate that she was on familiar enough terms with Elb to pass judgment on him, and then looked pointedly bored. Elb did not look once in our direction.

"Hey, ladies and gentlemen. How the fuck are you?" A few desultory cheers at the swear word to which Elb himself chimed in cheerfully, smiling and nodding his head. "Hey, hey, all right." Guess it was a wonderful bit of stage business to start things off with a profanity. Establish the proper rebellious atmosphere with the young men hiding their growing apprehension of a miserable life in a plastic cup of beer.

"Fuckin' great," said one young drunk loudly, but not too loudly, just loud enough to show his friends that he could say it.

"Good to be here tonight. Good to be at Fendra's with you fine people who like to party." I looked around at the crowd, which hadn't changed its enthusiasm level too much, and smirked. "And it is my very great pleasure, as President of Moon Management and Promotions"—Cara rolled her eyes to the ceiling to indicate in what low regard she held Elb's promotion company— "to introduce to you good people the best rock 'n' roll band in Toronto"—no response except some drunk spilling his beer in his lap to his friends' great amusement—"the best rock 'n' roll band in Ontario." No one seemed too enthused at this promise either, but Elb was doing his best to whip up some cheers by smiling and moving his hands a little and repeating, "hey hey. In Canada. In the fuckin' North American continent, yeah, all right"—someone inspired by the profanity accidentally said "yeah" too loud to his friends and Elb was so desperate for feedback he wasn't about to let it go—"in the free world, in the Western Hemisphere, on the planet Earth."

"The planet where?" said Cara, just loud enough to be heard and to make her three companions smile and quietly laugh.

"In our solar system, in the Milky Way Galaxy, in the universe, in any universe, in the violent god-force that drives your fucking rock 'n' roll hearts." Marty yawned and quickly glanced through the open door behind him as he readied his drumsticks. The audience seemed to be warming up to the swear words and ignoring the rest of the introduction, although one or two guys looked like they thought Elb's patter was arrestingly intellectual. (Toronto to the god-force of rock 'n' roll, yeah, man, intense.) "Black Dog."

The lights in the club went out as the band members entered the stage. I couldn't see their entrance because my eyes hadn't adjusted to the dark yet, but I could sense the three of them as I heard the door slam and felt it shut out the rest of the world. And I knew instantly that this shift into the dark marked a shift into their stage personas and that we were all now locked into an intimate other world together. There were a few quiet screams for fun coming from another table, screams for the sudden dark rather than the band, and then Les hit a chord on his keyboards that sounded how thunder might sound in a cyclone on acid and triggered a red garish stage light crashing a promise of something visual across the stage and receding before sight could catch up and Jade started playing a quick low hypnotic rhythm on his bass whose tones seemed to spring and fall in maddening gyres from Les's chords and pulled everyone into the music, into the music's consciousness, and Marty struck up everyone's pulse into a faster life beating on his differently toned drums, an old forgotten pulse that drove thought crazy and by the time Xander was wailing some melodic line like an evil banshee screaming visions out of hell the club was paying attention.

I mean the club was gone. There was no help for it but to be there in this higher pulsing energy that created a sacred space in the closed room. And the music kept swelling timelessly and bringing us away from ourselves and the red light finally won against the intermittent darkness and settled on Jade.

Who was not the merry, easy companion I remembered from my night walk. He was wearing a dark robe lined in a single moon and three stars, his dark hair loose and wild, his eyes circled in black stage make-up like a sorcerer's. He started half-singing, half-chanting a hypnotic poem to a hypnotic melody in counterpoint to Xander's playing and underscored by Marty's drumming that locked everyone irrevocably into this other world. I mean the music brought us into a new realm like helpless captives, but Jade's voice locked the gateway back or chained us in or something and we were his. The place could have burned and we would have remained in the music and raised a new world out of it. And now the binding spell was accomplished, and now the performance began.

They played without stopping. No song introductions, no breaks between sets. Worlds don't stop when their creators need a rest, and this dark spinning world of music was restless and relentless. And people were dancing, just sliding out of chairs and dancing without thinking about it—dancing alone, as couples, in groups that folded and split into other groups. Sometimes Jade would break from the band and descend to the dance floor, playing to the whirling bodies. Playing and singing and dancing with and to various members of the audience, responding and commanding in turn, playing some of them into slam dances, playing some of them prone on the floor, re-ascending the stage to play with the other band members, who all wore black like Marty. And talk about stage persona. This was not four twenty-somethings from Canada playing out and having fun on a Friday night. Jade played and sang and acted as if he really were a sorcerer out of another time, and interspersed his hard driving bass with delicately articulated medieval folk riffs before Xander would scream them out of the way with a rock guitar solo that would bend summer lightning into glaring ice or Les would pulverize all hell on a scathing keyboard solo that took all the rest of the music into higher reaches of sky and Marty—Marty used his drums the way a shaman might; his beats formed an ancient river carving canyons through the audience's newly opened hearts. I don't listen to much rock music, not since I grew up anyway, and I was unexpectedly and absolutely in awe.

Because this was rock and roll. Fierce and dangerous as love or hell. This was theater as music as poetry. This was sound spilling rivers of blood opening memories for buried lives.

The audience loved it. They didn't know enough not to. Here were musicians performing as characters performing as musicians and bringing everyone into the experience. Forget your miserable jobs and nagging families. Forget society devouring your best self. Forget your limitations. Don't you know all play is revolution? All happiness an act of subversion? Go dance a world in your own image. Forget your ugly prison cell world, my pretties. For ten dollars I'll lock you out of your lives and make you sing and weep and dance rainbows like the new-born gods and poets and revolutionaries you know in your heart's aboriginal dreamtime that you always are. I am here to love and heal and save you for your poor tortured brighter selves.

And he did. Jade was dangerous lover and pied piper and court jester and sea wizard all at once—and his music transformed every one of those dead-end kids into something special—relentlessly opened their hearts into a forbidden knowledge of their own power. And there were moments in the music when Jade would speak his finely crafted poems to dancers over the rhythm of his bass and Marty's drums, poetry that moved even me, or stop playing to take someone in the audience by the hand and sing or scream out a line to that person until that person was compelled by the rhythms to scream out something—anything back. And then—then he would slay people—I don't know how to describe it, but he would fix on the closest dancer, perhaps some newly baptized drunk who had just slam-danced a stranger for the first time in his life, and jump in the fray at the moment when the kid had just bounced his beer-sweaty chest off another and was all unbalanced, and he would playfully stalk him while playing some rhythm so compellingly and commandingly out of sync with the slammer's unsteady drunken movements that it would force him to fall prone on the floor, and then Jade would lean over him with his guitar, looking serious and concerned with a hint of a whimsical smile shadowing his lips, and graciously play him to his feet.

And how much was mutual pretense between artist and audience and how much was a dangerous command Black Dog exerted through their music I couldn't tell and didn't want to know. But Jade wasn't all commanding pied piper. Half the time he was responding to the crowd. A group of dancers' movements would seem to dictate a rhythm to him, or someone would start singing and Xander would pick up her melody and Jade would thrust it home to her on his bass like a courteous compliment. And at one point he set his bass in a rack and just sang, while I swear the other band members had him in their control. Les would send him into convulsions with geometric patterns of crashing chords, or Marty's rhythms would make his body and voice shudder, and Xander's playing would command melodies from his lips as his playing had commanded melodies from the dancers. And he was graceful and compelling and as beautiful to watch in these moments as in any of the others. Then he would take up his bass and resume playing and resume control and an audience member would dance frenzies for him and he would lengthen and echo her body's rhythms in low caressing tones.

Cara was howling and clapping through the entire performance, her hyper-buoyancy never changing one iota with the mood of the pieces. She screamed a lot and so got the other women at our table screaming with her. And although they looked delighted at the sanctioned release, Cara immediately turned it into a competition over who could be the most demonstrative and least inhibited. And after a while I honestly couldn't tell if she were high on the music or high on the public demonstrations of her own emotion. And somehow, in all the music, I also noticed Beth, who was leaning wide-eyed and entranced against a back wall, following Jade's every movement like a fluttery moth drifting into an inferno. She couldn't take her eyes off him if she went blind for it. But then, neither could I. Or anyone else.

They stopped at midnight, or rather, they held the music swaying with the time, and all of the room careening between the beauty of the dragon's cave dream-world they held us in and the living death of going back to our Monday jobs. But the swaying was tortuous, slowly mounting and building for a solid ten minutes of rising storms and broken scales until your mind wanted to crack and scream for completion. And then—and then—and then—they exploded into a fifteen-minute finale that shrieked and pounded like a desert whirlwind into a rock wall of promises of utter fulfillment. Pounded us down into the strange brief death of utter satisfaction.

But Black Dog wasn't finished. Xander segued into a classical guitar melody that pooled and ebbed like a low sonic sunset that slowly drained the finale's killing heat. Les backed him with whimsical strains that felt like shadows casking whatever surreality the band had just ambushed us with. Then more darkness as the stage lights dimmed. Resolved chord. Fade. Single candle. Spreading silence. Single ensemble crash.

"Thank you. Good night." The only emotion in Jade's voice was profound respect for his audience. The rock 'n' roll wizard had just armed us for a long and perilous journey into the rest of our sad and maddening lives on earth. He was acknowledging our courage. At least, that's how it felt.

Black Dog left in darkness. It was a better tribute than applause that nobody in the place seemed too eager to turn on the house lights and make the final break with the show. Everyone sat on the floor where the dim stage lights were now turned on them, dazed where they had been dancing. Or they sat on the tables, frozen in the position Jade had left them in, too stunned and sated to ask for more.

And then a slow reluctant return. Reality falling fast and wider than life. The dullest broke from the trance first and wandered sheepishly over to Elb's table and pretty soon an extensive crowd was over there buying out the store. If the price had been blood I suspect most of them would have paid it. Beth was slowly coming to herself. Then she was very slowly clearing tables and glancing at the closed backstage door.

"How'd you like the show, Pete?" Cara asked smugly, as if the music were her own creation or an experience she was used to living but was probably too intense for me to handle.

"What show?" I asked with my innocent, dumb, country boy expression, as if I'd missed something.

"Yeah, well I guess you just don't get a lot of that from reading classics." She was needling me about my dull life and holding up her exciting one for me to admire.

"You should try the last few chapters of Kerouac's *On the Road*." But Kerouac's genius notwithstanding, it wasn't much of a defense. Not that you "get a lot of that" from most music either—but take the very best performance by the very best musician and the very best novel by the very best writer and let's see who can get a roomful of people out of their dull lives screaming and crying their heart's emotions without mercy. Hint: It ain't gonna be the writer.

Cara stubbed out her cigarette. "Kerouac, Kerouac. Every Beat for forty years been reading Kerouac. In the history of the world more people have died for music than died for novels. That's what Ma says."

"Well, that's one measure of artistic achievement."

"Actually," she said seriously, "it is. But," changing her tone into something shrill and brightly braggy, "the boys'll be needing me." She sang this loudly so the other women could know and envy her relationship to the band. "But hey, nice knowin' ya, Pete." I took it my usefulness as an irritant was at an end. Then our table companions smiled brief good-byes and one wandered over to the throng near Elb's cash box while the other two lengthened the line to no purpose by just waiting in it for their friend.

"Hey, Beth," I called the still half-entranced waitress.

"Uh." She rallied herself and came over. "Uh, hi. I guess you moved, huh?" The place was closing and her voice had changed to an I'm-almost-off-duty-now-politeness that nonetheless imparted dreaminess from the show. "Did you like the band?" she smiled through the energy they'd left behind.

"They were 'really good.'" There was still energy from the music between us. I gave her some money. "Here, go buy a couple of cassettes and keep one for yourself. Along with the change for your trouble." I figured it didn't hurt to keep friendly relations with Cara's new friend.

She glanced at the bill. The change was a sizable tip for a few minutes work. "Are you sure?"

"Sure."

She did so, her job giving her the privilege of cutting through the considerable crowd. I kept thinking about going out back and getting re-acquainted, but a lot of people were now spilling out the back door to mingle with the band and I felt awkward approaching them through a crowd. And the fact was, this really wasn't the most opportune time to question Elb because he was also surrounded by people. But it was an opportune time to let him know I was watching him to make him nervous about what I wanted. So, when Beth returned with my cassette, I pocketed it in my shirt, ostentatiously patted it, and leaned back smiling, letting Elb wonder why I was now buying gifts for Cara's new friend.

"We're closing," Beth said as if she had to say it but didn't want to be rude to me.

"Gotcha. I'll leave after the crowd." And because of the tip, she didn't harass me about it. And so just to be a problem, I waited until the place was nearly clear and watched Elb quickly count his money and give some to Guido. Elb couldn't get out of there fast enough. "Thanks for letting us leave the amps and stuff set up for tomorrow," he said while quickly heading out.

Then just as Elb went out the back door and was still in earshot I called, "Hey, George, good take tonight," just to increase Elb's confusion.

Guido was pretty laidback about me still being there and he showed absolutely no surprise at me knowing his name. Then I realized that as the owner of a popular club he was probably used to everyone knowing his name. "Hope you had a good time," he said amiably. "We're closing now. Come back tomorrow."

"Thanks, George. Give my regards to Claude and tell Nick I said hi."

"Hey, you know Nick? Nickie Nariano? Hey, Nickie's a good man. What can I do for ya? Wanna a T-shirt? Good shirts." Elb had left the box on the table and Guido, like most mob types, had no problem giving away goods that weren't his. "Wanna cassette?"

"Sure." Can't beat Italian generosity. Helped myself to one of each. "When's Claude due to stop by? Nickie wanted me to talk to him."

"Don't know. Don't know Claude. Elbie knows him. Ought to talk to Elbie out back. Nick's got some people comin' in tomorrow."

So with that bit of information I left.

And that night, in a public camp site outside of the city, I played the cassette tape over and over in my car until my battery was fixed to wear down. And somewhere in the music I slept in hard moonlight and dreamed.

Fifth Business After

Saturday morning, September 5, 1992. Camp site near Toronto.

I woke to autumn sky so deep and vacant it cradled me in sharp relief, the way emptiness loans presence to the merest speck of matter. There was also something like a dream river of music running through my morning stupor, so for a few seconds I thought that somehow the cassette was still playing. But as my eyes slowly focused on a throng of dark branches, I began to realize that the "dream river" had fled to wherever dreams go. I kept trying to find it in the September sky, but the sky showed silent and wide as the eternity of space it blocks. Then a mourning dove sang me back to reality and I found myself entangled in my sleeping bag, lying torpidly on dead leaves and earth.

Drive to York. Toronto has a brilliant back to carry the sun on; its skyscrapers are fierce rivers of light. The city felt like a new morning. Toronto by day is a small town that goes on forever into city. And on first entry you briefly believe accomplishment can still happen here because the rest of Canada feels refreshingly underpopulated and so any efforts at success have better odds at getting noticed here than anywhere else. I understood what Jade meant about being "world famous in Canada." But as I remembered the working-class crowd at Fendra's, I knew my impression was all sun and nonsense. The city's beauty shimmered in windows kissing heaven, and the buildings were as forceful and inviting as a hero's life, but youth here was no different than youth anywhere. Dismal kids shriveling into adulthood; buried in such a splendid spot of concrete and dazzling light.

And then, 13 Oak Street, York, was a slum. The only slum in the city, as far I could tell, because even the poor sections of Toronto are kept better than some middle-class neighborhoods in American cities. I knew the place from several houses away because the colorful van was parked outside, but the van was parked at an angle that left no room for another vehicle in the driveway besides the beat-up car in front of it, so I parked on the side of the road and walked. The neighboring houses, although clearly poor, were neat and trim enough, with fresh paint and little plots of grass and flowers, but Elb's home base was a wreck of sloping roof and concave walls that reminded me of a fairy tale cottage gone sour. The place looked fit to collapse if you said the right word on a windy day, or if you said the wrong one in the wrong mood.

Its square plot of yard was overrun with fat, spiny weeds and nasty looking toys. There was a rusted used-to-be-red wagon that looked like it hadn't moved in thirty years. Its handle was twisted, and it contained a load of dirt and rocks and crawling lice. And leaning against the back of the wagon was a dented "flying saucer," the sort of thing that used to be popular in the sixties for sledding down hills and getting injured on trees. A purple plastic bucket spilled rotting sod and old rainwater, the kind of putrid water you often find in sealed cans and bottles in the woods and that your childhood friends make you drink on a dare. There was also an old yellow kickball, partially deflated, and there were coffee cans with holes for bugs to breathe through like we used to make as kids, and angry insolent coils of metal like rusty snakes strangling clumps of dying buttercups. I imagined that you could tug the metal pieces out but the roots would remain fixed in old rocks and hell and you'd cut your hands to shreds before pulling anything free.

Here be the remains of dead summers, I caught myself thinking, and wondering what poem that came from before remembering that it was one of Jade's lyrics on the cassette.

The whole thing was fenced off with loose coils of barbed wire and labeled with a sign that looked like it might have been stolen from a museum and that read in neat, stenciled letters, "Love, Hugh McCrae." I immediately thought of my second parking ticket in Rome, and of "Hugh McCrae" not showing up in the Toronto phone directory. Over the neatly stenciled words was a scrawl of red crayon proclaiming, "Danger. Keep off or die. Order of Lord Claude Hopner."

This was the place all right.

So I was utterly fascinated before I even reached the doorstep, where I immediately stopped short to enjoy the family argument that was spurting through an open window. I was safely hidden from sight of the combatants by oily plastic shower curtains that looked like they had hung limply in that one window for years. The windowsill was made of grime that somehow held the shape of wood, and in the grime someone had written the words "for fun" and drawn one of those Mr. Yuck faces you usually see on poisonous household products to scare kids with.

I silently congratulated myself on last night's mind games because Elb's voice of cultivated superiority was now fractured with high desperation, "—then stop the freakin' games, Cara. I've got enough problems today without your bullshit comin' at me first thing in the goddamn morning."

"It's not bullshit—Ma said I could have a party." Cara was still as coolly grandiose as she had been last night.

"Oh yeah? So then what do you call the latest *bullshit* about a fan club?"

"What do you care? You're not a member."

"You're not even a fan," said a second young woman.

"Shut up, Juno. Last I knew there wasn't even a freakin' club. Then Cara goes off and invents one and starts inviting in the neighborhood. What the hell was that all about?"

"Promotion," Cara mocked. "Gonna go into management and show the big boys how it's done—"

"Promotion—" he spat. "Then go promote yourself a brain before—"

"—Besides I like Beth. She's a sweet girl." It sounded like Cara said this to irritate her brother more than to defend her new friend. It worked. He groaned. "Don't *you* like her? I can make her like you," she half-sang, half-boasted.

"Shut the fuck up. You don't even know her."

"So what's your point? I like a lot of people I don't even know."

"Yeah," said the young woman named Juno. "Ma always says it's easier to like people before you really know them."

"Oh yeah? Well do you know that guy she was talking to, the one that asked about Claude and that you had to go and bullshit with all night, was an American FBI agent?"

"So what?" asked Cara casually. "I thought you liked the FBI. You're the one always calling them in."

"Would you lay off it? I'm not always calling them in—"

A raspy older woman's voice interrupted this fascinating exchange. "Shut up all of ye or I'll call everyone in and back up the birth canal with the Pill for a paddle out." Everyone quieted down. I could hear fierce rhythmic scraping against something metal, like a spoon stirring a large pot. "Now then. As if we ain't already got battle casualties desecrating the front yard I cain't beat the Middle East and all its cousins for asking a simple question and starting off another war in my kitchen for the sake of a sibling argument—Beulah it's disinfectant and it ain't for eatin' lest ya want to go blind—and seein' as yer name ain't Homer or Milton, what's the point in losin' yer eyes to yer appetite—and speakin' of blind, why weren't you and Juno watchin' the place last night 'stead of hiding upstairs and lettin' in monsters to hang curtains in my good kitchen and wreck up the yard—"

"We weren't hiding," wailed Juno. "We were lighting candles for Jim Morrison under a map of Paris in Cara's bathtub and we didn't know—"

"—And you didn't know my wretched house nearly caved in like Mother Hubbard's Russian shoe on sticks—Jeeminy crickers if yer gonna light candles for Jim you ought to know about keepin' off the crumb bum monsters who get themselves attracted to such things. We already did that one on July 2 to remark when he died off into Africa anyway."

"They better not be the candles I was saving for Jade," whined Cara.

"We wanted to try it again for the Fall to see what would happen." Juno's tone was more defensive than explanatory.

"Yeah, well ye seen what would happen. Dog done is done and if this painted broth ain't enough to disinfect the damn things—" Something liquidy and hard hit against the curtains from inside, dripped onto the sill, and hardened into more grime. Mr. Yuck and the words "for fun" resisted the mixture like a garish crayon drawing resists black paint. A few droplets came through the curtains and hit my arms, freezing and pinching like brown scabs. When I scraped them off they felt like ice pellets. "Damny dins deevers and a dirty egg if I'll touch those things without one good washing and they freeze my best attack, ought to make Juno and Beulah hang 'em out in a thundercloud for clearance."

"Why do you think the monster hung them there, Ma?" asked Cara, her voice emphasizing that she greatly enjoyed being in favor over her siblings. "If I were home he wouldn't have dared."

"If you were home, you wouldn't haven't dared do much 'cept insure your brother a miserable life. He did it to show he could do it while my two dimwit daughters were upstairs honoring Jimmy in September ever heard the like. Off one night to mend Elbie's latest screw up and have to miss my boys playing out and next thing you know we got monsters all over the damn place worse than an election year—" Another splash. The curtains made a quick wheezing sound, caught fire, briefly stank like a horrible industrial waste, and melted. The window scrawlings closed themselves in ashes. I moved out of sight. "There. That'll make 'em safe. Now, as to the obscenity in my front yard. The only bigger embarrassment to life I've seen in over twenty years are my four lazy children without the wit to do more than gape at their own violation."

"I ain't gonna touch it," said Juno, which I took to mean the disaster of broken toys in the front yard. "Make Elb."

"Elb was doing his job last night for once."

"But you can't burn rust," Juno pleaded.

"You can burn anything so long as you're smart about it, which you generally ain't. You been a stupid teenager for decades."

"Then aren't I due to grow wise, Mama?"

"Stupid teenagers never grow wise. They just grow into stupid adults with the power to define intelligence."

"I thought they grew into Elb," needled Cara.

"Speakin' of smart—was Nick there last night?"

"Nick's supposed to come tonight with some people," reported Elb. "That is, if Cara doesn't scare him off."

"Shut up! Enough on Cara. And at one point in the morning about a thousand years ago I wanted to hear from Les how it went last night before you two got going. Now Les, speak."

There was a length of silence.

"Come on, Les, Momma wants you to say something," badgered Juno.

And then, "All right," said Les gloomily. "Is this porridge?"

"What do you think it is?" the older woman asked impatiently.

"Dog food. And old socks."

"It ain't old socks. It's cheesecloth for flavor. And it ain't dog food. It's Maypo and Pepsi and you'd better stir it so it don't stick."

"Beulah's *eating* it," Les said in disgust. "And it smells."

"What should she do with it? Take a bath? Juno, now *yer* gettin' it all over your face. You'll have acne by tomorry and I ain't got time to dry out your skin."

"I like it," said Juno. "Besides, Les won't eat it."

"All right, then, make Les some Chinese tea and lemon drops the way he likes it and let him tell his Auntie Lu how it went last night for the zillionth time."

Les started to mumble something, but Elb cut him off as if he didn't hear him. "It went five hundred and three dollars and eleven cents. That's how it went. And Cara stole fifteen of it buyin' beers for the cop."

"I didn't steal it," corrected Cara. "I put in twenty to start and took some back."

"Elb, if you don't stop thinkin' like a weasel you're likely to turn into one. Magic's magic and if your thought becomes form and you start growing real teeth and a tail there ain't much I can do 'cept buy you a cage. Cara, buy beers for the boys from your own dole and stop eatin' your brother's profits, you'll give him an ulcer before he's twenty-five. Les, stop making faces over the pot and lighten up. The cops ain't chasin' after you."

"I am light," said Les glumly. "It just doesn't show."

There was another unexpectedly lengthy silence at that point so I decided it would be a good time to show up and make these interesting matters worse. I knocked forcefully on the worn and splintered door and got a piece of wood in my knuckle. "I'll get it," Juno screamed excitedly out of the collective silence that sounded like some intense preoccupation happening inside. I heard a chair slam to the ground and quick running footsteps. Then the door yanked open to reveal a woman in her early twenties with the eyes of a fourteen-year-old and a noticeable scar down her forehead. She had traces of mush on her lips and thick blue eye shadow smeared messily on her eyelids. A bright plastic girlish barrette that matched her bright neon green sneakers held some of her hair to one side, but not enough to prevent most of it from falling in her face. There were stairs ascending behind her and a little door to her right that looked like it led to the kitchen. "What." It wasn't a question so much as a breathless expression of disappointment and irritation. I wasn't whoever she had been expecting.

"Answer properly," yelled the raspy voice.

"What do you *want*?" Juno now sounded like an impatient young professor in a philosophy class, looking for an impossibly abstract answer to an impossibly abstract question that she really didn't understand.

"Claude Hopner." I flashed my badge for effect, even though my law enforcement trappings are fairly meaningless north of the border.

"I'll get him."

I heard Elb swear.

"Hey, Claude," yelled Juno. "Looks like you got a visitor." Then she ran away from the door.

A woman with a face that didn't have a definable age took Juno's place. She was dressed in dirty red slippers and a torn bathrobe that partly exposed pajamas with a faded elephant print, and she had long oily hair and hard unrevealing eyes. Eyes that would tolerate all the world and forgive no part of it. Her eyes met mine suddenly and intently, and then they softened into something that reminded me of pity, or of the eyes of a young Madonna still posing out of the Italian Renaissance, before they hardened again. "I'm Claude Hopner," she rasped, "but you can call me Mother Penny."

"I'm Pete Morrow," I said easily. "Can Elbie come out and play?"

"I didn't know Elbie had any friends," Cara commented from the background, while Juno laughed.

"Shut up, Cara! Some of the most successful people in life don't have any friends. But if ya get a real one, ya might as well flaunt it 'til someone complains. Well, come in." Penny was now looking at me through old familiar eyes like she knew me, and then she sighed impatiently as if I was one more unlooked for intrusion into her day.

"Am I bothering you?"

"No more than any of my other fine children. And it ain't like you ain't been passing through before," she grumbled. "Although it's been at least a century or two since you've been around, and even if ya don't care to remember it, ya might as well stay for breakfast. But Jeepers the Cricket if it ain't one kid it's another in the Lady's name and will they ever stop coming before the ogre turns his dinner bowl on Doomsday?"

Having made a career out of investigating crazies, I knew from experience that entering their world would elicit more useful information than trying to drag them into mine. So I decided to proceed as if this were a normal visit to an old friend I hadn't seen since the Act of Union, and follow where she led. We entered an absolute mess of a kitchen when Mother Penny broke her grumbling to scold me in the identical tone I'd heard her use with her children, "Yer welcome to come around again, but let's hope ya get it right this time."

"This time" seemed to refer to whatever I supposedly got wrong centuries ago, so I nodded in polite agreement.

"Hey, Pete, long time no see," greeted Cara. Her words struck me as both underscoring Penny's and acknowledging our encounter last night. But what struck me most was her lack of surprise at my being there. Neither she nor Penny acted like it was out of the ordinary for me to show up. I wondered if they were used to random visitors.

Another girl with a raised scar around her left eye, whom I took to be Beulah, was silently making playdough Gumby dolls on a piece of newspaper. There were newsprint imprints on their bodies and she was printing inky pictures of pierced hearts and torn daisies from their bodies back onto an old gray cracked table. Juno was watching her and giggling as Beulah patted the playdough and smiled. Les was leaning over the stove and looking grim.

"Hi, Les. How's tricks?" He glowered. "Great show last night." He didn't exactly ignore me and he didn't exactly respond. He contented himself with staring at a steaming pot on the stove as if it were a mortal enemy.

"It's a pot of plenty," said Penny, "so make yerself welcome to it. Here's a bowl ain't gotten used lately." She handed me a green plastic cereal bowl with a Mickey Mouse face on the bottom, so I screwed up my courage and slopped some of the pot's contents into the bowl right under Les's nose to show him by contrasting his aloofness how "at home" I already was. Cara grabbed a plastic spoon that Beulah had stuck into one of her dolls like an overgrown penis and gave it to me, so I thanked her and forced myself to sample the slop. Found that Maypo and Pepsi wasn't a half-bad combination. Sweet and thick like camping food. And rapidly filling. "Hey, Les," I said as I stood next to him eating out of the bowl with the plastic spoon. "This is great stuff. You should try some. Put real fire in your playing."

Penny folded her arms across her chest and looked immensely gratified. "Well, Lester," she crowed, "if it ain't someone likes my cookin'."

"Happened to be in town, thought I'd pay a call," I added conversationally.

"Most kind," said Penny, still beaming over my compliment. "Yer might as well. Juno, go boil some more sody pop. There's Mountain Dew. Throw in some Easter egg dye if there's any left."

"Hey, Elb," I said by way of greeting as I took the chair next to him at the table and spooned more of the warm slop in my mouth.

"Yeah?" he asked thinly, dismally trying to hide his nerves under a courtesy ready to snap, and twitching his mouth like he half expected me to feed him a live toad. "Ran into your friend Nick the other day. Gave me your address. Said you could enroll me in the Utica NPA. Been angling for a mafia membership for a while and thought maybe you could write me a reference—"

"I'm going," said Les. "Just dropped by for a visit."

"Say hi to the boys," said Cara, cheerfully unaffected by my opener. "Give Jadie my love."

But Les had already wandered out the door.

"He's been playing keyboards since nunneries first introduced the clavichord and he still acts like life can touch him," said Penny, shaking her head.

"That's because he doesn't know how long he's been playing the way we know how long he's been playing," lectured Cara grandly. "He'll get over it."

"No, that's because life can touch him if he isn't careful," corrected Elb testily.

"What do you know about life?" needled Cara.

"So speaking about *life*, Claude," I leapt gracefully into the fray, addressing Penny, "where do you hide your namesake? Is Mr. Hopner at home?"

"No, he ain't never at home."

"Yes, well, of course. I understand from Elb that's sort of the point with Claude. Which is too bad, because I was kind of hoping to meet him. Hey, Elb. Meant to thank you for calling me into Rome. Nice to be included on your guest list but it seems a little strange that you'd want me there to shake up the guy who's been getting you gigs and everything. Care to tell me what gives?"

"Why would I call you?" asked Elb uncertainly.

"That's what he just asked," insisted Cara. "Why don't you tell him how you thought you could manage better than Ma?"

"Manage what?" I asked her pleasantly.

Penny waved a hand to silence her daughter and answered roughly, "Manage what's supposed to be his business to manage if he'd get a leg along his life and do it." She looked terribly put out. "Tell ya what, Petie." She sat down at the table and lit a cigarette which was rolled in pale flowery paper and stuck it in a slender cigarette holder, as if she was taking time to consider something. Then she took a long drag and when she exhaled the smoke smelled faintly of cheap perfume. "Ya been around forever like my other kids so ya might as well know. Gotta boy for ya. Since ya keep sayin' ya know him ye might as well for real. Named Nick. Nick Nariano. Married a girl named Marie Nunzio."

"Good family."

"Well, it might be a good family and it might be fish. But I ain't got the problem keepin' things clear like Elb, so here's the digs you're lookin' for." She glanced at her son. His expression withered into a revealing stillness. "Elbert here gets set to meet Nick in lovely Rome last August to discuss family business."

"What business?"

"Life," explained Cara.

"Beauty," said Juno. Beulah tore the leg off one of her playdough dolls and looked up blinking through the red rim around her eye. She was dropping oozing piles of colored clay in random patterns on the paper.

"Beulah, don't be a ballywag. Make table pictures or give it up for goulash. Now—why don't you three girls go upstairs and plan your party? Then everybody's doin' yard work." Cara led the way out and upstairs. Elb just sat staring at his mother in dismay, afraid to stop her and afraid to talk, as Penny blithely smoked and continued, "Anyway, Nick's set to get my boys where they properly belong. Get them heard by the herd."

"Boys? You mean Black Dog? They got heard loud and clear last night."

"Yeah," she smiled. "My babies. But now we're talking radio and record store distribution."

"How long has Black Dog been a band?" I suddenly asked, thinking about the apparent time discrepancy that had occurred to me last night.

"Long enough to know they ain't gettin' where they should be at. They've all been bumbling through various recordings with various people and various combinations of themselves for three years now and sending out demo tapes to no avail. Finally got 'em all working together and they've got a new recording of Jadie's stuff that's divine."

"Yes, I've heard it."

"Bring dreams worth hearin' to a drunk's broken lips," said Penny. "Fills an empty life higher than cheap wine fills the last free afternoon of an old teenager's life. But it'll bring dreams nationwide in the USA if Elbie here don't screw up again." Elb was watching his mother and not breathing enough for anyone without a mirror and feather to really notice. "Nickie knows some people to get it into the stores and on the air."

"On the air. Didn't they used to call that payola?" I half-jested the question as if I might be offering subtle encouragement.

"Probably still do but what the duff?" she answered seriously. "Who the hell with half a brain gets caught?" Then she looked half-affectionately at Elb through slitted eyes. "Well, chances are." He chafed a little under the implied insult but said nothing. "Now. What Nick does is his business and it's not like we have to know anything about it. Prove the station manager took a bribe of bootleg whiskey or a few grand under the table to play a song once in a while. Ain't our problem. And then if he did take himself a gift, prove it wasn't a gift of friendship and not a quid's pro quo for playin' a record."

She was right so far. Any agency that cared to follow this up would have to do a sting and go through twenty channels to get a judge's permission to bug conversations and then get someone to say in so many words what the exchange was for. And a few grand here and there wasn't enough missing tax money to push it at any one radio station. Item. When a crime gets too evenly distributed, it usually achieves a certain immunity to prosecution. "So Elb, what piece of this is your promotion company getting?"

"That's personal."

"Elbie! Pete's only lookin' for fate like the rest of us. *You* ain't doin' nothin' wrong and you ain't got nothin' to hide, so let's give 'im his satisfaction. Now, I bungled and scraped to pay to record the demo up in northern Ontario. Took in a lot of boys for that one—studio costs bein' what they are but it's my body, my money, and my love gift, so who cares? And we got cassettes and CDs and so what if Moon Management sends free copies to American record stores via Nick's people. Lots of businesses send free samples."

"All right, so what?"

"And whose gonna refuse free samples from a good business family like the Nunzios? And let's say the store gets a cut of sales to stay happy. Pure profit for them. Moon gets what's left. And if Moon turns half of what's left over to Nick, for services rendered, so what?"

So what? Other than payola and a little impossible-to-prove extortion at the retail level, and a Canadian company doing a little money laundering for the Mob, the whole scheme really was a "so what." "The IRS will catch on sooner or later," I threw out, not sure whether I was challenging or warning. "Technically, Moon Management will still owe income taxes on money earned in the states and sales taxes on anything sold in the various states."

"Yass, 'cept we ain't sellin.' The stores are. And the CDs ain't have to be on the store's books as received. Just in the store to sell with everything else. Profit on those particular discs don't have to be recorded as particular—just lost in the noise or not set down at all, lest the store wants. And the ten dollars on a thirteen-dollar disc sent up north to Moon no one has to keep a record of. The U.S. can't possibly figure out that one as income tax on Elbie and how the hell would Ottawa ever figure he's gettin' money back from the states. The stores don't have to report to Canada. Then Nick's people get their share. And everyone gets to keep what they earn."

"Gotcha." I could appreciate any well-crafted tax evasion scheme. But there was a sudden shadow gnawing in my gut and pushing my interest away from the legalities of the case. I found myself saying, not as a protest, but as an expression of morbid curiosity, "Black Dog is a great band. Why do they need the Mob to promote them? Why don't they rise on their own merits?"

Elb shot a helpless look at his mother, who calmly dragged on her cigarette and studied the ensuing cloud of smoke before speaking. The sounds of the bright city outside drifted into the cloying mess we were sitting in. It felt like minutes went by in the smoke and I could hear the kitchen tiles decaying like so many wasted lives before she spoke again.

"Grow up, Pete, and take a long hard look at the life we'se got. You ever known anyone who rose on his own merits?" She looked hard at me as if she was really expecting me to consider her question. "C'mon, really think about it and tell Momma true." She took another long slow drag and said huskily, "Think about all the people you know that have risen in their profession and then think about why they've risen." As I was considering the question, she rambled on, "Sometimes people who have merits rise. Anything can happen once or twice. But most times of the once or twice, if you examine the situation, they ain't risin' on their merits, they're risin' through connections and they happen to have merits. The merit alone don't buy them much except an excuse for their patron's preference when the real reason is politics. Plenty of merit drivin' cabs and feedin' horses."

"Sometimes merit will get you a foot in the door." I was thinking of my own luckless entrance into the FBI and all my subsequent awards, which in both cases I had arguably merited.

"Give ya a riddle. Got two boys. One of talent and hard to work with. One mediocre, embodies the company culture, and has important relatives. Who gets the job?" She looked at me searchingly and I thought about Crensch getting this murder case and me being asked to solve it. I didn't answer. "All rightie. Ninety-nine times out of ten it's the second and you know it. Connections matter, not merit. Black Dog has the merit, now they have the connections."

"They're young. They could keep trying."

"This new scheme is 'trying,' ain't it? Goin' through the Mob ain't exactly givin' up."

"No, it's more like a lifetime commitment," I said. "But I meant you could keep trying through legitimate means."

"What's illegitimate 'bout payin' for services rendered and splittin' profit?" Put like that I had no answer. "For how many years should they try, Pete? They've all been trying for three years in different ways. You ever apply for a job for three years running that you're more than qualified for and face constant rejection and keep going?"

"No, can't say that I have."

"Who trods a life along for years beggin' for work he's already qualified to perform? Go on, and my boys are beyond qualified. So what do they have to wait for? And who benefits from the waitin'? You don't tell typists and plumbers and auto mechanics to keep tryin' for three years to get a job. And they don't. They can't get a job in one thing they train for another and no one tells 'em boo 'cause ultimately no one else cares so long as they ain't bein' bothered with it. But you do tell musicians they should put up with rejection for years as a normal course of events. And if they do it they get rewarded by people callin' 'em lazy and selfish and tellin' 'em to get real jobs. And if they don't do it and kill off their music to get these real jobs, their reward is people generally feelin' relieved about the killin' and decidin' there wasn't any talent there in the first place, 'cause after all nobody you know personally can be a genius lest you start feelin' too bad about your own life—talent has to be elsewhere and unreachable and not quite real to make everything fair and everyone comfortable with hisself. 'Tis torture plain and simple ought to be a penalty for that when yer worried 'bout a little payola." I looked at Elb, who sort of shrugged as if he was used to this particular tirade and then held back the movement under his mother's watchful stare. "Why don't we all grow up and start pretendin' we're adults?" I had no answer. "Why is it always harder for artists?"

"I don't know. Never thought about it. Guess artists are supposed to suffer?"

"Shut up, Pete. Ya sound like ya read too many books. That's a lot of Romantic claptrap Lord Byron invented on a rainy afternoon in Italy when his mistress had the cramp and he was bored. I know. I helped him and I've rued that one ever since. He couldn't get fucked so now all his brothers are. 'Supposed to suffer' is a great excuse for the suits to exploit anyone that can make 'em feel somethin' besides horny and hungry. Pete—is anyone *supposed* to suffer? Is that like some rule? 'Cause like most rules, it benefits someone who ain't you. If artists are supposed to suffer, people don't have to pay them for work well done, and they can justify ignoring them and make a virtue out of it by claiming it's supposed to be that way. And this new recordin'. Jadie's stuff. He sent a demo around a few months ago when I got them all playin' together through the grace of Claude. Brilliant music like Chopin with guts if Chopin had written rock 'n' roll. Nobody at the labels was much interested in brilliant music, of course, but I could have told 'em all that before they started if anyone bothered to listen to me."

"Why not? I would think a band like that would be grabbed up right away."

"They don't sound like everyone else. They're better. And A&R types are threatened by anything different, because if it doesn't sell they can't cover their ass later. You see, they might have to explain to each other why the chance they took didn't work—which means explanations become more important than product. And if you lack both guts and imagination, it's easier to say, 'Well, we thought they'd sell because they sound like fifteen other bands that sold moderately well over the past ten years, so how were we to know?' than to justify why they supported something different. Mediocrity rises because it's safe. Mediocrity's safe because it allows everyone to justify decisions based on past failures and doesn't threaten anybody."

"Why don't they sound mediocre to get started?"

Penny looked aghast. "Why don't they die? Pete, ever hear a mediocre band that got better? If they sell as mediocrities the business will keep them as mediocrities and they'll never play beauty." I remembered the covers they did in Rome. They couldn't sound mediocre if they tried. "So, with or without the labels, my pets' music will find its way into the hearts that love it. They'll promote and distribute themselves. With Nick's help."

"How'd you meet up with the Nunzio's? Why are they promoting Black Dog as opposed to another band? Or are there other bands?"

"There might be other bands later," said Elb, anxious to spread the credit.

"Fact is," said Penny, "you always lose money on other bands. Look at the major labels, if you can stand the eyesore—some have hundreds of bands on the artist roster and 98% of the bands are going to lose money and get subsidized by one or two others. Doesn't every A&R dick dream of knowing in advance who the one or two mega acts are going to be? Then you could drop the rest and increase profits. Well, Moon Management has the one band that matters, the one band that will sell and no drain. We could stand to make more money than the labels, our operating expenses being so much lower. That part is my love gift to Elb."

"What's Claude Hopner's involvement?"

"Look, Claude's Claude. He's the guy you blame things on. That's why he's a Romantic and we've got him ridin' the cow that leapt over the moon and inventin' cures for diseases that ain't happened yet. No one has to know what he's doin' at any givin' time."

Kind of like my present assignment, I thought.

"Elb and the boys didn't have to know it until a few weeks ago, but we're all in the game now. Claude's Claude, but I get to be Claude and make him happen when he has to happen. When we need a contact person or I need to push Elb into the right clubs and rehearsal situations, since he won't listen to me direct—" she prodded him with another hard glance—"it helps to have a Claude. Girls figured it out a long time ago, but girls is generally better at figurin' stuff like that. Anyway, we're keepin' Claude in the family because if things go wrong the party concerned can go hunt Claude down and leave us out of it."

"Sounds like a great guy to pin a murder on," I brightly observed, hoping to elicit further interesting chatter.

"Oh, yass, the goshdarn murder," said Penny without my probing further. "That was me if ya care to know and that was different business." She blew smoke like a trail of quiet pride. "Swiped the old man's baby fat and made it burn like a stink bomb. Tell me," Penny looked like she was anxiously begging for praise, "Didja like my trinkets? Tasteful as a tootie bar, I thought, but Elbie wasn't sure about the bubblegum ring in the trout even though I had to send Beulah to stand by the gum machine in the discount store for an hour feedin' it quarters and mayhem 'til she got the right colors out." She looked at him with disappointed, pleading eyes and sort of playfully begged her son, "Elbie, and your old mother thought for once she was lending a creative touch to an act of killin', and all you did was sniff and tell me my jewelry looked cheap."

"Oh?" I said, not entirely sure at this point what to say.

"Well, I thought it was kind of cute," she said. "What did you think, Pete? Was the greeting card a nice touch? I worried the mouse might nibble it so I fed it a dinner mint first but I wanted things festive to drive the point home."

"Why'd you kill him?" I wasn't exactly sure I believed her but I wasn't exactly sure I didn't. All of the details she was throwing about had been in the papers, so she could have been like a thousand other nut cases claiming responsibility for the sensational crime of the week. But I wanted to see where her story was going.

"Why? 'Cause Elbie cain't listen to his mother and the old man likes to be killed. We've been at war since agriculture forced civilization into existence and screwed everybody up. We've got our jobs through eternity, and mine sometimes involves killing him. Naturally, he always returns." Elb squirmed. "You see, Elbie was going to Rome anyway to meet with Nick. Well and fine, I says, let's get business goin' but don't bring the boys because I know Hugh will be down there this year. Just know it the way Kool-Aid turns milk sour. An' I was right."

"Hugh?"

"Hugh McCrae, the old man I killed. Tryin' to be a commander only makin' himself not noticed, the monster."

"Elb's name is McCrae. Related?" I remembered Elb telling me in Rome that Rinkowski (Hugh McCrae Rinkowski of parking ticket fame?) offered to call him his son while showing off photos of people he killed in Viet Nam.

"Violently related. Ain'tja Elbie?" Elb looked miserable. "And that's unfortunate but that's Elbie's name and there's nothing I can do for it but he's still my son and I love 'im anyway no matter who sired him. War's war. Now, so at the last minute my ever-lovin' son lies to me and says Claude got them a gig in an old army camp. Well I know it ain't Claude, 'cause I'm Claude when we need him to happen, so I makes the boy promise he'll go meet Nick for business and leave my pets here where it's safe. Don't trust Hugh around them. No tellin' what bad crowd he'll get them in with. Old Hugh had a nerve to call Elb in the first place, claimin' to be the commander and promisin' money to bring the band on the base and Elb'll eat money like a mulch cow eats the neighbor's hay in June. It's what he wants. And my smart boy who wouldn't recognize a monster if he swam down one's throat, for his ol' momma's done her best to keep them away, brings my pets down to play for that awful monster, and gets smart tellin' 'em to hold back and play covers—just in case Hugh is around and as if they could hold back, the idiot. And then he calls you in to have the cops present as an extra-security, thinkin' if his mother knows anything after all that will save him from trouble. As if cops know how to kill monsters."

Elb hung his face stiffly over his chest, as if he wanted to collapse into himself.

"Well, when I learned that the band was on its way to Rome, I followed in my car and snuck through the woods without Elb's notice. And I made up my own piece of security by killing the monster for what he was. Done it smart and fair and square and had some decorative fun. You want to see some leftover fat in a candle? You wanna see how I tattooed his foot with a gramophone needle?"

"Sure."

"Juno may have burned down the candle," Elb reminded his mother. "I know Beulah broke the needle."

"Well and a day." She got up and drew a plastic bag out of the freezer. "Here Pete, look." It looked like frozen fat, whether human or not I had no idea. She replaced the bag. "But of course he ain't dead. Just killed." I was trying to make up my mind what this distinction meant, when she added, "As you can see by the Christmas display out front."

Being on foreign soil I couldn't arrest her, even if her story was true. But I could start the paperwork on extraditing her if Fearless decided the case was worth solving and a foreign citizen worth the expense of preparing a case against and trying. It might be. No congressmen to embarrass. "You want to come back to Boston with me and make a statement?" Since I couldn't arrest her, I figured a friendly invitation would be informal enough to be legal.

"I'm always killing him. It's what he likes. I've been doin' it for centuries. There's my statement."

"Well," I said. "If what you say is true, you know I'm duty bound to extradite you."

"So extradite me. And prove I done it. And prove I said it. And prove Hugh McCrae's dead without a body for snappers—a good trick. Anyone even know who Hugh McCrae is? No. 'Cause he's emptiness and nobody. An ancient monster that slithered out of the primeval chaos. And then prove I ain't crazy."

That would take some difficulty.

"And take some fat home with you in a cake but who ya gonna match it up with?" True, I had no evidence a court would believe. And the Fifth Amendment would protect her. I wouldn't be able to start any process until I saw Fearless on Tuesday, so I might as well hang out in Toronto and see what else I could learn. Especially since the Mob was coming to Fendra's tonight and I might run into some old acquaintances.

"How did you make the body decompose?"

"Secret brew. Twelfth-century alchemy. Swiss, but I added some corn flakes for color. It was easy because it's natural for Hugh to de-compose, if you think about the word."

"So let me understand. You killed him because you thought he represented some sort of threat to Black Dog?"

"Gotta better reason to kill somethin'?"

I thought of all the nut cases and all the reasons for killing I'd collected over the years. "Not really," I said honestly. Then I added as if it were a suggestion, "Some people just kill without a reason."

"Some people are just plain stupid enough to live without a reason. Ya ain't got a reason to kill, ya ain't got a reason to live. Plain fact of the day if yer honest about it. Elbie, listen up." Elb slowly and reluctantly raised his head. "Ya see, if you really have a purpose in your life you'll kill to defend it. That is, if it be a real purpose and a life that matters. People who tell ya it's noble to die for a cause are idiots who'll favor yer enemy for ten cents and a kind word. Or most times just a kind word. Some folks'll lay over and die for everyone who says boo and cain't see further than to want heroes to do the same. It's nobler to kill for what you believe in than die for what you believe in. So I killed a monster for four brilliant musicians who won't even eat my cookin.' That's the way I am. So sue me."

"You know, I'd really like to interview the band members."

"Suit yourself, Pete. Ya think I don't know what ya came for?" She promptly wrote down everyone's address and phone number. "Should have talked to Les while he was here. He'd tell ya."

"Thanks." I got up to leave and nodded at Elb, who looked at me but still wasn't saying much.

"Baby." Penny hugged him and stroked his hair. "It's all right now." And as I was going out the door Penny called out behind me, "And Petie. I know where yer off to and why you came but please don't get hurt this time. That part ain't pretty."

Stave Five

Saturday afternoon, September 5, 1992. Disoriented.

First stop was Jade's. The address Penny gave me was in Thornhill, just north of the city. And so all during the drive north I got to suffer the grand inconvenience of knowing my real motivation for coming here better than I really wanted to.

Item. I was curious about Black Dog's history because I kept running into so many inconsistencies concerning it, and inconsistencies are generally good things to chase during an investigation. But what I had argued myself into believing in Fendra's was a decisive business reason for talking to Jade was dissipating into raucous reality now that I was actually following up on it. Because there was really nothing I had to ask Jade about that I couldn't just as easily cover with Marty or Les, who lived closer to Penny's place, or, if I must head north, with Xander, who also lived in Thornhill. And ordinarily I'd do this sort of peripheral digging over the phone first to see if there was anything actually worth a follow-up visit.

But nothing ordinary seemed to be making an entrance today. So here I was, heading north with all inefficiency, playing the cassette tape I'd bought last night like an obsessive teenager, and telling myself more times over than anyone in a normal state of mind would that I really did have solid business reasons for knocking at Jade's door, and that I really did have all kinds of serious discerning investigative questions to ask him that I just hadn't bothered to think of yet, and that after all I was only intending to make it a quick professional interview and leave and perhaps I would drop in on Xander too so I could fool myself into believing that it really wasn't like I was just going to Jade's. The music greatly enhanced my sensible frame of mind.

Lent me much confidence in negotiating the city traffic. Got so busy convincing myself that I was only doing my job that I nearly caused three accidents.

For after experiencing last night's performance and eternally going over our conversation in Rome I couldn't ignore what was really drawing me to Thornhill. Damn my life if I didn't just want to spend a day listening to Jade play music and tell me stories. And if I showed up at his door and flashed my badge, did I really believe that he would accommodate my wants?

Come on. Why didn't *I* just grow up and start pretending I was an adult? Instead of an awkward adolescent burdened with some kind of disorienting infatuation?

Item. I barely knew him. We'd had a conversation he had probably forgotten and that I now felt half-embarrassed obsessing over. I'd had an unsettling dragon dream I still couldn't shake. I'd seen him perform. Twice. Music like a dash of madness.

In other words, I had no real business showing up at Jade's residence, but I also knew that reality wasn't doing much to stop me, and I was unable to stop myself. *Got a better reason to kill time?* I kept repeating in my head, and then winced when I realized my thoughts had taken on Penny's no-nonsense vocal inflections. And winced harder when I remembered her telling me she knew where I "was off to" but not to "get hurt this time." As if in her crazy reality, I'd somehow been "here" before.

Got to Thornhill. City map useless outside of Toronto proper. Needed directions. Stopped at a gas station, took the cassette out of my tape deck and dropped it in my pocket with the cassette Guido had let me steal. Black Dog's music had become an absurdly private affair for me in last night's woods and I felt like I didn't want anyone to know what I was listening to. Resented losing my night-feeling to strangers. Resented losing anything fine. Got directions. Pulled away and felt my storm-ridden anticipation turn and settle into the same strangling nervousness I couldn't shake last night. Drove unfamiliar streets. Neck so tight it numbed my head like a piano wire noose.

Anyway, I found the street address with little difficulty because my inexplicable eagerness now made everything around me appear brighter and sharper than usual so I got there faster than I expected. The name on the mailbox said Elise McClellan, so I wasn't sure old Mother Penny had been any more honest with me than her son usually was, but there was nothing for it except to ring the doorbell and wonder if I'd been fooled. There was no car in the driveway except mine. There might have been a car in the garage, but the garage was closed up and there were no windows. No one answered the door. I heard no movement inside. Felt something like disappointment coupled with strange relief that I wasn't going to interview Jade alone after all. Rang the bell one last time, mainly because I was sure it wouldn't elicit any kind of response.

"Just a minute, I'm coming," called a clear voice accompanied by hard descending footfalls that threw waves of tension through my chest, a voice that was plainly being disrupted from something far more important than answering the door. I thought about flashing my badge, decided not to, and was on the verge of changing my mind again when Jade opened the door and we stood face to face. "Yes? What do you want?" He was easier and more natural with the question than Juno had been, but he also conveyed an air of being busy and wanting to quickly get through whatever business I might have. There was no hint of recognition in his face and I suddenly felt very sad and foolish and awkward, as if my dreams and memories and anticipations of the last few weeks had suddenly been made public in all their horribly immature intensity. Then it occurred to me that since we had only met once, in the dark, he wouldn't necessarily recognize me because I was wearing camping clothes and hadn't bothered to shave.

So I took out my badge after all and said, "Uh, hi. I'm Pete Morrow. Do you remember me? We met in Rome a few weeks ago—"

"Over a murder, wasn't it?" Jade spoke amiably, getting right to the point for me, and leading me to suspect that perhaps he did remember me after all.

"Yes, that's right." I put away my badge. "I don't want to take up a lot of your time, but your Aunt Penny gave me your address and I hoped you might be willing to answer a few questions for me."

"All right. Questions. For you." He sounded generously accommodating, but I got the impression that it was dropping his aunt's name that really bought me access into his busy schedule. "That is, if you don't mind coming upstairs with me. Xander's here, and I've got some stuff running on my computer that I don't want to leave." I thanked him for the invitation and followed him through a comfortably furnished living room with an upright piano in the corner. The room was maniacally neat. Even the light bulbs looked dusted and the wall sockets gleamed like they'd been newly scrubbed with cleanser. There was no evidence that anyone ever really walked on the plush carpet. A long roll of clear plastic protected the carpet and made a sort of walking path for us. "Do you play piano, too?" I indicated the upright, which was polished and shiny enough to reflect a gnat's heartbeat at a hundred yards.

"Some. I mostly use it for composing when Les's gear isn't available." We went up some carpeted stairs and down a short hall and entered a large loft-like room on the second floor that had been contrived by removing the wall between two normal size bedrooms. "It feels pretty empty," Jade explained, "because a lot of my amps and stuff are sitting in the club we're playing at this weekend and Les normally stores his gear here but that's all at the club now, too." I immediately noticed a little keyboard connected to a computer station in one corner. There was a hot plate near the computer and three standing guitar racks holding different basses. The walls were covered with shelves full of books. I took a moment to study them. Classics, including the entire Bohn Library series of Victorian translations of Greek and Latin works, a reprint of a seventeenth-century treatise on herbalism, a *Complete Works of Shakespeare*, and a book of color plates of Hieronymus Bosch paintings.

Xander was sitting on the floor and leaning against one of the bookshelves, cradling an acoustic guitar and playing some pretty Spanish-sounding melody with his eyes closed. He was utterly oblivious to our entrance but his presence prevented me from feeling alone with Jade, and I caught myself feeling mildly dismayed. Jade went over to the computer and entered something. *A pleasant room*, I thought as I stood there listening to the music, with neat, white painted wooden floorboards and a bright, soft throw rug like a Moroccan tapestry in the middle bearing the picture of an Arab on horseback slaughtering a she-lion in the desert. The Arab holds the spear of death in one hand while gently cradling a lion cub in the other. And back in the room large windows let in blue September along with a feeling of light and space. I noticed a little green plant sitting next to the throw rug in a pot covered with bright purple aluminum foil. The plant bore delicate white flowers and looked like it spent a lot of time talking solitary plant talk to the shrewd northern sun.

But mostly I stood there and envied that rare feeling of both work and fellowship happening between Jade and Xander, because mostly the room felt like their work and friendship were all pretty much the same thing.

But they were both now for all intents and purposes ignoring me so I wandered over to study a poster of Van Gogh's *Café Terrace at Night* while Xander continued playing. His music washed me into the painting's familiar street scene, where I felt like I was sitting among the empty tables, wrapped in the comfort of evening. And I knew that if I stayed charmed long enough the painted figure forever standing among the painted tables would bring me anything I was brave enough to ask for. Then I just kept surveying all the weird suns like stars or drifting cornflowers crying their light through the darkness exactly the way Van Gogh taught them to.

Then I remembered where I was and left the painting. I watched Jade. There was nothing of the rock 'n' roll wizard about him now and somehow the contrast with his stage persona made last night's performance even more impressive. He had removed his make-up and stage clothes of course and was now wearing ordinary jeans and a T-shirt. He had tied his long hair back in a neat ponytail, which gave him a no-nonsense air of being "at work" but also accented the classic features of his face when I caught him smiling in profile. And there was absolutely no consciousness about him of having overpowered his audience last night or of being thoroughly capable of doing so again. I decided he was far too easy with his own power to be conscious of it.

Jade finally called his buddy out of his trance with a hint of good-natured rebuke. "Hey, Xander, we've got a visitor. Remember Pete Morrow? From Rome?"

"Uh, sure," said Xander suddenly. "Oh, wow. Did you get that solo in the computer, Jade? Thought I had something there. Hey, Pete, what brings you to Toronto?"

"Claude Hopner invited me. Made me an offer I couldn't refuse."

Jade chuckled softly and appreciatively.

"Yeah, there's a lot of that going around," agreed Xander enthusiastically. "That's why we're here."

"So," I asked, "how long have you two been with Black Dog?"

"Forever," said Jade.

"No, really. Elb gave me the impression you were new to the band, that Les and Marty were playing with another band last winter and hooked up with Xander for the first time last March. But then he seemed to imply that you two have been playing together for years. Then your aunt tells me you've all been making demo tapes with different people for at least three years, and that various forms of the band go back that far. And now I see you have a CD out and promotion plans in the works and I hear you've been playing around town for a while."

"Well, various permutations of Black Dog have been around," said Jade matter-of-factly. "And I have known Xander forever."

"I was playing with Les and Marty as a power trio last March," said Xander, "although the three of us have played in other bands as well." He thought hard, as if the question required all his concentration. "I think officially the four of us have been together a few months now. The CD is our first recording as a foursome together, because the three of us needed a bass player and Jade brought in some songs and then we made the recording and then we became a band." He got more and more excited as he spoke, as if he wasn't too sure of things to start but had suddenly gotten into the process of discovering something new and now rather enjoyed it.

"Music's a fluid thing," said Jade. "I don't suppose we really have a clearly defined origin. Black Dog's always sort of been around in one form or another." He glanced at Xander. "Elb's really like the newcomer. He's the business guy."

Well, their explanation made the most surface sense and accounted for the most discrepancies so far. "So how did you and Elb meet up?"

"Cara saw us playing last May and introduced us to Elb, and Elb got us gigs and money for recording via Cloudy Claude."

"You mean your aunt?" I tested.

"Yes, I suppose so. That's Claude's identity this week." They both chuckled as Xander put his guitar away.

"Hey, Jade," he said suddenly, "if you don't need me, I'd just as soon go home and work out before the show tonight. That is, unless Pete here has more questions."

"I'm all right," I said generously.

"Sure," said Jade. The word was a friendly dismissal to Xander but the trace of doubt in his voice felt like a response to my comment. Xander picked up his guitar case and left. Jade closed the door behind him and went over to the hot plate while asking me courteously, "Would you like some tea? It's Chinese, Les's favorite. Water's already boiling."

"Then I can hardly refuse."

I noticed a shelf of black candles and seashells. The candles were burning in the airy light and emitting a soft fragrance of patchouli that was more apparent now that the door was closed. Jade noticed my interest in the candles as he handed me a warm mug and sat down on the throw rug, indicating that I should do the same. "Cara gave me those last night," he explained. "So what else would you like to know?"

Now that we were alone, and I had gotten through my important investigative business, I really didn't know what to say to Jade. Want to talk about dragons again? Want me to tell you a lie? The whole thing of me being here suddenly threatened to feel really stupid, and well, wrong. I settled for a banal, "I liked the show. I was there last night."

"Thanks." He smiled graciously.

And then there was a horrible silence because I knew that the only reason I was still there was that I was somehow expecting the intimate feeling of our night walk to be renewed. And even while I was hoping that he would renew it because I had no idea how to, I was painfully conscious that I was disrupting his work. And that I was sitting on tapestry images of desert violence and lightly sipping a tea which tasted like childhood memories of autumn wood smoke with an absolute genius whose music could bend the September sky with a few careless flicks of the wrist. And that on some days, like today, he was simply ordinary.

I watched Jade raise his mug and drink with me like we were old companions. The silence between us was suddenly comfortable and showed no sign of breaking. Then I was thinking once again about that damn mythology course I'd once taken, the one I remembered in the guest house in Rome, and how when gods take mortal form they always prefer the ordinary peasant to the king. But if Penny was, in Elb's words, "something like a witch," then Jade was, in my opinion, something like a god. And I was something like a trespasser. I knew my feeling was outlawed.

Item. We cannot honor our own deities lest some dullard get jealous and menacingly point out all the reasons we shouldn't honor anything.

I suppose if Jade had been more conscious of his greatness I would have been less in awe of him. As it was, this unassuming near stranger could pluck a few wound steel strings against a wooden box and make my deadened heart feel something holy. If there's a better definition of deity floating around out there, I haven't felt or found it.

I looked into his dark eyes. "Yes?" he half-mocked before glancing towards his computer station.

"Jade," I said his name and felt like I was taking an undeserved liberty, and then because I felt foolish and crazy for feeling that way, I glanced through the window at the sky and asked him the question I'd already been asked twice that day, "What do you want?"

"What do I *want*?" He considered the question seriously, as if it wasn't an impertinence at all, but he didn't answer it. Instead he took one of his basses out of a rack and began playing it unamplified, improvising some medieval-sounding melodic line that would have made a fine accompaniment to the piece Xander had been playing. The autumn sunlight fell on his face and arms as he played. "That's what I want. That's the line."

"I mean, in general."

"I never mean anything in general."

"All right, I'll play your game then—"

"I certainly hope so." He smiled. "Isn't that why *you're* here?"

I felt my chest constrict, my breathing stop, and my head go lighter than a broken bag of dead leaves. A few seconds passed before I steadied myself to speak. "I mean, I'll say this in particular." My voice was now colder and more legalistically paternal than I meant it to be, which made me feel even more screwed up about everything. "Penny let me in on your band's promotion plans. Far as I can tell, you and your bandmates haven't done anything illegal, meaning anything my government would particularly care to push against, but you know you're dealing with people who have. You do know that, don't you?" He didn't answer. His fingers were too busy for conversation. "Jade, here's some advice where it may not be wanted. You and your friends have a great band there. You don't want to start your musical career under a cloud, excuse the pun."

"I want to start my musical career." His tone was far too reasonable to argue with. I tried anyway.

"Once those people start doing business with you, they don't stop."

"I hope not. Longevity is a very good thing for a musician, devoutly to be wished."

"They'll demand higher and higher percentages."

"That's Elb's problem."

"And of course Elb's problems can't possibly affect you," I said sarcastically, "since he's only your manager and all," and then bit my tongue for saying it because he shot me a curious "why do you care look" and I realized I had no business caring. It was my job to do surveillance on this payola venture and definitively solve a murder case, not drop in unannounced on Jade's work and tell him how to live his life and issue warnings like a local cop lecturing a high school kid for speeding.

"I never argue with getting what I want," Jade said simply. "Life's more fun that way." Then his voice suddenly became conspiratorially playful, "Hey, Pete, check this out. What does *that* cloud look like?" There was now a patch of cloud bright and visible through the windows. Jade rose to put one of the candles on the window ledge and then lay on his back on the rug to better contemplate the sky.

"A cumulus cloud. There's a storm on the horizon."

"I think it's a Spanish galleon."

"Or a spotted dragon," I offered helplessly, unable to resist getting what I wanted, this new word game that I sensed him creating. Even though I knew that part of me was playing along instead of really playing.

"All right," he said easily, taking my request. "A dragon ship sailing to an old Viking kingdom, where age-old fighters spin tender broth from rainbows and oily shoe leather—" He paused while we fell through silence together and the dream made landfall. "A dragon ship to break into obscure shores of meaning and leave us stranded where all signs point in all directions. What do you see?"

"—the sky is green here—" and it was green, from what I could see through the dream's intensity.

"—green like a forgotten summer, boiling over backwards—"

"—green—"

"—green like the surge that kicks open a missing sky before an ocean sunrise–"

"—green like the moss on a stone hut, I guess, or a forest floor—"

"—a slow creeping hut. Where an old woman like a dark moon bestirs herself to welcome you. She's wearing forest shadows in her hair. She blesses you with porridge and wisdom and hands you a sword of light—"

"—perfect in my palm—"

"—what do *you* want?" he whispered.

I was so far gone into this living poem that Jade and I were co-creating, so happily blinded to the rest of the world by whatever was happening between us, that there was nothing else I wanted. But I heard myself say, "Water from an ancient river to wash old dreams in—"

"—you must give her a cup of blood to get a cup of water. Use the sword—"

"—I can't make myself bleed—"

"—then come quest with me. Into your desert. Where sand is the color of the morning sun painted in boiling oils—"

"—the sand pulls and sucks at my barren feet—"

"—are you falling through sand, Pete—"

I thought of my nightmare and said nothing.

"Come now, what are we reading—" Jade continued.

"—runes—"

"—runes. Deep in an old book of traveler's tales. Someone got lost and discovered distant alphabets trapping secrets in the east. What do they say?"

I read the imaginary runes. "The pearls of the north are born in decadence—"

"—yes, but don't they spell images of other books, and wands, and flowers singing like old wrens in the stunning heat of a strange, large noon? And you and I are strolling through fountains of bright Indian palaces and I—"

"—and I can hear you playing a sitar, and night stars singing winds out of tune—"

"—ssh." At first I thought Jade was cruelly silencing the word-music by suddenly ending our game and then I realized faltering footsteps on the stairs had really broken up our revery. The door rattled open, which jarred me into reality, but Jade didn't move. A thin woman of dowdy neatness with a sweater wrapped around her faded and much washed skirt and blouse entered the room like a bitter secret quietly eroding an otherwise pristine life. She was doing surveillance.

"Good afternoon, Mother," said Jade.

"Thought I heard a strange voice." She was ferociously hesitant, tamely annoyed. Her face was almost vehemently emotionless, save for a rigid, jury-rigged smile that appeared to be for my benefit. Life had been one long disappointment. She wanted everyone to share it with her.

"Pete Morrow, my mother Elise."

"Hi." Elise put out the candles. "Is my son bothering you?"

"No."

She studied me through pale blue eyes while speaking to my host. "You shouldn't burn things in the middle of the day, Jade."

"I know."

"So why are you doing it?"

"Because I shouldn't. Pete, I've got some work to do here but why don't you drop by the club again tonight? Come round back at eight or so and we'll get you in for free." He paused and asked playfully, "Shall we have the first dance?"

"Thought we just did," I said graciously. Elise watchfully ushered me out, so I made sure to remain in the hallway to eavesdrop.

"Playing out again tonight?" Elise asked in a tone of flimsy brightness.

"Always."

"At least I heard you say it's a club this time and not a two a.m. rendezvous on some lonely Lake Ontario beach." She was making an insincere attempt at humor. Jade didn't say anything, but I could hear him softly playing his bass. "Jade, do you really need to play out every week? You're always holed up in your room composing or you're always out playing. Couldn't you devote some time to going back to school or looking for a job?" He continued playing. "What were you *doing* with that man?"

"Entertaining him."

"Entertaining him," she mocked with less pretense at good-natured humor and then asked shrilly, "Oh, and did you get *paid* for entertaining him?"

"I don't know. Sort of, I guess." He was too busy playing to dwell on the issue.

"Jade, you've got to start thinking about your life—"

"Why?"

"Why?" she sighed in exasperation. "Because you're in your mid-twenties and you have to ask, that's why. There's nothing wrong with playing in a local band as a hobby, but not all the time. I love music too. But not all the time."

"Then you don't love music."

"I do, Jade," she insisted. "But not every minute. Only God can love every minute. We mere mortals need a break." Jade's fingers were not taking a break. They were playing scales. "Music has its place, but you need to grow up and see that there are other things in life."

"Like what?" He wasn't being sarcastic. He really wanted to know.

She didn't answer the question. "Why do you have to play so much?"

"I like it. It's mine."

"We can't do everything we like, Jade. You've got to start realizing that."

"What's in it for me to start realizing that?"

She sighed in exasperation. "You don't have to have a band. You can play here at home with your friend Xander and 'like it' just the same as playing out all over the place and it's still 'yours.' If it's only a question of 'liking it' you can play by yourself when you come home from a decent job, can't you? I do. A lot of people do. There's nothing wrong with that. I'm not saying you have to give up music, but there's nothing wrong with cutting down your involvement in the interest of earning a living. If you don't have time to practice you can always go to an occasional concert and listen to somebody else play. You can listen to records. You can listen to the radio. You can go back to school and study about music and get an education degree and teach. Like I do—" In the space of thirty seconds Elise had relegated Jade's brilliance to standing on the sidelines and applauding somebody else's achievements, and not being satisfied with that travesty, to sacrificing the exercise of his own talents to teaching somebody else to establish a musical career. I didn't much like her agenda. It smacked of sabotage.

"That all sounds rather complicated," replied Jade good-naturedly. "Isn't it easier to skip all the nonsense and just play?"

"Nonsense." Elise's voice was suddenly wry and soft. She couldn't resist her son's humor and vision, but her version of maternal concern still rose uppermost. "I wish it were nonsense. But it's reality. I can't support you forever as you live in randomness, arriving here without warning and then disappearing for months or years without notice or means of contact."

"So don't support me," Jade said in a "fair enough" voice. "You begged me to return, so I did. Say the word and I'll take it elsewhere. Again."

"Take it elsewhere. Where would you go? Where *do* you go?" asked Elise with the gentle sarcasm of pointed disbelief. "You don't have anything resembling a real job."

"If I took it elsewhere that wouldn't be your concern." Elise sighed audibly over his logic. They had had this conversation before. Her footfall told me she was retreating from the room so I started down the hall to the top of the stairs when I heard Jade say nonchalantly, "Anyway, got an aunt in York. Name of Mother Penny."

An odd, overlong, piercing silence filled in around the playing. The kind of silence that greets the news of a beloved child's death. I could feel it invade my body. I could practically hear Elise blanching. Then a tiny gasp. Then a squeaky, threatened, defeated sounding, "My God." More silence. Although I couldn't see inside the room, I got the impression that Jade was watching her distress with bemused curiosity. "Since when?"

"Since her son started managing my band. Penny's pretty cool about stuff like music. Doesn't mind if I hang out."

"Doesn't mind if you hang out." Elise repeated slowly, her voice so thick that it encumbered her own words. "Oh my God. My God. And her *son* is managing your band. How?" she asked weakly.

"Adequately. So far."

"That's not what I meant. I meant how . . . you've seen her? Oh my God." Elise started to cry a little. That is, I could hear tears in her voice.

"She's made me feel welcome. What's the deal? You know her?"

"No. No. No. No. No. No, sweetheart," her voice broke and softened. "You mustn't. I don't know her. Not for years. And here she is again." Her voice sounded squeaky and pleading. "What does . . . does she tell you anything about me?"

"That if you knew about her you'd react this way, even if she did help you out of a bad spot once. What's the deal between you? She says you're welcome to drop by the house sometime if you care to."

"There's no 'deal' Jade. She's just something I don't care to think of as part of my life."

"Suit yourself. Respecting Penny, I have no problem 'thinking about my life.'"

Elise cried out a little gasp at having her own words thrown back at her. "You mustn't go to her. Promise me. You can stay here. You can do whatever you want here."

"I always do whatever I want. Right now I want to practice."

"Please, Jade, I mean it."

"So do I."

I heard her footfall again so I quickly descended the stairs and slowly paced the living room to ensure that I would surprise a shaken Elise. She was all nervous and rattly and needed to be alone somewhere. "You're still here?" She clutched the polished banister and forced friendliness into her tone but she clearly wanted me out so she could be alone.

"I'm very sorry to bother you, Mrs. McClellan, but as I was leaving it occurred to me that you might be able to help me out with something."

"Yes?" Her eyes met mine and her voice sounded coolly polite like Jade's sometimes did, only her tone was sharply dutiful as his never was.

I flashed my badge for no good reason except overkill. "I'm FBI. United States."

She gasped and glanced upstairs. "I hope there's no trouble. My son didn't tell me you were—"

"No trouble. Don't worry," I said easily. "Only it just occurred to me—you know a woman goes by the name Mother Penny? Sometimes calls herself Claude Hopner?"

Sharp intake of breath. She looked upstairs again and shook. "I—uh. What is this about?" Then, "I don't know. I might know her."

"She lives in York. Thirteen Oak Street." She nodded dumbly to indicate she knew the address. "What can you tell me about her?"

She swallowed. "I don't know her that well. I might have known her a long time ago. I don't know what I can tell you about her." She started walking aimlessly. The walking was something, anything, to mitigate her nervousness.

"I'm investigating the murder of Hugh McCrae," I threw out. Elise shook so badly she had to sit on the couch. "You know him?" She was crying again, and she wasn't bothering to hide the fact. I softened. "May I sit down?" She nodded and took some tissue out of her sweater pockets. Up close, Elise smelled faintly of old lavender, the way very old women sometimes smell in the middle of a spring morning in their Sunday best. "I'm sorry. You're clearly very disturbed and I didn't mean to frighten you. There's no trouble here. I've just reached something of a dead end and I was hoping you could help. If you don't want to answer any questions, I won't insist." I rose to leave.

The tactic worked. "It's just—it's been a long time. Ancient history, I suppose."

"How do you know Mr. McCrae?"

"We used to be—I can't explain." She tried to collect herself and kept shuddering as a result. "I used to know him. Years ago. I don't know—we used to be," she looked sick, "sort of together." She swallowed a little. "Sort of married. I don't know. I don't know." She sort of whispered the last two phrases as if she was afraid of her own words. I had to be very careful to get whatever she was keeping to herself.

"Used to be married? Are you divorced?"

"No. He's just . . . gone."

"I'm sorry," I said sympathetically.

"Don't be," she said through tears. "I'm not."

"Oh." I let her find words because I couldn't think of any.

"He's really dead? How do you know?"

Actually, I didn't know. Hugh McCrae was getting to be as big a mystery as Claude Hopner, and as to whether McCrae was posing as Rinkowski or dead or alive or just "killed," or whether Penny was actually involved in the murder, I was pretty much clueless. I certainly needed something more concrete than Penny's bizarre story, which I hadn't made up my mind to believe yet, and I was hoping Elise could provide some much-needed perspective. So I reluctantly told her a little bit about the case but omitted the gory details because of her present state. "Was he Jade's father?"

"Oh God, no! Oh, no! That was my first husband. He's really dead. I think."

"You mean you don't know?" She sort of shrugged like she wasn't sure. "What was your first husband like?" The question was probably irrelevant to the case, but I was curious about anything concerning Jade.

"What was he like? He was a sailor. He came out of the sea and he died there. Jade was very young." She blew her nose. "So was I." That seemed to end the subject, but I pursued.

"What was his name?"

She looked scattered and offended. "Michael." Then she closed her eyes and breathed slowly, as if to shut out the world or retreat into her own. I didn't think she was going to offer me any more information, but she surprised me by continuing. "He told me his name meant 'Who is like God?' but that the answer was too awful to share. No matter how much I begged for it." She opened her eyes and looked steadily at the floor. "I'm sure he had other names. I know he had other lives, because after he died, I discovered that he had scores of abandoned wives and children all over the planet."

"What were his other names?"

She took so long to answer I began to think she was dismissing me, but as I made a motion to leave, she said without emotion, "I called him Dionysus. After the god of ecstasy, the vagrant who spent much of his time at sea." Then her detachment took a sudden swerve into bitterness. "So, Mr. Morrow, who is like God? Michael McClellan, who charmed himself into my life with songs and tales and long starry nights on a Halifax beach, only to leave a nasty hole in my heart that Hugh McCrae slimed himself into like vomit filling a mold."

"Does your son know Mr. McCrae?"

"No. I suppose it's better for Jade if he doesn't know any of them. It's a bad part of my life and I don't want it near us." She turned to me suspiciously. "How did you get our address?"

"Penny gave it to me."

"Damn the woman. She's nothing to us."

"Is Penny capable of killing?"

"Yes," she said without hesitation.

"Would she have a motive you're aware of for killing Mr. McCrae?"

"I try not to be aware of Penny or her motives. Hugh was odd. Killing him is an odd kind of hobby with Penny. She's tried to do it before but he turned into a rock. A fossil, I mean." I suddenly decided that Elise was as oddball as the rest of them. It just didn't show up as quickly in conversation. She glanced at my face and noticed my decision. "Look, I don't know what to say. He's gone and Penny did it. Now you say he's dead. Ask her about it." She was through with the conversation.

"One last question, if you don't mind. Do you know a man named Claude Hopner?"

"No." She wiped her eyes. "I've told you what I can. I hope you solve the case. I've got things to do now."

"Of course." I stood up. "Thanks. Here's my card." I scribbled my home address and phone number on the back. "Give it to your son in case either of you want to contact me about anything." The card I had already given Jade didn't have my home address and phone number on it and I wanted him to have it without me really giving it to him. Not that I expected him to call, but I liked having the possibility in my life that he could if he wanted to. I liked knowing that if my phone rang I had the space of a few seconds before answering when I could wonder if it was him. Elise looked carefully at the card and said they'd be glad to help in any way they could.

I started for the door. "Mr. Morrow," Elise called out suddenly. "Do you like to read books?"

"Yes," I said, feeling the oddness of her question and remembering the extensive library in Jade's practice room.

"I used to read a lot," she said shakily. "Sometimes that's how it starts, you know."

"That's how what starts?"

"You love stories, and then . . ." her voice trailed off and thick tears took back her eyes.

"You love stories," I prompted.

"No," she said. "I don't know if I love them. I still *collect* them. But sometimes I think they should be burned."

We did have the first dance. That night at Fendra's Beth plied me with Storms because I was officially "with the band" and this time I drank them. Jade was a wizard in dark eye makeup and a dark moonlit cloak. He danced briefly and intently with me. Our movement was a storm of grace.

And then he honored Nick Nariano with a dance, calling him by name. Nariano glanced back at his mob associates like he wasn't too sure about this venture but he rose to the occasion anyway, did an awkward tarantella type thing for about half a minute, and sat back down to drunken howls. The Mafiosi, none of whom I recognized except for Guido, were sitting two tables away from me.

I was cautious about being recognized, but not overly concerned. My past work had involved the older, Boston branch of the Nunzios. The new Utica branch that Nariano had married into, possibly as a means to impress the old guard in Boston, was far more likely to know me by reputation than by sight. Also, I hadn't dealt with the Nunzios in several years, and I was in a dimly lit club, unshaven, and wearing camping attire. I decided if my presence did cause flutters among the *criminali*, that alone would be information worth knowing, and I'd be sure to hear about it via Elb or Penny, who evidently enjoyed sharing the details of her illegal pursuits with me.

Elb was with them, pretending to ignore me, and looking much as he did last night in his dark hat and white silk shirt. Before he introduced the band, he had been studiously laughing at all Nick's jokes and now he was taking absurd pains to half rise and applaud Nick's little dance as Nick settled back at the table and the music careened elsewhere.

But the rest of the night was for the audience proper, and those kids got their money's worth. Even Beth got shyly dragged onto the floor where the rock wizard softened his music to acknowledge her sweetness and they both looked terribly sweet together, moving in a ruthless naivety like young lovers dancing in a careless spring.

He playfully lunged at her with his bass across his thigh like a troubadour and she lithely stepped back from his lunges in perfect time, with the brightest, most happily entranced smile I'd ever seen. And then she ran smiling and blushing back into darkness while he sadly tilted his head to gently mock loss. Then he suddenly turned to carry the band through an interlude that would scathe hellfire out of heaven.

And when the music closed into darkness and the band members made their exit through the back door, I saw Elb in the aftermath earnestly trying to discuss something with the table of drunken mobsters. Elb was doing his best to nurse a single beer so he could stay sober without looking like a prig. But his business partners were all three sheets to the wind on house Lambrusco and seemed to be having a fairly good time of it. Which was healthy for all concerned, I supposed.

"They're different. But I had fun. You have fun, Nick?" said one of them, a little afraid of having expressed his enjoyment before his boss did, but confident from Nick's behavior that the boss would agree.

"Yeah, I had fun," said Nick. "Beats placin' bets with Sammy LeMano's wife there." Laughter at some in-joke.

"No wonder he can't get it up," someone crowed.

"Hey, the band's got costumes like a clown," Nick threw out. More laughter, because it was supposed to be a joke to top all jokes. Guido looked especially pleased. "So, Elb, son. Good boy."

"Yes," said Elb politely.

"We get your records played, you guarantee sales? I mean I don't know nothin' about rock 'n' roll but what if it don't sell? The boss don't like to be out money, ya know."

"Claude Hopner's got money to insure your start-up expenses. You've seen he's good for it." Elb managed to sound both strident and placating. "But they'll sell, Nick. Look at those kids." The merchandise table was swamped, because the door was locked against fans spilling out back. Cara was running the table and doing her best to let everyone know that she knew the band. Given our distance across the semi-dark club, it wasn't clear whether she knew or cared I was there. "Just multiply that scene in record stores across the country."

"Yeah, I know a couple of record executives at SBC ain't gonna be too happy with us." More laughter. "That might be worth sending a message alone. For honor's sake."

"Would you like to meet the band?" asked Elb.

"Nah, that's all right." They were all too drunk to move. "Hey, Elb, gotta ask you a question. Suzie Q there, the Thai princess of Rome, gave me this a few weeks ago—" he turned over something I recognized as the calling card I'd left in the Thai restaurant. "You don't know this guy, do ya?"

"No," said Elb, making eye contact with Nick. "We've never met."

"You're sure about that? You wouldn't lie to your pal Nickie, now, would you? 'Cause if we're gonna be partners in this, we're gonna have to be pals. Trust. No one gets hurt."

"I never lie," Elb lied.

"Well Suzie Q there says this guy was asking about you. Thought you'd like to know he has a history with our family. Helped put two of my wife's uncles in the slammer for life a few years ago and if he's snoopin' around our business again, some of my partners ain't gonna feel too happy 'bout things." Nick paused. "You sure, now? 'Cause he was asking for you. Wonder how he could have gotten your name."

"I don't know. Maybe Claude knows him."

"When are we gonna meet Claude?"

"Claude was supposed to show up tonight but he sent some money instead—for assurance. He, uh, won't be met. Has a thing about it."

"Kind of like a silent partner," somebody joked.

"Yeah, well," said Nick, taking the check that Elb slid across the table. "I'll meet his money. Say hello to your beautiful mother for me. Tell ya what, kid, I'll start puttin' my people to work for you. We'll get your records played—then we'll see what happens when the money rolls in."

"The band's got another CD in the works. We ought to be able to use three hits from each one consecutively—three months on each hit—we'd end up dominating the air waves for eighteen months solid." No one but Nick seemed to be much listening. "That'll make anyone a superstar by today's standards."

"Sure. If we start seein' a return on the first hit. You got yourself a deal." Nick kissed Elb on the cheeks to a great deal of raucous laughter and Elb smiled good-naturedly at the gesture because under the circumstances he could hardly do anything else. I understand the old-time mobsters never used to kiss newcomers. Kissing is another screen image they've all stolen out of the *Godfather* movies for lack of any good reading material to imitate.

"Let's just keep it in the family. Keep it clean. You can start shipping CDs down to Utica next week. Hey, Cara—nice legs, nice legs." Cara flashed her legs under her skirt in a sarcastic gesture and gave them all a look of contemptuous superiority before adopting an overly done business demeanor with the next customer.

They all drank another pledge. Then Guido noticed me. "Hey, hey you—come here. You're the guy here last night," he called, to Elb's visible horror, and Cara's suddenly rapt attention. "Hey, here's a guy knows Claude. Says he knows you, Nick."

"Who are you?" called Nick suspiciously. "I don't know you."

At that moment I could have ruined the entire deal by telling the truth. At that moment Jade's musical career literally lay at the discretion of my Storm-drunk tongue. I gave him what he wanted. I lied. "Huh?" I said in my dumb southern boy voice. "You ain't the guy I'm lookin' for. Lookin' for Nick."

"I'm Nick." He seemed angry about it. "Ask anyone."

"You ain't Nick. Stop playin' games. I know Nick, and he ain't you."

"Hey, maybe it's a different Nick," someone said brightly.

"Nick Harshbarger, sometimes comes here. Classy guy. You wouldn't know him."

"Harshbarger. Don't know him. Hey, want a drink?" Nick was suddenly back in a festive mood. Elb looked like a corpse on leave. I was certain Elb's expression would betray him so I immediately did what no professional in my position would do. I got up and left.

But I suppose in retrospect it was as much business as chivalry. I knew if I wanted to push it I was now in a position to elicit whatever information from Elb I might find useful in the future. But if I killed the deal with a word there'd be no evidence to nail anyone on later. This payola thing was interesting to track because there was no telling what else might turn up, but it needn't go further than a personal hobby yet. I left Elb to recover.

And being drunk on Storms, wandered out the front door and around back to the limited access lot where the band was hanging out.

And together we tore Toronto to shreds. I think. Or the city got to me and I was the one being torn all over the place for a night and a day and another night. And taking life from every minute. Our wanderings were spotted and spacious. Rummaged through still open bars and still open strangers. Old bars full of old men and opinions hung drying since afternoon. We entered and drank to oblivion. Gone. Wasted. None of us knew who we were anymore. Marty had a knack for finding bottles in the crevices of old alleys and under benches and outside the doorsteps of abandoned houses. Or the old men gave him beers.

Marty was wandering more than we were, zigzagging over benches and leaving the group. He kept stopping passing strangers to give them directions as to where we were going. And he would do so excitedly, waving his arms and looking earnestly concerned for the stranger's welfare, as if the stranger needed to know where our random motions might take us. So straight about it he killed me.

"Excuse me, sir," he'd say in that slightly too high, slightly too loud, slightly too clear, greatly-too-uneasy-with-his-own-absolute-politeness tone of someone asking for directions, "We're going to go north on Yonge Street for three blocks, take a left onto Breadalbane, take another left onto Bay Street, and then go south three blocks to the Metro Toronto Police Headquarters and right onto College Street to the Toronto General Hospital," or some such thing. Most times the stranger would listen with an urgent look in his eyes, lock onto phrases like "police" and "hospital" and ask if we needed help. "No," Marty would reply, "we're just going to do it." And then Marty would casually rejoin us and we'd start walking somewhere.

"It's one of his games," Xander eagerly explained. "Most people ask for directions. Marty just gives them." He sounded enthralled with the social inversion. "Sometimes people give him money."

"And sometimes he buys beers," said Les.

"Nooo. Hey, Marty, how'd you know there'd be a six pack on the bottom of that newspaper dispenser?" I asked him as he pulled six bottles of Moosehead out of a *Toronto Star* machine.

"I'm psychotic. You jealous?"

I shrugged. "Seems like a useful trick to know. Wondered if it would work in Boston." Everyone laughed.

"Actually, I put them there," explained Marty, handing me a bottle.

"Why?"

"Like to scatter bottles around town when there's nothing else to do."

"You and Claude both," said Les.

"No," jested Marty. "Claude keeps wanting to stuff them with genies."

"Yeah, Marty has neat hobbies," boasted Xander. "*I* don't even always understand what they're about. But they always make you think."

"It's not illegal to think—I mean drink," Marty kept insisting as he passed around the bottles.

"Not like committing murder," said Les.

"Depends on whose," I said to be one with them, quaffing whatever was offered.

"Yours," said Jade smoothly, in a mock-menacing tone. "We have made you captive in the dragon's lair." I liked being drunk with him. I liked the comfortable eye contact we kept making. But it wasn't just us that night. It was all of us, and since his bandmates were in a talkative mood, Jade remained comfortably diffident within the chatter. Although his expression revealed that he was responding to all the ribbing, for some reason he wasn't saying very much. I liked the contrast. Three will o' the wisps dancing around a still, mysterious pool. A dark silence more alert than withdrawn.

"Planning a murder tonight, Lester?" I grinned. To my surprise, Les grinned a beery grin back. "Yeah, I'm gonna hang Marty. From the CN Tower."

"Oh, wow," teased Xander. "So was I."

"Hey, hang me and go sober." Marty amazed me by knocking out a loose brick in a building and removing a large bottle of Strongbow hard cider. "I know where all the beer gets hidden."

"Yeah, in your snare," said Les. "I mean, in your head."

"No, on Jade's tongue," insisted Xander. "That's where the poetry comes from." Jade smiled charmingly at the compliment and made a mock showman's bow.

"Ah, he does it with mirrors," said Les.

"In all your happy dreams," I said to the four of them with the affection of drunkenness, and blessed myself for being able to say it as I passed the bottle to Xander, who swallowed and passed it to Jade. And then I silently blessed them for taking my words as a matter of course, or for not really paying attention to what I meant so I could say what I meant without feeling foolish.

For the band wasn't trying to lose me or bring me in. I was there and they were there and Jade seemed quietly all right with it so the rest of them were. Item. No one offered me information on the Rome murder or anything else, and I didn't ask, because I couldn't bring myself to trespass against the sacredness of our communion. It was a natural coming-together for a night. My first.

Marty kept passing bottles around to wild pledges. We drank to the CN Tower; we drank to Queen's Park as we sat passing stories under a tree there like Canterbury pilgrims flying at a verbal jam session.

Les told tales of Juilliard. "They used to put razor blades between the piano keys to encourage accuracy in playing."

"Did it work?"

"Sometimes," he said drily.

We made up glaring nursery rhymes. We drank to the Queen. We drank on the steps of the Parliament Building under gracious arches that looked like the facade of another century and Jade was moving pictures through words and beer and we were all doing our drunken best to help. I don't remember the pictures, but one had fire and burned when we spoke it. We were a shadow government holding court and trying the night. Innocent and dark as stars turning out into space. No one could touch the little circle of our feeling. We called down storms and pretended to see them. And then we ran loose all over the city and at one point it rained and we drank to the Royal Ontario Museum. Or maybe that was Sunday, and we took shelter in the museum's planetarium where the rain scourged the roof and so made the sound of whatever the universe constantly expands into. We sang old songs. And then we drank to the arctic plain of Canada stretching into the planet's empty night.

I don't know where we went and where we were. The afternoon was spare and gray except for us. The city was kind. I think we ate spaghetti and clams. I think I paid. The night came again all moony before I left. We walked through dreams and sang. Marty displayed his insanity without apology and Les kept trying to get me lost in logical propositions that resolved themselves in dry-witted jokes and Xander kept shadow boxing with visions in the air and Jade—Jade was simply with me more often than not, keeping the spirit of everything I ever wanted holding and intense.

Stave Six

Tuesday. Late for work. Being a government job, nobody noticed.

Except Marcie, who was bending Kanesh's smiling ear about her Labor Day weekend at the Cape with her Harvard clod's cousin when I strolled into the reception area at nine forty-five. Ordinarily Marcie wouldn't have bothered to notice me any more than any other arrival into her sunny domain, but a three-day weekend on the Cape with the Cambridge crowd had pumped her chock full of social impertinences and she was eager to share them around. "You're late, Peter," she interrupted herself to chide in her irritatingly cutesy voice, "must have had a good weekend." She clearly wanted me to waste the rest of my morning asking about hers, it being the first day back and all. I didn't oblige.

I was still full of my own weekend, bursting with an honest light depression I wasn't used to having and which for some reason I wanted to keep close and nurse. The depression partly explained my lateness. I was carrying a hard inner blank about the weekend being over, or rather about the loveliness of my rough and tender Toronto spree being over for me but still continuing for the members of Black Dog. Item. My happy accident was their way of life.

Driving to work and listening to Black Dog's cassette tape, I nearly missed my exit knowing that up north there were four lives of single-purposed excellence around which everything else fell squalid and flat. Four lives always beautifully amusing themselves like they were born for it. Right now Jade and Xander would be painting music that nobody could touch and here I was slouching into another fine day at the field office. But it wasn't just their music. It was the fact that they were always naturally and bravely being what they were, and what they were just happened to be the greatest rock and roll band in the universe. Their music compelled because they did. And so I was falling in love—with rock and roll, I mean. Even at a distance I was utterly charmed.

But here I was lightly and utterly depressed. Show's over. The audience is on the road and on to the next venue, feeling markedly worse for the contrast. Only the band remains. It killed to have been there in the best of my spirit before returning to reality in a space suit of cold bureaucratic flesh. Like Wordsworth I had "crossed the Alps" without knowing it. And now I was sorely missing what I never had. Why didn't I live like them? Why didn't I have a heart of autumn sun in a comfortable room of books and paintings and music? Instead of Fearless and Crensch and the lawful pursuit of murderous psychotics.

I had always been living to miss something fine.

"Didja have fun, Peter?" Marcie insisted on impressing Kanesh with her workplace savvy by capsizing into my awful musings. Kanesh tried to use my entrance to extricate himself from the rest of Marcie's weekend report by making a motion of following me to my dismal office, so I decided to linger by the Corinthian leather couch and leisurely read the wanted posters. Since it was only nine forty-five, I saw no reason not to defer my dog catching duties awhile longer by extending Kanesh's discomfort. What the hell? If I couldn't hang out with my favorite rock band, I could still amuse myself by trussing up the office social rules in enterprising ways. Since Kanesh had made it clear he wanted to talk to me and I had made it clear that I was graciously busying myself until Marcie concluded her interesting conversation, there was no way he could find relief until I left the reception area and gave him a tangible excuse to break off and follow. In other words, I decided it was as good a time as any to see how my buddy Jesse James was doing.

"So what did you do, Peter?" insisted Marcie to my back.

I turned and responded cheerfully, "Got a lot of reading done."

Marcie looked slightly confused, as if reading and fun were subjects she couldn't quite reconcile, or as if I'd suddenly thrown a large monkey wrench into her bubblegum and glue paradigm of life by having a different conversation than the one she'd planned for me, so she dropped her jaw and murmured, "Uh huuh." Kanesh looked understandably grateful for this second opportunity to smoothly extricate himself, so I quickly turned my back again and Marcie resumed her chatter and Kanesh had to remain politely trapped because he was too full of his new PR role to be openly rude to anybody, especially the boss's secretary, who after all might do him important favors like typing up press releases. Marcie's chatter always annoys, but I suddenly didn't mind it as background noise. Actually eased my transition back to work.

So I turned once more to briefly smile approval in Marcie's direction as if I were enthralled with her latest seaside adventures, because I saw no reason not to encourage the status quo. She paused long enough in her banter to smile back and then continued tormenting Kanesh, who had to stand there listening to her full report with a big smile plastered on his face in case Fearless emerged from somewhere and happened to see his golden boy looking justifiably annoyed about anything. I smiled at him and waved.

The only thing I have come to detest more than Cape Cod itself is hearing about somebody's weekend there. Me, I tried it once and got rapidly cured. I was looking for Thoreau's Cape Cod, for a lonely beach like a politely stark Emily Dickinson poem, and a Wellfleet oysterman with a face like a ribbed sandbar who wouldn't mind sharing his quaint New England weatherlore with an interested landlubber over an afternoon's thick coffee. I found idiots getting Winnebagos stuck in sand dunes, cheesy Provincetown pictures of that imbecile sea captain that somebody really ought to shoot, and enough cops to populate the rest of Maine. The cops were all busy causing traffic accidents. Came back quite refreshed of my delusions.

The worst part of the weekly "Morons on the Cape" bonanza is that none of them have the good taste to keep quiet about it at work. But then no one's ever boring in private. And so Kanesh had to spend a morning listening to Marcie spew decades-old generic accounts of "so we went with so and so's cousin . . . and it was really nice, and we saw (surprise!) the ocean . . . and . . ."

I wondered what tales and word games Jade might play on a truly lonely beach. What those secret night rehearsals near Lake Ontario felt like under a full billowing moon.

Anyway, my man Jesse was still causing havoc, bless his original soul. There was even a newspaper feature article about him tacked up on the wall next to his wanted poster, which is kind of like the ultimate honor in our business, as it denotes a certain widespread popular appeal. The article had been reprinted from last week's *Phoenix Sun* and issued from Washington to all field offices because it contained more information about the case than the combined resources of the FBI did, which wasn't much.

Seems ol' Jess had successfully knocked off yet another freight train, only this one wasn't empty. It was full of milk cows on the way to slaughter under the auspices of some government program designed to strike at poor families by keeping the price of milk artificially high. Jesse had somehow managed to drive the cattle out of their boxcars and backwards over the Arizona desert and into some rock cave like the infant Hermes once drove Apollo's. Which meant that the animal rights crowd was now mooching in on the free publicity and claiming the guy as a folk hero. The feds eventually found the cattle unharmed with the help of a local tracker, but by that time Jesse himself had disappeared into Phoenix to do an in-depth interview with a local reporter on the steps of the local field office. Had a leisurely lunch. Waved at all the special agents. Wore his full outlaw regalia with a cloth covering his face. Everyone thought it was a special historical event. Even got his picture taken with the mayor. Seems that Jesse recognized the mayor coming out of the field office and called him over for a photo opportunity on a human-interest story regarding the Old West. Reporter had enough of a sense of humor to oblige. Jesse was carrying a sign that said, "Drug Free Drugs," which I thought was a rather ambiguous statement under any circumstances but didn't seem to faze the mayor, who was beaming and holding up the other side of the sign with a thumbs-up gesture. He was running for re-election.

But despite the confident claims of the animal rights people, Jesse himself wasn't saying too much about his own motivation for perpetrating crimes that went out of fashion a century ago. After the mayor went back about his business, the reporter asked Jesse, "Why do you live like an outlaw?"

"I don't know," he answered. "Just nervous I guess."

"Until now you've always robbed empty trains. Why?"

"Why not? It's somethin' to do. Besides, I hear I'm pretty good at it."

And that's about as clear as his self-assessment ever got during the interview, although he spent a lot of time showing off his Colt army and discussing the details of his costume, which he claimed to have made himself using nineteenth-century tools and materials. The chap was actually quite knowledgeable about the period of history he seemed to be living in. More so than most of my colleagues. I noticed the field office had moved him up to number nine with a silver bullet next to his name, which was John Fever. He was replacing some disgruntled ex-graduate student from MIT who had been sending letter bombs to former professors and federal judges and finally killed himself for spite so the FBI could take credit for solving another showstopper.

I was inwardly laughing like hell and enthusiastically cheering the guy on. Kept reading under Marcie's background banter.

"Do you think you made a mistake coming here?" asked the reporter.

"Yes."

"Well, then, aren't you concerned that you might get recognized standing here in the open in front of the FBI Building?"

"No."

"Why not?"

"Since government agencies generally cain't recognize their own mistakes, how the hell are they going to recognize one of mine?" The reporter noted that his interviewee waved at a passing agent who returned the greeting. "I ain't worried none."

"Is John Fever your real name?" asked the reporter.

"Well, lessee. Sometimes it's my real name. On the days I need a real name, 't serves. Other times jest call myself Desert Cloud."

"Desert Cloud?"

"Or Desert Claude. Or just plain Claude. Claude Hopner'll do in a fix. Ladies like it."

I felt the back of my head freeze into utter stillness under my hair. I read the line over three times while suddenly catching an absurd desire to pretend I was really more interested in Marcie's weekend than the wall. Not that anyone would notice my reaction, or if they did, think to attribute it to the news article, but I felt horribly self-conscious about my suddenly personal fascination with this story, about knowing in my gut that if there was a real Claude, Jesse was him. Made sense. Being a frontier outlaw seemed to be very much in his line. Typically, the FBI had not deemed his self-proclaimed alias important enough to list on his poster, which had been updated the same date the article was sent out. Or what was more likely, the lackey who compiled the new list didn't bother to read far enough to get the alias. There was no picture of Mr. Fever on the poster and he was not described physically. In the newspaper photo, his face was covered with a bandana and his eyes were grinning over the edge of the cloth like an actor from an old-time western movie. He had his gun pointed playfully at the camera. He was clearly enjoying the comment it made in juxtaposition to the political sign he was holding with the hapless mayor.

Marcie was still jabbering and Kanesh had his back turned to me so I quietly took the article down and stuffed it in my pocket. Not that anyone except Crensch, who was convinced the wanted list spelled out some kind of cryptic plot, ever paid much attention to the wall postings, because doing so was kind of like admitting you had no better way of wasting time that should be devoted to your case load, but I wasn't proud. I was also fairly certain that Marcie wouldn't have bothered to read the article when she tacked it up, and even if she had she wouldn't have noted or remembered a detail like Hopner's name. But why take a chance on Crensch or Fearless noticing, since both had heard the name mentioned on the tape I thoughtfully destroyed. I was damn glad I had the foresight to remove the note which bore Hopner's name from the corpse before the police arrived to make a record of it. I wanted Claude Hopner, whoever he was, to be exclusively mine.

Then I freed Kanesh by being rude. "Hey, Marcie," I interrupted her account of what she ate when she went out, "Looks good. When did you change the postings?"

"Just now. Mail arrived just before you came in."

"Oh," I said as if a different subject had just occurred to me, "is the boss busy?"

"Don't know. Hasn't come out of his office all morning."

Good. The coffee machine was probably still keeping him captivated. "You didn't happen to see Crensch yet, did you?"

"No, *I* haven't seen Sidney," said Marcie, proud to be helpful with so little effort.

"Well," I joshed with Kanesh, relieved at Hopner remaining my special province, "Crensch is sort of the type who isn't supposed to be seen. Might get found out." I winked the way Crensch often did.

Kanesh laughed appreciatively, partly because he now saw it as part of his PR role to be everyone's Ed McMahon and so demonstrate what an engaging fellow he could be even though he was a serious fed, and partly because Crensch was a laughingstock around the field office and any jest at his expense required laughter or the risk of being thought of as his friend. Then I left the reception area and gave Kanesh the tangible excuse he needed to break off from Marcie by following me. "Hey, Morrow." He burrowed into my thoughts like a worm in a perfect peach. "Gotta talk to you. I'm arranging a press conference a week from Friday to kick off our new anti-drug campaign, 'Say No.'"

"No."

"Ha. Ha. Ha. We thought it was a great slogan. 'Just Say No' is getting a little worn and overused now but 'Say No' is short. Punchy and to the point, don't you think?"

"No."

"Well, everyone kind of likes it. Doesn't give the kids time to think or question. And you can apply it to anything. Because it's simple, you know?"

"No."

"Well, it's the sort of thing everyone can understand. And we can make it one word: SAYNO. Kind of catchy. Congressman Laffer might be there. He's running for re-election. Might even use it in his speech. We're getting balloons printed up, and signs. DSS wants to jump on the bandwagon, too." He backed off a little from my look of contempt. "State-federal cooperation and all that," he quickly explained. "Add a human touch. You want to be in it?"

"No."

"Why not? Swell our numbers. Have a good time for an afternoon. I'm sure Fred will give you a release. Going to be cable, local news. Besides, we need someone who can write up a press release."

"No."

"Give you a spot on the platform. You can talk about your experiences with runaways and drugs." Kanesh suddenly saw that my experiences with runaways was still an issue between us since he returned Mellie to her murdering father, so he suddenly tried to keep things light. "Uh, we're going to have family games to show kids they can have fun without drugs."

"No." Any kid that needs to be "shown" by government officials how to have fun is beyond saving anyway, I thought. The rest get to be political prisoners for an afternoon. I lost him by entering our "library"—two or three shelves in a closet devoted to federal statutes and bundles of useless government papers. Wanted to grab whatever reading material I could find on the payola statutes and settle in my office to get some personal research done before Fearless got bored enough with the coffee machine to harass me about my absence on Friday. Also wanted to consider this new discovery concerning Mr. Hopner, or dream of desert clouds.

My office door was unlocked, but as the cleaning staff sometimes left it that way, I thought nothing of it as I pushed it open into the familiar deadly swirl of asbestos. But bad as the four-day accumulation of cancer dust was, I immediately closed the door behind me. For sitting at my desk and making a great show of doing my job by sifting through a pile of photographs of missing pets that Fearless had deposited on my desk last Thursday was the corpse-commander from Rome.

He was humming a tuneless version of the "Star Spangled Banner" and admiring the photographs with some degree of zest, although he also seemed to like looking up at the gaping hole in my ceiling. He was no longer in military uniform. He was wearing an old shiny business suit with a wide brown square-cut tie like people used to wear in the fifties. And he sported an old rusty WIN button from the late seventies, for "Whip Inflation Now." His face was smoother in the cheeks and sallower around the eyes than I remembered it, but it was his face. No doubt about that. He looked like an old-time salesman, like one of those older men with a spotty past you sometimes find peddling useless products for obscure companies and who cheerfully take three hours of lunch on a rainy day to do it in. I knew he would smell musty when he spoke. But right now he smelled vaguely of cheap alcohol-based cologne gone bad. Very clean and old before his time.

He had a Styrofoam cup of coffee and as he raised it I noticed fat fingers bursting through old costume jewelry rings. One ring was horseshoe shaped with missing diamonds and looked like a carnival prize. A thin, brown felt hat that went out of style in the forties and never even came back during the most tasteless nostalgia crazes was lying in front of him. The corpse looked up through clear eyes that didn't focus, then they gathered themselves into a fairly convincing version of recognition, then he smiled like he wanted to sell me some junk product he would demand me to believe in because if someone believed in it, it would bolster his own sense of self. I wondered briefly if he were with the United Way. Or a local "pro-life" organization. Both camps sport reps that feel like older men creepily emerging from a closet of abandoned mothballs. And neither is shy about appropriating other folks' office space.

"Hey, hey." Mr. Corpse stood up and wriggled his fingers as if he was pleasantly surprised with my presence or as if he were clumsily dropping something I couldn't see and the dropping was supposed to be understood as funny. The gesture vaguely resembled the greeting of a Rotary Club hanger-on from half a century ago.

"Hey, hey," I responded in exactly the same tone of voice. "Aren't you supposed to be dead?"

"Hugh McCrae," he named himself for answer, extending his hand.

"Pete Morrow." I didn't take it. Hugh McCrae kept looking strangely flushed and dizzy with whatever his job was, as if he was about to give me one of those once-in-a-lifetime opportunities companies harass people about every few months and I was terribly lucky and insightful just to be there to hear about it. I half expected him to ask my yearly income and whip out reams of papers and numbers and calculations for the next two hours to show me "what I could afford to pay" in case I was panicking to get in on some terrifically useless money-draining deal.

"Just come out of the closet?" he glanced at my legal books and then at me with a hey-you're-a-good-fella-and-we-know-each-other-already smile. I made no response. "Hey yes, yes, Mr. Morrow. Special Agent Morrow. Yes. Ahum—bit of a cough." He touched his throat and waited for a few seconds before continuing. "Need a lozenge." He kept his hand to his throat and stared at the ceiling as if he was expecting something internal to pass. "Wait. . . . wait for the bubble to clear." He kept waiting. I took my chair back and deposited my books in a desk drawer so their subject wouldn't become anyone else's business. "Had an operation. Cleaned me out and"—he waited further with his other hand curled in a fist against his chest as if he was going to pound hiccups out of himself—"there." He burped. "Can't really talk until the bubble comes up."

"See you got put back together." I indicated a metal folding chair near the door for him to occupy. He took up his hat and sort of folded down into the chair. I noticed liver spots on his head under patches of thin grey hair.

"Rubber. Rubber bands. They put a band in to clip back my stomach to my liver. They put in compartments like a cow's and the air has to rise sometimes. Now," he burped again and seemed recovered.

"Still fighting inflation?" I said, cheerily indicating his WIN button.

"Well, personal inflation, you know—it's a button, could mean anything. But hey—that reminds me. Been reading something very interesting. You know they say the universe is mostly empty space. Between particles of atoms is all space. We're mostly space. Between giant exploding stars is also a lot of empty space."

"So?"

"Well, they also say the universe is constantly expanding. So, you think about it, everything is getting emptier by the hour."

"Are you worried about it?"

"Oh, no. Too old to worry about something like that. Got a joke for ya. New one. Bet you haven't heard it. Where does a gorilla go to dinner?"

"I don't know."

"Anywhere it wants. Ha! Ha! Anywhere it *wants*."

"What do you want?" I asked cautiously.

"What do I want? Well, I'll tell ya. I *want*. That is, I want to change your life." He extended his forefinger to me as if he were singling me out for a special award. "Yes-siree. Got a way to do it, too."

"What are you selling?"

"Bonds. Insurance. Securities. Souls."

"Souls," I said seriously, leaning back in my swivel chair and pressing the tips of my fingers together. Figured that after what he'd been through he might know about souls.

"Well, I'll tell ya. Souls are always a steady sideline. Got a few. But bonds are where I clean up. Now I can get you a cheap interest in a junk bond to steady you out into a perfectly straight life. More straight planked than dried plankton. Square. An old L7 as they say. Hey."

"How's that?"

"Get you a job and family. Never have to worry about striving for success with three or four kids depending on you to put food in their whiny mouths and a company forcing you to put in ten-hour days for show when five-hour days would do as well. Life's done. No more higher worries. After two decades of that, even a latter-day Leonardo da Vinci would only want to retire and die. And of course, I get to collect the interest on the wasted life. Bonds. Ever marry, Mr. Morrow?"

"No."

"I did. Lost my poor wife may she rest in peace. Dear, dear, Ellie. Sad case." He took out a lint-flecked handkerchief and loudly blew his bulbous nose. His nose was rough and riddled with dead skin. It turned white and blotchy when he blew it. "Very good wooman. Knew greatly how to live. Quiet, you know. Say a prayer for her in church every day. To Father Joseph."

"You believe in God?" Figured I'd be remiss not to ask, considering the circumstances of his recovery.

"Of course. I deal in want. Where there is no want, there is no God. God is a great levelling force. Brings us closer together. My wife. Anyway"—he wiped the cloth over his face like he was soaking up grime from a fetid swamp, then he instantly recovered from his grief—"need insurance? Got a debt plan so far and deep you can't get out, will insure you stay anchored into a miserable work so grating it not only makes you forget what you were born for, it makes you despise the former self you once were. Would you like me to insure your life?"

"No."

"Security then. You're just the man for high stakes security, Mr. Morrow. I can tell. I've got a plan in the form of a vitamin pill. Make your animal longing for security, back in the lower lumbar regions of your brain, override your higher longing for excellence of mind and the risk that accompanies it. One a day with a light meal will make you break into physical convulsions at the very thought of change. As an extra, you'll always know how to vote. Selling plenty. All a deal."

"I'm sure. But why am I being honored with your deals?"

"Thought you might be interested."

"I'm not."

McCrae seemed a little hurt and taken aback that I wasn't. "Everybody else is. Just sold two bottles to your boss, Fred Pallader. Ten cents on every dollar goes into Congressman Laffer's re-election campaign fund."

"Why are you here and what do you want from me?"

"Well, Mr. Morrow, I really want you to help me." He twirled his hat and pointed his finger at me. "Talked to your boss this morning. Tells me you're good at missing persons. I need someone who's good at missing—*persons*. Ha! I'd like you to find my poor wife. She needs me."

"I thought you said she was dead."

"No, I said may she rest in peace. In life. Her legal name is Elise McClellan."

I pretended the name meant nothing. "Why don't you find her yourself? Hire a PI?" I asked casually.

"Well, she's Canadian, you know." He said this in a low voice as if it was a distasteful fact of life.

"So?"

"Got immigration problems going north of the border right now."

"What kind of problems?"

"Well, I'll tell ya. There's a fierce girl up there, an old witch calls herself Penny, doesn't much like me around. Better lay low." He winked.

"What if I can't help you?"

"Well, your boss mentioned another man—a Mr. Sidney Crensch." He pronounced the name carefully and loudly. "Special Agent Crensch. Got connections up Quebec way. Might be a help—"

"I'll help you." I really didn't like Mr. McCrae, whatever his deal was, but I liked the idea of Crensch tracking down Jade's mother and inserting himself into my Canadian business even less. McCrae's painstakingly loud pronunciation told me that he somehow, inexplicably, knew this. Started wishing Penny's "hobby" of killing Rinkowski/McCrae, or "the monster" as she called him, had left a more permanent impression.

He smiled. His face looked like a horrible greasy slab of old white bologna and my stomach convulsed because I was looking at it. "Thought so."

"Under the condition you keep our relationship confidential," I added quickly. "Anyone else gets involved, I'm uncooperative with whatever I get—understand?" I didn't know if the return threat held any meaning for him, but since he clearly preferred dealing with me to dealing with Crensch, I thought I might use his preference to my advantage. That is, to keep him quiet about things. "What can you tell me about your . . . wife?"

"Elise. That she's dying into nothing special. That she needs me to make a family again. Now you have a name. Now you can find her. Hey."

"Of course."

He stood up and gave me a card. Plain white. Cheap looking block letters read HUGH SASQUATCH McCRAE, SPECIAL ASSISTANT, NATIONAL DRUG ENFORCEMENT CONGRESSIONAL COMMITTEE. It bore a Washington, DC address and phone number. "Here's my office. We'll be in touch. Gotta hop a freight train down through New York way. Stop for lunch at an old Brooklyn diner went out of business thirty-five years ago."

"Hope you don't get robbed," I said drily.

"Eh," he made a clumsy hand motion as if he wasn't too concerned about it. "When you find poor little Ellie, tell her . . . I miss her."

"Sure."

He slowly lowered and raised his head in a gesture that almost seemed respectful. Then he plodded out of my office like a badly-acted monster in an old-time horror film.

The asbestos felt thicker than my life's long dullness after he lumbered off. My arms were cold and I did not move. There was a cobweb drifting like a dead wind across the emptiness separating the seat from the back of the metal folding chair where McCrae had sat. And there were several things clear. Needed to interview Penny again to get her reaction to this unexpected visit. Also Elise, to get hers. Which meant I needed to go back to Toronto. Which didn't break my heart. And I would certainly be remiss not to take in the Claude Hopner "party" scheduled a week from Thursday for whatever that might yield. Probably ought to interview everybody. Like to get an introduction to Claude himself, if possible, and armed with this newspaper article and an account of this morning's office guest I might persuade Penny to provide one.

But I also needed to keep an eye on Crensch while making Fearless think I was making progress towards solving this increasingly unsolvable case. Talk about expanding emptiness. Hoped there wouldn't be governmental pressure to find the corpse's "killer" because clearly there wasn't even a corpse; the body had inexplicably turned to dust at the morgue. Or rather, there was a corpse, but he'd now re-emerged as Hugh McCrae, whom Penny bragged about killing while claiming that he "ain't dead." And I didn't want Sasquatch to lead anyone in the government towards anything in Toronto because Moon Management's tax-evasion payola deal with the Mob needn't brook premature interference should another fed trip over leads in that direction while looking for Elise. That is, I decided there was no reason Jade and his bandmates shouldn't succeed through the only path open to their merit, and I for one didn't want to be party to some government worm with an accounting ledger getting in their way.

Not that I had any idea as to what I was looking for because now I was only following whatever was there. Logic ceased. Oh yeah, payola—that's right. The mob thing could get interesting in its own right. Follow it. It's an excuse to carve out another rainy northern weekend sometime. What a lovely, strange corner of earth to set up shop in.

Sasquatch had left his Styrofoam cup on my desk. The coffee was cold and smelled like stagnant water. There was a dead dragonfly floating on the top with one twisted wing. What a card!

"Morrow, get in here—" growled Fearless from his office through my now open door.

"Sure, boss," I called, quickly and uncharacteristically obedient, because I was suddenly grateful for an excuse to get out of the atmosphere remaining behind my recent office guest and into piercing normality. "Like some coffee?" I offered, entering his office with McCrae's cup in hand. "It's kind of old," I warned him as he threw a pill in his mouth and drank it down anyway, dragonfly and all.

"Bought these heartburn tablets from an aide to Mr. Laffer." He coughed and hit his chest. "Money goes to a good cause."

So the pills McCrae was hawking about were real. "Hey, boss, got a little heartburn myself. Like to see those."

"Got an extra bottle," said Fearless. "Five bucks."

"Deal." Evidence was evidence, even if I still had no idea what this evidence was evidence of. Besides, the congressman was already getting his percentage from Fearless's transaction so it wasn't like I was helping the campaign. Dropped a five-dollar bill on his desk. Fearless gave me a sealed bottle.

"He was asking about missing persons. I mentioned your name." He indicated that it was all right for me to sit, even though I was already sitting.

"Yes? Is he a missing person?" I asked innocently.

As usual, my obscure point sailed right over Fearless's head. "No, Mr. McCrae was here for the congressman." Fearless didn't seem too aware of McCrae having a specific case in mind, or of him asking me to solve it, so I figured McCrae must have inquired in a general way. Fearless had no idea that my brand-new hobby was keeping McCrae's wife from him while pretending to find her. McCrae was just a congressional aid with a general interest in missing persons paying a courtesy call in election season and pushing pills for his boss on the drug committee. Not at all the sort of thing to spark a fed's curiosity. "Chatted all morning."

"Glad you're not busy." Someone threw one quarter in the cup near the coffee machine and poured two whole cups of coffee before noticing that Fearless was keeping tabs. I went out and relieved the guy of the extra coffee without paying because I felt like I needed something warm in my throat after talking to Sasquatch. And so I had the pleasure of robbing Fearless from complaining about the missing quarter because he clearly had other things to discuss with me. Subtle acts of defiance sometimes reclaim one's power. "Paid my fee," I reminded him as I returned to my seat. Fearless ignored the comment and started telling me all about what a fascinating guy Mr. McCrae was.

"Collects Elvis sightings. Even has a theory about Judge Crater."

"Hey, how come you never put me on Judge Crater?" I asked. Crater was one of those unsolved files that make great copy on the cheesy tabloid news programs. The good judge allegedly vanished August 6, 1930 and was declared legally dead June 6, 1939. The case was still open because, after all, he probably still owed taxes. Then it occurred to me that for all anyone knew, Crater was McCrae. Name worked out. Sort of.

Anyway, Fearless seemed to appreciate my humor in spite of himself. "So. Speaking of missing persons, Morrow, where were you Friday?"

"Had some Petscam business in Boston to chase down. Saw the ocean."

"Yeah, all right." He didn't believe me, but it was even more trouble to write up an official report than to complain about my coffee, and there was clearly other business at hand, so he dismissed my absence by pretending it never happened. "Been getting phone calls about the situation-in-Rome." That was the way he now referred to the army base weirdness I was supposed to be solving, because "situation-in-Rome" was what Crensch always called it, as if it were all one word. "Got any leads?"

"Odds and ends. Nothing that feels right yet."

"Well?"

"Well, never dealt with the death of a missing body before. Gotta feel my way through it." Thoughtfully sipped the coffee. The warm liquid contrasted sharply against my surprisingly stiff throat and I shuddered and gagged a little. McCrae had left a profound physical effect on me. I kept thinking of the first time I was in the woods alone near Pittsfield and my eyes tricked out a dead animal that had looked like flowers from a distance. I drew back then in the instinctive way I was drawing back now. That's the kind of shudder McCrae left running through me.

"Think it might be a mob hit?"

"I'm pursuing that direction. But it's a delicate pursuit, as you know. Give me a few more weeks, leave me alone with it. Something will break."

"All right, let me ask you this." He glanced towards the machine. No one was there. "Isn't there anybody Crensch could, say, just arrest?"

"Probably. He's done it before." Crensch wasn't too particular about who he arrested. I was thinking about the time he brought in an ROTC student for impersonating a cop.

"I'm serious."

"So am I. Why don't you call his father? I'm sure he knows all kinds of folks that need to be arrested. Being in his line of work and everything."

"Come on, Morrow, cut the crap. What about someone *you* know?"

"Are you suggesting a clean-cut upstanding law-abiding guy like me consorts with criminals?" I asked in mock-horror.

He chuckled. "Someone that has a healthy rap sheet and that might be in on this thing. Someone we could nail for something minor. Any of your leads dealing or possessing?"

"Dealing or possessing what?" I asked in my too-innocent-to-be-true voice.

"*Drugs*, Morrow."

"Oh, yeah, I forgot. Must be the drugs." I rattled the pill bottle.

"Look, maybe you could run a check and see if you know any likely candidates who owe money on overdue parking tickets on federal property. I don't care what the excuse is, we need to grab someone for now."

"Why do we have to make a premature arrest?"

"Because the sensationalism of the case has caught up to us at last." He looked greatly annoyed. Perhaps the pills didn't work after all. "Look, Morrow, we've got to do something public. Utica's Mayor Dunn is running into trouble. Looked like he might win against Congressman Basher, the economy being so bad now and everyone wanting a change in Washington, but the mayor of a dying city who once served without distinction in the state assembly isn't getting perceived as the political outsider he claims he is." I made an expression of mild surprise, which Fearless ignored. "Now the congressman is making an issue of the murder-military-impersonation-bizarre stuff in his district, feeding off a public outcry about military waste—like military waste has anything to do with the murder," he grumbled at the side issue.

"Perhaps it's a pun," I informed him without really realizing the brilliance of my perception. "After all, it was a military waste."

My wit was too subtle for the pre-lunch coffee break. "Basher may still be voted out, but he's turning this thing to his advantage by claiming it's the mayor's fault."

"Maybe it is. Maybe he did it. I'll run a check on him. What the hell do I know?"

"It's not funny, Morrow. You know Utica's a mob town."

"Nooo. Really?"

"You know it might have been a mob hit. I mean—you think so, right, and we were asked in to put some heat on a private allegedly getting drug supplies from the Nunzio family, and after I released that much information to the Utica papers last Thursday—"

"Why are you bringing in the press?" I asked with a sharpness that surprised even me. The whole case had been relatively quiet since the initial burst of journalistic excitement, and now Fearless was causing his own publicity problems.

"To help out the congressman. To make him look like he's keeping us busy. Anyway, the mayor is no longer perceived as having the Utica Mob 'under control.' And there's rumors re-surfacing that he's in their pocket."

"You mean he isn't?"

"And Basher's promising quick action. Which we have to give him."

"Why are we suddenly Basher's private army?"

"Well, who knows he might get re-elected after all. Besides he's on the Congressional Drug Committee with Rep. Laffer, Laffer's endorsing him, and Laffer's run looks pretty secure. He could pass a favor along, especially since we're now helping his campaign by making our anti-drug thing an on-going media event."

"Check. To keep in Laffer's good graces it's now OK to disturb the Utica Mob. If Utica's crime rate goes up before election day Bashband stays in office, and we helped, and he owes us one. And since Mayor Dunn has to prove he isn't mob supported, he can hardly blame us in public for doing our job. And if he gets in office, with the right spin we could even let him take credit for leadership or something. And if we bust someone who isn't too central to anything anyway, it's not like we're really going to do much damage to Dunn's buddies, so the mayor could be persuaded to see our noble efforts at law enforcement as nothing more than a wink in his direction, and possibly be grateful to us that we didn't work harder than we had to." I sipped more coffee. Fearless was full of pout and grimace. "Gotta hand it to you, boss. I never would have thought of approaching things in quite that way. But it's damnably clever strategy."

"Look, Morrow. Save the analysis. The fact is that the situation-in-Rome has resurfaced as an issue in Basher's district."

"Because Basher made it one."

"Whatever. One radio station is having a 'name the killer' contest and giving away serial killer collector cards as a joke."

"Hey," I said lightly, inwardly wincing at my unconscious imitation of Hugh McCrae's favorite word. "Have to get some. See if I recognize anyone."

"Another station is giving away replicas of the items the police took from the body."

"Including the trout?"

"Plastic." He waved his hand in high annoyance. "But that's the rock 'n' roll crowd. I expect you to see the issue. Everybody wants to know who did it—no one believes the body just 'disappeared.' The local press is calling it a cover-up and using it to create election year fights, the religious nuts are saying it's the work of Satan—"

"I vote for the religious nuts. They always have the best story."

"The liberals organized an anti-nuclear protest this past weekend and threw pig's blood on a runway at Rome air force base."

"Why? There's no warheads there. There wasn't even a murder there."

"Yes, but the base is local and everyone knows where it is. And the protestors were claiming that if the army's so ill-run that mysterious imposters can take over without notice then someone somewhere will push a button and blow up the world."

"Maybe someone will. Wouldn't that be lucky?"

He sighed. "Look. Utica was a zoo this weekend. Even CNN picked up the demonstrations. The animal rights people brought spray paint to protest the pig's blood. The family values crowd suspects drugs and wants to test everybody on the base—the anti-tax crowd doesn't want the government to pay to test everyone on the base so they held a rally—everyone's got something smart to say except us—"

"So, what else is new?" *Whatever happened on that base touched off everybody's pet fears and obsessions in a big way*, I thought.

"Even the gays held some sort of sit-in—" he said distastefully.

"Well, why not? It's Labor Day. Guess everyone had a good time."

"Haven't you been watching the news?"

"I've been reading all weekend."

"Well, read a newspaper once in a while. This thing isn't going away. I'd like to put your name in the Utica paper with a list of some of your better-known accomplishments in solving bizarre killings. To make it look to the public like something significant is being done."

I suddenly felt hollow. "What about Crensch's name? He's the one officially on the case."

"Using your name in the paper is Crensch's idea. He thinks it's a ruse to lift attention from him so he can work better in secret. Any questions?"

"Why is it every time I go for coffee you try to get me killed?"

"What?"

"This is delicate, and at one time you thought it better not to let the Nunzios know I was in it. Why do you now want to warn the Mob I'm coming?"

"I already told you. To make the public think we're serious. It's only for show."

"I thought Crensch was only for show."

"Look, if the Nunzios are worried about you, they're not worried about Crensch. You tell him who to talk to and what to say. He'll do it undercover. You can survive drawing a little heat if you stay in the background and research."

"So Crensch knows I'm involved."

"Like I said, he thinks you're 'advising' him and that he's still in charge of the case."

"So Crensch knows I'm involved."

"Everyone knows you're on drug duty, which brings me to—"

"It'll be harder for me to gather data."

"Not if you tell Crensch what to look for."

"It'll be harder for me to gather data."

"Look, Morrow, we've got to do it. You're the only one with enough of a rep to make the proper impression on both the public and the Mob. Now that the murder has hit the national spotlight again, the Boston papers might run the story. You've got an image here of standing up against other government agencies—"

"Which I used to be rewarded for with vacations and everything."

Fearless frowned. "So your name will show that we at the FBI are not really buckling under to government pressure to solve this thing."

"What? Given the facts, why would anyone think we're buckling under to government pressure?"

Fearless wasn't one for stupid questions. "We are just disinterested servants of justice and the people and we're just doing our usually competent, disinterested job. That's the line. Got it?"

I got it all right. We were "disinterested" but Basher could whip us into quick action to look good for the voters. "So why bother with the drug-duty charade?" I asked.

"Well, that was my next point. We're going to put a spin on the story that the murder was drug related. Which it might have been. And that you," he hesitated, "you are now helping to spearhead our new drug task force."

"Meaning?"

"Meaning drugs are a new income source for the Utica Mob, courtesy of the Nunzio takeover. An income source that presumably means more to them than keeping the killer protected. If the Mob thinks you're on the drug trail, Crensch might be able to make deals to get the murderer, or someone just as good as the murderer, whose arrest would make everyone happy."

"So we've got all bases covered. If the Mob wants to sacrifice a troublemaker, we'll do them the favor of taking the guy off their hands, and maybe they won't rock things too much before election day."

"I thought you'd be overjoyed to be relieved from tracking dogs and cats and back into real work."

"Why don't I just go after the killer?" As soon as I said this I remembered Jade telling his mother, "That all sounds rather complicated. Isn't it easier to skip all the nonsense and just play?" Except I didn't sound as good-natured as he did when he said it.

"Because it's election year and drugs are an issue and we need people over on that side of the house. Looks good to the public to increase our force."

"Yes! So now I'm the local drug lord. I mean drug czar. What a bargaining chip!"

"Well, co-drug lord, if you have to put it that way. You and Piekarski are in charge. Just be at the press conference next Friday to show your smiling puss. Kanesh makes it all look good for the press, you do what you can to help Crensch crack the case—everybody looks good. For the record, drugs are your sole official concern now—"

"Yes, boss," I said mechanically, like I had swallowed a fistful of downers. "Drugs are my sole concern."

"So start going to all the meetings—"

"But what if my habit forces me to miss work and stay home and adopt anti-social attitudes and everything? Could happen."

"Tellin' me you got a drug problem now, Morrow?"

"No, a conflict of interest. Meaning I'd like to stay alive to save families and kids from drugs and everything. Wouldn't it be better not to remind the Mob what I look like?" Actually, I was thinking about Nariano and his buddies in Toronto, who didn't know what I looked like yet and really didn't need to.

"Look, the Mob already knows what you look like. It's not a choice. We need to go full force on drugs right now."

"What if I just say no?"

"What if I just say if you're not there, you get suspended. I don't need the headache right now."

Well, a week's about right for making the party, I thought. Just take off next Wednesday afternoon and I'll be on suspension anyway. Good deal. Besides, if they do mention my name and I'm not there, it will send questions and confusion into all the right places. Like McCrae's Washington office. When in doubt, keep them guessing.

"What about Petscam, sir?" I asked in a tone of serious concern.

"I've already put a rookie on it. Turn over your files. In the meantime you've got a week to familiarize yourself with our drug operations while you continue to quietly pursue this situation-in-Rome business." I got up and started out. "Chat with Crensch, take him to lunch, start making friends with the guy for chrissake, at least until the two of you come up with something solid."

"Right. Hey," I said cheerfully on my way out, "maybe I'll even buy him coffee."

When I returned to my desk, I noticed that McCrae had left new photographs under those showing missing pets from last week. Four different shots of a horribly mutilated black dog. And each one bore a different name, scrawled in a hollow heart and pierced with a broken arrow: Marty, Les, Jade, Xander.

Stave Seven

On the outside, the week crawled vacant and dreary, just like all my other weeks. On the inside, hell broke out its loose change and tempted my thoughts with exploding nickels.

Meaning I managed to get to the field office every day and be my usual lightsome self. Conducted my business affairs in public as if my life contained no new intrigue. Kept watching myself as if I were somebody else. Pleased with how well I performed.

But at the same time I kept falling into greater colors of weirdness.

Fearless released the article about me to the Utica paper, with the saving grace that I got to write it subject to his approval. Not that my input mattered where it mattered. There was no way I could disguise my identity or history, since revealing those things was the point of the exercise, but a staff writer from the paper re-wrote the whole thing for maximum distortion and controversy anyway, making me out to be some sort of miracle worker turned brilliant maverick federal investigator with an excessively improbable history of solving bizarre crimes that no one else this side of Sam Spade or Poe's C. Auguste Dupin could touch and that no one this side of a Japanese comic book could believe. Quite a puff, to Fearless's obvious dismay, and not too far from the truth, to everyone else's.

It was one thing to present my enviable credentials and let the public remember on their own that I was the guy who decked a social worker last June. For Fearless wanted to imply our grand disinterestedness without having to actually remind anybody of my little act of rebellion. It was quite another to be presented as the type of guy who could solve half a dozen psycho slayings before breakfast and three dozen more before lunch on a slow day. I was roundly praised as the "Holmes of the Hub" and "the nemesis of the Boston Mafia." A headline before my resume accomplishments read "brightest fed in the country." Which to my mind is kind of like being the hardest working member of a government union, or the most caring social worker in the DSS, but it really ticked off a lot of my colleagues anyway, as most of them lack my subtle perspective on things like that.

Although it was fairly clear to me that a lot of the praise was more a result of the staff writer's personal agenda than his personal admiration. Like most young journalists looking for advancement, he was full of his byline and hell-bent on impressing his editor with his ability to boost sales by injecting yet more sensationalism into an already sensationalism-saturated case. And he clearly had his own agenda, which went way beyond anything necessary to make the impact Fearless wanted. In the quest to throw more "governmental cover-up" stuff at his readers, he uncovered my celebrated tiff with DSS and took it upon himself to drag out all those details again. Sprinkled throughout the article were the ravings of some self-styled "psychic" who also claimed to work for the government on "unsolvable cases." Superfluous references to secret government drug experiments from the sixties. Old speculation on Dunn's alleged mob links. Space aliens and communists. Mexican faith healers. Jack the Ripper. Chappaquiddick. Every rumor that ever happened about anybody *and* every dirty whisper ever buried down the collective kitchen sink.

All of which was calculated to be much more interesting to the average out-of-work newspaper reader than a thoughtful piece on the economic recession. Which isn't a bad business strategy, actually, because face it, folks are basically lazy. Given the choice between muddling through on a greatly reduced living standard or expending effort to understand the causes of their misery, most people will muddle through and wait for someone else to "do something." It isn't their own suffering folks object to so much as having to think to understand their own suffering. I suspect it took the human race so long to evolve because it takes less energy to starve than to discover agriculture.

Item. Successful news writers know how to market reality. People will pay good money for outlandish, titillating, irresponsible speculations on missing corpses and "secret military research" and the staff writer was more than willing to further his career by accommodating. Filled up two columns of space with his ambitions. Slanted the article somewhere between the *National Enquirer* and normal journalistic hysteria. But I suppose that after the frenzy of the Labor Day Weekend protests, there was no way anyone could write rationally about the whole thing, anyway, because the "unsolved mysteries" tone had already been firmly established and the public expectations set. I sure as hell had nothing rational to say about it.

At least they didn't run a photo.

But the article found its way onto one of the national news services and the *Globe* picked it up and hell knows how many other newspapers, which meant I had to assume that McCrae had seen it. Also had to assume the Nunzios and all their associates, including Nick, now knew beyond the shadow of my calling card that I was involved in the "situation-in-Rome" and that I had more than a passing interest in their drug dealings.

My colleagues' resentment manifested itself in no one saying too much about the article when it appeared in the *Globe*, even though I noticed Kanesh nearly wet his pants while he was reading it because he collared me with copy in hand to confirm that I would be at "his" press conference. I told him ambiguously that I was under orders to be there, which he interpreted as cheerful assent, and I went on with my business of acting normal.

And of course, I got the requisite nuisance calls from people who suddenly knew all about "the vanishing corpse," which was how the media had dubbed this case. I listened patiently out of habit, because on rare occasions someone who really does know something calls about a publicized case and offers enough interesting material to send you on your way to a solution, but this time it was all stuff and nonsense about a one-world government plot and latter-day Nazis acting as hit men for a joint conspiracy concerning the Trilateral Commission and the Knights of Columbus and was I aware of some crank who was now all the rage among the right wing paranoids for proving that Emperor Hirohito actually planned WW II. I forwarded them all to Crensch.

Which kept him happy, I suppose.

Crensch spent a lot of time skulking around my office door and then pretending he wasn't there. And since it was now an open secret that we were partners on the same case, he decided he had to keep up appearances by suddenly pretending he didn't know me. Which meant that whenever we happened to pass in the hall, he would look pointedly straight ahead and sharply whistle "La Marseillaise." As I saw no reason not to do the same, we got on pleasantly enough.

More pleasantly than I did with my other colleagues, who after a few days of hearing Kanesh and Fearless speak of me as a "key member" of our upcoming "press brigade," broke their silence to rib me about the slant of the newspaper article, which was probably an emotionally safer way to fulfill what Fearless had made a social imperative than referring directly to the journalist's thick praise. Piekarski especially had all kinds of chummy names for me, which were meant to acknowledge the public flattery and show he wasn't a total chump while demeaning my accomplishments in a good-natured sort of way. Which is a common strategy for covering professional jealousy when silence no longer does the job. So lest I get the idea that my resume mattered more to my new co-commander in the drug war than the hocus pocus surrounding my present assignment, Piekarski dubbed me "Ghost-Buster" and "Body-Snatcher" and "Broom-Rider." I returned the compliments, of course, but when I was alone at night "Broom-Rider" bothered me in a way I couldn't explain to myself.

None of my old mob associates called. Not that I was expecting a call, but there was always the chance of getting a colorful phone threat.

There was no news on Hopner. McCrae didn't call, which was just as well, and I, of course, had no desire to renew contact with him.

But I did have a strong desire to understand what his deal was. Especially since he now had full access to my life and professional accomplishments via the papers. But a phone call to Laffer's Boston office under the guise of being an interested voter yielded no more information on the congressman's staff than government offices generally yield to interested voters. Which means that nobody I talked to on the phone knew anything, but everybody invited me to drop by and volunteer to help with the campaign.

Which wasn't a bad gimmick, actually. Walked in off the street, never gave a name or explanation beyond being "seriously concerned with the drug issue" and "wanting to donate some time," and I was "in" for an afternoon. Two things about political campaigns. Folks'll never question your credentials if they think you agree with them, and none of these outfits ever refuse free labor. And when I volunteered to "file things," the other volunteers gratefully let me have a go at it because it's generally more fun for political hacks to harass people over the phone with questions they don't really want honest answers to than to sludge through office work.

Two file cabinets. One without a lock. Checked that one first. No personnel file on McCrae. Wasted no time prying open the lock on the "super secure" file cabinet that another volunteer told me I "probably wouldn't need to get into," but she could give me a key if I "had to." No file on McCrae here, either, but there was a file redundantly labeled "NDECC—National Drug Enforcement Congressional Committee" that looked promising. So I helped myself and took a leisurely walk to the Boston Public Library where I made copies of the contents. On a sudden whim I borrowed half a dozen books on witchcraft for night reading. Figured it couldn't hurt to glance at them as reference material, now that I was slightly less inclined to smile at the notion that Mother Penny was "something like a witch." Clearly she was "something," as my travels up north revealed, and in the light of my recent experiences, I decided that if Elb believed his mother was a witch, I really couldn't hold it against him. I still didn't know what I was looking for but after McCrae's little office visit I supposed a little reading on the occult made as much sense as anything.

Also borrowed whatever I could find on payola, since the Bureau's statute books weren't all that useful or clearly written.

But a little reading through my copy of the NDECC file at home revealed that all of the committee members had copies of their personnel files stored in this file except for McCrae. The committee itself seemed to be a patch job of losers meeting once a week over a shrimp bar to impress the folks back home. Crensch's father was on it, which was interesting. I learned that Hugh S. McCrae was indeed an aid to Congressman Laffer, and that he also occupied some hack appointment job as "special assistant" to the NDECC. Which gave him a certain amount of unchecked power in the drug enforcement game, as the committee members could get voted out of office or shuffled off into some other trendy group, but McCrae would remain quietly behind the scenes, out of the reach and knowledge of the voters. He was just there. No indication of how long he'd been in government, but the penciled in words "from National Security Agency" occurred once after his name, along with the words "Pentagon assignment," as if someone had been idly taking notes on his past. NSA is one of those government wastelands where nobody knows what anybody does because no one really does anything.

It occurred to me that his position probably made him privy to the movements of base commanders. McCrae could have made it his business to delay or interfere with orders and set himself up pretty in that poor excuse for a defense installation near Rome. "Why" was a question I didn't want to touch. It also occurred to me that if there was NSA or Pentagon information on him it was well out of my investigative reach, unless I wanted Fearless and therefore Crensch to learn about my queries, because the elaborate justifications I'd have to make up for the requisite forms and permissions would have to go straight through Fearless. Not to mention the possibility of McCrae discovering that I was digging out his history, because there was no telling who talked to him in these organizations.

For besides the "evidence" I kept turning up, there were unfamiliar emotions I kept experiencing that I just didn't want to share. None of my private research was government business, as far as I was concerned. It was my private "northern life" I was chasing down and it didn't need exposure any more than a runaway teenager from an abusive home. Anything I found I wanted to keep.

The article prompted Crensch to leave off skulking and slip into my office, although he waited a few days until after it appeared in the *Globe* so he wouldn't be too obvious about having read it. He closed my office door and occupied my metal folding chair. I let him stare at me while I pretended to be engrossed in writing a report. After two or three minutes of glancing over his shoulder at the closed door, he furtively told me it was time.

"Time for what?"

"Who do you think we should bust? Got any ideas?"

"How about you, Crensch?"

He smiled and jerked his head to acknowledge my double meaning, then he got serious again. "Gotta few. But we want to get the right guy to make the right impact. Screw Paller."

"You mean 'screw Pallader'?" I corrected him.

"Right. He's a buffoon. Screw getting just anybody for PR reasons. Let's make some real noise."

"What do you suggest? You've been on the case longer than me."

"You think there's anyone I can make a deal with?"

"Probably," I said drily.

"Tell me who to make a deal with. Who to talk to. Someone I could approach, and promise you'll go easy on the drug trade in return for fingering a likely suspect. And I don't mean some loser that's ticked off his mafia boss. Let's get the real guy." He turned the metal chair around and leaned his folded arms across the back the way "partner cops with a derring-do idea the chief might not like" often do in the movies.

"Like I said, how about you? You're a real guy."

"Come on, Morrow, I'm serious." But he looked fascinated with the concept.

"So am I. We could bust *you* and tell the press that the government has secret hit men in the ranks of the FBI who infiltrate military installations on behalf of the French Consulate—"

He looked like he was seriously considering the ploy, so I broke off before I got myself in deeper trouble than I'd already planned on getting myself into. "But won't the Mob suspect something?" he asked.

"Nah, they'll probably arrange a secret escape for you from jail. They'll be so grateful to you for being their fall guy they'll probably even have a secret ceremony to induct you into their ranks."

"Yeah." He looked thoughtful. "But I don't think it'll work."

"Why not? Once you're a made man you're a made man."

"No one would believe it." After the news article, I wasn't so sure there was anything no one would believe. Crensch confirmed my doubt. "So, my sources tell me there's a psychic on it now. You know about that?"

"Oh, yeah," I said enthusiastically. "The psychic. She's really good. Predicts the winning lottery numbers every week. Maybe you ought to check her out."

"Could be. Could be. Could get rich." It was supposed to be a joke.

"Didn't say she predicted them accurately. Only that she predicted them."

"Well, she might be worth a trip to Utica anyway." Damn! I didn't want Crensch poking around in Nariano's backyard.

"Uh, Sid, come to think of it, I do know someone who might be helpful." I glanced furtively at the door, coughed, and whispered, since that was the sort of stuff he was sure to mistake for sincerity. "I agree that it's wasted effort to make a show piece out of arresting someone on a deal or arresting someone on a whim. I'd also like nothing better than to find the actual killer and bring him to justice." Considering the corpse was now alive I figured that was a safe enough goal to bestow on him. "I'd like to know who the hell was impersonating a military commander in the first place. But that's slow methodical work, especially if it *is* mafia business. The last thing to do is go stamping out fires as they happen which serves no purpose except to keep the boss happily blowing in every political wind."

"Yeah, damn straight."

"So, why don't you hint you've heard things from your congressional connections? Let the boss know we must keep things on the quiet side. And for the time being," I paused significantly, "let everything we discover be our secret."

He loved secrets. "Sure. Keep it zipped. Just you and me together. Now, where do we begin? You know the Nunzios. You're on drugs." Crensch meant that I was on the drug committee, but he was oblivious to the double entendre. "Who can we make nervous in the drug trade that might also know something in the murder trade?"

"I'll let you know in a week. With the takeover in Utica, there's bound to be a few personnel changes, and approaching the wrong person with the wrong word can destroy a case like this. Let me work a little more in drug operations until something begins to look familiar. In the meantime—why don't you go hang out in the North End, drink espresso, see what you hear?" That could actually be useful. The whole Boston Mob knew me and wouldn't say anything to or around me. None of them knew Crensch, and he was good at hanging out and getting secret titbits of uselessness, and whatever he did bring back to me I could make an educated guess concerning.

"Don't wear the uniform." That was how we referred to our standard white shirts and suits. "Just go in civvies and don't be too outgoing with the men, except to pay an occasional compliment to the older ones. Old Italian men never forget a compliment and will repeat their own praise for decades. But be especially nice to the mommas in the kitchens, because they're generally not used to it, and if the mommas come to like you, their daughters will come to understand that you're all right. The mommas won't say much. They probably don't know much, because if they're working kitchens, their husbands are probably low-level mobsters who own the place and all Mafiosi keep the women out of 'the business.' The upper-level mob wives cook in splendid isolation at home and never go anywhere except church."

"Perhaps I ought to try church."

"Probably a waste. You won't strike up enlightening conversations there. But the North End daughters who wait tables might chat with you if you encourage them." Maybe. The girls might talk, but often in a way that needed a lot of shifting. They tell you all about their boyfriends' new cars. You figure out on your own the boyfriend is a courier for a *capitan*. "Make yourself a regular someplace and if you make it known you're short on both cash and intelligence, you might even get some job offers after a while."

"Couldn't refuse. Couldn't refuse." Could see him stuffing cotton in his cheeks already. Really it was his kind of assignment. He had already risen out of his chair, risen to conquer Little Italy.

"And, hey, Sid. Don't bring the Uzi. It's gauche. Real mobsters don't use them." I winked like this was a compliment. He winked back. Then he slowly opened the door and slid sideways into the hall lest anyone see him.

Then of course there was a pre-press conference drug meeting of the "new task force," which was really all the old faces plus yours truly who was no longer observing but was now in a position of authority along with Piekarski.

"Hey, Morrow, find the missing corpse?"

"Yeah, in your ex-wife's bed." Mr. Family Values liked that one. Laughed like a bastard and kept laughing after everyone else stopped to prove that my little sally didn't affect him. Asked me to call the meeting to order.

"Order."

Piekarski made up for my brevity with a "save the youth and families of America" speech and a few bizarre references to "loose exhibitionist lifestyles" that drug use was supposed to encourage among preschool children. Then he spent an hour discussing the exhibitionist press conference arrangements with Kanesh and five minutes bantering on the same old gossip concerning the Boston-Providence drug ring. Since I had skipped one or two of the meetings I was supposed to observe, I quietly supposed that I might have missed some useful information, but I hadn't. A few agents opined about losing surveillance on a local dealer that the Boston cops seemed to have driven away and how nobody knew who his replacement was.

I said a few meaningless words about needing to stop the drug trade in Utica by determining who the Boston supplier was, and how the supplier was probably associated with the Nunzio family, but the only benefit I got from this was stifling the idle chatter because I was supposed to be the guy with all the mob experience and no one else really had anything too useful to offer in that line.

Speaking of drugs, I really wanted to figure out what kind of pills McCrae was pushing for his boss, but sending them off to the lab our field office was assigned to use was right out for obvious reasons. As I sat in the meeting, I thought I could do worse than ask a local street pusher. Then one night I got an inspiration to ask Penny about them when I went back north.

Did a lot of night reading. Learned all there was to know about payola. Mainly that the government pretty much didn't care. In theory, it was punishable by a maximum fine of $10,000 and one year in prison, but nobody had ever done time for it. Especially since the FCC ruled in 1979 that "social exchanges between friends are not payola," which pretty much made the whole game unenforceable and proved Penny's point about not getting caught.

How do you prove two people *aren't* friends, *aren't* exchanging gifts of friendship? I had thoughts of Jade all week. And the band. Every evening I stared over the top of my borrowed witchcraft books into the fire and traced pictures from the poetry that a dark northern musician had given me. Tried my damnedest to figure out if we were friends or what. And what McCrae wanted. And then my thoughts were all images of Toronto and my upcoming defiant return trip.

My occult reading was less than useful, although occasionally an allusion to a magical principle rang true to something I felt about Penny, the way an echo of a line of poetry sometimes rang true to a feeling or experience in my life. But mainly the books were just incredibly poorly written, and pretentious, and stupid. Well, the older ones weren't bad because they read more like elaborate Victorian hoaxes than anything else, but they weren't terribly useful as research tools. But the recent ones presented witchcraft as a kind of self-help affair in costume.

Write your troubles in the sand and let the waves obliterate them, advised one. Salt water is a cleanser. You'll feel better. Write your troubles on a piece of paper and burn it, advised another. Fire is a cleanser. You'll feel better. Speak your troubles to a rock and bury it. Earth is a cleanser—and so on. And mixed in was a curious apologetics, in which magic was supposed to be so powerful you couldn't safely write about it to the uninitiated but also so mundanely metaphorical you weren't supposed to take it too literally. A cosmic dog and pony show that seemed to have nothing to do with the history of witchcraft proper, as I was beginning to understand it with the help of the one or two reasonably responsible studies I did find. And my own frequent fire gazing.

Anyway, nothing in my reading gave me insight into Penny, Elb, walking corpses, or Black Dog. I did decide that, compared to Penny, modern witches were "something like" witches. They had the imagery sort of right, if nothing else. Penny probably *was* a witch, if the word still meant anything. I'd ask her about it. Along with the pills.

But despite my cynicism, when I looked up from my books and into the fire and thought about Jade, it still bothered me that Piekarski was calling me a "broom rider." Not that I felt "oppressed" or anything, but that I *felt*. Anyway, the way my life had been going, I decided I needed more convincing sources on witchcraft than those publicly available, so I resorted to scrying my hearth embers while Black Dog's cassette played on my stereo.

And damn if I didn't have a recurring dream in which I was offering pigeons and silver to Aphrodite. I was in an empty temple overlooking an ocean with dark waves like the night sky. Somewhere stars were laughing at me but I couldn't really hear them. Aphrodite was supposed to hear my petition and rise from the waves. Only I couldn't keep my mind on the goddess because I kept seeing Jade's face whenever I thought I was praying to her and so all my dream offerings were to him.

The nights went by in dreaming, as I said. And one night the phone rang and I had the prickly pleasure of wondering if it was Jade until I answered and the caller asked for a wrong number. And another night, while I was burning Hugh McCrae's name in a black candle for fun and to see if I would "feel better" for doing it, the phone rang again and I let it ring to prolong the hope it might be Jade and to my very great surprise—it was Cara.

"Hey, Petie, that you?"

"In a sense."

She paused as if the pause was supposed to mean something. Or as if she was too cool to speak right away and wanted me to pay her court by waiting. And of course, what could I do but pay court by waiting? "Sooo," she breathed, "whatcha doin'?"

"Readin' classics. How'd you get my home number?"

"Jadie gave it to me. Left it in bed. One helluva forgetful guy." Her pointed casualness nettled me, but I couldn't think of anything to say so I let her continue. "Yup. We had fun. Went over to his place just to hang out and watch the band practice, think his mother would have had a French cow if she knew I was there. And next thing ya know, well, we're all in the sack."

"What sack?" I asked to be funny, and to cover a catch in my throat I didn't like having. "You get the sack, Cara?"

"What sack? Oh, God." She giggled like she was terribly high or wanted me to believe she was terribly high and therefore not really responsible for whatever she wanted me to believe had happened. "I'm so fucked up. Well, not all. Everyone else went home. Just me and Jadie. Anyway, got your number, gotta call. You comin'?"

"For a lovely lady like you, Cara? Sure. I'll cum." I have no idea why I said this.

"Oh, Jesus, Pete. Come on," she said in a tone of annoyance meant to sound like false modesty, but which really sounded like delight with my flirtatious wit. "Oh, Juno says 'hi.'" She suddenly changed to folksy banter to prove how little she cared for my compliment. "I mean are you *comin'*?"

"Comin' where?" I played dumb.

"*Comin'*, Pete. To my party. For Claude. What's today? Monday. Gotta know. It's in three days. Ya see, I gotta make plans."

I did not ask about the band. For some reason my tongue wouldn't let me betray even a normal friendly interest. "Will Elb be there?" I asked instead.

"No. Ma says it's girls only. But it's our party and for you we'll make an exception. You're good people. Be there six sharp."

"You got it."

She sang a few snatches of an old folk song in a not-bad Bob Dylan imitation. Then she stopped and added, "We'll watch the moon die—"

"What, again? I thought we already did that in Egypt."

She took my remark as a tribute of interest. "We'll weave garlands and talk to it. We'll do it up right. We'll play Pink Floyd songs. You can stay here if you want. I'll put you up with Elb." I chuckled. "He'd really like that," she insisted.

"Will I get to meet Claude?"

"Anything could happen."

"Gotcha."

"Oh—" she seemed to break off to have a conversation with someone in the room. I heard, "Yes, Bethie, he'll be there." Then, "Bethie's here. Bethie from Fendra's. She's coming. Says to say 'hi.' And you'll get to meet Selene. She's a . . . dancer. Good people. Ma knows her. Ma says 'hi' too."

"Warm regards to the whole family." It was as close as I would let myself get to mentioning Jade.

There was a screamy sort of giggle in the background and Cara clicked off.

That'll be fun, I decided, rooming with Elb for a night, courtesy of his favorite sister. But I'll bring camping gear anyway. Just to prepare myself for whatever wilderness might come.

And for three nights I kept looking for dreams in the fire and asking myself what the hell was I really doing and feeling and why my life was going this way. But I didn't do anything to stop the way it was going. Thursday morning came. The sun rose outside my dreams. I woke simply and drove furiously into a midweek weekend up north.

Stave Eight

Thursday, early evening, September 17, 1992.

Thirteen Oak Street. Cara was a moon. But I didn't know that yet as I pulled in behind Penny's beat-up car, wondering where the van was. Eight hours of nearly non-stop driving hovered behind me and made the day feel like it never happened. Then I turned off my engine and sat looking at the quietly sloping house for a moment with that peculiar traveler's sensation that I wasn't really here in York yet and wouldn't be until I opened the car door and got out.

Travel days never exist like real days anyway. Short distances always seem more physically certain than long ones to me because I don't lose my healthy perspective on reality driving to places I already know. But long trips numb me to passing time and so when I finally arrive at my destination, I'm out of my usual life and thoughts for a noticeable while. I sat in my car for almost a minute before I remembered the white paper bag on the seat next to me and something like self-acquaintance briefly returned. Just to be a good guest I had bought some wine and cheese at the duty-free border shop, but as my housewarming gifts brought me back to myself they also brought me uncomfortably out of the coming evening. My party contributions felt familiar only because they weren't yet a part of where I was going, and so for a few seconds they highlighted my own distance from where I was.

But then I left the car and the area was with me. Sunset beginning in one corner. Dropping but not yet red. Sky still September blue. Day into night and the neighborhood held the time like a valley carved into the now comfortably uneven moment. Geese flying in the early evening distance anchored and accented where I was. I walked up the driveway noticing that McCrae's rusty yard display had been removed and that the space it left was all rough autumn grass. The missing van made the place different than I remembered it. And sometime before I reached the door the local north enclosed me and I was there.

I entered the unexpectedly quiet house without a strategy and without knocking. No sign of Penny. No sign of anyone downstairs. But the kitchen *felt* noisy, as if it had recently been abandoned and would soon be full of Penny and her crazy family again. The noise was merely on break—crouching visibly in the dirty pots and scattered dish towels. Went upstairs telling myself there was no reason to feel silly for blowing off my command appearance at the press conference tomorrow in favor of a girls' rock 'n' roll party. But I did feel silly. Silly enough to have to keep consciously persuading myself that since I was here now I might as well see it through. That skipping the whole adventure for a campsite or an immediate drive home would be a sorry waste of an excellent investigative opportunity, if not worse. Then I went upstairs and knocked at Cara's door. Louder than I meant to.

Juno answered. Hair still partially held to one side in her neon green barrette, but the barrette was now doubled with a bright pink ribbon tied loosely over a yellow rubber band. The ribbon was one of those long neon yarn "ties" I remembered girls favoring in the early seventies. Her eye shadow was smeary and green, a shade or two lighter than her neon sneakers, and she was wearing glossy pale pink lipstick that shone like acrylic sugar and honey. Her jeans and T-shirt looked pressed and newly washed. "Hi, Pete," she said brightly. "We're getting ready. Come in." She was clearly more surprised by my early arrival than by my arrival *per se*. She eagerly held the door open for me and as I entered Cara's abode, all my self-consciousness vanished. I immediately felt welcome and expected, one of the "good people" on the party list.

Inside, the party felt like it was already beginning to happen, even though Juno was apparently alone. All the shades were drawn, making the place dim but not dark, and the shades were sheltering the room from everything outside. Some of the shades had yellow-green glow-in-the-dark designs stuck to them, rubbery butterflies and spotted mushrooms and oversized grinning flowers, the kind that were popular among kids in the sixties who were too young to be hippies proper but still wanted their bedrooms to look "cool." There was a plush comfortable rug holding the floor that looked like a carpet remnant, and "bean bag" type chairs and reclining pillows scattered around, as well as a couch with tattered arms smothered in bright crocheted throws. The place wasn't orderly, exactly, but it was somewhat better maintained than Mother Penny's chaotic domain. If I had to describe it in a single word, I would call it *youthful*. But mindfully youthful. Youthful without being young.

A few candles were lit on small end tables and in bowls on the floor to catch the wax drippings, but more candles were unlit. There were rock 'n' roll posters and magazine pictures of rock stars tightly covering the walls like wallpaper, that is, where there wasn't crushed black velvet paintings of various band logos or psychedelic landscapes with hidden faces winking at you out of melting orange skies and mountains. Some posters were copies of album covers. The tables reminded me of little shrines with candles lit under a grouping of several posters of a single band or personage. The Beatles when they were new in their invasion and still getting along. Hendrix setting his guitar on fire. Jimmy Page solo surrounded by posters of Led Zeppelin, with a note under a lit red candle that read, "still burning for Pamela."

I lingered there because I recognized the handwriting as being the same as that on the "Hopner's Sardines" note I had taken from McCrae dead, a note that I had stared at often enough. Around the base of the candle was a necklace bearing a turquoise phoenix with proudly spread wings, clutching an unrevealing pearl. I couldn't tell if the phoenix was falling into one of its many deaths or rising from one of its many rebirths. Juno noticed my interest.

"The note means the *candle's* burning for Pamela," she explained. "Not Jimmy Page. Cara must have lit it." Did that mean Cara wrote the note on the corpse, I wondered? Was she with her mother when the "killing" took place? Maybe Hopner's Sardines was another Toronto rock band. "The necklace is a replica. Beulah made it." I made a mental note to ask about Pamela when Cara arrived, along with Hopner's Sardines, to gauge her reaction.

At another table was a poster of Bruce Springsteen sending greetings from Asbury Park, NJ. And next to him was one of Rimbaud—I mean on second glance, Patti Smith, whose poetry I suddenly remembered hearing with thrill and pleasure in my own adolescence. All over the room were faces I recognized from the sixties and seventies and newer ones I didn't recognize at all. Then, in one corner, a relatively barren table that didn't command much notice at first caught my attention. In the center was a single unlit gray-blue candle standing upright in a silver holder. A red carnation tied in a black ribbon was lying to the candle's side. Over this table was a conspicuously unused space of blank wall surrounding a small, embroidered copy of the banner I'd seen tacked up on the backstage wall at Fendra's—a dragon guarding a black dog holding a ruby, the dog positioned over a dagger and a rose. Diagonally down to the bottom right of the banner was an enlarged photograph of Black Dog in stage costume.

I didn't linger at this particular shrine, but I remained aware of its presence as I went over to another wall to inspect a fairly decent stereo system set up on a cheap pressboard entertainment center. Two speakers that were clearly too large for the acoustics of the small room were on the floor. The shelves the rest of the system didn't occupy were full of LPs and CDs. There were also makeshift shelves next to the entertainment center and orange crates scattered around which contained more of Cara's extensive music library. "That's Elb's," said Juno, referring to the stereo. "Cara borrowed it."

"I see." I got the impression from the elaborate hook-up that it was "borrowed" rather permanently. The stereo's radio was on at very low volume, tuned to a local rock station, and the radio signal sounded clear and comfortable the way signals sometimes do when you're warm inside and darkness or storms are falling without. The song was Neil Young's "Like a Hurricane."

"You're early," said Juno. "Want to help set up?"

"Sure." I handed her my bag. She peered inside and looked delighted with my choice.

"Oh, wow, wine and cheese." She jumped a little excited childish bounce on the tips of her feet and put the goodies on a table that was under a variety of posters and didn't seem to be dedicated to anyone in particular.

"Where is everyone?"

"Beth's bringing pizza," explained Juno. "Might be getting it. Beulah's downstairs making decorations. Cara might be with Beth, I don't know. Great—I love port wine." She inspected the bottle. "We've got crackers in the kitchen." As I followed her into a narrow cubbyhole of a kitchen, she said, "Cara says you already know Beth." The statement didn't demand a response so I didn't make one.

There were more magazine pictures on the kitchen cabinets. Buried in the mix I recognized a color sketch of Chopin. He was sitting at his piano, but his face was turned away and buried in a large white cloth, as if to mask his consumptive coughing. Elegant nineteenth-century ladies were crying and dipping silken kerchiefs in the blood on his piano keys. "That's Ma's," explained Juno, coming over to me. "She gave it to us. Ma used to know George Sand and everything."

"She help Chopin get his start, too?"

"I don't know. I think she might have helped George get hers." Juno was crunching on a stalk of celery. "Then I think she might have brought them together." Juno smiled, all breathless teenager recounting a favorite love story. "Ma helps everybody." Then her voice turned suddenly childish, "But you ain't gonna find me dipping my hands in blood nowadays. No way. Probably get AIDS. Do you like potato chips?" She was dumping bags of snack food into wooden bowls.

"Sure." I helped her.

"Do you know 'Funeral for a Friend/Love Lies Bleeding'?" I didn't. "That's what Cara calls the Chopin sketch. Do you like Elton John?"

"Don't know him."

"Neither do we. But Cara thought we might make it a seventies kind of thing, because sometimes Uncle Claude is a seventies kind of guy. And *Good-bye Yellow Brick Road* is a great LP, no matter what anyone says. Those songs are on it."

I had nothing to say to yellow brick roads except that I felt like my life was on one. "A seventies kind of thing," I teased. "Should have brought my gold chains and disco records."

Juno scowled. "Not quite," she said like any recalcitrant teenager out of any high school class between '74 and '78 voicing discriminating disgust with anything uncool. Then she took out an overlarge clear plastic tube of thick lip gloss and applied more to her already too shiny lips. "Tastes like cherries." She offered me the bottle. "Want to try? You can lick it off." I declined. "I was going to get my hair feathered and wear a guy's big blue varsity sports jacket lined with fake lamb's wool like 1974, but—"

The door opened and Beulah silently came in, trailing tissue paper moons gilded with silver thread. Among the moons were tin foil stars noisy in sequins and she began to tack them up on the ceiling in long pale glittering garlands. I could smell Elmer's Glue and that sweet, thick paste you only use in kindergarten to make a mess of your hands with. "Don't put holes in the posters or Cara will have a fit," Juno admonished. Beulah didn't need the warning. She had expertly made thumbtack holes in the ceiling so her interior decorating wouldn't mar Cara's wallpaper. Then she left the room, went downstairs, and returned with her arms full of articles of clothing. "She made those," Juno declared while Beulah nodded and smiled. "We're going to have costumes for later. Who would you like to be?"

"I don't know."

"We didn't know either, so Beulah made stuff to choose from."

"Do you ever speak, Beulah?"

"No," Juno answered for her sister. "Beulah only speaks when she has something intelligent to say. Kind of like Les," she teased. Beulah seemed to blush a little, but she quickly turned back to her decorations so I couldn't tell for sure. I decided that Beulah was an attractive girl, despite the scar around her left eye. "She makes things. She makes Black Dog's costumes. Made Jade's wizard cloak." I felt an inward jolt at the casualness with which Juno said his name, and congratulated myself on my face remaining bland. "Which is a truly excellent cloak," Juno added. I glanced my agreement at Beulah, but her back was to me now. "Made the candles, too. And scented them with her own perfume."

While Juno was explaining her sister, I heard the door crash downstairs and loud footsteps ascending to the apartment. Beth entered first, carrying three large pizza boxes. Cara held the door open behind her, carrying a large grocery bag under one arm. I didn't recognize Beth for a few seconds because she was wearing dark glasses that were a little too large for her face. The contrast looked intentionally comical without being too intentional, if you know what I mean. Beth was outgoing and eager to please because she was really shy and ingoing, and so the glasses weren't showoffy but more like a flattering obeisance to Cara's own coolness. I could tell immediately that Beth was trying to please her way into acceptance and that acceptance was easily forthcoming because Beth herself was so easy to please. "Ma always says Beulah could spin storms out of morning dew if she put her mind to it," Juno insisted with the kind of adolescent excitement that begs a compliment for oneself by praising others.

"So why'd you pop out her eye?" asked Cara like a cold wind against the praise as Beth bounced into the kitchen with the pizzas.

"Because my scar was opening and I couldn't see," said Juno dolefully, rubbing her forehead. This little exchange appeared to be for my benefit, although Cara hadn't greeted me yet. "But that's ancient history," she whined defensively. "Ma fixed it and now Ma says she makes things fit to open a shop in Yorkville someday. If that's what she *wants*," Juno added like a dutiful amen, glancing at Cara.

Cara responded by warmly kissing Beulah's cheek as if she were a baby, and singing a line from an old Elton John song that I did recognize. Then she shoved her bag of groceries at Juno. "Eggrolls. Dip. Pasta salad. Beer. Deli bread. Apples for later." Juno took care of the food by distributing it around the various altars. I noticed that Black Dog's got the apples, but I didn't like to notice their altar too much in the presence of Cara, lest she notice me lingering over Jade's image. Some things are too private to share.

So I went over to Led Zep's. "Hey, Cara, did you pick up any Hopner's Sardines?"

"Didn't know you wanted any." Her voice betrayed no discomfort; her tone said that naturally she would have gotten Hopner's sardines if I'd wanted any. There was also no hint of greeting in her tone. My presence seemed to be taken for granted by everybody. She flopped down on her couch and lit a cigarette.

I pretended to notice the note under the burning red candle for the first time. "Who's Pamela? Is she coming?"

"I doubt it. She was a GTO."

"A what?"

"A divine groupie." Cara coolly blew smoke. "Kind of a happening without notice. Wrote a book, Pete. You might feel something if you read it. Not a bad book, either. Reads like a wounded angel beating her heavy metal voice against an unyielding sky the morning after the apocalypse nobody noticed. You like Petrarch?"

"Yes."

"You'll love Lady Pamela." There was a knock on the door. Beth emerged from the kitchen with plates of warm pizza as Juno ran to answer.

"What do you want?" Juno asked. Then, "Do I have to say it every time? It's a party," she groused over to Cara, who ignored her by exuberantly blowing another cloud of smoke and studying the open door with the brightness of a happy vulture. A tall, bony, desultory girl with dyed blond hair showing dark roots slunk in.

"Nothing," the girl answered Juno vaguely. She didn't really appear to be speaking directly to anyone at all. "Hi, Cara."

"Hi, Selene. Didja sell any?"

Selene smiled grimly like the greeting wasn't all that funny, but also like she would take a certain amount of ribbing from Cara that she wouldn't take from anyone else. In fact, she carried herself like she was in the habit of dealing exclusively with Cara, but even as she entered the apartment, Selene seemed to inwardly keep her distance from Cara and everyone else. She was wearing a black sweater studded with cheap imitation colored stones. Tight black jeans and boots. She sported too many tarnished silver rings and too much make up for any natural prettiness to show. She was far too thin to be healthy. Selene reminded me of some runaways I'd known, the lonely crazy types that never seem to be running to or from anything, or even really running. The kind who seem to know in the cradle that no experience is ever really worth having.

"We're going to kill you tonight," said Cara.

"Cool," Selene answered without emotion. "Got any weed?"

"Got any weed? Got any weed?" mocked Cara. There was something in Selene that seemed to resist too much friendliness in Cara, something under her face that preferred to be let alone, and something else in the involuntary curve of her mouth like an embarrassing weakness that liked to be in this particular company sometimes without having to degrade herself by admitting it. Selene's question was not so much a question as a greeting needing to prove itself. I couldn't help thinking that if Selene had been five years older she would have been two years dead. Because I honestly couldn't imagine that waxen face and those tinny colorless eyes breaking twenty. And the self-consciously grizzled way she moved her young limbs told me that she probably couldn't imagine living into her own adulthood either, but that she sort of liked it that way. She probably needed the justification of early death to be at the party at all.

Beth offered Selene some pizza in a tone of voice suggesting sweetly veiled apprehension. I could not imagine Beth and Selene alone together or even having much to say to each other without Cara's influence. Beth actually seemed a little afraid of her, in a way I couldn't quite figure out and in a way that didn't seem to show beyond an almost physically palpable gratitude for Cara's presence. Selene declined with a shake of her head and sort of quietly huddled into the corner of the couch Cara was sitting on. Cara gave Selene a cigarette as Juno helped herself to the offered pizza slice when more young women entered the apartment, this time without knocking. And for a while the pizza and the wine and the altar food was shared around because more guests kept coming until the party numbered about a dozen young women besides Beth, Selene, and the three sisters.

Not everybody knew everybody else so Cara kept making introductions while the autumn darkness slid under the shades and softly clad the room. At which point

I noticed that some of the party guests kept politely glancing at me in the candlelight. "Pete's one of us," Cara confidently assured one girl, "he's a friend of my mother's. Good people. Even knows my funny Uncle Claude," she teased me, extending a paper plate of appetizers.

"Where is Claude?" I shot back.

"And you still have to ask, Pete" she responded brightly. "Where do you think he is?"

"Think you must have him hidden in a desert cave somewhere. All the better to rob trains with," I tried, when a loud girl with a busy giggle disrupted my sly investigative technique.

"Put on *Use Your Illusion I*," she demanded.

"No, U2," called someone else.

"I thought this was the seventies," pouted Juno.

"We can make it transitional," said Cara, turning to put the paper plate on an altar. She would have sounded like a genial maternal hostess if her voice had been a shade more teasing and a shade less show-offy. "How about *The Wall*?" She didn't wait for a response from any of her guests, but fumbled through one of the orange crates.

"How about *The Dark Side of the Moon*?" insisted Juno in an attempt to bring things back to the proper decade.

"Yeah, *The Dark Side of the Moon*," echoed someone else.

"Hey, damn good choice. For once," acceded Cara. "I know I've got Elb's copy here somewhere." She threw on a CD and as the familiar dark strains entered the room—familiar to me because Pink Floyd was one of the bands I used to listen to as a teenager—Beth and Beulah quietly cleared away the now empty pizza boxes and food remnants while Juno pranced around lighting all the unlit candles, including Black Dog's, to which she gave no more ceremony than the rest. When she lit their candle I noticed that even though most of the other food had been eaten the apples on their altar remained untouched.

Throughout this time Selene remained in her corner of the couch, sometimes watching the guests, sometimes defensively withdrawn into somewhere else, sometimes both. I tried to draw her out as the after-dinner preparations were being made. "Hey, Sell-Any," I teased. "Cara tells me you're a dancer."

She looked up with a hard, indifferent expression, stared in the general direction of an empty corner, and shrugged. It was not a shrug of modesty. It was a shrug that said that her dancing had nothing to do with her.

"Care for a round?" I held my hand out to her to see what she would do. She didn't exactly assent. She didn't exactly refuse. I didn't even notice her standing up but suddenly she was sort of dancing in front of me in a kind of small defiance against nothing, executing little formal movements like exercises out of a high school dance class with a little more grace than one might expect from her bony frame, but not much more. I dropped her hand and she danced solo to David Gilmour's pointed vocals, and kept dancing as a few of the other girls joined in singing, and then to the delighted cheers and claps of the rest, who to my mind seemed thoroughly unable to distinguish her near-mediocrity from excellence. Although I must admit that Pink

Floyd isn't easy to dance to. Then Selene tripped and fell on her back and her face broke into a disarming smile—her first real smile all evening, and she laughed while the entire party clapped and sang. She didn't bother to get up right away, either, but lay there idiotically giggling at the applause. So when the strange alarms of the next track started I extended my hand and helped to pull her into a sitting position. Despite her dancing, her hand felt clammy and cold.

"No," said Cara, "Let her stay. Selene is supposed to be the fallen moon."

"Who are you supposed to be?" I asked. Beulah had been marking up Cara's face with grease paint in the corner while Selene danced.

Juno sang a line from an old Who song. The girl with the busy giggle, clearly drunk now, joined her singing for a few seconds.

Beulah moved away from Cara, revealing a black glittery face with a silver-blue crescent moon painted in a soft curve across part of her mouth and stretching upwards across her right jaw and cheek. "I am the rising moon." She donned a black robe full of silver stars from Beulah's costume pile. "I am the night sky."

"I still want to be the seventies," insisted Juno.

"Then take off your goddamned neon sneakers."

"Can I be like the sixties?" asked a timid girl with mouse-brown hair and thick glasses and poor-looking patched clothes who didn't look like she had the strength to really "be" anything. "Joyce the Voice at a Rolling Stones concert?"

"Beulah's got a maxi-skirt and love beads. And a Captain Beefheart hat if you want it."

Then everyone started speaking at once. "I want to be Janis. People say I look like her. We have the same sign."

"I want to be anybody."

"Can I be Alice Cooper and put on dark eye make-up—"

"—No, Kiss," somebody else jumped in. "Kiss for makeup in the seventies—Kiss, I'll stretch my tongue." The other girls stared at the last speaker like she was overenthusiastic, or like overenthusiasm was actually possible here, which I thought was funny. "I always liked them," she cheerfully explained. Beulah was somehow able to accommodate everyone's taste with her costumes and grease paint.

"Beth?" prodded Cara, lighting up some marijuana to pass around. "Choose your poison, girl."

"O, yeah, Poison," said someone who had wanted to "be the eighties but really didn't care."

"I don't know." Beth spoke in a shyly indulgent tone meant to be an affectionate tease for the enthusiastic frenzy of the others, "I'll just be myself—"

"—Yourself?" chided Cara. "At a costume party for Claude? What would the dear man say?"

"Claude can't even be himself," added Juno. "Like my mood ring? If I hold it in a flame it turns bright purple."

"All right, or maybe a rain cloud," said Beth, in a voice suggesting she would choose a costume after all but not one that would compete with everybody else's rendition. Beulah ran over and sprinkled some silvery glitter and cobweb stuff that looked like clouds on Beth's hair and brushed some gray and pale pink powder on her cheeks. While Beulah was working her magic, Beth glanced at and then quickly away from Black Dog's photograph.

"Pete?" asked Cara in the middle of Beth's glance, so as to draw my attention to it. "Is there anyone *you* want to be?"

"No thanks, I have a life," I said good-naturedly.

"No you don't," corrected Juno, catching herself before Cara's withering look. "Well, he doesn't, does he? I mean, that's what Ma says."

"Shut up, Juno. Pete's here, ain't he?"

"I'd prefer to just watch," I said to make peace.

"Ooo, Pete's going to be our audience," said Cara. "OK, the incredible Mr. Life will go sit in the corner while we hold hands and dance around Selene." Selene started to get up. "Selene, stay put in the middle, we need your energy."

I settled myself onto the couch. It was cold where Selene had been sitting earlier. The party guests, in their various costumes, all formed a circle around the fallen moon, who was now sitting up and smoking the joint Cara had given her and clearly trying her best to look unaffected by the proceedings in spite of the fact that she sort of seemed to relish the attention. There was no longer any music playing, and the silence was strange and edgy as the women slowly moved clockwise. No one broke her handhold unless the reefer came her way, and I briefly wondered how more than a dozen people expected to get high by sharing a single marijuana cigarette until Cara produced a large plastic bag of more marijuana and several set to eagerly rolling their own joints, which broke up the slow dance. Beulah got up to gather the apples from Black Dog's altar, which she placed in a used potato chip bowl still lined with salt before an indifferent Selene in the center of the circle. Then she placed the burning gray-blue candle on one side of the bowl and the carnation on the other. Selene stared at the candle flame because it was there and passed along her joint to someone in the circle because it was time to. "Lie down, Selene," ordered Cara. "You're supposed to be waning."

"Are you scared," whispered one of the guests, her voice more cheerfully excited about the possibility of someone being scared than serious about giving warning.

Selene didn't answer. Her eyes looked maybe a little uncertain, but the rest of her was sort of snapped and quiet. I noticed a little charcoal censor in which people threw their roaches, and Beulah and Juno kept burning marijuana, so the sweet pungent odor filled the room, enough to get me a little high and hazy because the air currents tended to bring the smoke over to where I was sitting. Then Cara started humming and filling the room with a high pitched Native American sounding chant, and then she started singing a chorus from a Black Dog song I recognized from my cassette tape:

make me a heart of solid moon
an aching sound of sky
dark breath of windstorms
and the eerie way love dies

"That's neat," said someone.

"My cousin wrote that," said Cara. "Now, let us bless the night and the time. Let us cheer down the moon on her fall. Let us join slow hands and join slow voices in a circle. Selene," she called.

"Seleneeeee," called everyone else, not in unity but whenever they felt like it. "Seleneee the fallen one. Seleneee the slain." Selene looked on in solemn wonder, a horrid wonder bone-grafted into wide-eyed stoicism.

"Selene the fallen dancer," chanted Cara. Selene giggled and looked around the circle with a lumbering trace of self-consciousness that no one else echoed. "Do you know us now? We are a band of merry maidens. We are the muses of a grand disorder. We are maenads and we are called to do our grand work." Beth had taken off her glasses and she now looked all flushed and enthusiastic. This was new and fun for her and I could tell she was greatly enjoying herself. "We are the three queens and the Lady of the Lake who hands over the sword of white samite that the king might rule. We are the three Fates and the three weird sisters of the blasted heath. We are the triple goddess. We are maiden-mother-crone. We undress blessings and forge soft hearts of swords—"

"Come on Cara, move it along," said Juno. "Don't steal. That's one of Jade's lines."

"I know. I know. He gave it to me," said Cara impatiently. "And besides, the moon's waning anyway. We are Claude Hopner's daughters, and we call upon this night to bear witness to our god's sweet birth. For this is the season of apricots. This is the smile of the Sphinx. This is the night the moon died in dark water."

"This is the night the moon died in the dark—" echoed Beth.

"This is the night the moon died—" took up somebody else.

"This is the night of the moon—"

"This is the night—"

"This is—"

"Is—Is—Isis—Mother—Mourning Mother—" And the young women started shrieking and howling and ululating names like Bacchus, Dionysus, Enlil, "whose word is gale and storm," added Cara; Ea, Lord of Ocean, Prajapati, Lord of Creation, Agni the fire and lightning who is energy, Hephaestus who molds and makes and was cast out lame, "Apolloooooooo, sweet Apollooo who burns . . . ." Even Selene got into it, although I noticed she had sort of shrunk back into the circle, and her howls were sharp hoots that contained no names. "Selene," admonished Cara, but Selene wasn't about to move back in the center again.

"All right, the moon is dead," said Cara, unwilling to insist on her return. Cara went into the center and put out the candle, so the middle of the circle was dark and the outside of the circle formed by the maenads' backs held the light of the other flickering candles at bay. Beulah's garlands of moons and stars looked like a softly glittering universe hanging over our heads. "The darkness does not answer our call. The names are lost," pronounced Cara a touch too grandly to sound as sad as she probably meant to.

Nobody did anything, but everybody seemed sort of breathless from all the howling.

"Hey, aren't we supposed to call the directions or something," I said to be funny and show off my occult reading.

"North," said Beth.

"We're supposed to weep for Osiris now," hinted Juno. Beulah already had two glistening tears running down her cheeks, but she was handing out black mourning scarves for everyone to cover their heads with.

"Rain clouds always weep," said Beth cheerfully, "but I'll try a scarf." She threw it over the gray glitter like a black cloud and briefly turned to face the girl next to her for an appraisal

"The weeping is in silence," instructed Cara, visibly annoyed. Selene immediately started talking to the girl next to her. "Think of a god's name or something precious you've lost," said Cara, "and cry long and loud. We have to make the moon's death last."

"My kitty cat. My poor kitty got hit by a car."

"Osiris, o sweet Osiris, come back to us with the Nile."

"I lost five pounds but I'm not sad about it. I mean -- chocolate, sweet chocolate I can't have anymore."

"Rainbows," said the rain cloud.

"John Lennon."

"Keith Moon."

"Lynyrd Skynyrd when they crashed," said Juno.

"Jim Morrison."

"Jimmy Hendrix."

"Elvis when he gained weight and ruined himself."

"Janis," screamed the girl who wanted to be Janis, "O, Janis, speak to me."

"Isadora Duncan, who knew how to live." Selene did not say this, but she looked up with something like interest and glinted her eyes.

"Kerouac," said Cara drily. "Novels."

"Charlie Parker."

"Rene Magritte."

"Disco," said Juno, to be funny. Cara shot her a look. "Well, it's dead."

"Canada on a Sunday."

"Canada every day."

"Quebec."

"We wish."

Only Selene added nothing to the list, but she looked amused in her obscurity and vaguely clapped her hands in time with everybody's chanting. Some of the women mock wept, most giggled, nobody worked up the good mourning frame of mind Cara seemed to want, and so the "weeping" died away into a discussion of how much there was to do in Toronto as opposed to Buffalo. "The eighties" was complaining that she needed to get home early and go to work tomorrow. If she missed another day her boss was going to fire her.

Cara called order by relighting Black Dog's candle and holding it aloft. Beth noticed first. Her eager brown eyes seemed to glow in the sudden brightness as Cara chanted, "Out of the circle of darkness, out of the womb that churns in silence—"

"Burns," Juno bouncily corrected, "*burns* in silence. Ma always says burns—"

"'Churns' is more violent and creative. 'Burns' is the downside," snapped Cara.

"Yeah," said Selene unexpectedly, to Cara's seeming chagrin.

Cara continued, "—we bring forth new gods and clothe them in our best desires."

"Hey, Cara, how do you bring forth a new god?" I had to ask, since no one else seemed to know what to do, either. Cara didn't look at me, but Beth did, sharply and dreamily, and then she looked up at Cara, her hair falling joyously around her shoulders in the candlelight, her mouth smiling, her eyes merrily echoing my question.

"Ladies. Sisters of the Moon. I'll tell you how to make a new god like Mother Isis did. I'll whisper the secret of birth—the awful secret my mother whispered to me. The great swallowing trick of the eye that blinds itself for seeing the light. The way to make a god." Cara satisfied herself that she now commanded everyone's attention. "Call what you want, one by one. Call your weakness, your inner wish. For what you secretly wish for you must regard as dear, what you regard as dear is precious to you, and whatever is precious to you is your best blessing to them. Make Black Dog fulfill your dreams and wants. Make Black Dog your dreams and wants, imagine them so, and they shall be a god." Cara held the candle before Beth. "An honest wish to bless my cousin's band with."

"Do it soft first, and gradually louder," chimed in Juno to the rest of the circle.

"Kiss the flame and whisper what you want," said Cara, who was now also holding the bowl of apples. "Whisper and push what is dearest to you into the flame and take back an apple for your wish." Beulah ran out of the circle and put the Black Dog CD on the stereo system. "Make it a good wish to send energy to my cousin's band."

Beth smiled. "All right, your cousin's band," she said gaily, and then whispered, "Jade." Cara's hand stiffened a little around the candle. I don't know if Beth noticed but she quickly added, "and Cara." Cara's hand relaxed and Beth continued naming all the band members to show no favorite, "MartyLesXander." Then she paused, closing her eyes as if she was about to make a wish. I wondered if Beth had met them. "Good luck."

The next girl whispered slightly louder, "I don't know what I want. Good luck, I guess." A lot of the maenads now wished Black Dog "good luck" because Beth had started it off that way and no one wanted to say anything too different. The wishes got progressively louder as the candle made the rounds of the circle, sometimes one maenad passing it to the next, sometimes Cara holding it and passing it along.

Then the candle got to Juno. "Have a hit record," she said, hugging her knees to her chest.

"Have a hit," said Selene flatly. "And luck," she added, nodding her head and passing the candle herself. I noticed she didn't bother to qualify it with "good."

When the candle got to Beulah, she touched a finger to her still teary face and softly brushed the salt water against the flame. The flame did not die. The gesture was sort of weird and touching. Then Cara completed the round and returned back to where I was sitting outside of the circle. She extended the candle to me over the head of another girl and I breathed in an ocean scent. "Pete? Make your wish. Bless the flame with your desire."

I didn't want to voice my desire to myself let alone to Cara and a circle of maenads. In my wish I wanted a sea wizard to make beautiful poems and stories out of my stupid life. But "I'll pass," was all I said. Cara gave me the last apple anyway.

Then she returned to the circle's center. "I am the rising moon, waxing in my power, sending divine energy to Black Dog." Jade's voice seemed to answer her out of the stereo, just before it faded into one of Les's piano solos. "May Black Dog rise—"

"Rise—" chanted the circle.

"Wax—"

"Wax—" chanted the circle.

"—and increase." Everyone screamed in the affirmative, although I couldn't tell whether some of the screams were relief at the ritual finally being over, because the wishes had taken up some time. Cara extinguished the candle with her right palm, leaving the outside of the circle flickering in the light of the remaining candles. "Keep the apples three days in sun to soak up the power. Then eat them as if you are feeding off my cousin's band, or feeding off your own desires. The apples will grant your wishes as they disperse Black Dog's power through you and through you to the rest of the public. Go spread the news through all the adolescents who flower in this season and help Black Dog to live. You are their audience. As you love them so shall the world. As above so below."

Beulah hit a light switch and the sudden glare of two cheap electric lamps dispersed whatever "party" feeling was left. The magic had been completed, Black Dog blessed and sent forth to conquer the hearts of the audience that the guests were supposed to represent. The guests were now quickly getting the message that Cara no longer had need of them. Beth and a few others seemed willing to linger by helping with kitchen clean-up, and Selene kept trying deliberately to get in everyone's way. So while Cara was busy trying to usher people out, I seized the opportunity to give myself a solo tour of the downstairs without the trouble of a witness. "I'll go unpack my car and find Elb's room," I told Beulah in an aside so there would be no immediate protest.

Downstairs was not empty. Penny was home now, sitting in a kitchen chair with a broken back and a ripped plastic cushion that she had dragged into the living room entranceway. She was carrying on a spirited political discussion with someone in the living room that I couldn't see from where I was standing. She had a corncob pipe in her hand and the smoke had a greenish tinge and made me think of burnt sunflowers.

"And then we'se got the goddamn French. If there were seven plagues to kill humanity on earth, they'd have to have an eighth of their own before they'd call death square—hi, Pete— sit down. Wants independence and wants Canada to pay the tune—"

As I pulled up another kitchen chair I could see it was Les she was ranting to, although he looked too tired to care. He was slumped in an armchair and staring at a TV documentary on Mongolian farming collectives. He looked comically like a wizened old man, but that was more the expression on his face than anything physical. Together Penny and Les reminded me of an old farm couple sitting 'round the wood stove after the cows had been brought home to winter, although Penny seemed to be affably and curiously indulging Les's pose, as if she was wondering what he was doing there but was happy to have him around just the same. Elb was there too, sitting on a footstool and doing his best not to break his attention from his cash box on his mother's account. Neither Les nor Elb looked particularly surprised or particularly happy to see me.

Penny continued. "Wants French-only signs but lets in English if it's inside and no one complains that the color's brighter than it ought to be. Wants tourists and Bill 178. Wants immigrants, but only from Mozambique. Break away and leave the rest of the world out of it or shut up about it—"

"Shut up about what?" I asked to assert my presence. "Hi, Les, play out tonight?"

"Strategy meeting," Les grumbled in answer to my question. He was still staring at the tube. His T-shirt read "Anarchy Without Tears."

"Proprietary," said Elb defensively, looking at his mother and closing his cash box when he saw me looking towards it.

But Penny was still off on her own tack. "Forget General Wolfe already and take yer independence like a man." She was shouting at a smiling Mongolian farmer in a 1950s propaganda newsreel. "Any woman who could screw around all the ways they got in lower Canada would at least have brains to charge admission—"

"That's not Quebec City, that's a farming commune near Uliastay," instructed Les.

"Lordy Lay if they don't keep changin' the goddamn programmin'," said Penny, "an' I'm supposed to keep it straight without a TV Guide—"

"Well, you could have fooled me, Mother," I said amicably. "Easy to confuse a yurt with the Basilica of Sainte Anne de Beaupre. Nine out of ten American college students routinely make similar mistakes." Of course I should talk. Sainte Anne's was the only Quebecois landmark I knew of.

"Nine out of ten American college students can't even spell yurt," opined Les, who seemed to be in something of a mood.

"What's a yurt?" asked Elb.

"No, it ain't easy to confuse nothin' with nothin'," insisted Penny, ignoring Elb and responding to my comment. "It ain't easy at all 'lest you think about it some and then some more. Then ya wonder there ain't yaks and yogurt comin' out of a Sunday downtown service." She looked to Les and Elb for help.

"I don't wonder," said Elb.

"We knows that Elbert and I wouldn't brag 'bout it but that's you. Now ya think about it. You too, Lester. What's a yurt? Round house of skins ain't goin' nowhere but another dull round for centuries 'til the wind eats it into wind—ya want a sheltered life, ya gits it—and it's all the same to every last stick and cow, and there's the end of change and ambition. Now what's a cathedral? Enough stone to keep ya down and hating yerself while the bishop takes yer money and threatens ya with God. Is it a ploughman's wonder I get it confused and there's a Mongolian maid throwin' hay like it ain't hers and she's happy to say so—why don't we put on hockey?"

"I'd like to play organ in a stone cathedral sometime," said Les.

"You will," said Penny. "A cathedral of mind and heart—"

"No, a real one," said Les. "Maybe Loudes."

"God couldn't stand the competition," I teased him. He flashed a smile of acknowledgement and quickly hid it. I knew Les was suddenly remembering our drunken spree of a little less than two weeks ago and so we were friendly once again in a dull sort of non-exclusive way. The smile told me he had just decided to tolerate my being there.

"How 'bout I set you up in a yurt?" asked Elb. "Marty could rattle sheep bells and Jade could set up a rousing shaman's howl—"

"Not enough Mongolian tugriks to keep the boss happy. And the acoustics probably suck—"

Cara cut off Les's response by entering the living room with Beth and Beulah behind her. Cara's grease paint was completely removed from her face, with the exception of two black smudges Beulah had left under her eyes. She was still wearing the black and silver robe like the night sky. Beulah glanced towards her sister, then stole silently up to the sprawled Les, and presented him with a pale pink paper mache moon drowning in silver lace. Les looked awkward as he took it, like he sort of enjoyed Beulah's antics in spite of his studied moroseness but only when her antics happened to happen. The rest of the time I supposed he was just as happy to think about Mongolian yurts as silver lace moons. "Hey, Elb," said Cara playfully, "You've got a night guest. I told Pete Life on your behalf that—"

"Looks more like Pete Light with all the grass you've been burning," said Jade, suddenly entering the living room from a dark hallway on the other side that I presumed led to the downstairs bedrooms. An entrance so sudden and unexpected there wasn't time for my feelings to go all strange about being in his presence.

Well, Jadie, all our burning is for you," teased Cara. "We sent our luck and love to make you and the boys famous." The way she stood before him in her dark robe and dark grease paint smudges reminded me of his own stage persona, and I wondered if that was Cara's intent. A priestess flashing something of her god's power by wearing his symbols.

"Thanks," said Jade. "Eternally grateful." He was looking at me when he said it. "You were there, Pete?"

"Sort of."

"See any dragons?"

"Saw what I wanted to see."

"Cool. I get high when that happens."

Penny sighed and tapped her foot impatiently. "Beulah, it's a pretty heart you've got there," she suddenly appraised the moon, "but Lester won't break his for it." I couldn't tell whether she was rebuking Les, her daughter, or both. Beulah smiled bouncily and her eyes brightened over a hurt. Les's face resumed its habitual look of annoyance as he ignored the delicate moon by holding it in his fist. "And yer mother's jus' bein' honest," said Penny helplessly. "So don't listen to her."

"Les never listens," teased Jade. "That's why he plays keyboards." He glanced at the edges of the moon protruding from Les's fist. "It's a pretty heart," he said to Beulah. The hurt she was smiling over waned a little, but not much.

"So, you two about ready to go home?" Elb suddenly asked in a spurt of hospitality.

"Nah, too busy feeling all the fine points of exploitation," said Les drily, glancing towards the cash box.

"Oh, an exploited artist," said Beth shyly, nervously, glancing at Jade and then keeping her gaze on Les as if she wanted to speak to Jade but was afraid to do so directly. It was clear she hadn't met the band members outside of a performance before and she was somewhat in awe of them, which explained her silence up until now. "Elb ought to take better care of you boys." She was trying to tease but she was not entirely sure she could presume to and the effect was raw and charming, even though her language skills didn't appear to lend themselves to anything more witty than repeating Les's sally without really understanding it.

Elb grumbled something about having to keep receipts straight and not being everyone's goddamned den mother.

"Never mind Elb," said Cara to Beth. "He doesn't." Everyone laughed except Beth.

"Doesn't what?" she asked, smiling because people were laughing, not because she understood why.

"Mind himself. Oh, never mind. It was a joke."

Beth nervously laughed and tried to extend her own joke. "Well, I hope you all will stop getting so exploited soon—"

"Thanks," said Jade brightly.

Beth got emboldened and further tangled up in her sweetly reckless words. "I mean, once you're all famous. We sent you luck and love upstairs tonight so you will be famous, but even if it doesn't work, just think how many great artists aren't recognized in their own lifetimes, and—"

Penny coughed and chomped on her pipe. "Where'd you learn that bit of cowbungie, girl?" she asked a trifle harshly. "Not from Cara, I hope. Or are the schools getting worse than one likes to know now?"

"I—I don't know," stammered Beth. "It's just what everyone knows, I guess. Lots of great artists never get recognized in their own lifetimes."

"Name three." Beth had hit a witch's hot button. "Name three." Penny was rudely adamant. Rude enough not to let Beth get away with stammering silence.

"Uh, I don't know. Like Shakespeare. We read him in school."

"Most popular playwright of his day. Had the Queen's patronage. How do you think folks knew of his work so it could survive past the seventeenth century? One of Cromwell's minions found the grandson of an actor with a long memory, or an old manuscript buried under a rock, and decided he had nothin' better to do with his life than promote somebody's plays?"

"You don't," I jumped in.

"Shut up, Pete, I'm givin' a test." She looked at Beth. "Well?"

"Uh, you know, like . . . Mozart . . . or Beethoven?"

"Mozart or Beethoven?" sneered Penny. "Mozart's father wrote the first book on violin playing and took his kid performing for heads of state all over Europe. Played for the Austrian Empress. Composed for the Archbishop of Salzburg, 'cause sometimes the Church'll screw up enough to support a great talent, though the archbishop himself was a case. Gave enough public performances in Vienna to keep his name and music around the right circles so it would survive. And let me tell ya about Beethoven. He had Mozart's endorsement, made a living for years playing out to anybody who was anybody in Vienna and it wasn't like nobody knew him when he died either. You know any great artist who really lived and worked in obscurity in his own life and got discovered later—"

"Emily Dickinson," I said. I felt sorry for Beth and wanted to help her out.

"All right, there's one," conceded Penny. "But one does not a great tradition make."

"Van Gogh," said Beth. "Didn't he cut his ear off—" Les and Jade gave her a strange look, half mock-insult, half utter genial bewilderment.

"I didn't mean *you* should," said Beth, making it worse.

"So what if he did," interjected Penny. "His brother ran an art gallery and knew all the promoters. It ain't like he was undiscovered, just ignored. The art collectors knew he was around and didn't care and if he'd been painting in rural Kansas with a Fuller Brush salesman for a brother we'd never hear of his paintings yet. It pays to have relatives in the business, even if you are dead."

"Sorry," said Beth meekly. "I didn't know. I just thought—"

"You didn't think. The 'great artists aren't recognized in their lifetime' is a line of rag and bone to keep all the mediocrities happy in their obscurity. Anyone's too lazy to write their great novel or symphony can content himself with being a 'neglected genius' and life begins to feel a little better. 'When I'm dead they'll find my scribbling under a rock and make me a saint'—oooh boy, can't wait—like some Calvinistic mysticism about maybe being one of the elected and not knowing it."

"But Penny," I sallied, "didn't you once tell me it's the mediocrities that get the recognition—"

"Yass," she chomped the ends of her hair in a fit and got a snarl tangled around her pipe. I noticed Jade was softly laughing appreciatively at my seeming to best her. I wondered how seriously he took any of this. "But just 'cause ye get recognition in your life doesn't mean your work gets to outlive your life. Just cause all brilliance gets recognized 'cept your heroine Miss Dickinson," she said pointedly to me, "don't mean everyone as gets recognized is brilliant. Ain't gotta be Einstein to see that."

"To see what?" asked Elb. He was filling out a ledger and only half-listening.

"That it takes more than cash receipts to be an artist," sniped Cara.

"And it takes more than an ugly face to be the chief slut among sluts," sniped Elb. I thought Beth was going to die. "And more than what passes for your lack of intelligence just to be stupid—"

"You oughta know, brother dear."

"Well, what does it take to be a brilliant artist?" said poor Beth in a desperate attempt to please everybody by fumbling out a subject Penny might like. Her face glowed with an insipid eagerness to bow to anything Penny might say.

"Well, it don't take no special credentials to create something beautiful," Penny said in a gentler tone of voice, whether in apology for her previous outburst or for Elb's thoughtless remark or because she was genuinely pleased with Beth's compliant interest, I couldn't tell.

"Les has no special credentials," said Jade easily. "He went to Juilliard." He was trying to put Beth at ease but I could tell that his words had the opposite effect, making her much more rigidly uncomfortable than everyone else's bickering. The very fact that Jade could tease Les about Juilliard set them apart more thoroughly and completely and utterly irredeemably than a hundred of Penny's speeches about merit and mediocrity. So much of the band's closed circle of friendship was conveyed in the simple easeful bantering indulgence of those words that I suddenly felt as if Jade had established what was after all a natural pecking order without intending to. You couldn't admire the beauty of their hard-earned bonding and the talent that cemented it without wishing to be part of the inner circle, and you couldn't wish without sadly knowing your own distance from your desires.

Beth did something very brave, in my opinion. She managed to rise sweetly above her poignant discomfort and clumsily tease Les on the familiar terms Jade had just given her. "So, Les, your bandleader there says you have no special credentials, what do you say to him?"

"That *he* ought to know—" Les was speaking to Jade, not Beth, although I wasn't sure Beth could tell. Les cut himself off mid-sentence and simply fell into a dry moroseness before the TV because he was getting bored with the whole thing but was too polite to actually send her off.

But Penny got suddenly touchy about Beth's attempt at familiarity. "Just 'cause ye don't have to have special credentials to be a genius doesn't mean everyone with no special credentials *is* a genius," she reprimanded her directly. So much for taking the well-meant bait.

"Oh," said Beth dully, her fragile courage to tease and be friendly now utterly obliterated by Penny's tone. "Well, I suppose I better go. Nice to meet you both. Uh, good luck," she said uncertainly to everyone in the room.

"Good night, Beth," said Jade gently, making an eye contact that brought her gaze shyly to his. "I'm sure we'll see you around again."

She smiled back as if she saw herself as having just passed some sort of test with him, despite her poor performance with Penny. "I'm sure, too. Good night, everyone. Cara." Cara nodded but didn't bother to see her friend out.

It was only as I watched Beth leaving through the kitchen that I noticed Selene had been hanging back and listening to the conversation, her face still thick and pale with makeup. She left with Beth. Not with her exactly, but sort of trailing her like a gangly oversized clumsy wind. "So, what happened? Why are you crying—" I heard Selene ask in rough curiosity as they went out the door.

"Hang the moon in your room for good luck," jollied Cara, indicating the crumpled piece of pink moon in Les's fist. She was both instructing Les and reveling in how easy she felt in this company compared to her new friend. "It's well made and well blessed. We've even got an angry planet for Marty, and a swelling nova for Xander, and—"

"Hang yourself," said Elb, ever vigilant for a quarrel with his sister. "We're busy."

Cara glanced at the TV. "I can tell. Anyway, so were we."

"Did it work?" asked Penny, softly and seriously.

"Honestly, Mother. Did it work?" whined Cara, not liking to be quizzed.

"Didn't feel nothin' in the vicinity of my bones."

"'Course it worked, Ma. I'm a great priestess. Just ask Jadie if he felt anything. And all my girls love rock 'n' roll." She said the latter while looking at her brother like it was some sort of rebuke.

"Yeah," said Juno, entering the room in time to echo Cara's dig, "we all love rock 'n' roll. Hi, Les. Hi, Jadie."

"I love rock 'n' roll too," protested Elb, his head once again in the open cash box, "but some people gotta make a freakin' religion out of it—"

"At least they're *makin'* a religion," said Penny. "Better than stealin' one from somebody else and gettin' it all screwed up 'cause yer too lazy to come up with something good on yer own—" I kept feeling Jade's eyes on me. I kept not wanting to look at them.

"Hey, Penny," I said, "speaking of stealing, I got a newspaper clipping you might be interested in." I produced the newspaper article about Claude Hopner and his train robbing spree, which I kept folded in my pocket. "You know this guy?" Cara and Beulah ran over to look. Elb looked pointedly disinterested. Les turned off the TV and wandered down the hallway Jade had come in from. He had left Beulah's moon on the chair behind him like a crumpled piece of used tissue.

"Well, I might know him," said Penny, suddenly all smiles as she read through the interview, chuckling and cackling. "Well, indeedy. Come here, Elbie, here's yer uncle in the flesh, 'bout time you got a good look at a masked face you oughta know."

"Thought *you* were our uncle in the flesh, Ma," said Juno.

"That's only a winter thing. And not in the flesh. Jeeminy, if Claude's in the desert now playin' sugar daddy to cows and waterin' the wind with some of Pete's brethren there." I assumed she was referring to the article's mention of Hopner waving at an FBI agent. Penny reminded me of Mother Goose reading a pretty storybook to her little ducklings.

"Hard to get gigs and help with financing at a distance?" I asked her, to see how she'd respond to me attempting to keep the conversation semi-rooted in reality.

"Naw. Easier to take some blame if blame has to happen. Claude'll be right as rabbit's rum. 'Sides, found us buried gold out there to front up a little cash for Nickie and the boys. But jem the mem if I didn't think he was goin' in for a Burmese pirate these last few weeks and the gold was from Tibet. Could have sent us a postcard."

"What's his deal?" I asked.

"Fun and confusion. Well, it's his life, his party. Like the party upstairs if Cara had her girlfriends speak their wants like she was supposed."

"Yes, Mother," said Cara, exasperated. "I know what I'm doing."

"Lemme see again." Penny was really enjoying the interview. "That Claude, if he cain't be one thing, he's another. Jes' like Cara's girls bein' who they want. Yuss, he's good people." She sounded round and satisfied as she handed back the clipping and relit her pipe with a flourish.

"He's also on the ten most wanted list."

"Well and goodness. More power to him. Cara, Elbie, Claude's on the ten most wanted list." She was really excited about this achievement. "Listen up, children. That's 'cause he's bound to be 'most wanted.' Now who wouldn't want to be Claude, Claude who's anything he wants? Have to pack myself into a shadow like a desert crow and go incognito to pay him a visit when we gits affairs settled out here. What do ya think, Jadie?"

"Think I'd like to get affairs settled out here." Jade sounded like he was used to Penny's personal madness, and completely at ease with it, while still managing to be all business.

"Huuuuh," she smiled contentedly. "Need a new broom of willow."

"So what's the rest of the news, Pete?" Jade asked.

I started to answer as Les wandered back in to glumly watch Elb count money. Something about having an audience suddenly made me want to get my other questions answered without one, to see what Penny might reveal apart from her family. "Penny, I should like a private consultation with you for the time being. Is your kitchen free?"

"My whole house is free in case ye ain't noticed," said Penny, remarking on Les's gyrations, "no matter how much folks we've got. Whatcha got to say that my other kiddies cain't hear, Pete?"

As during my last visit, I decided my best strategy for getting useful information was to proceed as if I were in her world. But the natural, no-nonsense way she implied I was one of her "kiddies" and my recent experience at Cara's party made that easier than it should have been. "Bought these pills off your friend Hugh," I took out the bottle. "Don't suppose you could tell—"

Penny set up a howl to wake the dreams of last week's dead. "Not in front of the children. Jesus, Pete, have some sense, to go wavin' around obscenities like Hugh's medical monstrosities. And here with such nice news about Claude. Gimme those." She grabbed the bottle and wrinkled up her nose. "They smell to me. And I know what he gets 'em from too." She squinted and appeared to read something off the glass. "P.S. Don't Read Other Side—keep out of direct sunlight—contents refrigerate at room temperature."

"My boss uses them to kill heartburn."

"Sure, they's kill anything your heart burns for. From love dreams to fried sausages and egg. That's the point of it. Then ye begin to fear anything different, lest it point out what ya really are. Tell ya what they really are, since ya came here to know."

She led the way to the kitchen. Her daughters clustered around her. Les and Elb remained behind with the cash box. Then Les strolled in and stood curiously behind Beulah and I felt Jade take up a position directly behind me; but I couldn't bring myself to turn and look at him. Probably because I felt like he was more interested in my reaction than in Penny's performance and I wondered how he would react to my feeble attempt to cultivate an air of mystery.

Penny rattled through a cupboard, humming an old Irish air, until she found a tarnished coffee can with multicolored wax dripping out of it like a melted box of crayons. She threw it with the dirty pans in the sink. Then she found a child's play oven with a little pair of pincers and some metal trays. The kind kids used to bake insects in by filling the pre-cut shapes in the trays with liquid plastic and heating the trays over a bare light bulb until a spider came out. Sometimes the shapes were edible, and I remembered a godawful lime mint taste under my tongue. "Yeah, this will do for Hugh. Beulah, get me goo," Penny chanted. Beulah took a tube out of a silverware drawer.

"Not Incredible Edibles goo. Creepy Crawlers."

"She's doin' an ID investigation," announced Juno.

"Hey, maybe Pete'll learn something," teased Jade.

Penny flipped a few pills in a tray with a caterpillar shape carved into it and shoved it into a depression on the top of the little oven. Even though the oven wasn't plugged into any outlet, a cheesy sort of stench rose out of it and the pills began to run together into something white and wriggly with too many needley legs and moist wings. After a minute of Juno exclaiming, "Wait'll you see, wait'll you see what she gets," Penny removed a living slug-like creature, held it in her fist as it crawled in and out of her bent fingers, closed her eyes and drew a heavy breath.

"Dr. Morse's Indian Root Pills, Sarsaparilla, dried leeches, Comstock's Dead Shot Worm Pellets, Taft's Myrrhline free of all injurious energy producing ingredients, Horsford's Acid Phosphate for mental and physical exhaustion, beware of imitations, for alleviation of childhood diseases, for alleviation of childhood, cleanly to use, causes no pain, will cure most troubles, never fails when used as directed, H. S. McCrae and Co., soul proprietor—" Penny broke off. "Got enough garbage here to fill Parliament full of truth and then some." She opened her fingers and violently shook the insect off her hand. It gave a sickening buzzy hiss like something crushed might hiss and then it flew down the drain under the dirty pots. She handed the bottle back to me. "Dangerous to carry, Pete, but there ya have it. Thass what's the pills are."

"Well, I'm licensed to carry," I feebly joked. "But I want to know what these pills actually do if you take them."

"Nothin'. They come from Hugh, who is nothin'. Made of dead medicine and ought to be illegal, if ye ask me. Now, is that all the monster had to say to you?"

"Well, not exactly," and I recounted to everyone present the conversation I had with Hugh in my office, including his request that I find Elise for him and his new job as an anti-drug congressional hack, but excluding the strange, threatening photographs he left behind. I wanted to observe everyone's reaction to learning that the man Penny took credit for killing still lived. What struck me was not so much that no one present conveyed much surprise concerning anything I had to say, but that within the context of Penny's friends and family I no longer felt surprised or puzzled by anything odd. I could have been giving a weather report or discussing a weekend on the Cape for all the strangeness I felt.

"So Hughie's gotta job in Congress and wants a wife," said Penny. "Hope you boys are listenin' up, Jadie 'special—"

"Why Jadie special?" asked Les, a hint of dry mockery in his use of the familiar form of Jade's name.

"'Cause it ain't *yer* mother the monster thinks to git," rebuked Penny before turning to me. "Ye ain't turned him on to Elise, have ye, Pete?"

"No."

"Yeah, he probably knows how to find her. Fact is, I'm here and I can feel him moving like a glacial frost snapping out my torrid zone. No, Hugh's afraid of Toronto now, 'cause he knows I been watchin' out for him after his last display. He'll be wantin' you to bring Elise south of the border. He'll be wantin' to marry her all over again. He'll be wantin' to git himself established in such way over Jadie's life, wants to take Jadie's real father's place, as if salt sea sludge could compete with good salt sea. He'll be wantin' you to make it all possible." She pulled the ends of her oily hair through her teeth and chewed. "Yuk, needs a bath." She spat. "Well, yer safe here, and yer safe anywhere so long as I'm with ye, and I can teach Elbert some charms"—she looked at Elbert's blankly annoyed face—"*give* him some charms. Maybe."

I noticed Jade was keeping studiously silent throughout this exchange, even though the topic appeared to touch him the closest. Cara pranced over to his side in her dark robe and encircled his waist in her arms and briefly leaned her head against his shoulder.

"Hi, cousin," she said sweetly, as if she only meant to be friendly and cute as she pulled back away to stand by his side but would have liked Jade to give some sign of a deeper bond between them. He didn't. He was all quiet toleration. Penny snapped, "This is serious, Cara, stop the monkeyshines—"

"Only mean to say I'd slay a monster easy," protested Cara. "I'll protect my cousin from anything. After all, he's family—"

"I accept the thought," said Jade graciously.

"Including bad sex—" spurted Juno at the same time. "Sorry, it's a joke."

"Nothin' here is a goddamned joke, kiddies," scolded Penny. "Hugh's in a war and so are we. It's an old war. It ain't that he wants to stop the music so much as kill what makes it matter. We're about to unleash magic and dreams to anyone in the world who cares to live them. That's what music's for, and that's our goal. Hugh's about to do his best to see that the dreams don't make it home to heal anyone's war-torn heart"—Penny fixed me with her deep maternal eyes—"that's his goal. And it don't ever end."

"Hey, Pete," said Jade suddenly, as if Penny's speech never happened, "speaking of war-torn hearts, where are you staying tonight?"

"Here, with Elb," I grinned. "Gotta move my camping gear into the house."

"Would it help you to interview my mother again?" asked Jade. "I've got no problem with you staying the night in my studio. If it would help."

"But he was going to stay here," whined Cara.

"Wasn't my idea," said Elb.

"I accept the thought. And the offer," I said to Jade as Penny impatiently tapped her foot and hummed.

She suddenly broke in, "Then Pete, make sure ya don't upset Elise too much by mentionin' things she won't understand. Livin' corpses ain't no fish in her tea. She won't talk to me, but if I was you I'd ask her 'bout herself and her feelin's more'n a regular interview. Get yerself an impression to work with. See which side of the war her heart is on and maybe give me a clue as well. Never could figure it out." She waited for my reaction, got none, and prodded, "Good exercise for you to try."

"Sure, Mother," I said amiably. "I'll woo her truth right out of her."

"Yass." She waved her arms. "Now go to it."

I left with Jade, who told me to follow him in his car. Before getting in my own, I asked him lightly what he thought of Penny's rant. "Do you believe her political analysis?"

"I'm getting paid to believe it." He smiled. "How about you?"

"I know the feeling. We G-men get paid to believe all sorts of things we probably shouldn't."

Jade laughed. Then he drove like new madness through unfamiliar parts of Toronto, speeding down one-way streets in the wrong direction and leading me full throttle through exhilarating near accidents and fun until we somehow made it in a staggering sort of safety to Thornhill.

Ninth

Friday, early morning, September 18, 1992.

I was dreaming of the Arab with the spear of death. I knew him from the throw rug I'd seen at my previous visit to Jade's studio. He was still steady on his desert horse, but he no longer cradled a lion cub or threatened a lion cub's dam. He had become more like the Arab from Wordsworth's poem *The Prelude*, for he now bore a stone in one hand and a bright shell in the other. The shell kept changing into a starry mirror and running clear water. The stone kept screaming for mercy in the waves. But then we were riding together, or else the wind kept rushing us into the desert storm ahead, where we trampled on dying flowers like indifferent gods riding on broken hearts.

Until the ground lurched and swelled and opened and we fell riding into an underground cave full of treasure I couldn't name. An old chest spilled broken crowns. It was guarded by a white python like a dragon in disguise. He said that he knew me, that he, too, had spent centuries slithering through dreams he couldn't feel. Then his coils crushed my limbs.

The nightmare lashed me almost into wakefulness except I willfully held back beneath the feeling of a warm band of sunlight resting on my eyelids and a dangerously seductive voice reading poetry to me out of the morning I was still lingering away from. The voice was Jade's. The lines were from the section of *The Prelude* that had rounded my poor dream:

Why, gifted with such powers to send abroad
Her spirit, must it lodge in shrines so frail?

Too tired to argue with the free gift, I sank into the voice, which was reading me awake with a further passage:

He, to my fancy, had become the knight
Whose tale Cervantes tells; yet not the knight,
But was an Arab of the desert too;
Of these was neither, and was both at once.

A few lines lost themselves in a dream fragment before I came to again to hear:

He left me . . .
With the fleet waters of a drowning world
In chase of him; whereat I waked in terror,
And saw the sea before me, and the book,
In which I had been reading, at my side.

At some point in the reading I opened my eyes and began to know that I was wrapped in my sleeping bag and lying on the Moroccan rug in the middle of Jade's studio, and that my surroundings felt like early morning. The tapestry Arab had his spear pointed to my chest due to the crazy night position I had ended up in, and I smiled a little at the thought that I was literally lying over the she-lion and so taking her place in the tapestry. I propped myself up on my arms and got into a half-sitting position. I couldn't remember the previous night yet or how I got here, because the poem kept taking me away, so I just sat there watching Jade read as if nothing else existed. But it wasn't until Jade reached the lines about the sea and the book that he seemed at all willing to acknowledge that his audience was conscious. Then he looked up from the volume, met my eyes with his, and smiled faintly and indulgently. "Good morning, Pete."

"How did you know?" I smiled back.

"Know what?" he teased.

"What I was dreaming."

"I'm a professional." He smiled back. "I'm supposed to know things like that." The light that had been resting across my eyes was a stray beam falling through the side of a blind that covered a window behind me. "Are you hungry?"

"I've got camping food. Enough for two if you care to join me."

"Save it. You bought last time." He was remembering the dinner I bought for the band during our city spree. "I'll be right back." Jade vanished before I could protest, so in his absence I pulled on my clothes and rolled up my sleeping bag and pretty much got myself together. Thought briefly about work and the press conference. Heard birds I wasn't used to hearing outside. Stopped thinking.

Then I remembered arriving here last night. Jade hadn't said much except that it was a school night and so Elise had probably gone to bed early. Quietly led me up to his studio, and pretty much left me to my own devices. And then I woke to poetry and a gentle sun.

I could see now that the studio was fuller than the last time I was here. I noticed Les's keyboards and Marty's drums, and all the amplifiers and electronic equipment from Black Dog's stage show at Fendra's. An inexplicable disquiet rose through me to think I had spent a night dreaming in Black Dog's nerve center. There was something ruthlessly intimate about being surrounded by their gear that overwhelmed and unbalanced me, for here was the machinery of my private transport to my own imaginary worlds.

But when I noticed Jade's basses, and stood for a few minutes alone with them knowing how intrinsically a part of him they were, how they were like the holy relics of the mystery play he always seemed to be carrying within, there was suddenly something beyond my morning feelings that I couldn't begin to explain, an almost unearthly delight.

Just before Jade returned with a breakfast tray, I noticed that before I woke he had lit a gray-blue candle on a corner bookshelf, under the poster print of *Café Terrace at Night* that Xander's playing had dreamed me into the last time I was here. But I was feeling the poster rather than really seeing it, for it was now in that balmy sheen of no-longer-strange-but-not-yet-familiar that remembered objects seen for the second time in someone else's house usually wear. The poster felt personal to me, like a secretly known companion piece to my last visit. The candle reminded me of the one on Cara's altar, except that it was thicker and it was draped in a green plant that looked like mistletoe. When the flame touched a leaf the whole plant did not shrivel and burn as I expected it to, but the leaf gave off the heady scent of northern forests and made me remember pleasant solitary camping trips. The fact that he had lit it, that the flame came from him, gave me a sort of involuntary thrill. I found myself drawn to the candle and I was watching like an idiot the flame burning the green leaves as Jade re-entered and laid out breakfast on the floor. I was so gone in my own strange emotions that the noise startled me and I knocked into one of his basses.

"Careful," he grinned. "Hurts when you do that."

"I'll bet."

He accepted the flattery by holding out a mug of coffee. "Come join me before it gets cold. You can look at my Wal later if you care to."

"What's a Wal?" I asked just before I noticed that Wal was the manufacturer's name on the bass's headstock.

"Law backwards." He said this seriously as I sat on the floor in front of him. Once again we faced each other over the violent desert tapestry. "You and the bass are both renegades," he added lightly. "Perhaps it's about time the two of you got acquainted."

"Looks expensive," I said, taking the warm mug.

"It is. Another love present from my dear aunt. Penny says she knows a witch in Britain who was able to get it at cost and bless it on a wuthering heath." He spoke the last phrase playfully. Then he sipped coffee and so did I. It tasted like crushed almonds and honey and I liked the sensation of simultaneously having the same taste in our mouths.

Jade was watching me so I felt like it was my turn to say something, although the pressure was clearly coming from me, not him. It was really all right to be quiet together, if that was my choice. But after about a minute, I heard myself say, "Penny is very good to you and the band. I'm sorry there seems to be some distance between your mother and her." Jade didn't comment. He seemed to know I was just fumbling around, and that it wasn't worth the coffee-laden moment to pursue the subject. But for some reason I kept pushing. "Is Penny really your aunt? I've never completely understood your relationship to her."

He relented. "Like I told you before, Pete, I've never been one to explain relationships. I'll leave that to Penny." There was sun all over his hands. I charmed myself into believing he could weave bass lines out of sunlight. "Penny is Black Dog's fairy godmother. She spins our dreams into truth and we love her for it. Aunt, Goddess, Mother, Benefactress, Sorceress, Witch—" he was trying to seduce me with words again. I needed to make some empty proof to myself by resisting.

"So, what's the latest news from the Mob?"

He laughed. "Really, Pete, do you ever stop working?"

"Do you?" I shot back.

"*Touché*. 'A hit, a very palpable hit,' as the Bard once wrote."

This time I relented. "That's ominous," I teased. "Osric was referring to Hamlet's skill as a swordsman just before the mad prince fell to Laertes's poisoned foil."

"And yet the hit was in question. And Laertes also fell to Hamlet, a victim of his own treacherous poison." He paused and added in a cheerful stage whisper with a melodramatic wink, "Law and chaos murdered each other." Then he looked around the empty room as if for spies, and added, "We'd best be careful." I cracked up.

"All right, you win. I won't be too legalistic about things here—"

"—I wish you wouldn't." He was still performing. "The Wal might talk."

"—but I would like to sweet talk your mother for a few minutes."

"It's a school day and she won't be home until late afternoon. Guess you'll have to wait through band practice."

"Don't break my heart." I grinned. But as soon as I said the word "heart" I recalled the threatening photographs McCrae had left on my desk with the hollow hearts scrawled on them and I choked a little on the coffee. "One more point of duty."

"Don't choke."

"What do you know about Hugh McCrae? Why do you think he's approaching me to get reunited with your mother?"

"I don't know. Maybe he's bored."

"It's not funny, Jade, I'm a little concerned."

His eyes met mine. "Why?" he asked easily.

I faltered a little. "Professionally, I mean." And I described the photographs. "Do you have any thoughts on the issue you'd like to share?"

"Thoughts." He adopted an air of high pensiveness that was pure theatrics, then he said slowly, "Maybe he's bored." Something in his manner subtly reminded me of the way I sometimes dealt with Fearless. I didn't like the position he was putting me in, and Jade seemed instantly cognizant of the fact, because he suddenly said seriously, "I really don't know him. I can tell you that Penny's waging some sort of cosmic war against him that she seems to greatly enjoy. Which is cool, I guess."

"Which is 'cool'?" I asked incredulously, setting down my mug.

"Look, Pete, I don't work for anybody's government, so it's not for me to interfere with anybody's 'pursuit of happiness.' Let her fight with McCrae if it makes her happy. It's not for me to spoil her hobby by making peace."

"Jade, let me tell *you* a story—"

"—Please." He managed to sound both eager and deferential; and I managed to pretend that I wasn't completely disarmed.

I sighed and let loose. "McCrae is 'murdered' while impersonating a high military official. His corpse vanishes to dust in the morgue, and the story becomes an election year scandal that touches off public protests on every controversy since whose religion got kicked out of Paradise first. Then your band's 'benefactress,' or shall we say, 'patron witch,' who happens to be jointly financing your career with some character out of a western movie set who's quickly making his way up the ten most wanted list, cheerfully and knowingly brags to an FBI agent about her high creativity in doing the deed. Then a congressman worried about re-election exerts pressure on the FBI to find the killer, and I get put on the case with the added spin of being a drug law enforcer as a means of bargaining with the mob family whom the public suspects of making the hit. The same mob family, I might add, that's promoting your band. Then McCrae shows up in my office, alive as a clump of cancer cells, to tell me he's a 'special assistant' to the same drug committee this congressman is assigned to and could I please find his wife for him, and it turns out that his long-lost wife just happens to be your mother. And as an added attraction, he's pushing some bizarre pills around that sound like leftovers from a turn of the century medicine show and leaving photographs on my desk which to my tired investigative eyes appear extremely threatening to you and your bandmates, notwithstanding your neo-pagan girlfriend's circle casting."

"Like I said, cool." I deliberately remained stone-faced while I studied him, trying to determine if he was putting me on. He wasn't. "I mean, isn't it cool?" he asked pointedly. "And I didn't even know I had a neo-pagan girlfriend. Is she clever? What tradition does she follow?"

"I don't know." I had to smile at his perspective.

"I mean how many people get to just fall into stuff like that? Twelve dozen poets and their muses' dams couldn't make all that up. Maybe you should write a novel."

"What a deal," I said halfheartedly. Then I said nothing for a while, because while I appreciated Jade's attitude, I couldn't wholeheartedly endorse it, and I was trying to sort through my tension before speaking again.

"Hey Pete," he whispered into my thoughts, "what are you dreaming about? Can I come along and play?"

"Sure," I said absently, "I'm dreaming about how every time I go for coffee, my boss tries to get me killed."

"Really? How exciting. Tell me more. We'll have to ask Penny to make *you* a charm."

"It's a long story," I grumbled.

"I love long stories."

"Maybe someday."

He looked disappointed but he didn't push. "Does that mean you'd like more coffee, then?" he indicated my mug. "Being a man of mystery and danger and all that, there's no reason you shouldn't feel at home here." I had to laugh. "Hey, I'll even descend to the nether regions of the kitchen and fetch it for you if you like. That way your life will remain safe in my elven grotto."

"Is anything safe in an elven grotto?"

"No." He grinned.

"Well, that's all right then. I appreciate the offer. On all levels." We were smiling at each other and I felt like Jade already sort of knew my life without me having to explain everything I didn't really want to realize right now. Just as he knew my dreams and my taste in poetry and music. And he wasn't holding my eternal blood-deep cynicism against me, merely understanding and relieving it. Or acting as if my deep life-wasting boredom wasn't worthy of me and he understood this as such a natural fact that it wasn't worthy of him to dwell on it either. So it wasn't embarrassment so much as a heady sense of superfluity that kept me from talking about myself.

That, and my irritating inability to fathom his seeming nonchalance in the middle of all this weirdness, along with my obsession with getting him to concede something to my limited outlook on recent events. Why had he invited me to stay with him if he *didn't* want to discuss McCrae or the Mob in private? Clearly he wasn't serious about me interviewing Elise, since he had insisted we not wake her last night and he must have known she'd be working today. In fact, Jade was so damnably diffident about the things that concerned me that while I was sitting there with him and Wordsworth and the morning light I literally began to feel that perhaps I had the wrong perspective on McCrae, that living corpses and their enemy witches were just plain folk like everyone else, and that I was the one who needed the attitude adjustment. It actually took some effort on my part to resist the mood and say, "Jade, doesn't your mother ever talk about McCrae? Weren't they once married? Surely you must have heard something about him?" He shrugged a casual denial. "Do you know 'which side of the war' her heart is on?"

"No, that's your job. Look, Pete, I'm not worried about Hugh McCrae. He's Penny's problem, if he *is* a problem, and I'd just as soon trust her with it as anyone. He's not real where we are."

"Fine," I said pleasantly, taking in the studio with an air of ownership, "then my loyalty and duty to my new client, along with my deep sense of family values, dictate that I get Mr. McCrae reunited with his long-lost family as soon as possible. When would you like me to re-introduce him into your household?" This time Jade choked a little on his coffee. "Don't choke." I offered him a napkin.

"All right, Pete," he said steadily, "Which side of the war are *you* on?"

"The winning side, guy," I said, making long eye contact. And then, softly, "Your side. Look, I've got no desire to mess up your life. That's not why I'm here. And I've got better things to do than act as Hugh McCrae's personal dating service. I didn't like the guy before he died, and I don't like him any better now that he's back. He reminds me of the 'dead tongues of dead lizards.'" That was a line from one of Jade's songs. A melancholy shadow of acknowledgement dropped across his eyes and mouth; something reminded me of the dream offerings I kept making to Aphrodite before I made this trip. Then the shadow left and Jade was giving me a different smile than before, a chagrined smile that no longer pressed me to accept his stunning word gifts because it implied such a stunning vulnerability. I went for the kill. "But in return for keeping McCrae hungry at a distance and not interfering with the Nunzios' still tenuous relationship with your band, both of which actions are already costing me professionally, I'd like to feel some sense of inclusion in whatever the hell is going on here."

He gave me a sudden long sideways glance. A slightly dismayed expression that told me he was responding to the veiled threat under my words gave way to a slightly elated look at hearing me confess that I had taken it upon myself to protect the band. I watched these conflicting emotions with some degree of satisfaction while wondering which one would eventually win out. But neither seemed to gain ascendance over the other and when Jade finally spoke, his voice was skittish with slow uncertainty. "Elb said you lied for us. That his man Nick got hold of one of your business cards and discovered that you were hanging out in Utica asking about Elb. That George Fendra noticed you in his club after we finished performing, before you went out partying with us, and that George told everyone that you claimed to know Nick and that you said you were a friend of Claude's." He waited, not sure whether he wanted to continue. "And then for some reason you convinced them all you were somebody else."

"So what if I did?"

"Nice work, guy." He saluted me with his mug. The gesture briefly covered his unease.

"Well," I said magnanimously, "I owed you a lie, remember?"

"And then you stormed the city with us. And then you were at Cara's get-together last night wishing us well."

"I do wish you well. That's why you still have a working relationship with Nick and you're not sitting here reading poems to Hugh McCrae." Jade looked a little sick. "I'm sorry."

"Pete," he said a little hesitantly, "I happened to read that newspaper article about you. It was reprinted in the *Toronto Star* and Penny showed it around the band. We actually had a band meeting about it." He was clearly waiting for me to comment, but my detective sense that I had hit a vital spot and Jade was about to reveal something important kept me breathlessly silent. That, and the fact that I was suddenly anxious to know what he thought of the things the reporter said about me in the article, despite my own dismissal of most of it as fluff. "I understand you are 'the nemesis of the Boston Mafia' and the 'Holmes of the Hub.' Congratulations."

"It's a living."

He seemed to shift subjects, but not being able to follow his train of thought, I wasn't completely sure whether this was a shift or a build up to his real meaning. "Elb tells me that Nick called him last week. Nick's father-in-law, guess he's some kind of big mob boss, saw the article too. Nick's a little concerned about your new position, whether it was going to cause problems for some of their other business interests in Utica. You know, promoters don't like problems. He wanted further reassurance that Elb didn't know you, seeing as the 'colonel' was 'murdered' the same night we happened to be playing on that base and now you show up in the press as being in charge of the case. The article mentioned that you found the corpse on a routine drug investigation, so Nick had a tough time believing that you and Elb didn't run into each other that night."

"What did Elb say?"

"Elb said he might have run into you. Had no idea. So many people in the club that he gave his name to that night, and he's used to drawing heat due to his appearance and all. Just 'cause he dresses like a rocker every cop in a ten-mile radius hones in on him and assumes he's on drugs. Worse than having an Italian last name. Can't even cross the border without undergoing a special search and all that. Apparently Nick believed him." Jade seemed to be begging a question.

"Nick probably believed him," I assured him, "because like most Mafiosi, Nick probably thinks like a reasonable businessman and any reasonable businessman would assume that no sane manager is stupid enough to sabotage his own band. Look, *I'm* not interested in making it public or obvious that I know anyone connected with Black Dog, and if Elb wishes to claim I randomly harassed him on the basis of the way he dresses, I've got better things to do than contradict a compliment to my fashion sense."

"Sure," Jade tried to sound nonchalant but only succeeded in sounding grateful. "And one of those better things is brilliantly pursuing McCrae's killer. Of course, McCrae isn't really dead so it's anybody's guess what you might do there." He stopped speaking.

I remained stolid. "So?" I said evenly. "What would you like me to do there?"

"Pete. What is stopping you from washing your hands of the whole situation by going to the press yourself and saying the vanishing corpse walks, he works for the US Congress? Wouldn't that eliminate whatever professional risks you alluded to by satisfying your boss that you've done your job? Wouldn't that also satisfy the Nunzios that you're not treating this business as the mob hit the paper claims it is and that you're not primarily interested in their Utica concerns? It would certainly make it obvious that Elb hasn't turned you on to any of them in exchange for some kind of award. I mean, Nick did ask about that. Anyway, then the case would be closed, wouldn't it? Out of your hands, anyway, with no further cost to you professionally. McCrae would be under public scrutiny, which might even be a good thing, and you'd be back in Boston and presumably leaving things in Utica alone and . . . there an end." He smiled encouragingly.

So this was the deal. Jade invited me here so he could play investigator and find out what side of the war my heart was on, and then to see if he couldn't persuade me to drop my interest in the case. Hence I was supposed to believe McCrae was nothing to worry about and cheerfully remove myself far enough into the background so I wouldn't jeopardize his promotion plans. Barring that, I was supposed to drag McCrae out into the limelight and hope the public attention might somehow render him harmless if Penny couldn't. And he thought he was going to sweeten the deal by buying me off with sunshine and poetry.

"Where's my proof and who'd believe me?" I asked in my best Penny imitation. "No one on the base ever saw much of him and those who did never got a good look, he spent so much time alone. And his face has gone through some changes. It's emptier now. Blanker and sallower. The sort of face you'd recognize but couldn't prove you'd seen before. And he seems to have a paper trail of long government service to cover himself with. Besides, this case is a controversy. I start pointing out a congressional aid as imitating a colonel without any proof save my own unbelievable story, and the congressman my boss is sucking up to will be rightly embarrassed, especially since this same aid is attached to his pet committee. And then you can bet I'll be off the case."

"Since when does a guy like you care about embarrassing congressmen?" asked Jade, the subtle emphasis in his voice leaving my other concern dangling like an unspoken rumor between us. "Especially if it gets you off the hook . . . professionally, I mean. You're just pointing out the facts and not taking responsibility for what happens."

"I'm a fed. I'm not supposed to point out facts."

"I know. But then, you never do anything you're supposed to do. That's why you're here."

He had me there. Jade knew the strategic reasons I gave were wrong. I certainly wasn't squeamish about embarrassing congressmen. But I was squeamish about being removed from my present assignment in favor of someone like Kanesh. "I care because if I get taken off someone less accommodating to your interests will be put in my place, and McCrae will have won a major victory in his 'war.' Right now I'm in a position to protect the band at some risk to myself. But the more I know, the better I can help you." Then I said, with some difficulty, because it was a line I normally used on recalcitrant suspects but right now I meant it too sincerely to speak it with anything resembling conviction, "I care about helping you."

"Why?"

I thought about the cassette tape, the dreams, the fire gazing, the stories, my complicated emotions concerning him, the things I couldn't bring myself to say. In fact, I felt slightly embarrassed, so I cast down my eyes and drained my mug without answering. By all rights I had no business "helping" or "protecting" any of them.

"Why?" he asked again.

"I don't know," I said, sounding more irritated than I meant to. "It's a hobby. Like Penny. Look, Jade, I shouldn't even be here. I'll leave and come back tonight when Elise is home, and then I'd best shove off back to Boston. I gave your mother my home number but since you gave my card to Cara—"

"Since I what?" he looked genuinely perplexed.

"Cara called me about the party. Said she got my card from you."

He subtly changed, but I couldn't read what the change meant. "What if she did?" He was studying me intently now.

"Here," I scribbled down my home number and address on the back of another card. "For God's sake call me. Not at the field office, all incoming calls get recorded and I've got this partner who needn't know any more than I tell him—and look, just call me at home. Call collect if you have to. But call me. About anything. Even if there's nothing."

He took the card without saying anything. Then, "Elb and Nick are setting up a club tour in the states to correspond to the release of our CD. I could be anywhere in the upcoming months."

"Then call me from anywhere." There was a sudden uncomfortable silence running through me, running through both of us, running through the sun beam scudding across the floor, for the sun looked different in our present mood. It was obvious to both of us that I had admitted more about myself than he had. I felt exposed and so I tried to pretend I didn't feel anything and that this was a normal day on my job. Then I tried to change the subject to something defensively boring, to set things right or something, but the words came out in a different kind of defiance. "Hey, Cara gave me this apple when I sent my wishes to your band last night. I'm supposed to keep it in the sun for three days 'to soak up the power.' But seeing as I never do anything I'm supposed to do, do you want to share it with me?"

Jade responded by taking the apple and cutting it in half with a breakfast knife. "Since I am the dragonking, I suppose I should properly make that offering to you," he said gallantly. "You know, if you cut an apple crosswise the seeds will form a pentagram?" They did. He held half out to me on his palm. "Will ye partake of forbidden fruit before they throw *your* religion out of Paradise?" I must admit, Jade was good. Everything suddenly felt more than all right between us.

"Am I in such danger here, friend?" I entered into his game as we ate the pentagram together.

"No, for the duchess is secretly sympathetic to your plight. She pays me well to shelter heretics, for she loved poor dead Charles to distraction, and hates Cromwell's rule. I trust my escort conveyed you comfortably?"

"I missed your guard, my lord, and came here on my own account, hearing of your mistress's sympathies, I thought to seek her protection."

"Then I shall order severe punishments to be meted to my men for their failure to find you. 'Tis dangerous for your lordship to ride unescorted in these parts, for you know there is a bounty on your head."

"I doubt that you yourself, skillful as you are, could have found me, Count."

"But it appears I already have." Jade smiled broadly, a smile that gently ripped through delicate feelings I couldn't help but luxuriate in, although I also couldn't help but feel intimidated by my own weird courage in continuing this crazy dialogue with him. I fiercely wanted to play this fantasy forever while at the same time I feared taking our play too seriously and looking foolish in my own eyes. "And I would be remiss in my duty to let you leave here alone before we discuss how vital you are to our plans—"

"But perhaps her servants are not to be trusted. Remember the Wals have ears—" I was using humor to guard against Jade's skillful siege against my defenses, and I immediately felt awkward for halfheartedly fighting an experience I really wanted to have, for fighting because my conditioning kept telling me I was supposed to fight anything charming.

"Not to fear. For I am the Lady's chief servant, and can personally guarantee everyone's sympathies. You are among friends here. No one enters or leaves without my orders."

A loud crash of the door downstairs stood counterpoint to Jade's assertion. Sound of a mad elephant stomping upstairs. No, two mad elephants, with clashing weights like hard footsteps. Enter Marty into the spell. Along with Cara. Exit the spell. Sort of. Because it wasn't as if Marty particularly cared or seemed particularly aware of our conversation, and Jade showed absolutely no self-consciousness or need to break away. The choice was clearly mine to break. I didn't.

"How might I be of service to His Majesty?"

"I have set my spies against your couriers, friend, and we know you are getting messages through to young Charles in France, who by all rights should be king. But if my spies are informed of your network, I fear Cromwell's are as well. Stay here for your own protection until we bring you under cover to Paris, where you can—" Jade's words were suddenly lost because Marty was amusing himself by wailing on his drum kit and letting out sharp little yelps and Cara was brightly howling with him but I ignored them both for Jade. Then Marty suddenly stopped and dove into his kit to make some adjustments. "Where you can help Charles organize sympathetic troops." Jade continued easily, as if the disruption never happened.

"But I am ignorant of French ways—"

Marty was intentionally ignoring Cara, who was chatting away about how hard it was to park the van in the driveway with both my car and Jade's and Marty's taking space, but Cara was not long for ignoring us. Since Jade didn't appear to be going out of his way to notice her, and Marty was now strategically invisible, she came over to where we were sitting and promptly joined us on the floor.

"Hi, cousin. Hi, Pete. Watcha doin'?"

"Hey, show some respect," I said. "You're talking to one of Charles II's most important spymasters here."

"Cool. I love Charles II. Ma says he was a great king. Loved actresses. Loved gambling. Can I be Nell Gwynn? Who are you, Pete?"

"Nell Gwynn," said Jade. "Pete's the actress right now. Playing a tense hearted gambler giving me a run for my time. You can be Colonel Carlis and hide in an oak tree."

"Hide in an oak tree. Hide in an oak tree. You think we poor witches have nothing better to do on your behalf than hide in an oak tree. Really, cousin, and I suppose we should paint ourselves blue and make libations and sacrificial offerings to you as well." Enter Les and Xander, with Beulah and Juno behind them and, to my surprise, Beth, meekly smiling and trailing behind all. Cara suddenly noticed the burning candle and ran to extinguish it so the room now felt different in a way their mass entrance didn't account for. And I felt an irrational prick of resentment because her action drew my attention back to *Café Terrace at Night* and somehow robbed me of my earlier private pleasure in the poster as an emblem of my previous visit.

"Maybe Pete should be Samuel Pepys and write it all down," said Les, who had apparently been listening to part of our conversation.

"Hey, who's Samuel Pepsi?" asked Xander, setting down his guitar case.

"He kept a diary of everybody's life," said Cara.

"Must have been bored," responded Xander reasonably.

"Same as I'm going to do," continued Cara.

"Watch your words, everybody," said Jade.

"Watch *my* words, cousin. You should be grateful for my spellcastin' words, even if you are a poet. Gave you boys a lift last night." Cara lit up a cigarette in a self-congratulatory gesture that reminded me of her mother.

"Hi," said Beth nervously to Cara. "Juno invited me to drop by. I hope it's all right."

"When did you see Juno?" asked Cara, pretending delight at Beth's presence while Juno looked immensely pleased with Cara's obvious discomfort.

"Uh, after I left last night I noticed I forgot my sunglasses, and I called about them, and Juno said I might come over this morning, so I did." She looked uncertainly at Cara because she was having difficulty looking at Jade. "I hope it's all right. I can leave if it isn't." I got the impression that Beth had probably been absolutely thrilled to come here with Juno up until the point when she was here. Now she was dying with loudly visible embarrassment and looking at her girlfriends for support. I could appreciate something of her inner vulnerability because it sort of echoed what I had been feeling this morning.

"It's all right," said Jade to Beth directly. He was responding to her discomfort. "Any friend of my cousins and all that." Les scowled over his keyboard stack, but I couldn't tell whether it was one of his usual frowns or if his equipment displeased him or if he was responding to Jade's easy welcome. Juno plopped herself down on the floor. Cara kept trying to look delighted with Beth's presence because she didn't want to contradict Jade's welcome or show her pique in front of the band, and because after all Beth had made it clear that her being there was all Juno's idea and therefore due to no fault of her own. Beulah quietly took out some embroidery and began pulling bright, shiny thread through a bound circle of cloth. The three sisters did not appear at all intimidated by either the studio or the band, rather they seemed quite proud of themselves for being special enough to merit access into the inner sanctum.

Marty emerged out of his kit with a six pack of Budweiser, looking even less pleased than he did while suffering Cara's earlier banter. "Only four bottles left," he announced pointedly. "One for each." Then he wailed loudly on his snare and cymbals as if to make an issue out of being there for business, stopped and glared at me and the girls as if his sudden stopping were likewise an issue, and called loudly for no apparent reason except to be loud, "Hey, Jade. We weren't expecting a family get-together today, so what's the deal with giving a free show? Won't Elb charge us money for giving away our time or something?" By not directly addressing the women, Marty probably thought he was being chivalrous, like maybe they couldn't hear him or had to absolve his rudeness for being indirectly launched or something.

"I'm not going to send them away empty-handed. Penny's doing a lot for us, so if my cousins want to hang out they've got a claim." Jade strode over to take one of the beer bottles.

"What about her?" said Marty, indicating a horribly tense looking, breathlessly silent Beth.

"What about her? I can't very well just ask Beth to leave without offending the others," said Jade quietly, but audibly enough to be heard throughout the room.

"What about Pete the Heat?"

"Pete's cool. Don't worry about it."

"I figured Pete's going to be here anyway so why shouldn't we come, Marty?" called Juno, obliterating all of Marty's thin pretense at discretion and jerking the issue out into the open. Juno had been making it her business to listen openly to this exchange while the others had been trying to appear as if they weren't really listening. "That's why Cara took off with the van so early and we had to beg for Ma's old car." Cara screwed up her eyes into narrow slits and stared at her sister as if to subtly deny that my presence had anything to do with hers. "Besides, we're all fresh from bein' last night's symbolic audience, so it might increase the magic. Hey Jadie, play 'Free Bird.'"

"Maybe later, coz. We're working on songs for our next CD right now."

"Your next one?"

"Yes, the one we hope to release after our current one makes us famous," said Jade as a gentle reminder to his bandmates to be kind to the ladies.

"Well, I've got a great idea for your next CD," chirped Cara, eager to help shift the subject away from our presence. "Ma taught me some seventeenth-century songs once. Here's one for good King Charles."

As soon as Cara started singing, Marty spoke. "You could clear the breakfast dishes." He waved at the remains of our breakfast on the floor.

"Come on, Marty, what do I look like, one of your freakin' groupies?"

"Yes," said Marty truthfully.

"Maybe Pete would like to help."

"No," I said, just as truthfully. "I'm busy packing for Paris. Gotta save young Charles. But I'll watch you, wench."

"I'll do it," said Beth timidly. "I mean, why not? I'm a waitress, anyway." She smiled at Jade. "Glad to help. Glad to be here. I'll even wash them for you if you like."

"What you want to warm up with, maestro?" asked Xander, stepping all over poor Beth's line because he was now strapped up and tuned and ready to play.

"Let's start with 'Night Currents,'" said Jade as Beth gathered up the dishes. "I want to work on that second guitar solo. Still doesn't feel right when Les goes into that B minor seventh - E minor progression."

"Maybe it's the progression," said Xander.

"Maybe it's the F# suspended chord," growled Les.

"What F# suspended chord?"

"The one Jade won't let me play. You know, the one that makes the whole interlude interesting to listen to?"

"Save it for the buildup in the last sixteen measures," said Jade. "If you're too 'interesting' in this section, you'll be competing with Xander's solo instead of complementing it, and I'd like him to get solid on the solo before making any changes in the background—"

"In other words," translated Cara, "it's Xander's turn to show off."

"Go for it, Xander," crowed Juno. "We're waiting."

Xander turned away with a half-chagrined, half-proud smile and responded with a quick rush of wild notes. Then Marty struck up a halting, uneven rhythm and the band got down to business while the rest of us spent a pleasant morning listening to something like a private concert, with Black Dog improvising for long minutes at a time, or stopping themselves to argue about a passage or a tempo. At one point Beth returned after washing the dishes and clumsily slipped in behind us, but no one took much notice of her besides me because the rehearsal held our attention so completely. And I'm not sure I would have noticed her if she hadn't sort of nervously knocked into me, because Beth was doing her best to beat the planet Pluto for not being noticed.

But I also got the impression that in spite of Marty's protests, we weren't all that much of a nuisance, because the band seemed to forget about us when they played. I also greatly enjoyed watching Jade singing and playing in his street clothes, because I had danced with his strange, dark wizard-self, and so I felt privileged to see the behind-the-scenes construction of what they did, to touch the raw secret before it became delicate mystery. The "performance" was that much more intimate for being incomplete. But finally Marty stopped in the middle of a take on Xander's solo and everyone else had to follow, staring impatiently until he protested, "Look, *I'm* not used to composing with a cheering section. Feels like somebody watching me get dressed. Can't the girls come back later?" He was looking at Jade, but he appeared to be seeking support from Les and Xander.

"We're family," argued Cara. "We did a lot for you boys last night. I'll leave when Jadie tells us to."

"Hey, Jadie," said Les, "tell her to." I noticed Beulah's hands go suddenly stiff over her embroidery as she bent her head in unnaturally fixed attention to her work, which appeared to be another Black Dog banner.

At the same time I saw Jade take one look at Beth, who was painfully aware of not being wanted and equally painfully aware of not having a "claim" like her friends, and I knew instantly that he was not about to "tell her to." He called a band break instead, which only served to emphasize that our little audience was an intrusion into their normal practice session. Beth suddenly decided to be a peacemaker. "Hey, Jade."

She looked terrified of actually saying his name and even more so when he broke from haggling with Marty to make eye contact with her and acknowledge that she had spoken by saying, "Yes?"

"I have an idea. You guys must be hungry. Juno and I . . . and Beulah and Pete and Cara and everybody—I mean except the band—can go for sandwiches, so you won't have to make yourselves a lunch. Save you time. Then we'll bring them back for you and leave you to practice. You're working and we shouldn't bother you."

"Thanks." He smiled all his charm in her direction. Beth had done his job for him. The gatecrashers had no choice at that point but to leave.

But Xander screwed up Beth's touching diplomacy by playing the opening of his solo and suddenly exclaiming, "Hey, I broke a string." He took off his guitar. "Hey, um—Beth." It was an effort for him to get her name right. "Do you know where Richler's Music is in town?"

"Uh, no. I'm not from Thornhill."

"I know where it is," said Juno. "I know where everything is."

"Why don't you go buy me some strings while you're out. Tell Richler GHS Boomers Medium 11-50."

"OK." Poor Beth looked like she'd just been plucked out of the potato patch and put in charge of the Third Crusade. She literally perspired in disbelief of her luck and sudden status as a gopher for the band. She looked at Juno, then she mouthed Xander's words to remember them as Beulah looked up from her embroidery. Beulah was glowing silent but unmistakable congratulations in Beth's direction.

"I know what he uses," intoned Cara. "We can throw it on my brother's account."

"Which means Xander'll have to pay Elb back for them later," said Les.

"With interest," added Marty.

"I'll buy the sandwiches, then," offered Beth, not understanding the in-joke and eagerly pushing her newfound standing. Poor kitten, it would cost her a week's salary to treat the band like that, but she insisted. People will pay out their own eyes and teeth to safeguard their sense of self-worth.

"Cool," said Marty. "I'm hungry." His tone didn't mean that. His tone meant "so go."

They did, quickly, and with an odd sense of relief that probably wasn't supposed to show. But they had barely left the studio before Marty began to busy himself with an angry sounding drum solo which seemed to be directed both at their leaving and at my still being there. But I remained behind by studiously pretending that I was too dull to realize that I wasn't welcome. Being in law enforcement has made me pretty good at that trick. And as no one cared to prolong the issue by saying anything directly, Les busied himself by playing sarcastic chords and keyboard solos against Marty's angry rhythms. At that point Jade tactfully led me and Xander downstairs into Elise's maniacally neat living room.

"Marty's in a mood," explained Xander for my benefit.

"Really? How can you tell?"

"He gets that way around Cara. He'll get over it once she leaves for the day." Xander settled himself in a chair, put his scruffy sneakers up on a sharply polished end table, idly picked up a TV remote control, and began cable surfing for lack of anything to do. He clearly had known Jade "forever," because his attitude conveyed the unmistakable sense of having grown up in Elise's house as much as in his own. Clicked through old sitcoms. Paused for thirty seconds of an info-commercial on tennis equipment. Clicked into a black and white monster movie, a news program, a soap opera—

"Hey, go back to the news," said Les suddenly from behind us. He had left Marty banging away in fury upstairs, but none of us had heard him approach because of the drumming.

So Xander sighed and clicked back to a dour-faced reporter who was explaining in a deeply self-righteous dour-faced reporter's voice that she was standing on the Boston Common, in front of the Massachusetts State House, to cover a press conference launching the new anti-drug program, SAYNO. Then she simpered and bellowed something about there being an afternoon of family events scheduled to show young people that there were healthy alternatives to drug use. The conference was jointly sponsored by the FBI—"Hey, that's you, Pete," said Xander excitedly, as if he thought I might not know—the Massachusetts DSS, the Committee to re-elect Congressman Laffer, MADD, and half a dozen other self-important single- or half-issue political groups whose acronyms I tend to forget. Everyone but the local cops, because not even Kanesh was that extravagant, although there was a generous serving of Boston police parading around in the background to make sure that despite the upcoming "fun" events no one enjoyed themselves too much.

"You get Boston news up here?" I asked.

"No, that's CNN," proclaimed Xander.

"How would *you* know?" drawled Les.

Kanesh must be fit to break his whistle over getting national coverage, I thought. Of course, the reality was that Laffer's people probably made some election-year deal with the press, but that wouldn't stop Kanesh from carrying off the credit at home.

The cameras were now panning through quite an array of dignitaries. Even the local clergy were there to add the proper religious perspective, shaking hands and looking duly superior so everyone would understand that they were doing the world a favor by showing up. Plenty of poor-looking women were waving their babies around and looking satisfied that the "state was finally doing something about these kids." Also a few slack-jawed men with tight, inexpressive eyes wearing used-up clothes. The type who are always between jobs and so are always making a job of hanging out at mid-day political events. No-lifers who call up radio talk shows six times a day. Some of them probably had no idea what the press conference was all about but recognized a political show when they saw one and weren't about to pass up an event they could grandstand about later.

The politicians and their flacks were recognizable because they were the only ones present wearing suits and dresses. They were falling all over themselves maintaining the right amount of distance from and identification with their shabbily-dressed constituents. One pol posed smiling with a screaming toddler while the toddler's mother beamed with the rare treat of being noticed by one of her representatives, even if it was only to have her vote solicited.

Then the camera switched to a podium which was all gussied up with red, white, and blue crepe paper where Piekarski and Kanesh sat flanking an empty chair that I knew was supposed to be mine. A banner proclaimed SAYNO. Kanesh was telling a gaggle of reporters that "Special Agent Peter C. Morrow, co-leader of the Boston FBI's new drug task force, was ill today and sent his deep regrets that he couldn't make it." Jade burst out laughing like a madman and everyone else followed.

"You really ill, Pete?" asked Xander.

"Sure. Plagued with musicians."

"We'll have to weave a circle round him thrice," sallied Jade.

"Hey, now you're getting personal," I said lightly, charmed by his reference to Coleridge's "Kubla Khan."

"I know."

Fearless was there, looking grandly humbled and just discomfited enough to show that he'd really rather be behind a desk somewhere, preferably in Washington, but that he nonetheless felt honored to take the mic in such fine company. Said my name several times and mentioned my interest in the case of the vanishing corpse, which I knew was his follow-up on the strategy of the newspaper article. A nationally televised press conference was an irresistible opportunity to appease Basher and Laffer and warn the Mob about how tough we were. He got to introduce Congressman Laffer, who stood up and cheerily waved and urged everyone in the spirit of the day to "Say no to everything." Except his bid for re-election, presumably.

But as Laffer made his way over to Fearless, shaking hands with constituents and preparing to deliver his speech, the camera flashed briefly to the far end of the dais, where Hugh McCrae was sitting like a bloated bullfrog in front of a still glass of water. Even if he had missed the newspaper article by chance, McCrae now knew I was supposed to find his killer, and as I sat there wondering what his next move would be, Laffer introduced him as his "chief congressional aid" and an "invaluable special assistant" to the National Drug Enforcement Congressional Committee that he was currently chairing, at which point Xander accidentally hit the switch to the monster movie, Jade grabbed it and clicked back, and Les remarked trenchantly that McCrae looked rather like the creature from the black lagoon. Which he did.

"Maybe he is a monster," Les continued. "Is that the same guy you were talking about last night, Pete?"

"Yes, that's him. The missing corpse." Marty, who apparently realized he no longer had an audience for his fit of drumming, had wandered down in time to catch me say this and to see Laffer showing what a regular guy he was by indulging in a bit blandly inoffensive chatter with his chief underling.

"Have a good trip, Hugh?" Xander giggled at Laffer's word choice. Hugh raised his right-hand palm outward and quickly bowed his head in a gesture of acknowledgement. "Mr. McCrae has been speaking on my behalf out west, in Phoenix, where he has been studying a new anti-drug program in the schools out there. Desert sun agree with you?" McCrae smiled and bobbed his head again. Laffer launched into a predictable speech about family values, which Piekarski looked positively buoyant about, and he had just gotten to the requisite fascist part about "our nation's families, our nation's children, our nation's future—" when CNN decided they'd given him enough free airtime and flashed to the news desk.

A grim-looking anchorman was reading, "A bizarre murder has taken place in the desert near Phoenix, Arizona. The victim's body was found yesterday by a couple on a camping trip, who immediately reported it to authorities. Autopsy experts believe the murder actually took place several days ago, although the body was remarkably preserved due to the dryness of the desert air."

Heard the kitchen door open and assumed that Jade's cousins were back, but when I glanced behind I saw Elise standing quietly in the doorway between the kitchen and living room, arms folded and watching the news. Didn't have time to question why she was home from teaching in the middle of the day, because the news story continued.

"Federal agents think the body is that of John Fever, an alleged train robber who has been on the FBI's ten most wanted list for several weeks. According to a reporter for the *Phoenix Sun*, John Fever sometimes used the alias Claude Hopner. The body appears to have been drawn and quartered, for the limbs were separated and neatly laid in a bundle that was wrapped in a transparent garbage bag. There were signs of cannibalism. Taped to the bag was a hand-written note which read, 'Welcome the kiss that devours flesh.' In other news, unemployment figures in—" Xander clicked off the TV. Everyone felt too cold and shuddery to stop him.

We all sort of sat there without venturing to say anything, although I felt a certain dull unspoken hope coming from the band that I would comment. Jade got up and went over to the upright piano in the corner and began to a play a little, softly and sadly. I got the impression he both wanted and was hesitant about speaking to me alone.

"Good afternoon, Mrs. McClellan," I said cheerily. By not reacting to the news story, I hoped to better determine what Elise's natural reaction was. But she didn't appear to have much reaction. Considering I had mentioned the name Claude Hopner to her as a potential alias for Penny the last time I was here, her blasé calm intrigued me. Also her indifference felt more defensive than disinterested, although this was a purely subjective impression on my part, the sort of educated guess my work experiences have made me excel at. "Glad to have an opportunity to thank you for your hospitality before I leave."

"What hospitality?" She looked vaguely alarmed.

"Pete stayed here last night," said Jade quietly. I sensed he understood my strategy and was trying to goad Elise into remarking on the reasons for my presence.

"I see." Her voice was tired and irritated. She was used to Jade doing unpredictable things like bringing American FBI agents home for the night. He'd hear about it later, but for now Elise tried to flaunt normality by briskly changing the subject. "Well, aren't you going to ask why I'm home early?"

"Why are you home early?" asked Xander.

"Thanks," she said drily. "There was a power failure at school and afternoon classes were canceled. So, aren't you all practicing?" Her question in no way suggested that she would have liked the band to be practicing. There was an ugly ghost of eagerness in her tone that faintly suggested that she liked the band's midday idleness and so would be pleased to know the reason for it.

"No," said Les suddenly, "we just had our own power failure."

"You've got electricity here," said Elise, puzzled. "Did we have an outage?"

"Broke a string," said Xander. Xander and Les's talk had all the obvious feel of putting someone off the track of some hidden real issue. I could tell that Elise sensed this, although she said nothing directly.

"Well," I spoke up, "I was just on my way upstairs to get my things and be off. Just took a little vacation up here, and Jade gave me run of the house for a night. Thanks again for everything."

"I'll help you." Jade stopped in the middle of a chord to follow me upstairs as I knew he would.

As soon as we were alone, I looked at him without saying anything, waiting patiently for him to make the first comment about the news story. He knew I was waiting. There was a faraway look in his eyes, like a dream rapidly coming to pass in somebody's lovely face. He picked up a bass and sat down to softly pluck it without saying anything.

"Jade, is there anything you'd like to tell me?"

He played about ten seconds of random notes before he spoke. "Once upon a time," he began slowly, "when time laid lighter upon me because there was more of it, a monster lived in my closet and kept my mother his captive queen." I chose not to stop the strangeness of his language. I wanted him to speak freely. "He broke my toys and ate my dog. Then one day my good aunt made him go away into whatever place monsters go."

"And you lived happily ever after?"

"I lived. Ever after. I don't really remember much of it. Only dreams sometimes."

"Jade," I said softly, sitting down on the floor with him, "what is it like for a poet to dream of Hugh McCrae?"

"My God, Pete," he said, suddenly offended. "Now *you're* getting personal."

"I know." I paused, feeling the impact of repeating our own phrases. He was feeling it with me. Whatever was happening between us had nearly been named. "Look, Jade. I can't help you with your nightmares. I wouldn't presume. Perhaps Penny can deal with the cosmic stuff, I know I can't touch it. But now you've got mob problems and I'm not a bad hand in that direction. If the Nunzios think your front money isn't forthcoming, or Claude's drawn heat, skip the promotion plans."

"I know."

"If they've shelled out money to you, they'll want payment now. Can Elb handle that?"

"That isn't clear. Nick put up some money for payola and distribution. Elb said Claude was good for it, and we owe back the loan and twenty-five percent interest when the songs make money."

"Was Claude good for it?"

"Possibly. Penny has ways of getting some money. Claude gets the rest. You've dealt with Nick's people. What do you think Elb might do or say to reassure them to still back us?"

"How did McCrae know Claude was your fall guy?"

"Who can say? None of us were ever completely sure Claude was a real fall guy."

"Who was Claude, another witch like Penny?"

"I don't know. We all thought he was half real. Then we came to accept him like a free gift. Then you brought in the newspaper story and—"

"Sometimes I think you're half real." I wanted my teasing to reassure him. "Look, I'll talk to Penny. But I'd better get close to home and see what kind of information I can turn up at the field office. My partner is eavesdropping on the Mob and I might learn more from him. Call me. I'm sure you'll probably be all right if you stay cool about it. Tell your bandmates to keep it all low key for now. Penny and Elb might have some problems."

"Pete. Does this mean you're further jeopardizing your job for us?"

Significant pause on my part. "Kind of you to notice." At that moment, Elise entered the studio. She had been listening. Her face was pale with it. I had been so intent on our discussion that I hadn't heard her approach. My face was probably pale with that. Or pale with what seemed to be a new and growing understanding between me and Jade.

She stared quietly and shakily at both of us, as I nonchalantly gathered up my things. I really did want to leave and get back to Boston as quickly as possible, and I knew I needed to talk to Penny again before taking off. I also needed to find out what side of Penny's war Elise was on, but I couldn't read her. Her eyes were soft but her body was accusatory.

"Your son is an impressive poet," I began. "I greatly enjoy his word games."

"That's all one hell of a word game," she said nervously.

"Yes, it is," Jade admitted, but the sound of the front door crashing open downstairs, and admitting the loud chatter of Cara and company, saved further investigation. Elise turned without a word to go downstairs, and we followed, taking a little time because I was carrying down my things. By the time we got down there, everyone was in the kitchen. Beth was passing sandwiches around, Cara was sitting on the table, smoking and throwing witticisms at the band members, and Juno was chattering near a silently smiling Beulah.

"Who are you?" Elise asked, although the tone in which she uttered her question implied that she already knew.

Cara glanced up at her and coolly paused to drag at her cigarette, so Beth answered. "Hi, I'm Bethany Dundas. Dundas like the street. This is Cara, Juno, Beulah. I got guitar strings for Xander, and we were just leaving so the band could get back to practicing—"

"We *were* just leaving," echoed Cara contemptuously, like the rightful leader of her little gang, but she made no move to leave.

"What are you doing here?" asked Elise, her tone a tense threat.

"Just feeding your son, Auntie."

"Get out." Her voice was ugly and fearful and did not belong in the mouth of a mousy-looking schoolteacher buried in a slightly out-of-date skirt and too many sweaters. It sounded slightly embarrassing, like weakness ineptly parading as strength. Elise knew the names Beth had provided, knew Penny's children, knew she didn't want them touching her life and didn't wish to know anything more. I thought she was going to cry.

"We're going," said Juno testily. "That was already the plan."

"Get out of my house. Get out of my son's life. Everyone."

"It's not her house," said Juno loudly to Beth as the girls left. "Ma got it for her."

I thought Elise would die at this overt mention of Penny. Instead, she waited until the front door slammed closed and then she went into the living room and collapsed crying on the couch. I followed.

"Is there something wrong, Mrs. McClellan?" I asked innocently. I noticed for the first time a little crystal sphere on a stand carved like bronze dolphins, and remembered reading that dolphins were sacred to Dionysus, which is what she called her first husband. It was soaking up sunlight on a window ledge. "Very pretty," I remarked. "Is that new?"

"Mr. Morrow," she said thinly, "do you need more help in your investigation? Is that why you've come here?"

"Yes, what can you tell me about Jade's Aunt Penny?" Figured this was a great time to bring up the topic and see if she would add anything since last time. The band members were talking in the kitchen. Elise looked deeply annoyed with their banter. "Jade's 'Aunt Penny,'" she repeated with ineffectual sarcasm.

"How long have you known her daughters? Do they come here often? Did she really buy your house for you? Do you have any papers—"

"Look—I don't want them here."

I tried another tack. "That Beth Dundas seems like a nice girl. Talked to her earlier. You know, sometimes I get the impression Beth needs friends and she's a little intimidated by Cara and her sisters. Got any thoughts on that?"

"Yes," she said, coldly irritated by my assault. "I wish Hugh was back in my life."

"Why?" I wasn't convinced she really meant this. She spoke too clearly and emphatically, like she wanted me to remember her words and hoped I might convey them to Penny or something.

"No reason. Except I thought he might come straighten out both families," she replied in a light teary sort of sarcasm that made it clear to me she didn't really mean what she was saying, but that she wanted to revel in a sort of martyrdom and get me to ride it along with her. "But he's dead, like your friend Claude Hopner, so it doesn't matter." She sniffed. "Well, Mr. Morrow—"

"Pete—"

"Whatever. I don't know what you and my son were discussing upstairs, or even if you'll see fit to include me, but I do know you have no jurisdiction in Canada and no business harassing my family—"

"Mrs. McClellan," I spoke respectfully, "I certainly—"

"I would appreciate it if you did not return here, and that you also leave my son alone, unless you work through the proper Canadian authorities. If you do come back, or if I learn you have been speaking to Jade, I'll write a letter of complaint to your superiors in Boston." She wasn't used to making threats and her voice sounded scrawny and timid. I had no idea what else she was going to do about the conversation she heard upstairs, but I didn't care for her strategy so far. While she was speaking, the band members returned unobtrusively upstairs and now the sound of Marty's drums was pulsing in the living room. She had the look of hidden annoyance. "Shall I see you out?" she asked in a sharp politeness, as if to say, "At least I am behaving properly, you can't fault me for rudeness." She stood up.

So I stood up, gathered my things to the sullen strains of Les's keyboards, and left.

Penny's house was heavy with a crowded, late afternoon moment that had stretched into an hour because nobody was paying attention to it. I entered without knocking, like it was still last night. Elb was sitting in a kitchen chair and looking uncharacteristically subdued as he held a card of wool that Penny was spinning through her fingers into geometric shapes. There were more woolen shapes in a battered looking wooden bowl on the table, along with little cloth packets and scattered gemstones and other objects I didn't recognize. The wool kept changing color, although that might only have been the way the autumn sunlight hit it. Penny looked up at me without surprise. "Hughey got Claude," she said. I noticed the TV in the living room was tuned to CNN. Something that smelled like cabbages and beets and fresh dill was boiling on the stove.

"I saw the news, too." I sat at the table. "Guess you won't be doing much desert traveling, Mother."

"No," she said stoically, "busy making charms. Talk to Elise?"

"Some."

"Whatcha learn?"

"Not much." I described our interview, including her eavesdropping on my conversation with Jade and her comment about Hugh and her threat to call the field office.

"So, she wants ya out of her life. Well that's the way of it with her, what can ye do? Jadie see the news too? How's my pet?"

"Practicing."

She nodded approval. "Fact is, Claude got drowned decades ago when he was Michael. Now it'll be a decade or two 'fore he's back again in another generation, if then." She sighed. "They does that."

"Does what?"

"Comes back. Take Claude. He's been comin' back since the first folk in Ireland where he was Cudeal, if you change 'round the letters, and sometimes Michael. But now we'se need charms." She turned back to her spinning and muttered something like an incantation.

"Wait a minute. Penny. Elise told me her first husband's name was Michael."

"Yass, and this time it was Claude. Jadie's father came as a seafarer. Now he decides on a desert dervish train robber and so who knows next time he might be a mountain goat. Elbie, gimme that bowl of myrrh." He passed over a clay bowl of incense which Penny promptly lit, filling the room with a new scent of myrrh and delicious red peppers.

"I don't understand. Claude Hopner and Michael McClellan are the same person? Jade's father died and came back? Like Hugh?"

"Thass what I said. They does that." She spun a little star shape and put it in the bowl. "Beulah should be doing this," she muttered. "Anyhows, if ye don't know it ye should and ye surprise me ye ain't figured it out with all yer readin', Pete."

"Don't worry about it," said Elb, suddenly supportive. "Half the stuff to figure here ain't worth it in the end." He coughed. His eyes were tearing a little at the incense.

"Sometimes I think you ain't worth it in the end, Elbie, but here you are and so ye might as well listen, though you've heard parts before. Jadie's father is a god. But he ain't always strong and he ain't always here in the same way. Some call him Dionysus, riding the dolphins at sea. Some call him Bacchus, leading his frenzied dancers into burning desert storms. Some call him in the cave of Mount Nysa where his father Zeus disguised him as a ram and he was raised by beautiful nymphs. Thass where I first found him."

"I didn't know you were once a nymph, Ma," said Elb, mildly interested in one of his mother's stories after all, or doing his best to assess the impact of Claude's death on his own business plans without letting on that he was too directly worried about it.

"I wasn't. That time I was practicing as a mountain witch, prophecies on the cheap for them's as couldn't get to Delphi. Knew the local nymphs far as they were worth knowing. Taught some en 'em how to nurse. Anyways, bein' there and knowin' my craft, I became his priestess. And he grew in his power and we became great friends, yes indeedy. Used to make wine together and drink it with garlands in our hair and yer mother looked quite beautiful then Elbie if she does have to say so herself."

"I'm sure you were quite a looker, Penny."

"I was." She looked pleased with my compliment. "Ye see, back then the gods were all a different bunch than the kind they's got now. An' they'd remember a kind deed and didn't find it beneath their dignity to hang out with mortals just the same as divinities. 'Sides, most of the time they'd be fightin' with other deities over a tree or some new river that one took a fancy to over the other. Dionysus was beautiful. Rewarded me with a long life for my service."

"I see."

"Well, he did," she said defensively, responding to my noncommittal tone. "I've been around. And it was quite a gift, comin' from him, as his life ain't usually all that long when he comes around. Had to get it off his father. Anyway, 'twas with Dionysus saw my first play," she said with a sudden child-like enthusiasm, as if she were describing her first visit to the circus. "They used to hold the festivals at Athens to honor him, called the Dionysia, and that's where the Greeks developed their drama, as yer readin' ought to have taught ye. Mostly tragedy. Ye see, it had to be tragedy to honor that one, beautiful as he be."

"Why?" Of course I had read Greek tragedy, but I wanted her answer.

"Because he is such dark and frenzied joy 'twould go against nature for him to last. The god who sings and plays and taunts the maenads to come dance with him in the field, who howls down the rising moon, who is ecstasy and dreams, ain't one for old age. So when he crests in his power his followers usually tear him limb from limb, and then wake from trance to weep in the cold, silent dawn until he comes again."

"Kind of like the ultimate mosh," said Elb.

"Yass, Elbie. So Dionysus'll come back. I ain't worried 'bout that. Only this time it was Hugh that got him and held his own communion feast, so not dyin' as he ought, it'll take him a while longer. Sometimes the old Titans win, and Hugh's an old Titan. And sometimes the old Titans steal down a bit of the gods' power, as Prometheus once tried with fire, and that always makes 'em especially uppity and restless for a spell. Never did get over that bein' buried down in Tartarus bit."

"Thought Prometheus would be your sort of Titan, Penny."

She spat on her fingers to show disgust. "Steals fire as ain't his, he didn't invent it, to spread around to those as didn't earn it and promptly used it to burn each others' miserable villages to nothin'—he ought to have been chained to a rock. Buried under a fossil—"

"But you're using fire to burn incense." Penny chomped the ends of her hair while Elb laughed at my point, so I decided to get back to the issue at hand. "Speaking of fossils, Hugh came back right away when you killed him on the base."

"Yeah, well, he was due. His angles were right. An' I thought killin' him on a base, would be like killin' him on a bass, would have kept him down some time and taught him fear of certain things. But it had the opposite effect, givin' him a bit of a power burst like cannibalizing Claude. Which explains why he managed to lumber it up here, which by my power he won't be doin' agin soon, now that I'm feelin' for him. But it's still just me and the girls and Elbie here and I'm fresh out of new killin' ideas."

"Well, perhaps your friend Dionysus will be Jade's protector, being related and all," I offered cheerfully. When Penny got going it was far more useful not to contradict, because she had an odd way of making odd sense of otherwise inexplicable situations, and I couldn't find a believable premise for arguing with a woman who could spin wool in her hands without the help of a spinning wheel or other device. What I mean is that with Penny, as with a Black Dog performance, one tended to believe things one didn't have the courage to mention in rational company.

"Read yer mythology, Pete. Dionysus ain't no one's protector. He ain't for safety and he ain't really too big on fatherhood. Likes the sex as causes it to happen, but that's about it. None of those gods had much track record caring for their children."

"But Claude was sending you money."

"Aye, 'cause we're friends and I'm his priestess. Where else should a god send but to his priestess? Ain't directly his business if I'm helpin' his progeny, but that's the way I am, as you know."

"So why did you once claim to be Claude?"

Penny looked impatient, and slightly insulted, as if I had unfairly accused her of a terrible crime. "'Cause I can be," she half-shouted as if I were stupid. "A priestess can channel and become her god's energy same as gettin' in a TV game show. Ain't no trick. But I ain't him. Sometimes I can get him and sometimes I cain't."

"Can Jade also 'get him'?" I was thinking about his seductive performances and my own strange ideas concerning music and divinity. "Is Jade him?"

"No, Jade's himself. Another lost child and on his own with Elise."

"What the hell would a god like Dionysus want with Elise?" Elb and Penny both chuckled in a rare display of shared mirth, although to me it seemed like a reasonable question.

"Danger, mostly," said Penny. "Dionysus likes to dally with destruction. Keeps his power bright, like night against a dying candle. Dark wine likes what's dark to him, and so them's as reclusive and might make a quiet, bookish bride sometimes get him the same as a wild one. Once visited a prudish old lady and gave her a sad bout of what the world called senility that her nephew locked her up for. But not until she bashed in her divine lover's brains with a baseball bat—"

"Uh, speaking of which," I interrupted. "It isn't just your god-friend that lives in danger. Have either of you concocted up an equally convincing theology for Nick Nariano? I mean for when he comes knocking for Claude's share of the bill and wants to know who and what your alleged money source has attracted?"

"We've got Claude's share of the bill," said Elb. "He sent us gold recently, and Ma here converted it to Canadian dollars."

"Nick will want payment."

"He'll get it."

"He'll want assurance there's more coming, your source being dead."

"Ma can get some."

"Ah kin probably get all, if I scrape," said Penny. "Ah know counterfeitin' if I have to. So Nick's puttin' some Nunzio money into promotion, I can match it back for him, as he wants, and he's seen we'se good for it."

"Why didn't he just take your money to start?"

"'Cause the deal was we wanted him to start. No sense in waitin' for what ought to be inevitable. He's just started this past week, and he's promising out money we'll deliver, and in some cases he's had to put up money."

"So he hasn't made you a loan proper?"

"No, but he's been promising out our money, so yes, we owe him, but that'll get matched."

All right, that made sense. Nick was using his connections in the entertainment industry and Moon Management was insuring his investment. Then I remembered Jade mentioning Nariano's twenty-five percent interest rate. "Is that all you owe?"

"Nope," said Penny. "Nickie sees his services as worth what we're payin'. Even as Steven. But he likes to make a profit, same as Elbie here, and so when my pets' songs start makin' storms out of nickels, we owe him—what is it Elbie?"

"Twenty-five percent of his initial outlay," said Elb.

"Right, ain't one for numbers."

"That's obvious," I retorted. "Last time we spoke on the subject you told me the discs were going to sell at thirteen dollars. Three dollars for the store pure profit, because they were getting the goods as "free samples." The rest of the dollars to Moon Management, and half of that to Nick in a fifty-fifty split."

"Well, thass the other part."

"What are the real numbers?" I asked Elb.

"For promotion start-up it's costing us three hundred thousand dollars, Canadian. Ma faked a life insurance policy for part. We'll owe an additional seventy-five thousand, that's twenty-five percent, out of our half of the sales profits. And we'll make that easy. And it's only a one-time interest payment on the initial loan of services."

"And of course the Nunzios are in this for long-term financial interest. What'll you owe them for the second CD?"

"We haven't discussed that yet," said Elb. "Probably an even fifty-fifty split because the overall profit is sure to be higher. I'm not worried about it."

"Money ain't the problem at the moment," said Penny. "Problem is, from now on if there is a problem, we don't have an Uncle Claude to blame and send the Mob off of us, off of my children and my pets I mean."

"And Nick'll be asking about Claude's enemies."

Penny fixed me with her eyes and said coldly. "An' ye don't think I can make up a convincing make belief for him. I knows my job, Pete."

"So do I. What will you say to him?"

"Ever know a successful man didn't have enemies? Claude made the most wanted list. Gonna be people who envy that accomplishment. Same as some people must be envyin' all the awards and high heroism that newspaper article bespoke of you. Think what Claude might have had after him. Small time hoods with delusions of grandeur that they're so important the government is out to get them. Thems who envy his flash and romance and gentleman-robber style. Thems who turned criminal robbin' convenience stores because some Hollywood movie once got 'em fixated on bein' a swashbucklin' folk hero outlaw themselves, as Claude certainly was. Those who envy his gold. There's enough stories for Nick."

"Penny, you expect Nick to believe somebody knocked off your financial partner out of envy for him as a great criminal?"

She stared at me. "Yass. Nick's a great criminal. He'd eat that one up faster than hell's pigeons on corn. Every would-be mob boss thinks he's Al Capone and Al Pacino rolled into one." Actually, she kind of had a point there. "And you're supposed to be the mafia maven and all that. Give ye a life lesson, Petey, 'cause both you and Elbie here are sure to need it. Now, did Claude have a great life when he was here this time to have a life? Think."

"No," said Elb, "he got killed."

"Pete?"

I thought about my private interest and illicit admiration for "Jesse's" publicized exploits. "Yes, I suppose he did. He had fun with it."

"Exactly. Now. You can tell someone he has a great life 'til the cows run away from Argentina and set up shop sellin' toothpicks on Mars, but if that person truly has a great life, why are you sittin' there praising it?" She expected an answer.

"Admiration."

"Don't restate the freakin' issue, Pete. I know ye for not admirin' much, so ye really ought to know better. Think. What is admiration 'cept hypocrisy and socially acceptable jealousy? Lots of people 'admire' Mother Teresa, but I don't see too many volunteerin' to follow her path. There's the hypocrisy. Lots of people admire successful entrepreneurs—listen up Elbie—but that's mostly 'cause they wish they was wealthy. There's no one poor who's truly glad someone else is rich. Perhaps neutral in some cases, but not glad. Let's grow up about it. Why admire, why praise someone else's life 'less ye want it yourself? If ye don't want that person's life for yer own then I guess ye don't really see it as great or admirable or worth havin'. And if ye do, how can ye avoid sayin' it's honest envy ye feel? And in some cases, envy goes into killin' body or spirit—usually spirit, but physical murders happen."

"Maybe a certain life can be great for someone else but not for me."

"If it's great, it's great for anybody, Pete. Maybe some people make false distinctions to justify their own bad choices, else how on hell's earth could they live with themselves? Well, anyways, that's the lesson. Now stay a bit and I'll give ya a quick lesson in how to charm. Cain't hurt as I knows you'll be around some and you'll both need it to deal with Hugh. 'Specially you Elbie, as me and the girls cain't always be there on the tour as we should."

"Maybe you ought to always be there," I said suddenly. "I mean, if you're worried about it."

"And maybe I will, but it stands right now that if I leave Toronto unguarded, Hugh will be snugglin' back into Elise's life, and no one knows but she may let him for spite. And there's tricks Hugh could try if he took on Michael's position that I'd rather not think about. And he's growin' more powerful. Yass, now that he's eaten of Claude and gotten stronger, he might go after the band direct, but not if Elbie here learns his charms."

"Yeah," Elbie said dully. "I'll learn my charms."

"What do you mean 'go after the band direct'?"

"I mean stop the records from gettin' played and the music from bein' loved if he can. What's more direct than that?" Penny searched my face. "Ssh, cha Petey, calm yer heart down I kin feel it poundin' same as another kid outta my womb. He won't assault Jadie the way he got Claude. He ain't in this to create martyrs, as he knows that's the sort of thing to enhance the dream. He'd get at 'em from behind the scenes mostly. Like tryin' to scare off the promoters by murderin' Claude so maybe the CD don't make it on the air. Ye see, he don't want to chance makin' up the legend of a brilliant musician murdered in his prime, sort of thing could increase sales and tempt the promoters back in it if Claude's killin' doesn't tempt them away—no John Lennons for him. Hugh's the enemy no real hero can cleanly fight."

I tried to speak but Penny wouldn't stop her lecture.

"Lemme ask ye another riddle. Got two boys. Both play violin like they invented music before the gods had a clue for sound. First boy murdered by a monster like Hugh on the verge of the release of his first recording. Second boy cain't get his stuff promoted 'cause the record labels have a closed-door policy and he ain't got an uncle in the business and if he pushes his music too hard at the suits they laugh at his dreams and reject him to make their own envy vanish with their power. Who's more likely to get his work recognized and loved and whose more likely to be told he ain't serious, ain't no real musician? And if the second boy drags it along for years, well who's really experienced the worse death?"

"I see your point."

"Told ya, I been around for a while. No real artist was ever killed off violently. Too much violence about real art for violence to be a danger. Naw, Hugh will do somethin' administrative wise. Might get some law passed with the indirect effect of makin' free samples unprofitable for record stores to take, somethin' no one'll ever hear of but will stop my pet's career just as cold as a bullet. Everyone weeps and loves the music of a fallen Orpheus whose killer is cleanly known. Everyone spits on the explanations and failures of a self-professed artist strangling in bureaucratic attitudes and hidden laws and red tape. 'Specially when we gots a media makin' it all look like alls that talented gets recognized sooner or later. But that's why we're spinnin' charms. And if there should be a physical danger, well there's a few in here for that too."

"Why don't you work them, Mother? As a back-up to Elb?" I asked. Elb sighed loudly.

"'Cause Elbie's management hisself. Elbie's in the most effective position to stop Hugh's tricks, if he'd only look to his job and do it." Penny's tone implied that she was admonishing both of us.

She then took a fistful of woven charms and herbal packets out of the wooden bowl and proceeded to teach us both what she called her protection spells, while Elb leaned his head on his arm and sort of stared through her explanations. I took notes and listened. Learned all kinds of ways of thinking and protecting what my heart had decided I would protect. Learned everything she cared to give me for the sake of my loving admiration and slippery half-belief.

Stave Ten

Saturday morning, September 19, 1992.

Nearly passed out in front of my door. The reason I didn't was because I actually passed out in my car sometime early Saturday morning while I was imagining that I was parking it in front of my garage. I discovered later that I really had parked it, but I was so tired in the moment from having been awake for nearly twenty-four hours that all my real actions felt imaginary. Of course, coming from Toronto didn't help make anything seem more real than it needed to. I remember thinking that I wasn't in my car anymore, that somehow I was already in bed and feeling grateful that I didn't have to get up again. Then my predawn woods were suspended in a rigid blur, and there was a dream that I wasn't strong enough to disbelieve flying out of my steering wheel, and then I woke to Saturday afternoon sunlight shimmering on my garage door.

Which meant there would be no one at the office I could get valuable press conference information from until Monday, but that I also had the rest of the weekend in which to organize my thoughts and rationally plan out what I needed to know and do to keep McCrae at a safe distance from my buddies in Black Dog. Checked my house as was my habit after a journey. All right. Everything undisturbed. Closet doors half open the way I had left them. Closet air exuding that lately unused, nobody's home stillness I always expected closet air to exude after time away. Clothes hanging familiar, making a remotely warm contrast to the upright air standing still around them. Half-waiting for my return like they half-knew I often lived in them. Unpacked. Hung up an unused shirt, closed the closet doors, and threw everything else in my laundry hamper except Penny's little gifts, some of which I pocketed and some of which I carried openly through my house because holding them connected me to her world, and to Jade.

Played my answering machine and got three frantic messages from Fearless about the press conference and what did I think I was trying to pull by not answering my phone. Promptly erased everything.

Sat heavily on my couch while the feeling of order and control over my house and private wooded domain led inevitably into knowing that I was completely back in Massachusetts. Grounded myself in the braided rug on my polished wooden floor, felt the absolute neatness of my wallpaper's straight-lined cut still and perfect against the paneling of my exposed hallway, watched the familiar pattern of gold rose wreaths on white welcoming me back. My walls hadn't changed in my absence, but coming home makes everything look different than you're used to for a while, and there was a high I felt thinking about Toronto that lent a warm, cloudy lift to everything I was experiencing in the moment.

Stared idly at my sliding back door. Its drawn curtains still had the half-evasive look of no one having been home for more than a day. Then I was hearing the barking of my nearest neighbor's dog, which made me think that nothing in New England had changed besides me.

Then I noticed the stack of witchcraft books near my stone fireplace, and remembered the charms and instructions Penny had given me, and all my thoughts were in Toronto again. Only this time upon return I felt like the city wasn't so removed and separate from my life here. That my northern experiences were becoming part of my normal existence, that I could contact Penny and therefore everybody else up there if I wanted to. That I had charms in my pocket. And I literally did.

I lit a candle and set it on my hearth. Put the charms into a large wooden bowl like the one Penny used. Placed the bowl near the candle and imagined the sea. Felt the moment of autumn evening and knew Aphrodite was in it. Then I took out a yellow legal pad and began to sketch out a viable plan of action.

Item One. Needed an acceptable, though not necessarily believable, excuse for missing the press conference. Needed to avoid suspension. At all costs needed to stay on the case. For once I wanted to be at work. Should be easy because Fearless had more at stake in me returning to the field office in a cooperative mood and seeming to make real progress on the "vanishing corpse" case than in throwing his authority around with another suspension. He'd probably actually be grateful if I found a way for him to save face and forgo suspension, so why not subscribe to Kanesh's line that I was ill that day and sent my deep regrets that I couldn't make it? Not like Fearless would be in much of a position to argue, especially if I told him I had already sent my personal regrets for being ill and missing the conference to Laffer. Easy deal. Tough to explain a lie to a politician.

Item Two. Needed to start showing real enthusiasm for my new drug assignment. Become a cheerleader for SAYNO. If I kept Fearless and Laffer and Basher happy here by helping to show how tough on drugs we were, maybe it would be enough of a sop to the pols' "tough on crime" stance to make their interest in the vanishing corpse case vanish. And if I nailed some non-mafia related traffic on the Boston-Providence ring, my new-found law enforcement zeal would be sure to keep the Nunzios in a happy monopoly over their Boston-based exports and less anxious about my potential to cause trouble—if only the goddamn press would stop making an "unsolvable mystery" thing out of the "murder" and Fearless would stop feeding the press to satisfy some public bloodthirst that we were busy on outrageous cases.

Item Three. Needed believable rationale for not putting pressure on the Nunzios' Boston-Utica drug business to yield up a killer right away. All right, Crensch was supposed to hint around that his congressional connections wanted things on the quiet side for now, but that would only last until Fearless got more direct pressure from Laffer or Basher. Had to consult with Crensch again on that point. I had no fear that he wouldn't drop the line I gave him, his love of intrigue would see him through that, but if he failed to convince, I could certainly feed Fearless dead ends for a while. He'd swallow dead ends like McCrae's pills. Or better, keep him perched and salivating on the edge of his longed-for promotion with promises of being "close" because I greatly needed to avoid being replaced or augmented with another "ghost-writing" partner for Crensch if I failed to make progress. And if interest dissipated after the elections, everything could then become a dead end and the case could get dropped into the inactive files.

Item Four. Needed to stop McCrae. Learn what I could about McCrae being at the press conference, his workings on the congressional committee. Maybe I could learn something from Crensch's father if I were careful enough in my approach. Definitely needed to keep him away from Elise. Penny and I were partners on that one. Also needed to keep him away from instigating the sort of deadly administrative measures Penny feared but at the moment I had no idea how. I put down my pen while my gaze fell on the candle and the charm-laden bowl. How? Voters have no control over the actions of elected officials, let alone their largely unknown appointed hacks. I was certainly in no position to stop laws from coming to pass. But I was in a position to study charms and witchcraft, at least until my own research yielded something better. What the hell? Power's power, no matter where it comes from, and Penny certainly had something of a track record in stopping Hugh.

Then another thought struck me. What if I could "prove" (i.e. make up) that the vanishing corpse was a mafia killing, that I knew the hit man, but that arresting him would embarrass some congressman who was happy to take campaign money from the Mob but whose source of funding would be made public if he didn't quietly call a halt to our investigation? Not a bad angle, I might be able to work that—but wait, what if I could "prove" that the hit man was McCrae himself? That would be interesting—certainly give the monster something to think about—certainly keep the Mob assured that I wasn't harassing them and that I had no interest in Elb—certainly get McCrae out of the way for a while. Why not construct the fiction of McCrae being his own killer, a fiction with far more advantages than the truth of pointing him out as the vanishing corpse? Yes! Jade had the right idea after all, except he wanted me to tell the truth. But the truth was too close to fiction to be believed, and besides, since when would the truth work to benefit a dream-spinner like Jade?

I must construct a solid, believable fiction on Black Dog's behalf. Then I could present my "evidence" and let Fearless and Crensch do as they saw fit. Then I wouldn't be off the case. To the contrary, I'd probably have to replace Crensch as the chief investigator and be on the thing for good, or at least until the whole thing was resolved in McCrae's being under surveillance in a federal prison somewhere. Which would presumably end his threat against Black Dog. Laffer and Basher might even like the spin of being so dedicated to justice that they have to advocate pushing the law against their committee's own aide. Election year honesty and all that. I might even be able to use my impeccable record at solving bizarre murders to springboard myself off drug duty and back into more normal human puzzles, like psycho slayings. Everyone wins. And if, as an added bonus, I could find proof that McCrae killed Claude Hopner—no—with the geographical distance involved I wouldn't be assigned to that case, and I really didn't need to call the Mob's attention to my interest in Hopner's death. I had no clue how to investigate that one properly without advertising that I was investigating but hey, if I could do anything to help my brother feds in Phoenix make the connection without leaving my fingerprints on it—well, leave that for now.

But how to believably pin McCrae's own murder on him? Motive? Opportunity? What could I learn from Crensch's father? Wouldn't hurt to take Fearless's advice and start getting intimate with the boy wonder since his father probably worked with McCrae on a daily basis. And there was my plan. Go to work. Sweet talk Fearless. Get the office gossip on the conference. Sweet talk Crensch. Direct the drug committee towards non-mob drug sources for good measure. Study magic. Nail McCrae.

Now that I had a plan, things were looking up. It was not quite late afternoon, three p.m., still light, dirt light, the near-late day that doesn't feel like night comfort coming yet but more like your life is really lasting too long. I let my thoughts slip into the luxury of staring at the candle and thinking freely about Jade without having to feel the irritation of knowing that there were other issues that needed my attention, and my mind drew an image of a poet. The poet was in a medieval castle, chanting daring verses to smiling well-dressed ladies. I closed my eyes and contentedly imagined him making an afternoon go quickly for them while they were anticipating the dark ball and feast of the night, when I suddenly heard a hooting and a rummaging coming from my bedroom, a closet door slide open, and heavy plodding footsteps as someone emerged and tripped slowly down my hall. I turned quickly in time to see Hugh McCrae himself tromping into my living room with a slight ungainly bounce to his feet like he wanted me to know that I was lucky to have him as a guest.

He looked thick and oily and yellowish in the afternoon light, like an old person's unbrushed early morning mouth laying wide open in a dentist's office that hadn't changed equipment in decades. There was an ugly sort of sleep laying thick on his face, but he was coming awake through it. He also looked taller and fatter than I remembered, and his sallow eyes were more self-satisfied than before. I thought of a cannibal I'd once investigated, and then I knew instinctively that the remnants of Claude's corpse were coursing through McCrae like the aftermath of an unholy communion. He moved with a jerky kind of strength, like an image from a silent black and white film run in horrible slow motion. The kind of film that, if you watch it alone in a quiet house late at night, repels like lurid photos of a nineteenth-century freak show.

Unfortunately, my gun wasn't handy, so I had to rely on looking tough and concentrating on preparing to physically kick the life—I mean the death—out of him. Not that shooting him would help anything important. If Penny couldn't kill him permanently, I had no reason to believe I would have any better success.

"Hey, Pete. Son." He quietly smacked his lips and shrugged his head a little to the side, like he was flatly embarrassed to be found in my home but really couldn't help being there after all. Galling, dirty little shrug, like he knew that he wouldn't have to make a long issue out of showing the socially expected discomfort of a trespasser because he also knew me for the generous sort who wouldn't mind old friends and monsters imposing on my hospitality. His face demanded with the musty proficiency of a life-long mooch that I was supposed to be a good guy and say a few words to relieve him of the necessity to look uncomfortable because such a look would take needless energy and after all, he was here now so what could I do?

"Heh, heh, heh." He cast down his eyes and flipped over a fat meaty wrist, smiling in a dreadful caricature of boyish impudence. Then his glance suddenly fell on my bowl of charms and he shuddered a little and gave a strange little hoot as he backed up a step against the railing that overlooks the little stairway leading down from my living room. Naturally, I took the hint and grabbed one of the little herb packets Penny had told me to spread in a circle around any territory—including my heart—if I wished to keep monsters at bay. I opened the cloth a little and he began to wheeze and tear and jerkily bob his head in reaction to the scent.

"What the hell are you doing here?"

"Please close." He coughed and whimpered and waved his fat nerveless hands around. I thought of a bloated rat trapped in an airless chamber.

"How'd you get in? Answer and I'll think about it." The scent was having a wonderful effect on him, though I smelled nothing more harmful than a light bath bouquet of lavender and orange.

"Hey." He hooted violently and clutched his chest, rolling his eyes like he was terribly hurt by my rudeness and wanted to shame me by letting me know that he had presumed that I was of a better sort than to rudely poison monsters. It was clear that McCrae wasn't able to talk much more in his present condition, so I closed the cloth and said roughly, "Tell me what you want and how you got here, before I make you eat it." He coughed and wheezed and snorted and looked most unhappy, like a punished child who thinks he'll get his sentence softened by coyly admitting to his wrongdoing. A grimace billowed through his old fat face. Then he sat on the floor and held a wooden railing to recover.

"Damn Chinese. Well, I'll tell ya." He shook his head like an old salesman accustomed to having to indulge a potential customer's oddball reaction to some shopworn rap. "Huh." He put his other hand against his chest. "Bubble." Waited with bulging eyes staring at the floor. Then he swallowed and the sound made a loud crack. "Got in through the sump pump," he wheezed. "Down in the crawl space where there's a hole in the concrete floor and sometimes the stale water and the flushed worms come up through and make the cement smell faintly of mudfish. There's old mashed potatoes and gum down there in a lot of people's houses, or dried playdough, which is one way to find it. Not in yours, though."

"I don't have a sump pump. How the hell did you get in?"

"Well, I'll tell ya. Every house has a secret path between the back of the closet and the basement hole. I just found your hole, Mr. Morrow, and moved in. Not like anyone was home."

"Where's your car?"

"Car, hey. Took a bus. Did tricks with my handkerchief and made balloon shapes for the old ladies when we stopped for gas. Made ghosts out of tissue and string. Walked from Route 20. Chatted with your neighbors. Sold a dirty packet of old thread to the widow-farmer over the hill that owns the cows and the goat. She wants to be young, you know. Didn't you dream of her once?"

"Stay out of my dreams."

Something like a horrible friendliness seemed to clamp down deep in the back of his eyes. "Been stayin' in your closet, scrunched way down in the back behind your old clothes—watched you unpack through an old pinhole in the wood and felt the wire hanger go through me when you hung your shirt. Hurt my kidney enough to make old bug juice come out—how did you get that toy?" He meant the herb packet.

"Been studying." I indicated my witchcraft books so he'd have some alternative explanation for my proficiency besides my brief apprenticeship with Penny.

"Hoodey hey—"

"What the hell do you want?" I opened the packet a little.

"Well, I'll tell you." He coughed as I closed it. "I like the back of your closet."

"Comfy is it?"

"Comfy and there's a hole there that I can stick my finger down, the way the Romans used to stick theirs down their throats to force vomit during a feast."

He sounded weirdly childish for a minute until he managed to recover a little from my second onslaught. "Pete," he said as if we were friends, "Son. I got no good place to live. You know, for my back. I want to live with you when I'm not in Washington. I need a good place to live. Until you get me my wife to live with. Got drowned out of my other place."

"No."

He dropped his hand from the railing and sort of clumped across the floor to sit cross-legged on my rug, pulling up an already too-short polyester pant leg to expose a faded argyle sock held up with a garter belt. The gesture bothered me because he was trying to be playful in a twisted way that made all playfulness seem tawdry. "Hey—ever play Duck Goose?" He sounded like he was just getting into a new business venture and wanted to share his enthusiasm with someone. "You get to be It. You touch someone's head, and he's the goose. Then the goose chases you around the circle and if he catches you, you end up in the soup. And if he doesn't, he ends up in the soup and you're still It. He he he. Until you get caught. New game."

"What's your point and how the hell did you find my house?"

"Quite a game, finding your house, but, hey, you know, here I am. Now selling subscriptions to defunct magazines. Know how to get old Reader's Digests, pre-read with bathroom stains, sent out of 1953-1956. Also selling special vitamins and breakfast powder on the side. Change your mind about changing your life?"

"I'm busy. What do you want?"

His eyes looked like two empty saucers, empty with queasy yellow stains like the residue of an ancient poison. They reminded me of a pesticide I'd once sickened from in childhood after playing too long in my supposedly pristine woods. "You busy enough to find my poor wife while you were gone?"

"No."

"Yes, Mr. Morrow, to play all day." Was he somehow reading my thoughts? Then he took out a dirty handkerchief and blew his nose. "Well, got some quiet information might be helpful in speeding along your searches. Ellie has a son, you know. Grown boy. Horrible thing not to have a father watching over his life, as I'm sure you can imagine. Imagine," he sort of spat the word, "imagine how he must have suffered growing up without a strong father figure making sure he doesn't get involved in drugs or anything nasty, you know."

"I didn't know." I did my best to sound as if McCrae were wasting my time with information I had no use for. His lips spread into a thick, toad-like smile that told me I failed to convince.

"Yes, well. A shame." He let the implied threat sink in. Then, "I just like things decent, Mr. Morrow. Clean, you know, and quiet and honest. To save the children, you know. Greatly concerned with the young people of this country. I'm an old man, older than you'd think. And I'd like my wife and family back. I give you until after the elections. Like to be settled before Christmas with my bride by my side. To tango, hey."

"What if I find her and she isn't willing?"

"Had a very good trip out west, Mr. Morrow." Patted his stomach and I felt nauseated. "Imbibed unexpected strength, observing Arizona's anti-drug program. Lots of concerned educators and public servants like myself touring the schools, teaching the kids to buckle under to life and say no, after a fashion. Think your local slogan will catch on nationwide. Mr. Laffer likes it. Well, took myself a stroll and had an old bubbling lunch, but still greatly felt like I was missing Ellie and like dear Ellie might be missing me. Anyway, I did miss her. Just get her down here. Out of Toronto. We'll arrange a truce. Government law for family values. Like to make her life complete. Do something for the wooman."

"She'll be thrilled to get a prize like you."

"She's never thrilled. That's why I always liked Elise." He looked wistful for a moment, almost teary, but he rubbed his eyes and quickly recovered from his bout of sentiment. "So, you need information on the vanishing corpse to solve your case?"

I didn't answer.

"You know, in marriage you are only allowed to have just one—friend—in your whole life and then you are restricted beyond that—just one, Mr. Morrow—the end. That's why the Church has always favored marriage and governments have blessed the family. More control for less energy—and it's all pretty much a sham, too. And arranged marriages are best because you eventually get used to each other in a business way and pervert the highest of human passions by mistaking that getting-used-to for 'love.' No nonsense about grand passions when a 'getting used to' under fear of social censure if you split can be called love, same as finding your soulmate for life. Third World still does it right, under the ancient refrain of 'you'll learn to love him later.' Of course, the men are never told they'll learn to love their wives later, they don't expect to ever have to give that much."

He was looking for a reaction. I was refusing to give him one.

"Well, Mr. Morrow, there's no need to miss any more press conferences. I can prove there's a girl won't let me into Canada who did it, an old Penelope, but I need your help because I'm not privy to the material evidence same as you are. Need you to be a friend, hey. See, when that imposter colonel was killed—this girl left some notes behind, and I know from the papers that the field office has them. Nicely. And I'm sure the handwriting matches some of my own collected samples. But how would I just know that? You're the investigator who can make the match. From your secret sources. Of course, I could send your boss and partner copies of what I have, to point them in the right direction, but I prefer you to initiate extradition and uphold the law you are sworn to protect." Clearly he wanted Penny out of Toronto in case I failed to get Elise out of the city. "I'll give you copies. Here." And he stood up and took some paper out of his vest and smacked the paper down flat on the counter that separates my living room from my kitchen with his spread hand. "In case they get lost and I need to send more to the field office. I trust you to use them in the most effective way possible."

"Could take some time," I said evenly. "I can't just extradite someone on the basis of a few copies of handwritten notes. Need to convince a hell of a lot of people besides you and me to make it stick."

"Elections." He shrugged. "Need her by then." Then he stretched. "Lumbago. Like the cheese. Well, I'll be going. Great doing business with you." He hulked himself down to my front door and stopped. "Hooh. The papers say the death was 'mob related.' To seem to be torn apart by the populace adds a certain charm. Mob? . . mob? Get it? Heh, heh, heh—the colonel was torn apart by the mob. An honor traditionally reserved for those of a more Dionysian persuasion. And all the protests on various single-minded, narrow issues, like a proper wailing and mourning, almost as if I were Bacchus himself. And finding my killer will get Mr. Basher re-elected and you know Mr. Basher's on the committee to stop drugs in this country. You are a true patriot, Mr. Morrow." And he lumbered himself out the door and down my stony driveway and sort of faded off like a smelly whisper down my wooded country road.

I didn't touch the papers. They were evidence. I leaned over the counter and noticed that from that angle the sunlight revealed an oily stain of a clear handprint where the monster had spread his hand on the top paper. Then I read the one on top:

> 9/7 like a lucky dice
>
> Dear Hugh Munster—
>
> You are a chump. Stay out of my yard and my nice kitchen or I will smash your bones into green frog jello and chopped carrots and feed everything

to the landfill for three solid years and we'll see if you like that. Ever been a casserole? WELL, you leave any more broken toys and prickly displays in my yard and you die (again) for sure. We don't light candles for ugly old monsters like you, and we greatly hope you choke on your own fists like a half-evolved lungfish dork. You are not a pretty mermaid so stop trying to pretend you are one. WE know better.

Your enemy forever,

Penny Rosalie La Rue Dupruis Starmaker, Esq.
13 Oak Street
Sign of the Dangerous Dragon
York, Ontario

The handwriting was cursive and perfectly matched that of the Hopner's Sardines note that I had thoughtfully kept. In fact, I took the Hopner's note out and made sure. Which meant Cara had written to the monster at one point in time in her mother's name, as this was also the same handwriting that appeared on the "still burning for Pamela" note on her Led Zeppelin altar.

So Hugh McCrae thought this was Penny's writing, and clearly thought or knew or guessed the writing would match those bizarre notes left on his own corpse. I'd need to take out the collected stuff at the field office again just to see for myself that the other two notes in our official keeping also matched the handwriting I had here, but that wouldn't be a problem. And before checking, I could also call and ask Penny who actually wrote all those strange notes on the corpse. Any excuse for calling Toronto, I thought. But since the party, I had suspected that Cara had contributed her penmanship skills to the killing, and now it became essential that I find out for sure.

But before calling, I donned a pair of rubber gloves, the ones I wash dishes with, and for overkill carefully slid the top paper off the second by pushing at the edge with a butter knife, so as not to obscure the handprint. The second paper had DIE DOG DIE! scrawled in large red crayon block letters across it and contained a snarl of greasy hair that looked like Hugh's. It was clearly an original. Only the top paper was a photocopy.

Called Toronto. Couldn't get a line through on the antique, vacuum tube, manually operated switchboard phone system that services my town 75% of the 80% of the time the law requires it to, which meant the local folk had a 40% chance of dying before they can call an ambulance in an emergency. Got the local Masonic Home, because our phone system seemed to have a built-in default for long distance numbers being routed there. Tried again, heard ringing, a very faint "Yass?" and something like "let me get a bone." The connection was so rumbly and bad I hung up, and my own phone immediately rang shrilly off the hook, rattling all the dishes in my kitchen cupboards and startling me. It was Penny. "Yass, Pete. Heard ya tryin' to get me. Had to break open a walrus bone in an egg, but it's all right now. Can ya hear it OK?"

"I can hear you, Penny. Need your help with something."

And I told her about my recently departed visitor and his attempt to get me to extradite her for the murder and then I read the letters to her. Penny kept exclaiming,

"Lordy" and "Lady Lu and the moony twins," and "I'll be dipped," but she mostly listened in silence, although she broke off once to yell at Juno about something. When I finished, she said, slightly defensively, "Well, it ain't my letter."

"It looks like Cara's handwriting."

She sighed. "Juno—did you girls send a whammy letter off to Hugh—" and then her voice faded off. There was some discussion. After a minute or two Juno grabbed the phone.

"Hi. We did it."

"You wrote the letter?"

"Well, I said the letter," corrected Juno. "It was a note. Cara wrote it down and mailed it. I wrote down the crayon one for him to die, like a spell. But it didn't work. He didn't die." She snapped a bubblegum bubble as if this was all old news to her and she was currently busy with much more interesting affairs.

"How did Cara know where to send it?"

"I don't know," said Juno in a tone suggesting she did know but that it was all too complicated to think about and break down and explain. "Just leave it somewhere empty like a newspaper dispenser at three a.m., or in an old soda can or railroad box. Or in a school during 'God Save the Queen.'" Then she turned quiet while Penny grumbled something in the background, and then she added less brightly, "Me and Beulah were only trying to make up for that time he came here when we were upstairs having our little ritual—" then Penny took the phone back.

"Think my children would have more sense than to send letters to Hugh, but there ye have it. Little girls passing nasty notes in their mother's name, nearly as good as playin' dress-up when she ain't home. Cara probably dropped it down a hole someplace so's it gets there. So what else ye got?"

"Got some thoughts about using the notes, but first, I wondered if you had any thoughts as to how he had found and gotten into my house, since it had been all undisturbed when I got home and checked it."

"I'se hate to say it, Pete," she said patronizingly, "but bein' undisturbed is all his sort of thing, so that ain't no way to tell. The mosquito that buzzes is not the one that bites, so silence could mean yer about to be bit or yer perfectly safe. Undisturbed don't mean much."

"Wonderful."

"Yass, well." She sounded impatient with my sarcasm. "Didja call him?" she rasped.

"No, I have his Washington number, but I wasn't—"

"No, Pete, didja call him? Didja do anything funny with his name?"

"Funny with his name? Such as?"

"Didja scratch it in a candle, or an old piece of 'luminum can, or shout it at a rerun of an old quiz show—"

"Yes, wait—last week, before Cara's little party, I was reading about witchcraft, and I scratched his name in a black candle, for fun, and burnt it as a way of ridding myself—"

"Were ye thinkin' of riddin' yerself?" she asked doubtfully. "Be careful, Petie. Hughey's the ultimate rid, so the 'gettin' rid' part could bring him on. Think. What was really in yer mind at the time?"

I tried to remember. "I had read some silly spell about writing down your troubles and burning them away in order to feel better—"

"—Thass how ye got him. Petie, don't try no more magic lest I give it to ye. Like the protection spells. Those ye can prob'ly work. But if ye ain't got the right frame of mind yer liable to work anything if ye ain't careful. You wanted to feel better, and his name was in it, and the want drew him to yer location. Might have even eased in the possibility of him being at the press conference."

"If I 'called him' nearly a week ago why did it take him so long to show?"

"'Cause his kind is slower than us. Takes him awhile to do most things. Look, you can get rid of him by burnin' down a black candle—I've done it myself, but not if ye put his name on it and not if your state of mind is wrong. Ye see, he likes to have candles burnt to him, likes to feel like he's worth a bit of worship now and then, so ye really offered him a feast. Huh." She sounded curious and intrigued. "Yer gonna have to use yer herb packets and protect yer house."

"I've got seven acres of land here, Mother. Mostly woods. Gonna take a hell of a lot of herb packets."

"Thought'll stretch 'em. Look, Petie. Gimme directions. I'll send my girl Cara to help you. With more charms. Along with Elbie. Elbie needs the experience of working protection spells."

"O, Penny, speaking of spells. Is Cara a good secretary?"

"Are youse serious?" She sounded amazed, like the idea of Cara in an office job was as incomprehensible to her as Penny herself was to most people.

"Yes, here's my thoughts on the letter. I've got some parking tickets with Hugh's signature on them. Also a copy of the voucher he gave Elb when the band played on the base, which has a handwriting sample. Could Cara change the names, witch the handwriting? Is there some sort of alchemy or something for that? Say—'Dear Colonel Rinkowski—signed Hugh McCrae, NDECC Committee Aid,' using the handwriting on my tickets as a guide. The paper already has his handprint on it, and he used to work in NSA, so there's bound to be fingerprints on record somewhere to match—"

Penny chuckled. She knew where I was leading, and clearly enjoyed the idea of transforming Cara's letter into a threat from Hugh to Rinkowski. But she wasn't convinced. "But if Cara changes her signature on the letter to match Hugh's signature on the voucher and tickets, she'll need to change the whole letter to match so it looks like the monster wrote it. But if we're going to get him for murdering his own self, then the letter needs to match the notes from his corpse."

"I can get the notes from the field office. No one has paid attention to the handwriting, so Cara could change all the writing to match the monster's."

"But you said he's got the original that my darlin' daughters signed my name and address to. Gotta plan to cover that one?"

"Yes, ma'am. That's what I get paid for. The handprint on the photocopy he left me along with the match in handwriting will be enough for me to justify calling him in for questioning. But for the pièce de résistance, there's pieces of hair, his hair, all over the second letter, the one Juno wrote in crayon."

"The monster rubbed out her curse with his hair and wanted to it show off to you." Penny sounded more annoyed with Juno than with Hugh.

"Well, no trouble throwing that in the evidence bag at work and shaking things around." Penny gave a little girlish squeal of excitement. She sounded like a teenager who just found out she made first cut for the cheerleading squad and had been asked to the prom by the star quarterback. "Of course he'll produce Cara's letter with your name, but where there's a copy with his handwriting, there's a presumed original with his handwriting also. Someone would have to find you to get your story on the two letters, because what the hell could Hugh say that wouldn't put him in a psychiatric institute? I can hear him telling the authorities about some centuries-old witch in York—"

Penny giggled. "So, let 'em come up and find me—it's all Cara's handwriting—don't match mine either, and she knows how to disguise her own so as nobody knows whose it is—"

"Well, that's the point. I'd probably be the one sent to track you down. Of course, I don't have to find you—"

"And I kin tell anybody else who might come on a chance that I ain't who I am and don't know Adam about it? Done that one before with the census people. Got lots of names and papers if I need 'em." She was very excited and started squealing again. "With Hughey tucked away in a prison ain't like we gotta even stay in Toronto no more. I kin join my pets on their club tour without fear of him gettin' to Elise. Let him try to be a father to my precious and steal back the power Jadie got from my good friend Dionysus. Petie, yer somethin'. Leave it to you to stop a monster through writing—"

"Penny, slow down. Will a prison hold him? He got into my house."

"Yass, it'll hold. He likes prisons. Prisons have held him before. Kind of like bein' a fossil chained to a rock. A proper underground cell will do him fine. Like a museum case. He'll be so cadgy there he won't be going after my boys. But I'll send Cara with enough herbs to protect your property 'case he tries to show up again before you arrest him. Oh, oh, oh," she could scarcely contain herself. "We're goin' on tour and Hugh's goin' to jail and will not pass go and will not collect two hundred dollars and Elise'll never know it. Shazooms! Get the paper strips. Scatter the hair. Cara and Elbie will be there this week or I ain't their ever-lovin' Mother."

Monday. Sauntered past Marcie's not-too-watchful eye and noticed that John Fever-Claude Hopner's wanted poster had been removed from the wall but that no one had taken its place. Wished her good morning, because to my mind I was thoroughly up for monster baiting and so it was a good morning. Marcie responded with an anxiously cheerful, "Oh, good morning" that sounded like startled surprise with my apparent good cheer. She graced me with a super polite, strenuously blank expression that told me I was in hot water for missing the press conference last week but that Marcie was showing how "professional" and "neutral" she could be by pretending ignorance of my public disgrace.

So I settled into my desk and began to draw up a game plan for a "serious" drug task force meeting about establishing a viable way to get some real action and/or information on this alleged Boston-Providence drug ring, when Fearless rang my line. I knew it was him, so I let it ring a few times before answering. "Get in here, Morrow. Now." He hung up. When I showed up in his office a calculated twenty minutes later, after not answering my phone the second time it rang, Fearless was gulping down three or four of McCrae's heartburn pills with his coffee.

"Good morning, boss," I sang out pleasantly, settling myself into the brown plastic padded guest chair reserved for pols and other favorites. "It's a wonderful day. Have I got some drug enforcement strategies for you. Can you say—"

"Where the hell have you been all goddamn week? Kept trying to call your house—"

"Secrets." I rubbed the side of my nose in my best Crensch imitation. "Hey, where's my silent partner?" I looked around the room in mock dismay.

"I oughta suspend you, Morrow—"

"You did. Already missed a few days. But hey, sometimes you just gotta do it—"

"What the hell is the deal?"

"You mean you don't want to know who killed the imposter colonel?" I shrugged. "OK. Might as well take five then." And I stood up to leave.

Fearless's eyes bulged and blazed; he looked like a pathetic old animal losing his grip on a long-hunted lunch. "You mean, you mean—Pete—you think you've solved the thing?" I kept walking. "Wait, wait, let me buy you coffee—"

"No thanks." I closed the door to emphasize my seriousness and sat back down in front of him. "I think I'm close to being close to solving the thing. Had to do some last-minute private research last week. By the way, I did leave a message in Laffer's office that I was ill and couldn't make it—"

"Sure, sure, good thinking." Fearless seemed wonderfully reassured by the strange corroboration of our lies. "What have you got? Crensch mentioned something about his father's associates on Laffer's committee wanting this quiet, but he wouldn't be more explicit than that. Mr. Basher seemed rather anxious Thursday to get an arrest."

"Well, I think I understand their reluctance," I said in that absurd tone of courteous respect feds are supposed to use all the time. Great to prepare Fearless for nailing one of their own. "But I'm not in a position to discuss it with anyone yet. You'll be surprised, is all I can say, and I'm one hundred and fifty percent convinced that in the end Mr. Basher and Mr. Laffer and everyone else on the committee will be exceptionally grateful to you. Which reminds me, I need to take a quick look at the evidence bag." Fearless obediently called Marcie on his desk phone and asked her to get it for me. "Thanks, Marce." I debonairly took the bag from her as she entered.

"You're most welcome, Peter. Anytime." She was no longer blank politeness because Fearless was beaming his excited little "I'm happy with Morrow today" smile, so Marcie was sweetly beaming too. Overdoing it to assure me she didn't mean her earlier neutrality and that I was supposed to make the bad assumption that she was just busy working on something important earlier. "Anything else?" I shook my head so Fearless waved his hand to dismiss her. She wiggled her little duck walk and closed the door behind her.

"How much more time do you need, Morrow?"

"About a week. Maybe two." Fearless was jiggling around so much he could scarcely contain himself.

"Could I tell Mr. Laffer one of my boys is that close?"

"Sure, boss. You can say that something broke last weekend, and I'm in the process of sorting through the evidence to make an arrest that will stick." That rumor ought to mollify Hugh when he heard about it through Laffer's drug committee.

"Mob?"

"I'm hesitant to say. You will all be greatly surprised. But it's a bit delicate right now, so let me explain things to my partner. Like to follow 'need to know' procedure for the present."

"Right. I understand," said Fearless breathlessly. Crensch's line must have worked beautifully.

"Oh, and I'll be talking with Piekarski about another drug task force meeting this week. Got some ideas on nailing down the Providence rumors. Can't wait to get cracking to clean up America."

"Sure, Morrow, sure. You pull off the vanishing corpse thing and I'm putting you in for a raise."

"Settle for getting my ceiling repaired."

Fearless laughed at my humble ambitions.

I had brought the Hopner's Sardines note with me to work. Upon return to my office a quick glance confirmed that the handwriting matched the items in the evidence bag, as Penny indicated it would. Of course I believed Penny, but I learned a long time ago that it never hurts to confirm what you believe. Anyway, it was obvious that Cara had written everything, so Penny was playing straight with me so far.

Carefully copied the two strips of paper in the evidence bag by tracing my hand over hers, not worrying about fingerprints since my prints were all over the evidence anyway from having had the bag in my keeping at one point in history. I got the "Coca Cola vintage 1929, drink of generations. Eternal youth and eternal fun" with little difficulty, but the "eat well, fishie Worms are free and don't you know that every act is an act of love" with the skull and crossbones after the word "free" took some skill because I had to cut a circular strip of paper to match that one, but after one or two tries I pulled it off. Threw in McCrae's hair to better associate him with my forged placeholder evidence, and whispered a little prayer to Aphrodite to bless my trickery while shaking up the bag. Then I returned the bag to Marcie knowing no one would examine the contents too carefully. After Cara worked her magic on the original strips that I now had in my keeping, I would simply replaced my forgeries with hers.

Then I trooped back to my desk and called Crensch on his line. Crensch never picked up his line unless you rang a certain number of times according to some arcane code that depended on the month and the day and his mother's social security number, but today I must have hit it lucky because he did answer in a hesitant voice after two rings. "Uh, Crensch."

"Hey, Sid, get in here," I said cheerfully. He instantly obeyed, furtively closing my office door behind him. "Close the door, Sid," I said after the fact. "Guess you heard I missed the press conference last week—"

"What press conference?" asked Crensch in his best I-know-nothing voice. I couldn't tell if he was playing war games or if he really didn't know about it or both. "Just got back in town last night," he said significantly. "Went to Utica after all. On a hunch."

Damn! "Why? Sid, we're supposed to consult each other on those things."

"You weren't here."

"Yeah, well, all the more reason you should have been here, in the North End, doing mob duty. No telling what you missed in Boston."

"Plenty of mob duty in Utica," he hastened to correct me. "Heard some things. Found the psychic they mentioned in that article about you." It figured Crensch would go for the psychic, being a man of mystery and all. "Not bad. Read my cards and told me I'd have a long, interesting life. I'm the Fool. The Zero," he announced proudly.

"How much did she charge you for that piece of information?"

"Fifty bucks. Threw it on a voucher. Bureau will pay."

"Hey, Sid, I could have told you the same thing for less money."

"Yeah," he took the ribbing. "But the Fool card means I'm the place where decisions get made."

"Thought you were the FBI."

He laughed like that was a very good joke and when he finished, I realized in an unexpectedly touching way that he was sincerely laughing instead of making a social statement. There was something pathetically human about Crensch, and it occasionally showed. "Anyway, asked her about our friend the vanishing corpse, and she said two things." He held up a finger. "One. 'Protect the sun from motherless children.'" He held up a second finger. "Two. 'Do but slay this dragon and we'll give thee all our goods.'"

"That's enlightening." So far his little visit seemed harmless enough.

"Never know. Could be. But here's the zinger." He lowered his voice. "Also looked up that Thai restaurant, the one on your voucher from your trip to Rome last month. Got a deal going called the Neighborhood Protection Association that turns over a percentage of income to the Mob. Learned all about a man moving in and running Utica by the name of Nick Nariano—big cheese in town. Nunzio family bringing drugs into Utica, generating income for the local Mob and keeping lion's share for themselves." I pretended this was news. "Nick's runnin' all sorts of activities. Taking over the big boss's duties."

"Married his daughter. Probably take over everything when the old man kicks. Did you drop your name?"

"Naw, not my real name." Good. Crensch was obviously a fed from three states away, but he also obviously wasn't me, so maybe the Nunzios would think I was distancing myself or losing personal interest in their business affairs. "Used yours." I inwardly went ballistic. Even though it wasn't clear that Nariano knew what I looked like—I had fooled him at Fendra's—it was now clear, thanks to Crensch, that he knew I had some involvement in this investigation. Began to envy Marcie's ability to appear blankly unmoved when the situation called for it. "Cause a little confusion, you know? Make 'em think. Took your advice, flattered the mommas, sat in corners, listened and learned."

"What did you hear?" I asked evenly.

"Well, a waitress at the Thai restaurant mentioned a place called Lazzani's as being 'for the NPA' people, down in the Eyetalian section of Utica. So I went a few times. Heard a very high-level mafia meeting last Saturday night. Very high level," he bragged, leaning forward intently so I would take in the full effect of his discovery. "Saw the head cheese himself—Nick Nariano. Got the whole thing bugged too." Crensch showed me one of those under the jacket recording devices you're really supposed to get a court authorization for a Title III surveillance to use but which are sort of a gray area in terms of authorization when recording public conversations in public places.

"So, what have you got?" I asked.

"Well, Nick's lookin' a little worried. Comes in, joins a table of mobsters. Free pasta for all. I even got some 'cause Lazzani's wife had seen me coming in a few times. Anyway, here it is." He pressed the play button. Loud crackles and hisses.

"Turn down the volume, Sid. The whole office doesn't need to hear."

"Right—" Crensch adjusted the recorder.

"—got a problem." Nick's voice sounded sharp on the tape.

There were a few seconds of silence, in which I imagined his table companions all stopped eating in case one of them happened to be the problem.

"That musical program from Canada we've got going—that band we're supposed to be promoting—heard their backer's partner got whacked out in Arizona. That Claude Hopner guy who never seemed to wanta meet anyone."

"Yeah, never had a great feeling about that guy," said someone else. "Always half-doubted whether he was real."

"He's real. He's real dead. Now, I've been promisin' out money and gettin' people lined up to start shippin' these CDs we got down here into stores and gettin' some airplay. And Salerno here has been gettin' my people to start settin' up some club opportunities. So I start gettin' a little uneasy to think I ain't goin' to get back the money from my boy Elbie that I been out promisin' people on his behalf. Gotta reputation here."

Crensch stopped the tape and broke in. "You know anything about Claude Hopner?"

"Yeah," I forced myself to say lightly. "I know he's whacked. What else is there to know?"

"Yeah, well I've seen his name on the wanted list. When he was calling himself Mr. John Fever. Very interesting."

He started the tape again and Nick continued, "So, I call my boy Elbie last night and I say, 'Hey, Elbie whatsa matter? What's this I hear about your money-uncle not feelin' so good?' And Elbie says don't worry 'bout it. He's got my money, forthcomin' this week."

"What if he ain't got it?"

"Says he got it. Says I'm gettin' it soon as I show up at George Fendra's place. Look, kid says he's got it and his mother's vouchin' the same. Talked to them both this morning. Willin' to find out Monday night if he does."

"An' if he don't?"

"Then he better pray his CDs start turnin' round more money than he thought, or he's gonna find himself at the wrong end of the music business." Lots of laughter around the table, including what sounded like Crensch's. I glanced at him.

"So I laughed along, you know, to show no harm," Crensch eagerly assured me.

"That was clever," I commented. "Nothing like drawing attention to yourself."

"I know," he acceded. "Sometimes it helps allay suspicion. They noticed me laughing but didn't invite me over, even though I was sitting right there, at the next table." He had talked over the tape so I made him rewind it and play it from the interruption.

Nariano broke into the laughter. "Like to believe the kid. We got a grudge match here with a few folks at SBC Records and I like to believe the kid's gonna help us get our own little entertainment thing established. Give a young businessman a break, you know. Show some muscle towards the bastards who put away my father-in-law's people, doin' nothin' but record promotion so SBC could sell a product and chargin' a fair price."

"Yeah, Nickie, what was the deal there?"

"What was the deal there? The deal. 'Bout ten years ago, some of the big boys at the labels wanted some of my father-in-law's boys to push their records to the radio stations. Independent promotion, they call it. Good racket. Drive up. Pay a call on the station manager. Here's five thousand. Here's the record. Play the thing. See ya later. Clean, simple, the end. Nunzios made quite a bit of money on that one. Then some asshole gets in there on a white horse, starts complaining we're busting the budget, next thing you know there's an industry wide powwow and nobody's using us anymore."

"So why didn't he get popped?"

"Got bigger than him, Sal. Whatcha gonna do, pop everybody? Look, all I know is what was told me, as I wasn't there. Understand they got him in the pocket by yankin' off records. Stopped a few rising acts by gettin' records pulled off the air. Which he didn't like. Hell of a lot easier to stop a record from gettin' airplay than to ensure a record'll make it on the air after ye leave town and nobody's watchin'. We showed our honor there. Guy started gettin' it from artist managers complainin' how come my kids ain't gettin' promoted. Guys like Elbie McCrae don't give a shit how their records get airplay, so long as they do. So he tried to shut us down. But his colleagues got nervous and started funneling us money via 'tour support' budgets and such, industry began to waver, and Mr. White Horse there ended up lookin' the fool and ended up elsewhere. Then the Recording Industry Association of America tried to get Congress in it, and that went nowhere, no one being too willing to cooperate with an investigation."

More laughter.

"And then," Nick was suddenly warming up to his story. "And then—the RIAA was tryin' some bullshit to nail us on payola or fuckin' mail fraud or somethin' so they can turn around and claim they'se as innocent as the Virgin Mary's butt of our business practices, so that went nowhere fast. And there was this whole thing on a news program about the Mafia bein' in the record business, which was mostly shit, as everyone knows there ain't no such thing as the 'Mafia.'"

Lots of loud agreement.

"You know what the Mafia is, Sal?"

I could imagine Sal shrugging or doubtfully shaking his head.

"I don't know what the fuckin' Mafia is. Godfather movies and Marlon Brando—what do I know? Maybe the feds are the fuckin' Mob. What's the fuckin' Mafia—some boogeyman the fuckin' FBI came up with to scare people with—there ain't no fuckin' Mob—so some New York Federal Grand Jury begins to subpoena some bullshit documents from the labels, and there's a Senate investigation bein' started by some guy whose wife doesn't like rock music anyway, so what does she care who's promotin' it—and the next thing you know there's a trial on racketeering charges and RICO statutes and a lot of hardworking businessmen are out of the record business. So I says, I says to my father-in-law who lost his people in that one—if you can't join 'em, beat 'em. We'll make our own little record business—Moon Management, and run the other guys off the map. And that's what we're doin."

He slowed down long enough for me to picture him drinking from his wine glass and assume that everyone else was drinking from theirs.

"Salute. Now, I don't know much first-hand 'bout the music business, but Sal's in entertainment, and I know how to make money, so me an' the old man, God bless his soul—"

Lots of loud cries of "God bless the old man" for everyone's favorite mob boss.

"We agreed I should help start up this little business here—"

"—But Nick," protested Sal. "Someone gettin' wind of this little thing of ours might want it stopped. Someone this Hopner guy's double crossed, who might be after his money. If the guy's a deadbeat best to learn about it now, confirm once and for all what the future's gonna be."

"Look, my name's on the line, so I'll go see personally if Elbie has the money. And I'll talk to the kid about not seein' anymore potential problems. He's a smart boy, he'll see my point. Right now I'm more worried about who whacked Claude Hopner."

Mindless chorus of yesses and sures. Then, "Think it was the Iselli's?" someone asked.

"Iselli's," he spat. "Naw, it ain't the Iselli's. They know enough to keep their noses in Reno gambling and out of our affairs."

"Not the Iselli's," that same someone confidently echoed.

"You know, this Hopner guy was on the ten most wanted list," said Nick. "Occurs to me that he might have attracted a jealous follower—you know, maybe some joker thinks if he knocks him off he gets to make the list himself. Not everyone can be a classy criminal like us guys." So Nick had bought Penny's line. Although he delivered it like a joke and his colleagues dutifully received it as one, something in his tone suggested to me that he was primarily interested in getting his ego stroked by finding himself a real-life outlaw groupie. Got to be an ego boost to meet someone you've been led to believe would literally kill you to be you. "Sal's got a point about the money. But the bigger point is does the guy who whacked him have an interest in our little business here—which is why I'm lookin' for someone to find out who did it—"

"Got a cousin in Phoenix—"

"Yeah, and I've got a cousin on Cape Cod, so what? Well, I'm busy managing business, but anyone who figures out what the deal is surrounding Hopner and if it's a problem for us gets a bonus and my favor. Don't go crazy in there, just gather the information and bring it back and I'll make the decisions what's to be done. Got it? And no screw ups."

Chorus of agreement. Tape ran out. "That's all I got," said Crensch, rewinding the tape. "I'll make you a copy. What do you think?"

"When did you drop my name?"

"When I was leaving, which was right after the part you heard. Said good-bye to the kitchen momma. Said tell 'em Pete Morrow says thanks. Oughta keep the mobsters on their toes."

"Yeah," I said thinly. "Next time use a name they haven't heard before, to keep your confusion going, Sid."

"Well, what do think of the tape?" He looked like he was waiting for me to praise his espionage tactics.

"I think it's completely irrelevant," I said slowly and deliberately. "I think I found our vanishing corpse killer and it's bigger than Mob."

"Bigger than Mob?"

"Might even be bigger than government," I added significantly. Crensch gasped excitedly, silent mouthing the words back at me. "But it's also very, very secret. I mean I'll be working through special government channels to get the suspect, and so it's best not to spread too much information around too widely just yet." If that got back to Fearless and via Fearless to the NDECC, "the special government channels" part would sound to McCrae like I was working on concocting a case for extraditing Penny per his instructions. I wanted to plant the same useful ideas with my partner that I had with Fearless, because Fearless was sure to quiz him for details in case he could scrape up any further information to wax enthusiastic to Laffer about. I knew chances were pretty even as to whether Crensch's love of secrecy or love of bragging of his secrecy would win out under Fearless's cross examination. "I've just been tellin' the boss that something broke last weekend. By the way, need your father's number."

Actually, given my current plans, I no longer had any reason to contact Crensch Sr., and it is of course a fairly simple matter to get any congressman's office number, but I wanted Fearless to hear from Crensch that I had asked for it. Liked the idea of building up in his mind a series of maverick Morrow making independent contacts with the folks on the NDECC, because it might put the brakes on him saying too much to Laffer if he knew he might jeopardize my own promisingly arcane plans.

But at my mention of his father Crensch looked momentarily taken aback, like he had suddenly been briefly shaken with a dangerous bout of normality. "Uh, I don't know it offhand," he said embarrassedly, which sort of surprised me. "I'm sure you can call information for his Washington office." Then he recovered enough to ask, "Why?"

"It may concern him since he's on the drug committee with Laffer and Basher. Well, look, as I told the boss, the whole committee will soon receive the very good news that the vanishing corpse killer has been found, that the Mafia isn't overrunning Basher's district, and that Rep. Basher can claim he's tough on crime and help himself to a re-election and the drug war can continue without interference."

"Yes," said Crensch. "Nothing like a straight fight." Then he said a mite sourly, "Then since I'm apparently out of the loop for now, what am I supposed to be doing?"

"Keeping things zipped. Keeping things confused as to who's chiefly investigating the case should any reporters get bored for a story," I tried to think of anything harmless that would keep him out of my hair. "I'll be consulting you as things come up, because there's no telling when I'll need your expertise again. But, Sid, psycho killings are my thing, you know, you can't blame me for getting excited. There just aren't any domestic espionage type surveillance angles to the case that I'm aware of that your particular experience would be helpful in." He looked slightly mollified. "Look busy. I'll be in touch. Take it as a vacation Fred doesn't have to know about until we—" I emphasized the word "—*we* nail the guy."

"Yeah sure," said Crensch, unexpectedly rising with his tape recorder. I was capable of solving the case, he wasn't, there was nothing left for him to say. I hadn't meant to crush him like that but those were the inescapable facts. Then he smiled like he was willing to pretend we were still partners in more than name only. "Guess I'll go protect the sun from motherless children and do some dragon slaying with a psychic on the side." He wanted me to laugh with him so I did. Willing to relieve the mutual discomfort. Not entirely sure why.

Stave Eleven

Jade sent flowers. An explosion of red carnations, like the ones Cara was passing around at Black Dog's Fendra's gig, was leaning against my door and strengthening the sunset when I returned home from work the next day. Overnight delivery from Toronto. Like another dream. In the middle of the flowery blast was a handprinted note that simply read "thank you." It was unsigned, but I knew the carnations were from him. Had no idea if Penny had conveyed the new game plan or if he had sent them in playful appreciation of our last conversation. Put one under my pillow. Put the rest on my night table. Got me through the week.

Because Cara and Elb didn't show. I didn't think it wise to call, in case Nick Nariano should be at Penny's when the call came in. After Crensch's bit of sport with my name in Utica I could imagine all sorts of reasons for Elb not wanting to pay me a visit, especially since he and Nick supposedly had a little *tête a tête* Monday night. And there was no telling how long Nariano would stay in Toronto, or when or if he would be hanging out at Penny's to hear all about how envied he was. Besides, I was fairly confident that if something was holding up Cara and Elb, Penny would contact me.

But she didn't. So while waiting for my accomplices to drop by, and making up excuses to account for their delay and constantly telling myself that I would call one of Jade's bandmates on Saturday and make discreet inquiries if I heard nothing by then, I busied myself with planning and calling up a drug meeting and convincing anyone who'd listen that I was ready to fight the good fight for law and decency in America.

Given my rep, it was something of a hard sell.

Not that anyone felt comfortable openly objecting to my new membership in the club. For one thing, since the infamous newspaper article had recently reminded everyone of my admittedly stellar professional accomplishments, no one could seriously complain about my qualifications. For another, since I was only co-coordinating the drug task force by Fearless's divine intervention, I couldn't really be faulted for having inappropriate ambitions of my own. But the fact that my background wasn't in drug law enforcement and my personality wasn't particularly suitable for the special brand of flag waving mysticism that flourishes on that side of the house, meant that no real drug enforcer was about to mistake my recently granted authority for anything real.

It was all very well for the drug people to have me on board to observe and admire their stalwart dedication to some heady delusion of cultural relevance. And as long as Piekarski was grandstanding about family values and I was dutifully skipping meetings, my new confrères tolerated me with all the duress of workplace politeness as an ersatz co-coordinator with no real power to accomplish anything. But now that I had decided on strategically making our local drug war a Holy Cause so the word might get out to the Nunzios that I wasn't after them or their Utica drug trade, I suddenly found that I was upsetting a comically rigid pecking order with Piekarski and company that was clearly more important to their sense of how life was supposed to be than a drug-free America. Everyone wanted me to opine about the decline of morals in America and how great it used to be in some mythical decade before I was even born, when no one committed crimes and sex hadn't been invented yet and politicians never lied and Russia was still the enemy and the schools were better and no one knew how to spell communism; but no one really wanted a Johnny-Come-Lately to get too good at the schtick too fast.

Item. The more insistently democratic one is in one's mysticism, the more one resents sharing it. Let me explain. I'm convinced that the only thing the pope hates more than reprobate-agnostics like me are folks who try to be more Catholic than he is. Take my own experience with religious nuts. If you want to see a violent religious nut at his finest, don't lock him up with another nut from a different persuasion. You'd think there'd be a good show there, but there usually isn't. After introductions are made and they each tell the other how "lost" he is and how God or Allah or Buddha loves him anyway, they'll get bored and retire to separate corners and pray for each other or something. Each has his own little empire of insanity and sort of respects the other's borders. But if you lock two nuts up from the same religion, who differ over say the placement of a comma in some chapter or verse of their sacred text, watch the fun. You'll be lucky if the cell is standing fifteen minutes later.

The more one proclaims how specially appointed one is to save everybody by spreading America, God, the Family, Socialism, the Environment, wacko spirituality, obsessively inconvenient physical fitness programs, or anything else, the more resentful one is likely to be of getting outdone by any poor bastard who foolishly converts to the cause. Nine tenths of any belief system is being able to imply how special you are compared to the unconverted. But no one likes to be honest about this, because part of the myth of being "special" is also "being innocent of your own high excellence." Other people are supposed to make you a martyr, are supposed to take the hint and "notice." Otherwise, if you do get to be a victim, it somehow doesn't count. The game is you can't say that you are *trying* to be different because then it sort of becomes OK to be martyred and no one has to feel sorry for you. You have to pretend it's the most natural thing in the world for you to throw around some crackpot's original agenda as if you thought of it yourself, and then pretend to great surprise and sadness when "ignorant people don't understand." Which is why so many of the appointed feel compelled to always ask each other, "I wonder what he thought of my bloody cross, my environmental T-shirt, my Republican bumper sticker, my arrest record, my expensive imitation third-world clothes?" Not that any of these people ever wave these crutches to ego around to get *noticed*, mind you, or are looking to *impress* anybody by being different, they just always want to know what somebody outside the clique thinks. Condemnation is validation. Probably because they've all seen movies or read books about special people being persecuted and, by God, if merely being persecuted is the ticket to being better than everyone else, they'll be five hundred mediocrities lined up for martyrdom in the space of about thirty seconds. The lazy man's path to success.

So if too many people adopt your peccadillo without recognizing your prior claim, then you're not special anymore and a lot of the fun begins to wear off. You might even have to get honest work if you don't scramble to form a splinter group, find a new hobby, or start a civil war. Being able to both have your hypocrisy *and* blow your horn about it to other insiders is the closely guarded privilege of seniority, and I was sort of expected to pay my dues before making it my role to become an advocate of right living and clean thinking with Piekarski's little contingent.

Although everyone attended the meeting so they couldn't be faulted, nothing much was agreed upon except that we would now officially call our "new task force" SAYNO after Kanesh's serendipitous phrase, and get jackets and idiotic hats made up with FBI-SAYNO logos on them to show who we were in case we should forget or something. Anyway, Kanesh immediately undercut my agenda by asking and getting permission from Piekarski "to say a few words about last week's CNN broadcast before we get started." And so for about twenty-five minutes Kanesh puffed himself up by reporting that as a result of the CNN broadcast several other field offices, as well as local and state police departments and some deeply non-thinking high schools across the country, had contacted us for information on our PR activities. Then he read some hokey "letter of commendation" from the folks on the NDECC for our dedication to the war on drugs. According to the letter, SAYNO was not merely this year's name for our little anti-drug office clique, it was "a movement, a vision, a way of life and being, a program to make all our tomorrows and children's tomorrows brighter." Kanesh waxed positively spiritual over the concept. "Congressman Laffer would be pleased to be able to say that our Boston field office is coordinating a nationwide SAYNO program," he crowed as he handed the letter around. "Not that we here in Boston would be overseeing actual cases elsewhere, of course, but that we might act to coordinate other federal law enforcement agencies with the media. Consolidate public service announcements and media events designed to provide the public with a pro-family, anti-drug, pro-America message."

"What does that have to do with law enforcement?" I asked.

"Well, like the congressman says, the first way to fight drugs is through the hearts and minds of youth."

"Whatever." I really didn't care what his personal problems were. "But if we need manpower for an actual bust or something, I assume you're available?"

"Sure." He didn't sound too sure. Kanesh didn't go in for anything too rough if he could help it. "But Fred thinks it's a fine idea for me to go full-time into propaganda work. I've already cleared it through him."

Figured. "All right, then give us a weekly report on your media activities." Assumed that nobody else wanted to waste time with it. Piekarski looked a little put out that I had taken it upon myself to confirm Kanesh as our official public relations hack. He started to sputter his own agreement just to make sure that everybody knew I wasn't taking too many important decisions on myself, so I ignored him and sailed forward with all the enthusiasm I could muster, "Maybe you can get some publicity going about our interest in this alleged Providence-Boston drug operation. Let's showcase our cracking down on that as our first major SAYNO project. Let everyone know we're serious about keeping drugs out of New England. Mention my name." Figured I might as well put Kanesh to some use, but Piekarski wasn't done sputtering.

"Of course *we're* serious about drugs—"

"Which ones?" asked a too-serious-looking rookie, who realized his mistake after everyone laughed except Piekarski, who then had to join in with his irritated bark to show his people that he wasn't too dense to understand the faux pas. Piekarski's token laughter served to end the unfortunate disruption.

"I mean Morrow here ought to start acting serious—" Piekarski exhorted.

"About drugs, Charlie?" I asked earnestly, to another sprinkle of involuntary laughter.

"We missed you at the press conference. Where you been? Out crystal gazing?" Everyone smiled uneasily at Piekarski's bizarre reference to the more questionable features of the newspaper article. I swear the guy was fixated.

"This isn't my only assignment," I smoothly responded, my subdued tone loudly implying that I had been placed in charge of a high-profile, impossible to solve case so everyone was momentarily reminded of my superior investigative skills. "But speaking of assignments, it seems to me that there's a lot of smoke, excuse the pun, and no fire, about these Providence rumors. I'd like us to get serious about following them up. If drugs are getting into Boston that way, I'd like to put our investigative resources into gathering some facts about it, so we can formulate a strategy for making a dent in the traffic. I called this meeting so we could get some details and iron out a viable plan of action."

But in terms of getting a viable plan or even a vague notion on how to spring this Providence deal, I might as well have been selling hats at the local department store. Lots of street rumors, lots of thrice-told "one that got away" stories, but all anybody seemed to really know, the only common thread I could gather, was that some recently formed New England drug ring of otherwise unemployed low-lifes was getting supplies in off the Rhode Island coast and dealing some new brand of cocaine that was so evil and addictive that it allegedly caused death and convulsions through merely thinking about its effects. Which was why we had to spend so much tax money putting people in already overcrowded jails to show the evils of drug use; death and convulsions not being enough of a deterrent by themselves.

I didn't care. Even if it turned out to be mob related, I knew it wasn't the Nunzios because a) Providence has its own mafia, ask anyone in the Rhode Island state government; and b) the Nunzios really do try to put up a semi-legit image and so they don't go in for the secret shipment on the coast routine. Although I have no idea why. It's not like the feds are quick to nail anyone doing that sort of thing. The Nunzios get their stuff from local basement labs like the respectable underworld shoppers they are, and it gets home delivered in ordinary trucks and cars, so no one much notices.

Anyway, despite my full-faith attempt to take my new position seriously, our discussion went nowhere at full throttle. The resolution of the day was that Kanesh going to put together a PR kit, two agents were going on the street to track down more rumors, and we were all going to get new jackets and hats.

That was about all I cared to cover, when Piekarski suddenly sprang his own agenda item by "filling us in" on some dingbat organization called Christians for American Decency that had recently sent him some poorly researched, badly written "encyclopedia" that allegedly covered the proliferation of "secret Satanic cults" in the USA. I had no idea why these people were honeying up to Piekarski, but knowing Piekarski's obsession with all things bizarre, it wouldn't surprise me if he put his name on their mailing list. Anyway, the chief dingbat, one Mr. Joseph P. Heppelfauf III (why do these guys always insist on putting numbers after their names?), who listed his occupation as an "internationally known Christian researcher and expert on cults," had gotten his start in life by reading some hokey news story about some unidentified children finding a severed goat's head in a field near Plymouth and was now doing his utmost to milk it for rent money and fame.

I remembered the story myself as a Halloween hoax from five years ago, with the goat's head turning out to be sawdust and fake fur, but that didn't bother Mr. Heppelfauf. He was hot on there being a real goat's head, and so there was. Everybody's got to have a gimmick. His other big break came by way of hearing about some pathological "human sacrifice" case that allegedly happened in some undefined location in Guatemala eight years ago, but what more does an enterprising young crank need?

"Hey, Charlie." I really wanted to leave. "If these cults are so prolific and dangerous and everything, why haven't we heard about them before now?" Signs of edgy agreement filtered through the meeting, although no one was too eager to second my question, because no one knew yet what everyone else thought. One thing about cults, "Satanic" or otherwise. People will do amazing things to safeguard the image the cult represents to them. So if SAYNO was now a congressionally blessed about-to-become-nationally-known-super-elite drug force, *no one* was going to risk his more-American-than-thou image by disputing Piekarski's latest infatuation. If being an acceptable American superhero was about to be defined as doing battle with Satan, then the safest thing the brave SAYNO contingent could do was look carefully neutral, hear Piekarski out, and let Morrow ask the hard questions.

Piekarski was unflappable. According to Heppelfauf, who quoted plenty of unidentified police officers, the local cops knew all about the local Satanic cults, but if you asked any of them about it, they'd all deny it because was too dangerous to say anything.

"Maybe it *is* the local cops," I sallied, which got the expected laugh from everyone except Piekarski, who merely looked annoyed and went on to tell us in all seriousness that this "expert researcher" had "proven" that New England was bursting at the seams with "secret Satanic cults" that practiced human sacrifice on runaways and burnt the bodies so nobody except self-proclaimed experts like Heppelfauf could tell that a murder had been committed.

There were about a million ways to get into these cults, too, and Heppelfauf apparently knew them all. Through rock 'n' roll, drugs, Dungeons and Dragons type role playing games, computers, vegetarianism, dysfunctional families, MTV, violent TV shows, the Democratic party, the local grocery store (check the shelves, do they sell well-known implements of evil like tofu and brie?), Christian churches Heppelfauf didn't happen to like, radical environmentalism (the spotted owl was the devil's friend), Native American art, feminism, the list was fascinating and endless. A couple of guys sat there taking notes.

The fact that no one could produce any credible examples of this "cult epidemic" was only presented as proof that these cults were more secretive and dangerous than a Beacon Hill subcommittee, even though these same cults were careless enough to leave severed goat heads lying around in open fields and clumsy enough in screening applicants to get infiltrated by morons like Heppelfauf, who knew all about the hierarchies of hell but couldn't seem to get a simple declarative sentence right.

Anyway, you had to be very careful because your neighbor might be in one. Your *mother* might be in one. *You* might even be in one, or have *started* one, and not know it. Did you have bad dreams? Probably a result of "screened memories" of unspeakable practices. Did your dog have bad dreams? He might be possessed with evil energies. And of course taking him to the vet wouldn't help. It was great stuff. Really got Piekarski into a fine frenzy, because it was obvious from the encyclopedia that when these fearsome Satanists weren't having themselves a human sacrifice or dining out on tofu and veggie burgers, they were probably having a night of rip-roarin' sex and Piekarski sure as hell wasn't going to let that go on, not if he could prevent it.

There was one story calculated to give the Save-the-Family enthusiasts a hard-on about some bagbrain who "forgot" her six-month-old baby in a public playground while gassing it up with all the other available bagbrains about the latest deal in floor disinfectants and how wonderful her baby was and how hard it is to be a new mother.

Sometime in the middle of the baby brag fest, our heroine finally noticed that her kid had disappeared, so she up and did what any self-respecting, red-blooded young Christian American mother would do—she prayed a lot and sued the park. Months later, the border guards at "a major airport" notified her that "known Satanists" had been caught attempting to leave the country with her child. When she arrived at the airport, overjoyed that someone else had managed to track down the wonderful child she preferred discussing disinfectants to watching, she stretched out her arms and cried in delight to pick up her blanket-wrapped napping infant. Then her cry turned to a scream of horror, because as she lifted the child its chest fell out like a trap door, and she could see that its body cavity had been hollowed out and stuffed with bags of heroine. The border guards, of course, had noticed nothing.

So there was our drug connection. I could see it coming.

Apparently, some "secret Satanic cult" had stolen the baby as a "perfect specimen of humanity" to offer to Satan. Which meant that if the story were true, which I doubted, the mother would get to quote that line and feel special for the rest of her life, because she had been singled out for suffering by the high achievement of having a "perfect baby." The reason I doubted the story was because Heppelfauf was the only person on the planet who seemed to know about this incident, although he failed to explain where he got his information from. And his claim that the incident was too horrific and sordid for the American press to publicize was of course as believable as the border guards not knowing they had a dead infant on their hands until the mother got there, but shock value is shock value and why ruin a good story with consistency? And of course, no names, dates, or anything else too definitive was mentioned, so no one could check this out. But believe me, if there's a story with a baby in it everyone obediently goes bonko, whether or not the story is true.

I wasn't convinced that Mr. Joseph P. Heppelfauf was capable of reasoning out his own name, let alone the intricacies of these "cults," but he had Piekarski going to town and back. The dead baby story pretty much made his week, that and Heppelfauf's allegations that these cults were chock full of "homosexual practices," whatever that means. Take a guy like Piekarski that's as full of "family values" as a department store sales flyer, and he'll be the first to want to know all about someone else's sex life, just so he can complain about it. And it's always guys like Piekarski that make you listen to them describe in detail how disgusting someone else's sexual practices are, so I wasn't surprised when he topped off the whole incredible performance by reading off a detailed litany of Heppelfauf's Satanic sexual fantasies, some of which sounded pretty disgusting, I had to admit. Piekarski really got into the reading, too, so much so that when he stopped there was a tangible embarrassed silence in the room. "Well," Piekarski sighed in loud disgust, as if it had been a painful duty to read this stuff to us, "I just want everyone to be aware."

"Why?" one of my female colleagues asked coldly. It was safer for her to sound openly offended than it was for any of the men.

"Just in case."

"Just in case of what?" I followed up.

He didn't like the question. "Just to better educate and warn the public."

"You mean we should educate the public about homosexual practices?" I asked in my best serious-fed voice. "Maybe Kanesh ought to put out a press release."

"Hey, Allie," lisped a witty colleague, breaking the tension by flipping his wrist around in what was supposed to be a stunningly original imitation of a gay man. Everyone laughed except Kanesh, who sort of smiled and made a half-hearted attempt to lisp back just to prove he wasn't gay or anything. Which made me feel like punching him.

"I mean there's more than drugs at stake," said Piekarski, silencing the high humor. "There's a breakdown of morality in this country."

"And it's starting with guys like Heppelfauf," I protested. "Look, we're not going to put our resources into following half-baked leads from some crackpot organization like this. I don't care if there's ten goat heads in Plymouth. We're supposed to be a drug unit—"

"Yes, but it's sexy," Kanesh suddenly spoke. "I mean," he added as he caught a scowl from Piekarski, "stories like that capture public interest, make us look informed and up to date on the latest public concern, looks good for Congress. There's a lot of people out there concerned about the breakdown in morality, and this is one way of showing our concern. We don't want to seem naive." I was stunned. Only the government would define naivety as not believing in some crackpot's personal problems. "I know that Congressman Laffer has been hearing a lot from concerned church and religious groups," Kanesh continued as Piekarski nodded vigorously. "He told us all about Christians for American Decency at the press conference. They give to his campaign. And face it, a lot of ordinary voters are concerned about violence, and these are the sorts of stories the press likes to run, and our ratings go up when we are perceived as cracking down on what the public perceives as a threat—"

Our *ratings!* I had called the meeting with a good faith plan to crack open an alleged interstate drug ring, and we were actually assessing potential projects with an eye on their relative media possibilities. "Sure, Al, everyone calls their congressman to ask him if there's some way he can get the government to prevent their children from having sex with a goat. It's the latest national pastime. Why don't we throw in a space alien, too?"

Kanesh seemed to consider.

"You should talk, Morrow," said Piekarski. "Just because your article made your reputation look as sterling as it isn't doesn't mean you can waltz on over to this side of the house and set up some incomprehensible agenda for stopping drugs."

"You mean like nailing down a few rumors through street surveillance?"

"You're not dealing with the psychos here, you know." Actually, I didn't know. Piekarski looked a bit "psycho" at this point. He really did. If I saw him at the scene of a crime, I'd arrest him on general principles. "After all the flashy work you've done on the nut cases, I should think you'd be the first to support investigating the bizarre stuff." Piekarski really wanted that goat. "*I* don't know how much of this is true," he bleated angrily, "but I do know that where there's cults there's drugs"—the rookie sagely nodded his head at this piece of logic—"and that some field offices have anti-cult forces and we don't—"

"We've got Morrow," said the rookie, who hadn't learned yet to save his ass kissing for Piekarski.

"So?" bellowed Piekarski before he could swallow his envy. "Well, since Morrow understands the crazies, there's no reason not to use his expertise to promote family values and alert people to protect their children."

Kanesh, sensing what Piekarski wanted to hear, leaped in to ask why SAYNO couldn't use its mandate to stop drugs as an excuse for nailing these New England cults. Brilliant! Of course! I couldn't fuckin' believe it. Then we had a vote! We actually sat in the conference room and *voted* on whether or not Satanic cults posed an actual threat to mankind. And because folks tend to value their careers, it was unanimously in favor with one abstention, mine.

Drugs had suddenly veered from the source of all evil to a convenient excuse for nailing anybody we wanted to, or anybody some congressman's pet PAC wanted us to, without the inconvenience of the first amendment getting in the way. Then Kanesh had the nerve to suggest that I use my experience in missing persons to track and recover runaways that joined the cults. The DSS might even help. I didn't dignify that with a response.

But since no one besides myself was about to argue with Piekarski and I was willing to make a splash doing anything that would lead the Nunzios to believe I wasn't an issue in their new business interests, I reluctantly agreed to the new agenda. If the Mob thought the mighty Morrow was out busting kids for spraying 666 on a post office, what the hell?

The upshot was that the two agents with the most street rumors were commissioned to go gather more intelligence, Piekarski volunteered himself to personally interview Heppelfauf to get all the juicy details firsthand, and SAYNO initiated itself as the SWAT team of enforcing American values. Not just drugs, but Satan and the family, too. I actually found myself wishing Crensch were there to contrast and soften all the overkilling reality. It was an incredible lesson in civics.

That was the afternoon Cara showed up. She was waiting for me when I got home from work, sitting on my front steps in a detached kind of coolness and passing a joint to an impatient looking Selene, who was leaning against her shoulder the way a furtively innocent lover with an old sexless crush might lean. When Selene saw me, she slumped up into something like a sitting position without really moving, stared down at her spike-heeled boots in a kind of vague denial, like she didn't care to concede that she was really there or really anywhere, and took a drag. As I approached them, she slowly handed the joint back to Cara to avoid making eye contact with me. They had driven in Penny's beat up car, plastered with odd bumper stickers like "Zen works for a living" and "Don't blame me for God." One sticker was wordless and bore the faded image of a pink butterfly. A newer one had the Black Dog logo with the band's name in Gothic letters. Elb was nowhere to be seen.

"Hi, Pete, wanna toke?" Cara squinted a jaunty smile up at me and offered me the joint, as pleased to be on my front steps as Selene seemed tautly keen to be elsewhere. I noticed a large cloth satchel strapped across Cara's shoulder, open to the late September day with charms, and caught a whiff of lavender-orange herb scent behind the marijuana smoke.

I declined the offer and greeted them cheerfully, "Why can't you two go off and get high in the woods like a pair of normal scofflaws instead of risking being seen by every passing car on the road?" Actually there was very little traffic on my woodland road and my town was blessed with a highly understaffed part-time police force so I wasn't too worried about it. "Or did I just get the job of teaching you how to get away with enjoying yourselves?"

"There might be monsters in the woods," teased Cara. "Besides, we're not supposed to be normal. You don't want us that way." Selene sort of grinned her empty grin to acknowledge the joint being returned to her. When she smiled her face briefly reminded me of a gaunt sickly jack-o'-lantern carved in the wrong direction. "And besides that, what's wrong with showing the neighbors you've got two lovely young ladies hanging 'round your door waiting for hours just to get a glimpse of the super sexy super sleuth, Mr. Pete Morrow?"

"Never argue with lovely young ladies. Now, where's your brother?"

Cara scowled. "Elb's busy. Brought Selene along 'cause she's never been to New England before. Hope you don't mind."

Selene made a screwy motion with the edges of her mouth and murmured a few incomprehensible syllables but still avoided eye contact with me as Cara energetically stood up. Selene followed like a dull, stalky mushroom rising out of rot. When standing Selene looked even thinner than she did at the party, but that may have been due to her exceptionally tight pants that wrapped her little frame like thick spray paint on soulless sheet metal. Her eyes were as void as those cardboard pinholes kids make in science class to watch the solar eclipse through, and her face was tighter than a heart attack wound up and bursting through strangling veins. I didn't care for her "being there," but I cared less for making an issue about it since there was work to do and for the time being I had no choice but to trust Cara's judgement.

"Enter, ladies," I said magnanimously, unlocking the front door as Cara politely threw the roach in my front bushes. "Can I get you drinks? Something to eat?" Cara ignored the question and sort of swaggered inside like it was terribly big and friendly of her not to let on that she was accustomed to hanging out in more dynamically freaky places than my standard issue, split-level house in the woods. As if she could be charitable enough to put up with normality for a while to humor a poor benighted "good friend" like myself who didn't know any better than to live in such a conventional sort of dwelling. Selene conducted herself stiffly and uncomfortably to sit on the edge of my couch like she was chary of having any kind of noticeable presence here while Cara strolled around my living room inspecting everything and making condescending compliments that were intended to sound grandly appreciative. "Ooo, braided rug, just like a rustic log cabin. Ooo, thick brown curtains. Light fixtures, straight from the local department store I'll bet. Like your stereo system. *Pioneer.*" She oozed a sneery sort of approval, subtly letting me know that her brand of audiophile wouldn't be caught dead with an off-the-rack, low-end system like mine but that she was too compassionate to say so directly. "Where are all your books, Pete?" She wasn't really interested, just overgenerously indulging my boring little diversions and showing poor Selene what buddies we were.

"Keep a little study at the end of the house, along with my gun collection. Would you like to see?"

"Would I like to see a little study at the *end*? Books and guns, books and guns—Pete, you're so funny—ooo, stone fireplace. Gift basket from Mother," she added approvingly, poking a little through Penny's basket of herb packets and charms, which was presently the only thing on the hearth as I had recently returned my library books. She set her satchel down next to it. "Great place to set up an altar."

"Perhaps I ought to invert a broom to Hestia or something."

She didn't like the possibility of me crossing the line to *actually* setting up an altar. Her comment was solely to let me and Selene know how witchy she was. So she said "Hmm" and strolled across my dining room, which opens in an L from my living room. "What a large table to eat all by yourself at. Oak?"

"What makes you think I eat all by myself?"

"You mean you've got a girlfriend?" she squealed in genuine enthusiasm. "Tell me about her."

"Secret."

"Oh, come on Pete, you can tell me." She knocked on the table, pronounced it "sturdy," and passed into my kitchen. "Ooo, kitchen cupboards. Dishes. Appliances. Lookit this, a barely used toaster oven for the Lady's sake. You know, I always wanted to bake a cake in an ordinary kitchen. Just to see how it would come out. Nothing in Ma's kitchen is at all ordinary," she bragged, "and you never really know what you're going to get. Does your girlfriend bake? It must be really nice to cook things and know exactly what's going to happen." She said this like she was humoring me for something intensely childish, and then walked back into my dining room. "Ooo, sliding glass doors and an outdoor deck. Pete, you're so . . . middle America suburban, isn't he, Selene?" As if it were a miracle to her that anyone she knew would own sliding glass doors, but that she was cool enough to appreciate all sorts of surprising things. "Bet ya'v even got a wifey in the closet you're not tellin' anyone about, pardner," she said in a perfect midwestern twang with a curious John Wayne inflection. "Wallpaper with gold rose wreaths, can you believe this? Perfect straight cut wallpaper. Bury a corpse, Pete?"

"What do you think?" I asked Selene, who had been looking around through expressionless, pot-locked eyes because she thought I was too busy chatting it up with Cara to catch her in the vulnerability of displaying interest in anything.

She shrugged. "It's OK," she said flatly.

"OK, Pete, we're on our way to the Cape so we can't stay," said Cara suddenly. "Where's the stuff? Ma explained the plan to me, but why don't you tell me again what you need done?" Cara was suddenly all business. Just a young professional witch making an efficient house call. But she really didn't want my explanation, because once the desired impression of high competence had been plastered over her friend, she sort of snapped in a teasy feminine way that sounded more quarrelsome than the "girlfriend-cute" she probably intended, "Selene, go be a moon, and take a wander will ya? Pete and me are working." Selene sort of looked a silent shrillness at Cara, tensed up her shoulders, and wandered out the sliding glass doors, a shriveled moon reluctantly crawling into orbit. But instead of wandering she deposited herself on my back deck and dangled her legs over the edge while gazing blankly into the woods. It was fine with her to not have to hang out with us. Cara began drawing all the curtains, blocking Selene from sight and considerably darkening the house. I leaned against my pantry, watching her.

"How's Beth?"

"Beth . . ." said Cara, her tone implying that Beth was sort of falling out of favor. I could guess that she wasn't particularly thrilled with either Beth's attraction to Jade or her recent acceptance as the band's errand girl. "She's around."

"And your brother? My sources tell me he and Nick had a little meeting last Monday." Cara turned from the picture window she had just curtained, looking momentarily taken aback by my intelligence-gathering. "Been crystal gazing," I teased.

"Yeah, well, I wasn't there. Pete, why don't you get the letter and the handwriting samples while I set stuff up?" She didn't want to discuss the meeting and she didn't like the fact that I knew anything about it. When I returned from my study with all the necessary documents, Cara had emptied her satchel all over the floor and was lighting a white candle on my hearth. "You want to burn some incense?"

"Whatever you need."

"It isn't necessary for this, but I like to. Got some French Tea Rose from Juno. It's not bad." She lit a stick in my candle and shoved it in the crack between my hearth and fireplace. A plump, overdone rose scent filled the room. I showed her the writing samples, with the hand imprinted letter safely wrapped in plastic and bearing no tell-tale fingerprint from me and explained what I wanted her to do. She seemed to already understand.

"Pete," she lit up a cigarette, "before we begin, I gotta ask you a question." She was suddenly all serious and confidential, the Big Sister Wise Woman about to give me some sympathetic advice about the ways of the world. She hesitated dramatically, as if what she was about to say might be painful for me to hear but as if she were nevertheless strong and sensitive and concerned enough about my knowing the painful truth to say it anyway. Her manner was a dimly abrasive game. "Do you care about Black Dog?"

"Sure," I said lightly. "I'd like to see them succeed. I'd also like to top off this vanishing corpse case and move on to other things."

"Good," she said with slow, irritating approval. "That's good. Then it's good to put Hugh away. I like slaying monsters, too. But it's just as good for you to keep a distance, you know. Black Dog is working with Nick, and he doesn't like your line of work."

"Why should he?"

"Just let me tell you, Pete. All I know about the meeting." So the meeting was suddenly a subject for discussion. Apparently she had just thought of the right spin to put on things. She exhaled loudly to suggest that she wasn't sure she should continue but that whatever she was about to say would be rigidly true. "The would-be *don* is nervous about Uncle Claude's recent little accident, and your showin' up in Utica has pushed him over the edge."

Crensch's dropping my name after the mafia meeting he recorded was certainly having an effect.

"Not that Ma wasn't able to push him back, but no one wants any more problems. I mean, you're good people and everything, and you're a nice guy and everyone likes you, but the word from Elb is that it would be better for you to keep your distance from the band. Told me to pass along the message." She lightly puffed her cigarette and then took it out of her mouth and held it over my fireplace, tapping out the ashes and staring at the burning tip as if she would have me believe she was staring into a distant universe. "Ma says the same. My cousin understands the score, you know, and he's awful upset by the possibility of you blowing the deal. Told me so himself." I thought about the bouquet of carnations in my bedroom and smiled a little at Cara's clumsy attempts at manipulation.

"So what's your point?"

She smiled briefly around her cigarette. "So, I'm telling you if you care about helping the band, you'll nail the monster but you'll stay away. I wouldn't call. I'll take messages back if you have any."

"I don't have any. Just doing my job. So, *witch*," I changed the subject by making "witch" sound like a compliment, "here are the writing samples. I'm sure you're very good at changing *writing*," I added drily. She ignored the implication that I knew she had a hidden agenda of keeping me away from Toronto and told me to lay all the papers flat on the hearth. I did so, keeping the handprinted letter safely wrapped in plastic. She skimmed over the parking tickets and the voucher and the notes from the corpse and Juno's DIE DOG DIE! letter, which I explained was useless.

"Right, so take it out of the way. I need milk and vinegar like kids use for 'invisible writing.' Shake equal parts together in a quart container." I did so and when I returned from the kitchen, she had taken little plastic jars like containers from a kid's chemistry set out of the stock from her satchel. "Got any instant tea? Lipton's?"

"Yeah, sure."

"Bring me the canister. Or bags." I brought out a fistful of tea bags and placed them in the little fire-glazed bowl she had placed near the candle. She tore open the bags and filled the bowl with dry tea. "Tannic acid," she explained. "Water. Never mind yours. Carry my own." She poured some water from a little glass perfume bottle into the Lipton's tea and held the bowl over the candle. Then she mixed powder from one of the jars with the rest of the water in the bottle. "Sodium ferrocyanide—salt, iron, and poison. Just a pun." Then she took out a flat mirror and sprinkled and washed it with a rag dipped in the vinegar and milk combination. Once the mirror dried she sprinkled powder from a bottle labeled "Ferric Ammonium Sulfate" on it. "More iron and salt," she chattered.

"What's this Cara? Chem-Craft alchemy?"

"Doin' it the way my dear old mamma taught me. Now, you want everything in front of us changed to the monster's handwriting?"

"Well, everything should match the tickets and voucher. Don't obscure the handprint on the letter, and change the salutation to Dear Colonel Rinkowski—"

"—And the signature to Hugh McCrae, NDECC Committee Aide. Gotcha. All right, stand back and don't look." I did so, turning my back so I couldn't see what she was working. For fifteen minutes I heard an occasional chant in an unfamiliar language, and the hiss and splutter of the candle, and snatches of popular songs. I wandered outside to check on Selene. She was still sitting and staring where I had left her, tracing the movements of a nest of ants with her forefinger. She seemed to be in her own trance because she didn't respond to the sliding door opening and closing, although she seemed a little startled when I spoke.

"Bored?" I asked solicitously, sitting beside her and deftly assuming the same posture.

She shrugged like it didn't matter. She might be bored for all she cared. I had no idea how to make conversation with her. "Do you like New England?"

"It's OK." She kept watching the ants.

"Yeah, they used to hang witches here," I teased her. "Better hide Cara in the closet." Selene did not respond. I wasn't sure she'd heard me. "Do you like ants?" I tried. "There's a lot of them around."

"They're OK I guess," she said obediently and then added unexpectedly, "Sometimes I like the babies." She really was an odd sort.

"How do you spend your time, Selene?"

"Hangin' like the witches. Hangin' out." Her smile was a sloppy defense. "Doin' nothin'. Whatever." I was clearly making her uncomfortable by acknowledging her existence in my household. I tried one last time to fulfill my duties as host.

"So, Selene," I asked while feeling the absurdity of my question, "do you go to school? Are you training for a job or anything?"

Her eyes tracked back over the ant pile. I noticed the pile was surging over a dead robin at the edge of the woods and that this seemed to be a high point of interest for her. "Just hangin'. I might be a nun. Or open a shop somewhere. Or get married. Depends."

Sure. She had no life or plan for a life. She seemed to want to watch the ants in peace. I saw no reason not to let her.

When I went back inside, the French Tea Rose incense had lost some of its pungency because Cara had put out the stick and what remained of the scent was being eaten by cigarette smoke. Cara glanced sharply at me. "You can look now." She stepped back and dragged on her cigarette, intensely proud of herself. There was a mess of tea on the tickets and vouchers, "to make the writing disappear and inform the notes and the letter. Hard working through plastic but I've got that. Actually changing the names needed the sodium ferrocyanide to wipe them out and then the ferric ammonium sulfate to write them in. Through the mirror and back."

I inspected the writing. The change was perfection. I had no idea what her explanation really meant, but it really was quite an impressive trick. "How'd you do that?" I asked for clarification.

"Little bit of witchcraft Ma taught me. She got excited about the plan and worked out directions how. Don't worry your pretty little head about it, Pete. There's lots I can do if I choose. The chemicals have an essence I was able to transfer. But it isn't like real chemistry. Had to have iron in it to hold. Now, me and Selene'll go work a protection circle 'round your property."

"You mean Selene's a witch, too?"

"No, but she likes to watch." So she gathered up her things and I followed her out the sliding glass doors. Selene wordlessly slid off the back deck to join us, wearing indifference in the pale brevity of her mouth and eyes. As soon as I started to walk the two girls around the perimeter of my woods, Cara made us pause and watch her take deep breaths and chant something to the protective Mother Goddess. Selene studiously picked bark off a tree, although something in the stiff way she held herself told me that she was secretly hanging on to every one of Cara's words.

"Hey, Selene," I joshed, "don't you like to watch?"

She smiled awkwardly and shrugged, her face suddenly sweating like I'd caught her in a hopelessly compromising position. Then she continued picking bark, occasionally pausing to run her foot over the dead acorns which were littering the ground. Cara started strewing herb packets and incantations. Selene doubled over in a horrible coughing fit that reddened her face and shook her tight frame to the core.

"Go wait inside if you have to be a baby," ordered Cara, annoyed with the disruption. Selene valiantly tried to tag along for a few more minutes before plopping herself down on a rotten stump and letting us continue without her.

"She smokes up all my pot," complained Cara confidentially, "and then she gets too sick to hang through the freakin' spell. Complained about her damn cramps all the way here until I'm ready to give her womb the whammy just to shut her up. Selene's whole problem is that she loves this stuff, but it would break her ass or something to admit it. Same reason she broke up with her boyfriend, could never admit she might like him or anything, even though he was just taking her on motorcycle rides and using her for sex. She still liked him, I know, and if she'd ever said anything to him it might have been different but that's the way she is. So now she has to have one of her famous coughing fits just to prove she isn't all that interested in magic, but she'll be asking me a billion questions about it later, just watch."

But before I could comment, Cara pulled back into sorceress mode, chanting and scattering protection and scaring the birds. It took her more than an hour to do the property with all the undergrowth we had to tramp through, so it was just past the edge of dark when we finished and went back inside. "That ought to protect your premises from monsters, Pete. Ain't nothin' gonna get through any of that," she boasted as she dropped a little herb mixture on my threshold and we re-entered the house. By the sounds of a mindless sitcom blasting through my living room floor it appeared that Selene had left her stump and found my TV set, which I kept down in my basement rec room because I so seldom watched it. "Selene," called Cara impatiently. "C'mon, girl, we're going."

I imagined Selene's dull face fixated on the set and stiffening like a bug absorbing sweetness from an old candy wrapper. I stood there unable to shake the image of Selene's empty-eyed entrancement with some committee-written dialogue that wasn't even amusing two decades ago. Felt markedly unwilling to go downstairs and disrupt her canned utopia. It would be too much like grabbing a moth-eaten teddy bear from the stillborn grasp of a dead child. Then I just felt very sad, although I couldn't explain why. "Sure you two don't want to spend the night?" I asked, suddenly wanting to offer something to the dead soul downstairs while knowing the witch who seemed to be her keeper would grandly reject it. She didn't disappoint me.

"No, we've got some ocean magic to work. For the band. Want me to make an extra barrier where the monster came through before I go down and get her?" It was more of a boast than a real question.

"That would be my bedroom closet." I thought about the bouquet of carnations near my bed and added on a whim, "Yeah, Cara, sure. Would you mind doing my bedroom for good measure? I'd feel better about things." So she high stepped it into my bedroom, sashaying her satchel around like a second butt. But she didn't see the carnations because they weren't there. She saw Selene, who contrary to my assumptions, was catnapping on top of my bed. Selene's right arm had knocked the vase off the night table. I crossed to the other side of the bed to see that the vase was shattered and the flowers and water had emptied out onto the floor.

"Selene! Wake up, woman!" Cara leaped on the bed and slapped her shoulder, half-playful, half-annoyed. Selene gurgled and coughed, sitting up and staring at the wreckage she had caused without a trace of recognition. "Pull yourself together while I do the closet."

Cara performed her incantation while Selene rubbed her eyes and mumbled, "I was tired. I guess I dropped your vase. I was watching TV in it." We could all hear a commercial blasting into the room, louder than the show it sponsored.

"We know," said Cara, turning from the closet. "You ready for the Cape now, or what?"

"I had a bad dream," murmured Selene.

"So? Whatcha see? I can get bad dreams."

"Mice." She grinned. "Joke."

"Eeyore." Cara grinned back like there was something weird and private about them, like she genuinely understood and cared about Selene when no one else on the planet could. Cara's smile was surprisingly sincere for a second before it stiffened into something fake. "Hey, Pete, where'd you get the carnations?" she asked in bright dismay disguised as interest. She was looking at the "thank you" note sopping with water.

"Friend sent them."

"Must have been quite a friend." She sort of swallowed her words.

"Well, it was quite a night," I offered. "Brought me new understanding about my role in things."

"Good, that's good," said Cara uncertainly, looking back at the note. "I'm glad for you, Pete. Really I am."

"So why did you lie to me earlier?" I pressed her.

"Lie to you? When did I lie to you? Selene, do I ever lie to people?" She was really overdoing her innocence. Selene just grinned and took a sharp breath through her teeth. "What did I say? C'mon, Pete, what did I say?"

"That your cousin wants me to keep a distance. Which isn't exactly what he said to me."

"I only know what he told me," she whined. "It's not my fault if he's telling you different."

"I'll bet it's not."

Cara pretended I hadn't said anything unpleasant to her genial state of mind. "C'mon, Selene, we've got more magic to work. Gotta make the shore by midnight."

Selene looked blankly down at the scattered flowers and back up at me. "Thanks for the ants."

"No problem." I saw them out.

But back in my newly silent home, the carnations withered as I held them, and didn't really smell right. In an hour they were dry stems. I burned them with a prayer to Aphrodite. Then my house took on a musty odor for a few days, and despite Cara's best intentions, my closet kept creaking like an abandoned house eagerly catching an old wind.

Twelfth

For a few days the musty odor ran through everything like an undertow. I felt its stagnant slap and pull whenever I was alone. It creaked through my house. It loitered in my walls. It surged blankly through my night readings.

I felt like Cara had somehow opened all my inherent decay, that is, all my hard-earned aversion to life, when she performed her "protection spell" in my closet, and I wanted to try my hand at fixing things before her screwup became an unwanted invitation for McCrae to return. I tried scattering herb packets in my bedroom. Also around my house. After my awkward attempt at magic the days died brilliantly into October, but I felt no cleansing.

Called Penny about it after a bad night of must-encrusted dreams. This was a little over a week after Cara's visit, on a Saturday morning at the end of the first week of October. I had scattered herbs the day before thinking that Aphrodite would make my "spell" more potent on a Friday, Fridays being sacred to her, but the clearing I wanted hadn't happened. I kept dreaming that I was choking on something sickly sweet, and I kept waking in a horribly perverse sweat, and a man with a freakish face kept chucking and bowing and telling me I had to eat my old dragon if I wanted to get better.

Told Penny about the decay. Penny didn't seem overly concerned. Didn't care to hear about much except my progress towards putting Hugh in prison. When I insisted on describing how the carnations died in the aftermath of Cara's spell, she sharply cut me off.

"—Pete, did she change the *writing* in a way you could use it, like she was suppos'd?"

"Yes, there she was utterly convincing." I told her how I had already switched Cara's work for my temporary forgeries in the evidence bag.

"So she did her job. What do you want? Is the monster in his prison, then?"

"Not yet, Penny. Soon. Any day now."

"So what's *your* freakin' delay? Pete, there's a tour comin' up I wants to go on." This was the first time I'd ever heard Penny whine.

"Management problems. Took me a solid weekend to write a convincing report. Dropped it on my boss Monday, and he's probably taking his sweet time testing the waters before authorizing the arrest of a congressional aid. McCrae is a congressional aid, remember."

"Yass, we knows that, Pete. What's the diff?"

"Means we can't afford mistakes—"

"—Which is why we'se countin' on you not to make 'em." She was scolding me the way she sometimes scolded Elb.

"Well, then it was essential that I construct my report in such a way that even the most dunder-headed prosecutor can derive an argument for not letting him out on bail. You know the press will be in it. Want to feed them as much outrage as possible to whip up the public against him, so I needed to provide a lot of easily lifted sound bites." I winced when I realized how similar to Kanesh I was suddenly sounding.

"How you doin' that?" she asked suspiciously.

"By throwing in all the grand mystery of the universe. Hammering on all the strange details of the vanishing corpse matter. Putting potential headlines in caps so the flunkies who skim these things and sell government sensationalism to reporters don't have to work too hard. Then there's the investigative issues that snagged things a little this week. I'm claiming I found the handprinted letter in one of Rinkowski's files but forgot I had it. Been carrying it in a briefcase compartment I never opened all this time, which no one will believe but no one can disprove. Then I heard of Mr. McCrae via my boss, and since his name matched the letter writer's, it reminded me of the 'forgotten evidence,' and I suddenly got suspicious. Sent the evidence bag to our lab to analyze the hair samples for a DNA matchup. Had to explain in triplicate why they weren't analyzed before, but the sticky part will be getting him to donate his own hair to see if there's a match. There are government records of his fingerprints on file, so the handprint may be enough but the DNA matchup is extra insurance, then—"

"Huuhhm, Pete, bureaucracies and procedure been protectin' that sort since the slaves started runnin' the Roman Senate. But we're tourin' out of Canada by the end of the month. Cain'tja just arrest him and make it go faster?"

"If I could we wouldn't be having this conversation. Look, chances are that since McCrae works in Washington I wouldn't be making the actual arrest anyway. My job is helping to compile evidence for the prosecution."

"And gettin' the public in a frenzy on our side to keep him locked. All right, then, we'se waitin' for it."

"Speaking of mob frenzy, what's happening with Nick?" And I explained how I knew about the meeting between him and Elb.

"You're good, Pete. One of my own." She chuckled. "Took care of Nick. He got paid. CDs are out—bein' distributed all over the continent even as we speak. May be gettin' some airplay up here in a few days. Tour's on. Startin' up here in town next week for a few consecutive weekends at Fendra's. Elbie, my sweet starstruck son, is gettin' us press. George Fendra's puttin' up money for some local PR, bless his heart."

"Yeah, Penny, do you know Nick's boys are looking for Claude's killer?"

"No, I didn't but so what? Let Nick's boys figure out what they can. Ain't gonna be much. Ain't yet seen any of Nick's boys too good at figurin'. My lord Dionysus Hopner is tipplin' ocean-wine in a shadowy Olympus bar right now and his killer's gettin' whammied up in jail. Fair is as fair does and what the hell they gonna find?"

"Right now, nothing."

"Thass right." She sounded strangely self-satisfied.

"But I'd love to help them find McCrae. For extra insurance. I can get an anonymous tip to my colleagues in Phoenix to shadow the Mob, and once Nick's boys discover McCrae did it, the feds'll be happy to move in and take credit. Then if the press gets the notion he's a cannibal, you'll never see him out of jail again. I'd put my money on the Mob finding him before the government does, if he is to be found at all without us seeming to interfere. Got an idea how you might set Nick's people on the right path?"

"The monster did it. That's the right path," she said helplessly. "But if that ain't enough to nail him on, I don't see where we're gonna go, 'cause there ain't much else. Gotta have all the bells and whistles and fancy DNA stuff nowadays for the government to believe anything. Used to be ye just offer up a bullock."

"Would that help my house clear?" I sort of joked. Figured she was right. If anyone was eager to nail McCrae for something Penny was, so if Penny had no idea how to send the Mob on his trail I was convinced that for the moment there was no way to do it and our current strategy would suffice. But now that the subject was exhausted, I tried again to get her to explain what Cara had unleashed in my house. "Penny, I need to know what your daughter and her friend Selene were doing to my property to make it feel like the spirit of Hugh has taken up residence. Some of my books actually have mildewed pages."

"Didn't know she went with Selene," Penny said slowly. "That one. Huuh, well. Look, Pete, I'm sure it'll settle as dust generally does. Girls is girls. Cara may have done something backwards, or some decay got released from where it had been hiding or living in your closet as a prelude to her clearing. Sometimes Cara gets over excited about things. 'Specially with the tour coming up."

I thought Penny was "overexcited" herself where the tour was concerned.

"But you'll get him, don't worry. Here, Jade wants to say hello. Not that he ain't been listenin' through a herring bone in a saltwater bowl," she added. "Gotta pair of boys here and neither one can say hello to the other's dreams and yet they both think the world would crack if they didn't—"

"Hello to your dreams," said Jade smoothly. "How's tricks?"

"Hello to yours, buddy. How you doing up there?"

"Better and better, Pete. Hear you've got some household must."

"Nothing I can't clear. Your new priestess is a lousy housekeeper. Left me with a bit of a mess."

"I heard she killed my flowers. Have to fire her." He was charming me by his easy allusion to the gift.

"So you *were* eavesdropping. Picking up my bad habits?"

"Yes, was I any good? You're the professional."

I laughed and admitted, "I told Penny the flowers died." Then I added, "Selene knocked them off my night table," just to let him know I had kept them near my bed, but I felt awkward as soon as I said it, so I didn't tell him how I burned them as an offering to Aphrodite. He sensed my discomfort and graciously changed subjects.

"Just dropped by with Les for a minute. Which means Beulah has been plying him with grapes and he's been eating them and complaining about the attention for about an hour. Lucky you called to save me from having to watch—"

I heard Penny's voice rasp loudly in the background, "Juno, can ye keep Beth out of the kitchen while Jadie's on the phone? It ain't her business so stop bringing her in it. Why don't you two go out and see where Cara went off to?" Juno wailed something in a voice of protest, but I couldn't make out the words because Jade was speaking over them, telling me how grateful the entire band was for my support, and then I heard the sound of a door loudly slamming.

"Penny says your tour's starting and you'll be out of Canada by month's end. That was quick. Don't you need to book clubs months in advance?"

"Depends who's doing the booking."

Yeah, the Mob could be amazingly efficient with some things. I wondered how many acts were getting bumped or shuffled into opening band position to make room for Black Dog. Then I remembered the years they'd been struggling and bumped around and tried not to think about it. Fair is as fair does. "Does that mean I'll have the pleasure of hearing you on the radio soon?"

"You'll definitely hear us out of Boston and Hartford and Providence. And New York, if you can get New York stations from where you live. Utica and Syracuse are in the bag. If you're in the Northeast, you'll hear us soon. The rest of the country will hear us relatively soon. Nick met Elb last week and Nick's people are coordinating airplay dates with our tour."

"Could Elb send me your itinerary?"

"Our what? We are about to become wandering minstrels following the wind and the stars and you want something like a tour schedule?" he teased. "I'll see what I can do. Our stuff has been getting shipped all over, but we're supposed to start heavily in the Northeast. Could be playing around New England periodically for a while. Supposed to be playing in Worcester on Halloween."

"Don't sound so happy," I congratulated him.

"Why don't you come hang out with us? Club called Morgan Le Fay's."

"Rather keep a distance from your promoters for now."

"Promoters got better things to do than go to gigs. Besides, my lord heretic, the dragonking commands you to enter our realm and partake of Paradise. I'm missing you in the night sky. I'm missing you in the heat of the lonely moon," he sang playfully.

"I'm missing you too," I said straight and bravely, without the mask of poetry, because it was a phone conversation and I didn't have to face him while saying it. "Call me when you get in town. We'll go out." I tried to sound casual, but I heard myself sounding slightly demanding instead, and I worried for a second that he might take offense to my tone.

But he pleasantly surprised me by saying, "Sure."

Did another scattering. A few days later, the mustiness dissipated and the creaking stopped. Felt my house gradually clear. But I couldn't honestly determine if the clearing was a result of my clumsy attempts at turning Cara's household magic or if the sudden decay had simply run its natural course as Penny predicted it would.

Item. The first day my house felt fully healed was the day I learned McCrae had been arrested for the murder of the imposter colonel and transported to a federal prison in Lewisburg, Pennsylvania. I decided that whatever actually caused the healing, it suddenly felt as if the monster was safely locked up with all my household decay, that the two were chained and connected, and I was now utterly free.

Learned of McCrae's arrest via CNN, which I was now making it a nightly habit to watch because reporters often get news of things like that before I do. Irked to see Crensch's name linked with mine and touted around like he was really half-responsible for cracking the case. Not that I was surprised, because Fearless had previously made such a public issue about us being partners on this one. What irked me was the story's content made it clear that Fearless had notified the press even though it took him one or two days after the broadcast to congratulate me on my fine work and make it official. Told me I had gathered enough hard evidence to satisfy the prosecutors and that although I might be asked to testify at the trial, I needn't gather any more. Thanked me for my efforts and told me to concentrate all my energy on the drug war. Then he popped one of McCrae's strange little pills.

I was pleased to learn later that bail had been denied, no doubt because of the intense public scrutiny surrounding such a sensational case. As I predicted, the NDECC publicly dropped McCrae like a hot fossil. Congressman Laffer deftly distanced himself by promising to throw the whole force of a government investigation against his former aid, Basher seconded, Congressman Crensch, who reminded me of someone doing a bad W. C. Fields imitation, roundly praised his son's investigative efforts, and McCrae was locked up to dry. Yes!

Crensch also disappeared. Figured he was celebrating his unearned success by going incognito to spy on college students in the Bahamas or something. Or maybe he'd been reassigned to the consulate. Wondered once or twice where he might be put next. Was sort of grateful it didn't appear to be SAYNO, then gave his absence no more thought because I had more immediate things to deal with, like keeping up my studied role of being utterly devoted to winning our local drug war by chasing Satan and striking a death blow for good old-fashioned family values. I had originally thought I could drop the charade once McCrae was in prison, but the press did me the grand favor of bringing up all the old mob rumors surrounding the case, along with all the other empty mysticism any discussion of the vanishing corpse seemed to require. Which meant I could safely rely on the media making the Mafia a third party to the thing whenever they needed copy.

Worse, right after the arrest, CNN did a special segment on "how the FBI found the killer," advertising to all the world for the first time that I had originally been sent to Rome to investigate the alleged drug deals of a Private Claude F. Hopner, now "widely believed" to be the same Claude Hopner who, in the reporter's brilliant mangling of the English language, "made the ten most wanted list for robbing trains and being cannibalized." Only Fearless or Crensch could have released that tidbit, and I had to wonder whether Crensch had shared his Utica tape with the boss. I would have been surprised if Fearless had remembered on his own the name from the tape of Elb's call that I had so competently destroyed.

So Nariano would not only still have reason to believe I might be willing to interfere with their Utica drug business under the misguided notion that they had any further goods on McCrae to offer me, but my sudden public association with Hopner was bound to make him antsy. Even bet that since he was sending his boys to find Hopner's killer, he'd be sending a few to shadow me in case my actions had anything to offer them. Especially since Nariano now knew that I had been present on the base looking for Hopner the same night Black Dog had been playing and the "murder" happened. I decided it was important for me to keep up my public persona as a local drug czar for the near term. At least until after the actual trial when the press interest would die down, which would be in a few months.

I realized one highly effective way of letting the Nunzio family know that I wasn't actively concerning myself with anything touching them was by constantly collaring Kanesh to use my name in all of his PR releases about SAYNO's interest in Boston-Providence traffic and hoping the local Mob would see for itself that Morrow was too busy chasing their civilian competitors and effectively giving the Mafiosi an edge on the drug market to hang around their North End doorsteps. Got him to throw in Piekarski's family values rap for more confusion. Perhaps my role playing was overkill, but I wanted to err on the side of Jade's interests if I erred at all, and I figured it couldn't hurt to play the media on this one.

Kanesh was happy to throw my name around everywhere, of course, especially since I had made another media splash with McCrae's arrest, and he figured anything media would impress Fearless, who would be happy to impress the NDECC, who was carrying on a hot and heavy romance with SAYNO anyway. The *Herald* ran one of his releases on the heels of McCrae's story. So it wasn't hard to get the message out that I wasn't concerned with the Nunzio's Utica trade, and I reassured myself that it was likely that Crensch's stupid ass generosity with my name in Utica, while certainly not forgotten by Nariano, might be viewed as no longer a threat, so long as I kept up the public illusion of my newfound zeal.

So despite potential snags, things were looking up. Devote myself to Boston drug problems, stay out of mob work, Jade was coming to Worcester, and life was mighty fine. Even work got tolerable because I was able to use my position to delegate all the scut work. Even Piekarski's threat to bring his high holiness Heppelfauf in to speak to us in the near future was more funny than annoying. Now that I knew a real witch or two, I kind of looked forward to Heppelfauf's rant for its enhanced comic value.

Jade called me from Penny's after the news of McCrae's arrest got reported. I was reading John Donne's crazy sonnets to one of my Aphrodite candles, which I was burning to celebrate my recent victory and sudden house-healing, when the greatest bass player on the planet demonstrated his perfect timing by ringing the phone as I finished the last line of Donne's sexual expression of his love for God. "Nor ever chaste except You ravish me," was still twisting through my mind in divine verbal figure eights when I picked up the receiver and heard a slightly hesitant, "Hello, Pete? How's your world?"

"Hello, Count," I responded cheerfully, still high enough from my candle reading and recent law-enforcement success to make a light reference to our word game before self-consciousness set in. Also damned pleased that Jade would actually call me.

"Thank you." He paused. "My lord." Then he let silence and his open acknowledgement of our word game convey his gratitude for the arrest.

I broke the silence by quoting Donne, "Let us possess one world; each hath one, and is one."

"Whatever dies was not mixed equally," responded Jade easily, quoting from the same poem. "Figured I'd find a tough guy like you reading poetry on a night like this."

"Sometimes it takes a tough guy to read poetry," I responded amiably.

"I know," he said seriously. I wondered if he was thinking of the morning he woke me with Wordsworth. Then, "Well, buddy, my good aunt is throwing a celebration to kick off the tour. The whole band is grateful to you. You're our hero and deserving of the palm of victory. Come be our guest of honor this Saturday. See a gig at Fendra's. Spend the weekend."

"Not sure about gigs—"

"Why not? If you're worried about my mother, she never goes. She'd sooner die, trust me."

Penny had clearly conveyed Elise's threat against me to Jade, although I wondered if he appreciated that if she did notify the field office of my interest in him and his band, it was more likely to put his career in jeopardy than mine. Didn't need Crensch making side trips to Toronto.

Explained the situation again, including Crensch throwing my name around in Utica. "You're slippin' up, guy. Thought you were paying attention the last time I called, when you were listening in on me and your aunt. Now that the press is linking me to Hopner, I'm not even convinced Toronto is a good idea. Your gigs would be a logical place for any guy with Hopner associations to hang out. Nariano's sure to have people at the club and some of the Nunzios know what I look like. For now I'd rather not be seen at your gigs."

"So don't be seen. Be cloak and dagger about it. Nariano didn't recognize you the last time you were at Fendra's. And from what you just told me, he thinks you're Crensch."

"Why take the risk?"

"What good is a gig without a risk?" he teased.

"*What?*" I was momentarily stunned. "That's a hell of a risk to your career, Jade."

"Joke," he said quickly. For some reason I thought of Selene and Cara. Penny grabbed the line.

"Pete, been listenin' in the bowl. And now my pet's got crushed puppy eyes that Momma has to take care of. Ya comin' up to meet his fancy or ye gonna stew down there for rats? It ain't always easy to ask, as ye oughta know."

My desire to see Jade fought valiantly against my judgement. "No gigs," I said noncommittally, knowing he was probably listening, feeling weirdly flattered that he was hurt by my refusal to make the trip.

"All righty, then, stay here while my boys play out. I wouldn't have ye here if I thought there'd be an issue. Ah kin keep the Mob from the door for a day or two."

"Rather not have my car seen in your driveway."

"So don't be seen, as Jadie's smart enough to say. Ain't need a wicker broom or basket to fly and rent a car."

"All right, tell him I'm coming. But not to Fendra's. I'll stay at your place while they perform." And drive Elb and Cara over the bend, probably.

"Youse coming, that's enough." She clicked off before I could tell Jade myself. Probably wanted to take credit for my own change of mind.

Late Saturday morning, October 10, 1992.

Stopped outside Penny's kitchen window and spied on Cara and Selene. They were sitting at the table and passing one of Beulah's paint pots back and forth, twittering like a pair of cruel birds. That is Cara was teasing and giving vague orders to Selene, who was responding with little smile-grimaces and private sounds like she enjoyed the special attention of Cara giving her orders but wouldn't go quite so far as to actually show her enjoyment through open obedience. But she sometimes dropped her grimace and smiled quite broadly and sincerely through Cara's banter, more than I'd seen her smile before. She liked being alone with her witch-friend. Cara kept giggling and dropping some powder in the paint pot that caused a vague sea breeze to escape from the window whenever she stirred it. Somewhere at the back of the sea breeze a tea kettle was bursting out tiny storms over the stove and when Cara told it to shut up it did, to Selene's great amusement and Cara's obvious edification. The rest of the house felt as silent as an old oyster's winter sleep.

But the instant I sauntered into Penny's unkempt kitchen, Selene sprang away from Cara, tightening up like an excruciating philosophical argument in a head-on confrontation with some inevitable inconsistency. "Hi Pete," she said in breathless friendliness, as if I was suddenly a welcome excuse to cut off her friend's banter.

"Hi Pete, how's tricks?" said Cara, seconding her friend in a kind of brightly phony innocence as Selene made an ugly blushing kind of giggle. Elb wandered in from the living room, looking irritably half-awake, his hair and clothes as mussed up as the kitchen, and told his sister to shut the fuck up. The kettle started screaming again. He swore at the kettle but the screaming only got louder. I had the feeling Cara was doing it.

"Hey, what did I say?" asked Cara. "'How's tricks?' What's wrong with that? Just bein' friendly. Just want to know. Pete knows I'm teasing—"

"How's tricks, boss?" I greeted him.

Elb courteously gave me the same greeting he gave Cara. Clomped up to his sister's apartment, each heavy footstep conveying his utter disgust with the world.

"Elbie's in his usual fine fucking mood," announced Cara. "And leave my altar offerings alone!" she screamed after him. "You screw with my Black Dog altar and I'll give your girlfriend herpes *and* a taste for gossiping about it."

Selene giggled at the threat. "Who's his girlfriend?" she asked with a contorted sort of interest, as a kind of distracted looking Beth delicately entered the kitchen from outside with a wrapped package in her hand. Cara sort of arched her eyebrows and looked at Selene as if to say, "there," and Selene mumbled a few low breathy giggles of acknowledgement.

"Hi," said Beth, struggling out an uncertain friendliness towards the two girls. I could tell instantly that there was a large unspoken strain between Beth and Cara that Beth was desperately pretending wasn't there, and that she felt but couldn't prove that she had been the subject of Cara's contemptuous glance. Neither girl greeted her so she turned to me, "Oh, hi, Pete. Didn't know you were coming—"

"—Hi," interrupted Selene.

"Am I early?" asked Beth nervously. "When Juno called she said to come around noon—"

"—Juno said to cum at noon," repeated Selene in a kind of drafty imitation excitement meant to be funny. She was certainly in an odd mood.

"—Juno said. Juno said," mocked Cara, all quick smiling enjoyment over Selene's pun. "Juno says a lot of things, most of them wrong. No, you're not early. The band's late, crashing upstairs in my apartment, where the party's to be. Always put up my boys after a gig. Should go see if everyone's decent. They might not be, you know. But first, come let me look at you."

"Look at me?"

"Come, come, come," ordered Cara in a too thick affability. Selene made gulpy noises like something laughing. "Let's see if you're ready."

Beth walked over to the table in embarrassing obedience to the witch's orders, doing her utmost to hide her discomfort under the practiced agreeability of her profession. "Were you talking about me when I came in?" Beth asked uncertainly, trying to tease the question as if it didn't really matter as Cara made an issue out of inspecting her poor looking jacket and jeans.

"Yes," said Cara. "We were." Admitting it was supposed to make it all right. Selene nodded seriously. "You pass, your clothes look fine. You know my brother likes you? He really does." Selene started laughing. "He was upstairs talking about you with the guys."

"Oh," said Beth, shrugging and making a face while rolling her eyes towards the upstairs, her posture suddenly hampered into an exquisitely tight neutrality. "I didn't know."

"You two ought to go out. I can fix you up. What do you think, Pete?"

"I try not to involve myself in matters of the heart," I said with exaggerated politeness as Jade sort of slouched into the kitchen. I hadn't heard him descend the stairs.

"I'm disappointed," he said carefully, "matters of the heart can be a lot of fun."

"Mornin' cousin," said Cara. "Last night was a lot of fun."

"Mornin', Pete," said Jade. "How doth your lordship on this many a day?"

"Excellent well," I replied. "Maybe you should call your next song, 'Matters of the Heart.'"

"That would be a great name," echoed Cara.

"That's what I call all my songs," Jade responded playfully, looking at me.

"Hi, Jade," said Beth in a voice too strong for shyness and too hesitant for poise, a voice that sounded too innocently pressured to be properly anxious. "You were awesome last night." She said this shakily, conscious of Cara's presence but more conscious of Jade's and determined to speak anyway.

"Thank you," he said, still looking at me, "I was inspired." Beth's eyes flushed. Cara studied her icily while Selene suddenly had sickly eyes like a distempered cat. Then they both studied me. Then Cara sort of shook her head and smiled up at her cousin.

"I couldn't believe it when you dedicated 'Storm Season' to me and then went right into that new song I like, 'Night Currents.' That's the first time you played that one out, isn't it?" asked Beth.

"My cousin dedicates all his songs to everybody," deflated Cara. "Who was that fat guy with acne you dedicated 'Poison Puppy' to?"

"I don't know. Some guy who liked it," he said this like he was sort of teasing me for liking his stuff.

"I don't like 'Poison Puppy' as much as your other songs," offered Beth, as if saying something negative might somehow make amends to Cara for having a song dedicated to her. "It's kind of sad and strange."

"So are some matters of the heart," Jade responded lightly, looking at her for the first time. Beth looked profound and grave under his glance. Suddenly Cara no longer existed. I could imagine Beth repeating that remark to herself for months, or writing it in her diary six thousand times or something. Words too sacred to profane by sharing them with any living being more distant than her own secret soul, words fit only to crown a dream or die a softly unspoken death inside one's dimly passing youth. Then he turned back to me. "Anyway, top o' my life to you, your lordship. Penny's making breakfast upstairs, and my mates are starting to rouse, if you care to join us."

"Called your mother," said Cara suddenly. "Told her you were here so she wouldn't worry."

Jade looked at her with cool irritation. "How thoughtful," he remarked.

I was not cool. I rode roughly over his words, anger squelching discretion. "Why?"

She ignored me and turned to Jade. "I can be very *thought*ful on your behalf, very Apollonian if I choose." If her tone had been three shades duller, it would have sounded like a threat. Instead, it sounded skillfully bright and teasy. "Anyway, I *thought* she might like to know where you were," she glanced at me, "and what you were doing." I figured Penny had told her about Elise's threat in a fit of wartime enthusiasm. "Just want to establish friendly family relations. After all, she is my aunt, sort of. Just trying to keep peace. What's wrong with that?"

"So what did the bitch say?" asked Juno with good-natured youthful curiosity, trouncing in from the living room with Beulah and yawning like she'd just woken up. "Hi, Jadie," she yawned again. "Hi, Beth." Beth looked sort of relieved to see Juno, but a nervous outsider politeness was making her unwilling to enter into this discussion of Elise. Beulah noticed the paint pot with dismay, grabbed it from a startled Selene, and went off in a huff to wash it out.

"Just having fun with it, Beulah, jeez," whined Cara. "It's not like I stirred up the whole fucking set." Beulah gently set the washed pot on the counter and stomped huffily upstairs. "Yeah, so tell your buddy Les not to take all my fucking blankets," called Cara with a spot of cruelty in her voice. I heard the door slam up above.

"Don't worry, she will," said Juno. Then to squirt more trouble around the air, Juno irritated Selene by plopping down next to her and asking Cara in a voice of innocent small talk, "So what did Elise the Police say when you called?"

"Not much," said Cara cryptically, "but I tried. I did my duty. Speaking of duty," she said to Jade. "You know it's my job to initiate you before your tour. You are not going off without a witch's blessing. Ma said I'm to have the experience—"

Elb trooped down unexpectedly and yelled at his sister, "Ma also says you and Juno are supposed to be helping and that Beulah shouldn't be doing all the work."

"I'm talking to my cousin," she whined.

"No, you're not," Jade dismissed her coldly. "I'm talking to Pete. Alone."

Cara got up, looking angry and stricken. "C'mon Selene." I noticed Beth's face was frozen in the moment, only her eyes were wide and alive, the rest of her unable to leave or stay. Cara nailed her. "Beth, ya gonna come up and make yerself useful, girl?" Beth seemed to shake herself inside and started to follow behind Juno when Jade suddenly surprised me by saying, "Stay down here with us, Beth. It's too early to be useful. None of my friends ever are."

"Sure, all art is quite useless," I quoted Oscar Wilde as the others went upstairs, all the while second and third guessing whether Jade really wanted to speak to me alone. Beth glanced at their backs as they left the kitchen, as if to provide mute reassurance to anyone in the clique who happened to look back her way that it wasn't really her choice to stay behind.

Then she glanced shyly at Jade and smiled with the most joyful self-consciousness I'd ever seen. I knew she was terribly charmed by his casual morning-after-an-explosive gig persona. Both of us were. I'm sure he was "awesome" last night. The residue of the latent energy of his last performance still made you helpless to watch, and Beth was probably feeling the privilege of seeing the contrast although she couldn't articulate it beyond the anxious joy of her smile. I remarked on the strength of his casualness. I wondered if she was noticing his dark hair falling over his shoulders the way I was noticing, and then I was sure she had to be.

But the sound of a vehicle and voices outside took Jade instantly outdoors, leaving us alone inside. I glanced through the window and saw him chatting and signing autographs for four or five young folks who looked like they frequented clubs. Beth saw it too. I settled back. "Watcha got there Beth?" I asked, indicating her package.

"Present for the band. Made it myself." She suddenly sat at the table. "I suppose everyone's upstairs." She glanced towards the stairs, not sure what to do, not sure if Jade really wanted her to be waiting here when he came back or what. I felt a little sorry for her and then, faintly embarrassed, because for God knows what reason, she suddenly began to confide in me. Got the impression there was no one else in the world she could talk to and for some reason, perhaps because of my foreign status, she had decided on me. "I won't be seeing them after the tour starts. Maybe I can write. I'm supposed to get a tour schedule when they have one, but I don't know if they do yet." She looked like this held cryptic significance. "I'll miss them. I had dinner with Jade one night."

"Just the two of you?"

"Uh, no, the whole band. And his mother."

"His mother?" I thought about her throwing Beth and the sisters out the last time I was over there.

"She was really nice to me. I was surprised. I kind of ended up there by mistake because Juno said to go meet her and Beulah at Jade's, that Elise wouldn't be home, but they didn't show and it was just me alone and the whole band was practicing there but Xander said stay so I did. Missed work. Which is why I shouldn't miss again today. I just wanted to give them all a present. Hope they end up really famous. Sure they will. Sang a song to me while I was there. 'Blood Thunder.' You know that one?" I nodded. "And Jade kept looking at me while he sang it. It was awesome. I'm getting to know him real well right now. I think he understands me. I'm sure he writes all his songs for me, although he probably doesn't know that yet."

Jade returned and Beth stood up, suddenly tongue-tied. Then I felt the three of us grow into a different quiet that brought us strangely together in her unease.

"Couple of folks noticed the van," he explained. "What do you have there, Beth?" he asked to break the tension Cara had left behind. "Sit down."

She sat next to him. "Present for the band. For you," she added shyly. She gave him the wrapped package and mumbled what sounded like an apology. "Made it myself. But it isn't magical or anything."

"Good," said Jade conspiratorially, deftly unwrapping the package, his voice still suggesting his recent irritation with Cara. But the irritation was soothing now, because with that one word Beth's face flushed like the afterglow of a sparse July night. She was suddenly spectacularly and unbelievably special, perhaps even favored. Her god valued her handiwork. That was worth her priestess's wrath. Jade carefully removed a bundle of black cloth, which unfurled into shining silk and bright embroidery in the kitchen light.

"It's just a simple shirt. I learned how to make shirts once in a sewing class," Beth explained, her voice both buoyant and halting, her eyes studying Jade's face because he wasn't looking at her. The material looked more expensive than anything I would buy for myself. More expensive than anything I'd ever seen Beth wear. "But I embroidered the Black Dog logo on the back." Jade turned the shirt around so we both could admire her handiwork. It wasn't as skillful as Beulah's, but it was utterly heartfelt. Must have taken her weeks. I imagined her sitting alone in her room whenever she wasn't waiting tables at Fendra's, playing the Black Dog tape I'd bought her, running the material through her fingers, snipping and cutting like the third Fate, pricking blood from her anxious fingertips, spinning her own dreams whichever way she wanted them spun. The shirt was her Aphrodite candle.

"What do you think, Pete?" Jade held it up for my inspection. I couldn't think. I just kept imagining him wearing it, his dark hair flowing into the dark cloth.

"It's beautiful," I said carefully. Then I felt sad. Like I was reading a tragedy and temporarily forgetting that I was real and home and only crying for a fiction.

There was a homemade card inside the package with a red heart on it. Beth gave it to him. "Love always, Beth," read Jade in his beautiful poet's voice, looking at her and smiling with such enticing appreciation that she blushed all over again and almost cried. "It is beautiful. Thank you."

"I hope you wear it. I hope you think of me when you wear it," she added shyly. "It's filled with my good wishes. Like we did at the circle for the Claude Hopner party. I hope I did it right. It's like my own private initiation. Or something. I stitched it by a candle dedicated to Black Dog."

"How could I help but think of you when I wear it? Thank you, Beth." He kissed the shirt. Then he kissed her cheek.

Then there seemed to be nothing more to say. The gift was at an end. Beth was bursting over the awkwardness of knowing this, and the more terrible awkwardness of wanting to extend this holy moment forever and not knowing how to do so. I heard her voice speak without her presence behind it, as if Beth was afraid of her own words and could not really acknowledge that she was saying them. "I'll miss you . . . and the band when you go."

"I'll miss you too," said Jade without hesitation. "You helped make our gigs at Fendra's especially enjoyable. We're all indebted for the many favors you've done us. Storms-in-the-Bottle and running errands over broken strings and driving Les that time—"

"—I like doing things for the band." I couldn't imagine Beth ever interrupting Jade except to stop him from cataloging her generosity. "I was just hoping to ask a small favor from you." I could see her pulse beating softly in her throat. "Will you send me your tour schedule?"

"I'll try. When we have one to send."

"I might be moving out of my mother's house soon. But if you send it to Fendra's, I'm sure to get it."

"I'll do my best. No promises. I don't know when or if we'll have a schedule."

Beth nodded. "It's just that I'd like to write to you when you're on the road." There was something desperately unsaid in her voice. I heard it because it sounded like something that I had lately been keeping desperately unsaid in mine.

"All right, I'll make sure to tell Elb to put you on his list." Mentioning Elb seemed to turn everything towards going upstairs. In another second or two there would no longer be an excuse for one-on-one contact unless Beth invented one, and she knew it.

"Jade, before you go," she swallowed. "I have to say it."

"Yes? Say what?"

"I love you." I sat there in a witch's kitchen listening to this twenty-something half-child say what I was afraid to say, feeling my own body falling apart with her words. I couldn't look at him. Then I couldn't look at her. Then I couldn't not look.

"I love you too," said Jade casually, but not insincerely, speaking in an openly generic way that could have easily included both of us as just her. It was clear to me that he was conveying his appreciation for a fan's devotion, while she was presenting her best offering to her god, but Beth glowed like a little bundle of dry kindling catching flame. I felt all twisted for her and for myself.

"Will you wear my shirt then? I'd like to see you in it. To take your picture."

"Sure. I'll wear it right now. Like a lady's favor to see me in good stead when I go off to war." He winked at me as he lapsed into the seventeenth-century English of our previous word game. Beth sat there enthralled as he changed shirts, and a few picks and a piece of wound wire fell out of his pocket. "Changed strings last night. Clipping," he remarked, and stood to throw them out, which effectively ended the whole subject. So much for Beth's love, I thought.

"Can I have them?" she asked quickly, her first confession making it easy now to ask.

"Sure, if you want them. The picks are worn anyway."

"Are they the ones you used last night? When you dedicated that song to me?"

"Yes, but I only use them in one or two songs for a cleaner attack, so I never think about replacing them until they're really worn. Here," he said, "they're yours. Use them well. And here, you might as well keep the old shirt too."

Beth smiled and cried as if she'd been given communion, and held the precious objects in her hands.

"Didn't know your attacks were ever clean," I teased Jade.

He smiled and shrugged. Beth asked if she could take his picture with her polaroid camera, and then she asked me to take their picture together, and she hugged him, and Jade warmly hugged her back as I took the snapshot. She sat all silent smiles with him while the photographs developed and then she gave him one to sign. He wrote "To Beth, Love Jade" across the back.

She read it and cried. "Love, Jade," she repeated. "Take care, Dragonking."

"Aren't you coming upstairs with us?" he asked suddenly. "As my guest?"

She looked torn. "I can't. I'm already late for work. Working a second job Saturdays now. So I can help pay for an apartment when I move out."

"When are you moving?"

"I don't know but my mother wants me out. Can't support her grown children forever, and she's moving in with her boyfriend soon so I have to leave. I just came over to say good bye." But she didn't sound convinced that an afternoon's labor for rent money was worth refusing Jade's invitation, so she followed by saying, "But since I probably won't see you again for a long time, I'll come as your guest." Her voice was simultaneously too solemn and too enthusiastic, and I felt sort of touched and bothered about her willingness to risk her second job in the poor Canadian economy for a few more hours in Jade's company, and then I knew I was mostly feeling sad for myself because I had also been risking my job for him.

"Great, two guests." We rose and went upstairs, Beth carefully placing her holy relics in her large handbag. To keep them out of sight from Cara, I supposed. She stood and smiled and extended her hand, which Jade pressed in a playful good-natured way that reminded me of the way he pressed his fans' raised hands from the stage, and then dropped it as we went upstairs.

Jade opened Cara's door for us, and as we entered the apartment, he explained to Beth and so to everyone sprawled and waiting for us in the living room, "You know the party's really for Pete. He's become one of Black Dog's personal heroes."

"No, I didn't know," said Beth, breathless and happy. Sharing the honors with me and facing Cara's barely concealed hostility did nothing to dampen Beth's pride in being there as Jade's "guest" at a family gathering while he wore the shirt she made him. I guessed that nothing in her life had ever been as sublime as this, and that made me feel even sadder.

Especially since no one in the apartment looked as enthusiastic about our presence as Jade sounded. Marty and Xander were seated on the floor near the stereo and hesitantly eating an oatmeal-like slop, and Les was leaning against a beanbag chair in a corner and complaining about the bowl Beulah was placing in front of him. Beulah snatched it away and took it into Cara's kitchen. Then there was a loud crash like Beulah had shattered the bowl and I heard Penny rasp, "then learn to make it right as he likes it before you start smashing things about it." Cara was lounging on the couch with Selene perched primly near her bare feet. "I didn't know this was a party for Pete," Cara exclaimed. "I thought it was just a family party for the band to celebrate the tour."

"Then what's Selene doing here?" grumbled Elb, who was sitting on the floor with no one in particular. Selene made kind of a self-satisfied stone face at Cara.

Cara smugly responded, "Nothing."

"Hi, Pete," said Selene.

"What she ain't doin' is startin' up a fight," called Penny from the kitchen. "Who's here is here and there's slop for all and then she can leave before the party gets goin' if she don't like parties."

"Yeah, Elb, there's slop for all," said Juno, emerging to lounge in the kitchen entranceway while Penny continued grumbling.

"Juno invites Beth and Jadie invites Pete and Cara invites that girl Selene and all I know is I'm still makin' breakfast for the whole circus when I've got three fine daughters who oughta give their mother a break 'fore we start packing for Buffalo."

"Sounds like one of them did give you a break," called Jade.

Cara glanced up and noticed Jade's shirt. "Where'd you get that, cousin?"

"Beth made it." Jade turned around so everyone could see Beth's handiwork, and Beth stood there uncertainly, waiting for public validation of her newly intimate association with Jade.

The crowning glory of any love affair is to have other people recognize it, I thought, and then knew I was thinking of my own secret love affair with the dark, with this Dionysian rock musician, and how unrecognized my dreams were. Jade stood there expectantly but nobody said anything about the shirt. Beth lost some of her newly won confidence as the silence worsened into a sudden surprising awkwardness broken only by the sounds of Penny's harsh humming and a few more crashing pots.

Finally Xander spoke up to relieve the tension, "It's really nice, Beth. Jade looks good in it." Les pointedly yawned and sort of glowered one of his signature dirty looks in Xander's direction.

"Thank you," Beth said hesitantly, looking at Jade to show Xander her willingness to confirm his comment. "He does look good."

"Jade always looks good," said Juno, sounding bored. She was still leaning leisurely in the kitchen entranceway. "Ma wants to know who hasn't eaten."

"I want to know how come I never get any presents?" Marty suddenly asked, splattering his question all over poor Beth. He might have been roughly teasing an old friend he knew very well, except that his croaky just-woke-up voice was further roughened by having a throat full of unswallowed slop, and there was a slight bullying edge to his tone that made me remember the temper tantrum he threw the day she and the sisters showed up at Jade's house during a practice. Beth started to speak, to bravely assert her position, but Les cut her off.

"'Cause Jade's out in front charming the chicks while you're buried behind your drum kit," said Les brutally. If Beth was bothered by being called a "chick," it didn't show. As far as she was now concerned, the word didn't even apply to her, only to all the unfortunate women who would never stand next to Jade at a family gathering. She had been granted a special status. "You want groupies hanging off your ass, you should have learned to sing."

"Or run interference through the dragonking's FM remote," said Marty before anyone else could speak. "I can slip the soundman a bill and charm the chicks into thinking the frontman sounds like cluster flies in heat."

"Why not? The rhythm section might as well match," responded Jade, finally able to get a word in edgewise. I could tell Beth was instantly reassured by Jade's retort, although she still looked like she couldn't tell whether the bandmates were clubbing each other in earnest. I wasn't entirely sure myself, because Marty and Les had a weird sort of air about them, but then Beth made a timid little reply that had the unfortunate effect of turning what could have been overlooked as band-teasing into something utterly serious and utterly irrevocable.

"I think you're all great," she said helplessly.

"Then how come you don't make me a shirt?" asked Marty, embarrassing everyone present by pointedly waiting for an answer Beth couldn't give, and making it even worse by demanding a second time, "How come?"

"I—" Beth fumbled and looked horrified, Marty having effectively just made her look like a liar and a hypocrite. Les looked up at her with withering curiosity. And although it's terrible to say it, poor Beth really was a liar, even though I'm sure it never would have occurred to her to think of it that way.

Fact is, she wasn't crashed out in love with Jade's bandmates, and she wasn't spending future rent money and hard-earned time away from two jobs making shirts for all of them. True, she had done them all favors, but the favors were clearly done for Jade's sake. I couldn't imagine her driving Les anywhere for the boon of his charming company. And in her ungainly innocence, she had thoroughly expected a few words of admiration would make the other three believe that they were as valued as their frontman was in the face of her material evidence to the contrary. She couldn't convince anyone present to believe in her mollifying illusion, and no one seemed to be in a mood to let the issue pass. Les kept cruelly studying her with a look that would mummify a fresh breeze, and Cara and Selene joined him for fun or spite.

"A fan's appreciation is a great gift to have," said Jade, clearly in a no-win situation as the envy seemed to be directed at him as well as at her.

"Thanks for the gift," said Les to him drily.

"What do you care if you don't get a stupid shirt, Marty?" asked Juno. "Nobody sees you anyway."

Xander leapt valiantly to Beth's aid and promptly kicked open the impending explosion. "In any band there's a focal point. We all know that. We all signed up for that at one point. Jade gets all the attention because he's the singer and has the best stage presence."

"So what if he's the singer? In most bands the bass player is heard and not seen. In most bands the bass player is buried in the drums, and buried in the mix, and just plain buried. Bass is supposed to be a supporting instrument. How many bass players front bands? I had a great drum solo last night. Didn't I have a great solo? If the wizard king there wasn't flashing his robe around and trance-dancing all over the middle of it."

"You had a great solo," said Cara. "But it wasn't you the crowd was reaching to tear apart."

"Oh, so that's why the guy from the newspaper only wanted to talk to Jade and was too busy to scratch down a word from us. 'Cause a few horny chicks in the front row have to get their weekly jollies by grabbing at his legs? Excuse me for impugning such fine journalistic excellence." Marty elaborately crossed himself like he was doing penance, just as Penny waddled out of Cara's kitchen buried in three different ill-matched bathrobes and wiping her hands on an apron. She had to shove Juno out of the way, who seemed to be sort of enjoying and sort of horribly fixed to her place by the discussion. Then she caught Marty's gesture and gave him a look that made Les's grimace seem tepid.

"Cain't you all shut up?"

"No."

"Ya got poor Beulah in there in tears, if any of ya bother to care, and my old face is set to be practically the same if I ain't keep seein' this part of the business before and knows how it's going to end."

"How's it goin' to end?" asked Juno pertly.

Penny kicked her in the shin. "Thass for a troublemaker go help yer sister." Juno moved back a few steps into the kitchen but did nothing to help Beulah. "Now, c'mon. Yer all the gods' gifts to music right now or ye wouldn't be here eatin' my fine mush so why don'tcha all get along and shut up about it."

"Why should we shut up about it?" asked Marty.

"Marty. It cain't be just any drummer with a personality problem in the band. You're special. You know you are. Even if you don't know you've been the one for war, clangin' cymbals and sistrums since the desert tribes started fightin' and bangin' down the moonforce on high holy days in old stone temples."

"Bangin' down the what?"

"Moonforce," said Les, so utterly evenly that it suggested grand irritation with Penny's bizarre speech.

She sighed. "It's your drumming that helps makes Jadie special. It's your cadences that bring on the trances that bring on the show."

"Imagine that," said Marty, "I've been drumming and perfecting my craft for twelve years so I could one day bring on Jade's fucking 'trances.' I feel much better now, folks and ladies. My life is complete. My talents rewarded. What do you think, Les?"

"Same reason I suffered through Juilliard. So Jade could compose my solos for me on my equipment and save me the trouble of creating my own. What a deal."

"You do create your own," rasped Penny.

"And Jade changes them into his whenever it strikes his fancy."

"It's a team effort," said Xander. "It shouldn't matter."

"But it does matter. It ain't me the crowd wants to kill," complained Les.

"How come nobody brings on my trances?" whined Marty.

"What trances?" needled Juno.

Penny's voice cut through the chaos. "Marty gets his trances same as everyone else only he don't know it and it don't show to dimwits, which means it won't show to most. But let's not get the bad feelings goin' before a tour. Ye want to show your trances? Jadie's got his downside the rest of you will never have. When you get famous, which ought to be soon, it's Jadie got the most to fear from stalkers and crazies who'll do their level best to tear him apart for dreams."

Everyone was suddenly wrapped in a very ugly, very embarrassed silence. No one made eye contact with anyone else. I took the opportunity to study Jade, whose eyes were stricken with utter hurt and confusion and who literally could not open his mouth to defend himself without making matters worse. And even in his hurt I found him beguiling, because I knew or felt what Penny was driving at, or knew that only someone as talented as Jade could make the human look of hurt captivating to watch.

Penny wasn't finished. "That's why the rest of you are jealous of what's carryin' your own careers into the spotlight. You all want to be loved enough to be kilt for it."

"Kilt? I just want to get laid," said Marty. He was looking at Beth. Beth was afraid to look at Jade so she looked at Juno, who smiled and shrugged.

Cara spoke, smug in her coolness. "So get laid, Marty. I won't stop you."

"Shush, Cara. And all my other ones, listen up. Some folks envy talent. Most don't know what it is and couldn't recognize talent enough to want it if they saw it. Most envy the esteem talent buys. 'Cause it's a herd animal thing to be liked better'n the top dog. Esteem is better than money, even if it comes by way of resentment. So attracting both seems much more rarified and fun than falling behind on the bills. All right. Then there's the opposite kind which is too stupid to want to be anything better. Don't know which is worse. Lookit Beth."

"Why?" asked Les.

"'Cause Beth will never get stalked. She ain't pretty or special enough to draw an obsession, which is mostly why she gets obsessed with someone who is. Which is harsh to say, but I've seen too much to mince up the words. It's harder for some folks to make a life than worship one, and so we'se got shirts for dreams. Not that I say it's a bad shirt, but let's see it for what it is before we start slinging around how nice it looks."

Selene softly hooted and said "yeah" like a compliment to Penny's insight. Beth glanced at Jade, saw all the hurt struck beauty I was seeing, and murmured softly that she had to get to work and left, two tears falling down her cheeks. Jade followed her, probably as an excuse to get out of the situation as much as to be a gentleman. I have no idea what he said to her because I didn't go with him.

Instead I heard Elb give a half-hearted defense of his cousin. "Jade brings in money. What good does it do to complain about it?"

"What good does it do not to?" asked Les.

The question stumped Elb as well as everyone else, so Cara jumped in, turning on Juno. "And I still don't know what *she* was doing here anyway." She was speaking of Beth. "Ma's right about public threats. We've got to start screening the band against strangers—"

"—If strangers aren't welcome here I'll take Pete elsewhere," said Jade from the door. He did not re-enter Cara's apartment. I took the cue and left with him, closing the door behind us.

"Where's Beth?" I asked as we went downstairs, sounding more piqued than I wanted to and regretting my tone the moment it was too late to call it back.

"She left. It's all right. I took care of her." Then on the way out he attempted to dispel my regrettably visible irritation by softly smiling and asking if I could bear being seen with him around town. I refused. Told him I wasn't thrilled about mob types seeing us doing up the city. Then I suggested we drive north to the campground I stayed in during my first trip to Toronto and that we might take a walk down a hiking trail I'd noticed up there. I also insisted we take separate cars as a precaution, and that he follow me. He reluctantly agreed, adding playfully that he hated to follow anything.

"Then pretend you're in pursuit," I tossed back as we entered our cars.

And then we had nothing we could say to each other until we were alone together in the northern October woods.

Stave Thirteen

Saturday afternoon, October 10, 1992. Campsite near Toronto. Off season.

Light. Leaves. Bright, dead, killing, exhilarating, fallen. Sky azure and endless, like the sky in a Shelley poem. Afternoon showing of autumnal warmth. The kind you know will exit into winter in a few days but is glorious while it lasts. Kept hearing the crack of autumn branches that always sound like they're about to break and drop and never do. Kept walking.

We had said nothing since leaving our cars and were still silent together, Jade strolling a little way from me along the trail with the air of being a guest in someone else's house, seeming to gingerly admire all the nature around us, but obviously not used to being outside the city. He was there for me, accepting the woods for my sake, honoring me by trying to see what I saw in autumn afternoons without asking me for explanations.

The trail rose gently and brought us out onto a pleasant ridge of old comfortable oaks cliffing over a lake. The shore below us was dull brown sand and gray rocks, the rest was framed by shimmering trees. An island of red and gold and purple underbrush sprawled across the middle of the water. Ducks lived there. *Fishing territory*, I thought instinctively. Then knew I was fishing.

We sat on oak roots shaped like dwarven chairs carved out of the hard living trees, and I felt the earthy comfort I always feel when I have a solid tree against my back. We were facing each other, then the water lapsed me into a dream of being with Jade in another life. Then I saw him glancing at the autumn waves and believed he was dreaming with me, and then the moment was just us and perfect. I spoke first.

"Hey, Dionysus. You superstitious?"

"I don't know. Would you like me to be?"

The question caught me off guard. "I don't know. Whatever works." My voice sort of trailed off because I didn't really know how to explain what I meant. How do you warn a god to be careful? Are there any myths for that? Any sacrifices? The ancients liked to slaughter an animal while asking their god to protect them, but what are you supposed to kill while asking your god to protect himself? Are you even supposed to ask?

"I suppose I could knock on wood and ask the tree sprite for a blessing," he teased.

"You may be in need of one." I tried to make my voice sound as easy as his. Nearly succeeded.

"Why?" He leisurely spread his arms to embrace the tree behind him, exposing his body to whatever words I might throw at him. Jade's sudden pose made me think of Guido Reni's painting *San Sebastian*, because as Jade smiled encouragingly at me, I saw all the silent sensuousness of Sebastian martyred to a tree and helplessly pierced with arrows, his loincloth draped so loosely it is already beginning its inevitable fall, his loins just one painful involuntary shudder from absolute exposure, the viewer already helplessly rending the cloth to take in the saint's throttled power with his eyes.

Glanced down at the water before plunging ahead. "It isn't just your fans that want to tear you apart."

"You mean Les and Marty?"

I nodded. "Among others." I was thinking about Penny's mention of stalkers and how dangerous Jade's dark seductiveness might be to himself as well as to his audience. "Sounds like they resent you."

"They're artists, they resent everybody." I had to laugh. "They get their moods. Besides, they're such excellent musicians they tear me apart every time we play."

"Are they good at it?"

"You've seen the show. You tell me." He meant for me to lighten my mood and laugh again, but I couldn't. I kept remembering the way the music seemed to control him in those moments when he wasn't controlling it. "If they weren't good at it, we wouldn't be working together," he said merrily.

"Jade," I said stiffly, "Do you have a hard time dealing with things?"

"No. Do you?"

I sighed. "Some things. Not everything. And not until lately."

"What's so hard for you lately?" he asked solicitously, leaning forward slightly.

"I imprisoned your monster. I've done and will continue to do everything I can to see that he won't get out to hurt you—"

"Done and will continue to do," he repeated in mock-seriousness. "Sounds like an oath of office," he teased.

"Or a pledge of allegiance," I acknowledged without thinking. "And I'm sitting here talking about it like it's the most natural thing in the world. That's one thing."

He laughed. "But I love it when you talk about it. Please go on."

"I'm paying regular visits to a real-life witch out of an ancient storybook. That's another."

"Is it so hard for you to hobnob with witches?"

"I've had dreams I can't explain. That's a third." I looked towards the island. It was hard to continue.

"Are you complaining?"

He studied me with the most earnestly understanding expression I'd ever seen, listening softly and respectfully while maintaining his pose of appealing vulnerability. He just kept looking at me like I was part of the painting I was imagining him to be. I just kept breaking to look at the autumn day. "My life was void and blank and dull and then somehow you came into it, and I have a hard time with that. With sitting with you here. With knowing you exist. With knowing there's something to dream about. It's been decades since I've known there's been anything to dream about." I was beginning to ramble so I stopped. Also beginning to cry. Didn't want it to show.

"Pete," he said softly, "do you see that willow branch being pulled under the waves?" I looked down at the water and saw what he was referring to. "I wonder how many storm winds it's had to bend before to save its life and now it's drowning anyway. Do you suppose it's happy?"

"I don't suppose anything right now—it's getting hard to know enough to suppose anything—"

"Then let me help you. I think I heard a fairy maiden laugh as she held it under. You can't see it now because her laughter turned it into a gold ring—"

"A ring," I faltered, then jerked myself into this new word game with a horrible gut-wrenching act of will, determined to take everything this poet freely offered me, summoning the courage to admit that this shared fantasy, this escape from the earth-bound dullness of existence–was all I ever wanted. But as soon as I admitted how much I had at stake in the journey, I feared failing to get there, and I lost my vision of the fairy ring he had created for us to imagine together. The glorious fall around us suddenly felt like a different kind of fall, the one from Paradise. "Help me, Jade. I can't see the fairy—"

"Sssh, relax. That's only because her ring makes her invisible in the waves. She's there, but only her dragons can see her. Only the water knows her call. Come, I'll take you to her palace, where she keeps a coral sun just for us, just so we can touch its sea colors and bleed for its prickly warmth and—"

"—drink deep from our life's blood—"

"—and turn ourselves into anything we choose. We shall be sea dragons; knights errant doing holy battle to win back the treasures of our past, raiding secret sandcastles where all the childhood heroes we thought were dead lie merely imprisoned. As we free them we become them. Pete, who did you want to be before the world broke you? Who do you want to be now, before the world—"

"—Stop." There was a mad rush of ocean drowning against my heart. I wanted to claw it away. Then I wanted to have it back to drown in. Then I realized there was saltwater drowning my eyes and cheeks. Had to wipe it away and pretend it hadn't happened, although I knew he had to be noticing it was there.

"Why stop?" he sounded hurt and puzzled. "Don't you like dragons?"

"It's just a stick and water. We both know that."

"So? You're right. I'm using my schtick to beat the water out of you." He grinned.

I tried not to laugh at his pun, but I felt my mouth involuntarily smile and knew he noticed that too. Then I laughed while a line from Sophocles's *Ajax* ran out of my memory and through my head. *With a god, you are always crying and laughing.* "Well, buddy, it appears that our friend the stick just got waterlogged enough for gravity to drag it into the muck. Not even the fairy could save it. There's nothing on that lake bottom but nature and beer cans." I knew I was suddenly the devil's advocate, society's sibyl, voicing the sort of objections I'd heard and been constrained by my entire life. I also knew I only wanted to challenge him because I wanted him to win, to destroy my arguments, kill *my* monsters, and free me from the reality I despised.

"Have you been down there?" he asked.

"No."

"Then how do you know?"

"How do you know anything?"

"You don't. That's the fun of everything. In strict truth and reality, you're only imagining the beer cans and the muck. Be honest." He smiled.

"Am I also imagining gravity?"

"Yes. But so what? I won't hold that against you. Everyone imagines gravity. But really, Pete, I know you can do better than that."

"'Imagines gravity.' But material bodies do attract."

He was smiling encouragement. "I know."

For the first time in my life I felt capable of blushing. "I mean physics . . . I mean—I don't know . . . ."

"Neither does anyone else, really. Why should planets and suns pull towards each other? Earth and fire are opposing elements. Pretty damn magical stuff that sort of thing should happen at all, if you ask me. If it weren't real, would anyone imagine it? For all we know right now gravity is some fairy maiden's eager fist beating galaxies into submission, and her rage happens to make some scientist's numbers come out right. But that's not her fault."

"A fairy maiden's fist," I teased.

"Can you prove it isn't?" he asked earnestly.

"No, but you can't prove it is."

"'Then take your choice,' said the serpent to Eve. And tell me who's got the best story."

"Rule number 2A," I said absently.

"What's rule number 2A?"

"One of my personal investigating rules. There's no such thing as proof. Proof is reality's wishful thinking."

"Reality can't think wishfully. That's reality's whole problem. And besides, there is such a thing as proof. A man tells a psychiatrist he's a rabbit. Can the psychiatrist prove he isn't?"

"No. Not to the man's satisfaction."

"Then the man's proof won."

"Won what?"

"Only the rabbit himself can answer that question. Since I'm not a rabbit, I wouldn't presume."

I laughed. "You're tough to do battle with."

"I know."

"All right, what if I leave proof out of it and say the man's belief won."

"Proof, belief. Same difference. Pete, what do you believe? Beer cans or fairy palaces? Right now. Not in some abstract future where it may be expedient to pretend to believe what other people want you to, but right now, in this moment, with the two of us alone. Look over the cliff, imagine what you can't see in the depths of the northern water, and tell me if your thoughts are really confined to old rainbow trout sucking on worms." He leaned back, Sebastian again.

I kept looking at him, at his words and dark hair and smiling dark eyes and arrestingly classical features, trying to know who he was right now. I kept seeing his performances and hearing all his poetry in his music. Bass lines. Lines of poetry. The ancients didn't separate poetry from music. Anyone touched or tainted with enough divinity to do one did both, because there wasn't a "both," there was only the compulsion of verse. Didn't "verse" once mean a "turning into?" Wasn't the first act of creation the universe, meaning the "One turning into," as in God turning itself into everything it wanted, as in poets turning one line into another, one section of music into the next, or the artist turning your own emptied life into whatever you wanted to be before the world?

Make me a hero so I can speak freely. I'll pay you with applause.

He belonged to another line. To the scattered procession of Dionysus's heedlessly illegitimate children, like passion flowers lurking out of the mad corners of old centuries, who for all their divine pretense couldn't be anything other than what they were, who could do nothing but strum lutes and mandolins and bass guitars and chant prose-poems to keep misfits awake and dreaming for generations. What was it like to be so *helplessly* powerful with an energy so attractive it keeps pulsing in open hearts through centuries? He was closer to the words I read at night than to me. That alone made me know he was already closer to me than my own words.

"If I were a Druid priest I'd sacrifice you under that oak tree. You're too dangerous to live."

"Is that your wishful thinking or somebody else's?"

I gazed across the quiet water. Bird in the distance like a lost sea pigeon. Then gone.

I knew I had some power here. It was entirely up to me whether I saw him again. He would come to New England and perform, but I needn't insist he visit me when he came. I could go home, go back to the drug war, see the McCrae case to its end and there an end. I could say what I wanted to say, get in my car, and make the long trip home right now. I would feel foolish, maybe even sick. I would be afraid of my own dreams for a while and music would make me feel desolate but at least I would know for the rest of my life that I had said it, that I was once moved enough to say it. If I needed to, I could always pretend that this conversation never happened, and comfort myself in knowing that no one would ever have to know how deeply my pretending cut.

But I also knew that no matter what Jade's reaction, I would never say this to anyone again. Cynicism had done its life's work with *éclat*, and I was resisting my feelings even now. I looked at him across all the autumn. Fall and winter turning.

"Yes," he said softly. "Say what you have to. We're alone."

Thought of all the books I'd read on fall days because the stories were better than anything I found in life. Hated the betrayal when the books ended. Needed the fiction to get through the social hypocrisy that tore me apart every day. Hated the need. Knew I would hate myself worse if I didn't have the need. Felt the same surge I'd only felt once before in my life, when a suspect caused me to make a snap decision and shoot to kill. Knew I was likely killing again, that I was risking the remnant of my true self that had somehow evaded society's jackboots.

"I love you."

Done. I'd never found anybody I could honestly say that to before, anybody I could honestly imagine enough to love. He was a painting, a myth, a melody that wouldn't stop, an actor remembered from childhood, love the way the bards sang about it. A last chance at belief before the absolute horror of nothing set in for the rest of my life, more cold and deadly than the deadly contrast of this moment. I'd said my prayer. *Please, god, have mercy. Don't say you don't exist.*

"Cool. I love you too." He said this so simply, so naturally, so enthusiastically, that my heart believed him before the rest of me did, and then I believed him because my heart wouldn't stop believing and the rest of me had to catch up, and then I was foolishly happy. He didn't say it the way he said it to Beth, but more like the way he would say it if I meant something to him apart from the rest of his life. "Does that mean we get to plight our troth like a pair of medieval lovers? Let's say we've escaped from the cruel families that would separate us to find each other in the freedom of the woods, that we are meeting to kiss on pain of death—"

I kissed him, lightly on the mouth, worshipping the place the words came from. Scared like I'd never been scared before and reveling in the newness and stunning beauty of my fear. Loving my freedom to fear something. He kissed me lightly back and I imagined sea salt on his lips and tasted salt on mine. We were so alone. Then I kissed him again. And really cried. Let myself really cry as I held him against the oak tree and he laughed and clung against me like one of those flowers I had imagined beaming out of the centuries, and we were whatever we chose to be and happy on the edge of our self-composed cliff.

Saturday night.

Words still holding me warm in Penny's crazy house. Everyone else at Fendra's. So happy to be alone and protective and thoroughly in love. *Yes!* Went up to Cara's apartment and stood before her Black Dog altar, fingering the fresh carnation on the table and gazing at the photograph of the band from which Jade's image gazed back. Kissed the image and wondered if the original were sensitive enough to feel it in the midst of his performance. Looked around the apartment but nothing else interested me. Touched the flower again and thrilled to how cool the petals felt against my warm fingers. Like an ocean bath, I thought. Like Aphrodite's kiss. Licked water off my fingertips. Went downstairs.

By the light of a black candle, I settled into Penny's torn living room armchair and imagined the performance I kept missing. Watched CNN.

Sort of. I mean the TV was on but I wasn't really following the news stories because I kept running over every living detail of the afternoon and thinking about Jade, and getting horribly high off knowing that we loved each other, that we were intensely in each other's lives, until an anchor grounded my attention by telling me that new leads had turned up on the "mysterious Claude Hopner investigation, thanks to the efforts of Special FBI Agent Sidney Crensch of the Boston field office, chief investigator on the case, who was interviewed this morning—"

—*What the hell? How did Crensch get assigned to a murder in Phoenix?* Grabbed a video tape and shoved it in the VCR to catch what I could of the interview for Penny's benefit and my own record. Penny's VCR made loopy squealing noises as it ran, but the letters REC were lit up so I assumed it was catching the story. Had no idea what I was recording over but decided that nothing could be as important as this.

As the tape clicked in a studiously grim reporter was sitting officiously next to Crensch's desk and reminding everyone watching that Crensch's "brilliant collaboration" with "nationally renowned FBI sleuth, Peter Morrow" had led to the recent notorious arrest of "an important congressional aide in the case of the vanishing corpse." Fearless stood puffing and glowing in the background with his hands behind his back as if his fine management abilities were really responsible for the success of the whole vanishing corpse affair but he was a swell enough guy to modestly credit his agents for rising to the occasion. Could have solved the whole thing himself if he weren't busy kissing ass and shoving paper. Figured he and Crensch both had to make a special trip in on a Saturday morning for this event, and wondered if that had been purposefully arranged to ensure that I wouldn't be around to screw up their interview. The reporter's send-up on the vanishing corpse and his unsuccessful attempts to get either Fearless or Crensch to comment on McCrae's arrest had allowed me enough time to shove in a tape and push the right buttons so I didn't miss any of the part of the interview touching on Hopner, but his perky interest in McCrae also made it obvious that I had been purposefully cut from participating in a press event that logically should have included me.

Which was fine in the sense that I would have done my utmost to avoid the interview anyway, but made me suspicious of Fearless's motives in keeping the interview a secret, as the reporter was clearly all over the vanishing corpse business and Kanesh, who was usually in the thick of any press activity, had been making it a habit to throw my name around lately. But I saved further speculation for after the interview.

For once Crensch was not full of secrets. He was clearly revealing everything he knew or thought he knew about Hopner, which also surprised me, until I figured that Fearless probably put him up to a full public disclosure to impress somebody in Washington with his field office's efficiency. Or to stave off potential budget cuts by showing the public how well we were doing our job of safeguarding criminals against cannibals.

"Is it true you believe that Mr. Hopner's killer was a woman?" asked the reporter, pronouncing "Mr. Hopner" in that oh-so-respectfully patronizing tone "sensitive" reporters tend to reserve for "alleged" axe murderers who haven't gone to trial yet and must be referred to in a tone of simpering fairness until proven guilty, at which point all pretense drops into a harshly pronounced first and last name.

"Yes, we're positive the killer was of the female sex," said Crensch proudly. "Strands of blonde female hair were found on the corpse's remains. The woman is suspected of being middle aged, possibly in her early forties, although age is uncertain as the test results there were inconclusive. Definitely female and blonde. We know that."

"Well, that narrows it down," said the journalist in what would have passed for an unexpected burst of wit if he didn't sound like he was presenting a serious analysis for his viewers' benefit.

"The handwriting on the note that was found on the garbage bag containing the remains also looks feminine," explained Crensch, as the camera showed a wrinkled piece of stationery with a pale pink border laid out on Crensch's desk that read "welcome the kiss that devours flesh."

"We got fingerprints. Ran the usual lab tests," declared Fearless, weaseling himself in for shared credit with whoever actually did the lab work out in Arizona.

"Welcome the kiss that devours flesh," the reporter slowly intoned for those of his viewing audience who couldn't read. Then he asked perceptively, "Is it unusual for women to engage in cannibalism?"

Crensch responded that the whole case was "highly unusual" and that he suspected mafia involvement. And out came his assertion of having "certain knowledge" that Claude Hopner had been a drug pusher for the Nunzio mob family, which was taking over Utica, and how he had gone AWOL from the Rome army base, although there were no records to prove this, mind you. Secret sources and all that.

Much of this business had been released in earlier reports concerning the history behind McCrae's arrest, but it was now indisputable that Fearless wanted these details kept before the public. I wondered again with a sinking feeling if Fearless had merely remembered the content of Elb's initial phone call, or worse, if Crensch had made himself a personal copy of the tape before I destroyed it and would recognize Elb's voice if he ever heard it again. Since Elb was claiming to be the base commander on the tape, and no one knew who the imposter colonel who became the vanishing corpse really was, I was concerned. Especially since Elb's name had come up on Crensch's Utica recording as a business associate of both Hopner and Nariano. Why wouldn't Crensch, like any other investigator, be doing his utmost to track down Elb McCrae, especially since he shared a last name with Hugh?

But they couldn't have investigated Elb's initial call too closely, because they were taking his lies at face value and presenting them as hard evidence. Which also told me they didn't have a hell of a lot of hard evidence about anything but were desperate to make it look like they did.

"Why is an agent from Boston investigating a murder in Phoenix?"

Damn good question. Then Crensch started feeding the reporter new stuff. "Hopner's drug deals on the base make it a logical outgrowth of my success with the vanishing corpse case. Been following Hopner a long time. Might be a connection between the two incidents."

Fearless jumped in, "We here in Boston are heavily committed to the War on Drugs, what with our SAYNO program and our heavy involvement and sponsorship of anti-drug events, and Hopner of course was a suspected drug dealer." Having put in his plug for SAYNO, he let Crensch continue speaking.

"We have learned through sophisticated surveillance techniques that the Nunzio family is also interested in tracking down Hopner's killer, and when the Mob is interested, we also tend to be interested. Got intelligence that Hopner might have been heavily involved in a mob-supported illegal payola record promotion scheme, so we're interested in following up that end—"

"Care to elaborate?" interrupted the reporter just when it seemed clear that Crensch was about to elaborate.

"Not at the present time. Other than that we know it's international and that there may be other links to the vanishing corpse, which we're also not prepared to discuss at the present time."

"No further comment on the charges against Mr. McCrae?"

"No comment," answered Fearless with a confident bureaucratic grin.

"Any thoughts on who the imposter colonel was?"

"We have no thoughts at this time," said Fearless confidently.

"No thoughts," agreed Crensch.

"Thank you."

The next story was about some priest from Chicago who was being investigated on child pornography charges. I turned off the TV and the VCR, then I played the tape back several times, trying to decipher what was really going on and why Crensch's new assignment had been kept so secret from yours truly. If he'd been traveling to Phoenix, it certainly explained why I hadn't seen him around the field office much since McCrae's arrest. But since Fearless knew I had done all of the work on that case, I couldn't understand why Crensch was given the Hopner assignment at all, especially since the murder happened practically on the other side of the country. Of course, why use federal agents from Phoenix when you could spend tax money flying Crensch back and forth from Boston? But government inefficiency alone didn't explain it, because the distance involved meant that the Hopner case wasn't something Fearless could just assign to one of his agents without orders from Washington. That concerned me most of all, because with Fearless's *non sequitur* mention of SAYNO and his obsessive push to brown up to Congressman Laffer it was an uneven bet that pressure was coming from the NDECC for him to solve the Hopner case.

But why would the committee care about an alleged small-time drug dealer like Hopner, even if he did enjoy harassing empty freight trains? Publicly they were all running as fast from their association with Hugh McCrae as election-year decency demanded, and Laffer's public promise to throw the whole force of a government investigation against McCrae could have been construed by Fearless as wholehearted interest in any spin-off activity surrounding the case. Crensch may have approached Fearless with his Utica tape and Fearless couldn't resist bringing his prize to the NDECC. Probably got Laffer's crony Basher all hot and bothered about mafia activity in his district that he could nail the mayor on. I didn't think the pressure originated with the committee because it had to have been Fearless and/or Crensch who released the first information about Hopner to the press after McCrae's arrest. That release could certainly have been calculated to make an impression and start things off.

All right, I could easily believe that the whole committee was now on a kick to distance themselves from the whole Rome business by nailing anything related to it. I'd seen that sort of thing before. But that didn't explain why Fearless was keeping me off the case and making a secret about putting Crensch on. Who stood to benefit the most by having Crensch find Hopner's killer without my assistance? Crensch Sr. wanting to turn his boy into a national hero? Maybe Fearless was desperately trying to impress Crensch Sr. by promoting his boy's career. Probably afraid if I were in it I'd do all the work like last time. Had to keep me off so the congressman's son would get a clear shot at glory. Only thing that made sense. Sort of.

The killer being female made no sense. McCrae may have been trying to frame someone else, or simply throw off any investigators, which generally isn't hard to do. Glad that someone got fingerprints. Hoped they matched my sample. Hoped I could find a way to show they matched so McCrae would get implicated in Hopner's death after all. Another bit of brightness was that if Nariano or his buddies saw the broadcast, the Nunzios had to know that the guy passing my name around and eavesdropping in Utica wasn't really me. He'd probably be inclined to chalk the whole thing up to government lies and harassment, which was fine. Let the Mob tail Crensch. Make my personal life easier.

Have to consult Penny about it when everybody came back after the show tonight. Warn Elb about keeping a low profile. Then I'd have to catch my flight home tomorrow morning and see Monday if there was any way I could get myself assigned to the Hopner case without generating any publicity about it and without having to explain my sudden interest to Fearless. Had to keep Crensch confused and distant. Had to go to work on behalf of the Mob and do my best to protect their promotion plans.

Item. When you love someone, it's easy to pass hours in speculation without even feeling the hours pass. Yet when waiting for a lover's expected arrival, time clots up stiller than a dead man's heartbeat, so I had no idea how much later it was when

I heard the van pull into the driveway, and Penny's loud parade of the usual suspects clattering into the kitchen. Jade entered the living room ahead of the others to find me, but I was already crossing the room to meet him. He was still partly in his stage clothes. I mean I noticed he had removed his robe and changed into jeans, but he was still wearing the dark tunic he sometimes performed in. We smiled at each other in a deliciously warm slyness. He spread his arms and we hugged each other openly and joyfully, continuing our afternoon's dream like it had never been disrupted. Then he kissed me on the mouth, freely and romantically, merrily making it obvious to the others straggling in behind him that we *were* kissing each other and that he saw no reason to hide it.

He sat next to me in the armchair and playfully leaned his head on my shoulder, which, as the chair wasn't really made for two people, sort of forced me to drape my right arm over his shoulders, which was fine. Penny clomped in with her arms folded across her chest, clucking and smiling and bobbing her head so her overlarge earrings jangled and pitched back and forth wildly. She was proclaiming, "Thass what I likes to see. That's as it should be and I'd a thought you'd two would never come down to it—"

"Oh, Jesus Christ," complained Marty, who had entered directly behind her with Les, "now we've got Jade here kissing up to cops. Do you ever leave off it?"

"No." Jade smiled.

Cara was standing pale and silent near the kitchen doorway, not really entering the room and not really leaving, trying to find words and losing them under Penny's watchful eye. It was funny, because Penny's obvious approval of our relationship kept her usually self-assured priestess-daughter fairly tongue-tied. She smiled tightly at us like she also approved, said nothing, and exited into the kitchen where we heard the bump and a lurch of a chair and a smash and rattle of change and Elb crying out, "Can't you watch where you're going for Christ's sake, you have to trip over my boots ya got some kind problem or what—" and then the sound of footsteps stomping upstairs as Elb came into the living room with Xander and slammed his cash box triumphantly on the table.

"Petty cash compared to what we're goin' to see as our CD takes off," he boasted, as he opened the box to straighten out whatever damage his sister might have done to his money supply.

"*Whose* CD?" asked Marty.

"Our project, our program, gettin' you guys off the ground," explained Elb quickly.

"That's better." Marty was still in one hell of a mood. Les was scowling and pretending not to notice us. "So when we leavin' for Buffalo?"

"Tuesday mornin'," said Penny. "Dawn. Gettin' the van all loaded up and stocked for my pets, and Nick knows a guy providing a bus. Regular caravan we'll have ourselves goin' and it'll be just like some old times I remember from a few centuries ago. Preparin' all your favorite goodies and bringin' along my travelin' cauldron for makin' more. I'm sendin' out my girls to stack up on Molson 'cause I knows *you* likes it, Marty." She said this last rather pointedly, as if to let him know that his preferences mattered to her, but she said the first part as a reminder to Juno, who had just bounced into the room. "Anything you want, I kin get it. It's what I'm here for." I felt kind of bad for Penny, as she sounded so much like somebody's mother looking for a spot of childish acknowledgement and nobody was giving her any. Then her tone brightened. "Skip centuries ago. We're goin' to have a traveling party likes of which been never seen. Right, cuddlekins?" She extended her hand to Juno, who went over to Penny and snuggled up under her breast like a warm little teddy bear.

"Right, Ma," she murmured.

The spontaneous show of maternal affection was captivating in its utter honesty. Penny could be brutal in her open assessment of her children, but she was after all an Earth Mother who loved them abundantly and naturally, it simply being her nature to love like nature, without weakness. "And Mother will get you and your sisters tambourines and bells for your feet so my girls will be the best outfitted camp followers any pilgrimage of grace has ever seen. Prettier'n what passes for the Three of Cups in a modern Tarot deck."

Juno drew back from her hug, smiling in childish anticipation and holding Penny's hands. "We'll be pretty enough to beat the band." Then the moment of natural intimacy had completed itself and passed.

"Yes, well, don't beat them too hard," I teased her, locking myself even closer to Jade than I thought possible in the confines of the chair.

"Hey, Jade," said Juno suddenly, as if the promise of prettiness had just made her remember why she was there, "where's the shirt Beth gave you? Beulah's upstairs. She wanted to see the back of it." I noticed she showed absolutely no reaction to us sitting together.

"Private. Gone." He looked steadily at Marty. "In the interest of keeping peace in the house."

Marty wasn't interested in peace. He wanted details. "So you gave it to some other chick?"

"Looks like he's giving up on chicks," said Les, commenting for the first time on our practically sitting in each other's laps.

"Not in public he ain't," said Elb hastily, counting out cash. "Don't care what you do offstage as long as you don't get caught and effect the cash receipts."

"And if I do get caught?" challenged Jade.

"Then I'll kill you," said Elb, for lack of a more creative threat. "We've got a lot of money in this now."

"Hey, Pete," said Jade, "sure you don't want to go out and roam the city, see what's still open—"

"Yeah," grumbled Elb, "that's the sort of thing I mean—"

"Elbie, it don't matter," said Penny. "A lot of guys like him on a level they'd never care to admit, and that pays in the bills just as well. Be yourself, Jade—"

"Yeah, Jade, be yourself," said Juno, dragging herself through the room and exiting into the kitchen. "Otherwise who cares?"

"I intend to, coz," he called after her, cheerfully confident, yet clearly irritated with the discussion.

We heard her lightly tripping upstairs as Penny said, "You'll be attracting all kinds anyway, sweetie, and that's as it should be, and you look so much better and sing with such an edge when the love light's on, who should complain 'cept them that don't know music anyway and they's got bigger problems than worryin' 'bout you. Your father Dionysus always liked it both ways and more, and no one's goin' to limit you here so long as I can help it. Besides, Elbie," Penny turned to her son, "the girls is all howlin' 'cause Jadie's got a touch of the feminine 'bout his spirit and understands 'em in his poems more'n most men. More'n you. If you had poems."

"I've got cash."

I felt bad for Xander, who hadn't said a word yet and was sort of awkwardly quiet about it. He tried to cover his awkwardness by sitting next to Elb and watching him count money, although I could tell his attention wasn't really on finances. His expression hovered halfway between the floor and an awkwardly silent tolerance that seemed uncharacteristically sophisticated and refined in Xander's usually openly honest face. His unspoken acceptance was as touching as Penny's maternal moment with Juno; it made me realize a natural nobility existing in their friendship.

"Hey, Xander," called Jade, trying to include him the general discussion. "You making sure management isn't robbing us blind here or what?"

"Sure, makin' sure, buddy. Hey, how come you never told me you two were a pair?" Then I realized Xander felt like he had been excluded from something important, and his expression, which I could only call sophisticated awkwardness, stemmed entirely from his feeling of being left out. Then I remembered how they had been life-long friends, and the emotional kindred I felt between them the first time I was in Jade's studio, and wryly thought the best friend was feeling displaced by his buddy's new lover.

So did Penny, who said, "Xander, if Jadie had a girl in his lap you'd be feelin' the same thing but to a lesser degree. Which only means ye need to learn to take girls more seriously than ye do."

"I take girls seriously," protested Xander.

"Good," said Les.

"And Jadie, don't ignore yer old friends for new. They'se important to have."

"If you can ignore a friend then you're not a friend," said Jade simply. "Right, Xander?" Xander didn't say anything.

"He's ignoring you," commented Les.

I wanted to ingratiate myself with Jade's bandmates, so I made an offering to the band by mentioning the news report about Hopner, the general interest in which instantly eclipsed the general interest in us. I candidly discussed my surprise at seeing Crensch named principal investigator and explained how I could help the band by finding a way to match up the known fingerprints from Hopner's corpse with McCrae's. "I'm assuming the part about the woman's hair has got to be something he threw in himself to confuse things. The fingerprints will help make the case." Then I rose out of the chair and ran the tape.

"Hey," Marty protested. "Our demo-video was on that. You recorded over it."

"Never it mind," said Penny. "It ain't like an only copy."

"It was the only unedited copy, before most of us got our parts cut down," he complained, but as everybody told him to shut up once the news broadcast started running, he didn't pursue the issue. Penny, however, suddenly reached over to me and hit the pause button on the remote.

"So, that's what they make ya work with, Pete," she commented on their still images. "That man Pallader ain't got much for his life to go on, but that other one Sidney Crensch got a bit of a sad case around him and I'd watch him close if I was you."

"I intend to," I heard myself echoing Jade's response to Juno.

"He sorely wants to be what you really are. I can always tell that kind. Just remember it." Then she hit play and settled down to watch the rest of the interview.

When the tape got to the part where the killer's note was on camera, Jade sat up with a tense expression and Xander suddenly cried out, "Hold it! Hold the tape!" I backed it up and hit pause on the remote.

"What is it, pet?" asked Penny.

"I recognize the handwriting. I recognize the paper," Xander said excitedly, turning to me and then to Jade. "Jade, it looks like your mother's. She always uses that paper."

"I know." His voice was flat, almost gutted.

"Claude Hopner was out in the Arizona desert. How could that be hers?" asked Marty.

"I know she was attending an educational conference on drugs a few days before the body was found," Jade thinly explained. "In the states. In Phoenix." He looked up at me. Everyone else looked at him. "I never thought about it until now."

I remembered what McCrae had said about visiting an anti-drug conference in Phoenix and that he told me he felt like he was "missing Ellie and like dear Ellie might be missing me. Anyway, I did miss her." I repeated the remark and added that it now made sense. Then I showed the rest of the tape.

Penny breathed, "Lordy lay. I should've figured Elise would be the one. And there she is just missing the monster and the monster just missing her in the desert, wouldn't you know it, she loved him after all. So Elise has it in her to be a maenad and tear apart the god she loves. After all these years there's the passion." Penny sounded weirdly relieved. "She loved your father when he came to her as Michael, Jadie, and was devastated when he went to sea and never returned. She must have seen him in his new manifestation as Claude, and known the right way to get to his heart."

"Yeah, on a dinner plate," said Les.

"Well, I'm glad she got to him 'stead of Hugh," Penny declared. "Thought the monster might have been gettin' a bit uppity 'cause it's the maenad's place to kill Dionysus, not his. And my wine-drunk lord is always gettin' it from his frenzied lovers. So maybe Elise has a good heart and one of kindness after all. Half-way feel like I ought to send her a note of congratulations." Everyone stared hard at Penny's strange enthusiasm. "Let's take the best side of the story and say Elise was protectin' her youth's first love from the monster's desecration by killing him first."

I remembered the comments I'd heard Elise make concerning Jade's music and suggested that her killing may not have been that well-intentioned. "I'm not sure it wasn't partly, if not wholly, an act of sabotage against you guys. She once overheard Jade and me discussing Claude and your business plans, so she knows of my interest in Claude and McCrae. What would it take for her to discover Jade's father in Claude? I noticed Elise keeps a little crystal sphere on her shelf, set in a bronze dolphin stand," I offered. "Is that the sort of thing you could find Dionysus in, dolphins being sacred to him and everything?"

"You know what he means, Jadie?"

"Yes. Always thought it was decorative."

"So what? You're decorative. Don't mean ya don't have a use."

"I know what he means, looks like a fortune teller's crystal ball," explained Xander.

"Yeah, right," sputtered Marty impatiently, "and Jade is the son of the grape vine and all that. Did your mother kill our financial backer now or are we playing some new game of mystery here?" The way he asked the question, his violent earnestness, the tenseness in the room and the absurdity of the context, made Les, and then everyone, including myself, laugh.

"My mother the murderess," chanted Les. "Sounds like it ought to be a TV series."

"I can't believe your mother would do that," said Xander as an afterthought.

"What? Kill Uncle Claude?" said Jade.

"No, that I could sort of see," said Xander honestly, as if he'd just been struck with an interesting insight into Elise. "I meant crystal gaze."

"She probably learned it from Michael. It ain't hard. But as to what Pete's sayin', I'm havin' thoughts agin' as to whether Elise is Caliban or Calypso. I mean it ain't so much rendin' him proper as knowin' in advance how he figured in you boys' comin' life—"

"—Look, are my crazy aunt's peccadilloes going to ruin my business venture or what?" snapped Elb. "I don't care why she did it, if she did it—"

"Thass yer problem—"

"I wanna know what's the strategy here if I have to explain it to Nick."

"Youse management and youse askin'?" said Penny. "Elbie, go figure out somethin' besides change. Ya don't explain nothin' to Nick. Yas don't tell him. And Pete here makes it his job to make sure that man Crensch doesn't find out the truth."

"What about the feds puttin' it around about our payola deal?"

"Lay low around feds," I advised.

"I'd freakin' like to," whined Elb, "but they keep showin' up on my doorstep."

"Look, Elb," I tried to mollify him. "You're right. We don't need the Nunzios to discover via a highly publicized FBI investigation that Jade's mother killed her son's financial backer. They're not going to like the fact that Crensch is on their payola trail, even though Nick seems smart enough to know that the feds are using that to bait press attention and in reality won't be able to do much about it. But if it gets out that Jade's mother committed such a sensational murder, and you guys are skyrocketing into media attention via Nick's help, you can bet the payola, the quasi-legal independent record distribution and the tax evasion angles of the case will get fleshed out—publicly. Especially if you do start making enough profit to make the legitimate labels upset, because they'd love to expose the competition to PR problems."

"What's a PR problem?" said Penny. "Elise ain't Jadie's fault and the fans won't care where the music gets distributed from. At that point rumors of mob involvement might be a spicy story to increase sales."

"Hey, yeah," said Elb, sounding a little more cheerful. "That is if Nick don't back out before that happens."

"Well, guy," I said, "then you and me are partners in making sure Nick doesn't back out. I'll keep my colleagues distant and guessing. You tell yours anything you have to. And in public, we don't know each other."

"I like that part," Elb agreed.

"And Jadie stays here and gets initiated on Monday, the moon's day, 'fore we take off," Penny added.

"I'll be all right at home," said Jade. "Can't imagine she'll be any different than usual."

"You talk to her since Cara called her this morning?" I asked.

"No."

"Do you have to go home tonight? Isn't most of your equipment at Fendra's, where George's friend'll be loadin' it onto the bus?" asked Penny.

"Look, there's a few things at home I need." He rose as if to go.

"I kin get you anything you need, Jadie. Clothes, anything."

"You haven't been home in two days and it's almost dawn now," I protested. "Why go back at all?"

"Honey, I know how to make things," Penny cajoled. "Beulah knows how to make clothes. I can get you all the lousy spendin' money you need. Ain't hard. You can just disappear like your father Michael did before he returned as Claude and leave Elise to her own heartaches."

"Got some stuff on my computer."

"What's on your computer you need?" Penny asked softly.

"It's only the sequencer and it doesn't have a hard disc so there can't be anything on it and it's Les's anyway," said Xander. "Didn't you bring disc copies of everything to the club? The rest of his equipment is in the van. He don't have to go home."

"Not unless Les wants his board," said Marty. "Which he might."

"I don't want it right now," said Les. "Not like I ever get to use it anyway."

I locked both my arms tightly around his waist in a firm hug. "And I insist, Jade. But don't antagonize her by simply disappearing. Call and feel out the situation. If she's seen the news she knows my government is looking for her, and if she remembers my name, she'll probably think the feds are after you too."

"They are." He smiled, hugging me back.

"She won't send them in your direction without implicating herself in the murder, but it's worth finding out her current state of mind."

"Yass, and me and Pete can listen in the salt bowl."

"My thoughts exactly," I agreed.

"All right, Pete," said Jade, releasing himself from our embrace, "just for you."

He went into the kitchen and returned with the phone, which wasn't attached to any jack. Penny gave me the salt bowl. "Set it in the middle so's we all can hear," she instructed. "Just dial, Jadie, ain't need a bone this time of night." He sat on the floor with the phone in his lap. Everyone watched him curiously as he dialed.

The phone rang twice before a quietly anxious Elise said, "Hello."

"Good morning."

Brief irritated pause. Then, "Good morning, Jade. How are you?" Elise spoke with bright sarcasm. "Been a while, hasn't it?"

"Yeah, I crashed with the band last night—night before last night I mean."

"So, how is Penny?" Elise sounded like a jealous wife asking about a rival.

"She's here," said Jade comfortably, "Would you like to ask her yourself?"

"No, I'd like you to come home sometime. I notice your studio's pretty much cleared out. Does that mean you're not returning any time soon?"

"It means I've loaded most of my equipment for the tour."

"And Penny's probably going along. Well, that's nice," she said snidely.

"So what if I goes along?" asked Penny in dismay. "Hugh's in prison and I earned it. What's her problem?"

"Would you like to come along?" asked Jade.

"What would I do at one of your shows?" Elise sounded terribly offended. "I have a job, Jade, I can't go traipsing all over the place in a *bus* with you and your band. No. I'd rather not."

"Tell her I kin fix her job," prodded Penny. "So that ain't the issue."

"Penny can arrange things—"

"—I'm not interested," she bellowed.

"Fine," said Penny aloud, "then stop belly achin'."

"—So that's just it, huh, Jade?" Elise continued. "You're bound and determined to go out there and be the big deal. Such a big deal you can't even come home and say goodbye and I guess I have to accept it. You know what I'm doing?" she sniffed.

"No," said Jade reasonably.

"Well, I'll tell you. Listen close. In case you care." There was a strange smashing sound. "You know what that is? That's your friend's keyboard." She smashed it again. Les started screaming at Jade and Penny told him to shut up and go smash Elise's face and do some good instead of squawking like a cut chicken.

"Ah kin get you another one."

Elise continued brightly, "But I'm sure it won't affect your wonderful friendship with Les because you're both so special and Les probably thinks you're so wonderful he won't mind. I don't even know what this is," she sort of sobbed. "Got more complicated controls than a piano, so I guess I'm just old-fashioned and it's beyond me. Command, Edit, Env 1, Env 2, ASR. But you left it behind so it can't be too important and you must not care." *Smash.* "Sooo—I don't know what to do with it. Since you're not here, might as well smash it."

Jade was speechless.

"Good thing you saved the discs," said Xander.

"You're going to make it and be the great . . . I don't know what. You're too special to be like everybody else. Gotta be different, I guess. See ya later, Mom. Thanks for raising me."

At the word "Mom," Penny grabbed the phone and shouted angrily, "Elise! It's been a long time and I know I shouldn't say it, but I got two words if ye care to hear it. If ye'd rather have Jadie crawlin' to kiss yer butt for gettin' laid with him a quarter century ago and more and if you'd rather have him witherin' his talents workin' some job whose payoff doesn't threaten you than seein' him excelling at what he is, then you ain't his 'Mom' and don't deserve callin' yerself by the name."

"I raised my son," said Elise coldly.

"I don't care how many meals ye made him on the fly while ye shuffled off to PTA meetin's and said what you were expected to say. He was there in your house and the social conventions told ya ye had to and convenience did the rest and all the other whining mediocrities of motherhood be tellin' you ye did yer best so ye couldn't think to find it anything but fine. But to my mind, if you only fed and clothed and sheltered him to limit his life later on, you ain't a 'mom,' yer a glorified butcher fattenin' the brown cow fer slaughter. Raisin' Jadie means raisin' who Jadie is, not tryin' to damp him down into who you are. Bein' a real mom takes a certain talent for recognizin' the *people* ye happen to have at a young age, Elise, and you don't freakin' have it, an' now I'll have to get Les a new sequencer and it would be fair for you to offer to pay for your own damage—" But Elise had already hung up.

"I love you, too, Mom," said Jade, trying to make a joke out of the whole bizarre conversation. Nobody laughed.

"Don't go home now, sweetie, you're with us. And you're with us too, Pete," Penny affirmed in case there was any doubt. "A child's a child." She went over to comfort Les, who turned his stony face away from her. "C'mon, Lester. Sequencers or strawberry shortcake, I can get 'em and 'tis all one. Write down what you want and I'll get ye one better."

"I want to be left alone."

Penny covered the snub by turning to me. "Tell me what you like, Pete, and Mother'll gather up some special treats for you too for when we're in town. Just like my other kids."

I kissed the top of Jade's head protectively. "You already have, Ma. Thanks."

"One thing I don't need thanks for is love running its inevitable course," snapped Penny, looking at Marty like she still wanted acknowledgement for the beer she had promised him earlier. "That one is all the gods'."

Fourteen

Tuesday, October 13, 1992.

Dreaming his kiss. Yes! Woke smiling to my woods. Glowing. Rising like a ghost from my bed, so happy to be alive I couldn't even feel my body rise, but there I was, standing before my closet and pulling on the day's uniform and not even feeling it because I was too busy loving October and still dreaming entirely of my lover. My . . . *lover*. Yes! Yes! Yes! My *lover*, who could charm falling stars into tender shooting leaves of sacred dream-holly singing staves through my heart. My *lover*, who was the greatest musician on the planet. Jade. Jade would be in Worcester at month's end for his Halloween show. So happy my life mattered. So happy nothing else mattered.

Couldn't move for happiness. Sat on my bed. Sighed with joy. Got a chill from my open closet. Satisfied myself that it was only October morning in my home recesses and not some monstrous must, but I lost more time mentally going over the disastrous results of Cara's housecleaning. Still, Jade was coming, and I knew my home was safe now. Checked it yesterday after driving home from Logan Airport through Columbus Day traffic. Checked it forever last night.

But thinking of Cara's visit led me to wonder about the "witch's blessing" that she was going to bestow on my lover. An "initiation," she had called it, without explaining into what. Didn't like them sharing magic together. Didn't see much to do about it except trust Mother Penny to see there'd be no harm done. Not that I thought Cara would harm Jade. She was far more likely to turn her aggression towards me, as I suspected she had during my house "cleansing." But I was annoyed at the thought of her presuming on the intimacy of whatever she and Jade were supposed to be sharing. Then I smiled, happy to realize that kind of annoyance was now my privilege.

Heard a Black Dog song on a rock station on my drive into Boston, which was cool. It was the one called, "Pierced with Love and She Will," which is sort of a violent love song to a dissipating rain cloud. It made me think of Beth wanting to be a rain cloud, and then I understood her choice, and then as I pulled into the parking lot to get through another work week, I suddenly remembered my own feelings the first time I left Toronto and returned to the field office. Contrasted them to my current happiness. Felt a little sorry for Beth, but only because I knew I could afford to. Which made me feel even sorrier, if you know what I mean, because really I had nothing against her. Certainly couldn't blame her for being in love.

But as I entered the wastefully empty building, I couldn't help thinking that Beth was now the one left behind to work her miserable jobs. Couldn't shake the image of her waking every day to know first thing that the god who made her dreams happen had left town for points unknown with no definite date of return. Beth couldn't even write to him or faithfully follow the news of the cities he was in because she didn't have his tour schedule. I pictured her staring at her photographs and playing her cassette tape and memorizing his voice and talking to his image. I saw her dreaming of him wearing the shirt she had made him, dreaming everything except that he had sought to mollify his bandmates by denying its existence. And Beth's poor little rain cloud dreams would be a small stinging comfort when her mother freed herself to live with some loser of a boyfriend by throwing her out to mull through the rest of her increasingly shabby life.

Beth would no doubt wait tables and dream about the adventures Black Dog was having on the road, wasting the last days of her youth waiting for their return, getting through the looming dullness of her new adult life by imagining that Jade was missing her, by believing that any minute he would stroll into Fendra's and return life into her dreams. And after the inevitable crash of reality, would she ever love again? Or would she shrivel into a bitter old heart, beating and hating?

Then as I rode up alone in the elevator, I thought briefly about that damn girl Mellie and her sandwiches. Wondered whether it was better to run away from torture, learn Greek, and get murdered, or to work out a dull life stupidly believing that someone else's self-created dreams are meant for you personally, only to die a slow, exhausting cynic's death when you finally learn that they aren't. But then I remembered his kiss on my mouth for the thousandth time, felt him and his words all over again, and was really too happy about the turn my life had taken to mourn Beth's at length. Yes, I could have been her. So glad I finally wasn't.

Settled at my desk. Tried to attend to my drug war duties. Only got as far as throwing away a memo from Piekarski informing me that Joseph P. Heppelfauf III was going to speak to us lucky SAYNO warriors at the end of the month before I was staring at my pale green cinder blocks and anti-drug posters without seeing them, too love-fallen to focus on work. Knew I needed to think about the best way to wrangle myself onto the Hopner case and wrangle Crensch off it while keeping a low profile on my sudden interest. The latter would take some fancy maneuvering, because with Crensch and Fearless now making the Hopner investigation a public deal, it would be delicate work to keep any *official* involvement mum from Nariano. But I knew that as long as McCrae was in jail and the case against him was tight, my priority was protecting Jade's career by keeping Crensch from learning any more about the Mob's promotion plans and keeping both Crensch and Nariano from discovering that Elise was Hopner's killer.

So, Mr. Morrow, what do you do for a living? Protect the Mob from the government. Protect criminals from both. Interesting occupation. Really fills up a life.

But I kept failing at my job, because all my nationally renowned investigative mind could do was look forward to Halloween. So I sat at my desk and helplessly thought about Jade without let up until Piekarski burst into my office.

"Hey, Morrow, ya want to discuss a drug deal with me or are ya broom-riding the weird stuff or what?"

"Broom-riding" was Piekarski's way of denigrating my successful history with oddball cases. "I'm broom-riding, Charlie. Gotta understand the enemy."

"Gonna be a great talk," he challenged me to show enthusiasm for Heppelfauf's upcoming visit. Then he lounged against my door frame to show that a straight and narrow kind of guy like him could be loose enough to lounge anywhere, which was supposed to be an assertion of his status or innate broad-mindedness or something. I noticed he kept his shoulders stiff while he pretended to pick his teeth. I yawned, leaned back, and put my feet on my desk, which he didn't seem to like. "Got some ideas on Providence."

"Yes?" I said, thinking that was how Jade sometimes responded. I was echoing his voice. I was in love.

"Deal might be a religious outfit they got goin' on down there. Supporting themselves dealing that new crack. Dangerous stuff. Got a hint they're bringing it up here to Boston."

"How do you know?"

"Rumors. Neighbors complaining about their headquarters. Figure there must be all kinds of illegal stuff going on." He sounded vaguely excited. "Firearms. Reports of gunfire. Been gettin' calls from neighbors and lots of other people."

"Sure it's guns and not a car backfiring?"

"No. Want you to *get* sure. Thought you'd care to check out the complaints." He handed me some papers. "See if they have a gun license. See what BATF might have on them. You know, the usual. Head guru goes by the name Lamar Toon. You might want to listen to the phone recordings first in case anything clicks with your street experience."

"You think there's mafia involvement in this ring?" I asked indifferently.

"You tell me, Morrow. You're the expert. I know it's a cult thing, so there's some of the weird psycho shit you've been into going around, and I know they recruit runaways. Place is probably chock full of missing persons. Check out every angle you can through the usual channels and see what you can find on them. Might make a big bust."

Sure. Religious weirdos and drugs in one package, along with community support. How could SAYNO say no? Felt a little sorry for the bastards because if any one of them had ever violated so much as a zoning law in another state, we'd have the excuse for the media event everyone wanted. "Well, it's something to do. Might as well kill a morning on background work." I started to shuffle the papers around so he would buzz off, but he kept lounging and looming in my doorway like he needed to colonize my office space.

"Lots of calls of support to SAYNO. Lots of families concerned with decency. Hey, Morrow, how come you don't have a family?"

"Because I'm not concerned with decency?" I asked in my too innocent-to-be-true voice.

"Just wondering. Ever go to church?"

"Always keep a place for God in my heart." I pretty much said this just to irritate him with an open piety he'd never believe coming from me, even if the statement was sort of true now. Piekarski gave me the old eyeball of uncertainty. He couldn't disapprove of the words but he didn't like them any better for that. I pretended to work, which really seemed to tick him off.

"Think it looks good for you as the co-leader of SAYNO to present a wholesome image." He said this weakly, like he really wasn't sure.

"Thought I did. *You* got secrets we don't know about, Charlie?"

Piekarski laughed his harsh little laugh. "Well, I like your recent bout of public enthusiasm for our little enterprise. Kanesh has certainly been making the most of it in the press. Which helps. I'm not complaining. But just remember this Providence thing is a SAYNO bust, not an excuse to highlight any one agent's heroism. Do the background checks. Play on the team. We'll win." So he didn't like Kanesh throwing my name around more than anyone else's. Probably didn't like being out-decented in the local papers by a cut-up like me. It wasn't fair. "Ya know what I mean?" He cast his eyes down like he wanted me to understand his question without embarrassing him with an answer.

"Yes. If this Providence deal is a go, you don't want me hogging all the public glory when you've been fighting drugs longer than I have, so you're emphasizing my role as a background investigator lest I get any uppity ideas about running the show." Piekarski looked like he just got caught by his local church committee with his dick up a prostitute's ass. I smiled. "Gotcha."

"I just meant we're a team, Morrow." He suddenly couldn't wait to get out of the conversation. Backed out of my office sputtering, "Ask Marcie for the telephone tapes."

Marcie was gabbing so I helped myself to a generous supply of recorded boredom. Didn't feel like hanging around the desk to listen to her latest weekend romance so, without stopping to sort out the SAYNO tapes, I grabbed the whole tray of recent, not-yet-filed away calls and hustled them away to my office. Figured it would keep me busy for a morning so no one would bother me and that maybe I would uncover some angle on Providence to get safely enthusiastic about. Played them at random through my cheap little tape recorder without really listening because my thoughts were utterly on Jade, and the canned conversations ran the dreary gamut from "My daughter's on drugs what should I do?" to "Why don't you arrest so-and-so? He looks suspicious when I spy on him." I think I was running one of Jade's songs through my head when I heard my name come out of the machine. Turned the volume to low. Backed up the tape. Hit play.

"Afternoon. Fred Pallader."

"Sidney Crensch."

"Yes, very interesting tape, Sidney. Uh, hold on. Thanks, Marcie." Pause, sound of static or rustling papers.

"Can't hold on too long," said Crensch.

"Then why are you calling me? Why don't you come down here and talk about it?" So Crensch was calling on his office phone. How the hell did an interoffice phone call get recorded?

"Rather not be seen," said Crensch, like no one was supposed to know he worked here.

"Not sure I want to discuss this over the line." Sometimes lines got crossed on inter-office calls and you could hear conversations if you happened to pick up the phone, although that was a fairly rare event.

"It's safe," Crensch assured him. "I figured out a special code for dialing out and back in," more static. "So no one can listen." Except the ever-watchful computer, which caught the full conversation off the in-line and which Marcie dutifully threw in the tray without knowing what it was.

Fearless sighed audibly, but with Crensch, what can you do? "All right, Sidney. I did inform the congressman of your discoveries. I can tell you the entire NDECC is very interested in any action we take against anything related to the McCrae case. Mr. Basher is especially interested in having us make a production out of going after the Mob in his district, especially with the elections getting close. Oh, spoke to your father." Fearless seemed to be waiting for a response, but Crensch remained silent. "He'd be proud to see you succeed on another national story."

Fearless sounded unsure of Crensch's aptitude for success, and the warm sentiment was probably supposed to elicit some reassurance. I figured once again that Fearless had talked to Congressman Lasher about the tape, and the NDECC was happy to have Crensch investigate the Hopner business. If Crensch Sr.'s boy wonder was pursuing spin-offs from the vanishing corpse affair it would underscore that the committee was distancing itself from its former aide. Anyway, Fearless didn't get a response. "So—the upshot is . . . you're the chief investigator on the Hopner case. Find his killer. Chase down this payola thing. Look busy for the public."

"And Morrow?" Crensch suddenly had that same excited tone he used when we first met and he bragged about terrorizing citizens with his Uzi.

"Morrow," Fearless sort of grumbled. "He's on SAYNO now. You can continue consulting with him if you want. I'll leave that to you."

"Find it odd he knew a few things and didn't share. Ate at a Thai restaurant pays protection money to a local mafia club—the NPA." Crensch savored the acronym, drawing out each letter like it was three syllables long.

"So?" Fearless sounded like he was busy and wanted to get back to paper pushing.

"So, the waitress tells me he asked all about Nick Nariano. Left her his calling card to turn over to Nick. So then I checked the phone bill—"

"The restaurant's?"

"Ours. Found some calls to Toronto the day he returned to work after finding the vanishing corpse. Checked out the numbers. Called a hardware store and nobody there knew anything. Very interesting. Called international directory assistance," Crensch pronounced the words carefully, like they designated some super-secret organization. "Called a bar. Fendra's. And Nick Nariano is promoting some musical band from Canada and was planning to meet their manager, one Elb McCrae, at this same bar. Elb McCrae and Hugh McCrae. Kind of wonder. Kind of wonder. What did Morrow know and why didn't he share it?"

"Well, why don't you ask him?"

"Rather keep it mum."

"Pete's always had his own way of working. He was probably more interested in finding the killer than chasing down some two-bit payola scheme."

I could practically hear Fearless biting his tongue as soon as he'd referred to one of Crensch's new projects as "two-bit." Crensch didn't like the reference. He got a little shrill.

"This is bigger than payola. Same names. And the Mob wants Hopner's killer. Lots of highly suspicious stuff here to just escape Morrow's attention."

"I agree with you that it's a little suspicious that he knew about mob involvement and said nothing, especially as he was originally sent to Rome to warn off the Mob," replied Fearless with irritation directed at both of us, "but that's Morrow. Probably stockpiling tips against a rainy day."

"There's odd and there's odd. Especially since he sends me after the Mob in Boston when the action's in Utica, then tells me to keep it all zipped, and then just seemingly pulls Mr. Hugh McCrae out of a hat. How the hell did he figure that? If Morrow's such a brilliant detective, how the hell did he forget the incriminating letter in his briefcase for so long?"

Fearless didn't answer. It wasn't in his career interest to pursue anything that would damage the integrity of my evidence against McCrae. Once you point the finger of justice against pols or their followers, you'd better be right, even if you were wrong.

"And he hasn't been, well, right lately. Once suggested I pose as a secret government hit man," Crensch quietly bragged. Thought I heard Fearless suppress a chuckle. "He missed the press conference where his prime suspect, Mr. McCrae, was actually present, and now to see him in the papers you'd think he's Mr. Drug-Free America and all gung-ho for the SAYNO show."

"Pretty strange for Morrow to suddenly behave himself, must admit."

"So," said Crensch, "I say we watch him." Fearless sighed. Loudly. He clearly had better things to do than play I-Spy on one of his agents with Crensch. "See if he's got any more secrets he's not sharing." Of course Crensch couldn't admit he wanted to "watch me" in case I had any useful information he could steal to help him on the case he was supposed to be solving. Yet I could certainly believe that Crensch also sincerely thought I was a shady character. That was sort of his job.

"What do you think you'll find?"

"Maybe he's doing something secret. Maybe he's playing funzies for the Mob. Just watch him and see."

"All right, you watch him, Sidney." Fearless sounded bored and irritated. He really didn't care. He just wanted to get rid of Crensch. "If you get anything else, let me know."

"Sure. Gotta keep things clean. No conflict of interest. Gotta keep everybody on the right side of law. Gotta go." More static obscured sounds of Fearless wishing him good day. End of tape.

Tape was labeled 10/8. A few days after McCrae's arrest.

I knew Crensch was righteously miffed at my cutting his involvement in the McCrae case. So miffed, in fact, that right now his sole agenda seemed to be to discover whatever the hell I had fallen into, and he figured that slinking his way through this Hopner-payola deal that I knew so many "secrets" about was the best approach. So he waited for the arrest and my full-time co-leadership role on SAYNO to form a logical breaking point to my involvement and ran to Fearless with his tape. Fearless ran to the NDECC for brownie points, and Crensch, who was now clearly more interested in getting real or imaginary goods on me than in solving the Hopner murder, got the assignment.

Fortunately, the boss was too busy for intramural intrigue and inclined to dismiss Crensch's excitement, but he was sure to start suspecting something if I suddenly got busy convincing him to exclude Crensch from the Hopner case in favor of my own involvement. Item. Keep going publicly on SAYNO while working in secret to keep Crensch in the dark. Watch him. Hadn't Penny warned me to?

Penny had said that Crensch wanted to be what I really was. I considered this as his motivation for wanting to destroy my career, even if it was my sleight-of-hand pyrotechnics that solved the vanishing corpse case he got half credit for. Never mind that my brilliant solution was all a fiction pasted together with magic. It wasn't his solution. Crensch had done his level best to be seen as an important super-sleuth by going to Utica, and had run smack into the wall of shame that comes from having one's self-delusions mocked by someone else's reality. That made him dangerous.

Compared my situation to Jade's and found one nagging difference. Les and Marty resented Jade's growing popularity because they were both as talented as he was and they knew it. I knew it. They already were what they imagined themselves to be, they just couldn't get anyone else to believe it. Theirs was a tragic rage, a merited anger that commanded thoughtful respect. But Crensch wasn't a sacrifice to the public's shallowness. He was a stunning victim of his own.

I found myself heartily wishing that Crensch was a more insightful, recognized investigator. He'd be a lot happier human being. But Crensch was a suffering wannabe trapped by his fantasies of himself. It was not my job to free him.

Anyway, the deal of the month was SAYNO. Ran the checks. Looked properly "concerned" when the mood was on. Found nothing obviously illegal but plenty of stuff we could push on. Some guy calling himself "Small Brother Mink" was running a "charitable house" that "ministered to" and "took in" teenage runaways, misfits, anyone willing to swallow his dogma and work for the "spiritual community." There were rumors and reports of drug deals I could send people in to investigate. There were firearms, but "Brother Mink," whose real name was Lamar Toon, had the proper licenses and no criminal record, so I didn't see what we were supposed to do about it. A few licenses were up for renewal soon but they were all legally valid at the moment. Meaning there was enough stuff to make an issue out of or ignore, depending on the political winds. Maybe I could get a holiday out of visiting the place myself, which was called "Bit o' Providence." Decided it could keep me busy for a while if I wanted it to.

Friday, October 30, 1992.

And then we got Heppelfauf. In the flesh. And not just SAYNO, but with the elections coming on, the whole field office was required to turn out and give this guy a welcome because Christians for American Decency was the latest deal in unregistered PACs and had bought off so many pols like Lasher. Kanesh made it a photo opportunity to show the local press what wonderful community relations the FBI had, which may also have accounted for Fearless swelling the numbers. It was supposed to be a pep talk on our crime fighting efforts and make us all feel good about busting fourteen-year-olds for smoking dope or something, but it felt like more of an opportunity for Piekarski to strut around more "evidence" of how badly our country's morals were decaying and for Fearless to show how supportive we all could be of any group who'd recently bought favor with the hacks and politicians he needed to impress.

So we assembled in our newly decked out meeting room, furnished with a freshly overpriced office carpet and replete with plush seated metal folding chairs, because we suddenly had to spend our budget to soak up more money next year. Us SAYNO warriors were entitled to the best seats, but I settled into the back row anyway to better amuse myself with everyone's reactions. Marcie was there, chatting it up about tonight's date and blissfully ignoring Piekarski's grimaces. She was loudly wondering how long this would take and when we could all go home.

A fiftyish, puffy, red-faced weasel whom I took to be Heppelfauf was up in front with a small crew of sorry-looking hangers-on. Despite Piekarski's enthusiasm, Heppelfauf probably wasn't sure if his gig would work on this particular crowd, so he had brought in a few reinforcements for moral support. Right now he was making an officious deal out of refusing Piekarski's solicitous offers of coffee and Danish. Then he was stuffing his face with half the tray while Piekarski made conspicuous small talk with all the new agents he usually never bothered to notice so the new hires would all have ample opportunity to congratulate the SAYNO co-leader for organizing this little affair and so Heppelfauf would be impressed with what a big time fed he'd hoodwinked into giving him a forum with all us wholesome law enforcement types.

Kanesh took smiling leave of the press photographer, banged his way up to the front, and tapped Heppelfauf on the arm for greeting. Heppelfauf had his back turned so it wouldn't be obvious that he was on his fourth Danish, and when he turned to give Kanesh a hand clasp he got sticky frosting all over Kanesh's hands, which was funny, as our shining PR man now had to wipe his hands on his suit while pretending he wasn't as the press photographer dutifully took pictures. Then Kanesh steered Heppelfauf over to me and gestured grandly to the photographer, who followed with his lens, much to Piekarski's scarcely concealed dismay. So I smiled and extended my hand for the photo op, seeing as our guest had now wiped his with a paper napkin.

Heppelfauf clearly had no idea who I was. Kanesh mentioned my recent press attention and "hard work" on SAYNO and Heppelfauf loudly complimented me on my dedication to justice and my strong sense of family values and told me how proud my wife and kids must be and how guys like me were saving our great country from ruin. Fearless judiciously saved me from responding by suddenly red-flagging Kanesh's attention so I got to settle back to watch the rest of the show undisturbed.

What I saw was that Heppelfauf clearly enjoyed the authority and prestige he exerted within his little circle, and just as clearly needed the unquestioning obedience and devotion of that same circle to feel like he belonged to life. I pegged him as a professional mooch who'd fallen into the easy deal of taking money and mindless adulation for playing father figure to his followers' worst natures. And his followers were beauties.

One was a militantly dowdy middle-aged woman who was seated in a chair up front and doing her best to look as if it would have been an emotional strain on her to stand. She had a tight, vindictive face that sported a mouth as dry and narrow as a line of scripture. Plastic-looking, heavily sprayed hair that didn't fit well on her head. Kind of hair that looked like a wig but sadly wasn't. Hair real enough to break, the kind you kept imagining someone poking pencils in. Penciled eyebrows and hefty cheeks bursting in a riot of spider veins. She had an ugly impatience about her and an aura of not having bathed in a few days. Carried an unmistakable air of living with deep emotional strain and deep exasperation with the world, and of being fiercely proud of both accomplishments. No nonsense about Danish and coffee for her. She was here on a mission and looked to have plenty to tell us if only we would begin.

She seemed to be the undisputed leader of a little posse of nerve-ridden righteousness seated to the side of her, which consisted of two other women and a querulous little man in thick glasses with a beaten face like a dried rat. The two women kept nodding their heads as if they might speak to us unconverted heathen out of Christian charity but wanted us to understand the risk to their immortal souls that such contact would entail. One took out a little prayer book and silently mouthed the words to show how devout she was. The man had managed to get himself a Danish but it was laying untouched on a napkin in his lap because the woman kept flashing the prayer book at him and pointing out passages with her finger, which had the effect of disrupting his attempts to eat. Figured him for the type who liked to throw rocks at teen age girls entering abortion clinics.

Heppelfauf was commiserating with Fearless on the danger of cults and Fearless was solemnly agreeing. Then Heppelfauf launched himself back over to the press, loudly expounding to the reporters on the monetary and chastity pledges all his members took, which set the women's heads nodding even faster. Which was amusing, because to judge from the sample he had with him, I thought chastity pledges more than a tad grandiose, rather like illiterates piously forswearing the pleasures of great books.

Crensch sauntered in stylishly late and took up his observation perch in the back at the opposite end of the row from me. He nodded at me from the end of the row and gave me a long salute. Saluted back. Then I put an expression of rapt attention on my face while thinking about Jade, who was supposed to perform tonight and tomorrow in Worcester. Wanted to get home early in case he happened to stop by.

Then Piekarski introduced Heppelfauf as a freedom fighter, which was an apt choice of words because he did seem to be fighting freedom, and Heppelfauf began by introducing the impatient-looking woman as Mrs. Edith Kipfer, secretary of his organization and "devout Christian." Mrs. Kipfer had recently suffered the tragic loss of her fifteen-year-old son, Egbert. Heppelfauf seemed pretty happy to tell us this, as if her loss was some sort of credential we couldn't fail to be impressed with, and Mrs. Edith Kipfer nodded with solemn exaggeration and then gave us all the once over through slitted eyes, as if she would dare any one present to say that she hadn't suffered.

Wonderful. A professional victim. Which meant that this could take hours. I kept hoping the "tragic loss" meant that her kid had gotten some sense and run away and changed his name but as the story turned out "recent" meant that he'd killed himself six years ago. She'd been making the rounds with her story ever since and had once appeared on some half-assed national talk show. Figured she ought to be about due for another personal tragedy if she wished to stay in the business.

Joseph P. Heppelfauf III then tried to impress us with his Cracker-jack-box credentials from some phony "internationally renowned Bible college" in rural West Virginia that I'd never heard of. Mrs. Kipfer gave us all a look of holy triumph as if to say none of us could possibly question *that.* She only served the best. But lest we get too awestruck, Heppelfauf hastened to assure us that "even though I'm an upper deacon and a licensed minister and an ordained elder brother in the Lord"—he flashed around some chintzy pin on his lapel—"even though they call me 'reverend' and 'most reverend' and 'most *high* reverend—' " A recruit sniggered. Piekarski looked around for the culprit but couldn't find him, so he settled his gaze on me. I kept looking thoughtful and pious and crossed myself just to tick him off. Heppelfauf continued, "—I know that human titles mean nothing in God's eyes. We are all the same. We are *all* sinners. Friends, let us open with a prayer."

He held up a fat, greasy hand, closed his eyes, wheezed a little, and raised his head like an old mule. His followers did the same without the wheeze, then they folded their hands on their laps and bowed their heads, while Heppelfauf intoned, "Yes, Father," about fourteen thousand times to let us all know God was talking to him and we were supposed to be in awe of his heavenly contacts, even though he just finished telling us what a hell of a humble guy he was. Then he put on one of those Holy Joe kind of voices that tend to excite little old ladies into giving up their egg money and launched into his bit, which really perked up the religious groupies at his side.

"We are sinners. We are dirt. We are nothing. We are putrid flesh, Lord. We are worms and less than worms." Everyone nodded in vigorous agreement as Heppelfauf worked them up into an orgy of self-abasement. "We are flesh and evil. We do not deserve to live. We do not deserve to exist."

"We do not deserve to live," echoed the suicide's mother with loud satisfaction.

"But we wonder in your presence, Lord. We wonder at your forgiveness. And we wonder at your love in dying for us." I had to wonder myself at the notion of an all-powerful son of God dying for this bunch. "We love you for suffering for us, Lord. We love you for dying for us sinners. For as you know, none of us truly matter."

"Does that mean I can leave?" I asked Piekarski, pointing at my watch. Really wanted to be home in case Jade dropped by before his gig. Marcie looked up hopefully. Fearless shot me an evil glance.

"Friends," said Heppelfauf loudly. "I am here to speak of mercy. I am here to speak of love. For God died to be merciful. God di-yied for love. But what is mercy? What is love?" A too-serious looking recruit actually tried to answer, but Heppelfauf rode roughshod over him.

"Let us start with mercy. Is it selfishness? No, friends, it is not selfishness. Is it a new coat? No, friends, it is not a new coat. We like to have a new coat on a winter day, but that isn't mercy."

Heppelfauf's followers all laughed knowingly, and Mrs. Kipfer whipped her head back and forth in devout agreement. Guess you couldn't fool them.

"Is it you, friends? No. Is it me?" He spread his fingers across his chest and paused dramatically before answering. "No, friends," he shook his head sadly and humbly, "it isn't me. Is it a groundhog? No. It is God's acknowledgement that we are sinners and in need."

His whole contingent was shouting "no" in unison with him and looking at us like they were inviting us to partake of their insanity. To my embarrassment, thanks to Piekarski more than a few of us did.

"I thought it was a groundhog," I murmured in pious disappointment. A few people laughed and tried to cover it up in front of Piekarski, who looked around to see who said it. This time he knew it was me.

"Shut up, Morrow, this is important."

This is government property and we're holding a goddamned prayer meeting, I wanted to say, but decided I'd better cool it to keep up appearances for the press.

"Friends," said Heppelfauf, raising his hand, "What is love? The love that di-yied for us. All right, but what is that love you ask? What is it I ask you? Is it hate?"

"No!" shouted Mrs. Kipfer and Co.

"Is it mercy?"

"No!"

"Yes, it is not mercy. And so I ask you again what is love?"

He happened to be looking towards the hapless recruit who had tried to answer him before. He waited, smiling. The recruit remarked that he wasn't sure. Marcie spoke up unexpectedly and suggested that love is when you "really" care about someone.

Wrong! Four dirty looks from Heppelfauf's camp followers told Marcie that she really wasn't supposed to answer. The pause had been a mere rhetorical device. "It is the love of Christ! Who died for your sins," he corrected her triumphantly, as if he was Christian enough to forgive a well-meant interruption.

Mrs. Kipfer was not so charitable. She drew back and stared at her mournfully, as if she would be most happy to know what Marcie had to say to that! Fearless was sitting next to his secretary in a smiling state of confusion, looking understandably relieved that Heppelfauf hadn't singled him out yet. Crensch looked like he was jotting down anything that might be a code word. He had his eye on Heppelfauf's pin.

"My friends," Heppelfauf spread his fingers again. "Love is Christ dead on the cross. Remember that. For whomsoever loveth the Lord is called to suffer in Christ, to suffer and die as he did. And what is Christ? Christ is light of light and truth of turooth."

"Amen."

"Say to me that Christ is not turooth, and love, and mercy, and I will insist ten million times over that he is, whether or not you care to hear it. But what is turooth?" He stared at Marcie, who wasn't about to get trapped again. "If I were to go forth into the streets and see a garbage truck, and return to my congregation and say, 'lo, my friends, I have seen a shining mountain of gold with angels singing,' would that be turooth?"

Mrs. Kipfer whipped her head in righteous indignation at the thought it could be otherwise.

"Or if I were to go forth into the city and see a shining mountain of gold, with singing angels leading the way to Jerusalem, and the prophet Daniel preaching about the Lord with a full brass choir, and I were to partake of God's holy feast, of the bread and of the wine, and I were to return to you and say, 'My friends, I am sorry to tell you there is no shiny mountain of gold, there is no holy feast and I have not partaken of the bread and of the wine, for I have been to the city, and I have only seen a garbage truck,' would that be turooth?"

Camp followers moaning and shaking.

"Or if I were to say that the unnatural evils of this age will prevail, that those who wish to destroy the family will succeed, that the followers of Satan who promote sinful lifestyles will multiply on the earth, would that be the turooth?"

Lots of adamant head whipping and cries of "no" over that one.

"My friends. It is a spiritual battle we wage. A battle of the flesh and of the spirit. That is turooth. Yes, indeed. We are out to protect the family from raging homosexuals, from drugs," lots of loud cries that sounded vaguely enthusiastic, "from abortion, from the devil—"

"Yes, Lord."

"From rock 'n' roll, which is destroying our youth. The devil's music that is luring our children to hell." This seemed to be Mrs. Kipfer's cue because she suddenly stopped moaning and whipping her head around and snapped immediately back into stiff self-righteousness. Looked so eager for the floor she could scarcely contain herself. Her mouth was already working up and down. "As our sister in Christ will testify."

Edith Kipfer nodded sagely. "My son, Egbert," she began, giving us all a look of contempt, "was killed by rock 'n' roll." She drew herself up with deep breaths and narrowed eyes, surveying the room as if she was silently reprimanding us for our inexcusable ignorance of the murderous effects of rock music.

"Praise the Lord," said the rat-faced man, who hadn't realized the show had moved on until the woman at his side nudged him and his Danish fell to the ground.

Mrs. Kipfer raised her head and sniffed. "He was a beautiful Christian boy. An honors student at his Christian school. Liked sports, when I let him watch them, but he was never one to participate in anything too rough. Could be your son. Or yours. Or yours." She pointed around the room at random, ending with Piekarski.

"Was Egbert your son, Mr. Piekarski?" asked a reporter next to the press photographer, pen in hand. Piekarski wasn't able to answer because the whole place, including Fearless, laughed uncontrollably at the thought of Mrs. Kipfer getting it on with Piekarski. It really was too funny.

Mrs. Kipfer's face crumpled into stone. "He was not Agent Piekarski's son. His father left a long time ago."

"Praise the Lord," said one wit out of the crowd, bringing on more laughter to Mrs. Kipfer's and Fearless's obvious irritation.

"And let me tell you my son, Egbert, was a beautiful Christian loving child. Always told me, 'I love you, Mommy,' every time I asked. Always did. Always obeyed his elders. Very obedient child. Always said he was a sinner right along with his please and thank-yous."

Heppelfauf clasped his hands behind his back and looked properly reverent.

"You see, I used to punish him by making him learn his scripture. And he would do it or go without supper. Then one day I got blessed. Egbert said to me, 'Mommy, I like to learn my scripture. I love Jesus. Please don't let me have dessert until I learn my Bible lesson. I don't like dessert anyway.' And I never had to punish him again. He would always insist on learning three verses a day. Beg to learn three verses a day. He was just full of the Lord. Sang in the church choir. Loved music."

She played us a tape of some choir singing a godawful hymn that made raccoons in heat sound melodic by comparison.

"That was my son." Then she passed around a photograph of a dorky looking kid condemned to a crew cut and horn-rimmed glasses, imprisoned in a red and blue school uniform. When I studied the picture, his eyes scared me a little. Strangling baby eyes that never had a chance to see their own world. But the really weird part was that on the back of the picture someone had drawn a heart pierced by an arrow shaped like a cross, which made me think of the photographs Hugh McCrae had left on my desk and which made me know in my gut that Hugh or someone like him had been involved in this deal.

As I passed the photograph along, Mrs. Kipfer continued in the tone of an outraged tattler, "Then one day, Egbert, my beautiful, Christian, obedient son, came home from school—and I caught him." She looked fiercely around the room. "I came home early from work and found my son had snuck some friends in the house. Friends who were not Christian. Whom he was not supposed to associate with, for the Lord tells us 'Light shall not have fellowship with darkness.'"

"Amen."

"These 'friends' were playing this awful music on my CD player with lyrics I could barely understand and wouldn't repeat. 'What's this?' I asked my son. 'Is it Christian music?'

"'No, mommy,' he said, 'It isn't Christian music.'" She closed her eyes and shuddered. "'It's rock 'n' roll.'

"Rock 'n' roll. Well, I immediately confiscated all the CDs, sent Egbert to his room to pray for forgiveness, and made all his friends go home. Then I played one myself to see what my son was into, as is my duty as a parent. Couldn't even understand all the lyrics until I read them off the paper sleeve inside. Words so disgusting I couldn't believe my son would be exposed to such things. Then I prayed for strength. Then I played the CDs over and over just to be sure and forced myself to copy down the words to bring to my church. I was so shocked I didn't know what to do except pray. There were songs about sex and songs about drugs and songs about violence and songs about Satanism and—" she sounded faintly excited "—incest."

Piekarski wanted to know the name of the record.

Mrs. Kipfer swallowed and held her hand in the air and shook her fingers around. "Well, there were many records. Legion, like the devil himself. All kinds of groups with horrible names. I have a list. Anyway, I knew I was in a battle with Satan, for scripture tells us the faithful will be tested, and I was tested. The very next day one boy's mother actually called and accused me of stealing her son's property. At first of course I denied having them. Then I told her she should be grateful I was trying to save her son from this filth, that it was my duty as a Christian to be a witness to Christ, and that our Lord would not want any child exposed to this garbage. She threatened to take me to court if I did not return her son's filthy property. And I would have gone to court willingly to be a martyr for Christ, except that when I returned home from work the next day and went to look for the discs, they had disappeared. Egbert told me his friends showed up while I was at work and broke in the house and threatened to beat him up if he didn't give back the discs."

"Amen."

"So you see, I had my house broken into and my son was threatened with violence, which is what comes of listening to rock music. At that point I began to investigate this whole rock 'n' roll 'culture.' I felt led to do so. Jesus had chosen me to do battle with Satanic forces. I watched videos. I went to concerts. I read filthy magazines and bought CDs. And let me tell you—it is dangerous. More dangerous than you think. Concerts are Satan's kingdom. I went to many so-called 'concerts' and I'll never forget what I saw. Drugs. Young girls shamelessly baring their breasts in front of the stage, in front of close circuit cameras, for all the crowd to see. And laughing about it. Ungodly shrieking music. Drink. Dirt. Profanity. Violence. What you hear on the radio isn't the half of what goes on at a concert."

Piekarski looked utterly fascinated.

"I tried to witness to these kids—metalheads—they like to call themselves—to tell them about the Lord—and they laughed and threw trash at me. Showed no respect for anything. In my opinion, concerts should be outlawed."

She took a minute to let this insight sink into our heads.

"But Satan wasn't through with me," she added, "because he punished my efforts to expose this evil by taking my poor son."

Lots of shudders from the prayer posse.

"Satan spoke to him through the music. The Lord was testing me. I would walk in on Egbert when he was in the bathroom or shower and catch him singing strange ungodly things that I knew came from rock music, that came from the CDs I was collecting. Then I discovered a notebook hidden in my son's room. Filled with filthy poems that no Christian child would ever write, and I knew he was possessed. Prayed about it. Brought it to Father Joseph here."

She meant Heppelfauf, who waved his hand and said, "No titles."

"Together we watched videos and listened to all the disgusting music I had collected and I showed him my son's notebook." Heppelfauf shook his head in distress. "And we read every poem together. Every poem. And we held hands and prayed. We prayed to the Holy Spirit for guidance. We prayed and invoked the power of the holy blood of Jesus Christ. And when I got home," she drew herself up and graced us with another self-righteous "so-there" expression, "Egbert was dead. Satan had killed him by forcing my son to stick his head in our gas oven. And there was rock music blaring on our CD machine, which was set to repeat one phrase over and over—'Do it.'" She waited for some response. "Rock music drove my son to commit suicide." She almost sounded like she was bragging.

The photographer snapped a picture.

"We're all very sorry about your son," said Kanesh grandly, pausing to smile for another photograph.

But Mrs. Kipfer had hardened her eyes to slits and was gazing in the distance. Too strongly martyred to make a response. Figured her clock had just about stopped.

"Well," said Heppelfauf, to break the silence, "I'm sure you will all agree with us and with Congressman Lasher who supports us that the rock 'n' roll industry is placing our youth in grave danger. That's why we're sponsoring a bill to hold artists and record labels responsible for any violence that occurs as a result of rock music. We can't outlaw it because Satan still has a powerful hold on the industry, but we can make the perpetrators pay compensation to the families of its victims. We are also joining with like-minded organizations to protest rock clubs and concerts and distribute pamphlets about their dangerous effects. We need to educate people. Research shows that rock music can cause measurable chemical changes in the brain that cause violent behavior, same as many illegal drugs. A researcher in England exposed mice to a nonstop onslaught of hard rock music and they suffered permanent nerve damage. It can kill an unborn baby, same as an abortion. Four documented miscarriages have happened at rock concerts in the last ten years. It can bring on demonic possession. It can destroy families."

"What can the FBI do to help?" asked Fearless, needing to brown nose so Laffer would get a good report but as unsure as the rest of us what Heppelfauf's latest obsession had to do with the agency.

Here was the punch line. Heppelfauf had a special "letter of merit" from Lasher. Told us that "Congress" and many other "high government officials"—meaning the congressmen and hacks he'd bought—were all "very concerned" and "strongly in favor" of cracking down on anything illegal in the music industry. Then he passed the vaguely worded letter around, which was also signed by the other NDECC members. The letter was full of strong polemic and vague resolutions against the "corrupters of our youth" and pledged full support of any investigation into "illegal activities" in the music industry. The sort of thing that was probably supposed to be a payback to make Heppelfauf look good to his supporters while keeping the pols from taking any stand that could hurt them on election day, as it is always safe to take stands against "illegal activities." Face it—teenagers don't vote, and the under twenty-five rock 'n' roll crowd barely does, whereas the Kipfers of the world are always at the polls. So what harm in adopting a vague "get tough" stance against the music industry, especially since they could always blame any failure to really get tough on some court's interpretation of the first amendment and use that as an opportunity for more invective?

It also meant that Crensch and Fearless would be riding their payola discovery without let up.

"We are also supporting legislation in various states to raise licensing fees for new clubs, and restrict zoning, and to enforce laws against record stores selling profanity to minors. For their own protection, minors should get signed parental consent to purchase this music, and both parents should be required to listen to a recording before giving consent, and those under eighteen must be accompanied by both parents to concerts."

Which would effectively shut down concerts and record sales, if it ever passed, which I doubted. The record labels could probably cough up more money and buy their own friends in office if they had to. This "bill" was probably meant to spur public debate and focus attention on Christians for American Decency and boost Heppelfauf's standing among other "Christian leaders." Something they could all rally around, lose, and feel victimized about.

Then I wondered what it is about religious fanatics that always drives them to pick on young people. Is it envy or cowardice or simple hatred or what?

Piekarski was all over himself pledging SAYNO's support of Heppelfauf's efforts, spewing on our behalf that we would issue FBI warnings about the results of too much exposure to rock 'n' roll. Then Fearless was thanking everybody and echoing Piekarski's pledge of support, which was quasi-legal as the FBI is supposed to remain officially neutral about everything. And as co-leader of SAYNO, I had to have my smiling picture taken with everyone and so get publicly implicated in the latest "concern" about the music industry. And the whole *shebang* ended with a reporter asking Crensch about the payola aspects of the Hopner case, and I did my best to look uninterested as Crensch said there was "a lot he couldn't discuss" and Fearless declared SAYNO's mandate to save youth from drugs "using whatever means necessary."

So much for trying to pass as an all-American drug czar with no current interest in Nick Nariano's business.

I am the enemy. Bang. Bang.

Stave Fifteen

Friday evening, October 30, 1992.

Made a simple supper. Sort of.

Took hours making it, because I wanted it to look as simple as it wasn't.

Made enough for two. Which was wishful.

Too excited to eat anyway. Stared at my homemade bread and carefully laid out grapes and cheeses and gingerly simmered west Indian curries for a while and hoped for a knock on the door. Imagined taking my love by the hand and leading him into my surprise pre-performance feast and speaking poems together and kissing him deep luck for his show tonight and knowing he would return tomorrow thinking of me. Then packed everything away untouched and just gave myself over to fits and dreams and clock watching. Evening was a slow surge into midnight. He would be working now. He would not come tonight.

Sort of regretted my afternoon impatience to be home. Then knew I couldn't be anywhere else. Played his tape, imagined his performance, stopped playing. Knowing he was in town, that I would soon see and touch him, that I could see him right now if I felt the risk was worth it, made me impatient with listening to a tape which, for a price, anyone else could listen to. I wanted the words he meant only for me. Couldn't wait to have them. Couldn't wait to live until they came.

Couldn't read. Couldn't do anything but wander out onto my back deck and listen for a car that never came and wander inside and listen to a phone that didn't ring and sit on my hearth and sift through my basket of herb packets until the orange-lavender scent was lightly in the room, scarcely tangible, only recognizable because I knew it was supposed to be there, like old potpourri leaves left in an open, forgotten place. Noticed I had absently opened a packet a little, and the opening was scenting the room. Then I just sat easy in the magic and felt or imagined night currents singing through my house.

For some reason it charmed me to think of Friday nights being Jade's work nights. There was a fitness in him working through the nights I had always held personally sacred to my private pleasures, that the world had always held sacred to the pleasure goddesses. Freyja, Aphrodite, Venus. Welcome, ladies. My hand was fingering another basket charm, a small vial of oil scented like the protective herbs, and for lack of being able to concentrate on anything else, I rubbed a little oil into a red candle, the way Penny had once described to me, as a way of working a probably superfluous protection spell. Carried the candle throughout the house, lightly scenting and protecting my dwelling and returned to my hearth to extinguish the flame with my hand.

Sat out on my back deck one last time, just staring into October night and feeling the Hallow's eve around me. Was it tomorrow, then? Saturday was Halloween proper. Midnight must have passed locally because I could now feel the autumn earth open itself to the soft merge of an ancient power like the vestige of dream time, a ruin of an energy once so strong that it kept returning now to split the year between harvest and death, still recurring the way it had to, like the dim tail of a once sunny comet. I was waiting in the dark of the day that the witches of old claimed did not belong to the year, that was not a real day but a bridge between the worlds, a hole in time that was the best condition for contacting the gods or speaking to the dead. What a weekend for a Black Dog performance. Jade must be slaying people tonight.

I told the night I wanted him. I told the night he would call in the morning. I'd fill a bowl with salt water and make him call.

Bed. Slept to dream of a harvest dance somewhere in old Europe, with villagers clapping hands and sticks and rocks together as Jade called down the moon and pronounced the secret names of old goddesses and worked rhythms into the soil from an instrument like a lute and I was there with him drawing rude animal figures in the soil and we knew that next morning the corn would be cut here and we would be moving on.

The clapping got louder and insistent as the moon rose red and angry and Jade had to argue with it so it wouldn't blast the corn. Then bells rang somewhere like a furious church tower and the folk kept running as the bells kept ringing and I came awake to my door pounding, my doorbell booming, and my heart whipping breath out of me.

Two-thirty a.m. Samhain. Pulled my robe around me like it was still a dream and centuries ago. Grabbed my gun like an instinct. Went to see who it was.

Kept house dark. Switched on the outdoor light while peering through the curtained window next to my door. Jade was standing on my doorstep, looking like a shadowy wanderer the night had blown in. He was now sort of leaning against my right-hand railing and quietly surveying blackened woods and sky and eerily lit dead leaves gusting across my front yard. I unlocked and opened the door.

"Trick or treat." He smiled.

"Go drive your car into my garage," I said quickly, surprising myself that caution still took precedence over all the witty things I had imagined myself welcoming him with.

"And I was expecting a lover's greeting."

"You just got one. I'll explain later." And without giving him a chance to respond any further, I turned off the light and locked the door. Went down into my basement-level garage and opened it up. He gunned his car and raced it in with a squeal, stopping half an inch before the back wall. I closed and locked the garage door from inside, shutting in his car from sight of the road as he turned off his headlights and emerged into utter blackness.

"What's the deal, buddy?" He asked as I took his hand and brought him into my unlit house and up the stairs into my living room.

"Gotta keep you a well-kept secret." We embraced each other standing. "Welcome. Anyone follow you?"

"Don't sound like a fed," he teased. "How the hell would I know? I thought I was following you."

"Have any trouble getting here?"

"Got directions from Penny this afternoon," he said. "But I got lost for a while on one of your famous unmarked country roads and when you didn't answer the door, I wasn't sure this was your place." I drew back a little from the embrace. "Did I say something wrong?"

"You mean for all you knew you were banging fury on a stranger's door?"

"Yes." We couldn't see each other's face in the dark. Suddenly wanted light so I went over to the hearth and lit the protection candle I had anointed earlier. Threw a little herb powder in the flame and then rubbed a little more oil along the sides. The orange-lavender scent went lightly then obviously through the room.

"Good way to get killed."

"You going to kill me?" He looked playfully at my gun, which I had forgotten I'd been carrying the entire time. The handle was visible in my pocket. I put on the safety and set it down.

"Jade. What would you have done if this had been somebody else's house?"

"Asked directions and left."

"You know, most of the folk around here are old New England farmer types who don't mind scaring away trespassers with a shotgun. Got a neighbor down the road who'd just as soon blast a long-haired stranger pounding at his door in the middle of the night as answer."

He smiled. "You care."

"Don't you?"

"Hmm," he sort of leaned into my chest and I let myself run my fingers through his hair. "I care about long-haired strangers bursting in on you in the middle of the night. This is a lonely place you live in, Pete."

"Not anymore. How was your gig?"

"It was a gig. It's over until tomorrow. Kept hoping I'd see you there."

"You tell anyone you're here?"

"No. Finished playing around one. Talked to some press people, fans. Going to have an interview published in the local papers tomorrow. Just left as soon as I could. They'll figure it out."

"I'm going to be in the papers tomorrow, too. As the grand champion of family values and the foe of rock 'n' roll."

Jade broke into a broad grin. "Cool. Maybe they'll run the pieces side by side."

I sighed. "Look, Jade. There's too much here for us ever to be open about. Based on the context of the article they're putting me in, Nariano will believe I'm out to nail his promotion plans." I explained our afternoon's diversion with Heppelfauf's fanatics and told him about my discovery of Crensch's attempts to get assigned to the Hopner case. Expressed my concern about future PR releases concerning Hopner and mentioned Crensch's determination to watch me. Jade was listening, his eyes fixed intently on mine, his face open and serious, but his body felt like it was elsewhere, like he was leaning on me for physical support and leaning heavily on his inner resources to look attentive. Figured he was exhausted from his gig. "I've tried to keep a public profile of distance from Nariano's concerns and my efforts have backfired."

"Happens."

"So from now on we must be secret. That's why I wanted to hide your car. Just in case. No public meetings. We must never, never be seen together. Not by the press, not by your mafia promoters, not by my colleagues. Our relationship shouldn't even be discussed by your bandmates or anyone else. Understand?"

"How romantic. My secret lover. Yes, Pete," he said softly, clinging closer and tighter to me and making a long eye contact I found utterly seductive. "I understand perfectly. We shall love each other in a dream. No more than thoughts on the wind. We shall make ourselves up as we happen and deny ourselves as we pass and look through each other as if we don't exist. Will that amuse you? To pretend that we are nothing more than blessed strangers?"

His mouth was close to mine as he spoke. I kissed him, briefly, because we were practically kissing anyway and felt his body yield a lot more than I expected it to. "You've got it," I said seriously, brushing my mouth against his and kissing him hard again for emphasis. "Officially we don't know each other." I kept kissing him in between the words. He closed his eyes and took the kisses. His body one long sensation like stormy seas dissolving between my hands.

"Keep telling me how we don't know each other, Pete," he half-whispered, clasping his hands behind my neck as if he really did need physical support and brushing his mouth on mine. "I love the way you lie." I softly stroked his forehead and pressed my mouth roughly against his for a very long time. He was swaying as if he was having trouble standing so I clasped him tightly against me and before the end of my kiss I had somehow gotten him gently down on my braided rug. I was still kissing and stroking his candlelit face as he returned kisses into me.

"I love the way you lie too," I said. And he did look beautiful lying there with the candlelight falling all around him. He murmured something half in trance already, which made me feel like I had more sexual prowess at my command than anyone had a right to. Felt flattered that I had such an immediate effect and wondered how much was lovers' theatrics.

"Hmm?" I said softly, kissing him again so he couldn't answer. "Hey, don't look so relaxed." He obediently stiffened his body and sat up a little as I took a large pillow from the couch and placed it behind him on the floor.

"Cara give you those?" His voice was a little stronger now, but stronger as if in response to my playful command, and not as if it was his own strength speaking.

"Your aunt made them. Work wonderfully well against monsters."

"Cara used something similar during our little initiation Monday," he remarked.

"What did she do to you?" I sat on the floor across from him. "Do I have to kill her?"

"She danced. She chanted. She sang my songs to me and showed off and burned things and made a deal out of bringing out my 'full powers and sensitivity.'" He smiled. "I'm now a witch *and* a son of Olympus."

"I could have told you that."

He leaned back in the pillow. "She burned something like that herb combination. Makes me feel relaxed and sensitive and open. She worked some magical command into it."

"Oh yeah?"

"Yeah," he grinned. "It's good stuff."

Insight. I threw another pinch on the flame, which temporarily increased the scent in the air. Then I leaned over the pillow and softly stroked his face and spoke a command in a soft, whispery voice into his wine-dark smiling eyes. "Relax." Then I kissed him in an excruciatingly hard violence, once and long, without let up, as his body utterly succumbed to mine. So well did Cara's magic or Penny's herbs work that by the time I was finished, I felt no muscle resistance, just a charming slackness lying in my arms.

"Jade," I said softly in his ear while gently stroking the soft shirt over his utterly relaxed chest. He murmured something that sounded like my name or like a conversation he was having with someone else in a dream. "I told you to relax." I said this softly in his ear, then I licked his ear and his body felt like a tide had just pulled out of a still shore. "Sssh." I unbuttoned one button on his shirt. "Guess you're right. This *is* good stuff. Makes you charmingly docile."

He seemed to smile a little and we fell together into a soft kiss as he shuddered beneath me and I kept unbuttoning his shirt and running my hand along his chest. "Are you enjoying yourself, my love?" His face was transcendent. Figured he was too gone to enjoy himself, but I was certainly having fun. Then I noticed how excited and hard I was feeling. How it wasn't any longer like I *wanted* to make love to him because I already was making love to him and thinking or feeling nothing but the sensation.

"Jade," I whispered, as he shuddered and moaned softly to my voice, and I reached my hand down between his legs. He was moaning louder now. He was utterly mine. "I want you to sing for me."

He moaned a soft little song in sounds that weren't quite words.

"Good," I said slowly, "now I want you to tell me a story."

He moaned in the cadence of prose—something about secret lovers naming stars.

"Very good. I want you to give me a poem."

He did. In a Celtic-sounding language.

And I stopped his speech with a kiss.

And his moan became a rock 'n' roll scream of ecstasy.

And I watched him and held the candle over him and he writhed and jerked in an ethereal violence as I placed my other hand just over and barely touching his penis, meaning that only when he breathed were we just touching. I was as hard as his music and greatly enjoying my discovery of power. Set the candle down on the edge of the hearth. The light fell and held him.

"You want to come now, don't you, witch?" Jade was too gone to answer me coherently. "And I can keep you wanting until that candle burns out. Could take hours." He could hear me. He moaned a little at the thought. I kept my hand steady to his loins and gently stroked his closed eyelids with my other hand. Whispered, "Do you know how hard I get when I see you like this? How many times I've imagined you giving me such a private performance? I'm your audience now. Give it to me." And I cradled his penis as he came, and I came watching his flawless body pass out.

Dazed and reverent.

Took the quilt and another pillow from the couch, threw the pillow near him, and wrapped him against the cold. Intended to cover myself also and sleep next to him, but I kept lingering to look at my work, at the dream I had temporarily become one with and mastered with a power not my own. Felt strange about my "discovery," yet I did not extinguish the candle and could not extinguish my thoughts.

I studied Jade's dark hair falling casually over his shoulders, pictured his dark eyes friendly with the fire of his inner life, and knew that he was self-generating, self-flourishing, and that his life had purpose. He lived music, would make sound from a stick and a shell and a star's light if that's all there was to make sound from. Then I understood that Jade didn't merely play music, he was always inventing it, and that is what made him so seductive and dangerous. Because at the same time you loved him you knew that the quality of your love marked him as your better, a stranger, a god's forgotten son.

But how long can you worship a god before you know your place in the pecking order? Perhaps that's what destroyed Semele, Dionysus's human mother who saw her lover, Zeus, in all his glory and so burned to death as he entered her. Not the god's power, as the myth implies, but the woman's irrevocable knowledge of her lack of power, her stone wall mortality, her human limits made manifest. I caught myself thinking of Elise, and then thinking that perhaps Semele exploded with the rage of not wanting the supporting role of being merely a god's mother, perhaps she wanted the impossibility of being a god herself. And so the king of the universe had to suffer the indignity of carrying the fetus to term in his thigh. Thwarted expectations, even unfair ones, can maim.

Know a god, know thyself.

It would have been kinder of Zeus to give her a lie.

I quenched the candle and laid down next to Jade, under the quilt. Held him, locking us together before my hearth, my Aphrodite altar. Cried. Slept.

Woke to Halloween noon and raining. Jade had gotten there before me. He had raided my kitchen, and was now arranging my "surprise feast" for me on my dining room table, complete with two white emergency candles he had found in my pantry and lit. The candle flames were comfort inside a gray day.

"Good afternoon, Pete." He smiled like a gracious victor might smile to a fallen enemy. "Looks like I wore you out."

I groaned good naturedly, watching him ostentatiously open a can of beer for each of us. Chuckled at the incongruity of Budweisers and *bhel puri*.

"Care for some tea?" He indicated the beer. "Some grapes and curry?"

I groaned again and went to the table. "I was going to surprise *you* with all of this."

"You did. Enjoy."

Felt like a messy, unwrapped package in my stained-with-last-night robe while Jade was fully dressed and full of the day. "Uh, better shower."

"Don't be long. Sound check's at six," he teased.

Grabbed the quilt, went into my bathroom. Threw the quilt in the hamper with my robe. Then I stood unclothed, noticing that Jade had already prepared my bath for me with warm water and incense. He had left one of my sandalwood incense sticks burning near my bath for welcome. He had also thrown a single red carnation in the water. Must have had it in his car from his gig. Washed and dressed quickly. Returned to the table.

"To you, hero." He saluted me with his beer can. He had filled my plate with bread and cheese.

"To us, Dragon Lord," I saluted back. The instant the cold beer hit my empty stomach, I realized how ravenous I really was, so I stopped drinking and started devouring the feast. "See, you've made yourself at home already. Nice work, guy."

"Least I could do."

"Have fun last night?"

"It was a gig," he said with an affected indifference that made us both laugh so hard we couldn't eat for a few minutes. Our laughter made a magic circle where we were, warm and intimate and comfortably just-us with the sound and feel of the dark rain outside the curtained windows. I loved everything. I watched him eat the bread and curry I had made, and I ate, knowing that I had survived a life plain to the point of tears for over three decades just to have this perfect moment. "Happy Halloween," he said.

"Trick or treat?"

"Yes."

"I love you."

"Noted."

"I love you." I loved saying it.

"Really?"

"I love you." And hungry as I was, I couldn't eat anymore, because eating just got in the way of holding him, touching him, talking to him and hearing him talk to me. But Jade insisted, saying, "Come, Pete, I'm not feeding you crushed diamonds."

"I don't understand."

"Aren't there old tales of Indian princes who loved tragically and so committed suicide by eating crushed diamonds? I understand it was quite the popular feast for unhappy lovers in mythic India."

"Are we to be unhappy Indian lovers today then?"

"Only if you don't eat."

"You sound like your aunt," I laughed, but I ate quickly to please him and to get it over with.

"Now." He led me by the hand to the braided rug, and we sat together on the floor. "Let me tell me you a story." He had a burning candle in his other hand, which he placed on the hearth.

"Please." I settled myself expectantly, taking his hands in mine. "Tell me everything." He pressed a sea god kiss into my mouth, which gave me a dream of the Mediterranean and which I kept returning. And when we finished, Jade tilted his head a little to the side and gazed at me with his intensely brown eyes.

"Everything." He was studying me. "Did you know that 'to seduce' and 'to destroy' once meant the same thing in Greek?"

His tone suggested a rhetorical opening to a story, so I did not answer, but as he was waiting intently for some response, I finally whispered, "I understand." Then something in me quoted Yeats, "Did she put on his knowledge with his power / Before the indifferent beak could let her drop?"

"Did she?" asked Jade, letting me lead.

"When Zeus disguised himself as a swan and raped Leda—" I looked into Jade's tender, smiling eyes and faltered, not sure how to phrase the question I wanted to ask.

He spoke softly. "Leda gave birth to Beauty, to Helen of Troy, whose abduction inspired Homer to compose the first epic song-poem in literature—"

"Whose beauty caused a war."

"So? The war's over." He smiled. "Only the poem remains."

"Sounds like a prayer."

"It isn't. It's a statement of *fact*," Jade said in a deadpan voice that sent us both giggling.

"*Fact*," I chuckled. "Like you would know, Count."

"Well, you can't have a war without a poem, can you?"

I felt his strong musician's hands pressing confident and warm in mine. "Jade. I don't know what to do about you. Or with you. Do you realize what you are to people? To Beth? To Cara? To the girls who grab your legs in the rock 'n' roll clubs and the masses who are starting to hear your songs on the radio?"

"Yes. I'm whatever and whoever they want me to be. That's what they pay me for."

"They pay you to live the lives they want and can only dream about having."

"That's entertainment." He shrugged. "Who do you want me to be, Pete? For you I'll work for free."

"What happens when your fans grow up? What happens when they start wanting for themselves, and realize they've missed their life, and begin to see that you haven't missed yours?"

"Then they stop paying me and I play to new fans who aren't afraid of the dream yet. What does that have to do with us?" He placed his hands around my neck and leaned forward into a kiss that I broke off.

"Jade, yours is the kind of beauty that inspires wars of the worst sort. Those religious fanatics I told you about last night—"

"The ones your colleagues seek to please by branding you my everlasting enemy—" Jade kissed me sensuously and I did not resist.

"Yes." I held his hands. "They know where there's power sure as a starving cat knows a king."

"So do I."

"They know what they resent. And they'll do whatever they can do to impede it. And so they blame the music for a young boy's suicide while they worship a God who takes joy in death—"

"Ssh, Pete. I'm not afraid of them." He laughed. "Cara told me there were a couple of old biddies protesting outside the club last night. Maybe they know these Christians for American Decency folks who came to haunt your workplace yesterday, maybe they've got their own deal. But Cara got all ticked off because one of them called her a witch while she was parading back and forth in front of them in black and blessing strangers with hex signs and handing out carnations. She brought a pamphlet backstage and read to us about the evils of rock music. We all thought it was funny. I read parts of it for laughs during our show."

"And so your fans no doubt felt good and rebellious and mightily enjoyed the notion of transgressing something."

"They were transgressing something. They paid to transgress. They paid for their transgressions." Jade spoke in a mock-preacher's voice.

"Do you have a copy of the pamphlet?"

"Sure, Pete, here." He took a crumpled copy out of his back pocket.

It was one of Heppelfauf's. Printed in bold letters across the top was the biblical injunction, "Thou shalt not suffer a witch to live," and the rest was a badly written rant accusing the rock music industry of genocide. I burned it with a curse.

"Hey, come on, guy. So they got enough media influence to manipulate your image into Captain America. It's not like you haven't paved the way. You're the one insisting on secrecy between us. What could be better?"

"I hate those people, Jade."

"Why bother?" He laughed. "I'm sure my aunt can protect you from the witch-hunters if you ask. And if not, I'll save you."

"I don't like them hanging around the clubs you're performing in. These are the same people we occasionally have to arrest for kidnapping and murdering physicians who do abortions or for torturing children in their basements. Some of them get crazy. A lot of serial killers get a childhood of abuse in their ranks. It's common practice for those kinds of groups to take license plates and trace down the addresses of young girls who use abortion clinics, who they continually harass with death threats we can't do anything about. The local cops all look the other way because they're afraid. The political winds are blowing in their favor right now."

"Pete, Pete, calm down. We're not running an abortion clinic."

"No, but they've already recognized your magic. They're calling Cara a witch. How long before they start harassing the band, now that they're on a 'rock 'n' roll is the devil's music' kick? And what will they find about your mother and Claude Hopner? That's the sort of thing that would greatly excite them, now that they have a few pols in their pocket and influence in the Bureau. They own the pols that gave Crensch the green light to investigate the Hopner murder and all that goes with it, including payola."

"Then they can fight it out with Nick's people. Might be amusing."

"Yeah," I sighed.

"Look, Pete, the fans got a few laughs at their expense. We had fun with it. No one took them seriously."

I looked into his beautiful face, like a new moon emerging from a new night, and ran my fingers through his beautiful hair. "Your fans. Jade, your fans love you, but they also wish they were you. Wish they were the one reading the pamphlet and playing bass like a happy little demon on vacation from hell. Wish they truly possessed the mystery and the talent to be persecuted. They're borrowing—or they've paid to borrow—your power, and for a few hours they get to feel important enough to be singled out as the enemy of some dingbat group of aging illiterates. Which speaks volumes about the rest of their lives. They'll dance and get high and get laid and break their hearts while listening to your music but it's themselves they imagine playing it when they prance with their air guitars in the fleeting privacy of their post-adolescent bedrooms. As long as you are not quite real to them, an image in the ether, they'll adore you. But one day they'll wake up to the reality of their meaningless families and soul-killing jobs and begin to understand that the image they've wanted to appropriate is a real human being who has a power they'll never touch—"

"Who's a real human being?" teased Jade. "And why should we care?"

"Because someday they'll hate you for it. And maybe turn to someone like Hepelfauf, who blesses their resentment."

"Do you hate me for it?" he asked earnestly.

"No." I paused. "I'm just lonely."

"Still?" he asked in a voice of soft concern.

"No." I looked at the cleanly lit candle. The flame had an iridescent center. "Just involved."

"So shoot."

"All right. Have you spoken to your mother?"

"No."

"Is Les still angry about his sequencer?"

"Hard to say. Les has been fairly quiet lately. Penny got him new gear, so he isn't complaining too much." The mention of Les seemed to bring up a certain discomfort. I could sense that the tension between his bandmates hadn't decreased.

"Your monster's still safe in jail, you know," I assured him. "There's one problem down."

"Then can I safely live here with you?" he asked, brightly shifting the subject away from Les without really shifting. "When we're in New England? For the next three weeks we'll be in Boston, Springfield, Providence, Hartford, Northampton—not necessarily in that order, with days off in between. Then it might be New York, New Jersey, who knows."

"Yes. You can stay with me whenever you like. I'll give you a house key so you can let yourself in. But, Jade, please be discrete. Have you heard anything from Elb or Nariano about this federal investigation into payola that's brewing, or about my ex-partner searching down Hopner's killer?"

"No."

"None of your bandmates ever discuss your mother's recent outbursts?"

"No, not with me anyway. Lately it's pretty much been all business. We've got to finish writing our second CD while we're on the road." He looked distant. "I'm lonely, too."

"I know," I said sadly.

"But come," he took my hands in his. "I'll save you. It's full moon in Thessaly, and it's our job to seduce and destroy. Loudly we climb over the Day of the Dead. Here we are in a city where old women carry charms in their mouths and everyone is a poet. Young women sit on the rooftops and blurt dirty jokes to Adonis as they plant fennel seeds in clay pots. Then they scream and cackle his name all over the city, and utterly convince themselves that they love the new seed that will sprout to die. It is late July and the new plants are to be left unwatered to enjoy three long sumptuous days of stifling sun."

"Why?"

"So they can have a funeral by throwing the dead plants in the sea."

"Are we here to save Adonis?"

"No. We're here to witness his yearly death. We are pilgrims stopping at holy places. Briefly."

"Why is the death of Adonis holy to us?" I whisper.

"Because he is beloved of Aphrodite."

"Jade—stop it!"

"Why? Don't you like my tale?"

"I don't like the implications."

"You tell one." He settled himself to wait.

"Euridyce loved Orpheus for his music. She died of a snake bite."

"Poor girl," said Jade, smiling.

"But because of his music, Hades and Persephone gave Orpheus a chance to reclaim his lover from the realm of the dead. Euridyce would follow him like a phantom made flesh back to the living, providing he did not look at her. But the singer violated the law by glancing at Euridyce and so Queen Persephone made him return alone to the living. And Hades took his lyre away and placed it in the sky where Orpheus couldn't have it and so he died mad."

"It's a good story."

"Maybe."

"Did he eat crushed diamonds?"

"Yes. Sure. I don't know." I looked into his eyes. "If you like, guy. If it would please you. And in the end, he ate plenty of crushed diamonds."

"I love you," said Jade.

I kissed him, and fondled him, and lost myself in his body for a dark rainy hour. We called and sang and moaned and whispered to Adonis of the Fields. The cold harvest rain made no answer.

Stave Sixteen

Sunday, November 1, 1992. Samhain proper.

Sunday afternoon was cool and full of thoughts. I was reading Yeats and imagining his love for Maud Gonne, and then I was out on my back deck cleaning guns. Heard a car pull into my driveway and someone get out. Confident keys. Side garage door bangs open like the entrant lives here. Hope he does. Overhead garage door slides up with a resolute crash. Car drives smoothly inside. Overhead door closes. Side door closes. Yes!

Did not go inside. Willed Jade to come outside to me.

After a few minutes, the sliding door behind me opened and closed. I smiled softly, and did not look up from my disassembled weapons as steady footsteps approached me on my deck. "Greetings, lover," I said.

"Greetings, Pete. How's life?" answered Cara, settling herself next to me with an air of contentious familiarity. She was alone. She was also heavily made up in thick eye shadow and rouge, the way Juno usually was. She was wearing black leather dress boots, leopard tights—one leg blue and one leg red under the spots, and a thin black low-cut mini-dress with open slits up the side, taut under a belt of wide silver hoops. Her cloth satchel was bulging at her waist. If she wasn't a witch and presumably able to maintain a strong body resistance against disease, she'd be flirting flu out of the early November weather, even if the day did look like it might be holding back an incoherent Indian summer.

But Cara held a peculiar, nearly material warmth in her exposed skin, an aura in her body that made me remember, from my own adolescence, the peculiarly exciting comfort of crowded, pot-laden concert arenas just before the lights went out and the first band entered to suffer the slights and slings of the crowd's impatience. As she took her place next to me it was like we were suddenly teenagers together, skipping school two decades after graduation, two active ghosts reliving a pleasant day out of our past now that the day no longer counted. Felt like it was still my own youth with her no matter how old I was. Also felt slightly mocking. Like Cara's magic.

She was holding a pink cigarette between her fingers. "Figured I'd stop by, pay you a call. See how my old friend Pete was doin'. Wanna smoke?"

"No. How'd you get in the house?" I asked easily, not pausing in my work.

She glanced at my Walther, one of the guns I keep at home for personal protection, and looked bored. "How'd you'd get in the house? How'd you'd get in the house?" She mimicked my words as if we were old friends. "Really, Pete, I know where you live. It's not hard to get inside. I get to borrow Jadie's car when I need to go out and get things for the band. Just held the keys in my hand and knew which one was yours. So I decided to stop by, to see how you were. So, how are ya?"

"Nice work hiding the car. Jade tell you to do that?"

"No. Jadie doesn't even know I'm here. I figured out for myself that you two guys would like things secret. Especially the way the local papers are writing about you this weekend as the purest thing since Jesus Christ sliced milk into wine. See the papers yesterday?"

"No, I was busy," I said drily. Actually, I had seen it this morning, but I wanted to hear her version. There was nothing in yesterday's *Globe* and only a blurb in the Worcester paper. But this morning, in a subtle effort to whip up voter frenzy just before elections, the Sunday *Globe* practically devoted an entire section to Christians for American Decency, Lasher, the drug war, rock ' n' roll, Satanism, and the FBI.

"Too bad. Everybody else did. The Worcester paper had a whole article about you yesterday. There's quite a write-up in today's *Boston Globe*. With photographs. You should check it out. Anyway, I know that no one needs to see Jade's car parked in your driveway. I'm not stupid, Pete. And I *can* keep a secret." She said the latter with an emphasis I didn't care for. "*I* wouldn't tell Nick and his boys that you and Jadie have an 'understanding'—"

"Then what are you here for, Cara?"

She shrank a little from my bluntness. "I just wanted to make sure everything's all right, Pete, to see that your house is well-protected against the nasties." She flicked some ashes from her cigarette off the deck and into the ground. "You know, my cousin's waxing into his full powers like an exploding moon right now. I initiated him into the mysteries of rock 'n' roll—"

"*You* initiated *him* into rock 'n' roll?"

Cara looked a little put out. "Look, Pete, there's lots you don't understand about me and Jadie. We're cousins, ya know. I know you two like each other. That's cool. As long as my cousin's happy, that's all I care about. Like to keep my family happy. Really."

"How old are you, Cara? Really?"

"Been around," she said sanguinely. "Ma says I finally took shape at Woodstock. Though I had a pre-life haunting sock hop gymnasiums and drive-in theaters back in the fifties, like a girl you might dance or neck with and never see again because I wasn't there again, just an energy flash or a twinkle in old Pop Culture's eye, as the saying goes. I don't really remember it, but I suppose I was the kind of girl who might have been taken for a Beat blown off course through straight America, who listened to forbidden music pounding across the continent at night on exotic radio frequencies and knew that was the power source Elvis drew his swarthy heat from. If you were a nice sheltered boy and kissed me, you might get sick inside for weeks afterwards wondering if you'd done something wrong and if I was 'nice.' But I'd be gone by then, just a foreign feeling in your bones. Ma says they made an urban legend out of one of my flashes. Still gets told at girls' parties. Over and over. Guys just tell it once, in grade school or something, but guys generally hear it at home first from their sisters."

"Oh yeah? Which legend?"

"Which legend?" She smiled softly. "Ever hear the one about the hook?"

I hadn't. "A musical hook?" I suggested brightly.

"A musical hook," she sneered. "Pete, a real hook instead of a hand, so you couldn't play music if you wanted. Most popular teenage underground oral tradition of the fifties and beyond. Can't believe you never heard it." But I could tell she liked the fact I hadn't, so she got to tell it.

"You see, a young couple was parking on the side of an abandoned road. They had the radio on, might have been Wolfman Jack, and a special news announcement came on about an escaped mental patient from a local asylum who had been out and about killing other couples parked on abandoned roads. This mental patient was supposed to have a metal hook instead of a right hand. The girl was scared and wanted to go home so the boy promised they'd only stay a while. And so they were necking and everything, when the girl heard something tapping at the window like a tree branch and began to scream, and the boy started the car and hit the gas and peeled out of there. And when they got home, they found a metal hook and a bloody arm on the door handle. You never heard that one?"

"I don't know. Maybe when I was a kid." Some of it sounded familiar.

"Well. Ma says I was the girl. Only I wasn't scared."

"Was Hugh the hook?"

She looked at me oddly. "Yes, I suppose he could have been. The story's hook," she darted. "But it was a heavy metal hook so who knows? Pun." She grinned.

"Juno got into a legend back in the thirties. She had a pre-life too. Ma says she was the vanishing hitchhiker. Known as Scarlett in upstate New York and Lucy down in Arkansas and all kinds of names all over. She was the one hitchhiking on an abandoned road one winter night. A couple of guys picked her up and she said her name was Scarlett and she lived in a house down the road. It was very cold and she was only wearing a thin summer dress so she borrowed one of their coats. When they got to the house, the boys turned around and saw there was no one in the back seat. They got out and knocked at the door but no one answered. So the guys returned the next day, looking for their coat. An old man answered the door and told them Scarlett was his daughter who had died eight years ago, and that other people had come by with the same story. They didn't believe him, but they drove a little way down the road and saw a cemetery. The missing coat was visible from the road, draped over a tombstone. The tombstone bore the name Scarlett."

"Sounds like the kind of trick Juno might pull," I said cheerfully. "Do you have any other siblings? Ones I haven't met?"

"Sure. I've got siblings *I've* never met. Ma likes to have kids occasionally, so here we are, her present batch. What do ya think? Are we beauties, or what?"

"How'd *you* get here? Out of your 'pre-life' I mean."

"Well, Ma finds boys. The right boys at the right time. Woodstock was the right time. Ma wouldn't have missed that party for the universe's approval." Her voice suddenly got self-congratulatory and thickly mystical. She studied the smoking end of her cigarette.

"Ya know something, Pete? My earliest memory is lying naked on the muddy ground and feeling the warm rain on my breasts and face. There had been a hell of a storm the night before I 'got here.' Thunder and labor pains. The dream of it was still with me. Someone wrapped a blanket around me, and Ma was there with food, a muesli of rolled oats and sesame seeds and wheat germ and honey. Courtesy of Hog Farm. Ma had a leather fringed jacket for me to wear, sewn with beadwork and peace symbols. And she gave me bell-bottomed jeans, and a peasant-style blouse, and sandals, and a big floppy hat. Someone gave me love beads and daisies and I was set. Taught me language."

She hesitated, squinting her eyes into the curling smoke as if it was an effort to remember. "No. I already knew language. It was the acid that gave me the words, and I was just there out of Ma's dreams, her own little dress-up hippie girl whom she took by the hand and led dancing through the crowds. I was alive. Like wow." Cara was really warming up to her story now. "And what crowds attended my birth, Pete. Tie-dyed vagabonds and sky-clad nature's children and outcasts and lovers and people out of a rainbow's myth. I was just one of them in the crowd. What a birthday party, huh?"

She had lost a little of her high falutin' pretentiousness, but not much. There was a genuine nostalgic enthusiasm under the story she was telling.

"Didja know that, for the three days it existed, Woodstock was one of the largest cities in America? The largest temporary gathering in the planet's history? America's youth were all there—if not physically, in spirit. How many, Pete? How many beautiful butterfly people attended my birth? The *New York Times* said four hundred thousand. Someone else said six hundred thousand. Was there a quarter million? Half? Were you there?"

"No." But I remembered feeling it in Pittsfield, on a summer afternoon thick with distant shadows. I was young and exploring the woods and suddenly the sky turned strange and festive.

"Gotta cool statistic for you, Pete. You know, in 1970 the US population was 203,211,926. It was. Check out the US census. So call it two hundred million, and say half a million came to Woodstock, and say one quarter of one percent of the nation's population showed up to the biggest party in world history. One in four hundred people. You run into four hundred people in your life, Pete? At least. You probably see at least that passing in one minute on a crowded city street. Every minute you'll be seein' someone who was there for the rest of your natural life. You see, enough of the population was there to make a measurable dent in the order of things. But let's get even closer to the matter. How many seventeen to twenty-one-year-olds lived in the United States on August 15, 16, and 17, 1969? Do you know?"

"I never counted."

"Eighteen million. 17,970,430 fucking people in that age group, to be as exact as the census. I looked it up. So we're talking 2.7% of a generation was there to be indelibly marked and *initiated* by the experience. One in every thirty-six. Nearly three out of every hundred. Chances were better than excellent that everyone with a claim to youth was either there or knew someone there. Because youth is generally tribal and clickish enough to know everybody. You know what I'm sayin' Pete?" she asked with a harsh urgency that reminded me of Penny. "The youth of America were at Woodstock—literally. So let's talk about initiations, Pete, and let's talk about who is fit to bless who. Do you know how the festival began? Really began?"

She didn't appear to be looking for a response so I didn't give her one.

"On the night before the first day of the celebration," she began huskily, "the fairy folk arrived over the visionary hills of upstate New York to make fires and magic. Real fairy folk emerging from outer history for this event, along with a few stray souls that got caught up with them and never came back to reality. The energy of the next three holy days was already hatching them over here out of fairy time to occupy the front edge of the event. They probably didn't even know they were here, they were just here, following the herds. And they were burning and chanting and pointing bones and whirling and swaying and buzzing with arms outstretched in low circles and throwing glow-in-the-dark balls and giving each other cheap plastic prizes for fairy gifts—just partying with all the popular effluvia of carnivals and happenings. Primitive as newly arrived Neanderthals. And then, at Friday dawn—I was born Saturday noon in the exact center of the festival's pulsing moment—but Ma said on Friday dawn, to mark the first day of the festival and send things off, there was a proper death. One. Like a sacrifice to mark the time with blood."

She dragged on her pink cigarette and watched gray clouds bending over my trees. Then she continued.

"Some teenage boy from New York had been sleeping under one of the trucks they used to haul shit out of the portable toilets. Downside of the universe. The underbelly of the waning moon before turning up again to fertile earth. Local farmer who didn't know he was about to perform the ancient sacrificial rite hitched his wagon to the truck and ran the kid over into the mud. Killed him at dawn. An unconscious offering to the earth. The next three days were most abundant. Gotta ask you another question, Pete."

"Sure."

"I know you love Jadie, but do you know what rock 'n' roll is? *Really* is?"

"Why don't you tell me, Cara?" I picked up the frame of my Walther and pointed it at a nearby tree, squinting as if the tree were a target. "What is rock 'n' roll? Really?" I kept my weapon steady, pulled the trigger, heard the soft click of metal hitting metal frame, set it back down, and proceeded to re-assemble everything.

"Really," emphasized Cara slowly, watching me work. "Once upon a time, there were chants and screams and cries that made blood thicken and visions come in all the hidden places of the earth. Rock 'n' roll started in some hell hole in Africa that no one can find anymore, probably doesn't even exist, probably gone away into fairy land, probably buried under some swampy shift in the current of a disease-ridden finger of the Nile, or under some stagnant, insect-infested backwater mire of the Lualaba River where nothing human will find it. They had the beat in Egypt and in Kush for a long time until civilization smoothed it out, and some of that got into Greece and points north before the sea storms took it. I mean the rhythms worked for visions, for shamans and priests bringing in god energy. I mean, Pete, the rhythms were there, the rhythms that make your body change and your dreams come and that speak to the places you're afraid of and remind you of the dust you really are while crying out the dream you could be. The underbelly rhythms—ya got those, the rest comes easy. And when the Egyptians and the rest of northern Africa lost the beat the beat kept going in the continent's underbelly, generation after ancient generation, pulsing in its ground source.

"You know, I think it had to be the Nile. But not the predictable rhythms of the Egyptian Nile everyone is familiar with. The unruly disorder of the jungle Nile, deeper in ancient Africa, the river no one thinks about. You know the Nile is the only river on the planet that rises near the equator. Its source is mud and heat, then it flows north, into the direction of magic. Ptolemy was right when he said the Nile starts in the Mountains of the Moon, because the most remote headstream of the Nile is the Luvironza River in Burundi, near those mountains, called Ruwenzori now. You know what Burundi is, Pete? You ever hear of the place, for all your reading?"

"Can't say that I have."

"It's near the equator, too. So hot that nobody has slept there in centuries, so sweaty and stagnant now that it licks against the steamy Congo Basin to dream of cooling. They export coffee and not much else." Her eyes locked into mine. "The kind of coffee that kills."

I said nothing. She blew a long trail of smoke and continued. "Burundi has dirt roads and trails, not much else. They export by boat from Bujumbura on Lake Tanganyika to Kigoma in Tanzania, from there to Dar es Salaam on the Indian Ocean. Or into the Congo. You see what I mean, Pete?"

"No."

"Even the stuff that gets out of that region today doesn't get here. You'll never taste Burundi coffee. It's rough and thick like the African Nile and if you drink it straight it poisons your tongue with a white paste. The people are very poor farmers and cattlemen. They live on blood and fish. Cattle blood, which they draw daily from the living cows. And that's where rock 'n' roll started. Somewhere in the damp prehistory of that region, among people who picked it up from fairies or fairies' relatives." She said this like a grand pronouncement to a geometric proof.

"All right, so how did it get here?"

"Through hidden souls in hidden people. The hidden ones brought it over in the stinking bottoms of slave ships, where the beat flourished in chains and high-pitched wails. The ones the ocean didn't swallow worked to death humming and chanting the beat down in the Mississippi delta, down in the mudflats and bayous and clinging southern heat. Kept it going like a private religion undercutting all the tame and monstrous hymns shoved down their throats with a bullwhip. Got regions of the delta still buried in mud out of myth ain't nobody knows about, and the beat got spread all over there in the swamps and backwaters. Into blues, you know.

"Listen to delta blues some time, Pete. The real stuff—go back to the source. It's got chromatic rundowns make your bones shake like skeletons in a funhouse wind, strange scales to make you feel another world passing through your body, which of course it is. Voices like forgotten heat. And the beat—the blues—spread and passed across the continent. Night waves tumbling thunder from Chicago radio and landing who knows where." Cara spoke with brazen reverence. This was sacred history.

"Then forward. It's the forties now with adolescence forming and some of us do hear the beat and the whine buried in the skywaves between midnight and dawn. There's a new world coming; we can spin and touch it when we dance with our pillows. Something's out there bringing in youth. And then down in the streets of Baltimore, where north and south meet and mix, young men gather on street corners at dusk and sing the beat—just sing the surge through their generation. Doo wop. Do what? Doo wop. Do what? Hello, the music speaks of mystery and difference and now it's getting out, pulsing from the inner-city containment and into the almost recognizable places of an emerging mass culture.

"And so comes the fifties and the genie's out, hoppin' and boppin' and Chuck Berry makes us all "Sweet Sixteen" like the title of his song. And faster and faster we all "Rock around the Clock" like the title of another song; comets in a tailspin until the clock goes dead. For years."

She looked at me searchingly. "The north saved us from atrophy. The north invaded the motherlode and kept it warm and brought it here to take dark root and stay. There was no American revolution. England won. Won it for us, led by the Beatles. And that's when I finally happened into life like a flower on a top, as Ma used to say. You know what else I remember?"

"No, should I?"

"Sunday morning dawn. I was awake and leaning on Ma's strong breast. Hendrix discharges his National Anthem to the ruddy sun and the emptying hills like a left-handed salute. The ritual is over. The city is coming down. The walls are falling and the beautiful citizens are spreading the energy back across the continent. There's steam rising from the ground as Hendrix plays, so many bodies had been there, steam like the earth making an offering to the priestly wizard pouring backwards music into the song of the land. Here was a crossroads and a blessing. Leave your guitar by a crossroads for a night and you'll play better'n the devil, the old blues masters used to say. Well, here was a psychic crossroads, here was the end of rock 'n' roll's childhood and exuberance and the start of its entrenchment. It crossed over from dreamland and took form when I did—forever, and so strong you can still hear the ancient blues howling the surge even under the most corporate, slicked up, commercial 'radio-friendly' productions. You can't kill the spirit. Not this one anyway. It's too loud."

She waited, and then said softly, "And of course Ma took me home, where I bathed and got younger and so I was also a child in Toronto with a brother and sisters to meet Jadie with. That was when Elise brought him there from Halifax, to separate him from the sea."

"That's quite a story, Cara."

"Yeah," she smiled stiffly. "It is. Jadie's good, but I can tell stories too. Girls generally can." A pause of small defiance. "Anyway, last Monday, I brought him into my circle and together we faced the South, the direction of fire and creativity. I made him look in a cracked mirror and know himself. And I wove magical protection into his basses, his heart, his poetry. You should thank me, Pete. Did you a favor. No one can hurt him now. He belongs to us witches."

"How romantic."

"Well, Pete, it's a job." She nodded and smiled. "So, what did you do all week?"

"Instigated my own protection."

"Yeah, I can tell. You've got witch-hunters all over the office and the press co-opting you for the other side. Thought you were *good* at this," she needled. "Well, if the monster gets loose—which I'm sure he won't," she added gratuitously, "you'll have to start doin' a better job or leave it to me to keep him at a distance. I'm Jadie's priestess. I'll protect him."

"Is that what you came here for?"

"Just came to chat, Pete. I'll leave if you want me to."

"What about the rest of the band? Are they 'initiated' now too?"

"No. Jadie's special. You should know that. Don't know what you did to him yesterday, Pete, but he was righteous awesome last night. Even for him. Just about burned the whole place down with his bass solo. Had chicks rippin' off their clothes and everything. Local radio station was there. Ma was happier than a Chinese New Year on stilts."

"Did she rip off her clothes, too?"

"Well, you know Ma. She enjoyed herself."

"How was the rest of the band about it?"

"They're all mostly business right now. Working on their next CD—"

"You mean, nobody is speaking to Jade."

"Well, Xander is. And we speak. Now that we have our own language and everything. But they're all fire on stage, you know."

"Yeah. Were Nick's people around last night?"

"'Course they were. What do you expect? Didn't see the big boy himself, but his boys were hangin' out, talking to the radio station people, havin' themselves a good time."

"Guess with friends like the Nunzios you don't have to worry about witch-hunters," I sallied.

"Yeah, them." Cara returned to her earlier jab. "Papers are sayin' you're their boy, Pete," she mocked in a singsongy voice. "Out to save the world from rock 'n' roll, out to nail payola—"

"Not exactly. That's my ex-partner's deal."

"Yeah, well the papers make it sound like you're in it. You're the head of SAYNO. You're out to save the family and nail the drug dealers and your office is in bed with Christians for American Decency—"

"It'll calm down after Tuesday's elections."

"Hope so. Elb's goin' 'round like he swallowed a cow with thumbtacks on her horns. Not that I care—"

"Oh? Is he worried about payments?" I smoothly changed the subject. "The way I understand it, Elb owes Nick the first seventy-five thousand dollars out of your half of the CD profits—"

"Hey, look," said Cara. "The CD is in northeastern stores and on the northeastern airwaves this week. Elb doesn't know what the returns are and neither does anybody else. The clubs were full here and in Buffalo and it all looks good. You know we might get our demo-video on MTV? The one for 'Pierced for Love and She Will' that the radio stations are playing now?"

"Yes, I heard it on the radio this week."

"It's a great video. There's a shot of my legs. Anyway, it's a great rock 'n' roll song so why shouldn't people buy it? A lot of the people in Morgan Le Fay's last night already knew the words, which is a good sign. Guido says it's selling great in Toronto. He's happy with the profits we made for him playin' at his place. And when the boys finish up number two, we'll be sittin' pretty. Because from that point on it's fifty-fifty on everything, minus the stores' cut, no matter what the profit. That's the agreement. So really how can we lose?" she asked, making pointed eye contact.

"I don't know," I said evenly. "Sounds like you've got it all under control."

"Pete," she threw her cigarette on the ground. "I've got more under control than you know how to dream of. You know what a rock 'n' roll priestess is?"

I didn't respond.

"No stories this time." She squinted her eyes towards the wind in the trees, making out her sharpening dream of grandeur against the cloudy sky. "A priestess brings in her god's energy. Makes him happen when he has to, as Ma might say. Remember the circle at my little Uncle Claude party, when I gathered my girlfriends together and we were the symbolic audience preparing the way for Black Dog to take the world? Well, a priestess is always audience, always listener. I'm the living representative of all the chicks and all the guys Jadie has to win. I'm the gateway. The front row Momma. The torch has been passed to me."

"Isn't Mother Penny interested in the job anymore?"

"Ma loves the job. It ain't that. It's that she loves developing her girls' potential, and she's happy to create another priestess for the work. No"—she smiled an odd little inward smile—"Ma's there for back up, but the project's mine."

"Congratulations. What's your point?"

"Well, I don't know how to say this, Peter, but you know as well as I do the thing Jadie loves more than you, me, or life is his music. His heart wants to get his music out there. He needs me now for that—"

"He's a brilliant musician, Cara. He doesn't need you to get out there—"

She got all tense and annoyed. "He didn't. He does. Pete, there's more to management than Elb raising wine glasses to the Mob. You see, me and Jadie have this magical bond now. When he plays, I feel it—all over his body and mine. I'm every chick that scrawls his lyrics in her torn jeans, every guy that jerks air guitar to his rhythms. As above so below. Let me tell you something, Pete. Jade might be a son of Dionysus, the maenads' god. But sometimes, just sometimes, the *maenad's* god. And right now, I'm the chief maenad. When Jade plays, I have to feel it, or nobody does." She let that sink in. "I'm the youthful spirit of the age, Pete. But there's more than that. I'm keeping Jadie protected with my magic, and goddess knows he needs it now, with Elise's little escapades and his relationship with you. But I could slip, ya know, anything could come out that shouldn't. I mean, I just want you to know. I don't mind sharing my cousin's affections with you, really I don't, but Jade knows what a help I am to the band. He knows he needs me. So I'm just sayin' Pete—he probably cares about you in his own way, but well, family's family. Some things go back aways."

"You finished?"

"Not yet," she said sardonically.

"Well, I am," I gathered up my guns and started for inside.

"Don't you have anything to say, Pete?" she asked, following me. She was a little thrown by my studiously cavalier reaction. I kept her waiting while I put my guns away, which only increased her uncertainty as to whether I had heard her latest threat. She looked most irritated at the possibility of having to repeat it as she followed me through the house. "You're awful quiet," she teased.

"Yeah, priestess," I said slowly, as if I were suddenly remembering something. "Does Jade know what a 'help' you're being this afternoon?"

"He knows how I feel. I don't care. He'll learn to appreciate me if he wants an audience." She looked a little nervous.

"All right, then, Cara. I do have something to say." It was an effort to keep my voice light, but I managed. "Thanks." I went into the "ordinary kitchen" she had once gone into paroxysms over and went through the motions of boiling water. "Like some tea?"

"Thanks for what?" she asked uncertainly.

"For offering to use your 'power' to keep the press and the fundamentalists out of my hair. I'm grateful." I made an earnest, charmingly familiar "thanks, buddy" kind of eye contact, which threw her for six or seven loops.

"Pete," she corrected. "I didn't offer anything. Figure you're man enough to handle your own problems."

"I mean," I said easily, "that if anything should 'slip' to the detriment of Jade or the band, whether or not you're actually responsible, I will do whatever it takes to kill you in the most hellish way I can imagine." I smiled. Sincerely, completely, and happily. We had an understanding. A bond. "Sugar?" I asked casually, without a trace of sarcasm.

She got ticked off for some reason. Left wordlessly. The self-proclaimed chief maenad of youth culture clomped pale and awkward out of my house, like a narrow broom slipping and clattering through fat and ancient grease-stained hands.

Phone rang about an hour later. It was Penny demanding to know why I sent her daughter home in tears. Had no idea what kind of story Cara had concocted so I recounted all the honest details of her visit. Then I demanded to know what kind of priestesses Penny was bringing up anyway. That pushed her voodoo button.

"Dedicated ones, Pete. Ye cain't do the work without the emotions that goes with it. It'll be hard for Cara for a while because she's new at it and there's lots for her to sort out. If there's problems then I'll straighten 'em. They'se *my* kids."

"Then start straightening, Mother. Your kids are giving me royal heartburn."

"Then don't get so *hoity-toity* 'bout it, Pete. Ye might see worse heartburn in the world if ye look for it—"

Car pulled into the driveway. "Sounds like Jade's here."

"Yeah, well that's fine. Pete, you keep Hugh in jail and yer man Crensch off of fingering Elise and uncovering payola and you keep yerself low and me and the girls'll handle the rest—" Jade unlocked the front door.

"Got my gear. Mind if I crash here a while?"

"Hide your car?"

"Yeah, forgot." He took off.

"Penny, why don't you handle everything? Throw the whammy over Crensch and seal up the monster's prison and charm Nick into loving all of you no matter what potential problems might present themselves in the near future. Make my work easier."

"They'se limits and they'se limits and I ain't Wonder Witch, as if what I'm doin' now ain't good enough for earth and beans." Garage door crashed. Heard Jade pull his car inside and start taking stuff out. "And suppose I did it all. Would ye cease to be makin' yer offerin' if yer Momma put a nickel in the pot for ye?" She had a point. "We're all doin' what we kin do to get the music out, and you know yer business better'n mine. I'll have a heart-to-heart talk with Cara 'fore we move on to Boston." Jade was coming up the stairs to the living room with a guitar case in each hand. Set the cases on the floor and went back down to the garage. "Here, talk to Beulah."

The phone conveyed Beulah's perpetual silence. I hung up as Jade brought a small amplifier into my living room. "Setting up shop?"

"Just the basics. This is my practice amp. Brought a drum machine."

"Welcome." I hugged him. "Need help with anything else?"

"No, the rest of my gear is on the bus, our combination traveling studio and girls' road dormitory when the coven isn't invading the van."

"So, where is your entourage camped out? You never told me."

"Motel one of Nick's guys owns in Worcester. Word is we're staying there until we play Boston next weekend, though we're spending most of our time in the parking lot on the bus working out our new stuff while Penny and Cara keep the fans at a distance."

"Nice place?"

"Perfect. Seedy enough to give Les something new to complain about and Marty something to wreak havoc on that's already too damaged to matter. Anyway, when I'm not fighting with my playmates, you got yourself a housemate for the rest of our New England tour."

"Cool."

"Would've come sooner but we were working out a new song today and Cara hijacked my car."

"Yes, I know. She was here." Told him about the visit, including my phone conversation with Penny. He seemed greatly amused by the whole deal.

"That's Cara. Don't worry yourself, Pete."

"I'm not," I said seriously, throwing my arms around him and playfully wrestling him down on my couch. "I never worry." Kissed him. "If the priestess slips in her duty,"—kissed him longer—"the priestess dies. Nice and traditional."

He laughed like I was kidding.

Tuesday came. Everyone got re-elected who was supposed to. Tuesday left and the drug war continued its mean-spirited banalities without a hitch. But my SAYNO duties were semi-tolerable because my lover was with me at night, making beauty for me like a new life to order and pressing back the rest of the world into meager unreality. By day I slugged it along for the good of oppression. By night I lived in a temple of my own device, wearing all the glorious freedom a dragon's mate could lay claim to.

Sometimes he'd be there before I got home from work with a strange supper of his own concoction laid out for me. Beet soup and cranberries, or a stinging vegetable stew, or a riotous lemon pepper chicken and red pasta. And whatever we ate we were always drunk soon after. Soon came to expect Jade would be home when I was, but I could never predict his arrival, and I got secure enough to mildly resent his work demands when he wasn't there. Then I resented his work when he wasn't working for me. I resented my work. I resented anything that got in the way of us seeing each other.

Sometimes I'd be certain he wasn't coming, then he'd show up after midnight and gently raise me from my bed with a poem before playfully pushing me back into my dream of him with a kiss that became hours of dark lovemaking. Sometimes he'd roughly jerk me awake with a single amplified bass note at two in the morning, which he let ring and ring while the windows shook thunder and we'd sing and tell stories all night. It's warm when your new lover comes to you in the dead of night and you create a private world together that no one else can enter. Warm. Living dreams, laughing in hidden corners of time, are *warm.* Warmer than a perfection of childhood. Any other comfort is frigid in comparison.

I didn't sleep much in those first weeks. I didn't care. Couldn't lose the time when he was with me. Couldn't let my thoughts rest from anticipating his next visit when he wasn't.

I was happy. Jade safeguarded my joy by making me cherish it. I would wake in the near dawn and there was the pulsing energy of my god at my side, like Cupid revealed to Psyche for more than a stolen moment. But unlike poor Psyche, there was no transgression. Jade did not hide behind a mask unless he took me with him—he was all revealed to me. I wondered if I should be so open, but then I already was. Nothing worth hiding, that was the pleasure—he accepted it all. We were the last lovers anywhere, so we did it up right.

We pretended I was sick so he could make me stay in bed while he fluffed up my pillows and fed me orange brandy and syrup. Then he sat on my bed and played medieval games with me that Penny gave him printed on English postcards. Fox & Geese. Nine Men's Morris. Draughts. We were always capturing each other's opponents. We were always embracing toy wars. We made up stories of the land of Counterpane. We had our own in-jokes, our own expressions that not even his bandmates and cousins shared. We were coven. We were band. Didn't even know or care it was November and winter coming. I sort of knew what season it was at work, but when we were together we knew nothing but ourselves. To me he was stormy and northern and dangerous. But more dangerous to lose than have. He told me he loved pleasing me. He told me he worried about me.

I asked him why. This was during my second faux sickness, when we were reading random poems to each other, so I wasn't sure if his worrying about me was part of the game. Counterpane had spun itself into a Sunday afternoon epic to rival the Brontë sisters' early sagas, complete with tragic lovers and empires rising and crashing in hard revolutions. We had created more interwoven characters to play than a Dickens novel. Jade grabbed my book of Robert Louis Stevenson poems and read, "I was the giant great and still." He smiled tenderly. "That's why."

"Yes?" I said in playful seriousness.

"Yes," he said solemnly. "You're doing so well now. You're getting so much better. Don't be the giant." He whispered this like a seductive warning, licking my ear while he said it.

"Don't tell me what to be, Count."

"You're learning."

"Besides, what have you got against giants?" I pinned him to the bed in a playful embrace. "*We* might be giants. We make love like giants. We create stories like giants. We are the giants of Counterpane who watch the leaden soldiers go among the bedclothes and into the hills of dreams and send ships in fleets among the sheets and plant cities all about to rise and fall at our pleasure—"

"Mmmm. Pete, the Giant of Counterpane is great and still. He watches his creation move and live. But he can only watch. He can create universes crawling like wrinkles through his bedcovers, but he has to be sick to make them happen, and he can't enter them."

"Maybe that's why he creates. His creation is a counter pain to his daily pain."

"Give up your daily pain. Don't go to work tomorrow. Don't go ever. Come live with me and be my love. Be my prisoner in the never-ending dream. Run wild with my poor lonely heart. Counter nothing."

"Jade, when I'm with you there is no tomorrow."

"I know. So be with me."

"Tempter."

"Yes."

"It wouldn't be hard," I said reluctantly. "But you have a CD to write to keep Nick happy."

"Who's Nick?" he teased.

"I know. I know." Kissed his hands. Sucked his strong fingers like a child sucks his first candy, with wonder and wanting more and knowing I would always want more for the rest of my life. "I'd love to be with you always, but in the long term it could kill us both."

"Kill us both." He grabbed the book again and read the last verse of Stevenson's "Bed in Summer."

And does it not seem hard to you,
When all the sky is clear and blue,
And I should like so much to play,
To have to go to bed by day?

He waited for an answer.

"Hell, yeah, it does seem hard to me," I said sorrowfully. "Let's go to bed by day." I playfully grabbed him.

"Never." He grinned. "Not you. I'll never let you go to bed by day. Never. Never. Never." He pressed my arms behind my head. "I love your stories." He kissed me. "I love your characters." He kissed me again. "You're mine. You want to play and play and play—clear and blue forever like the sky—and they're going to try to make you go to bed and I'm going to be your champion and stop them—"

I interrupted him with a pitiless kiss. He struggled a little because he still wanted to speak, but I kept kissing and pressing his body down on the bed so he couldn't until he was helplessly tendering himself to the sensation. I heard him moan a little, so I relented slightly. "Sssssh—" I said, keeping my mouth posed over his.

"Pete," he whispered, "are you trying to silence me?"

"Yes," I said softly against his mouth, kissing him harshly without letup to underscore my intent.

"Why?" he asked softly when I finally stopped. I had misjudged my power. He still had breath to speak.

"Because you're talking rot." This time I kissed his mouth and stroked his thighs and refused to stop until his body jerked into an orgasm. "So there!" I teased. "But I love you anyway." I lightly kissed the top of his head.

He sighed and held me. "They'll kill you at work," he said earnestly. "They'll butcher you with bureaucracy and sever you from your beautiful, ancient soul."

"They haven't yet."

"They will. You're starting to enjoy yourself and it's bound to show. Isn't that like the ultimate crime, Pete? The one all the governments murder for? Being happy?"

"The Bureau won't kill me for working with a smile. IRS does it all the time. Some of those guys get fined if they don't."

"All right, maybe they won't kill you. But if you're not careful, they'll pass a law and make you enforce it." He said this in such a deadpan voice we both nearly died laughing.

"The only law here is my law, poet."

"Pete." He wove his fingers in mine. "Would you rather be the giant or his dreams?"

"What kind of question is that?"

"It's the only question. It's your question. Would you rather be the poet or the poem?"

I pretended to give deep consideration. "The poem."

"See?"

"That way I could sneak up on the poet in his dreams and grab him by the balls and not let him go until he had spent himself on me. Invent me, Jade. Write me. I'm yours."

"Invent you. Pete." He smiled. "God couldn't invent you. You're too perfect to invent. Come, invent yourself."

"I thought I was."

"Pierced With Love" went into heavy rotation in Boston and Providence and everywhere else in the northeast so they extended Black Dog's New England tour for a month, with a couple of side jaunts down to New York. Which was most excellent, as it meant that Jade would be coming to me by night at least until the new year. I tried not to think of the emptiness beyond January. Only the resounding youthful joy of now. And I tried to get through my SAYNO duties with the minimum of fuss, duties that had pretty much narrowed themselves down to listening to Piekarski get excited over Satanism and rock music, which he now listened to religiously, and having endless look-busy-because-there's-nothing-better-to-do chest-thumping strategy meetings for nailing Lamar Toon, who probably had no idea what sort of name we were inventing for him in the field office.

Not that "Small Brother Mink" appeared to be a Satanist proper or anything. All anybody could make of his cult was that it was some potluck mixture of Christianity and Buddhism with a dash of pop psychology thrown in to remit the more glaring inconsistencies, so no one was entirely sure Satan even entered into it, although Piekarski did his best to make a case. His "expert sources," meaning Heppelfauf, suggested that Small Brother Mink was an anagram for Satan Beelzebub Moloch, the first letters being the same and everything, but we never got anything more definitive than that and after a while the project got to be a tough call because no one could actually prove that Toon was doing anything illegal. There's only so much you can do with rumors that don't check out.

The local police said there were drug dealings near his cult headquarters, but what the hell, if you want to get technical about it, there were drug dealings near ours. The dealings on Toon's street included this super-duper new crack, but no one ever saw him or his people sell drugs. When it came out that Toon himself preached against drug use and advocated "purifying the body" through macro-biotic diets, Piekarski looked most annoyed with the information and decided in a brilliant piece of perspicacity that his preaching was no doubt a ruse to allay suspicion. Which actually reassured a few of my colleagues that Toon wasn't totally innocent, but didn't get us much further towards making a case.

Even the runaway issue was badly in need of some backhanded government propaganda, because no one, including myself, had any evidence that he was breaking any federal laws. He was taking in minors, which technically isn't a federal issue anyway, although if the minor had broken a state law by running away from home and had crossed a state line, you could probably trump up a harboring a fugitive charge for harassment purposes.

But as Toon claimed to be some sort of minister who was helping to save kids from drugs by keeping them off the streets, and had gotten a sympathetic journalist to believe him, it was tough going to press charges in that direction, because, as Kanesh pointed out, we'd have to anticipate some media fun with SAYNO persecuting a fellow drug warrior. And as I pointed out, the religious aspects of the case meant we'd have to be careful to not violate anyone's first amendment rights. If you wanted to join a cult that believed Toon was the 320th incarnation of the Buddha's Divine Light, as he claimed, the government wasn't supposed to be in the business of stopping you. Not that we couldn't make something out of Toon taking in minors, but we'd have to work through the Rhode Island state agencies to find evidence of anything criminal.

Rhode Island was certainly eager to push things along, because their social agencies hate competition as much as anybody's, but the state couldn't find anything beyond a few young women of legal age living there with their own preschool children, which wasn't a crime anyone could do much about, as Bit o' Providence was properly licensed and zoned and everything as a multiple dwelling. The state investigators tried to find evidence of teenagers working for Toon without proper working papers, but the youngest "cult member" they could conjure up was a properly licensed for work seventeen-year-old whose mother supported Toon. Then it became clear that as far as anyone official could tell, Toon's teenage runaways were all eighteen and nineteen-year-olds, legal adults. Everyone "knew" there were younger members, but no one could find any. It was severe. The guy even paid his taxes.

But Toon was still an irresistible mark because being a wacko cult leader, he was disliked enough by the community to make him the most media-friendly local candidate for an all-out raid. Folks are willing to believe anything about a fringe religious leader, so that alone gave Kanesh some leeway to dream up an acceptable spin. Part of the issue was that SAYNO was applying for a special budget from Congress, and

Piekarski had high ambitions of eventually bootstrapping our little gang into the prestige of a separate government agency like BATF with himself in control, so he needed to cut a fine figure for the public. Of course our friends on the NDECC were on our side, but there had been some serious talk lately of shutting down the BATF and streamlining other law enforcement agencies, so we needed to show our congressional godfathers and the public how hot we were at arresting drug lords.

"Kind of like an audition," was the way Kanesh put it.

Anyway, Toon had guns, which would make him suspect to the liberals. He had invented his own religion, which would make him anathema to the right wing. He collected misfits and runaways, which would scare the hell out of middle American families with guilty consciences that would stay awake nights worrying that their kids might prefer Toon to themselves. We could keep claiming that he was suspected of being "associated with" local drug use, which would inflame just about everybody. We could claim the state had "suspected" and "investigated" him for child abuse, since, if pressed, we could stretch the investigation into Toon's alleged illegal employment of youth into "abuse." Then we could make sure everyone knew there were preschoolers living in the compound. If we were lucky, judicious exploitation of that angle alone would provoke loud public demands to "do something," at which point we could step in like heroes.

So in terms of raw material, you couldn't find a better gull if we planted one of our own, which was a half-serious suggestion someone made during one meeting when it had become crystal clear that nailing Toon with anything resembling hard evidence would take more thought than was collectively possible at the field office. Sometimes the nuts obey the law. Then what do you do?

Piekarski thought we should send a couple of agents down there apartment hunting. "Get some undercover guys to infiltrate this thing and send reports back. Someone who looks like cult material."

I looked at the blankly dutiful faces around the meeting room. "Shouldn't be too hard," I said blithely.

"Hey, Beisweiler and Zogney," barked Piekarski, as if they were sitting across town instead of in the same room. "Think you two could pass for a couple of teenage girls, lost on the town, runaways from Kansas or something and in need of a place to stay?" Beisweiler shrugged. Zogney looked at Beisweiler and shrugged. Everyone else looked relieved that they wouldn't have to miss weekend football games in the pursuit of justice.

"Yeah, Beisweiler would be great," said someone. "She could pass for a kid."

Beisweiler looked annoyed but gamely said, "Sure, I'll do it." Zogney seconded.

The two of them passed for kids for about thirty seconds as far as I could figure. They were back at the next meeting.

"What happened?" interrogated Piekarski.

"Toon was a little uncooperative," said Beisweiler resentfully. "We knocked on the door and after a long time a woman answered it. She let us in. We gave her our story and asked for Lamar Toon and she kept saying she didn't know him. She appeared to be taking care of four or five dirty looking children. Then Zogney here asked for Small Brother Mink. The woman left us alone for about twenty minutes.

When she returned, she asked us what we wanted. We said drugs. Then she left again for about five minutes. Then she came back and took us to a room on the second floor where Toon was. He asked us what we wanted and we said we wanted to buy drugs. Crack.

"'How much money do you have?' he queried. I told him two bills, and he responded, 'Let me understand. You two street puppies are offering me money for crack?'

"I clearly replied, 'Yes. I'll give you two hundred dollars for one gram of cocaine. Just a hit.'

"He then informed us that it's illegal to buy or attempt to buy drugs. 'Zero tolerance,' he stated." Beisweiler sounded miffed.

Zogney picked up the story. "He left the room, which appeared to be a little prayer room. We waited about ten minutes and searched the room but found nothing but religious books and papers. Then, to our great surprise, Toon returned with four Providence police officers who arrested us for attempting to buy drugs. And as we were leaving in cuffs, the Bozo Buddhist leader told us it was illegal to search his premises without a warrant. So then we had to spend the afternoon proving who we were before the locals let us go."

"Stop laughing, Morrow," said Piekarski.

"Hey, Charlie, the guy's slick. Whatever he's into won't be candy to catch." I looked at Beisweiler. "He knew from word one you were feds."

"How?"

"The papers always call him Brother Mink. Only us government types would ask for him by legal name. And the recent friendly visits from state agencies have made him wary."

Piekarski waved me off. "What else did you see in the compound?"

Beisweiler and Zogney looked at each other. "Nothing worth noting. It's just a big boarding house."

"See any guns?"

"No." Zogney paused. "But the children seemed badly cared for. Dirty. Like they weren't getting their proper baths."

"All right," said Piekarski, "let's make a formal complaint to Rhode Island Child Protective Services and see what they can find."

Everyone seemed satisfied that the Rhode Island social workers would be doing our job for a while. I cheerfully suggested that if the only thing we could get on Toon was that his tenants' children weren't getting proper baths, then I supposed the most appropriate thing for us to do was to consult another governmental agency about it. Maybe we could even petition our friends in Congress to budget an agency for regulating and investigating children's baths. That ought to provide some hack jobs. The meeting was adjourned without comment.

And outside in the hall, as I was seriously thinking about whether there really wasn't some way I could quit my job and live with Jade forever, I passed Fearless's partially opened door. The coffee machine was full of old afternoon. Paper towels shoved under the pot and stained with grounds. The ugly other side of the morning's jolt. Heard voices in consultation. Fearless's agreeable rumbles, Crensch's pointed inflexions, and, in a shock that stiffened my suddenly clammy chest and limbs, the coldly smooth salesman tones of Hugh S. McCrae.

Stave Seventeen

Wanted to eavesdrop but with people spilling into the hallway from the meeting and everyone rushing out of the offices to go home and Kanesh making a bee line for Fearless's partly open door, I had to force myself to walk casually to my office without looking as if the universe was any different than usual. Felt like I was straining through hours to get there. Felt like I was taking a lifetime to unlock my door. Just got it open when Piekarski bellowed down the hall, "Hey Morrow—when ya gonna look in your crystal ball and give us some predictions about what Providence is going to do next?"

"I'm no good at predicting Providence," I replied curtly, quickly closing my office door to shut him out. Soon as I settled on my thoughts he opened it. Piekarski was a rude bastard. Guys like him generally are.

"On your way home?" He bulldozed the question like a midnight cop harassing a coffee shop whore.

"Workin' late."

"Yeah, on what?" He nosed over to my desk. If it wasn't SAYNO stuff, he had to know all about it.

"Secret," I said easily, meanwhile wanting to kick his smiling ass. "No rest for the wicked."

Piekarski strutted around my office, sniffing approval at my anti-drug posters, reading all the stupid slogans aloud, slowly, as if he'd never seen them before, as if nobody else in the field office had the same stupid posters on their walls and I had surprisingly good taste for sporting them on mine. "Hey, why don't you talk to Beisweiler and Zogney about the religious books?" he barked. "You're supposed to know all about the nut stuff. You might get a usable angle on Toon."

"Thought you were the religious guy, Charlie. Why don't you talk to them?"

Piekarski grimaced. His subset of the right wing was pro-family and pro-church-on-Sunday and everything, but it was never "religious." Have no idea why they all hate that word, but it always seems to draw a scowl. "Like to send someone back to steal some copies."

"Need a warrant to steal books," I said absently.

"We'll get one."

"Need probable cause. Owning religious material isn't enough of a crime." I was speaking in an automatic kind of way because my mind was all stuck up with whatever was going on down the hall.

"Might be a crime. Might be Satanic. Could put you on a consultation team with Joe Heppelfauf and his people."

"I'd rather work alone." I gestured at the papers on my desk. The double entendre was too subtle for him. He didn't take the hint.

"We ought to have a progress report on everything while the Rhode Island Child Protection people do their thing. You're the report guy, Morrow. Just organize and tidy up what we've got so far. Gotta start makin' a case. Gotta be something there we can use."

"Yeah, Charlie, leave me alone with it for a while. Take some thought to dream up a progress report on Everything."

"Yeah, right, but don't take too long. You goin' to your car?" Piekarski didn't want to risk riding down the elevators alone, now that the building was pretty much cleared out, but he wouldn't come right out and say it. "Everyone's leaving."

"So leave. I'm not stopping you." He looked blankly puzzled. "Gotta tidy up here, Charlie. Later."

He looked at me suspiciously. "Since when you work late?"

"You can't win a war in an eight-hour day."

"Yeah, well don't kill yourself." He didn't mean it. He just didn't like me putting in more time than he was. "Tomorrow."

"Right."

Left my door wide open. Heard Marcie, Crensch, and Fearless greet Piekarski. Heard McCrae get introduced. Heard the group leave through our serious double glass doors. An iron-fisted quiet like sluggish asbestos made its rightful claim through the building, the city, my shortening life. Time swam thick around my flashing heart-beats, like my body was pulsing ahead of the crush of hard minutes.

Heard McCrae's slow, heavy footsteps return and become a plodding approach to my office. He was returning into the wasteland emptiness of the building as I knew he would. He was lumping through the quiet like quiet was the only thing on the creaky old earth that couldn't stop him. Felt something in reverse enter my office like it was almost forward and right. Saw a large face loom like a bloating nightmare.

"Hey." The monster grinned and pointed.

"How was prison?" I hear myself ask.

"Found a hole." He eased himself down on the metal folding chair. "Woo." He was thick and padded with fifties-style brown coats, dry cleaned over and over into a disgusting green and gold sheen of fuzz. His face was fat and cold and flatter than I remembered it. A bleached toad. The coats were keeping in the cold of his body. Everything about him was in reverse. "Met some people. Jail folks, hey."

"How'd you get sprung?"

He didn't answer. He glanced at the anti-drug posters that had so amused Pie-karski and read aloud in a voice like a dull slow echo of Piekarski's irritating approval, "'Drugs are for dopes and dopes are for drugs.' Nice design. Straight." Then he stared back at me in a silently bulging offensiveness, torturing my discomfort at not knowing why he was free. An overgrown toad face relishing my dead-fly ignorance.

"Drugs are for dopes," I repeated emptily, as if we shared a language. McCrae opened his mouth into a tight little hole and began to make careful noises in a high perky intonation, as if he would stop the lecture the instant I questioned him so I'd better take whatever information he was giving me now or never ask again.

"Well, I'll tell ya. It's like coming back from anything, you know. Death was easier but this time I got my lawyer—smelly old thin one who don't work so good anymore." He wiped his dry, cold face with a cloth that had one of those old-fashioned colored tinfoil Christmas decorations in it like a dead star glinting up out of the past, the once bright colors embalmed like dead dreams trapped in a humiliation of tarnish. "But he used to do real estate transactions for me. And taxes. Any old thing ya don't need to be a lawyer to do 'cept by law—to file papers away and stamp in the usual manner. Wills and probates and long, tired affidavits. Anything redundant and thoughtless and slow. You know, to keep his life precluded by inanity. And this man, good man he is, brought me a file to cut through the bars. And do you know what the file was made of?"

I didn't answer.

"Say no if you have to."

"I don't have to."

"It was a file of papers, Mr. Morrow. Good papers. First there was the business of the missing corpse nobody thought of. The *corpus delicti*, they say."

"The morgue in Rome saw the corpse. There are records. The government prosecutors know somebody was murdered on that base."

McCrae stopped as if he would go no further. I was not supposed to say anything if I wanted his story. So he sat there, saying nothing, to punish me for speaking. I sat wondering why his release hadn't been on the news, and then realizing I'd been so preoccupied creating worlds with Jade that I hadn't watched or read any news lately. Love was keeping my thoughts very much out of the real world's way. Jade was too distracting for his own good. Never again.

As my mind drifted into self-accusation, McCrae smiled. "*Nobody* was murdered on the base. That's the fact. My old body's gone. Unidentified. So who does the United States accuse me of killing? No name, rank or serial number, hey. Just a pile of dust. Can't kill dust. I must be accused of killing somebody. I must have a motive. Well, that's the first thing in the file. Federal judge ruled with no known victim, there's no crime to have a trial over."

"Why didn't that come up at the arraignment?"

"Election year publicity and physical evidence. If it weren't for public pressure and the physical evidence—because nobody argues with the *physical* evidence," he jabbed his index finger toward the ceiling, "and the *press*, the *press* pressed me like a fat sensuous bug by getting all your flag words out to the public from your painstakingly written report"—he jabbed his finger towards me—"hey, I might have been free then. You slowed me, that's all. Which I like, hey. Being slowed.

"But second. Second, I change my body a lot. Get sick you know. Like wasty cheese. I get cheese whey like sweat and over time I'm a lump turning inside out. Heh, heh." He shook his head. "Ya know, I'm never really anything. Just churning slowly 'round in my place like a crabby liquid oozing out of a garbage dump. Well, my lawyer had 'em match my fingerprints from my arrest to the fingerprints they took for my NDECC job. No go. Perhaps there was a mistake and my prints got mixed and matched with somebody else's on those government papers, but anyone could see now that they weren't mine, even if that unknown somebody else's did match the prints on the unfortunate letter to the corpse. So that unknown somebody else, another nobody working somewhere in government, and having some knowledge of the movement of military commanders, might have killed another unknown nobody who is now dust. Which all has nothing to do with me, Mr. Morrow.

"Then third. Lawyer asked for newfangled test. D . . . N . . . A. Well, my body changes that too, like a dinosaur sloughing dried up scales, and my new hair isn't what it used to be." He leaned forward to show the dry and cracking sandy hair of an old man, the kind of hair that should have been gray like the snarl he left on Juno's crayon letter but was now clinging like a dead crab to a grotesquely youthful past.

"Fourth. Scrivening my handwriting was a good trick, but tricks decay over time. Nature wins. Like a peach left too long in the back of your refrigerator."

"What?" I asked.

"The handwriting went back to what it was, along with the names. The magic didn't hold. So my lawyer—he says, go take a good look at that letter, the one with the handprint that don't match and the DNA samples that don't match and put on your specs he says and take a good look because my client is being wrongfully held, and the judge had to say there's insufficient evidence. Got out last night and hopped a bus to get here. Shared a stale baggy sandwich and Cheezits with an old woman with bad breath and broken shoes. She was a good mouse, hey."

I couldn't think of anything to say.

"So I'm a free man." He smiled. "Wanna buy into a home delivery service?"

"Why are you here? Are you going back to work for the NDECC?"

"No. That's set into spin and they'd be touchy about reinstating me. Once tainted, always tainted, even if you're innocent. Like I said, nature wins. But ya know, well, got my own project now for a brown cow. Yessirree. Yippee. As I was sayin', in prison I met some folks. Johnny Nunzio. Good boys. Good Mob. Johnny remembers you."

"Nice of him to say." Johnny Nunzio was one of the guys I put away on that interstate trucking deal a few years back.

"Johnny Nunzio," he repeated. "And his cousin's brother-in-law, Paul S. Campobello. Good boy got sent up on some racketeering charges, some record industry scam he took the fall for to save a Nunzio boss a few years ago."

"So what's your point?"

"So ya know, hey, fine talk. Liked my jail, Mr. Morrow. It was a good jail. Pauley's gettin' out soon. End of the year. For Christmas maybe. Gotta job lined up workin' for the family. Record promotion, he says."

"Does he talk to his old mob associates from jail?"

"Does he talk?" giggled McCrae. "He talks, sure. He talks to me. *I'm* an old mob associate, heh heh—get it? *Mob* associate. None of his old friends come to visit much. The deal when he went in was a good job in record distribution when he got out. Reward for taking the fall. So Pauley—Pauley talked to me and Johnny—we were watching news on the nice color TV the jail provided in the rec. Interview with Sidney Crensch mentioned your name as a partner on an earlier case"—of course, he meant the CNN interview that I recorded in Toronto—"and since you were a mutual friend between me and Johnny we were talking about you. 'Do you know Pete Morrow,' I says?

"'O yes,' says Johnny. 'Hey, I know that guy.'

"And since Pauley had a professional interest in this story on Claude Hopner and payola, he jumped in and we were talking about that too, especially since the scheme was linked to the vanishing corpse, which I had an interest in. Now I says . . . I says I know this Claude Hopner fella, know him a long time, and I bring out the towel and cry a little and say I know what the love I just missed—*missed*—Mr. Morrow, missed in the desert, did to him that made me hungry. So I says, hey, ya know, Pauley, I know who took Claude out, it's my wife Elise McClellan and my old friend Pete Morrow knows her son. Seein' as Pete couldn't find her for me, when you get out, you might try up Canada way. And he's asking how I know and I say, just mention the name McClellan when you get out, and you'll see."

I just kept staring through him. Couldn't swallow. "Doesn't sound like your style, Hugh."

"Well, it's an old style. Primitive warfare. Got my hand in the arsenal of democratic despotism, and in some circumstances throwing stones from the bottom works better than detonating the newfangled warhead on top if you understand that the principle is the same. You know, Pete." He blinked. "I'm a Titan." For a second his voice echoed the desperate self-righteousness of Mrs. Kipfer, but then it reverted to his own inane cheerfulness. "I ruled the first Mob with my many brothers and sisters. The monsters in mother's deep. Antaeus, Cecrops, the Centimani, Ceto, Charybdis, the Cyclops, Erechtheus, the Erinyes, Ladon, Nereus, Oceanus, Phorcys, Pontus, Thaumas," he named them off on his fingers. Then he pointed to my gaping ceiling and preached, "Many were Giants, in the good old days before the gods." Placed his hand across his chest as if he was about to recite the Pledge of Allegiance and briefly bowed his head like a salute.

"I know all about mobs, Mr. Morrow, organized and otherwise, and I know that regulations and laws and such devices are nothing if not organized assaults from some mob. A certain mob doesn't like someone making too much profit in a business, so they get costly regulations passed in the name of some bogus safety concern to eat up profits and time. Old time mob used to just call the guy a witch and stone him before they stole his property, but the end result is the same. Another mob doesn't like sex, so they pass a law ensuring that anyone who has it without risking conception and trapping their lives up in unwanted children for decades will suffer. Another mob hates public acclaim and tries to regulate what artists can say and do. Another mob hates enjoyment in general and tries to regulate anything smacking of fun to death. So pretty soon no one can do anything but hate the smallest signs of happiness and success and pass laws against it. Because that way you can kill without crowning martyrs and keep your hands clean, you know." I remembered Penny had once said something to the same effect. "So the NDECC is one way, and the Mafia is another. It's all religion."

"And is the Bureau a third way?" I asked thickly, hating to have to ask and knowing I would hate myself for not asking. "Did you come here to show my ex-partner how to solve the Hopner case?"

He kept grinning with an obscenely beatific expression, and a slight shaking of his head, as if he was mocking his own smile and encouraging me to do the same. He kept it up for minutes, smiling and shaking and saying nothing. His face was a slimy angel's. There was nothing I could do but sit and sicken and watch until he spoke again.

"Hey. Well. Just came by to see Mr. Crensch and tell him about the letter myself. So he gets that dirty girl's proper address off it in case he wants to look her up. Just wanted to wish you a happy season, Mr. Morrow, to you and yours. Hope you all have a Happy New Year and a Christmas." He stood to go but made slight swaying motions back and forth in the thickness of his coats.

"So what are you going to do now?"

"No more questions, Mr. Morrow. I'm zipped."

"Are we going to be in touch?"

"Ah, Mr. Morrow, we're always in touch. You know that." He smacked his lips. "I'm sure we'll be working together for quite some time. Got a job to bring us in touch, to keep me supporting my old friends in government in my humble way. Good job." He pointed a finger at me. "Old friend Father Joseph Heppelfauf getting me on board his Christians for American Decency—fine organization—to help with youth up Canada way. Starting my own chapter. Advising on the occult. Saving young people from drugs and evil, you know."

"Merry Christmas," I said icily.

"Yes, Merry Christmas." He leaned on the doorjamb. "I'll be around." Then he left, and I sat there in my ugly office hearing him hoot as his feet dragged away down the hall, hearing the glass double doors close, and the wasteland silence of the building fill my life.

The same questions kept goading through my drive home. Especially couldn't stop wondering whether McCrae had dropped Crensch any information concerning Elise, or if he had his own reasons for wanting the Mob to find her before the feds did. Had no idea why he wanted to turn Crensch on to Penny, unless he thought there was enough evidence there to nail her on the vanishing corpse murder. Maybe he had no idea that it was Cara's handwriting on the notes. Or maybe he did know better, but wanted to destroy Jade's career by making sure that even if Nariano chose to keep it in the family that Elise murdered Claude, he couldn't do the same if Penny or Cara got arrested on murder charges. Any of these arrests would demand a public investigation into the payola scheme that Crensch had asserted on the CNN broadcast tied both cases together. Elise wasn't directly involved with Moon Management's shady promotion deal so her arrest might not yield much. Penny was.

But that still didn't make sense. If he wanted to turn the Mob against Black Dog, he needn't implicate both Elise and Penny. Either one would do nicely if done right. Also Penny was so experienced in this sort of intrigue it would take more than the letter to trump up enough to arrest her on. My government would have to figure out who the hell she was first, and that could take them longer than it was taking the union to fix my ceiling.

Maybe the monster just wanted to focus enough official attention in that direction to cause problems. Or maybe he primarily wanted to torture me. Because actually, other than torture, there was no other reason for him to pay the Boston field office a visit fresh out of jail. Dropping Penny's address was just an excuse, because he had to know that both Crensch and myself would probably be receiving copies of the letter with instructions to follow up on Penny's address in the next few days via the appropriate channels, seeing as we both had been officially on the vanishing corpse case. Also, he clearly wanted me to know that he was on his way to Canada to work for Heppelfauf. Maybe he was discussing his new job with Fearless. Planning ways to keep in touch with SAYNO. Maybe he was really seeking Elise out on his own, to get "himself established in such way over Jadie's life" and "steal back the power Jadie got from Dionysus" as Penny had once feared, but if that was the case, why was he putting the word out about his intended bride to the Nunzio family? And again, why did he see fit to come here to tell me about it?

So my thoughts were stumbling me in the door, and I didn't even notice that my love was leaning easily against a thick couch pillow and playing his bass unamplified. Which was unusual, because he usually turned his amplifier loud enough to rattle the house foundations when I wasn't home. He scattered my speculations by his sudden greeting as I was emptying my pockets on the counter that divided my living room from my kitchen.

"Hey Pete, miss me?"

I turned around and said something fairly incoherent.

"You're looking as hollow-eyed and haunted as a ghost without a motive to come back and live."

I sat next to him on the couch. "Where's your car?"

"In the garage. Where it's supposed to be." There was a hollow ghost in his voice. Sort of.

"Since when do you leave anything where it's supposed to be?" I tried to tease, but the words came out strained. I usually had to remind him about hiding his car.

"Like to keep you guessing once in a while." He grinned.

"Glad you're keeping quiet." I leaned back and watched his face, trying to determine if he was pretending he hadn't heard the news of his monster's freedom. He knew I was watching him. Covered his knowledge by plucking a string hard and getting an ugly loud buzzy sound.

"Hear that? Fret wear. Play so much that I've worn down the twelfth fret on my A string so it's lower than the fret for A#. See? Makes the string buzz like a tired wasp against the thirteenth fret when I play the twelfth. Same problem with the ninth fret on my D string. When it's amplified you don't hear the buzz, but I'm going to have to do a little fret filing before it gets worse. Like to keep my gear in good repair." He was sort of rambling in a way that was unnatural for him. "I can usually compensate if the buzz gets bad enough to get picked up by the amplifier, but I prefer to have the whole fretboard open to me. I'd just raise the action but I might have to sacrifice some smoothness in playing—"

"Of course," I interrupted absently. "Jadie, will you do something for me?"

"Sure, my lord, anything. I am always at your service." He knew. He was trying to hide behind a word game.

"Lay down your bass and let me hold you," I said directly.

"All right." He set his guitar in its stand and moved over to my side of the couch, where I held him as tightly against my chest as he had been holding his own broken instrument. He closed his eyes and leaned his head against my shoulders. Felt his body was nervous like a scared little bird. Sort of gently rocked him back and forth like I was comforting a child on the waves.

"I know why you're here today," I said simply. "I know why you're quiet." He didn't respond. He just kept holding on to me. "Jade," I said gently, wanting to tell him about this afternoon but entirely unwilling to do so. He was already hurting, and something in me didn't care to admit that I had come home straight from a meeting with his nightmares and was utterly powerless to fight them. I softly kissed the top of his head. "We can always go away. To some tropical island, to some hidden mountain in the west. Tahiti. I don't know. Some foreign place the Mob won't bother us in. I'll build us a log cabin, and we'll grow wildflowers. We'll grow carnations and roses, and you'll play and sing and make poems for me every night. We'll swim in midnight oceans and worship Aphrodite, and have long stories by evening woodfires"—I held him tighter—"and it will only be us, forever and safe—"

He pulled violently back, looking strangely dismayed.

"What's wrong?" I took his hands in mine and pressed them. "We'll be happy in our own hearts' country. We'll love each other and be blessed." He moved away from me. "Wouldn't you like that? I've got enough savings to—"

"To put me in jail instead of him?"

"Jade. What jail? What are you talking about?"

He hurt me with a look of utter distrust. "Do *you* want me to join you in quiet country retirement? Do *you* want me to play for you and no one else? To be so absolutely alone in our mountain cabin that no one besides yourself need even know I exist? Would you like that?"

"Isn't my admiration enough for you?"

He paused before saying, "No." Then he looked searchingly into my hurt face and said, "Would you prefer me to give you a lie?"

"I don't know," I answered honestly.

"All right, I'll give you one. I would love to have my music silenced from the rest of the world. I would love to play only to you and the unyielding stars. I've worked so hard for that, for the final reward of only having one response from one person forever and ever without end. Thanks for the invitation, Pete. Let's give the monster what he wants. Let's retreat into utter obscurity—"

"Isn't that what you once told me you wanted? Didn't you tell me 'don't be the giant' and that they'll kill me at work for being happy and so why don't I just give up my job and go traipsing off to fairyland with you?"

"That was different," said Jade. "You hate *your* job." I groaned some incoherent protest. "I only meant travel around with Black Dog," he said quickly, to mollify me.

"Hang out with us for a while." His recovery failed to convince. He wasn't ever this sloppy.

"Sure, Jade, pack up your things." He looked uncomprehending. "I said pack up your things, guy. We're going." I knew I was playing a game of chicken, but in the moment I didn't care.

"Going where?"

"Worcester. Springfield. Wherever your entourage is camped out this week. Lead the way. I'm joining the tour."

"Pete—I—"

"Come on, let's go. Got my keys. I'll throw some clothes in a duffle bag while you move your gear." I resolutely turned my back and started for my bedroom.

"Pete—wait," said Jade thinly.

"Why?"

"I mean, what about Nick Nariano's promotion plans?"

"Right." I turned back to him. "Poetry is all very well, but you don't really want me scaring your promoters away." I spoke coldly. "And I thought you really meant you wanted to go away with me somewhere, to be your 'prisoner in the never-ending dream' and all that—"

"My music is my never-ending dream—" he protested.

"Then leave the world and play for me. What do you care?"

He didn't answer. He looked at his bass and fingered some patterns on his fretboard without plucking any strings. Playing and not playing. Deliberately shutting me out.

"Sure, Jade," I snapped, "Gotcha. And I was silly enough to think you were enough of an artist to love the music for its own sake and not care how many empty people are willing to kiss your ass for the sake of a few chords."

"I'm enough of an artist not to care to hide it. For anyone." He stood up and put his bass in his guitar case. Something in his tone and gesture reminded me of the way he reacted when I overheard Elise telling him to give up his music ambitions in favor of a safe, predictable teaching career. I immediately felt all wrong about the way this exchange was going, and the way he seemed to suddenly and easily cast me as an outsider, but for some reason I couldn't let on that I felt that way.

"Where are you going?" I demanded.

"Home," he said wryly. "Got some tracks to lay down." He grabbed his case and started down to the garage.

"Now?" I knew he was lying. He was never here when I returned from work unless he'd been working with his bandmates on the new CD all day. Refused to follow. Heard the garage door slide open. Followed. Heard car pull out as I went down the stairs. Missed him.

Stared for I don't know how long at the empty winter road outside my window. Needed to talk to Penny but didn't care to call their Nunzio-run motel. Kept staring and thinking about protection herbs until the phone rang. Then the ringing shrieked suddenly up into a squeal so I knew it had to be her.

"Hello."

"Pete. Didja see the news this morning?" rasped Penny anxiously.

"Where you calling from?"

"Where should I be calling from? We'se been basically in Worcester, Pete, case ya didn't—"

"—Is the line secure?"

"Ain't no one can listen. And it ain't like I'm callin' ya at work. I'm usin' it through a toy phone in the van. It only calls out, ya can't call this one in. Hold on—" Heard bright tones of a computerized children's melody, a disconnect, then "yass OK I got it back. The boys is out eatin'—which I ain't too happy about considerin' my cookin's better than the local places, but we've got a bigger problem now, if ya ain't seen the news—"

"Yes, I know." Told her about this afternoon's office visit, but decided against mentioning my argument with Jade. Then I started to spill out all my questions but she cut me off.

"Pete, Pete, I ain't no sphinx to give ya answers ya cain't understand. So I ain't got none but this. Here's the gist of it. Hughey says he's finding his way back north to start himself a religious operation and he's payin' ya a house call to make sure you know about it. And he's sendin' the Mob on Elise, though I'm convinced he's after her himself. And he thinks he's goin' to turn yer brothers in the law loose on me for a murder charge. Good luck on that one. Well, I ain't thinkin' it's primarily to scare ya, though there might be some of that. He's primarily boastin' 'bout what he's goin' to do, like an old time Teuton poundin' his chest before battle. Ain't no victory worth it if ya can't boast to yer enemy beforehand about what yer goin' to do. And he ain't got courage to tell me about it direct so he figures you for a go-between."

"How'd he figure me for that?"

"He knows you got him framed through witching the writing. How many witches got a motivation to do that one for kicks? So he knows ya know me more than to say, '*Zoe Kai Psyche*' and keep walkin'. And he's old enough to tell what you like. He's been doin' that for centuries. He kin see the sea in your eyes. He knows ya, Pete. He found your hole. Ya got somethin' ya like, he'll take it away. And if he sets up shop with Elise, he'll be doin' his best to steal back Dionysus's power, you watch. That's all what his kind does—"

"—Right. So I've heard. So what are we going to do about it?"

"Well, I ain't leavin' Jadie. Not now. Not with monsters on the loose, I gotta stay close to my pets and that's that. Gonna have to send the girls back home to keep a weather eye open for the Titan's tricks. Thass one thing."

"I don't trust Cara playing guard duty in Toronto."

"Ya trust the other two to keep the cops from my door and send them on a new track? I ain't sendin' Elbie. He wouldn't know what to do if Hughey told him how, and he has to stay here where Nick expects him to be. So we ain't got much choice 'less ya wanta call off the tour, which, considerin' Nick's investment, ain't much choice at all."

"But, Penny, you're the only one in the whole circus that has a chance of keeping Hugh out of Toronto."

"And if I do, my pets is here tourin' without me and he's free to do havoc up close if he likes 'cause I hates to say it Pete but you ain't much for stopping him."

I chafed because she had a point and it stung. "So what do you expect your daughters will be able to do in Toronto? The last time you left them alone, he strolled into your front yard."

"That's the youngest two alone. Cara's the clever one. She'll keep him out with their help." I didn't respond. "Look," she protested, "they could kill him for a while if they'se lucky and that might solve the problem with him. Depends on how strong he is right now. Cara knows how to kill him so she might as well. Or else they kin work some binding spells in the proximity to dampen down his power. If they gits there first, they can block up Elise's property with charms. They can lie to whoever comes knockin' on my door on a murder charge that they don't know me." She waited for me to assent but I remained silent. "Cara especially ain't afraid of monsters. I'd trust that one to storm straight into Elise's house and pluck out Hughey's crumbly heart if she had to. That girl won't stop at nothin' where Jadie's concerned."

"So why didn't Cara's work on the letter hold up? Why do you think the handwriting reverted?"

Penny got all angry and excited. "'Cause I told her to use salt, iron and poison through a backwards mirror. But Hugh McCrae poisons salt, as it comes from the sea, and he is cold unmoving iron. So ya need a certain level of skill to not get it confused between the mirror and reality, and she is new at it. Should've done it myself but she needed to learn."

Reminded Penny of Cara's little threat. "Mother, with all due respect, do you think Cara knew exactly what she was doing? Could she have 'reverted' the writing at a distance to free the monster?"

Put out kind of silence. "Ya sayin' I cain't train nobody for the work—"

"I'm saying your eldest has her own agenda."

"Shaddap about Cara. Ya trust her or ya don't, and I'd say right now ya have to. The girls go back for a bout of monster killin' 'cause there ain't no other way I kin see and that's that."

Given the choice between the girls or Penny staying close to the band, there was no choice. "And what about Nariano getting the word to think that Elise killed Claude?"

"Look, if he gets word he'll send someone to talk to her. Sure they'll want to know why and if it means an interference in their business but crimey so long as they're gettin' their money and Elise ain't a rival family tryin' to hex their long-term plans what should they care? They'll just take her for a nut and maybe put someone on to watch her. Sure they'll probably want it hushed. But it ain't like Claude's death has cost them any money far as I kin tell, and the song's on the radio and the tour's on so they're in it now. Ah kin get them to trust me for it. An I got plenty of stories to make it right."

"It's Crensch I'm worried about. He's tailing them. The issue is keeping my brother feds from discovering Black Dog's illegal promotion scheme and if they find

Elise they won't stop with her. They'll discover what's driving Black Dog's success, believe me."

"So make sure they don't discover it, Pete." She sounded highly annoyed. "What can I say?" Then she hung up.

So I had no choice but to consign the monster's Canadian foray into the hands of Penny's capable daughters and trust her assertion that Nick's discovery of Elise's guilt was containable damage if only I kept Crensch out of the way. Maybe I could encourage Crensch to chase down Penny once we were duly notified of the letter, because Cara would easily lie him away from her doorstep and it would waste time and distract him from tailing the Nunzios for a while. But there was still a significant chance he'd pick up mob rumors about Elise and go that route. Her foreign citizenship would slow the investigation but not stop it. And it still bothered me that McCrae wanted the Mob to chase Elise and the feds to chase Penny, because I couldn't figure what his game was. All right, there was nothing for it but to trust Penny and concentrate all my efforts on keeping Crensch from solving the Hopner case.

Of course, I hadn't even been watching Crensch's machinations as closely as I should have been, mostly because SAYNO was keeping us out of each other's immediate way so I couldn't safely determine what Crensch was doing on the Hopner case without making it obvious that I cared. Routinely went through the tape bin but found nothing helpful. Learned from office gossip that he was eavesdropping in the North End, so I had the impression that he was trying to tag behind the Mob's investigation while convincing Fearless that the Mob was tagging along his. Also had the impression he hadn't gotten any further in his search for Hopner's killer because everyone at work, including myself, had noticed that Crensch was suddenly extraordinarily arrogant and hyper secret, full of being in charge of a nationally exposed case. If he had anything real, I was sure he'd be bragging about it. He'd taken to sauntering by my office several times a day to glance inside and spy. I'd taken to leaving my door open or closed at unpredictable times to give him something to keep tabs on.

Made a fire and let my thoughts revert to my recent tiff with Jade. Hated that. It was November 30, and I knew that after the first of the year Black Dog would be leaving New England and playing clubs down south. Jade had said another song from their first CD was going to get some airplay then. He thought it might be "Poison Puppy." Their video for "Pierced with Love and She Will" had been in heavy rotation for two weeks and I had moved my TV set upstairs and snaked the cable line through just so I could watch it.

Despite Cara's legs, which framed the first shot of an impoverished city street like a pair of black stockinged burglars, it was a great video, with Jade leading the band through a scene of urban devastation. It ended with a shot of a girl dying in crucifix position outside a church as the priest took up a collection for the poor. *That ought to frost Heppelfauf*, I thought wryly. Not least because the video was so brilliantly executed, with Jade's voice of love and pathos pounding out ironic commentary on the destitute lives depicted in the street scene.

It was odd that our argument kept running through me at a low level, while my thoughts were on other things besides the argument, sometimes like it hadn't happened. Even reached the point of thinking so much about McCrae's visit that I couldn't think of it anymore. It was just there like a cancer in my body, and I wondered if this was how the terminally ill sometimes felt when the effort of remembering mortality occasionally succumbed to an exhausted denial. Got me through a lifeless night.

And then, two days after the monster's visit, we were duly and properly informed of the letter, and Crensch got right on the hobby of convincing Fearless to start all the paperwork he'd need to go "investigating" in Canada, and I tried to jump on it on the basis of my involvement with the vanishing corpse case, but Fearless told me my SAYNO duties were now a higher priority. Crensch could handle Canada by himself. So that was that.

Called Cara in Toronto that night to give her a heads up. Juno answered, chomped gum while I spoke, and interrupted me by speaking back in a tumble. "Just got here yesterday. Cara isn't happy that Ma sent her home. Neither is Beulah. I'll give everyone your message." Then she hung up.

Jade hadn't called or visited since our argument. I was more annoyed than angry, as the days left before Black Dog was to quit New England were ticking away, and once or twice I was tempted to call the motel but caution held me back. Then the phone squealed and rang on the fourth night of silence. Grabbed it.

"Hello," I said noncommittally.

"Uh, hello . . . uh, Pete?" said Xander, a little uncertainly, as if he wasn't sure it was all right to call.

"Yeah, Xander, how are you?"

"Good. Hey, how are you?" he asked, gladly relieved to cover up his hesitancy with friendliness.

"Good," I said. "What can I do for you, buddy?"

"Hey, uh, can I talk to Jade?" he asked quickly, not liking to have to ask.

"He's not here. What time did he leave Worcester?" I asked casually, not liking to let on that we had quarreled and that I was therefore more than happy that Xander seemed to be implying that Jade was on his way over here. "Can I take a message?"

"Yeah, yeah," said Xander, sounding vaguely overexcited. "When he gets in, could you remind him that tomorrow's Friday and we're supposed to be driving down to New Haven for a show? Uh, we didn't think he'd forget but we wanted to make sure."

"All right."

"Yeah, and I really want to talk to him about some ideas I've laid down on some new tracks. Put down a bunch of stuff yesterday. I mean, if he can get here tonight, that would be great."

Something inside me clutched. "Didn't you see him yesterday?"

"No. Haven't seen him all week. We figured he was at your place—"

"—He ain't here," grated Penny's voice suddenly. "Ain't been here since Monday. Ain't he been with you, Pete?"

"No," I said uneasily.

"Why not?"

"I don't know—I thought—"

"So where is my pet if you ain't there to watch out for him with the monster on the loose?"

"I don't know—"

"—Yeah, close enough for government work."

"—Penny don't hang up." Got angry. "Couldn't you have done something witchy to trace him?"

"We didn't know he was missing until just now."

Something in the way she hissed the word "missing" made me go sick inside. "Penny—he left here around seven-thirty Monday evening. We'd had a disagreement—"

"And ya couldn't see fit to tell me with a gig coming up and important people gonna be down in New Haven to see my pets? Don't know what I kin do four days after the fact but now Mother's gotta try 'cause there ain't anything else for it—"

"Penny, please let me know what you come up with." But she had already hung up. Sounds of strange birds twittering on the line. Then dead.

Spent one of the worst nights of my life. Picked up the phone twice to call the motel, thinking that if I got Penny on the line I could ask her to call me back on the toy phone without my having to reveal anything compromising, but I knew it would only make matters worse if one of Nick's cronies was listening and learned about her private line. On the third time I called anyway and asked for Penny, having no idea what I would say but being desperate to say something.

"Who's that?"

"Elb McCrae's mother. Might be out back in her van."

"Who you? Watcha want?"

"Need to talk to her."

"Give me message. I'll see if I can get her."

Hung up.

Spent the rest of the night in a state of torture. Nothing beats imagination for concocting sickly night terrors when we have nothing to do but leisurely consider all the fine horrors that could possibly happen to someone we love. Switched on the news, like I had been doing all week per my resolution during the monster's visit, and although none of the stories were any different than anything else I'd seen this week, my heightened agitation made them difficult to watch, because I kept stupidly imagining that the next story would report some murder victim that someone would identify as Jade.

Where the hell was he? What if he did run into McCrae? Would McCrae ever be upfront about his violence enough to hurt him directly? How? I shuddered to think of all the ways, and found myself in the absurd position of praying to Aphrodite that the monster was indeed too sleazy and underhanded in his attacks to confront Jade directly. I wanted him here safe. I was ready to go to Worcester myself just to be with Penny, damn Nariano and the rest. I was pacing out of helplessness and angry resentment and then I was pacing out of just plain fear. Every time I heard the wind in the trees, I told myself it was his car. All night long.

Drove to work the next morning without seeing anything around me. My stomach felt heavy and sick and my hands felt shaky and cold. Heart beating in my head because I couldn't feel anything but nerves in my chest. And in that august condition I somehow made myself put the final touches on my Providence report. Emerged from my office to make copies and had to listen to Crensch officiously tell Marcie about all the secret channels he was working through to start his investigation in Canada. He was so gleeful about getting this lead on an important case that he even forgot to hush up around me. Marcie kept bobbing her head and wishing him luck.

And I kept feeling like nothing around me was real and I was dragging through my workday like I was dragging through heavy water for a rain-soaked corpse. Spent the afternoon doing nothing and of course that made everything worse, because I had time to mindlessly resent the green cinder blocks of my office for being the same as they always were while my life was unraveling. Sometime in the afternoon I listened to Piekarski complaining about how slow the Rhode Island Child Protective Services were and why weren't they coming up with "anything good" yet and had I come up with any angles? My body was stiff, my voice cold and weak, but I got through the discussion. Had no idea of anything I said.

On the way home I pushed my radio scan button looking for news and it locked onto a local talk show that had Heppelfauf and Mrs. Kipfer on as guests. Caught the tail end of the rock 'n' roll killed Egbert saga and the same torpid fascination that causes people to stare through repeat showings of gruesome accidents made me listen to the rest of the show.

Heppelfauf was trying to drum up support for Christians for American Decency by parading around their latest fetish and proclaiming that it was a "known fact" among "Christian researchers" like himself that many rock bands were "Satanically possessed" and that rock singers had been known to go into trances and call in the devil himself. Wouldn't want his own kids in the front row when the spirits descended onto the stage. Knew of one boy who went to rock concerts frequently and ended up possessed.

The talk show host clearly had Heppelfauf on to bait him, and was having quite a good time, but to his obvious disappointment as well as mine, most of the callers seemed to be sympathetic to Heppelfauf's madness. Because to listen to most of them, you'd think crime didn't exist before innocent young children discovered rock and roll, and now we had serial killers and who worshipped the devil and everything. Heppelfauf had probably told his followers to be sure to call in. Not that everyone bought the "singer is the devil" line, but most liked the idea of censorship and felt that the government should "do something" about violent music and entertainment. Everyone's "kids were at risk." Everyone was worried about "crime and drugs." Everyone had a three-year-old daughter who shouldn't be exposed to rock music.

The talk show host tried to ask the callers if they listened to much music, if they bought CDs, if they went to concerts. "Music should be relaxing," said one indignant woman who pledged support for Heppelfauf's bill. "It should be for background. I don't listen to it a lot."

"I used to play the organ, in church, so that was enough for me," shrieked someone else. "I don't want my *ch-eye-eld* getting shot for drug money or God-forbid-having-sex because of a rock 'n' roll song."

The host brought up the first amendment and an angry sounding man insisted that the first amendment was never meant to be used to support violence to our kids. "You can have free speech, but only up to a point," he declared without a hint of irony. One woman was sure she'd feel safer if certain forms of music were regulated. She liked Heppelfauf's bill because it made the music industry responsible for crime, and it was about time somebody took responsibility for these kids. She had three children of her own. She shuddered to think what they might be exposed to.

So did I.

But I shuddered the rest of the weekend without word of Jade. Almost drove down to New Haven to see if he would make his gig but I had no idea what club they were scheduled to play in and I didn't want any Nunzio associates to recognize me. So night and day of quiet agonizing nothingness slogged by. Couldn't eat or drink. Lay on my couch and stared through a horrible minute by minute watch as the sun changed its patterns on my floor while the second hand of my wall clock kept moving nowhere. Jade's practice amp and drum machine were lifeless reminders of their owner. Slept about two hours. Had caustic dreams. Felt guilty upon waking. Then raw and cold and anxious. Kept dying.

Phone rang early Sunday afternoon. Didn't even hear it at first because by that time solitude had completely bent my mind into my most exquisite fears. When I heard myself answer with a rough "hello," I was semi-aware of standing in my kitchen near the counter that separates it from my living room, with the receiver in my hand and without remembering getting there. Breathless with the sensation of the top of my head splitting off and cold fog smothering my slamming heart while I listened to a soft, hesitant silence and then an even more hesitant, "Hello? Is this Pete Morrow?"

In my distracted condition I didn't recognize the voice right away. "Yes, this is Morrow. Who wants to know?"

"Uh, Beth. Beth Dundas. From Toronto?"

"Sure, sure. Yeah, Beth, what can I do for you?"

"I got your phone number from Juno," she said nervously. "I hope it's OK. I'm only calling because Jade came to visit me last week—" felt all my strained apprehension exploding into fury "—and he mentioned that he stayed with you sometimes. I don't know how else to get ahold of him so I was hoping he'd be there."

"He's not here, Beth. I haven't seen him. When did he leave Toronto?"

"Uh, yesterday." So he missed Friday's New Haven gig.

"So when did you see him?"

"He came by work last Tuesday afternoon and he talked me into skipping out because George wasn't around. So I did. Showed him my new place. I've got my own place now, Pete, it's a little room I'm renting over the bakery I work in on Saturdays."

Beth sounded unusually chatty and confident. Her voice was buoyant. Bright and happy with the new confidence of an intensely happy love affair, the same happiness I knew had entered my voice and demeanor and that Jade had half playfully warned me the government would persecute me for. Jade had probably spent the week with her and she was all in a happy fit for having been with her dream.

She kept chirping, "It's really good. It's a really good place. I don't have to pay rent in exchange for working Saturdays and some mornings before Fendra's opens and just for being there at night so there's somebody around. My boss is really nice about it. Juno brought Beulah over this morning with stuff and helped me decorate it, so it looks cool. She said they had to quit the tour. Beulah looked like she'd been crying and Juno said she wasn't too happy about leaving Les—"

"—See Cara?"

"No. Juno said she's in a horrible foul mood about having to come home and she's not talking to anyone except Selene. She said there was some trouble on the tour that they were sent back to take care of, but she wouldn't say anything else and Jade never mentioned anything like that to me. He just said he needed a hiatus, needed to get away and just play for one person who could thoroughly appreciate his work without the distractions of anyone else—"

"He said *what?*"

"That he just wanted to be alone with me. In a log cabin on a mountain with wildflowers, somewhere where he could just play and sing for me and no one else."

I wanted to kick Jade's butt into Lake Ontario.

"Pete, I'm so happy. He was so sweet. He just came into Fendra's last Tuesday without warning and snuck up behind me and said, 'Would you like to go out dancing with a storm in a bottle?' and at first I was scared it was some creep, 'cause Fendra's attracts a lot of guys with problems, and then I saw it was him, just like I had been imagining for weeks it would be, only it was real. And then we went out. We went out everywhere. He took me ice skating and dancing and out to eat in an Indian restaurant and I kept missing work and he kept saying, 'Don't worry about George, I'll talk to him,' but I didn't care about George. And he stayed with me, and we ate breakfast together at three a.m. and sang to the city streets and Pete, he bought me a rose from someone selling flowers on the street corner and I still have it and it was the best week of my whole life and I'm so happy. I can't stand it I'm so happy. Everyone's seen his video and people kept stopping us and asking him for autographs and once I heard someone say, 'Isn't that Jade McClellan from Black Dog? His girlfriend is really cute,' and I looked around and I didn't know who said it but I felt so proud and I couldn't believe I was really with him. Then Juno came by this morning and she didn't even know he'd been in town."

I was too stunned to interrupt any of this, and like a masochist asking for seconds I heard myself say, "So, what else did you do?"

"We had dinner at his mother's."

"Whose idea was that?" I knew I was in interrogation mode, but Beth didn't seem to mind answering my questions. On the contrary, she seemed to be enchanted with the opportunity to talk about Jade.

"His. He wanted to see her."

"Was she happy to see you?"

"I guess. I don't know. I've been seeing Elise since the band left. Jade doesn't know it, but I've been taking piano lessons from her on Sunday afternoons. Just for fun. Just for myself," she added quickly, lest I think she had other aspirations. "It was her idea. She suggested it when I had dinner at her place that time before Jade left town. And at first I was shy about taking her up on it, but I'm glad I did."

Of course. What groupie wouldn't seize the opportunity to take music lessons from her idol's mother?

"Only I don't have a piano to practice on. Elise says I need a lot of practice and I'm kind of old to be starting music for the first time, and I have clumsy hands, which I know I do, but I keep telling her I don't expect to play like Les or anybody. Someday I'll learn one of Jade's songs and surprise him with it. Someday. It'll be a long time before I'm that good. Anyway, she lets me play hers on Sundays when I'm not working one of my jobs. There's a broken down out of tune one here in the bar so when it's not busy—"

"—You're calling from Fendra's?" I asked suddenly, sick at the thought of George Fendra hearing any of this.

"It's OK," she hastily assured me. "George doesn't mind if we come in and use his phone when the bar's closed, as long as the answering machine picks up the other line, which you can't call out on anyway for some reason. He's really nice about it. This phone is a line the phone company doesn't know about or something, so he never gets charged." Or gets a bill with my number to ask questions about, God bless the Mob. "I can't afford my own phone yet. There's nobody here but me. I was going to practice a little before going to Elise's—"

"So is George upset about the days you missed?"

"A little. But he's a nice guy. Jade talked to him Friday and George was so funny. He said, 'I didn't know you two had a thing. Young people in love.' And he sang part of some old-fashioned Italian song, and I was so embarrassed, and so happy in a way, because although Jade didn't say he loved me last week, he said it that one time before, when you were there, and he didn't say anything when George said it, so I guess it was all right. And then George said suddenly, 'Hey got a call from my friend Nick sayin' you supposed to be playing somewheres tonight and nobody can find you. He know you're here? Maybe you better call him.' And Jade smiled at me and said, 'No, no one knows I'm here. It's our secret. I'm sure the gig's been cancelled.'

"We stayed at my place that night—actually we stayed there every night—and lit candles and he told me stories and it was oh—just really nice. But he left yesterday and I just wanted to make sure there wasn't any problem and he got back all right and—I guess I just wanted to talk to him. To say hi."

"Well, Beth," I said stiffly. "I haven't seen him."

"OK, well if you do, will you tell him I called? He knows he can call me at Fendra's during my hours or he can try downstairs at the bakery in the morning, but my boss there doesn't like me taking personal calls. I'll be at his mother's today."

"I'll tell him."

"Thanks, Pete. You're good people." Beth hung up. I hung up. Stared at the phone, at the rude air in front of me and at the cloying stillness of my house. Walked out of the kitchen and crossed to the other end of my dining room. Carefully and deliberately rammed my fist through my exquisitely strait-laced gold-wreathed wallpaper. Bled.

Monday blurred by like nothing. Crensch skulked through the halls and "worked through channels." I just worked and skulked through an ugly day. Left early.

Home. To my numb surprise, came home to find Jade's car parked in my driveway. Pulled up behind it. When I took my hands off the steering wheel, I could see they were shaking but I couldn't feel them. Got to my door without real thought, having no script or story to follow, just dragging myself into what was bound to be one hell of a little chat but having no idea of strategy or goal or what I really wanted to say. Found my front door unlocked. Opened it in slow motion and made myself fight my body's stiffness to saunter inside. Slammed the door behind me like the place was still mine.

Up the stairs and into my living room and there was Jade, deftly moving his heavy practice amp across my living room floor with one hand. His drum machine was tucked under his other arm. His eyes showed briefly that he wasn't expecting me.

"Move it." My voice was rougher than a bum's life in a February recession.

"I am," he said simply, lifting his amp off the floor and bending over a little with its weight as he tried to maneuver past me.

"No. Move your fucking *car*." I grabbed his arm at a pressure point near his wrist and expertly forced him to drop the amp, which made an awful thud as it hit the wood floor. He protested but I kept holding his arm as I grabbed his drum machine with my other hand. Then I released him. "*Now*. Or I'll move the damn thing myself." Which was a fairly stupid threat to make as I didn't have the keys to make good on it, but one of the things you learn in law enforcement is that sometimes stupid threats work when uttered in the right tone of voice. And this was law enforcement. Kept his equipment hostage as he went outside and drove his car into the garage. So many issues and all I could think about was hiding his goddamned car. Phone rang while he was out.

"Yeah?"

"Pete, where's Jadie?" It was Penny. "My pet got back Saturday midnight, praise the Lady. Took off half an hour ago without sayin' where. Figured him for your place. Did he make it safe?" Casual as a hell shadow. As if it wasn't necessary to call me when he first got back and disrupt a pleasant weekend.

"He's here. We're busy." Hung up.

Jade returned as I banged down the phone. "Who's that?" he asked lightly. "Anyone I know?"

For an answer I grabbed his arm and slammed him onto the couch. "Sit down," I ordered superfluously. Instinct and training told me to keep standing, to keep up the appearance of authority, but I relented by forcing myself next to him and sort of pinning him in the corner of the couch without releasing his arm.

"Come on, Pete, that hurts—"

"—It better hurt. It's fuckin' supposed to. *I* hurt."

"C'mon, guy, watch the wrist—"

"If you don't start behaving, I'll break your goddamned wrist. Solve a lot of problems." And I increased pressure while his beautiful face winced in pain. "All right." Dropped his arm but I still had his body pinned with mine. "What's your fucking problem?"

"Pete—"

"—Hugh McCrae is out of prison, headed towards Toronto like a bad case of dying foliage reversing the natural order of the Fall—"

"—you're speaking poetry—" he tried to protect himself by smiling appeasement.

"No, I'm not." Grabbed the front of his shirt and shook him.

"—Yeah," he said, quieter now, "didn't know he was heading north until Penny said—"

"—Shut up. There's a hell of a lot you don't know." Shook him again. "You got it? You're gonna listen to me until I'm finished." But I was so angry I didn't know what to say, so I let go of his shirt with another shake and stood up. He was rubbing his arm now in the space I left him and looking stunned, but I could tell that I now had his attention. Paced the floor to let the violence dissipate a little. "How's your arm?" I mumbled.

"Sore," he said matter-of-factly. "What's *your* problem?"

Sighed. Stared at the spot where I'd pounded the wallpaper the other day. "I'm in love with a dragon with shit for brains."

"So?" He was still rubbing his arm, but there was a hint of merriment in his brown eyes that I didn't care for.

"*So?* Damn you, Jade, I ought to kick your rising rock star ass back across the border. Do you have any idea what you've accomplished this past week? What you've put me through? When you talked to Penny, did she also tell you that McCrae was in my fucking office last Monday? That he's told your promoters that your mother killed Claude? That Cara's goddamned letter reverted with Penny's address on it and it's now part of evidence? That Crensch is heading into your hometown to do some detective work on her involvement with the vanishing corpse and there's precious little I can do to stop him? That Crensch has been chasing down mob rumors and it's only a matter of time before my government shows up on your mother's doorstep and starts investigating everything connected with your band? That your cousins are back in Toronto trying to save your ass, and I'm sick of the family values charade I have to put on at work to save mine, and yours, and—" You can only scream for so long before you have to stop. Jade was absolutely expressionless as I caught my breath. "You know your buddy Xander was worried about you, in case you fucking care. He thought you were here screwing off from your band commitments—"

"Yeah, I talked to Xander—"

"—Why bother, when you couldn't see fit to talk to me? And you've been back since fucking *Saturday*?" He started to speak. "Never mind how I know. I thought you were working with your bandmates until I got a call last Thursday and it turns out no one knew where the hell you were, not even Penny."

"So? That ought to make some of my bandmates fairly happy," said Jade lightly, doing his best not to respond to the real issues at hand.

"Or was that part of the game, to make me worry about you—"

"It was your game, Pete."

"What the hell do you mean by that?"

He smiled softly and mockingly. A smile that would have entranced me on stage but in the present circumstances only made me want to hit him. Restrained myself. "If I was playing a game, you set the rules—"

"—Did I fucking tell you to go traipsing around Toronto with Beth?"

He showed absolutely no surprise at my knowing how and with whom he had spent the week. "You made me think about my life. You questioned whether I was enough of an artist to love the music for its own sake. So I went north to see if I could happily play in splendid isolation to an audience of one, and not care 'how many empty people are willing to kiss my ass for the sake of a few chords.' And I found my solitary audience and played my heart and soul out to her and her alone in splendid obscurity. Since you wanted an artist who is capable of leaving the world, I left the world. Anything to make myself worthy of your dream." He looked me directly in the eyes. "As long as I'm fulfilling your fantasy, what do you care who I do it with?"

I was so furious I couldn't take enough breath to scream, so my voice came out like I was choking on broken glass. "You talk to Nick? Is he happy about the New Haven gig you blew off? Or does he think your no-shows are setting new professional standards?"

"Are yours?" I didn't answer. "I have no idea what Nick thinks. That's Elb's job."

"Was Elb happy you blew off the gig?"

"He's never happy."

"Are you happy?" I was screaming now because my voice had broken loose and I was fairly maniacal at this point.

"Saw my mom." He said this in the same irritatingly easy tone he once used to tell Elise that he had an aunt he could stay with if she wanted him out.

"Yeah, I heard. Your girlfriend called here looking for you." He didn't react to my word choice. "That was a bright move, Jade. Was your mother happy to see you?"

"She was thrilled." Jade's eyes met mine. He looked vaguely amused. "Tried to poison me."

"*What?*" I grabbed his shirt again and shook him. The material ripped a little because I was standing and pulling upward with some force. "Is that funny?"

"She might have thought so, I don't know. Didn't work. Poor Beth nearly got it instead." He was getting comfortable and almost playful with my anger. I released the shirt. There was now a sizable tear down the front.

"Are you telling me the truth?"

"As far as I can. It wasn't too original on her part. In fact, it was all very much like the movies. Which was pretty funny, 'cause she's never been much for movies." He was breathless from my last assault and trying not to show it by jollying me. "She wasn't too secretive about it, either. She keeps rat poison in the cupboard and I noticed her put some in the sugar bowl. And when she brought out the tea things, she only put sugar in one of the cups and then she made an issue about giving it to me because she and Beth didn't take sugar."

"Surprised you didn't fucking drink it, being poisonous and all."

"Are you sorry I didn't?" he quipped. "Really, Pete, what do you think of me?"

"I think you're a self-destructive jerk," I said coldly. "So what saved your life?"

"Beth. She grabbed the poisoned teacup and announced that she did take sugar now because I did, and she was trying new things and that Elise had put more in than I usually liked. Which was true, because my mother was probably doing her best to make sure. Beth insisted on serving me herself and she was so proud and flustered over the honor she grabbed the tray and spilled the other two teacups before she could put sugar in any of them. So I did the decent thing and used my considerable manual dexterity to spill the poisoned tea she was planning to drink in her lap. Which was all pretty funny."

I stared at him. "I'm not amused."

"My mother was. She laughed hysterically at the spills. So I mopped Beth's clothes with a towel and we left."

"I'll bet she loved that."

"She did. Hey Pete, you want me to spill poison on your clothes?"

I did not answer. Looked glumly at his equipment. "So. You moving out?" I asked, my voice straining into a hurtful indifference I didn't really feel.

"You want me to?" he asked seriously.

Sat next to him without comment. "No, Jade, I want you."

"Yes?"

"Shut up! You are not going to hurt me again, you got it? You brought me dreams to play with and you can't have them back, not now. I don't care how many girls you lay when you're on the road and who you play to and what kind of bullshit you have to prove to who, so long as you don't endanger my dreams. Got it?" He looked uncomprehending. But then, I wasn't entirely sure what I was saying either.

"Pete," he said softly, "I'm not in the business of endangering anyone's dreams. Least of all yours."

There were unmanly tears welling in my eyes. The storm had left them. I blinked them away. Held him tighter than my taught chest held my cracking heart. Held him fit to break my heart against. Damn it, he *was* fit to break my heart against. "They're my fucking dreams—" I half-sobbed, like a child who just got his favorite toys stolen.

"Whose would they be?" He managed to pull away enough to make eye contact when he said this.

I pulled him hard against me. "You gave them to me and you can't take them back. Ever." I was crushing him so hard he couldn't breathe. "Ever ever." He was gasping for air against my chest, and I was gasping for words. "They're all I've got. You're all I've got. You're going to stay close to Penny, and you're going to stay in touch with me, and you're going to stay away from Elise, and you're going to stay out of trouble, and you're going to do your fucking job like you're supposed to." His body was shuddering for air while I was speaking but I didn't care. Finally let him go as he gasped like he'd been dying under water. "Or I swear to you, Jade, it won't be primeval monsters and envious bandmates and your crazy mother you'll be in danger from. Because if I hear about any more trouble, if I hear that you're endangering my dreams, I'll come to one of your performances, I swear to all the gods I will, and I'll fucking kill you myself." Weird thing was I knew I meant this but I wasn't sure how I meant this. Then I kissed his lips, lightly.

"I love you too, guy," said Jade easily, smiling. "Does that mean I can spend the night?"

"Of course, my love, whatever you desire."

Kissed his fingertips, like a lawful knight in a medieval romance saluting his mistress before a terrible battle. Then I took both his hands in mine, and gently traced their lines like I was telling him his future. Marveled at their supple lightness.

Rubbed the place I'd hurt. Kissed the forming bruise.

Stave Eighteen

The god slept with me every night before he left for points south. Tenderly pressing his mouth on mine, he'd still my breathing until I'd pass out tasting grape clusters. And then he brought me down into piercingly desolate dreams. And then it was one long dream divided over the twelve remaining nights before Black Dog was to leave New England. Because for those nights I only remember one long mirage that I kept living through.

Mostly I was a twelfth-century French nobleman, and I had great wealth and social standing, and I was related to the king, and I was greatly to be feared in war, yet every night I retired to my coldest chamber and wept to the moon while a sad-looking *jongleur* cajoled me on his lute or my favorite jester broke his old heart with the effort of trying to make me laugh. I wanted old stories. The kind of stories my mother, the late queen's sister, used to tell to comfort her princely nephew for his mother's death, but never bothered to tell to me. And all I could do was sit on my cold stone window ledge and watch the barren moon make her slow descent while her horns tipped my fields with a strange silk that looked like silver. And all I could feel for in my weeping was a memory of something English and strange that I knew as a child but couldn't feel anymore. Something old and odd I kept weeping to find.

We played this game awake, too. Jade made up the script and assigned roles. I was King Morpheus the Dreamer or somebody like him. Jade was any dream I wanted to happen. Tirelessly. Upon command.

Since there were twelve nights left before what remained of Black Dog's caravan was to move on we took to calling them our "Twelfth Nights." Each night Jade brought me a little gift like in the old song about Christmas's twelve days. Semi-intangible gifts like old bass strings and broken charms and candles inscribed in new languages that quickly burned themselves out. It was dragon time all over again. But it was dragon time with a dusky vengeance.

Something had clearly changed in the nature of our play, although I couldn't explain, not even to myself, what was essentially different now. Perhaps it was just the aftermath of the fight interfering with my perspective. Perhaps we were just in a queer new dream of Jade's invention that I hadn't mapped myself entirely through yet. But it seemed that Jade had suddenly gotten just a shade too professional about things. Not so I'd notice, but enough so I'd *notice*, if you know what I mean. That is, I might think I was noticing and then spend hours wondering if I was wrong. I know I kept feeling slightly indecent about our games without knowing why, and without really knowing if I were really feeling indecent or merely imagining that I was. He smiled too perfectly on cue, spoke too smoothly, responded too eagerly to my requests. He was too—*solicitous*, but not in any way I could call out and question him on. Certainly not in any way I could object to.

I knew he had always taken pleasure in entertaining me, but now there was something more purposeful than playful in his acting. Of course he always played to a purpose, but I suppose what was different was that he seemed to be playing more to my randomly stated purposes than his own. He had become more of a blank canvas. Sort of. I mean he played all right, played his roles beautifully, and gave me one or two breathtakingly beautiful private concerts, but he always seemed to be taking his cues from what I wanted. He refused to lead.

His bruise slowly healed. I don't know. It was like we were lovers, like our fight never happened, but it was also like he had business to get through and roles to play, "lover" only being one of them. I was getting my wishes granted in spades but something in my heart kept complaining about it down where I couldn't hear the words too clearly. I felt most unreasonable, like an unfeeling nobleman desperately commanding someone else's poor Fool to give him a lawless emotion. I suppose there was a strong unspoken understanding of limits. He knew he was there to keep my dreams alive. And I knew that after our fight I'd best shut up about it, because we both knew that this dream-keeping was what I really wanted and would kill to keep.

The other change was that there was no more guessing. When I came home from work he was always there. When I woke in the morning he always rose before me and made me cinnamon-scented coffee. He always saw me off to work in the dark. So for twelve days, as a prelude to work, I drank cinnamon coffee while driving into winter sunrises. Morning sky was another of his kisses, crashing orange and open over the city, fiercely.

Days below zero. Strange nights like hellfire.

In my absence Jade drove to Worcester and laid down vocal tracks and fought with Les over the final mixing and production work on the new Black Dog CD. Elb wanted him to get a wrap on things before the band moved on for the rest of their tour because Nick wanted to start getting copies pressed, the current plan being to start getting airplay for new CD songs sometime in late June to capture the summer buying season. Or rather, to "capture the summer and create the season" as Jade sanguinely explained.

Jade also mentioned that "Pierced With Love and She Will" would run its course after the holidays, and that "Poison Puppy" was due to get airplay from late January through March along with a new video Nick was arranging to have them shoot down in New York. Then they'd release a third as yet undecided track to radio to keep Black Dog's name before the public until the new CD came out. Elb planned to use releases from the new CD to keep the band on the air for the rest of the year.

I wondered how things would sit with his bandmates once the imminent need to complete the new CD was no longer forcing them into maintaining a semblance of an off-stage working relationship, but I said nothing about it, basically because there was nothing to say and because Jade never cared to bring the subject up. Besides, I knew that refereeing band infighting fell more squarely in Penny's domain than in mine. My only responsibility was to keep Crensch from discovering Elise and to fight the drug war without blushing. Jade's only responsibility right now was to perform in the clubs Nick sent him to and to promote Black Dog's music. I assumed that his bandmates were still ambitious enough to see that as a common cause.

As the last dawn ushered in the last day of the old year, we were making slow sultry love to each other, and I was so intent on the experience that I had already forgotten that I had already decided to be late to work. He was leaving today. Black Dog was playing a New Year's Eve gig in Manhattan, where they were going to stay to shoot their "Poison Puppy" video, and then they were heading south to Baltimore. Figured it might be months before we saw each other again.

Needed to hold him against me. Needed to hear the phrases he made up just for me. Poems to carry me through the rest of winter. We rose from bed holding hands. Walked aimlessly through the house. Felt the day all snowbound. Dressed in silence. Then I helped him load his equipment into his car.

When the mundane business of living was finished, we shared a strange tea that tasted like peppermint and hibiscus that Jade made up instead of coffee. Then I made him wait for me as I washed the mugs and put them away, because there's nothing sadder than washing up the dishes a loved one has just used after he's left for a long journey and you don't know how much time you'll have to survive through before he'll come back. It feels too much like a burial. Then we were standing before my hearth and holding hands again, because parting was imminent and there was nothing left to do to prolong the moment. Outside, the sun was already pulling the day along. We were fighting to keep things early. We knew we were losing.

"Don't be late for work," Jade teased, glancing at the clock that mocked his admonition. It was nine already.

"Don't get into trouble." Felt the emptiness of his leaving swell through my gut. Tried to squelch the feeling in a tight embrace. Didn't work. "I don't want to have to worry about you. Listen to Penny and do whatever she tells you to. She's got your best interests ahead of her own. No more missed gigs. No more New Havens. Keep Nick happy."

"He's happy. Elb talked to him. The CD's finished. He knows that's where his money is."

"Write to me. Call me if Penny can rig up a secure line but don't use a regular phone if your promoters might be listening. Don't go home."

He smiled into my eyes. "I am home."

"Right." I stopped the lecture and ran my fingers through his night-black hair. Imagined the rock 'n' roll sorcerer he was on stage, the strange intensity of all the emotions his performances ripped out of dying hearts. Felt all the forbidden emotions ripping from my own. Kissed him for a long time. Owned him. "I love you."

"I love you, too." He smiled.

"Come visit me in my dreams."

"Always, my lord."

We kissed again. Even as we kissed I felt the day advancing outside. Five minutes, and then the emptiness within would be jabbing at me from without. I was suddenly conscious of wearing my white-shirted federal "uniform" and of Jade wearing his jeans and dark T-shirt with a musical equipment manufacturer's logo printed across his chest. "Hartke Systems. Transient Attack." He leaned his dark head tenderly against my white-shirted chest. What a strange tableau our kissing must have made, I thought as we held each other.

"Take care, Count."

"So should you, my lord."

"Don't worry about me."

"Don't worry about you," he mocked, sounding a little like Cara but without her irritating condescension. "I'm leaving you all alone and unprotected before the tender mercies of your government and I'm not supposed to worry? Pete, you may smile and smile and be a singing villain, and get caught at it behind your desk, and your Uncle Sam will mete out strange punishments to your happiness. Remember, he *wants* you. To fight his war. I fear that I will fail in my job to shield you from his wrath."

"I can handle my government. Uncle Sam isn't Uncle Claude," I said ruefully.

We were now standing at the door that separated my basement from the garage. I didn't notice our descending, but here we were. Jade leaned his back against the door and threw his arms around me. "I promise you something. I swear it by Bacchus and all his manifestations. If I find out your Uncle Sam isn't treating you right, I *will* come back—I'll be *forced* to come back—and save you."

I laughed. "You're always saving me."

"Oh, it's a serious promise, Pete. I may be off to war, but I've still got to protect your dreams. I will conduct myself accordingly." He kissed me briefly.

I looked into his stunningly sincere eyes. "Thank you, lover."

"My pleasure," said Jade. "Good night." Said it just the way he would have closed a Black Dog performance. And then he was gone and there was only the closed door to look at.

For no reason except the way the moment felt, I stood by the closed door and listened to him leave. Wrenchingly listened to him back out his car, heard him pull the loud garage door down, pull out of the driveway, and head off to New York. And I kept listening after the last sound of a sound had faded into the bald day, even though there was nothing to hear but my own imagination filling in the end of his driving. Then the furnace clicked on and the sudden queerness of standing where I never spent time standing in my house, and the sensation of wind brushing my windows upstairs, and the odd cry of a winter bird outside made me utterly lonely. Returned slowly through my emptied house, the emptiness washing out of my belly and into everything around me. Knew it would be a lurid winter.

Late to work, of course, and still feeling hollow. Entered the serious double doors. Crensch. Crensch was all brightly suited up for travel and clutching his briefcase in both hands while swinging it in wide, showy semi-circles about his waist like a shiny new status. He was the rat's meow. Even had his shoes polished. Never seen him look so chipper as he high stepped it past me toward the doors with Marcie calling out behind him, "Have fun up north, Sidney. Hope you solve your case." Crensch bobbed and nodded like an old horse that had just unexpectedly escaped the glue factory and won first place in the county fair. Then he bounced out of the doors, stopping briefly to acknowledge my existence with an oddly genuine smile of greeting and the friendly words, "You're late."

Ignored him as he tripped off to join a cluster of union types waiting for the elevator.

So. Crensch was off to Toronto where he would be able to wreak havoc with my life beyond the muted wilderness of his diverted dreams. The fool probably didn't even know yet the full extent of the damage he could do to me up there. Which was the worst of it. Crensch merely wanted to destroy a career I despised to shore himself up against a living reminder of his own incompetence. That's a common enough way to do business, I suppose. But through no fault of his own he was stumbling into the destruction of the only part of my life I loved. I greatly resented that kind of victory being handed to Crensch, not least because he lacked the native intelligence and drive to earn it.

But what did I want from government? A worthy opponent? Hey, I couldn't even get my ceiling fixed.

"Oh, Peter," Marcie's voice fluttered into my thoughts as I was leaving the reception area, "Charles wants to talk to you. Says it's important. So does Fred."

"Right," I said absently, increasing my pace. Settled at my desk with my SAYNO papers, and kept thinking. It greatly worried me that Crensch had discovered my office call to Fendra's, because I knew he'd be stiffing his nose around the bar and talking to George. But there was absolutely nothing I could do about it except trust to Cara's ability to throw him off and hope that he hadn't picked up any mob leads on Hopner's killer. Paul Campobello was probably out of jail by now, but I hadn't heard anything from Penny or Jade about him spreading McCrae's information around and leading Nariano to Elise.

Considered whether there was some secure way to reach Beth because maybe she could put Crensch off from George, but Beth seemed too simple to trust with that delicate kind of prevarication. Although, on the other hand, she also seemed to be strong and steady beyond herself where Jade was concerned. I mean, who wouldn't lie for Jade? But Beth didn't know the whole story enough to lie effectively about anything, and I saw more danger in filling her in than by trusting solely to Cara and her sisters, who already knew enough to keep Crensch away from everything explosive. Which of course was supposed to be my job, but as Penny had hurtfully pointed out, I wasn't having much success there. Sat and stared at my SAYNO work. Devoutly hoped her daughters would show me up. Remembered derisively that I had once threatened Cara with death if anything should slip to the detriment of the band. Right.

But I figured it wouldn't hurt to give Cara or Juno a warning call tonight. Despite Cara's antipathy toward all potential rivals, they might be able to offer some insight into the wisdom of warning Beth about Crensch. I knew that if Crensch followed standard procedure, he'd settle into some cheap motel tonight and wait until he got "briefed" by all the proper Canadian authorities who knew less than he did. Safe to assume he wouldn't hit 13 Oak Street until tomorrow afternoon at the earliest, or maybe even as late as Monday.

Nearly eleven-thirty. Stared at my papers to waste time. Missed Jade. Could drop in on Piekarski or Fearless. Could go to lunch. If I felt like eating. Phone rang.

"Hey, Morrow, gotta brief job for you. Related to the vanishing corpse business and this Claude Hopner murder case." Fearless sounded both too friendly and too reluctant, like he was trying to hide something from himself and wanted me to help.

"Sure, boss. I'll be right there." And I was. Like a greased shot. "What can I help you with?" I asked as I entered Fearless's office and settled myself in the usual chair.

Fearless said nothing about my coming to work late, so whatever it was he wanted, he *really* wanted. "Just some clean-up work. Crensch is off to Canada, so I need you to write up a full report for our records on the developments since Mr. Hugh McCrae was cleared. Just a formality to keep our facts straight and to keep an extra record of all the clearances we had to get to send Crensch up there."

Praise Aphrodite!

"Didn't Crensch do all that before he left?" I asked in a deadpan voice to cover up my inner excitement at being suddenly privy to Crensch's investigations.

Fearless winced. "Seems Crensch isn't much for report writing. Since you've been on the vanishing corpse case, much as you've botched it, and this Hopner thing is something of a spin-off, you're the only other agent qualified to do the job." He stopped and said almost resentfully, "Otherwise I wouldn't ask you to." Wondered how long he had wanted to me to do Crensch's report writing for him and if that was the reason I hadn't gotten any official reprimand on how splendidly I'd "botched" the vanishing corpse matter. Because considering the turn it had taken, I had to look like the biggest fool in the Bureau in the eyes of the NDECC, and yet until now Fearless had said nothing about it.

"Don't mind," I said cheerfully. "SAYNO's running slow while we're waiting for Rhode Island to find something on Lamar Toon for us." Fearless made no response to my statement beyond a nervously distant scowl. Wasn't sure he even heard me because he looked like he was greatly preoccupied with unusually weighty matters he didn't really want to discuss but saw no way not to bring up. "Guess I'll need to see all his notes and paperwork," I said easily.

"Yeah, it should be on his desk. I told Marcie to give you a master key so you can take what you need." Got up to leave. "Uh, Morrow," the scowl drew deeper, "close the door for a minute." I did so. Fearless sighed and plunged into it. "There is a report that Crensch started to write on the Hopner business. Here." He gave me seventeen neatly bound pages. "It's not really satisfactory, and well, I'd like to have your opinion on it sometime."

"All right." I took the bundle under my arm.

"You know, the vanishing corpse business is the next best thing to a dead issue now," said Fearless like he was groping his way into something more important. "Don't know why that address in the threatening letter you produced for evidence long after the fact happened to get overlooked, Morrow, but it did," he continued pointedly, "so Crensch is doing the formality of dropping by to see what he can find. So we can put in the record that we've tried everything. But the fact remains there's no body, and it would take an act of God to convict anyone in court. But we've got to put some kind of official closure on it, offer something to Congressman Basher to tell his people. Make sure everyone understands there's no body, there's no legal grounds for a conviction, that we tried, that it's not our fault."

"Sure," I said noncommittally. If that's how my report was supposed to read, fine. Wouldn't be the first time the government took months to stumble upon the obvious. Figured it was just as well to close the vanishing corpse case. Also just as well that Fearless didn't seem to be expecting any breakthroughs there from Crensch. Make it that much easier for Cara to turn him away.

"Sidney's main concern in Toronto is evidence gathering on the Hopner case. You'll learn this from his notes, but it seems Hopner was financing some tax evasion scheme involving a Canadian company that's working with the Nunzio family to promote records—CDs—in the states. May involve payola and other federal statutes violations. His father, the congressman, wants him to succeed at this. He's thinking of running for senator next election. Always makes the House without a problem, understand he barely has to campaign, but now he's looking ahead because the senior senator is retiring and he wants to establish a stronger image for himself.

"You know that there's a Crensch family thing for standing for law and order and decency. Congressman Crensch is very committed to family values and the NDECC members are all interested in any illegal, prosecutable activity surrounding rock 'n' roll right now. Drew their support in the last election from a lot of citizens' groups who feel that rock music is destroying the world, and the congressman would welcome an opportunity to look serious about it, like he's paying back favors. I know you're familiar with one of those groups, Christians for American Decency?"

"Yes, I've met them."

"Right. Well, they gave a lot of money to Mr. Crensch and Mr. Lasher and they want some bill passed that's supposed to hold performers and record labels responsible for any violence which occurs as a result of a rock 'n' roll performance. But that bill will never pass, there's too much money in the music industry for that to happen and it's so poorly written that nobody would know how to enforce it if it did. It'll be a wonderful grandstand for both sides, but the congressman thinks it will end with the record industry voluntarily policing itself for a while and his supporters complaining to him about not getting the job done. He would like something concrete he can show his people. So if Sidney can solve this Hopner case and nail the Nunzios on some illegalities concerning record promotion, it will look very good for him."

I knew he was only telling me these things because he expected me to keep these considerations in mind while I wrote the report. He normally wasn't quite this explicit about his political motivations, preferring me to understand without him having to explain. Also took this for Fearless's long overdue account of the real reasons Crensch was going to Canada and I wasn't. I shrugged noncommittally. "Well, boss, what can you do?"

"Morrow. Gotta ask you something before you leave and I want an honest answer." He puckered his face up so tight that I knew something good was coming.

"I'll be as honest as I can be," I said solicitously.

Fearless looked like he was about to spit a snake. "Do you think Crensch is stable for this kind of work?"

I pretended to consider. "No."

"Got reasons?"

"He takes himself too seriously," I suggested.

"That it?" Fearless looked annoyed.

"No, that's only half of it. The other half is that he knows he isn't worth taking seriously. That's a deadly combination. Sometimes police cars get wrecked and everything."

"Yeah," sighed Fearless, "What can you do?" He was clearly unhappy with my bringing up the police car incident from last year but he was unable to object to my point, which for once didn't seem to go sailing over his head into hyperspace. "I mean have you noticed anything— how can I put this—more unorthodox than usual in his professional behavior—*lately*?"

"You're asking me about unorthodox professional behavior?" I asked seriously. Fearless sort of smirked. He wasn't enough of a dunderhead to miss the irony of the question. Instead, he said, "I'm asking you because you've worked with him. Would you say he gets a little—*overzealous*—about things sometimes?"

"I've been too busy with SAYNO to keep tabs on Crensch's overzealousness," I said breezily, figuring that would be an opportunity for Fearless to fill me in on Crensch's wanting to keep tabs on me, which I wasn't supposed to know about. "Why? Would you like me to keep an eye on him?" I asked innocently. It was too much to hope that I'd be sent to Canada, but I had to try.

"No," he waved his hand and looked annoyed. "Don't need you spying on Crensch." I could tell by the way he said this that he had probably forgotten Crensch's voiced suspicions of me from two and half months ago, which didn't mean Crensch wasn't trying to find something to nail me on. "I need Crensch to solve his case load and keep Dad happy. Anyway, take a look at that report and tell me what you think."

"Sure thing, boss."

But he stopped me one more time before I got to the door. "Uh, Morrow. Two words of advice. One. You know the NDECC has an interest in SAYNO. Likes having a serious guy like you in charge. But this screwup of yours on the vanishing corpse didn't make you or me look very good."

"I understand, boss," I said contritely.

Fearless wasn't listening. He plowed over my words. "So you and Piekarski better get your act together on this Lamar Toon thing. What's saving your butt right now is that Congressman Lasher's convinced you're on the verge of a major drug bust. You botch it, you might be shoveling files around in Guam for the next five years. And that's not just me speaking. Got it?" I nodded and turned to leave but Fearless wasn't through. He said in a milder tone, "You've done some brilliant work, Morrow, but there's some mistakes past excellence doesn't make up for. Two. *I'd* personally appreciate it if Sidney got this Hopner thing solved. He's got authorization to plant some bugs, and he's going to be sending tapes of anything he gets down here. Like you to listen to them closely."

Better and better. "All right. Wouldn't be the first time I've played silent partner to Crensch."

"You're not an *anything* partner this time, Morrow. Understand? It's his case, first, last and final. I never asked your opinion on anything and you're only listening to the tapes because you're writing up the investigation. And if anyone asks, *you're* writing up the investigation because Crensch is too busy doing the real work. Nobody wants your fingerprints on this right now." He paused and studied my face. "Seems that Crensch once thought you knew something about this Hopner thing that you were keeping to yourself." Turned out he remembered the phone call after all, or Crensch had recently reminded him. "I don't know if that's the case, and frankly I really don't care if you've got some *irrelevant*"—the way he accented the word it sounded vaguely hopeful and entirely irritating—"*irrelevant* insights into the Nunzio family's involvement with this tax evasion-payola thing that you haven't offered up. Maybe you didn't realize you had anything useful," he suggested for me, "or maybe Crensch is confused."

"I vote for confused," I said evenly.

"But if you can pass anything through me to him that'll make him look like a hero, I strongly suggest you do so."

"All right," I said without expression, "I'll see what I can do to make Crensch look like a hero." *Not even Jade could make that bit of fiction believable*, I thought wryly.

"Don't you get it, Morrow? If Crensch figures out that you knew anything about this rock 'n' roll stuff and that you didn't report it, you've got a major career problem and I've got another headache. It's called obstruction of justice. Now notice I'm not asking you directly whether you've known anything about this business. But I'm telling you to wise up to the impression you've already made with the NDECC on your last little romp with a major case, and to think long and hard about the way you want to play things next."

"I want to get to work," I said as smoothly as I could manage, making once again towards the door.

"Right," said Fearless as I got it open. "Then get to work, Morrow. Keep me posted."

Stole some coffee under his watchful gaze. Felt like a reflex.

Got the master key from Marcie before she took off for lunch. Immediately made myself at home in Crensch's office, which looked a lot like mine except that his ceiling was intact and his cinderblocks were painted a horrid glaring white instead of a sickly pale green. Also, his overhead lights buzzed. But he had the same desk and squeaky chair. Same dirty computer terminal. Same ugly posters. Since the papers on his desk and the report Fearless gave me were mine to study, I found it expedient to put them aside for afternoon reading and search Crensch's office while I had the opportunity. Figured if I kept the door closed and my research confined to the lunch break no one would notice how much time I was spending in there.

Crensch's desk lock was easy to pick open with my own desk key and a paper clip. Same with his file cabinet, which I searched first, although it didn't contain anything of interest. The bottom two drawers were surprisingly empty, the third drawer contained only his government-issue tape recorder. The top drawer was stuffed with files of every trivial memo that ever made its rounds through the field office, from old coffee fee reminders to meeting notices. Had no idea why he saved them. Seemed to collect memos from the entire building, too, because he also had files with IRS memos and immigration memos and human services memos and union memos, whatever he could pick up in his travels. Even daily receipts from the little newspaper and candy store outside, which told me Crensch had apparently cracked the mysteries of its randomly open hours.

Couldn't access his computer files without his password so that was out. All right—desk. Nothing useful or interesting here. Some pens and paper clips and a stack of our high quality one hundred percent bond paper with the FBI logo on the top. Too many rubber bands, many of them broken. Wondered if they were a collection. Drawer of extra files, all empty. An empty drawer—did the guy even work here? Then, I opened the bottom drawer, which Crensch had somehow rigged up with a separate lock that was trivial to pick, and I found something I can only describe as awkwardly obscene.

A vaguely Native American-style blanket, the sort of thing the Newton-Brookline crowd might pay top dollar for at a museum gift shop and pass off as an original to one-better their friends, lined the inside of the drawer like the drawer was a holy shrine. Crensch had pasted blanket strips to the front of a large, hardbound sketch book, which I promptly removed. Under the book was a pile of goose feathers and glass beads. Some of the feathers were dyed a horrible neon pink or blue, and in the middle of the pile was a cedar box with a mass-produced machine-stamped "carving" of a buffalo head on the lid. The box contained a tarnished silver and turquoise ring of no discernible pattern or personality except that the ring looked lonely, like a stolen reminder of another world that Crensch had no claim to.

Then I opened the sketch book, which was labeled in big block letters MY WEST and was full of Crensch's original drawings. At least I assumed they were his because he signed and dated all of them. Learned how my esteemed colleague spent his slow days at work. Learned more about the Idaho congressman's son's dreams than I really cared to know.

Let me say I'm no judge of art. I know what I love—sometimes I even know why I love it—but most times, especially if I really love a particular piece, I prefer not to know why at all. Basically because once you know something like that, it's like eating the fruit of the tree of knowledge of good and evil. The gate closes, the angel whacks you with her fiery sword of insight, and you can't go back to Paradise. It was weird, but as I stood there staring at Crensch's sketches, I remembered that when I was a teenager, I hated religion. Not because of hell, but because it promised eternity in exchange for soul-killing constraints. That was when the limitlessness of art became a comfort, and I began to love the fierce grace of imagination trespassing on reality without end.

Anyway, I did not love Crensch's sketches. They weren't beautiful. They were not skillful or clever. They weren't even all that interesting. And there was nothing arresting or original in his vision—all of his sketches had a certain flat copycat quality, lacking in the confident playfulness and acute vision that draws and holds. A group of hunters pointing their spears at a buffalo. A plain of teepees with mountains in the background. An old chieftain's face done up in warpaint and feathers. All the sort of thing you'd seen a million times before. Once he surprised me with the sketch of a nude woman carrying a hunting spear and riding on a horse under a full moon, which conveyed an unexpected charm, but for the rest they were unremarkable.

But they weren't awful. Certainly better than I could have done, which isn't saying much, but they did show that Crensch had some ability. He could draw a passable human face, although most of his faces looked the same. He did have a mildly interesting sense of perspective, and one or two of his desert landscapes held my eye longer than mere competence would have. But not too long. Then I noticed they were copies of postcards he had stuck in the book.

Like I said, I'm no judge of art, but I've camped out west enough to know that these sketches were powerless; they could not make me see their subjects in a different mind than my own. Crensch was not about to take the art world by storm and in his case I couldn't imagine anyone finding that unfair. But I also couldn't imagine why Crensch never went to art school or chose to develop his talent in some way. Because it seemed to me there was enough raw stuff here that had he worked diligently from an early age he might have blossomed. And he was certainly crazy enough for art school, so temperament wasn't the problem.

Also wondered if he'd actually ever bothered to learn anything about Native Americans or if he was drawing everything from postcards. Kept feeling like an intruder as I flipped through the sketches, because they were none of my business and clearly had no bearing on the Hopner case, but I was morbidly fascinated all the same. Wondered what Jade would think, hated myself for wondering, and didn't care to explore why. Hey, it wasn't my fault Crensch was an amateur—to his credit he wasn't bothering anybody with it. But I still felt like I'd walked in on a eunuch trying to masturbate. And even though I felt embarrassed for opening the door without knocking, I couldn't help but rudely stare.

When I turned the last page, I saw an envelope stuck in the binding. Since it was open, I took the liberty of reading the contents. It contained a four by five-inch sketch of a flowering cactus with a large sun in the background, executed more than a little stiffly, I thought, and dated about the time Crensch began working at the field office. The back read:

> Dear Mom,
>
> Putting down my roots in law enforcement like a cactus in the desert. Soon to crack my first big case.

Wondered what the hell that was. He hadn't been on any big cases until now. Kept reading.

> Hope you are well. Tell Dad not to worry about anything, I am doing fine. Boston has a lot of nice museums. You would like them. I am thinking of joining a local professional artists' group and of entering my sketches in a local contest.
>
> Your affectionate son,
>
> Sidney

Any Boston artist group would tear Crensch to pieces in about thirty seconds and spit him out for seltzer water, I thought wryly. Then I wondered if he had been naive enough to bring his work before a group of professional Boston artists and how he held up under the snubbing. Felt a little sorry for him. Then I read the other piece of paper, which seemed to be a response to the first.

> Dear Sidney,
>
> I'm returning your letter. Your mother died in the hospital last night. She never gained enough lucidity to read it. You needn't come to the funeral.
>
> As to your "sketches" I heartily advise you to grow up and remember why you're in Boston and to stick to your job and leave "artist groups" alone. To be blunt, you lack your mother's talent and it's about time you accepted the fact and got serious about something in life. I know she would agree. Let me add that I find your naked savages personally embarrassing and an affront to the decent family values I have spent my life trying to promote. If you must doodle, I strongly suggest that you keep your "art" to yourself.
>
> Let me know when you solve your first big case.
>
> Dad

Read the note three times in weird sort of hollowness. Put everything back where it belonged, locked the drawer, gathered the papers on the desk, and went to my office for my afternoon's work.

All right, so I now knew the explanation of Crensch's seeming estrangement from his father. But the fact that Crensch wasn't a good artist, wasn't an artist at all really, but clearly considered himself one, kept sticking between my thoughts like last year's dirty snow sticks in the cracks of an otherwise pristine mountain peak. I sat there wondering—imagining—what Crensch's personal suffering and demons must be like, and all I could come up with was utter revulsion. That, and the certainty that I didn't really want to think about it because I couldn't stomach knowing. Thinking of him, trying to psyche him out the way I had trained myself to psyche out any other opponent, was like steeling myself to swallow a nest of dead rats while chewing and sucking on each one slowly—I couldn't do it. I couldn't even think about doing it. I did not have the psychic constitution to put myself in his place.

Although I suppose there was plenty to pity there, I couldn't pity him. Then I realized for the first time that what I felt for Crensch went beyond mere contempt for his splendid incompetence as an agent. What I felt for the man was an irrational, instinctive, murderous hatred.

And it wasn't just because of his mediocre sketches and utter ignorance of his own lack of talent. Ultimately, that was not my business. It was because I knew that, given half a chance, he'd destroy Jade's career as effectively as Hugh McCrae would, and then he'd go back to his postcard copying and "artist groups," without any more clue as to what he'd destroyed than one of his badly drawn dull-witted buffaloes trampling over a great and living warrior. That made his ambition to destroy my career, which he did understand and appreciate, finally unforgivable. That made everything worse. That was something to hate him for.

So I read his papers in hatred.

Learned that besides visiting Oak Street to close the vanishing corpse business, he indeed planned to talk to George Fendra. He suspected Fendra was "associated" with Nick Nariano and the Nunzio family and the record promotion "operation."

No mention of Elise McClellan or Black Dog, but that was only a matter of time once he got to Toronto and picked up on Paul Campobello's rumors. That is, if Cara couldn't turn him away from the city. That would be a trick, though, because it was clear from my reading that the plan was for Crensch to be "recording" and "monitoring" and "investigating" and "coordinating" and screwing things up in Toronto forever, or at least until he got enough evidence to make an arrest and solve his big case. But hey, any witch with the power to put the damper on Hugh McCrae ought to be able to take care of Crensch. Had to believe it.

Anyway, I learned that he was going to try to bug Fendra's, as well as George Fendra's private residence. Good luck getting listening devices into a mafia home, I thought. But Crensch was all set with broad permission to monitor other places should any more information emerge to make it necessary. Had no idea how he'd listen to several bugs simultaneously, unless he used transmitters on different channels and sat in a van at some central location, scanning until he got something. Of course everything would be recorded, but clearly everything would not be heard as it happened. But transmitters gave such weak signals he couldn't be too far away physically to receive anything useful, and there was no guaranteeing that the places he needed to monitor would be near each other. Then I realized that other US and Canadian authorities were permanently involved as "investigators," so no doubt other agents would be on hand to set up listening devices. Meaning that even if Cara could ditch Crensch, there'd be a lot of other losers around to take his place. Better to keep Crensch in charge up there—at least that would keep me privy to the tapes.

I was mildly surprised at how big a deal this murder case had become, but it sort of made sense. Ottawa probably felt it was losing its share of tax plunder from Moon Management, and tax evasion is the sort of thing governments will lavish all their resources on to nail. Crensch was the nominal head of this "international operation" because of his interest in the murder case, but it was clear to me that what the two governments wanted was not so much Hopner's killer but a piece of the spin-off money action that seemed to surround Hopner. I had no idea how much money Black Dog's new CD was making. I wasn't even convinced Nick or Elb knew, but Crensch had the right people in both governments believing that there were hundreds of thousands of tax dollars at stake. That this was some sort of shadow music industry that he had stumbled across and that it would generate millions of untaxed dollars over the years off our innocent, impressionable youth. He clearly had no idea that Moon Management was one band and one record. Didn't even know yet that Moon Management was the name of the operation.

Well, Elb should certainly know about this, but I had no safe way to contact him unless Penny called me. I'd have to rely on Cara to pass the message. Fortunately, Crensch didn't appear to have an interest in wiring Penny's house. Not yet, anyway. That really was being viewed as a close-the-vanishing-corpse-case duty call. But he was still hung up on finding Elb McCrae, although he didn't appear to have a clue how. Knew the name from his Utica tape, but that was still about all he knew. Basically seemed to be pinning his hopes and "investigation" on uncovering something at Fendra's. All right, I'd have to warn Cara. Maybe she could do something preventative there.

Then I read the seventeen-page report Fearless had asked me to take a look at. It was truly bizarre, even for Crensch. Hell, it was truly bizarre for government, let alone Crensch.

Crensch wrote like a bad parody of Piekarski, which ought to have won him a gold star under most circumstances, going on and on about our "mission" to clean up America and the danger to our youth from drugs and rock music and the "liberal conspiracy" to hide behind the first amendment. But that was the least of it.

The first paragraph was a florid invocation to the "unbounded power for good and right living" the FBI could "exert over society and the world at large" were it to simply exercise its "rightful noble mandate" to "enforce the Law." Then he spent a page or two on how we agents must appear to the "poor, struggling, decent American public" as "angels of light" who guard innocent "citizens and children" from the terrors of the "dark criminal element." And then Crensch zinged it up into an explosively passionate wail on how "the Law was Truth and Truth was Law" and on and on into this high-strung quivering exertion of meaningless eloquence on why we needed to attack the rock music industry through whatever means possible and how the Hopner case was the door into the world of "Satanic magic" that must be eliminated for the good of society—I mean it was a hoot, if it wasn't so personal. It was so bad that even Fearless wasn't about to let it get loose from the field office and hurt somebody. Then I got to the last neatly typed page, which was a copy of the King James version of the Lord's Prayer and saw that Crensch had scrawled in handwriting across the bottom after the typed words "forever and ever without end" the phrase "Exterminate all the brutes!" Reminded me of Kurtz in Joseph Conrad's *Heart of Darkness*. Except Crensch was more bathos than human horror. Which, I have to admit, was worse.

All right. I'd confirm Fearless's well-founded suspicion that Crensch was two degrees short of a triangle and counting. Keep the boss convinced he needed my clear-headed coolness behind this case, whether or not I was "supposed" to be offering input.

Wrote up the sort of report he wanted. Did a bang-up job. Just about finished it when Piekarski came grubbing along into my office. Said he'd been "looking for me all afternoon."

"Why didn't you try my office?"

"Fred said you were busy."

"He was right. Gave me some extracurricular stuff to push around."

For once Piekarski didn't seem nosy about it. He was too bent on flapping his mouth to care. "Yeah, well I got some dope on Toon for you, Morrow. I'm calling a meeting on Monday to spread the word, but you and me have to coordinate our game plan first."

"What you got?"

Piekarski puffed out his cheeks and let out a very big, very slow, very whistly breath of air, as if to say he had finally gotten ahold of some Very Big Stuff, due to the fact that he was a very big drug warrior and all that, and I was just an all-flash kind of guy who couldn't be expected to come through when the heat was up. Clearly had some heavy stuff to tell me, the implications of which I couldn't possibly understand. I kept looking mildly expectant. "Local cop catch him dealing in a school yard?" I finally prompted, to get him to say what he had to say and get out so I could go home.

"No," said Piekarski, "I wish. But it's good. Rhode Island Child Protective Services found a sixteen-year-old selling flowers and pencils for him without working papers."

"So? That's not our problem. That's a state violation."

"So?" said Piekarski gleefully, scarcely able to contain himself, "That's also child abuse."

"Child abuse isn't a federal crime."

"Sure, Morrow, but we can use it. Toon has broken a state child abuse law. That means Rhode Island authorities are now legally justified in removing all children from the premises. That ought to shake loose some tongues."

"Didn't the investigation uncover anything worse than a sixteen-year-old working without papers?"

"Doesn't have to. Look, this is how we work things, Morrow. This is how you get a drug bust rolling. Kanesh sets up a press release on the children being removed because of evidence of child abuse. We can say that now. He is a child abuser—never mind the details. Get the public against this guy so his followers feel some social pressure to bolt. Most important, the unwed bimbos that follow the cult don't get their kids returned until they turn over some direct evidence on Toon's crack dealings. And if the bimbos remain silent for that bastard, they can be threatened with abuse charges just for knowingly keeping their kids on his premises, because under Rhode Island law, they're technically accomplices. Hell, they can be threatened with not seeing their kids again. Something will break now."

"Nothing like a little state-supported kidnapping to get the job done," I said drily. I hated this stuff.

"Whatever works, Morrow," said Piekarski defensively. "We have to crack this thing. I want us to be present when the social workers interview the women. Get every detail."

"So when will that happy event occur?"

"Week, maybe two. Let the press tar Toon. Let the women worry for a while without word of their kids. Let the kids feel separated from the cult for a while—they might offer up some useful information—who knows? By the end of the month I'd like to get enough probable cause to get a warrant for ransacking the place."

"Sure." Didn't like the tactics. Didn't see much to do about it. Had to keep my job because I had to keep an eye on Crensch's investigation, and if I balked at SAYNO with any degree of effectiveness, the NDECC would have me out. No question. *Oh, Jade, my love. For your sake I willingly become what I hate.* Then I added bitingly, "Hope to hell Lamar Toon is guilty."

"Of course he's guilty," insisted Piekarski, "he has to be. There's probably all kinds of shit going on in his premises we don't know about, and we finally found a way to cash in."

"If there isn't—" I didn't finish the sentence because Piekarski interrupted me.

"—If there isn't, Morrow, we'll just have to make sure that there is. This thing has gone on far too long for us to come up empty-handed now. Right?" I nodded dumbly. "Follow the news this weekend. We'll have a full meeting Monday." He turned to leave. "Stay clean for the New Year. Don't ride any splintered brooms before we take down Bit o' Providence."

"Wouldn't dream of it. Satan could be watching."

Piekarski shuffled off, laughing. He was in a revoltingly fine mood. He was no doubt thinking I was quite the wit.

I went home thinking of Jade's parting promise and the nature of the war my government was drafting me to fight and of how coldly intimate our new distance suddenly felt.

Stave Nineteen

Thursday evening, December 31, 1992.

Called Oak Street. Phone rang about sixteen impatient times before Juno answered. "Hullo. Penny's Hole. What do you want?" Her voice sounded thick and crunchy, like her mouth was half-paralyzed with a pound of reluctant caramel candy.

"Hello Juno. It's Pete—"

"—Just a minute let me swallow." Heard a large gulp. "OK. Fried ice cream from the store for New Year's. Chocolate eggnog flavored. No one else wanted any."

"I need to talk to your sister."

"Which one?" Another gulp, along with the scraping of a spoon.

"Cara." As if she didn't know.

"Her Royal pissed-off Highness is still incommunicado. But I can tell her everything," she assured me.

Dubious with that bargain. Like Penny, I had more confidence in Cara's ability to grasp what needed doing than in Juno's. Had hoped Cara's animosity towards me wasn't going to be a barrier to sharing crucial information that could only help Jade. "I'd really prefer to talk to her myself."

"You can't. She won't talk to you."

"Can you put her on the salt bowl to listen?"

"She won't listen. But you can talk to me."

"All right," I sighed. Reluctantly detailed all I knew about the state of affairs in Toronto. Then asked, "Have you or your sisters seen Beth lately?"

"No. Beth works a lot."

"I wondered what you girls thought of getting her to throw Crensch off the track when he shows up at Fendra's. Getting her to notice where he plants his bug so she can show George and he doesn't say anything he shouldn't."

"I don't know," said Juno carelessly. "We could ask."

"Of course we could *ask*—but it would mean giving her information about Black Dog's mafia associations and I don't like sharing things like that around on general principles. I have to trust to your judgment on this one. Would Beth be likely to do more damage than good?"

"I can hang out at Fendra's like I have a job. George doesn't care. Beth doesn't have to know anything."

"Cool. Thank you. But Juno, if you do that—for the goddess's sake—don't greet Crensch at the door when he comes to your place. Because if he later sees you hanging out with George, he'll get suspicious and he'll be back at your place for more. Right now he's making a routine call and he doesn't expect to find anything useful. He'll ask about the threatening letter your mom's name is on because he has to. Have Cara tell him Penny doesn't exist. That she has no idea who she is or if she is. Have her convince him that some misfit chose your address at random. And remember, she doesn't know who the hell Claude Hopner is either—or Hugh McCrae, or me, or anybody he happens to ask about. And then of course she mustn't be seen at Fendra's. And it would be best if you didn't mention Penny's name when you answer the phone. Got it?"

"Sure." Juno sounded bored.

"All right, give me your progress report. Has Hugh McCrae arrived? Has he found Elise? Is he establishing Heppelfauf's religion all over the city?"

"Yeah," said Juno, as if she just remembered something. "He's here. He's with us."

"*What?* Why didn't you tell me?"

"Why didn't you ask?" she said in a pouty, irritated adolescent voice. "Cara captured him when he got off the subway."

"How?"

"With an old piece of dusty string licorice, the kind you used to be able to get with squishy vanilla inside. I had to help. We've got him locked in the closet. Beulah feeds him dog biscuits under the door. His power's pretty much drained out."

"Are you serious?"

"You want to talk to him? Here, wait. I'll go upstairs." After half a minute of pounding footsteps and a slamming door I heard Juno yell defensively, "I can't help your dirty looks, Cara. Pete wants to hear the monster." Then there were more footsteps and a faint *chump chump* kind of sound and a low, painful hoot, like an injured old factory machine from the last century still in strained painful use. "I can put him on if you want," Juno offered, suddenly terribly interested in showing off their prize.

"No, that's all right," I chuckled at the sisters' efficiency. "So what are you going to do? Keep him in your closet indefinitely?"

"Surprise Mom when she gets home. We haven't told her."

"You mean she hasn't asked?"

"Oh, she's asked. But we're not telling her. It's a surprise."

"So what have you told her?"

"That the monster is all tied up and powerless. Which he is. We just wanted to show her what we did when she comes home."

"Is Cara talking to your Ma?"

"No, I'm the only one who's talking to anybody. Sometimes Selene comes over to see the monster and Cara talks to her. That's about it. She's still pretty pissed. Beulah just cries a lot and makes orange salads. It's really joyful around here," she complained. "Can't even play a record without getting yelled at."

"Why don't the three of you just kill the thing and rejoin the tour?"

"Because then Mom couldn't see. Besides, we're sort of stuck. If he's dead, he'll just be a rock for a while and pop back anywhere at any time. This way we have him and we know."

"Well, congratulations on your victory," I said blithely. "Didn't think it would be this easy. Have your mother call me on a secure line when you talk to her again."

"OK." She sounded like she could as easily have been responding to someone in the room as to me.

"Call me after Cara deals with Crensch. And Juno, whatever happens, make sure he doesn't search your premises and find your prisoner."

"We're not stupid," she whined. "Gotta go watch *Star Trek*."

Why bother? I thought drily as she hung up. Couldn't be for the escape value.

Then it was night in an empty house to miss Jade in. Had to get used to knowing he wouldn't be there. Turned on MTV and watched until they ran his video, which only made me feel lonelier. Turned it off and sat in my silent house, which made it worse. Turned it back on to take the kill out of the loneliness, and learned from an irritatingly hyper VJ with a splendidly limited vocabulary that MTV was going to do a live broadcast of Black Dog's New Year's Eve performance. Wondered why Jade hadn't mentioned it, and then the VJ announced as if in answer to my thoughts that they were all very excited to get this last minute go ahead for Black Dog's show. Apparently MTV had been planning to broadcast different bands from clubs across Manhattan for their "MTV Rock 'N' Roll New Year's Eve Party All Night Party," or some such thing, and Black Dog had just joined the roster and taken the prized mid-night slot. Nick's boys must have been hard at work. Anyway, gave me something to look forward to for the next few hours. Rigged up my VCR to output the sound through my stereo system and to catch the show on tape.

Fire gazed. Glanced at a badly translated medieval romance and yearned for the real thing.

Then I had a weirdly poetic thought about Cara. Decided that as long as she had a monster in her closet, the high priestess of rock 'n' roll couldn't be near her god, that she was in effect as much Hugh's prisoner as he was hers. Then I wondered if that was the sort of thing Hugh might enjoy, and if he also thought about it in that way. I mean Penny had once said he liked prisons, and dog biscuits in a closet wasn't such a bad deal for a man of his tastes, as I understood them. The monster might actually be fairly content with his lot right now. He might even be hanging out at Penny's place from his own inclination as opposed to the sisters' power, and reveling in the sordid fact of his mere existence separating them from the band. But of course I couldn't know and it wasn't productive to worry about it. Could only believe that one major problem was under control. Could only concentrate my efforts on the next one.

Caught the eleven o'clock news from Providence. After a couple of stories on the usual political obscenities, the newscaster reported in a voice of understated glee that state social workers responding to "anonymous local complaints" had found "direct evidence of child abuse and potential neglect" occurring at the "Bit o' Providence compound of known cult leader Small Brother Mink, whose legal name is Lamar Toon." Then a camera showed about half a dozen heavily armed Rhode Island police officers converging on the compound with two smiling social workers whose healthy self-regard was clearly enhanced by their armed escort. The cops forced entry by battering down the unlocked door with their shoulders. Had to do something tough for the cameras no matter how stupid it looked to the trained eye, I supposed. Next thing I saw were six or seven crying children being forcibly separated from their angry mothers by two policemen with batons. One woman uttered an impressive string of profanities and got whacked on the shoulder for her trouble. Then the camera cut to the rest of the police, who were grabbing flailing arms and legs and hurling squirming children into a large paddy wagon that looked like it doubled for harassing homeless people into shelters.

While the kids were being abused, one of the social workers, who, as far as I could tell, hadn't even entered the premises or looked once in the prisoners' direction, confidently told a reporter that the "children appeared neglected and would be in state custody until further investigation," adding pointedly that "Child Protective Services has already uncovered evidence of abuse on the compound, and federal investigators may be joining the investigation." Her partner smiled in proud agreement.

Nobody asked, and nobody offered, why, if they had such hard evidence of abuse, Toon wasn't being arrested himself. Instead, the reporter filled up time by reminding the anchor that Toon was indeed a religious wacko who believed he was the divine prodigy of a three-way celestial marriage between Buddha, Jesus Christ, and Mary Magdalene, that neighbors had complained about him having guns, that there were "rumors about drugs," that he preached a modified version of the sixties' free love philosophy, and that one of his former followers had reportedly left the cult and tested positive for AIDS.

None of which was strictly illegal, of course, or even anybody's business, but the reporter had hit enough panic buttons to convict Toon in the public arena before the government could scare up enough evidence of anything suspicious enough to put together a reasonable search warrant. Of course, the point of this whole charade was to get the evidence we needed to make a drug bust, so a premature arrest on "child abuse" charges that would only reveal a teenager working without papers would blow the whole operation and needlessly embarrass a lot of us government types. Much better to get the public to imagine the worst and cry out for blood. Which explained why no one came out and said Toon was an abuser, merely that "abuse occurred on the compound." Passive voice is great stuff. Just as effective as an outright accusation for publicly tarring the cult leader but with the extra benefit of leaving us the option of not having to arrest anyone in particular right now.

But that didn't account for the reporter failing to ask the obvious, unless some background deal had been made. Which it had, as I learned Monday at the SAYNO meeting. Turned out the instant Piekarski had gotten the official results of the Child Protective Service's investigation, Kanesh glad-handed it around all the Rhode Island news channels, telling anyone who would listen that this child abuse prime-time event we were about to orchestrate was all part of an ultra-secret, ultra-delicate, ultra-major "drug operation" that promised to be a story of "national interest." The deal was: Film the event, let our lackeys do the talking, don't ask too many questions, throw out this pre-prepared list of rumors, and we'll give you front row seats for the drug bust. Kanesh was actually granting most-favored-reporter status to the journalists who agreed to go along with the program. Which meant, as our PR guru half jokingly informed us, that we were now obligated to provide the press with a good show when the drug bust went down. Piekarski didn't think "that should be a problem."

But I'm needlessly getting ahead of myself because Monday's meeting merely confirmed what I suspected as I sat in my late-night living room taking in the hastily produced docudrama that passed for news. Since we couldn't destroy Toon honestly, we had to resort to destroying him with believable fictions, and like it or not, I was on the writing committee. Stared at the story's close as the reporter finished dutifully spreading our propaganda. Heard the newscaster thank him. Watched the paddy wagon speed away into night like the final shot of a bad police show. Then back to the news desk for sports.

Switched over to MTV to wait for Black Dog's spot.

Sat through about thirty minutes of some headbanging band I didn't recognize that was playing behind a second terrifically dim-witted VJ, who was on location. Most of the camera's attention was on the VJ, who kept showing how hip she was to be chatting mindlessly on her mic from the mosh pit while bodies slammed into her and the band's lead singer screamed his obsessions in her face. Looked like a great job. I mean, if you liked having an audience for that sort of thing.

At about ten minutes to midnight, the "Party All Night Party" returned to the same feverish VJ that had announced Black Dog's upcoming appearance earlier. Only now he was calling himself my "'Party All Night Party' New Year's Eve Host—right here, all night long." Babbled about how excited he was to have Black Dog joining them live, and took so much time about it I wondered if they'd get on before next New Year's Eve. Conveyed the irritating sense that he thought he was cooler than the band because he got to announce their spot. But he finally shut up and the "Party" cut to Black Dog in mid performance of "Flowers of Evil," one of the more scathing rockers from their first CD.

It took me a few seconds to recognize the melody in Xander's angrily mysterious guitar solo, because they were playing a radically different arrangement than their recorded version, but the difference only seemed to excite the crowd more. I know it excited me—it was a brilliant difference. Xander was playing his solo without Les's usual keyboard accompaniment, so his guitar stood out more than it did on the recording. He was using a starker, more insistent sound and stretching out his riffs and phrases into long spacy tone-poems that felt like Einsteinian nightmares. Strains bursting with time the way time might burst into an unrecognizably foreign nature at the speed of light. Melodic variations that felt slow until they took you inside the music, where they suddenly felt explosively fast in the way they held you from moving anywhere else.

Marty was off in one of his trances that nobody but the initiated could recognize, laying down an enthralling primitive rhythm that led me into something like a half trance as the ancient drum beat pulsed through my speakers and into my night.

The dream went on between Marty and Xander, while Les sat scowling at the girls on his side of the stage who were holding candles up to him and screaming. Thought he would've relished the recognition. Then the camera caught Jade standing to the side behind him, giving Xander the stage for his solo, and I understood who the screams were for and why Les looked so put out.

Shot of Xander with an exaltation of groupies throwing red carnations at his feet and some drunken guys playing air guitar around the groupies. Low pulse of bass like the lash of a planet quaking. Screams like worlds giving birth. Then another pulse. And there was Jade, who had so tenderly kissed me this morning, closing Xander's strangely beautiful solo by striding across the stage like a haplessly powerful storm-wizard pounded to death and brought back by the blast of his own rhythmic authority, a sorcerer who took a wrong turn in his meditations and ended up bringing in a new year with his own rock band. Made it to the mic, where he sang like a wrecked Fury wounding the empty universe with his voice.

The energy in the club must have been incredible, because the energy was exploding out of my TV set as Jade turned his mic toward the crowd—toward his worshippers—who were pounding the air with their fists and wailing out his words as Les shuddered out the bass line like matter-of-fact mathematical thunder falling from his keyboards while Jade held out the mic. "Flowers of Evil" hadn't gotten any airplay, so it was glaringly obvious that the club audience had bought the CD and listened to and memorized every word. But even if they hadn't, the power of the music was swelling words out of them like their empty souls were trance-dancing at a witch's Sabbat instead of a darkened Manhattan club.

I must have been dancing, because I found myself holding a red candle from my altar up to my TV set, as if in trance I were in the club with him, or in whatever dream he was colonizing the club for. Then I heard the magic drawing me into him through the poem he was chanting and the bass runs he was using to rape the words for meanings too deep to feel in ordinary language, making the English he used sound like pre-verbal rock rhythms straight from the seed bed of the ancient Nile. Men and women were holding candles and wailing like they taught the first torture victims how to scream. What fantasies was he plundering from them? What beauty was he finding in their hearts to scare them with? Some had their faces made up in dark eyeshadow like his, and he descended from the stage to kiss one or two of them like a high priest initiating new converts to Dionysus.

Now go—dance and destroy a world, any world, so long as it isn't yours. Howl dawn from your own blasted heart. Stay with me forever or for a second of your poor life—I bless you—I mark you—you are rock 'n' roll.

He did not have to say these things when so many hearts were saying them for him. Goddess how I wanted him to kiss me in his stage persona like that. Every time he kissed, I found myself feeling this morning's orgasm rip through my body all over again, as if we were still physically together, as if I were his helpless screaming audience, utterly in his control.

One girl ripped her shirt off on camera and grabbed him, so Jade kissed her, clasping a bare-breasted pagan beauty in jeans and nothing else against his muted strings for the world to see. It was incredible—everyone grabbed at his cloak and touched him and screamed and chanted his name and he ascended the stage and walloped his bass back into the familiar part of "Flowers of Evil" and everybody cried and screamed and sang across the midnight boundary into the new year.

My mind was rocking outside of my body, my thoughts were there like a gasp of wind in a sea storm, and I had the sensation that I couldn't catch up to wherever I really was. He wasn't even there and he was making me feel everything I was capable of feeling all at once. I think I was howling as my fist held the candle to my TV set, as I felt the scent of Penny's lavender-orange protective charm burning from my candle as the song ended. I had anointed the candle for one of our sex games the other day, and now I was reliving the game and the scent was holding me the way it had held Jade. The incense wouldn't let me disentangle my thoughts from the song and I just kept staring at the unspeakable event Black Dog was creating as Xander and Les collided chords into Marty's cymbal crashes and Jade let out a final scream.

And passed out.

Thought it was part of the act, but as I sat there in the wavering light of my candle, the camera kept rolling, and he didn't get up. Which added to the mystery, if not the charm. Wild screams of applause. Marty and Les exchanged looks of quiet annoyance. Les exited in disgust. Marty coolly sipped a can of beer, as if to say he didn't give a damn. Hit his snare a few times which sent cries of "solo" through the crowd, then he stood up, flexed his muscles, and poured the rest of the beer over his head to loud cheers, threw down his sticks and stalked off. Brief glimpse of Xander looking confused, then the camera cut to the crowd, which was swaying back and forth with candles and lighters held high. The screams got louder and the audience began to chant, "Jade! Jade! *Evoe*! *Evoe*!"

Apparently he still didn't get up because the chanting continued as the camera panned to a smiling VJ who was trying to describe "the most incredible performance—you just had to be there" while the fans around her linked arms in a human chain and swayed to their own chant. Then the camera caught Xander again, who was now leaning over to revive his friend while the VJ's voice kept babbling over the chanting about how people had claimed the music was making them hallucinate, how she swore she could see her dead grandmother rising out of Xander's guitar solos, and then the camera swung back to the audience where there seemed to be a disturbance.

Kept gripping my candle as I heard screams rising through the chant and saw a sudden angry muddle of smoke. Knot of loosening panic out in the crowd that couldn't break through the dazed and chanting human chain in front or behind it. Then it looked as if someone had managed to set something or someone else on fire and the crowd was now trying to make room around the event while keeping close enough to stare and scream. Close up shot showed somebody furiously trying to beat the fire out of the back of some other guy's jacket with a crumpled shirt, and at that point it became obvious to enough people swaying in the tightly locked chain that someone's clothes were burning that the cries of "Jade" turned into cries of "fire." Started a good old fashioned death stampede where the crowd of two or three hundred souls tried to ram themselves at once out of the club's single entrance.

Saw some bodies go down. Then a few more as the camera kept lavishly running on the carnage. From the angle, it looked like the film crew was now on stage looking down at the crowd. Then the camera hit the stage again where Xander was assuring the VJ that everything was fine while trying to get a still unconscious Jade to sit up. Camera stayed rudely on Jade's face and shoulders for long seconds, then showed two or three rent-a-cops throwing scared kids off the stage and back into the crush on the floor, which only made the panic worse as everyone fought everyone else to get out of the club's only available exit.

The camera panned back to the VJ and the cops on stage. I noticed I had put out my candle, and at that moment Jade recovered a little. Xander quickly helped him stand and led him offstage as the VJ eagerly told us what we'd just seen, adding her hope that "the creative force behind Black Dog would be all right." Then the camera showed another grotesque view of the crowd trampling and screaming to get out the only door. No more smoke and fire, just a murderous herd instinct killing to get away from an imaginary threat. Then, without warning, it was back to "our 'Party All Night Party' New Year's Eve Host" who quickly switched to another band in another club.

Tasteless as the live coverage had been, the sudden cut-off of direct information was worse. Sat staring at the extinguished smoking candle. Red wax hardened and cooled on my hand, forming a shape like a dead butterfly as the TV blared music I wasn't hearing to happy dancing bodies I wasn't watching. Turned it off with the remote. Didn't want to be there.

Phone's sudden ringing sent a shock through my body. Ran to answer it, desperately hoping it was Jade or Penny. Close.

"Hey, Pete," said Cara. "Happy New Year."

Tried to control my voice but I only succeeded in making it sound thin. "What's the deal, Cara? You talking to me now?"

Sound like tight slow breath being exhaled. While she made me wait for a response, I pictured her with a cigarette, holding fire between her ring-studded fingers, whistling a long cool line of smoke over the phone. "Yeah, I'm talkin' to ya, Pete," she finally said. "Happy New Year."

"Happy New Year." Didn't want to ask her why she called or if Juno had delivered my message. Cara clearly had her own reasons for contacting me and I figured I'd learn more if I just let her talk.

"Just had to call and say 'hi.' See whatcha doin'." She was clearly waiting for me to make some kind of expected response. I didn't. Made her wait before I spoke.

"Right now I'm talking to you," I said smoothly.

"Yeah," she said, a little too casually. "Did I wake you up?"

All right, so Cara really did want to know what I was doing tonight. Probably wanted to know if I'd seen the spectacle on MTV. "Dozing," I lied noncommittally.

She sounded a little disappointed. "Sorry to wake you up, Pete. I didn't know." She paused. Not to make me wait, but because I had thrown her an unexpected piece of script. She had clearly hoped I'd been watching Black Dog's spot.

"Yeah, so am I." I responded languidly to her apology. "What can I do for you?"

"Uh, nothin'. Talked to Juno. Got your message. Everything's cool here. Everything's under control. Me and Selene are just hangin' out burning things. Having monster flesh for New Year's."

"Sounds lovely." I yawned.

"Yeah, well, ya know. Got a prisoner, gotta treat him right," she bragged. "So, Pete. You burning anything for the new year?"

"Only in my dreams."

"Better watch your dreams," she said in a dark tease that reminded me briefly of Jade's voice. "Never know where they could end up. Yup, me and Selene been sittin' here, just following our dreams. You want to talk to Selene?"

"No, I'm tired, Cara. I don't really feel like talking," I said irritatedly, hoping to prod her into getting to the point.

"I don't feel much of anything tonight," Cara sort of boasted. "Don't feel anything. Isn't that sad? Me and Selene are trying to feel something, but we can't."

"So why are you calling me?"

She sighed, highly annoyed with being pushed into anything resembling an honest directness. "Because, Pete, remember, if I don't feel it, nobody does." I remembered her saying something like that during her last visit as a kind of implied threat against the band. I pretended I wasn't making the connection. Kept silent. Let her finish. "Well, gotta go play with the monster. I guess I'll be seein' ya, Petie."

"I'll be seeing you too," I said coldly, but she'd already clicked off.

So what did Cara have to do with tonight's debacle? Did she cause it? Did she push the energy in the wrong direction? She had asked if I was burning anything. I stared at the candle and recalled my dreamlike connection to my lover throughout his performance, and how, the first time he visited me, burning Penny's protection charm had nearly made him faint. He revived tonight when I killed the flame. I suddenly felt in my flesh that I had worked magic without meaning to. Or that Cara had been working magic through me.

Cara might have pushed Jade's energy back against his audience to cause panic, might have called down Pan Himself for all I know, and tried to use me as her proxy against him for maximum spite. And yet, despite her attempt to damn us both, Jade walked off the stage in the arms of a friend. The protection charm worked. Perhaps I was developing more "power" through my fire gazing and meditations than I knew about.

I was staring at the phone and hoping it would ring as I thought about these things. But I stared through morning and no one called to disturb my conjectures into anything that made less sense.

Followed the news all weekend. All the local channels kept repeating the government smear job on Toon, with the help of various local town idiots who once had the wit to put their names on some media roster so they would get calls for stupid TV interviews and be able to impress their mothers by publicly showing their astounding lack of insight into real life. Most of the town idiots were introduced with the ambiguous phrase "expert on child abuse," which is not the first way I would choose to be presented to the public, but I suppose that's my problem, because the shrinks and the wannabe shrinks that the news folks paraded out to fill in two or three minutes of air time with titillating speculation seemed to relish the title. And of course everybody knew everything about cults and child abuse and child abusers except whether or not Toon had actually committed any crimes. That was left to public prejudices to safely determine.

But the news story that held most of my attention concerned Black Dog, and thanks to the MTV coverage, this one made the national media. Turned out to have been quite the stampede. Three people dead. Seven injured. And the slant of most of the stories was, "Is rock 'n' roll dangerous? Should it be regulated?" Which meant that Heppelfauf's idiotic bill got lots of media attention and Heppelfauf himself got to make appearances with Mrs. Kipfer and brag about the death of Egbert. Also meant that Black Dog now had a solid name for itself outside of rock 'n' roll circles. CNN kept running the MTV clips of the performance and the death crush of the crowd.

Heppelfauf got lugged out onto a Sunday night interview where he provided running commentary on all the "secret Satanic signals" Jade was allegedly sending out to his "followers" and how the "black dog" was a well-known Satanic familiar, and how this "sad, tragic" situation was only "one small indication" of all the evil inherent in rock music. The interviewer did a lot of smirking, but he was too politely "neutral" to prevent Heppelfauf from making a fool of himself.

So Christians for American Decency got lots of free airtime for fundraising, and Heppelfauf went through his tired bit and waved his hands a lot, and by the end of the interview every loony tune Christian fundamentalist in the country was no doubt bobbing and tottering to the Great Man's invective against Black Dog and rock music. Now that Heppelfauf's target audience was prepared to bolster his ego by laying siege to Congress in his name, and to sacrifice their kids' college tuition money to his girth, what did he care if he alienated everyone else with absurdities? A buck's a buck. He knew where the horses were buried.

Besides, people were dead, so who could argue with that? It wasn't like most people cared about rock music anyway, so it was pretty much Heppelfauf's battle to win. He urged parents not to let any of their "precious children" go to rock 'n' roll clubs, forgetting to mention that clubs only admitted legal adults. Urged that Black Dog be made accountable for the deaths. Urged support for his bill. Urged people to join Christians for American Decency. Urged prayer. Urged donations. Mrs. Kipfer looked eagerly morbid on cue.

So Heppelfauf and Kipfer were a media hit all week and all I could do was survive through work and wait for my phone to ring with news from Jade or Penny. Which it didn't.

All right. My week. Monday looked to be one hell of a cheerful day. Piekarski and Kanesh ran the meeting and confirmed all my speculations about the Toon affair. Informed everyone who couldn't figure it out from the news that "we now have Toon by the balls" and that we'd soon have a major drug bust to impress Washington with. Everyone seemed to approve of the strategy. I made a half-hearted attempt at waving the flag, which probably came across as more parodic than patriotic, but nobody seemed to notice. Then Piekarski decided that me and him would be present when the social workers grilled the grieving mothers in a week or two and that Kanesh would make it a news story so we could keep stringing the issue along before the public. Fine way to kick off the new year.

Wednesday. Got my first care package from Toronto. Fearless slipped it to me in the privacy of his office. "No transcripts. Just a tape. Won't waste your time telling you what you can hear for yourself. Give it a listen, get back in here, and tell me what you think we should do." I liked the desperation in his voice. Really liked the word "we." Crensch was blowing it. Made my week.

Went to my office, closed the door, and put the tape, which bore Monday's date of January 4th and the words "Oak Street," into my fine tape recorder. Hit the button. Waited breathlessly.

Crackles. Crensch was wired and his mic was muffled so the signals on the tape weren't that clear, but I was able to make out and transcribe the following.

Loud knocking. Waiting. More loud knocking. Humming. Sounded like the tune of "Row, Row, Row Your Boat." Pictured him bouncing on his heels and looking "unobtrusive." Wondered what he thought about Penny's strangely sloping house. More knocking. Couldn't believe Crensch would hang around that long on a routine visit, when all he needed to do was truthfully report that nobody appeared to live at that address. Dead end—end of case—onto the mob investigation. That's what I would have done. Hell, that's what anyone would have done. But Crensch hung around in the January cold for at least twenty minutes.

I kept fast forwarding, but being afraid I'd miss something important, I rewound the tape and made myself listen. More crackles. Whistling. Crensch said, "Test." Then more knocking and crackles, and suddenly, underneath the empty noise, a faint sound of a female voice. So faint on the tape I had to rewind and play it several times over to make it out. Sounded like Juno screaming from inside, "Get the door, Cara, it looks like him." Then a faint, whiny, "'Cause I'm not supposed to answer it—"

Crensch humming. Could almost see him standing a little straighter, like a nervous high school buck psyching himself for his first date. Probably even straightened his tie.

Door slammed open. Must have struck him someplace good because I heard a sharp "ouch." Then Cara's voice.

"What do you want?" she asked coolly.

"Good afternoon, ma'am. I'm Sidney J. Crensch Jr. United States FBI—"

"So?"

Crensch lost his thin suave. "I'm here on a routine investigation—one with international implications—"

"A what?" interrupted Cara, clearly contemptuous of his temporary show of ego.

"A routine investigation . . ." Crensch's voice trailed off a little, seeming to lose the confidence to repeat the more grandiose part of his introduction. Tried to recover. "I'm looking for a woman—"

"You're looking for a woman," Cara repeated with devastating matter-of-factness, as if she just wanted to understand what his problem was so she could get on with her life. I pictured her leaning against the splintered doorjamb like a classic prostitute leaning against a streetlight, tasting weird smoke through one of Penny's cigarette holders, looking like she was too dirtied from real life to let bumblers like Crensch waste her time. She was brilliant. Really made Crensch seem like an awkward john that wouldn't know which end went up if he were holding it.

"Uh, yes ma'am. I'm looking for a woman." He hesitated over the phrase, perhaps Cara had thrown him one of her supercilious looks. But then he pulled himself together enough to say, "A woman named Penny Rosalie La Rue Dupruis Starmaker, Esq." He drew the name out with slow significance, as if he were rattling off some code word for entrance into a secret boys' club. It was embarrassing.

"Who?" asked Cara, making him repeat himself.

Crensch got the name screwed up the second time. "Understand she lives at this address, 13 Oak Street." Cara did not respond. "Sign of the Dangerous Dragon," added Crensch significantly.

"No one but me and my sisters lives at this address," said Cara truthfully. "And none of us are named Starmaker."

For anyone else, that would have ended the visit. All Crensch had to do was believe her and close the case. Some nut put 13 Oak Street on a letter and that's that. And maybe he would have believed her and gone on to his real work if Cara hadn't abruptly asked, "Would you like to come in and look around?"

Under normal circumstances, most investigators would have said "no," closed the case, and gone on to the mob investigation. But Crensch had to say yes. The whole thing was being recorded, and he had to claim he'd done everything possible to follow up on the letter. He coughed a little, shuffled his feet, and finally said doubtfully, "Sure. Thanks."

Sound of entering the premises. Sound of door slamming closed. "There's my sister Beulah tearing sheets," explained Cara. "Aren't you, sweetie? The sheets are for Hangman. The baking soda, vinegar, and number nine red food dye is lava for a volcano. Don't touch it or it might explode."

"Ah," said Crensch uncertainly.

"Beulah's a little artist and likes to make things. We call her the third fate."

"I see," said Crensch, trying to sound as if he did.

"How's my little sister?" purred Cara. "Keeping busy with her toys?"

"What happened to your eye, Beulah?" asked Crensch, gawkily attempting to make friendly conversation so he could show the backup team he was "investigating."

"You'd have to ask my other sister about Beulah's eye," replied Cara. "But she's off someplace." Good. So Juno had the wit to stay out of sight. "Kitchen. Living room." I sensed that Crensch did not venture far enough out of the kitchen to notice that there were more downstairs rooms off the living room. Probably glanced into the living room from the kitchen doorway and assumed that was all there was to the house. Juno was probably keeping herself in one of those unseen rooms. "Care to come upstairs?"

"Anything you want to show me down here?" Crensch asked stupidly.

"No. I live upstairs." Crensch made no answer, but the sound of footsteps treading up to Cara's apartment filled the tape. Door opened. "My place."

"I see." Wondered what he thought of her assortment of candles and altars and magical paraphernalia. Cara offered no explanation, letting Crensch make of her apartment whatever he wished. "This is my friend Selene. She's a dancer. She's very famous."

"Hi," said Selene.

"Hi," said Crensch. Floor creaked like he was walking over it. Faint giggles laced with Selene's breathy hoots. More creaking. "Uh, nice posters," he commented. "Psycho-delic." More giggles, louder and nasty. "Very nice. Very nice."

"We're drinking peppermint tea and telling fortunes," said Cara loftily. "You got a fortune?"

"Uh, I don't know. I'm sure I might. I'm sure I—"

"—Everybody's got a fortune," interrupted Selene.

"Yeah, everyone dies," cackled Cara. "Someday you'll die. And then what?" she waited for a response. While she was waiting, Selene made a noise that sounded like *ping*.

"Uh, I don't know," Crensch tried to answer the question. "Then I guess I would have had a happy life." He sounded like the schoolroom idiot trying fake his way through an unwelcome quiz.

"But would it have mattered?" pressed Cara. "I mean once you're dead, would it have mattered whether or not you had a happy life? Would it have mattered whether or not you had even lived?"

Crensch actually said, "I guess." Then, "I don't know."

"Maybe to a daisy," said Selene. "Or some lettuce."

"Or some lettuce licking the dirt," agreed Cara. "But so what?"

"I never think about it," said Crensch.

"And we thought you were an *investigator*," teased Cara. Crensch had nothing to say to that little dig. There was an uneasy silence.

Then, "Hoo hoo," whimpered Hugh McCrae faintly.

"What's that?" Crensch sounded relieved for an excuse to break the silence by changing the subject.

"My little black dog," Cara answered carelessly. "We were about to have him out for tea."

"Where is he?"

"In my kitchen. On a leash. Won't come until I call."

"Hooey, hooey," pleaded McCrae in a high, cracking falsetto.

"Quiet, Hughey," ordered Cara. "You'll get fed later. You might even get a fed."

"Fed a bone," giggled Selene.

"A blood bone," said Cara. "Kind you take from a corpse and make peppermint tea with."

Crensch gagged and coughed.

"Joke," said Selene.

"So, Mr. Crensch, you want a fortune? You want to join us lonely ladies for tea? We set an extra place for my dog, but you can have it. Sit. Sit. Sit."

Crensch hesitated before he said, "No thank you, ma'am. Guess I've seen enough. Have a good day."

"We always have a good day, don't we, Selene? But come, sweetie, stay with us and I'll tell you your fortune." She paused before adding in her deep voice of pseudo-mystery, "Your *secret* fortune."

Crensch couldn't resist being told his secret fortune. "All right. I'd be happy to, ma'am. For a little while." More creaking. Chair being pushed around.

"Welcome. But first, tell us all about your work. I'm sure it's very interesting," Cara flattered in a thickly seductive voice.

"Can't. Secret." Long indifferent silence. "It's very secret," repeated Crensch, hoping for an admiring response and perhaps a little more flattery and turning up nothing but clinking teacups and Cara singing snatches of nursery rhymes for several minutes. "So, um, Penny LaRue doesn't live here?" he asked to break back into notice.

"No," said Cara. "I live here." Selene giggled. "Drink your tea, Sidney. Then I'll tell you your fortune."

"Can't wait," said Crensch.

"Why?" poked Cara. "Your fortune will always be there."

"True," he dopily agreed.

"But Selene first. Give me your palm, Selene. No, wait, girl, you have to finish your tea first. Gulp it down. There. It's dribbling out of your mouth. Use a napkin. Now. C'mon Selene. You've got to *hand* it to me." Giggles. "All right. Your palm's a mess. I don't see anything."

"What's wrong with her palm?" asked Crensch anxiously. "It's got red lines all over it."

"She cut it up with thumb tacks," said Cara. "Pretty job. All right, let me see your tea leaves." Sound of cup scraping across the table. "Selene, you goon! You're not supposed to drink the leaves! You've swallowed your own future. Now what will you do?"

"Joke," said Selene.

"Joke," said Cara. "All right, let me see Mr. Crensch's palm. At least that bone's clean." Another long silence.

"What do you see?" asked Crensch a little nervously. "I haven't cut it, have I? You want my tea leaves? I didn't drink them."

Cara's voice suddenly got all husky. "I see a long, long wasted life. I see eighty-five years of long waste. I see you like to paint but all your pictures are dead. I see Arizona."

"Wow."

"I see a long, cool western desert. You're bound in white. You're looking for something. You won't find it. It's in a cloud."

"It's in a cloud," repeated Selene.

"Protect the sun from motherless children." Crensch quoted the Utica psychic he had interviewed during the vanishing corpse investigation like he was suddenly saying a prayer.

"You should," said Cara. "You're somebody's son. You're a motherless child. You should protect yourself. You should make sure nobody takes what's yours."

"Do but slay this dragon and we'll give thee all our goods." Crensch was really getting hot now with the Utica psychic references. Wondered if he even remembered he was wired.

"Did somebody say 'dragon' Selene?" Breathy hoots from Selene. Long weak hoo-hoo whimpers from McCrae. "We are slaying dragons. Like fairy knights out of romance."

"Down," said Selene.

"Clown," said Cara.

"Joke."

"Uh, so you two girls are a couple of dragon slayers getting the goods?" asked Crensch, like he thought he was being clever.

"Sure," said Cara grandly. "That's why we're here. But your palm says you're not a dragon and you've got no treasure to guard so you don't have to worry about us."

"Sure," said Crensch. "I'm not a dragon."

"All right," said Cara seductively. "Show me your tea leaves and tell me who you are. Gaze into your mug with me. What do you see in them?"

"Uh, I see images. I see a bear. I see myself in Arizona painting a desert. I see paintings running from my hands, so fast I can't catch them. And a shape like Mickey Mouse. With a tail."

"Mickey Mouse with a tail," repeated Cara.

"Squeak," said Selene.

"What does it mean?"

"Means you found the magic palace and you're done with your fortune," said Cara. "Hey, Hughey, get out here. Now, boy."

Enter a wheezing McCrae. Sound of Crensch pulling back his chair. "What? I—I uh Mr. McCrae—I'm so surprised—it's good to see you, sir—what are you doing here?"

"Well," said McCrae thickly, in a voice like the old Jolly Green Giant commercials, "hey, hey—I—I'll tell ya—it's good to see you too, Mr. Crensch—I'm here—investigating."

"Tell him everything, Hughey," ordered Cara. "I command you to leave no stone untouched, you old fossil."

"Where's your little dog?" asked Crensch.

"Ate him," burped McCrae absently. I remembered Jade telling me that when he was a child, McCrae ate his pet dog.

Everyone laughed. "Go on," said Cara, "you know what to tell our guest. And you better get it right or I'll stick you back on cotton candy and pepper doughnuts."

"How long have you been in there? Why didn't you come out for tea?" asked Crensch, now trying to cover his embarrassment with affability.

"Feels like I've been there twenty years. Well. It was a hole. Came here to do my own investigating," said McCrae. "Wanted to know what this 13 Oak Street was." Cara and Selene giggled.

"What did you find?" Crensch asked in his best "investigating" voice.

"Nothing, Mr. Crensch. Found nothing. Nice girls. Kept me here. Made me stale tea in an old shoe. Now it's time to leave. Gotta job up here in Toronto now. Did I tell ya?" I imagined him pointing a finger. "Establishing a Canadian office for Mr. Joseph P. Heppelfauf III's organization—Christians for American Decency. Now the north. Yessirree. Got some old relatives to look up."

"Think it's time we let you see them?" asked Cara.

"If you please, miss, I should like permission to go."

"Soon. But take a look at Sidney's sketches first."

"How'd you know I had sketches?" asked Crensch, obviously flattered.

"I know everything," said Cara mysteriously. "Want to see them, Selene?"

Selene made a noise that sounded like *kaweet*. Sound of paper crackling. Crensch spoke. "Just a little sketch of the border crossing I happen to have with me. Border guard. Drew the car in front while I was waiting. On the back is a pet fish I had when I was young. Not my best effort. Tried to give it a leash and wings."

Hugh McCrae commented, "Very nice. Very nice. I can almost feel the flat fins of your flat fish, Mr. Crensch. In my old heart. Which is my gall bladder sac. You draw pretty as a picture. Yessirree."

"Uh, thank you," said Crensch, obviously pleased. "It's my secret passion."

"I can tell. You know what I like about your secret passion, Mr. Crensch? If it's a car or an old fish, you draw a car or an old fish, just as it is with nothing added. I like that. Solid and square. You could make a fortune doing sketches for nickels."

"O yeah?" said Crensch perking up.

"Why not?" said McCrae. "You could stand outside an art museum and sketch people's kids for gum money. Why should you care for Rembrandt when you can draw like this?"

"All right, Mr. McCrae," said Cara, "you may go. Work your wonders. Selene, why don't you show him out, show him around town, help him find his relatives?"

"Sure," said Selene with a weird sort of shrug in her voice. "Poor monster. Come, pet."

"Later, Mr. Crensch," said McCrae.

Sound of leaving.

"Well, Mr. Crensch," said Cara, "anything else you'd like to know?"

"No," said Crensch. "I'm satisfied. What a nice guy that Hugh McCrae is. Too bad he got mixed up in such a weird case."

End of tape.

Brought it into Fearless as if it all meant nothing to me. "Well, Morrow?"

"Sounds like the vanishing corpse case is closed," I said deliberately.

"No clue, Morrow. Any other bright ideas?"

"Yeah, sounds like Crensch found a couple of live ones. Look, boss, it's his case. I think there isn't much to say until he hits the Hopner stuff."

"I meant his running into McCrae."

"So, McCrae couldn't find anything, either. He was curious about the address in the letter and he was in town on business and who can blame him for stopping by.

Now he's off to help Heppelfauf convert Ontario. He's not our problem. He's probably more than happy to see for himself that we tried our best with the vanishing corpse case. I say leave him to his work and let's watch Crensch in his."

"Right, Morrow. And how to explain to the Canadian authorities that our guys go in for tea leaves and fortune telling with the local bimbos? Crensch is in charge of this case and if he looks really stupid, we look really stupid." He had a point. No doubt there were lots of Canadian law enforcement types guffawing over the American boss's peccadilloes.

"We don't explain. We pretend. We dress him in the emperor's new clothes. If it comes back to us, we hint that it's all part of some secret plan. Then Crensch'll look like the hero you want him to look like because everyone'll be afraid to let on that he can't penetrate the secret. Don't worry, boss. You can count on me to realize your dream."

Fearless scowled. Ordered me to get some real ideas on Hopner, fast. Dismissed me before I started making sense.

The low point of the week, though, was when some lucky shill for a tabloid news program's "human suffering as entertainment" division managed to wrangle an interview with Les. The interview aired Wednesday evening. Apparently, the "journalist" had caught up to Les outside of whatever motel Black Dog was staying in and had persuaded the usually aloof keyboardist to do a live extended interview at one of the New York TV stations on what the media was now calling "the New Year's Eve Massacre."

I just happened to catch the beginning of it while cable surfing for news. Les was slouched in a chair on the opposite side of a little round table from the journalist, looking quietly dour as the journalist introduced him by saying that she had hoped to have Jade McClellan instead. He didn't look any happier while she spent about a minute praising "Black Dog's bassist-singer-songwriter-front man" who "by all accounts was the true creative energy force driving the band, and who's music reportedly caused some people to hallucinate as if they were on a drug trip." Then she finally turned to Les and added in a tone of near apology that she was, however, "still happy to have the opportunity to talk to Lester McGuire, the band's able keyboardist."

Les corrected her coldly. "I'm also a songwriter."

"I'm sorry," responded the interviewer, with just a trace of glibness. "So, did you write your current hit, 'Pierced with Love and She Will'?"

"No. I played on it." Les looked like he wanted to kill someone slowly. The interviewer sensed this and remained superciliously silent. Les struggled with the need to prove himself. Need won out. Usually does. "I wrote a lot of ideas for our CD that never got used."

"I see. Well, as you know," she continued brightly, "we're not here to discuss your talents as a songwriter—"

"—Why not?" Les sort of bellowed. He looked a little drunk. "You started the interview by discussing songwriting."

"I'm sure people are much more interested in how you feel about the New Year's Eve Massacre."

"I'd rather discuss my songwriting."

"Surely you're not deluded enough to think anyone cares about your songwriting? Three deaths. Seven injuries. Two of them still in critical condition. How do you feel about that? Do you have anything to say to the families?"

"How do I *feel*?" He tossed his head and made a show of seeming to consider the matter.

"Yes."

"Disgusted. There should have been more deaths."

Interviewer could scarce contain her glee. She'd found a gem of an interview subject and she knew it.

"More deaths?" she repeated sanctimoniously.

"A lot more. Wish the whole place had burned down. Wish we'd killed them all."

"You wish the whole place had burned down. You wish you'd killed them all. Why?"

"Piss off more people. Get more attention for the band." Les was drunk.

"So is that what Black Dog is all about? Death and destruction?"

"Pretty much," said Les without a hint of irony. "That, and egos."

"Why did Jade McClellan pass out during your performance? Some people are claiming it was trance-induced ecstasy. Was it drugs?"

"No," said Les. "It was ego. Jade enjoys showing off."

"I don't understand," said the interviewer, adopting a tone of snide sympathy guaranteed to needle Les. "I'm sure many of his fans were quite concerned."

Les was visibly angry. "That's the whole point. Jade's the mystical witch and the center of the band and everybody's supposed to wonder where he goes in his dreams and be 'concerned' about him. He's very special, he wanted attention, and he got it."

"Don't you want attention?"

"I just love the music," Les sort of complained.

"Then you must be concerned about Jade yourself, since it's his music you're playing."

"It's our music."

"So why do you care who gets the most attention?" asked the interviewer softly. It was a fair question, but something in her quiet, super-polite tone made me want to slap her. She was clearly more interested in making Les squirm than in following up the story about the deaths.

"Because I want to get credit for my work. What's wrong with that?"

"You do. You're a good keyboardist. What's wrong with that?"

"I'm a brilliant keyboardist."

"So?" She waited for him to hang himself.

"So? So ask me about my fu—" [expletive deleted] "—songwriting."

"What would you like to tell us?"

"That I have a lot of originals we never use. That Jade isn't the only creative force in the band."

"And I'm sure that's the way you like it," she said to cause another explosion. "You get to play behind a very talented young man. You're very lucky. A lot of keyboardists would kill to be in your position. What's wrong with that?"

"I don't play behind anyone. *I write songs!*"

"Do you think rock music is destructive?"

"No."

"Name some keyboardists you admire." Les mentioned a few names I didn't recognize.

"Are you happy they're getting credit for their work?"

"Yes, sure. They're good keyboardists and songwriters."

"All right, then why do you need to take credit? Sounds like there's enough keyboard players out there who deserve success and are promoting the art. You must be very happy for them. I mean, if you think they're good, and they made it, and you just want to promote the art, why should you care? You must be very grateful the job's being done."

Les threw over his chair and started screaming profanities. The camera kept rolling.

"Please, Mr. McGuire. You want to be understood." Les stood gripping the table edge and swaying back and forth. It was weird. "Do you just want to be the star of the band? Is that it? And you'd kill your audience to get there?"

"Yeah, so? It was my band before Jade ever joined. What's wrong with honestly saying I want to be the star? Jade wants to be the star, but since he is the fu—" [expletive deleted] "—star he can get away with the 'I only do this because I love music' line that's supposed to make him sound all humble and everything. But since I'm not the star, I get massacred for admitting to having ambitions I haven't fulfilled yet. And if I 'just love music' it gets used as an excuse to put me down as a sideman. But if Jade 'just loves music' he's a hell of a guy for it and gets to pass out on stage. Why is it a crime to admit that I want my own—" [expletive deleted] "—band? Why is it no one's ever supposed to be honest about this business, and say they do this for attention? So what?"

The interviewer shrugged, happy to let Les go on.

"We all want to be famous. That's why our manager, Elb McCrae of Moon Management, Toronto, has worked so hard with Nick Nariano and the rest of the Nunzio mob family to promote our CDs in the states. You think we'd be selling ourselves out as mafia pets if we just loved music?"

"Care to explain?"

No, he really didn't. He swaggered out. He'd done his damage. They played a commercial for pain relievers. I helplessly put my fist through the wall.

Stave Twenty

Of course the media had a field day with Les's temper tantrum. But then, so did everyone else without a life.

Perhaps he was to be congratulated. I mean in terms of getting credit for his work and garnering some much needed attention, Les couldn't have picked a better time to make his victory speech. The New Year's Eve Massacre and Heppelfauf's various public appearances had pretty much made rock music the issue of the week anyway. And I'm sure the sudden surge of fascination with "rock 'n' roll as an evil force" was greatly bolstered by everyone's residual irritation from the nonstop winter break barrage of their kids' CDs. So circumstances obviously helped.

But no matter what the current controversy, the first few days of January are always a particularly rosy time to offer oneself for public sacrifice. There's lots of post-holiday invective dragging around that needs to be discharged at something. Lots of people are grumpy and dissatisfied with themselves for breaking their New Year's resolutions and for getting older without accomplishing anything, so it's a great relief to be able to tear into somebody else who might have a shot at glory. All kinds of folks have fresh family quarrels to remember from the party season and nothing else to really look forward to until summer, so being able to get loudly self-righteous over a public display of anger like Les's is something of an unexpected treat. Extends the festivities.

By the Wednesday of his interview, the massacre story hadn't exactly died, but it was dwindling from hard news into predictable commentary. In fact, by Tuesday it was only Heppelfauf and his crank cronies who were keeping it alive, and if Les hadn't agreed to do an interview, the whole affair probably would have fallen from media scrutiny in favor of some new atrocity. But face it, in terms of anger and self-destruction, Les had pretty much done a strip tease with a flesh corrosive, desperately easing the pressure of his personality by leaving nothing to entice but exposed muscle, and forgetting that starving jackals will slather and tear at what they can get.

Which meant that angry Les, who was both drunk and ballsy enough to go before the public and demand the same respect for his considerable artistic achievements that Jade got for his without having to stoop to ask; melancholy Les who probably really did love his own music as much as Jade loved his; soul-killingly talented Les, who Penny, with her centuries of expertise, could claim was one of the gods' gifts to music; was now the star joke of the radio talk show crowd and the newspaper columnists and the media commentators. And since the media has had a long-term love affair with righteously clucking over public displays of temper, the story got picked up like a hot date all over the country. Even made a bit of a name for Les's sadistic interviewer. A few months ago no one had even heard of Black Dog—now everybody was an expert on the band and had "followed them all along." And now, of course, nobody could miss them because any media maven in need of copy or commentary kept bringing them up.

Who could resist the band that killed? The band that was being backed by some reputed mafia figure? The band that was led by an alleged witch? The band that otherwise normal people hallucinated to? Here was the band the born-again wackos hated, and it's always great fun to drag them out. Here was an angry young man who dared to express socially maladjusted honesty. Here was a character who thought he was somebody special. He even threw a chair on TV. Like I said, it was a field day for the imaginatively impaired.

Speaking of imaginatively impaired, the only faction that took any of Les's claims seriously at first was Heppelfauf's. Christians for American Decency was more than happy to keep bringing up Les's interview while asking for money and support for their bill. Everyone else decided he was crazy. Which he was. Which didn't mean, of course, that Jade wasn't a witch.

Have no idea how Nick Nariano was taking things, but I did notice that "Poison Puppy" started getting airplay all over the place. Whether Nariano wanted to cash in on the publicity or the radio station managers were acting on their own was hard to tell. I knew Jade was under the impression that "Poison Puppy" wasn't supposed to hit the airwaves until closer to the end of January. It was obvious that they'd filmed their new video immediately after the massacre, because that was getting airplay too. Made marketing sense, I supposed, although some people were commenting on the band's "callousness" and "insensitivity" to be working immediately after the tragedy, even if they weren't the direct cause of the deaths. Could only hope the video's airplay meant that Les hadn't completely destroyed Nick's goodwill.

The only person in the world who seemed blissfully unaware of "Black Dog the mob-supported band" was Crensch, who was supposed to be our new expert on these things. But what can I say? Sometimes government works.

So it was a hell of a week. No direct word from the band. No sign that Crensch had been driven to do anything intelligent. Probably "consulting" with his Canadian experts about the payola case, now that the vanishing corpse business was closed. Probably trading compliments with McCrae, who was no doubt doing the same with Elise. For all I knew the three of them were living together in blessed harmony.

Tried to call Toronto. Cara hung up on me. Kept calling every night. Brought out a salt bowl and went over my limited knowledge of phone tricks. Broke open a chicken bone wishing to make Juno answer and talk to me. All I got was a nasty sounding disconnect.

Then early Sunday evening I was jolted by a boldly turbulent call from Beth. "Pete?" she asked shakily, immediately launching into a breathless string of fidgety explanations before I could reply. "—I'm supposed to be working, but it's slow out there and I had to call you because—"

Held my breath while she was speaking, because I didn't know whether Crensch had managed to tap Fendra's secret phone line yet or not. Then I figured that if he had, since Beth had just dialed my number, the deal was up anyway. "Where's Saint George?" I asked cavalierly.

"He's not here tonight. He's never here on Sundays. Pete—I—I have to talk to you—there's a bug on the other phone, the answering machine phone—I know there is—I'm sure this one doesn't have a bug because it's hidden in a closet and it's the one nobody knows about—Juno showed George the bug on the other line and he left it on—Pete I'm so confused—I've got to talk to you—I'm scared—everything—Juno's gone—everyone's gone—I've got to talk to Jade—is he there?"

"No."

"Pete, where is he right now?" she sounded sweet, shrill, and hysterical all at once. Shyly demanding. Only Beth could sound that way.

"I don't know. Supposed to be heading south. He doesn't have a real tour schedule."

"I know. Jade is never real." Her voice smiled a little, then it got frantic again and the words tumbled out like a determined little spring rain muddying the ground without end. "I saw what happened last week and I was so worried and Juno wouldn't tell me anything and his mother—"

"—Beth. Slow down." I interrupted her in a voice more harshly confident than I felt. "You're on a safe line. No one is listening. I can't help you if I can't understand you, so you must tell me everything. Slowly. In order. Take your time, it's all right. If you need to go wait on a table I'll wait for you to come back, or you can hang up and call me back. I'll be here." Put a long tape in my answering machine and turned it on to catch everything. In my present state of mind I didn't trust to memory.

"OK." She said it like it was an effort now to speak, pausing like she was struggling against a pitiless inner chaos just to claim her thoughts, let alone order them. It was hard for Beth to recognize her mind right now. Her heart was too open for that sort of meeting to leave it unsullied. "OK. I'm sorry. Pete. I know you are a good friend to Jade. I hope you can help. I'm scared. That's all I can say. I'm scared." She swallowed her voice and tried to speak slowly. "I know something is wrong. Last weekend Jade passed out during his New Year's Eve performance. Did you see it? And now everyone's talking about the people who died, who got trampled to death in the club, as if Jade doesn't matter."

I felt myself smiling a little at her fiercely innocent loyalty. Poor Beth.

"All right," she continued, "so I was very worried, and I called Elise, and she didn't seem at all concerned. She said 'it was just like Jade' and 'she didn't care for his theatrics' so why should I? I thought it was strange that his mother didn't care but Juno didn't know anything about it either and I figured if his mother and cousin didn't know it had to be OK—but I was so worried, and I lit candles for him and prayed."

Abrupt silence. Whether she was hesitating or sidetracked by a customer wasn't clear. I waited long seconds for Beth to resume.

"So then I took my piano lesson at Elise's last Sunday and she didn't say anything and I didn't say anything because I didn't know what to say. But I played my lesson really badly because I was distracted and Elise said it was close to right, even though I know it wasn't, and that I need to work on my left hand. Then she gave me an old acoustic guitar—not a bass, a regular one—but she said it was Jade's and he used to fool around with it—so I thought, 'OK, I guess everything is OK or someone would hear'—I mean she didn't seem worried—so I took the guitar home with me but I have no idea how to play it. There's like a little lesson book inside I haven't had time to look at because I'm always working. But I'm sure that Jade would be really surprised that I have his old guitar." She stopped speaking as if she had confused herself and needed space to sort out her story.

"All right, Beth, go on." I didn't know what the guitar had to do with anything, but she sounded so distraught that I didn't want to disrupt her flow. Just let her tell me everything. I'd sort it later.

"OK. So then I was working Thursday night and I saw on the news on the bar's TV a clip from Les giving an interview and bad-mouthing Jade and throwing over his chair. And I got really angry, because I thought Les was behaving like a jerk, and George saw it too, and he said, 'That boy better watch his mouth. For a smart boy, he ain't actin' too smart' and then when it was over George said, 'Whatsa matter with him, he's supposed to have it good right now and don't he like his life?'"

It wasn't like Beth to parrot her boss, but I sensed that she was desperate to make sure I understood how egregious Les's behavior was by mirroring Fendra's reaction. "Were those his exact words?" I asked evenly. "About Les not liking his life?"

"Yes. And I totally agreed because how dare Les say those things about Jade—he says Jade has an ego, well Les has the biggest ego I ever saw—and then Les calls Jade a witch and says the band's in the Mafia. Well, so what if Jade's a witch? I don't care. And then George asked me if I believed in the Mafia and I said didn't know but I believe in witches because Jade's cousins are definitely witches and he said, 'Who you think believes your boyfriend's in the Mafia?' and I started laughing because who *would* believe it? You can definitely believe Jade's a witch, he's got the looks and the dark attitude—at least *I* think he does—but who would ever guess he belongs to the Mob? I couldn't see Jade as a mobster. It wouldn't fit. So I decided Les was being a jerk. And I said to George, 'If anyone belongs to the Mob, George, it's you—you've got the looks—' and I was only trying to tease him but he didn't think it was funny and he told me to go wait the tables and he was kind of mean about it. Anyway—so wait—"

I waited three or four minutes.

"I'm sorry, there was a customer. Anyway, Friday afternoon this man comes in—and he seemed fairly nice. We were talking and he introduced himself and said he was from the United States FBI. So of course I asked him if he knew you and then I told him how you used to come to Fendra's and everything and how my boyfriend sometimes stays with you when he's in New England."

My heart juddered like a ripped bag in a hurricane.

"He said you were good friends and he gave me his card—wait a minute—Sidney J. Crensch, Jr." She waited for me to say something.

I forced myself to respond neutrally. "Yes, I know him. What did he want?" Might as well get the whole damage report.

"He said he just wanted to talk. I think he was lonely. He seemed nice. Ordered a beer but didn't drink it, due to regulations. He was funny. Asked all about you—how we met and how often you came to Fendra's and if you knew George—hold on—" I waited while she took care of another customer. "OK—are you still there?"

"Yes."

"And he asked me all about my boyfriend and I told him all about Jade and Black Dog and what a great band they are and how they used to play here and he acted really interested—he was really nice. And I probably shouldn't have been talking so much because I did have to keep getting up and waiting on people. Anyway, I did my job—I worked—I wasn't just talking—and Sid—he said to call him Sid—just wandered around and looked at things and waited until I wasn't busy to talk some more. He seemed very interested in me."

"I'm sure he was."

"Oh—and he asked about that man you asked about that Cara gave the party for—Claude Hopner. And I told him how I didn't know him personally but that I thought George did business with him once and that he might have been Jade and Cara's uncle and how you came to the party. And I told him about the party, and about Cara and everything—he wanted to know all about Cara—then while I was getting a drink for someone, Sid tried to call out on our answering machine phone and I had to tell him no one but George was allowed to use that phone—which is what we're supposed to say—and that there's a pay phone in front he can use. So he said he didn't have any change and could he use it for a minute and before I could stop him he was sitting behind the bar and taking the whole thing apart and saying there was something wrong with the line but he could fix it so what could I do? Especially since I was the only one working because I had to open and I was busy because the bartender was late and I had to make all the drinks for people myself, which I'm really not supposed to do.

"Anyway, it was after that that Juno dropped by to say hi and she was asking me what was going on and we were talking when George came in with Andy and Ray, our bouncers. So I introduced George to Sid, who was sitting on the floor behind the bar—and I was scared 'cause when he stood up he put the phone back and we're not supposed to let anyone use it—and George started having a fit and told Sid"—Beth took a deep breath here, as if to steady herself for what she was about to say—"'you'd better get the fuck out of my honest business just tryin' to make a living Jesus F. Christ now get the hell out or I'll have my buddies take you out'—and Andy grabbed his collar 'cause Andy'll fight anyone, he doesn't care. And Sid looked scared and left and I felt bad for him because he seemed like a nice person and sometimes Andy can have problems—especially when George tells him to."

She went quiet again. I had the impression that she found it uncomfortable but somehow necessary to repeat Fendra's words.

"And then?" I asked, having to hear the rest, knowing that Crensch had probably been wired and that all of Beth's revelations to him were now government property.

"And then"—I could sense her struggling with her mind again to get things right—"and then—George kept having a fit at me and asking me why I'm talking to a guy like that and what did he want to know and I was crying and all upset because I knew I was supposed to be working and I *was* working, I didn't neglect my job, and George kept yelling 'what he wanta know about me—what you tell him about me?' and I kept saying 'nothing' because I didn't want to make George more upset—and I told him the truth—that we mostly talked about Jade and about Jade's uncle Claude Hopner and about you—I mentioned your name and said that you were another American FBI agent we both knew and that Jade is good friends and stays with you—and George quieted down a bit and wanted to know what I said and so I told him everything because what could I do and he told me to get to work and stop talking to strangers."

I couldn't speak because I couldn't breathe.

"Then Juno tried to make things better by saying, 'I think he bugged your phone. He was taking it apart before.' And George checked the phone that Sid had fixed and—Pete—you'll never believe it, but he did put a bug in it and George started swearing a blue streak and slammed the phone against the back of the bar and then he said to just leave it so we did. So that was Friday. Pete—hold on—"

I waited about ten minutes of eternity. Speculated through nerve-strangled logic on whether or not Crensch had been wired for his conversation with Beth. There was always the slim chance that he wasn't. Tried to hold onto the hope that he wasn't. That Fearless already believed he was disturbed, and that although Crensch could certainly bring back some wild tales to Fearless, he couldn't begin to prove anything unless they were recorded. If they weren't recorded and I stayed cool, the stories couldn't hurt me. Had to remember that. But if the conversation was recorded, there wasn't much I could do to deny them. Either way I'd have a hell of a lot of explaining to do, which I really wasn't up for. At least I had a warning, and the rest of the night to strategize, which was better than nothing.

Then I felt something wet and hopeless in my eyes and I tried to rub it away and I couldn't speak. Hated my life. Had to keep thinking. Figured that at least Crensch's phone bug couldn't do much damage as it would only record Fendra's answering machine. And now that Fendra's suspicions were up, Crensch didn't have a prayer of getting in his house or that of any of his associates. Not that he probably ever did. So further "investigating" in Fendra's was out, unless Crensch could put aside his ego and delegate the job to someone who had more wit than he did. Who knows, maybe he'd be smart enough to know that he'd just blown the whole deal. That he wouldn't get much deeper into the Mob's business than he got from talking to Beth. But since Beth had blabbered about Cara's Claude Hopner party, for all I knew the Bureau would re-open the vanishing corpse case. And at the moment I couldn't figure out what to do, couldn't even feel all my hopelessness yet, because Beth wasn't finished.

"OK—we can talk. Pete—last night, about ten thirty, eleven, a lot of George's business partners came by and had a drink and George closed the bar early even though there was a band and sent everyone home except me. So I thought maybe he wanted me to wait on his friends and I wanted to do a good job on account of him being so angry all week, especially on Friday, so I stayed like he asked me to. And I made drinks for everyone and waited on the table and I was just going back to the bar with my empty tray when I . . . accidentally recorded something, and I—"

"—*What?* Slow down, Beth. Take it in order, you're losing me here. Did you do something to the bug on the answering machine?" Tried to keep the panic out of my voice. Not sure I succeeded.

"No. I mean . . . I was carrying a little cassette player in my front pocket so I could listen to a homemade tape that Jade gave me while he was here, and I put in my earphone and pressed play, but I didn't pay attention to how close the tray was to the bar and it must have knocked against my pocket and hit the record button, because it recorded a lot of what George and his friends were saying. And I'm really scared for Jade."

"Beth." I could barely control my voice. "I want to hear what you've got. When do you get off work?"

"Last call is one a.m. But then there's clean-up. It might be two or three in the morning when I get back."

"Call me when you get home and play the tape for me. I don't care how late it is. I'll be here."

"I can't. I don't have my own phone yet."

"But you live over the bakery you work in, right? Isn't there a phone there you can call me collect on?"

"Yes, but I don't think my boss would like it—"

"—I will pay for the call."

Hung up on her to force the issue.

It was two-thirty in the morning when she called me back. Turned on the answering machine to record. "Pete? It's Beth. Did I wake you up?"

"No," I said truthfully. I had pretty much been sitting by the phone all night coming up with no new resolutions. "I'm very glad you called."

"Pete, it would have been all right from Fendra's. Really. Nobody listens. Anyway, here's what I've got. It starts when I bumped my tray." Sound of an object, which I assumed was the recorder, being placed on something hard, like a counter or a floor. Sharp click of a button. Then the voice of George Fendra came through my phone.

"Hey, Beth. Come here and sit down and tell my good friend Nick all about what you tellin' me the other day, 'bout that Sidney Crensch guy comin' by to bother us and how your boyfriend there is such good friends with his buddy Pete Morrow that he stays in his house—"

And then someone I presumed was Nariano said, "Come on, Beth, you can tell me—we're all friends here, right?" Several voices echoed "right" as Beth stopped the tape.

"Pete—I don't know how to explain it, but it didn't feel right, like there was something wrong or maybe some trouble and at first I didn't want to say anything because I thought maybe George was in trouble so I just looked at George and asked him—"

"—It's alright, Beth," I reassured her. "We can talk after you play the tape."

Click of the button. Beth's recorded voice sounded uncertain as she asked Fendra, "What do you want me to say?"

Nariano responded. "You're a good girl and George here been doin' you a lot of favors and we just want to know what you told that fed that came askin' questions here the other day."

Then Fendra spoke. "Tell him."

The recording segued into an extended barrage of silence. "I accidentally erased part of it. I'm sorry."

"What did you tell Nick?" I asked thickly.

"Everything I told you before. And Nick kept getting angrier and angrier and swearing and pounding his fist and when I mentioned that I knew you and Jade knew you he got really angry and wanted to know how often Jade stayed with you and what he said to you and I had no idea and couldn't tell him because I really didn't know. Said some terrible things about you, Pete, and how you'd once hurt his wife's family and how it wasn't going to happen again and how Jade 'had no goddamned business associating with feds and Les had no goddamned business advertising the business' and 'how that boy Elbie was worse than useless and his head ought to roll' and I suddenly got the impression that for some reason Nick wasn't happy with Black Dog and so I made myself speak up and defend Jade and the band and Nick told me to shut up he didn't want to hear it and I felt horrible—"

Beth started to sob. I could hear tears running through her words.

"—like a piece of dirt—like I was nothing—and I started crying and I got all upset and angry and told them they weren't good enough to carry Jade's guitar strap and Black Dog was the greatest band in the world. I didn't care if I lost my job. But when I said it everyone looked shocked at me talking to Nick that way and then Nick looked around the table and just laughed and said, 'who you think is making Black Dog? Santy Claus and Saint Mary?' and everyone laughed when Nick did and I didn't understand so I just shouted, 'they're making themselves because they're brilliant and great and wonderful and everyone knows it,' and Nick got angry and told me to get out now and George said I'd better leave. So I pretended to leave but I snuck back behind the bar and I listened."

"That was brave."

"I couldn't leave—I had to know what they would say about Jade. Pete—please listen I'm so scared—they weren't like normal people. Even George was acting different than he usually acts. OK. I heard Nick say he had to think about things and then everyone was quiet for a long time. I was afraid to breathe. After a while I almost thought they'd left. And then, here's the rest of it that I caught."

Beth fast forwarded the tape and pushed play. I heard Nick speaking. "Heard a story from my boy Pauley Campobello who just got out of jail—needs a job—that he heard some jailhouse rumor 'bout who killed that Mother Penny's old friend Claude Hopner, the one this Sidney Crensch joker said he's chasin' down on his TV interview to find some bullshit payola tax evasion scheme. Boy Pauley says this Hopner guy was killed by a woman named Elise McClellan, who I find out happens to be Jade Black Dog's blessed mother I swear to Christ."

Several people laughing. Nick told them all to shut up. Then he said, "So Pauley has no idea whether Elise McClellan killed Hopner or not, but that's the word from jail. Any of you got a better story?" There was a pause, as if no one knew what to say. "Pauley, he talked to her husband in jail, who's some government clown in on some charge that he killed that disappearing colonel near Utica they were all trying to blame the Mafia on at one time. Not that Uncle Sam was desperate for a fall guy or anything. Yeah, so he got cleared or somethin' and now he's out."

"So what he's out?" asked Fendra. "We don't know him."

"So nothin'. Unless the feds re-open the case and start crawlin' back up our butt about it. Wish they'd get real jobs instead of chasin' us for murders we don't know nothin' about. But he was also sayin' to Pauley that Jade Spades there was friendly with Pete Morrow, and it turns out it was Morrow and that joker Crensch had a hand in puttin' him away on that murder charge that didn't stick. So Georgie here calls me last night and says Crensch is up here buggin' the phone and payin' him a visit and what can he want?"

"You think he's lookin' for another fall guy?"

"Maybe. But the girl said he's askin' 'bout Claude Hopner. And remember, he had that TV thing a while ago that he was after Hopner's killer and after us. So we got a problem. Got some musicians don't know when to play and when to shut up. Got a piano man goes shitfaced on TV tells everyone who made him somebody. Got a singer rattin' on his family to the feds."

"Why you think he's doin' that?" asked Fendra.

"Why? Who knows why? Maybe he don't like his mom. Maybe he don't like her husband. Maybe he just got problems, all that long hair affecting his brain. Maybe the whole family's screwball—his Aunt Penny there ain't right."

Someone said, "How we know his mother did it?"

Nick answered. "We don't. It's a rumor. That's the point. But if she did it what can we say? Claude Hopner ain't cost us a nickel dead or alive. He ain't the problem. Elbie got us our loan of services back plus interest and everything else they owe—we're fair and square there. All right. So whatever that first CD makes from here on in it's an even 70/30 split on the rest and we keep it that way for a while. So I'm sayin' look—if the feds get this Elise on Hopner's murder so what so long as it ain't gettin' to our business. If Crensch finds her out don't have to mean he finds us—who's Claude Hopner? I don't know Claude Hopner? You know Claude Hopner?"

Everybody said they didn't know him, including Fendra.

"And if there's publicity about the murder—so long as it stays on the murder—could sell some records—the kids like that sort of stuff today. That's why I had my people workin' their ass off to get that video made and out and that new song on the radio right after last weekend's little party picked up attention. Besides, if she did it ain't like another family or anybody musclin' in." Another pause. "And maybe she just don't like outlaws. Ya know, some people get jealous. So she's a crazy girl and her son is worse than crazy. Think this through. No one kills and cannibalizes for business. It's sick and it ain't right. She's just crazy. Maybe she ought to be in jail. Who knows?"

"Yeah, who knows?"

"But there's an awful lot of rumors pointin' to her son gettin' too friendly with that bastard Morrow whose got no business interfering in our business. That's got to be stopped. 'Cause let's say this Crensch guy finds Elise wasted old Claude—is it going to point an investigation to us? Specially since piano man there went and opened his mouth on national TV. Gotta problem. Black Dog's makin' us money and they stand to be makin' us a lot more. Feds want to stop it and the boys in the band ain't smart enough to know who they're workin' for."

"Waste the feds."

"Naah, there's always more feds. Can't waste the bullshit paperwork and wastin' one of 'em only makes the rest come down on us harder."

"Waste Elise—"

"Naah, ain't gonna kill the guy's mom. What does that do? Just make another investigation we don't need and she ain't done nothin' to us. So maybe she had a problem with Claude Hopner. Ain't our problem. Keep an eye on her, sure, that don't hurt. See if anyone goes pokin' into her life, see if it's going to go further, see if she's crazy. George, you can manage that."

"Sure," said Fendra.

"I say we pull in the reigns. No more interviews. No more travelin' unsupervised. No more nothin'. From now on Black Dog stays up here in the Northeast, in Utica, Worcester, Boston—our territory. George here gets an option. Got a club or two of my own in New York, but that's it. The band is playin' in our clubs. Had enough problems with that fiasco on New Year's Eve had to shell out to Lammelli to keep peace don't need another problem. Then we put some people on the boys to keep an eye. Good job for Pauley there."

Murmurs of approval.

Nariano continued, "I'll tell Jade personally to stay the fuck away from Morrow if he likes his life. That the guy's bad news. I'll tell him who to talk to he has to talk. Hate to have to find another singer to keep the business going. And I'll tell Les personally to stay off the fucking tube he's there to play music no one cares what he has to say. My wife's cousin took a few piano lessons once—Les could be replaced if he don't wise up. Elbie ain't doin' his job so we do his job. We close ranks, the money goes to Switzerland or Donald Duck, we don't know nothin' about it."

"Sure," everyone agreed.

"Here's to rock 'n' roll."

Beth stopped the tape. "That's all there is, Pete. I almost didn't go to my lesson yesterday because I was scared—and I'm calling you because I don't know what to do—and there's more—hold on can't believe it sounds like my boss is coming in. Bakers start early but I'm not supposed to be here until he opens at seven—"

She hung up. It was three-thirty.

Hell of a week for Beth, too. Stood with the phone in my hand, listening to the harsh dial tone, trying to get my bearings. Had to get my bearings. It was Monday morning. This meeting was late Saturday night. All right, so Nick Nariano didn't give a damn about Elise or Claude Hopner now that he was committed to the band and it was making him money. Penny had been right about that. There was a time earlier in their business relationship when that sort of revelation would have had an impact, but Nariano now recognized that his profit wasn't coming from Claude. Also recognized that since his initial expenses were recouped everything was pure profit from now on, and 70% of a skyrocketing business was worth preserving. Seemed like the whole trick was still doing my limited best to make sure Crensch didn't uncover anything definitive enough to nail Nariano on. And frankly, after Beth's revelations, I had no idea how to accomplish that. Because even if Crensch could be counted on to botch things, there were a whole slew of Canadian authorities who weren't as reliably incompetent.

Please, Aphrodite, speak to me. My dark bass god who holds my dreams is now a prisoner of the Mob and both our governments are poised to form an unholy circle 'round his name. Lend me your favor.

Got to go to work later and act normal. What can I do? See what Fearless confronts me with and confess to doing some unauthorized side work? If Crensch had bugged his conversation with Beth I could just say that sure, I've spent time with some of the band members, but if I had anything real from them why wouldn't I have come clean and hell, maybe Crensch ought to check out Elise, hadn't thought of that angle. But I knew that with the pressure Fearless was under the case wouldn't stop there, and that Hugh McCrae was likely popping back into Elise's life, and—damn it, Morrow think—

What if the tape, if there was a tape, never got to Fearless? What if I listened to it first, wrote a safely fictional version of events, and then discovered my blessed machine had destroyed the source? It would certainly buy me time. Eventually Crensch would get to Fearless with the facts and eventually the Canadian authorities would corroborate them—I'm sure they kept copies of everything—but destroying the tape upon arrival at the Boston field office might buy me a few more weeks of surveillance before I got canned, which might yield an opportunity to quietly block the investigation, although chances there were slim. But what other option did I have? Knowledge might be power, if I was lucky. Didn't give a damn about the job anymore anyway except as a vantage point.

On the other hand, delivering the tape would probably force my hand in terms of delivering the Nunzio family to what passed for justice, because ultimately I couldn't explain Beth's conversation with Crensch except by telling the truth, or telling enough of the truth to do damage. Considered resigning from the FBI and making my resignation a public issue to show the Nunzios I wasn't trailing them, to show that whatever Jade might have said to me couldn't hurt them. Be easy to resign in protest over the way this Toon affair was being handled. But it was too late. Crensch had been around dropping my name. Our names had been linked over the vanishing corpse case, so even if Crensch nailed the Nunzios, Nariano would now have to believe I was involved at some point. In either case, I wouldn't put it past Fearless to attach my name to the matter just to cover his own ass with NDECC over the obstruction of justice issues.

I could already hear the subtext in Fearless's meager little brain. *Promote me. I managed this sly undercover work with Morrow's secret cooperation from the beginning. None of my agents are outlaws. Let's forget the vanishing corpse. Morrow had to botch it to preserve evidence on this bigger tax evasion thing.* Fearless would come up with some bootlicking way to get himself to Washington. That was a given.

And then, with no more money to be made from the band and Nariano knowing that Jade was talking to me more than he should have been—

Started screaming and kicking my walls and the furniture. *No! Goddammit! No!* The Mob would not waste my love because of me—*No!* Crensch would not solve his case—I'd fucking kill him first. I'd take Jade and go away to another country—Japan, anywhere. We'd just leave the world. We'd just leave the fucking world—I just wanted to hold him and be left alone in a dream of our own making and I was nearly sobbing and going half-crazy with concern and rage and helplessness when the phone rang. Knocked myself hard against my kitchen counter grabbing it. I started my answering machine tape again to catch everything.

"Hello."

"Pete, it's me," said Beth urgently, sounding more terrified than anxious. "We can talk again. My boss started his morning baking and got a call from home so he asked me to come down and watch the kitchen while he's out. I still have more to tell you."

"So tell me."

Excruciating silence. Then, "Why does George's friend Nick hate you?"

"It's a long story. Right now I want to hear the rest of yours. Please. Start talking."

"I told you about Saturday night and how I think Nick is really mafia and that he has something to do with Black Dog—"

"He is and he does. You're dealing with dangerous people."

"OK, Pete, you know all about dangerous people, I guess. OK. They were saying Elise murdered Claude Hopner, and Jade"—she broke down— "I know Jade is in trouble with them—I know he is"—she cried a little—"and I know he didn't do anything." I let her cry. Understood. "Pete—there's so much—and George surprised me by coming in after I called you from Fendra's last night and before that there was more—"

"C'mon, baby," I said gently, "It's all right. Take it in order. The only way you can help Jade is to pull yourself together enough to talk to me. Remember, I'm a professional. I know how to deal with outlaws."

"Pete—you're such a good friend." She blew her nose and choked a little. "All right. So yesterday I was supposed to go to my lesson before Fendra's but I work in the bakery Sunday mornings now and it's part coffee shop and we always get newspapers and I just happened to see one on my break and it showed a photograph of Juno and Cara's house only there's been like a major fire—a gas explosion it said—and there was nothing left but ruins. And I was shaking so bad that I screamed when someone tapped me on the shoulder and it was Juno and then I saw their car out the window and Beulah and Cara were in it and I said, 'My God, Juno, what happened?' and she said, 'I stopped by to tell you we're going back on tour. Ma wants us with her now.'"

Goddess be praised was Penny wising up? Figured she heard about Crensch's visit and arranged the explosion to create an inarguable dead end. Crensch wouldn't be back at her girls' doorstep now. Wouldn't even find them again in a hurry. *Yes! Good job!*

Beth continued. "So I asked her why they were leaving so suddenly and she said they'd been having problems in Toronto and I asked her if she'd heard from Jade and she said she hadn't but she thought Jade was OK and that he was supposed to have played in Baltimore last night and that the band was heading down to Fairfax, Virginia and they were supposed to meet them down there and I remembered what Nick had said about Black Dog staying in the Northeast but I didn't say anything to Juno about Nick because I wasn't supposed to have heard that part of the discussion and I don't trust Cara if Cara found out so I just said, 'Are you sure they're going to Virginia?' and she said, 'Yes, they were supposed to leave Baltimore early this morning and play in a club near Fairfax tonight, but who knows what will happen when we get there?'

"So I said, 'what happened to your house?' and she said Cara blew it up but she had to go because Cara was having a fit and she only stopped to tell me not to tell anything more to Sidney Crensch and that I shouldn't have been talking to him on Friday—like now she tells me. And they wouldn't have stopped at all because Cara didn't want to except Penny told them to tell me not to talk to anyone about the band and that I should find another piano teacher besides Elise. So I said 'OK,' thinking 'how can I afford to pay a piano teacher and what could I say to Elise about suddenly just quitting' and then I asked Juno to give Jade my love and ask him to write and she said she would and then they took off so I'm all alone."

"So why are you talking to me if Juno told you not to talk to anyone?"

She choked a little. "Because . . . because I have to talk to someone and you are the only person I can trust and that's why I called you last night because I thought maybe there was a chance Jade was really heading back to New England instead of Fairfax and that he was with you or you knew where he was for sure—"

"Like I said, I don't know where he is, Beth. But I know he's with Penny and I'm sure his cousins will find him. Juno's right. Don't talk to Crensch. I wanted to warn you myself but I thought Juno would take care of things and I thought the less you knew the better. Crensch is trying to get enough evidence of illegal activities to arrest Nick and his friends, which means Black Dog," my voice skipped a little trying to find words to give her, "could get hurt."

"What do you mean—hurt?"

"I mean they'd have a major career setback. Need new backers protecting their interests. Fast." Marveled at how steady I sounded with my own euphemism.

"Why didn't—"

"I made a mistake. I followed a need-to-know policy and I didn't count on Crensch sweet talking you. Look, the damage is done. Tell Crensch nothing further. Lie. If you love Jade, you're working for Nick. Understand?"

"Are you working for Nick?" she asked with a scared sort of tightness that made me feel dirty, like I'd just broken her stunning innocence into running blood and pus.

Paused. "Yes. I am."

"O my God—Pete—I thought—"

"For now, Beth," I lied. "It's a role. And Nick can't know about it. It's part of a bigger case. You've got to trust and work with me. Understand? You've got to be my eyes and ears in Toronto and tell me everything."

"All right," she hesitated. "That's what George said last night after I called you. He surprised everybody by showing up on a Sunday night, and when he came in he was all friendly and promised me a raise if I would spy on Elise for him. He knows I'm taking lessons because of when I practice in the bar. He said to hang out with her. He said I could even skip work to go to her place and then come back to tell him everything. Pete—did she really kill Claude Hopner?"

"Yes. But I don't think she will hurt you. Just act normal. Go to your lessons. Report to George. Report to me. If Crensch ever shows up at Elise's get out of sight—no need for him to find you there and make a direct association with Fendra's. That's the main thing we need to avoid right now. Otherwise, Beth, the best thing you can do for Jade right now is to keep both George and myself informed about Elise, keep your calls to me secret from everyone, and don't let Crensch or anyone else intimidate or charm you into a conversation concerning Black Dog or anything else. You don't know about Cara's house blowing up except what you've read in the papers. You don't know about Jade because you haven't seen him. I'm ancient history and primeval gossip. You might try to find yourself another boyfriend to get seen with—to put up the illusion of distance." *That was great advice coming from me*, I thought.

"A boyfriend—" sighed Beth. "I couldn't do that to Jade. He'd be so hurt. And I work so many hours when do I have time for a boyfriend? Pete—I'll do everything else you say. Promise. But now let me tell you the rest."

"There's more besides the house?"

"A lot more. This is before George asked me to spy. I went to my lesson yesterday afternoon before going to Fendra's, although at first I was afraid to go because of what Juno said and because of everything else I'd heard. But I was more afraid not to go just in case I should hear something more about Jade, or in case Elise might think it was strange that I suddenly wasn't showing up, but I was really uncomfortable about going. All right—so I don't have a car and I usually take the bus to Thornhill and walk—and the bus was late so I was late but I got there and I rang the bell like I always do and I heard Elise playing piano inside and then—guess who answered the door you'll never believe it—"

"Who?"

"Selene. Remember Cara's friend Selene? She's living with Elise now. In Jade's old room. I'm serious. And Pete—she was there and it was so weird because I didn't even know she knew Elise—and I can't explain it but the whole thing felt really odd and wrong—and she said, 'Hi Beth,' and I know she doesn't even like me and I said 'hi' because what could I say and she let me in and then Elise stopped playing and said in an odd, cold voice like she was mad at me for being late, 'Hello, Beth, are you ready for your lesson?'

"And I said, 'Sure, I'm ready.' So she let me sit down on the piano bench and she told me about Selene living there with her new boyfriend and I just started playing and Selene was like sitting on the couch and she was really still and holding a pillow tight and chewing on the corner and staring at me and making me nervous so I played terrible and the place smelled funny—it was perfectly neat and clean like it always is but the sunlight was full of dust and it smelled like Elise was burning cabbage and dead animals and rubber—I don't know what—it smelled so bad. And I kept stopping to cough because the smell made my eyes run—and every time I stopped playing Selene would yell loud and clap and she was really obnoxious and I wanted to leave because I hated her being there and staying in Jade's room because there's definitely something wrong with Selene—"

"I've noticed."

"All right, so I got through one song, 'Blow the Man Down,' and I was supposed to play an exercise for learning a scale, but Elise said 'no more lesson today Beth, you've done fine this week' and I knew I did really lousy—but she asked me to come have some potato soup in the kitchen and Selene said, 'Come on, Beth, meet my new man' and so I stayed to be polite and, Pete,—there was a really strange man sitting in the kitchen I didn't like. His name was Hugh— Hugh McCrae—and I can't explain it but he felt really wrong to me—"

"It's OK, Beth. I know him. He is wrong."

"I could tell Elise was afraid of him. I didn't like him. I don't know what he was doing there. He was reading a newspaper that was three weeks old and he kept telling me I played like an angel and I kept saying you want to hear an angel listen to Jade's friend Les play sometime he plays like God, and Elise didn't seem to like that because she said in kind of a mean voice like she wanted to change the subject, 'He's all right.'

"And then Hugh McCrae started telling me how much he liked to listen to piano exercises and old-fashioned tunes that everybody knows and how much he liked the way I played and how I should never be embarrassed to mess up because everybody knew the song anyway so my mistakes didn't matter and I felt like they did matter and I said I was glad Jade never took that advice or he wouldn't be where he is today and nobody said anything. And then Hugh McCrae wanted everyone to sing 'Blow the Man Down' from my lesson, and the three of them sang it together. And they all started giggling like it was the funniest joke in the world and I asked Elise if she'd heard from Jade and she said no, of course not, she never hears from him, and then she explained to Hugh McCrae that Jade was my boyfriend. And Hugh said it must feel splendid to play the way I did and go out with a talented young man like Jade, must give me such a grand sense of life and all it held for me and there was something about the way he said it I didn't like, and then Selene interrupted and—wait."

I heard Beth fumbling with something. "I like to record my piano lessons and I'm sure I caught some of this on tape." More fumbling. Then a button click, and wildly mismatched voices belting out "Blow the Man Down" as if it were a curse. Sound of fast forwarding, and then Selene's rough voice explaining, "Hugh is my boyfriend. We met at Cara's. He was staying there but he got a little sick so I helped him move."

Beth stopped the tape. "I felt grossed out because Hugh is at least three times her age but you have to know Selene to believe it. Anyway, it gets worse."

The tape restarted to Hugh saying, "My girl found me a very nice place for us to stick to. Like fat flies on tarpaper. One with very fine food that people left for us, praise the Lord" and Beth abruptly stopped it again.

"It just feels gross to hear it. Selene told me how they had been staying in a corrugated tin shack by the dump so Hugh could get better because he didn't have any other place to go and he didn't want to bother anyone until he got over his sickness and got strong. And then I couldn't eat the soup—I forgot to tell you it was the soup that smelled like garbage—so I just asked Selene, 'How did you end up here?' and Elise sort of smiled primly and started to say something but Hugh interrupted and said . . . are you ready for this, Pete? It's . . . ." Beth sounded tearful again. "I can't explain it." She started the tape to Hugh speaking.

"Well, my old girl Smelly Ellie here has been calling my name for years, although she hasn't realized it until now. We used to be married you know. Yessirree. Stuck together like . . . like birds of a feather."

Selene giggled and said "birds."

"What happened?" Beth's voice on the tape was strained, her usual politeness quavered with unease.

"Well, I'll tell ya. Had to go away to do some underground work. With the worms you know." Selene sort of giggled again like she was McCrae's personal laugh track, and McCrae continued, "My old girl Elise here and I struck up a bargain yesterday when I moved in. A bargain basement buyout right out of 1952. Hoo skidoo. Thought she'd gotten rid of me and would be scared to have me back, but you know—but so often with these old girls 'no' means 'yes' and hey that's the kind of lie I like—where the girl says what she's supposed to say until she says what she means. Where it all follows a certain expected pattern and we all know what's up."

"Yes." Elise sounded like she was primly smiling behind her words. "We all know."

Then McCrae again. "So Ellie didn't want me back, but you know it was a Saturday and I used to visit on Saturdays and I say to my girl 'hey' I say, 'remember me out of your widowed past and I'm sorry I missed you in the Arizona desert but I was there you know on similar business' and Elise stood there shaking with her mouth tightly screwed into that lovely twist of a smile but I knew that my knowing her desert affairs would get to her. Like toe jam gets to a clean foot.

"And so I said—'Hey, presto I'm back like Easter Sunday and this is my girlfriend, Selene the Moon, and this time I've got a great deal. Got something to sell I know you want.' And she just clutched her door and stared. 'So come on, hey,' I says, 'let's just let our past be the past and isn't it a grand day—so plain to see everything in?'

"And Elise here, she kept staring, so I told her, 'I've got an offer you can't refuse. To unmask old Dionysus, that pretender god of wine and song, for who he is. The outcast who seduced you when he came from the sea, playing a sailor called Michael. The one who left you to emptiness and entropy. That is, to my own titan self. The grifter god who got with the desert, enjoying himself as Claude, before you killed and dismembered him in a reckless attempt at a communion that I finished for you like a well-earned meal. And now the ragged result that 'Michael' left you with seduces others with the musical skills that you taught him, and leaves you to air and wind like his father did. Wanna buy some justice? Wanna buy some fun and excitement?'

"And Elise here stood there and cried like I was selling relief from pain, and she said, the way she used to say it way back when, 'Come in, Hugh, I know you now.' So I did. With my pretty girl, Selene. And here we are. Snug as bugs in rugs."

"And Pete,"—Beth stopped the tape to comment again—"everyone laughed like he said something terribly funny and all I could say was 'that's nice,' and then Hugh smiled this big ugly grin and pointed at me and said 'that's nice and splendid' and I asked Selene if she knew Elise before now and she said no but they were housemates now and they smiled at each other like—it was ugly, I can't explain it. So here, listen."

I heard the tape repeat what Beth just told me, and then Hugh saying, "So what is your boyfriend doing while you play such splendid piano lessons and wait tables and sell doughnuts?"

And Beth stopped the damn tape again.

"I'm sorry, this is hard. I was so upset when he said those things that I fidgeted with my recorder in my pocket and accidentally stopped recording. Elise had apparently told him how hard I work and I said that Jade was supposedly playing in Fairfax, Virginia and how much I like their new 'Poison Puppy' video—have you seen it, Pete?—I'm starting to like that song now even though for a long time the imagery bothered me until I got to know Jade better—and so Hugh started telling me how great Fairfax was because everybody went to church and how he was working for some Bible organization—Christians for Canadian Decency, and starting a chapter out of Elises's house and then Selene says she's a Christian now and they were all wearing crosses, including Elise. And then Hugh asked me if I knew the Lord.

"So I said, 'No, I work too many hours to have time for religion.' And Hugh wanted to say some prayer, and after he said it he kept quoting the Bible at me about how Jacob had two wives—so I figured Elise and Selene were like his own private harem or something, it was all really sick, and he kept smacking his lips and saying, 'As to my house, we will follow the Lord,' like he wanted me to say something but I didn't know what. And then he asked me if I talked to Jade a lot and I said I did but mostly when I was alone and he wasn't there to answer and Hugh said how 'dandy' that was and how it was 'just like a prayer' and he was 'most impressed with my simple little heart' and I said 'I guess' because I had to say something but by then I was really just trying to find a way to leave."

"So is that the end of the tape?" I asked for clarification.

"No. There's more when I made myself start recording again. But I was going to say I had to go to Fendra's and just leave when Hugh pointed his finger at me, only now his finger suddenly looked all twisted, and I didn't notice that before, and he said, 'Well I'll tell ya something, Beth Dundas. I am the Father. I am Jade's protector. You remember that. You take it to your simple heart and keep it frozen there forever and ever without end. Amen.' I got really nauseous when he said that, like my bones were going to vomit, and I just sat there trying not to be sick when Hugh kept going, 'You tell Jadie all about it if you like. Tell him who his real protector is and see how he feels about that.' Then Elise smiled her awful smile and slowly whipped her head from left to right over her soup bowl, as if she was immensely pleased or impressed with what Hugh had just said. I just looked around the table and pressed record and asked him what he meant, because I couldn't believe any of this and I wanted to share it with Jade. Here." I heard Beth click the button, and then Hugh McCrae's voice.

"Well, I'll tell ya what I mean. I'm a poet. Oh, yes. I've got words of my own. Old words. So old they don't mean anything anymore. You see this is a good Christian household. And by living here I've got the authority of the good Christian Lord, for the good book says a man has authority in his own house as if he is the Lord. To be plain and honest, I have the authority to be believed in. Just as Jesus was when he told stories. And hey, to be frank, I'm working for a good Christian organization that supports some fine politicians. Good folks. Folks I used to work for. Still chummy. Don't mind who knows. I'm being plain and open and I've got nothing to hide.

"Now, Beth Dundas, there is a certain family out there—the Nunzio family—I believe you might know some of them through your work, the world being so splendidly small—this family knows some secrets about my dear old wife and if that family wants to know more well—you can tell them I'm here to satisfy their curiosity. Tell them I've got credentials. My boss, the most holy Rev. Joseph P. Heppelfauf III, funnels a lot of money that supports the war against this family's business competition, which leaves them a clear monopoly in the drug trade, and they like that. In fact, they sometimes send money along to these same politicians via the Church. All very fine. So let's say that as long as I'm here, I'm selling insurance that they'll leave my precious wife's desert doings alone. That's one thing I mean. Plain dealing as dirt in the sun."

"We like dirt," said Selene.

Beth spoke over the phone while the tape was running. "I swear Elise touched her cross when Selene said that." The recorder continued playing Hugh's monologue.

"So Elise definitely believes in me, believes in my authority, because she knows she needs me as her protector and head of the household. She knows I certainly won't let my wholesome little music teacher get torn apart by the Mob. Now, Beth. The other thing I mean, is that I know the United States FBI is following the Mob, sticks and stones in hand. I know they are because you have to start rumors somewhere and so I started them. True rumors."

Beth talked over the tape again. "And, Pete, he jabbed his forefinger straight up towards the ceiling to emphasize the point, like he was preaching at me."

Hugh's voice continued. "But where are the federal agents going to go without evidence? Without hard facts. Now, sometimes the feds make up their evidence and make up their hard facts and sometimes that works, but in this case it must be truth, must be truth that kills. And so I can drop a word of truth whenever I like. I can wait a day, wait a month, wait years. But at some point I will say, 'Hey, FBI. Pledge my heart and hope to die like a Boy Scout. I live with Elise McClellan and I know all about her family secrets,' and presto—what happens—the feds move in to take my wife away on a murder charge and then of course they'll start looking into her son's doings.

"And if Jade should be an accessory to violating some American or Canadian statutes that no one really understands, well there are enough inexplicable legal complexities to silence his music. No martyrs—just abstract, dirty little legalities. And the residue, the hellish residue, is—'how come you never hear Black Dog records anymore, did they get lazy, and then—Black Dog who?'—forgotten, like the music never happened. Beautiful way to end a life pumping gas for the next sixty years, and being treated like the dirty sea he came from. Maybe he ought to wait tables and learn to live like you do, my dear."

Beth stopped the tape. "Pete, I couldn't help it but he sounded so smug and mean that I think I started crying. I just hated everything."

"I know how you feel." I couldn't think of anything more to say, and after a few silent seconds in which it felt like Beth was waiting for something more, she started the tape.

"You see, I can put my wife in prison same as another old girl once put me and use that device to put her son to justice. And Elise here, who likes her prisons well done, who's been in one her entire life, says prison's a bargain when it happens to put her son to rights because she's a good mother and would like to see him earn a clean living at a decent job. My dear Elise, oh holy mother so full of maternal concern, I offer you fun and excitement—I offer my lady the very deep pleasure of destruction, when destruction happens, and I offer her the opportunity to choose her own time, to tell me when it's time to say the Word."

"Hugh is good to me," said Elise.

"Well," said Hugh, "I like protecting the band from destruction. I'm much more involved in Black Dog's welfare than Jade's own father ever was. I'm the only one who can do it right. When the battle's all said and done, I am ultimately the protector. That's a spiritual victory, praise God. So Beth, spread the Word—spread the gospel to everyone you know—that I'm here to talk about the death of Claude Hopner and I'll talk when I'm ready and until then I've got my alibis in order as to where and when I saw my virgin bride in Phoenix. So, what do you think of that while you're working off your bones in your little jobs and playing your delicious little lesson tunes while Jade makes the charts? Would you like to play with us?"

Selene sort of chirped, "Hugh's going to make me a dancer. Maybe you can play accompaniment for me."

I heard the familiar soft hiss of a tape reaching its end. "That's all. I said I had to go to catch my bus and I just got up and left because I really couldn't stand being there. And now you and George both want me to keep going back."

"How much of this did you tell George last night?"

"None. I didn't even tell him I went to my lesson. I wanted to get ahold of Jade or talk to you first. Pete, I trust you. I'm afraid of Nick, and Hugh, and now of this other agent, Crensch."

"Tell George everything. Tell him when the heat comes down on Elise for killing Hopner, it will be because Hugh dropped the word. Not that Nick cares about that business anymore, but it might deflect some attention from Jade."

"But, Pete, I don't understand any of this. Why does Hugh hate Jade?"

"For the same reasons we—you love him. Beth—let me think for a minute." It was so late it was early. We'd been talking nearly an hour and I was full of that semi-natural high one gets from staying up too many hours. I'd be in wretched physical shape for work, but at the moment my thoughts were working better than usual.

"All right, Beth. This is my take on matters. Keep it confidential. You might not understand this, but Hugh means Jade no violence. At least not physically. In fact, I think if Jade met with any physical violence right now Hugh would be most upset, for reasons too complicated to explain, but basically he hates the kind of romantic adulation that would accompany Jade's martyrdom. Especially now that his music is getting known, well, an early death would help make it legendary. Hugh likes things sordid and quiet. Likes to destroy the part of life that matters and have his victim live to suffer."

"You're right, Pete. I don't understand," Beth said timidly, and then added unexpectedly, "Most people live to suffer, and work jobs like waiting tables, except when there's music."

I couldn't tell from her voice how she meant this, but the insight kind of surprised me, coming from Beth.

"Sure," I agreed. "Most people waste their lives. Why should Jade be special?" She didn't answer. "I don't know, Beth. You do what you do. What Hugh does is destroy artists, and the best way to do that is through the most mundane, unromantic, boring means possible. He has a longstanding grudge against the gods. He'll purge the divine and leave the merely human standing like a bad joke to ruin even the memory of whatever was once beautiful. Can you imagine Jade without his music?"

"No. I can't. He wouldn't be Jade. He wouldn't be anything."

"All right. You see, Hugh has calculated correctly that it will be very difficult for the FBI and the Canadian authorities to get the kind of evidence of tax evasion and payola and extortion that a court will need for a conviction. Wire taps help, and discussing those sorts of illegal activities on tape helps, but you really need to trace the money and get ahold of records of financial transactions to get a charge that will stick to the higher ups like Nick. My government doesn't want to nail a few flunkies for strong-arming record store owners or intimidating a few radio station managers. They want to make a show about busting the bosses to impress some politicians who are suddenly beholden to the anti-rock 'n' roll crowd.

"The problem is some of Nick's friends do directly and indirectly support these same pols, so it's an even bet that the government will end up having to make a big production about nailing a few fall guys, but it will be a while before that happens, because it will be a while before the right people in government figure that out. Right now the feds think they want Nick but that's because they don't know any better. And Nick knows he can't always count on the political winds blowing in his direction. Especially since he believes I'm involved and he knows I've taken down members of his family before. But in the end, when the plans get made, Jade would make a splendid scapegoat. Right amount of notoriety.

"What Hugh doesn't realize is that Nariano is smart enough to distance himself from the whole Hopner affair and stay clean, so he's counting on the murder investigation spinning off into some definitive charges against Jade related to his mob involvement. Some arcane tax violations he could go to prison for and be forgotten about. He also doesn't realize that Crensch may already have stumbled into the rumors about Elise, although Hugh thinks he can keep the heat off as long as he likes with presenting alibis until the truth moves him to speak."

"Doesn't he think that if there is an investigation Jade could get hurt?"

"Probably not. He doesn't know what we know. But he may think he can buy off Jade's safety the way he's buying off Elise's, through Heppelfauf's influence. Or he may think when the time comes, he can persuade the right people that Jade will be more useful as a fall guy in jail. That's the only strategy that makes sense and explains his actions right now."

"Pete—what should I do?"

"Let Hugh think he can do his worse by turning in Elise. Let him enjoy his game, his 'protectorship' because the longer he waits, the less damage he can do there. He knows you're Jade's friend so he's happy for you to tell Jade about it—to play psychological warfare and in that way let Penny and the band know who's winning. That's why I suggest you don't tell Jade any of this if he does contact you. Hugh only wants to use you to torture him. I'll handle that part of the story if I get the opportunity to speak with him or Penny. Hugh also knows you work for George so he's happy to let George and the rest know that he's closely associated with Heppelfauf and that Heppelfauf helps to buy them a monopoly in the drug war.

"I doubt that Nick cares, because I doubt Nick has ever given half a thought to Christians for Anything Decency except that they're not happy with Black Dog, either. Anyway, their political alliance with the Nunzio family is accidental, but Hugh can use his new position as a Christian fundamentalist salesman to help convince Elise that he's protecting her from the Mob, which explains why he made it an issue."

"What will you do?"

"Whatever I can. All right, buddy, is there anything more you have to tell me?"

"No, that's everything for now."

"What's your number at the bakery?" She gave it to me. "All right. Since you work mornings I'll call you there before I leave for work if I don't hear from you for a while or I need to talk to you. But I want you to call me from the bakery from now on. Never call me from Fendra's. Do you understand? It's too risky. And I don't care what time you call me, so long as you call me at home and not at the field office—never at the field office—"

"OK."

"Go get some sleep. Stay in touch."

"I will. If I can." She paused, then added in a strange quiet voice, "What a life this all is," and softly hung up.

I hung up. Slept an hour or two without dreams. Woke heavily into a meagre dawn.

Stave Twenty-One

Monday, January 11, 1993.

Monday wasn't morning, just the rest of the sentence my thinly hyphenated sleep had broken. Got to the field office before Marcie did and played guard duty with the desk. Got lucky. Collared the special delivery of the tapes I needed to intercept and intimidated the courier into thinking I was authorized to sign for them. Then I fudged Fearless's signature and closed myself into my office to write pretty little reports.

I knew Crensch would be calling in sometime, but I also knew I could stall the ramifications of any verbal report he made by reminding Fearless that Crensch was crazy. The fact that one of the tapes delivered this morning contained only Fendra's answering machine giving out the month's entertainment schedule would be a help there. That one I promptly left in Fearless's mailbox, making a mental note to include a lot of comments about its uselessness in my reports. The other two I let my machine chew up after I creatively transcribed the contents. Then I left the damage in his box with my eloquent apologies. One of the tapes was the expected recording of Crensch's conversation with Beth on Friday. The other was a recording of the mafia meeting Beth had overheard.

Which meant that I needed to warn Beth to let George know that Crensch had bugged the tables while he was wandering around in the bar. She could "accidentally discover" a listening device while cleaning and call George's grateful attention to it. That would do wonders to keep the law out of Fendra's permanently, because I knew Crensch had no chance of getting another device planted in the bar. George would be checking everything and everyone constantly, and Crensch would be left sending home bad recordings of Fendra's answering machine.

It was still early enough to reach Beth at the bakery, but I didn't need her number showing up on the field office's phone bill. I'd made that mistake the last time I called Toronto from work. So I locked up my office and went to find a pay phone. Of course as I got on the elevator, Piekarski and Fearless and a handful of other agents, including Beisweiler, got off, so I had to look enthusiastic about life and work and announce that I forgot something in my car to explain why I was leaving the building at such an early hour. And Piekarski had to reciprocate by letting everyone know that he wanted to talk to me later about "important business," which may have been true or may have been his way of impressing everybody with his authority. Ignored him with a smile.

Found a pay phone three blocks away. Called on my credit card and got a very tired sounding Beth. Felt for a minute how tired we both were, how our common exhaustion was a bond from last night, and knew she felt that too. That was the best and unspoken part of our exchange. For the rest I told her about the table bugs and what to look for and she promised to take care of everything this afternoon.

All right, back to more writing, which pretty much filled a dutiful day, with one dismal interruption from Piekarski, who really did need to see me. He had great tidings of joy. Seems Lamar Toon's gun licenses were about to expire, and some cooperative brother law enforcement agent from the BATF had assured Piekarski that Toon's renewal application for a federal permit would get lost, making Toon eligible for illegal weapons charges. Also, we were on for Friday for torturing the bereaved cult mothers with the help of the two social worker thugs I had seen on TV. Kanesh was keeping the press informed of all "publicly suitable" information and it looked like we might have a major raid going with warrants and everything by the end of the month or early February at the latest. Then he asked me if I'd seen the morning paper.

"No, been busy writing the morning paper." Indicated the reports on my desk. But Piekarski was so hot on whatever he was about to say he forgot to be nosy about what I was writing, which was just as well.

"That rock band that's been in the news. Black Dog. Some Satanic name. The one that caused all those deaths down in New York and that Joe Heppelfauf has been speaking out against." He occasionally liked to refer to the "most reverend" Heppelfauf as "Joe." Basically because nobody else did, and Piekarski liked to imply that he for one was a plain-spoken all-American kind of guy who didn't bend the knee to titles, while at the same time he was also moral and right-thinking enough to claim the privilege of being on intimate terms with an increasingly famous religious preacher like Heppelfauf.

"I'm sorry, I haven't been following the story," I said blandly. "What's Joe got to say?"

Piekarski wasn't about to accord me equal first-name status. He was too Christian for that sort of charity. "The *reverend* thinks their leader is a witch and that he probably practices black magic. Might even be a high priest of a secret cult. According to today's paper, seems a lot of other people think so too. You should check it out. I've heard their music," he added, like he'd just discovered some exciting new pornography to get disgusted with, "and I tend to agree. Listen to it too long and you start having thoughts."

"Does it hurt?"

Piekarski ignored me. "They're not even American. I understand they've come down here from Canada."

"So?"

"So you tell me you ain't been following the story, Morrow? Last week one of the band members went on TV and claimed to be working with Nunzio family. Figured that might interest you."

"It might interest me," I commented, as if it were a purely academic issue. "But I'm not chasing the Mob right now. What does this rock band have to do with the war *I'm* supposed to be fighting?"

"Nothing right now," he admitted. "But you did a number on the Nunzios at one time. Think they're promoting this new band?"

"Anything's possible." I shrugged. "But that's Crensch's business now. Why don't you take it up with him?" Piekarski had no idea I was writing Crensch's reports because Fearless didn't want it widely known and neither did I.

"Crensch," Piekarski sort of spat the name. "What the hell does that guy know about anything? He probably had trouble *finding* Canada. Everybody knows Fred only sent him up there to keep him out of trouble. Ya think Crensch is going to figure out that this Black Dog band might be the key to his first adventure with the Mafia?"

"I have no idea, Charlie, and right now it's not my problem." I said this with an unbelievably straight face, considering. "I want to clear up these odds and ends for the boss so I can put some time into preparing for our Friday morning onslaught."

"Yeah, Morrow, right, but you're missing the obvious, as usual. Crensch is going to fuck up. We know that. He's going to blow the whole deal, and Reverend Heppelfauf's people are going to go protesting to their politicians about it. Now, what happens if SAYNO becomes the clean-up act? We use your mob experience, and my drug experience, and our unofficial mandate to promote family values, to get the real dirt on this band. We do Crensch's job for him and we end up looking like heroes. All these rock 'n' roll types are mixed up with drugs, so we can easily make a case for the whole project falling in our purview. Besides, we're gonna need a new project after the bust. Keep up the success rate."

"I think there's enough drug activity to keep us busy without chasing down some rock band from Canada," I said carefully. Liked the possibility of getting closer to the case than I already was, but not if Piekarski, Kanesh, and the rest of the SAYNO team were going to be officially on it too. Crensch was easier to sabotage, and I desperately didn't need one of Kanesh's media announcements about SAYNO's involvement.

"Come on, Morrow. We're here to make SAYNO number one. It's the perfect setup to make an impression on the public, and Fred already likes the idea. Talked to him this morning. He's not happy with Crensch's progress up north, and he sees us as a kind of insurance policy if things don't work out. Don't see how we can refuse."

"So what does that have to do with my work right now?"

"Talk to Fred," said Piekarski like he was giving me an order. "He wants to see you anyway."

"Yeah, soon as I finish this stuff."

Piekarski shoved off before I finished speaking, looking most pleased.

It was hard not to kill him. Wondered if he noticed.

So I finished up my propaganda work, bright and pretty, and stopped unannounced into Fearless's office, papers in hand. He was on the phone brown nosing someone so I made him uncomfortable by dropping into the visitor's seat and pointedly listening to his end of the conversation until he hung up. "Yes, Morrow, what is it?"

"Heard you wanted to see me, boss. Here's my report on the latest business from Toronto."

"Yeah," he took the papers and scanned through my transcript. "So what happened to the tapes?" he asked as if my note hadn't explained everything.

"My tape recorder ate them. Isn't the first time. Really need better equipment."

"All right." He pressed the sides of his mouth to show annoyance. "Tell Marcie from now on you can use mine if you have to, or borrow the one out of Crensch's office. Don't need any more mishaps."

"I was able to transcribe the contents," I said cheerfully. "It was only when I played them a second time that I had a problem. But I didn't find any of them particularly useful," I added by way of consolation.

"Yeah, I was afraid of that. Worth reading through?"

"No," I said honestly. He dropped the stack on his desk and sighed. "How do we get Crensch pointed in the right direction?"

"Not sure there is one. The Nunzios are good businessmen. Know how to make a lot of stuff look legal that isn't. Crensch needs to start by finding a reliable informant, and cultivating that sort of thing takes experience and time."

"Talked to Piekarski this morning. He seems to think SAYNO can handle it."

"But wouldn't it offend the congressman if his son was displaced?"

Fearless gave me a very deep scowl and hid his desire to respond to my admittedly rude question by pretending that something had suddenly caught his interest near the coffee machine. So I glanced back at the machine too, which embarrassed him because he now had to ignore the tacitly shared fact of there being nobody there. So he looked at his watch and sighed as if he was late for something. What torqued him the most, what caused his flabby cheeks to flush and his Adam's apple to bob like he'd swallowed an angry toad, was my utter lack of insolence. I had studiously kept my tone as open and honest as Beth's touching innocence. I was being terribly helpful. Right now, Fearless hated that sort of thing.

"What do you think of SAYNO doing some backup work to Sidney's investigation? I mean after you guys resolve this Lamar Toon affair down in Providence?"

I guessed that if I hadn't asked about offending the congressman's sensibilities, there would have been that hint of pleading in Fearless's voice that I'd heard concerning this issue before. Instead, he was too intent on pretending he wasn't angry to give himself away. I studied the ceiling, studied the wall, looked thoughtful as hell. Then I spoke like the idea had just occurred to me, thanks to his brilliant suggestion, "I suppose I could go up to Toronto and look around for kicks."

Fearless looked a shade uncertain before he said, "That's not what I asked. I meant, obviously, if SAYNO took this thing over, you'd play the key role, but I'm *only* considering transferring this to SAYNO, not to another agent. SAYNO is the NDECC's pet force." The obvious implication was that I wasn't, and that Fearless didn't want to have to repeat the warning he gave me before. Then he swallowed and coughed like he didn't want to say whatever he was about to say and bravely continued, "A transfer to SAYNO might ruffle fewer feathers and might make some people in Washington happy, considering some of the stuff that's coming out to the public now, which I'm sure you've been following."

He waited for an acknowledgement so I nodded and said noncommittally, "Piekarski mentioned the same thing earlier."

"Right. Well, it would certainly solve a lot of political problems"—he waved his hand as if such silliness were something he'd, of course, rather not deal with but what can you do if you want to make a living at law enforcement—"if Sidney got assigned to SAYNO. SAYNO does all the work in Boston that you and Piekarski find necessary, and Crensch, of course, remains your man in Toronto. Be a splendid case to follow up the drug bust with," he added quickly. "Teamwork. Make everybody happy."

"Make everybody happy," I repeatedly pointedly. It was clear that the decision had already been made. I knew that nothing I said at this point would stand in the way of good politics.

"Well, that's it," said Fearless, dismissing me in a tone of affable near-apology. Then he brushed his hand over the reports I had given him and shoved them aside. Just as I was leaving, he told me to keep up the good work.

Bought a newspaper on the way home. Bought three, actually. And between the papers and some focused fire gazing and what I could gather from some brief news reports on television, I was able to piece together the details of what Piekarski was all excited about. Here's what happened. Near as I can imagine.

Black Dog had been scheduled to play a fairly large club called Grimalkin's, just outside Fairfax, Virginia, on Sunday night. Presumably they hadn't gotten word from Nick yet of their newborn status as prisoners.

There had been enough local radio advertising to attract the attention of the good Christian folk of Fairfax, and apparently there was much Sunday morning preaching on the "thou shalt not suffer a witch to live" injunction. One enterprising preacher actually held a special service about the band's growing reputation for practicing witchcraft through rock music, charged a hefty "prayer fee" for admission plus "whatever else the Lord tells you to give," and raised nearly five thousand dollars for an hour's work. Ran the two Black Dog videos for everyone's edification, then ran them again while everybody prayed. Mrs. Kipfer was on hand to speak.

The Fairfax chapter of Christians for American Decency decided to protest Black Dog's arrival by blocking traffic outside Grimalkin's with the aid of the local police. Meaning the police were conspicuously absent while the church folk kicked off their block party by waving crosses at cars and doing their best to persuade the drivers to run over somebody. The height of the afternoon's fun was crowding around old women stopped at red lights while one or two of the younger gang members pounded on their windows with Bibles and terrorized them with badly done descriptions of hell. Gave one seventy-two-year-old grandmother who was driving home from church a heart attack, and the ambulance damn near didn't make it through the crowd in time to save her. She was listed in critical condition.

The police chief later denied all knowledge of the protest to excuse himself for letting things get out of hand, but he was contradicted by the assertions of several local business owners who claimed they made complaints all afternoon and got no response for hours. Many were forced to close shop early. It was only when the traffic blockade threatened to keep their Christian brethren from arriving at a nearby church, which was supposed to be the designated center of the gathering, that the "prayer leaders" moved the festivities to the church's parking lot, which cleared the streets for a while. Being January, you'd think they'd have all gone inside the church and kept their ignorance decently behind closed doors, but you need to have an audience to "witness to the world," so Christians for American Decency held a public prayer meeting in the street-fronted church parking lot, to which they had pretty much invited half the state of Virginia and from the sound of it got a nearly one hundred percent acceptance rate.

So many people arrived for the outdoor afternoon service the crowd spilled out along both sides of the street and took over one or two privately owned parking lots near the club. The "service" went on for hours, stopping for pedestrian-harassment breaks and starting as more and more arrivals came along to make donations. A Christian couple got married. Another couple "re-affirmed their vows." Every fundamentalist preacher in the region who valued his career had to show up and lead a prayer, and one or two local politicians even put in an appearance to endorse Heppelfauf's bill.

The Great Man himself arrived late, flanked by the press and a few goons, after his stooges had warmed up the crowd for him. Heppelfauf gave a marvelously incoherent speech about rock 'n' roll being the devil's chief weapon against the Christian Family, and how it was the duty of every Christian "who loved the Lord" to "destroy the devil's music." My impression was that by six pm or so, after the shops had all closed and the normal traffic had died down, the "saved" pretty much owned that section of town.

Everyone brought their kids. Everyone paraded their "innocent children" whom "the Lord commanded to protect" back and forth for hours in front of Grimalkin's and proudly lectured to them about the evils of rock 'n' roll. "You see that building? That's where the devil lives. If you go inside, the devil will take you to hell."

When the club owner showed up around six-thirty, he was greeted with jeers and hisses and bizarre cries of "Not our children! Save the family! Praise the Lord!" The owner had the foresight to arrive with his private security, and the uniformed security guards did manage to clear the sidewalk and parking lot in front of the club so the patrons could get through later, that is, if they could get their cars down the street. However, the periphery of the property was now surrounded by an angry mob of Christians, ferocious with a day's worth of fiery preaching and good fellowship. The prayer leaders competed for popularity by taunting the security guards. Kept singing hymns through bullhorns while their followers joined in, everyone trying to outdo each other with cries of "yes, Lord" and "praise Jesus."

Mrs. Kipfer was given a prominent position near the front of the crowd line next to her host preacher, where she waved around a large blown-up photo of her son, Egbert, which bore words scripted in a design like splattered blood, "Another child aborted by rock 'n' roll." Others had signs with Bible verses condemning witchcraft, and a few waved American flags. Homeless veterans showed up to beg for coins. Somebody opened a stand and sold "Christian T-Shirts." Somebody else with an even better sense of enterprise collected money in a can for "special prayers."

Some of the protesters were in such a frenzy over Black Dog's expected arrival that they behaved like bad parodies of sincerely love-struck groupies. Grown men and women rolled around on the cold winter ground and called on Jesus to save them, although nobody specified from what. Many spoke in tongues. Many more shouted out "interpretations" of the tongues; contradictory assertions bothered nobody's conscience for long. One woman saw an angel in a tree. Someone else saw Elvis with his face on fire like the devil praise God! A third person saw Jesus's face on a garbage can.

At this point Black Dog's gaudily painted van pulled into the parking lot, followed by the bumper-stickered car Cara drove. The crowd went ballistic—screaming for Jesus and hiding the kids from sin and grabbing squalling toddlers to defiantly wave around in the air to prove how devoted they all were to Family. Cara got out of her driver's seat, defiantly threw a cigarette into the crowd, and cried out, "How ya all doin', motherfuckers?" which got loud gasps and self-righteous prayers from all the men who use Christianity to help them not deal with women, and outrage from women who were mostly raised in the liberal seventies and liked the novelty of being old-fashioned and ladylike in the presence of profanity. Everyone was outraged that their precious children had to be there to hear such language. Was there no respect for the family anymore?

Cara cavalierly strolled over to the van, her sisters now behind her, Juno bouncing along and popping bubblegum bubbles and Beulah softly smiling and soft shoeing it and winking at people at random. A chant of "witch" went up from the crowd. Cara entered the van last, turning to bless the multitudes by tracing a pentagram in the air with her forefinger, followed by the letter A with a circle around it for Anarchy. Then she closed the door. Once they were safely inside and no longer a threat to God-fearing Christians, someone bravely threw a rock, which put a mark on Elb's expensive paint job.

No one came out of the van for several minutes. I imagine Penny was strategizing how to get all of Black Dog's equipment into the club without mishap and how much of a protective circle she could cast against the crush of fanatics. All I know is that they pulled the van as close to the door as they could, which was still a good twenty feet away because of Grimalkin's stairs and grassy border, and that they handed equipment out to the security guards who brought it safely inside, to jeers and boos and cries of "traitor, traitor go home and die."

A few more rocks hit the van but no one seemed willing to throw anything but insults directly at the guards. As soon as the guards finished bringing in the equipment, two of them came back out to the van and did the best they could under the circumstances to escort everyone into the club. Juno, Beulah, and Elb went first, flanked on each side by guards. The cry started up again, "witch, witch, witch," and one angry woman shook her soiled baby around.

Penny got out next, without waiting for the guards to return, with Les, Marty, and Xander following. Penny probably figured she could protect her pets better than anyone, and probably didn't notice that Jade and Cara were still in the van. They were greeted with loud boos and more cries of "witch." A lot of people clapped and chanted, "I can tell you're going to hell." Les raised a clenched fist and pushed two fingers up like devil horns in a mock salute. Somebody threw a bottle of "blessed water" on the pavement, which emboldened someone else to throw a rock over the heads of the group instead of at the van. Marty responded by shattering a partially full beer bottle in the crowd's general direction, which frothed and foamed and seemed to shock and surprise people for a second. Penny probably wasn't interested in screwing around with ignorance, because she didn't once break her stride, even though the water landed in her general direction and splattered her legs.

But according to one report she loudly hissed, "Your God's a Luddite and his mother was a Chaldean whore and if he don't like innovation, tell him he can rape another virgin and start another war and that maybe he ought to get a real job someday asides from eternally torturing his kid on a cross—" but apparently she was inside the club before she finished this interesting speech and the crowd was chanting too loudly to hear much of it.

No one else got out of the van. The guards didn't emerge from the club, so they must have thought everyone was now inside. Penny surely noticed by then that Jade wasn't with her but she didn't come back out so she must have thought that Cara could manage the situation, although Goddess knows why considering recent events in Toronto. To this day, I don't know why those two remained behind, and my best guess is that it was Cara's contrivance, that she was manipulating a situation in which she could speak to her cousin alone, perhaps to offer her own story of the northern battle front. Why Jade let his cousin manipulate him is anybody's guess, unless he had something to prove by facing the hostile mob while clinging to the traitor that fed and freed his monster. That would be like Jade. She probably wanted the reporters to see her walking alone with him, arm-in-arm, the proud witch-priestess and her own dark lord defying the infidel with their passion. That sort of thing would appeal to Cara's romantic vanity, especially if her picture ended up on TV and me or Beth were to see it.

I'm not convinced the crowd was generally aware that anyone else was still inside the van, even though they had already seen and harassed Cara as she entered it. Fundamentalists are not a particularly bright group. Nor are they particularly brave. For as soon as Penny's cluster went into the club and the crowd began to realize that the guards weren't coming out to order them back, they pressed closer into Grimalkin's parking lot, positioning themselves to "witness" to the poor lost souls who would soon show up for the rock 'n' roll show. The crowd began to pass the time by pelting the van and the car with rocks and screaming for God to take notice of their faith. One guy actually got up enough courage to go up to the van itself and scratch "Jesus Saves" in the paint with his rock before he dropped it, screaming that it burnt his hand.

I don't know. Maybe it did.

Anyway, when Jade and Cara finally emerged together, the crowd had gotten much closer to the van, and so the first general reaction was a sudden gasp and backwards crush, along with one or two panicked cries of "Oh my God, it's him," as Jade came out of the van. Cara locked her arm through his and mocked the crowd by smiling and bobbing her head at them, as a loud angry chant of "burn, witch, burn" erupted from the less panicked back portion of the protesters and everyone else took it up for safety.

From what I saw on TV, Cara began merrily half skipping, half dancing to the rhythm of the chant, joining in herself with a mocking "burn, witch, burn" that only infuriated the crowd more, while Jade kept just a hint of smile on his lips for the public and did his best to keep walking to work while Cara did her best to slow down their progress by skipping out and dancing in front of him. She probably wanted to be seen as long as possible.

The chanting got louder, and someone threw a rock that missed Cara's back as she was facing Jade and blocking his progress in one of her little dance steps. So Cara responded by stopping, taking Jade's hands in hers, kissing his fingers in an elaborate gesture, and dropping them to perch up on one foot and spread her arms like she was a woman on a cross. The movement took all of three seconds, enough for someone to send a rock flying right at this hated Pagan couple and nail Jade in the head as he tried to stride past Cara's antics. He went down with surprise, I thought, while Cara's magic apparently turned back a second rock heading straight for her. At least, that's what my tape of the news story showed as I watched it over and over—a rock headed towards Cara seemed to curve out of its trajectory and end up back in the crowd, although nobody remarked on this feat. I saw Cara help Jade to his feet, there was blood streaming down his face now, and walk him proudly inside, like they'd just been coronated.

I think she loved him best when he was hurt.

All the further news I got of that incident or of anything else that week was that Black Dog did manage to play Grimalkin's Sunday night and that they were "continuing their tour" despite the difficulties they'd been plagued with. Called Beth on Thursday morning and learned that she'd shown George the table bug and that he thanked her and destroyed it, that she'd heard the news about Fairfax, didn't trust Cara, and had gone to Elise's Tuesday night on George's insistence but didn't get the impression that Crensch or anyone else had been digging around. Hated it there. Only stayed a few minutes.

"Fill me in on the few minutes."

"Nothing much. Hugh McCrae and Selene were sitting on the couch together and holding hands. They were all watching television and Elise asked me to stay and watch with them, but I just went home and looked out my window at the street. It was raining and I thought about things. It was weird not working at night and having time to watch the rain and just be alone and think. Then later I went to Fendra's. George wants me to go back to Elise's tonight." She made a sound, sadder than anyone else could have made, because it was so thoroughly hers. I wasn't used to hearing Beth sound sad. "I've got to work now. Can I call you tonight after midnight?"

"That's tomorrow, but sure. I'll be waiting."

Another all-nighter with Beth would put me in fine form for the social worker interview tomorrow, but what I could I do? The only other delivery from Canada this week had been more hits from Fendra's answering machine, and Crensch surely had to know by now that he'd lost his table bug there. I should think he would have been immediately at Elise's door, his only other lead, but if he had he was keeping it a secret from Boston. So Beth was my only source of information right now.

She called me collect around one-thirty am.

"OK," she greeted me like we were continuing our earlier phone call without interruption, "They were holding a Bible study, led by Hugh McCrae, and it was in Jade's old studio, and there was like a little reception with snacks downstairs, and it was filled with born-again Christians with problems. And I have to tell you first that Sidney Crensch was there—"

"Did he see you?"

"Not at first, I don't think. There were a lot of people. I saw him first, talking with Hugh McCrae and laughing and showing some papers to him and Elise. This was upstairs in Jade's room before the meeting. I remember what you said about not having him see me there, so I was going to go downstairs and just leave and tell George I saw him, but Hugh noticed me in the doorway and waved his hand in the air and called me over.

"'Hey, Bethany Dundas, hey. My little friend Beth. Hey. Hey. So gosh darn glad to see you back here. Come over here, Beth. You're welcome, praise the Lord.'"

Beth's voice conveyed an unfamiliar mix of sarcasm, anger, and unfocused resentment that I found unsettling because it was so unlike her. McCrae's greeting had only happened hours ago and Beth was too unsettled to forget it.

She continued speaking. "And Elise turned from the paper she was looking at and called out. 'Hi, Beth, come on over and meet someone.' And everyone was looking at me, including Sidney Crensch, so I had to go over and say hi."

I was losing the battle fast. "What did Crensch ask you?"

"Nothing at first. He was showing Elise and Hugh some sketches of the cross and of the wise men in the desert and they were saying what a wonderful artist he was. Other people came over to praise the Lord and look, so Hugh said, 'Our Brother Sidney here doesn't create art himself, of course, God creates art through him. We must all remember that pride is a sin. How wonderful to be an empty vessel for the Lord' and everybody seemed to like that a lot and so they all praised the sketches because now they were God's and not Sidney Crensch's at all. It was stupid. And I don't know if you remember but there's a poster on the wall, with tables like a cafe—"

"Yes, I know the one. It's Van Gogh's *Café Terrace at Night*."

"Well, it's Jade's poster, and it had Jesus stickers all over it, and Crensch took another sticker and stuck one of his cross sketches on the poster, like he was trying to be funny and pretend he was a born-again Christian to get in good with Elise or something. Selene had made crayon markings around the stickers, and she called them her 'magic circles' and I just hated them all being there because it was like they were destroying the spirit of what used to be Black Dog's special place. And all the books that used to be in there had Bibles on them, I don't know. It wasn't like his room anymore.

"Anyway, Selene asked me right off, 'How's Fendra's? How's the bakery?' and I said 'good' and Hugh McCrae started making a speech about how 'grand' it was for someone like me to live and work in a little bakery serving the public every morning and how Jesus washed everyone's dirty feet and then Crensch asked me where the bakery was and I didn't want to tell him but Hugh leapt in and said, 'Hey, let me think. Let me think. Little Beth Dundas works at The Coffee and Cakewalk on Bloom Avenue, just off Dufferin Street and lives just upstairs. Christian brothers and sisters have to watch each other lest they stray.' So I just nodded because I knew he got the address from Elise and Crensch said he'd have to stop by sometime."

"Be aware. Check things. He probably will."

"Sure. So then we had this prayer to start things and Crensch was trying to pray louder than everyone else like he wanted to fit in but it kind of only made him stand out more but nobody seemed to notice, and Selene kept trying to shake my hand in the 'hand of peace' greeting but I wouldn't let her. And then—Pete—I'm sorry, but I couldn't stay there and spy and I don't know if I can ever make myself go back—not even for lessons because the whole thing was about what an evil person Jade was and how brave their Christian brothers and sisters were when they threw rocks at him in Fairfax and how sad it was that Elise was such a good Christian and it was surely a sign of her spiritual strength that the Lord was 'testing her through the evil of her son' and they seemed to get a lot of money out of it.

"And then I realized that probably the main reason there were so many people there was because Elise was Jade's mother and they were all curious. And they all seemed to feel superior to Jade, like they were so moral and he needed to be 'saved' and they prayed for him but I didn't because I have my own way of praying at home.

"And then Hugh said that this room was the studio where so much evil music had been created and how truly blessed it was that we Christians could re-consecrate the room to the Lord simply by being there and doing nothing, because Jesus loved us and lived in all our souls, and that we didn't even have to do anything to be loved because Jesus loved us just for being there, and how our prayers and hymns and loving presence would help reclaim the room and the music for God—and I'm sorry Pete—I couldn't stand the smugness from these people and I didn't want to 'reclaim' anything so I just left. I told George I saw Crensch there and about the prayer meeting and everything, but I also told him there was no way I was going back."

She waited for my response. "Please, Beth, I know it's difficult for you but I need you to be there for me. Right now you're my only source of information."

She said in a weird tone of determination and plaintiveness, "I'm not going back. I'm not double spying for you and George." It was hard and new for her to say this. "George got mad and told me not to come back to work if I wouldn't cooperate and so I guess I'm out of a job. I don't care. When I'm around those people, I hate everything, and I don't see how being there with his obvious enemies and saying prayers against him is going to help Jade."

"All right, Beth. What do you think is the best thing to do under the circumstances?" I waited.

"Under the circumstances, let Elise and Hugh and Selene go be Christians and have meetings. I don't care. My being there won't stop anything. I don't want lessons from her. I'm no good at music anyway, except for listening. Let Nick keep Jade guarded. At least he'll be safe and nobody will be able to throw rocks at him anymore."

"Beth—we've got to do our best to stop my government from investigating Black Dog's mafia promoters. That's the issue here, like I explained to you before. You're in a wonderful position to keep me informed about both the Nunzios and Crensch, if you'd only agree to keep a lookout for both me and George. Why do you want to make it more difficult for me to do an already difficult job?"

"I don't," said Beth. "It's just that I have my own difficult job, too. I—thought about a lot of things the other night while I was watching the rain."

"I'll pay you to work at Fendra's."

"It isn't that, Pete. I know if I don't work at Fendra's I can probably get more hours downstairs in the afternoon and I'll have more time at night—"

"—Time for *what*?"

"I don't know. Isn't that sad? Just time." It was a great effort for Beth to complete her thought. "I love Jade. I'm worried about him. I can't tell you how much. It's just that—I wish my own life mattered too. Not that it doesn't. I mean, I know it's important to wait tables and serve coffee and make people happy. I know everybody matters and everybody is important, whether you're a coffee waitress or a famous bass player, but sometimes—I would like to—I don't know—it's hard."

"Beth—you *do* matter. You're the most important element in this whole operation right now. I'm very grateful for your help so far."

I understood her so completely I failed to convince.

"My help. Pete—I can't go to Elise's and pray against Jade. I won't. I can pray at home. I don't care that George fired me. I've had enough of being a waitress at Fendra's, anyway. You know, I think Elise has problems, but my mother has problems, too. Maybe not as bad. I don't know. But no one will make a federal international case out of it. I've just got a lot of things to sort out now, Pete. You can call me at the bakery if you want."

"Sure," I said quickly. "I think I'm beginning to understand. It is hard."

"Yeah," she sort of sniffed, "I'm sorry. Good night."

"Good night, Beth." After she hung up, I wondered if she had been apologizing, or just feeling sorry for herself and her situation, or if somehow she knew I really did understand her blossoming *angst* and was therefore genuinely sorry for me. Maybe she was just sorry for life. Couldn't blame her. It was hard.

Friday, January 15, 1993.

Had the pleasure of killing. Twice over. First killed a morning by jaunting down to Providence with Piekarski. Then I kept killing Piekarski's profligate self-regard. He was ticked because Fearless's political decision to deputize Crensch as SAYNO's man in Toronto meant that Piekarski couldn't use SAYNO to bring home the glory to himself, despite his own lecture to me a few months ago about "teamwork." He had a point, considering SAYNO's whole definition and agenda had evolved out of Piekarski's particular bent, and in fairness, if SAYNO's next big case was saving the American family by destroying some Canadian rock band, it really was Piekarski's game.

So he bitched about Crensch for forty-five minutes, and bitched about Fearless, and I just kept driving and annoying him by throwing out all the lines he had used at our "drug enforcement meetings" about the country falling apart because nobody respected authority anymore and how Fearless was the boss so it was our duty to follow and respect his orders and how Crensch's father was an elected official so we had to respect him too and how teamwork was the watchword and how we should all be proud to be fighting evil in any way we could. Which finally shut him up for about five minutes, because he wasn't equipped to argue with his own idiocy. But Piekarski was more resourceful than I gave him credit for, because he soon launched another attack.

"Hey, Morrow, ya think Crensch is a flit?"

"I think he flits a lot. Easier than working."

"That's not what I meant," grumbled Piekarski, irritated at having to explain his meaning if he wanted company for his resentment of Crensch's new position. When guys like Piekarski really dislike someone, it's soul purging to get someone else to agree. It somehow puts them right with themselves for a little while. "Do you think he's a fag?"

"I don't know, Charlie. Why don't you ask him? I'm no good at spotting those things."

"Yeah, that's what I figured." Puffed himself up as an expert or something. "Just look at the guy. He's not married, doesn't have a girlfriend—"

"You're not married either, Charlie."

Piekarski didn't much like the reference to his divorce, but I sounded so determinedly friendly about it that he couldn't make up his mind whether or not I was insulting him so he just continued, "Yeah, well, you've *never* been married."

"I'm married to my work," I said easily. "But that's the second time you've noticed. I'm touched."

Piekarski backed off. But not for long. He was hot against Crensch right now and he needed me as an ally.

"Yeah, well I'm not convinced Crensch there is married to his work. If the guy was a workaholic, I could sort of understand it. Likes to pretend he is. Likes to make everybody think he's a goddamned superhero, but when it comes to anything dangerous, all he knows how to do is eavesdrop. Could you see that guy in a shoot-out?"

"Saw him shoot out a street with an Uzi once."

"I mean in anything real. I mean could you see him busting down Toon's door? What the hell is Crensch doing in law enforcement besides keeping his old man happy?"

"Maybe he's keeping his old man happy. Respecting authority and making obeisance to the family and all that. Maybe he's cheerfully giving up his true calling to please his dad. Surely you of all people can appreciate Crensch's sense of family values."

My reaction greatly upset him because he had no way to respond without looking like a hypocrite or a fool. Wondered which he would choose. He chose fool.

"Yeah, well, if Crensch is going to join the team, I hope he's paying close attention to the way we do things when we finally bust down Toon's compound. Wait'll he sees there's more to the drug war than hoping that somebody gives him some street gossip he can repeat to the boss and then hoping that somebody else sorts it out for him. Maybe he'll start asking himself if he's got the balls for SAYNO work—"

"—Before he hogs all the credit," I threw out to keep things honest.

"Right," grumbled Piekarski, without making eye contact. "Just another reason to make the bust a good show."

When we got to Providence we were delayed for two hours trying to explain our business at the reception area of the Department of Social Services. First we had to wait in line with about two dozen resentful-looking "clients" because there weren't any signs for the Child Protective Services Division and the armed guard wouldn't let anybody wander around the building unsupervised. Piekarski tried to cut the line to state our business to anyone who could wave us through, but he was thoroughly snubbed by a resolutely overbearing woman who seemed to relish putting an equally overbearing macho cop like Piekarski in his place.

Which was sort of funny, I have to admit, because the *hoi polloi* in line had all looked vaguely alarmed when Piekarski shoved them out of his way, loudly advertising that he was "FBI. Boston. SAYNO Team. Here for a pre-arranged drug investigation." But when the woman told him to wait his turn and waved him to the back of the line like an annoying bug everyone looked vaguely amused. Especially since he now had to walk back through and stand behind everybody his ego had just been pushing around.

"You can't fight government," I said cheerfully as he joined me behind a dirty-looking woman who was clutching a bag of clothes and dreamily ignoring her three dirty-looking kids who were grabbing at anybody they could find.

He pretended he hadn't heard me, which didn't work because the woman acknowledged my comment by turning her head and flashing me a quick knowing smile. I smiled back. Piekarski looked away. An elderly woman caught his glance and asked him for food stamps. Twice. I wasn't about to help him out, so I stood there smiling and saying nothing while the line slowly moved. Piekarski did his dismal best to look tough. Kept failing. An old drunk with a matted beard and yellow teeth kept asking him for money and telling him he liked his shoes.

Whenever Piekarski spoke to me in an effort to shut out his new friends, I ignored him and studied the woman behind the counter. She clearly thought she was doing all the world a favor to occasionally disrupt her conversation with a co-worker to fill out forms for people and answer the phone. When she didn't feel like working, which was often, she'd bark a lot of arcane orders in a way that was supposed to impress the folks in line, although a lot of them were too spaced out from drugs to notice. However, the drunk would occasionally repeat the orders to people at random in a fairly good imitation of the woman's voice, which greatly annoyed her. Which also meant that when the fellow finally got up front he was punished by being made to wait and then brought protesting to the back of the line. His having to wait, of course, only increased our own waiting time.

When it was finally our "turn," the woman made us wait at the counter for about twenty minutes while she bellowed and lectured to her co-workers. Her assistant, who struck me as an otherwise unemployable wannabe paper pusher who thought herself quite the deal to be working for the State, kept asking if she could "help us" and if we "wanted food stamps" and then wandering away to another room in the middle of our explanations. This happened two or three times until her boss grandly took our names and ordered us to wait some more. About forty-five minutes passed during which I saw other dedicated state employees filling out crossword puzzles and complaining about projected budget cuts. Every so often a "client" got called out of the line and worked over.

However, after the woman made three phone calls, we were finally ushered through a maze of hallways and into a horrible little office that smelled of too much cleaning solvent, where we waited another ten minutes before one of the social workers I had seen on the New Year's Eve news story about the police stealing the children from Toon's compound came in to greet us. She said her name was "Meg." Her last name was "not important." It was all very secret-secret and everything, more secret-secret than the Kremlin, more secret-secret than Crensch on holiday, and it seemed to me that she had something to prove to us FBI types by showing how "classified" the social services people could act when circumstances called for it.

She and Piekarski had spoken on the phone before but they hadn't met face-to-face until now, so she ID'd him with a smile, which was funny, because for some reason she forgot to do the same to me. Then she said she would "lead us" to the Child Protective Services Division, where two of the women from Lamar Toon's cult who had lost custody of their children were now "ready to be interviewed." For a second I thought she said "ready to be executed."

But she didn't "lead" us anywhere right away because first she wanted to "brief us" on the "context" of what was going on. The two women, Mary K. Gonzas and Sheila Baker, who still preferred to be called by her cult name, "Mother Bunny," were quite distraught and ready to talk. Both had already agreed to undergo extensive counseling and therapy at taxpayer expense as a condition for having their children returned. They understood that the first step to healing was getting out of denial so they were both willing to make official statements about drug use and drug sales on the compound. Piekarski beamed like a bastard. Couldn't wait to get to it. Meg looked terrifically pleased with herself. Us insensitive, ignorant FBI types were actually consulting *her* on human issues and being forced to listen to and adopt her agenda. She was saving the world. She was very important.

As she led the way down another corridor, I kept thinking about state use of psychological torture to get people to say anything the state happened to find amusing, and how this was like a seventeenth-century witchcraft trial. Wondered if three or four centuries ago I would have been a reluctant inquisitor with Jade on the other side of the questions. Then I wondered who would have broken first.

Meg eventually stopped us outside a closed door. She knocked a strange little cadence on the door, which she said was a "warning signal" and then she went in first to "make sure everything was all right." Five minutes passed before she gave us entry into the star chamber.

First thing I noticed was the other social worker I had seen on TV. She was seated at a little round coffee table. In front of her was a stack of papers and manila files. I took that to mean that she was the boss, especially since Meg sat away from the table. Since this other social worker remained steadfastly nameless throughout the interview, I mentally called her the Queen. Meg began to introduce us to the cult women, who were so broken and shadowy you didn't even notice them at first, but the Queen interrupted the introduction to assert her authority. Then she made the introductions herself and got our names wrong. Then she pretty much ordered to us to sit down.

As I said, you didn't even notice the cult women at first. Mary Gonzas was an olive-complexioned, Hispanic woman with less presence and more impenetrable pathos than a dead child's skeleton. Her English was as broken as her spirit. She looked malnourished. Also scared. Or rather, if she'd had a shade of strength she would have looked scared. As it was, she was too weak to look anything. There was no light in her dull eyes where you expected to see light, and her facial features were all too large for the rest of her body, making her decidedly unattractive. A moth-eaten, pie-tin face on a popsicle stick body, like a once-loved doll trashed by a no-longer-loved child.

The backs of her hands had yellow spots and shook like they were filled with palsied bees. She didn't look up at either me or Piekarski, although once or twice she glanced at the floor near the Queen's chair as if she feared that the dominant social worker wielded absolute power of life or death. Maybe Mary Gonzas had enough presence of mind to believe that basic survival demanded the occasional appeasement of a glance. But even her glance lacked the anemic conviction of a beggar's. I think her eyes merely moved in their sockets on an instinct she had no power to stop.

Sheila Baker—Mother Bunny—had a round, pale face and covered her hair in a tight little black and blue checkered scarf. Her cheeks held an unhealthy looking flush and her eyes were red with crying. She kept asking the Queen for a Kleenex, and occasionally, if she begged enough, got rewarded with an impatient, demeaning look and one half of one yellow tissue, which she clutched against her face for comfort until it was soaked to shreds. Meg asked us cheerfully if we wanted coffee.

"Might as well," I replied.

So we drank a remarkably good coffee, chocolate flavored, courtesy of the state of Rhode Island, and the Queen turned on her tape recorder and Piekarski turned on ours and took out some papers and I made sure to ask the prisoners whether they wanted an attorney present. They didn't. They signed a form stating they didn't, although I wasn't sure Mary Gonzas understood what she was signing. Or if she was signing, because she didn't write out her name so much as make a few scratch marks with a pen that I gave her. I explained for the record that the question was a formality because the two women weren't facing any criminal charges, they were merely aiding in a federal investigation, but Queenie cut me off and commanded Mother Bunny to "start talking." She also stole my pen for her own use.

Mother Bunny looked up at the Queen, hesitated, and then said quietly, "What am I supposed to say?"

"Tell us about the drugs," badgered Piekarski. "Ever see Lamar Toon use or sell drugs?" I was poised to take everything down in writing.

Mother Bunny looked at me, looked at the Queen again, sobbed a little, nodded, and said uncertainly, "Yes. There were drugs." Then she looked at Mary Gonzas, who looked down at her own space of floor and nodded. Throughout the whole ordeal Mary Gonzas said little, letting her cult sister do all the talking and nodding in agreement whenever somebody intimidated her more than she already was. How much English she understood, how much of any of this she understood, was anybody's guess.

"What kinds of drugs? When? Who'd he sell them to? In what amount?" asked Piekarski, getting right down to business.

"All kinds," said Mother Bunny helplessly, like she was guessing. Piekarski told me to write down "all kinds." I asked for clarification.

"Marijuana? Cocaine? Heroin?" Piekarski demanded. Mother Bunny nodded. Well, slightly nodded. You almost had to imagine her head dropping in agreement. I wrote down Piekarski's wish list.

"Anything else?"

She looked at the social workers. "Uh, pills?" she sort of asked. "Like valium?"

Wrote it down.

"Great," said Piekarski. "You'll swear in court, you'll both swear to a judge if you have to, you've seen these drugs being used on the cult compound?" The women nodded, Mary following Mother Bunny's lead. "When? We need dates and times."

"All the time. Anytime. Every day."

"All the time?"

"Sure," said Mother Bunny, confident of having the right answer. "Every morning. Every night. We smoked a lot of pot. Did drugs every night. Small Brother Mink—"

"Lamar Toon—" corrected Queen Bee.

"Lamar Toon, we used to call him Brother Mink, made everyone take drugs."

"Even the children?" asked Piekarski.

Mother Bunny nodded and cried.

"*Your* children?"

"No, not my children." She was looking at Meg when she said this, as if Meg was the "good cop" who knew she hadn't abused her own kids. Meg showed her sensitivity by looking stiffly and importantly at Queenie. "I wouldn't let my children. But other children, sure. They all took drugs."

"Then how were you able to protect *your* children?" asked Queenie, with a hint of menace.

Mother Bunny shook. It was hard enough for her to find the lies her government wanted. She was terrified of now being seemingly trapped in an inconsistency. "I—I would take them myself. To save my children," she said eagerly.

"*All* of them?" asked Piekarski enthusiastically, conveying a repellingly bright enthusiasm Mother Bunny mistook for an accusation.

Mother Bunny started crying. "I just want my children. Whatever. I'll say whatever." She didn't want to go any further with the charade.

Meg nodded sympathetically. "You and Mary both tested negative for drug use," she offered encouragingly. She probably meant it to comfort and encourage, but after she spoke, it was obvious that she had pointed out a major problem in the witness's story.

"Uh, I don't know. Maybe I didn't take the drugs every day. Sometimes I hid them up my dress or put them down the drain. I don't know what you want me to say."

I felt embarrassed over the whole thing and resolved to do what little I could to get the torture over with. "All right, you'll swear you've witnessed drug possession and that you've seen illegal drugs given to minors. That's all we need there. Let's move on, Charlie." I wasn't thrilled with helping her lie, but then I wasn't thrilled with much lately.

Piekarski asked her when and to whom Lamar Toon sold drugs.

"To everyone. He gave them away."

That was the wrong answer. We needed to get him on selling. Piekarski insisted in a nasty whiny tone that he didn't believe her. Toon must have sold drugs to finance the cult.

"O yes, he did. On the street. To junkies. To anybody. To kids. Sold cocaine and pot. I don't know when—pretty much sent people out to sell everyday whenever he needed money."

"And you saw this?"

She nodded.

"Where did he get his drugs from?"

She looked at Mary Gonzas. Mary Gonzas looked back and retreated into herself to stare at her shoes. She made a long, low animal-like whimper. The only time I'd ever heard a sound like that before was when I found a dying raccoon in the woods that had managed to crawl away after getting hit by a car.

"Did he make them?" prompted Piekarski. "We've got other witnesses that said he made his own coke." Actually, we didn't, but it was an old trick that worked on the two frightened women.

"Yes, he made drugs. He made his own. Has his own laboratory for that. Grows his own marijuana under lights like a hippie."

It was as good an answer as any. I wrote it down.

"All right," said Piekarski, "You'll swear there's a drug lab on the premises?" She nodded. "Why does he make the children take drugs?"

I spoke up to save the women further discomfort. "Charlie, 'why' doesn't matter right now. We already have enough here for a search warrant. If the witnesses are willing to sign they've seen drug sales and a lab what more do we need?"

"I don't know why." Mother Bunny answered the question anyway. She really wasn't good at this. She cried and asked for another Kleenex. Queenie refused so I grabbed the box and threw the whole damn thing on her lap. She let it slide to the floor. "I don't know. He makes everyone."

"Are the children forced to do anything else?" asked Piekarski eagerly. I pushed the papers over for the witnesses to sign, trying to end matters.

"They're forced to work and to learn. We have teachers who give them spiritual instruction in walking the path of light."

"The path of light?"

"The way, the truth, the gateway to Heaven," Mother Bunny said by rote. The phrase was something to cling to. It seemed to help. It was awful.

"What if a child disobeys?"

"Nothing. I mean—I don't know."

"Are they physically abused?"

"No."

"But they're drugged?"

"No. I mean yes."

The Queen broke in. "Some children have complained of being forced to get undressed by Toon. You know about that?"

"No, not my children. I don't know. Maybe the others."

"Does Toon practice Satanism?"

"Charlie, you can't ask that," I protested.

"Why not, Morrow?"

"It could be construed as a First Amendment violation. It's not a crime to simply be a Satanist. We've got to limit our questions to actual crimes. And for the record, child abuse is a state, not a federal concern. It won't help us make our case."

Piekarski got annoyed. "Does he ritually sacrifice children?"

Mother Bunny looked like sickness chasing after death. "Not my children. I don't think so. Just drugs," she nodded. "We don't have a sacrifice. Brother believes—" Queenie looked at her. "Lamar Toon believes we're all sacrifices. We're all children of the light. We all come from God to be willing sacrifices."

"Including the children?" insisted Piekarski.

Mother Bunny looked at Mary. "Including us all in blessed love," she hoarsely whispered and looked down.

Piekarski told me to add allegations of child sacrifice. And technically, I pretty much had to because the witness had been bullied into saying it, but to cut short Piekarski from asking for all the gory details these two tortured prisoners were incapable of creating to his satisfaction, I stood up and made them sign the papers. They both signed their names tearfully, "in blessed love," although Mary sort of printed the words in a child-like handwriting with Mother Bunny's help. Then I gathered up the documents and started to leave, knowing that my action would force Piekarski to follow.

Queenie seemed affronted by my lack of social skills because I didn't formally close the interview by kissing her ass and "deeply appreciating" her agency's cooperation. Hell, I didn't even bother to tell anyone to have a nice day. So all she could do was officiously order Meg to "show us out" before we went through the building without an escort. It was a small victory, but Piekarski had to go along with the program. As we left, Mother Bunny was crying and clutching her Kleenex box like it was one of her stolen children, and the Queen was taking it away and yelling at Mary that she'd "never get better if she didn't change her attitude."

Meg brought us outside the building, confidently explaining that it could cause a lot of trouble if we wandered around the Division unsupervised. We might disturb some of their more sensitive clients, she added importantly, hoping we understood. But when we got to the parking lot, Piekarski, unhappy with me for depriving him of a long-anticipated hot tale of sex and Satanism, graciously shared his lack of understanding by slamming the car door on her chatter and rattling impatiently through the window, "Come on, Morrow, time to see the judge." No small talk for him. He could be as strictly "professional" and "by-the-book" as I was. Especially with a crushed libido.

But so could Meg in a state-mandated kind of way. She needed something friendly to say to close things so she smiled and told us to have a good weekend. She said she hoped the judge would "go our way."

I thanked her. In the name of blessed love.

So what else?

I didn't get through the next few weeks. They got through me. I know that weeks passed through me like the bodily memory of a sword thrust holding back my strange dying. I remember a blemished winter. I remember my life leaking through my awareness. Here's the list of what I recall.

One. Prepared to siege and destroy Bit o' Providence. Took up the better portion of my life. Piekarski got his warrant, but he waited until his BATF buddy sent word that Toon's gun license renewal had gotten "lost" so the FBI could throw in illegal weapons charges on top of everything else. That was especially important, because SAYNO needed an excuse to give the media a full-blown paramilitary operation that could be broadcast to the country, so we needed to invent an enemy who was dangerously armed. Kanesh leaked Mother Bunny's "confession" to warm things up with the public and hinted there might still be children inside the compound suffering all kinds of unspecified horrible things. Waiting for the gun licenses to expire took a few weeks, but when all was said and done, we were on for February 12.

Two. Scoured the media for news of Black Dog. Knew they were back in the Northeast. Assumed they were under the Mob's watchful guard. No one contacted me via one of Penny's safe lines. Assumed there were reasons. In the middle of my nights I kept getting caught in this phrase that of course Jade never wrote safe lines, and the words were stuck in my mind like a song, and it hurt me to get rid of them.

And one morning someone spray painted some lyrics from "Poison Puppy" under a bridge in Newton. My gut clutched every time I drove by it. I don't know why I mention this, except that when I get a memory of those weeks passing I keep seeing the image of that damn dark decaying bridge with neon green words starkly declaring to winter, "the way I imagine / it ought to be hidden." It marked my days. I had dreams about that damn bridge. Still do.

Three. Beth fucked up.

I remember learning that Beth neglected to check *all* of Fendra's tables for bugs, because there was at least one left to record Nick's next business meeting. This meeting occurred near the end of January. The only reason I got the tape before Fearless did was that the courier happened to arrive while I was waiting for Marcie to finish flirting with a new hire so she could take a few seconds to give me some reports I didn't really want. I was thankful that she wasn't paying attention because I was able to initial the receipt for Fearless and keep the package without her noticing.

Played the tape at home that night. Here's what I learned.

Nick wasn't happy. Despite Black Dog's faster-than-light rise to national madness and their ability to sell out all of his clubs—to the point where unhappy fans shut out of two filled-to-capacity venues rioted and Nick's promoters had to extend shows three and four nights in a row—CD sales were falling. Nick thought he made the right decision when he pushed "Poison Puppy" out to cash in on the growing controversy surrounding Black Dog, but despite his efforts to push up sales, his people were telling him sales were plummeting. He talked to Elbie. Got nowhere. Then he talked to Elbie's mother, who didn't much appreciate the business aspects of business and felt they should just be happy the music was out.

Penny didn't much care for the new "arrangements" by the way, which I took to mean the new lock and key arrangements, but Nick didn't much care for what he called her growing "attitude." Told her she and her brood could take a hike if they didn't like the way he was running things. Black Dog wasn't their band anymore. Who the hell was making them? Who the hell was delivering what they all said they wanted in the first place? Shut her up. So he was through with Penny. She could hang around and be the boys' nursemaid, he didn't care, but he didn't need her.

He talked to some other people with experience in this sort of thing. Seems everyone who was going to buy the CD did so when the first single came out from it, and "Poison Puppy" didn't draw in any new people. A lot of people loved the band, but who's going to buy the same product twice? Bad marketing decision. Waste of resources and money promoting that song, never should have done it, but hell, live and learn. Not the band's fault.

So here was the deal. Now that Nick had broken even on his initial investment and wanted a quick profit to plow back into the business, he was going to release the second CD, the one scheduled for late June. That would sell. Especially now, since the band was very hot. Might even get them to open for a more established band on a major arena tour this summer if he could find some record label execs that weren't dickheads. Which was a pretty big if. Meant they would have to come up with a third record for when this one ran its course, something for summer release, but he was sure they would. Even if they were playing out in his clubs all the time, they had their days to write in and besides, what else do they have to do? They ain't going nowhere. Everyone laughed.

Speaking of which, George spoke out about Beth's report on Crensch being at Elise's and her subsequent refusal to cooperate. Nick told him to get another spy over there, but he didn't sound too worried. A murder case could sell CDs, and what did Elise know about the business? She wasn't Penny and if her son keeps his mouth shut everything should be all right.

And of course everyone thought Nick had brilliant ideas, so the meeting convened with plans to get the new CD out immediately and get a new video filmed for one of the cuts. Maybe film a live performance with screaming girls and everything at one of Nick's venues. Help advertise the venue as a fun place where people could have a good time without problems. There was no direct mention of the Fairfax incident. Important thing was profits.

I suspected Nick needed to prove to the old man that despite one bad decision he could bring in money. Made me think of a decisive Fearless. Then I decided Fearless didn't have to know this tape existed until someone else told him about it.

I did wonder why, since Crensch had clearly miked more than one table, he hadn't been sending back useless tapes of drunks having mindless conversations. Especially considering we still kept getting the answering machine on a regular basis, which was just as useless, despite Crensch indicating in one of his reports that it was the opinion of "his team" that the band schedules might turn out to be of value in the payola-tax evasion investigation. Maybe someone had decided that random drunken babbling from Fendra's patrons wasn't worth writing home about. Maybe Crensch was keeping the tapes.

But mostly I was too cold to wonder anything.

Four. On February 2, a few days before I started hearing a cut from the new CD get airplay, Crensch made the headlines by arresting Elise McClellan for the murder of Claude Hopner. I have no idea why or if Hugh McCrae chose that date to drop the word and terminate his "protectorship" but my suspicion is he didn't. It was too good a time to bring more attention on the band, and there was no way he could have known about the CD's imminent release. Not even the King of the Titans can win against governmental intrusion. Crensch's evidence, as I understand it, didn't rest on anything McCrae gave him. He had sweet talked Elise into giving him a lock of her hair in exchange for one of his wretched sketches. Could Rapunzel have done better from her own prison? The DNA test showed that it matched the hair sample found near Hopner's body. Elise's fingerprints and handwriting matched the note's.

She confessed when confronted with the evidence. She gave no motive. Then she prayed to Jesus for forgiveness and hung herself in her jail cell with an old plastic girl's belt filled with straw flowers that McCrae gave her. He emerged from a crack in her cell, gave her the belt, and watched her die. Then he left. At least, that's what I saw while fire gazing.

I kept living her death, kept getting morbidly obsessed with those last heartbeats. I fire gazed and knew that in the end, the woman dreamed and Dionysus did not know her. Only the monster knew her, small and dense in the hole in her cell where the monsters come through. As the belt cut away her mortality, she dreamed of giving birth again, of holding the sea between her legs like an extended orgasm from heaven. But there was no pleasure, only a spiny lash as the nasty water retreated from feeling. In her last second she was a music teacher the sea had marked, and there was sparkling blue and green like hidden hysterical suns rising to burn through her shallow ocean. Then gray like a bad film. Then gone.

It sold records. But McCrae had to feel it as a triumph because of course everyone wanted to talk about the scandal and nobody wanted to listen to the music for what it was. By bringing Elise the belt, McCrae had made life bigger and more compelling than art. So the music was out there but it was damn hard for anyone to really hear it. It sold, but Jade's soul was publicly reduced to a mere guessing game for "clues indicating the songwriter's family pathology." Jade did no interviews. Nick wouldn't let his boys speak to the press.

Heppelfauf made out like milk. "Yes, Elise McClellan's house was his Canadian headquarters," said one of his spokespeople. It would continue to be. They were praying for her soul. Perhaps it was all God's wisdom. Perhaps her son would repent of his evil. Have faith. Send money to the Egbert Kipfer Memorial Fund. People did.

Which meant that McCrae and Selene were still shacking up and needed a handout. Deathbirds in love. I knew them constantly, like I knew the interchangeable families of missing children that had nothing for lives. Selene was another Elise and also the strange empty daughter she never had. On and on humps the monster on damaged virgins throughout the generations. It was early there. The monster would be making his new bride feel good and complete for not dancing. He would justify her sins. Later they would breed missing children. Later still she would feed him her body's dust like wine.

Stave Twenty-Two

Friday, February 12, 1993.

First thing we did was check our guns. It was supposed to be a once over routine, but when some BATF reinforcements showed up at the field office, we had to check everything again, and then they had to check everything they had presumably checked before, so everyone could show his weapons to everyone else and our respective leaders could compete for issuing the most idiotic orders. This was around four a.m. The raid was scheduled for six-thirty. The city was dark around me.

Early mornings suck. I love the night. The infinite fall and promise of darkness, the near illusion that the dark will go on forever if I can only find the right fiction to read and ride. Love sunsets. Pathos. But wake for early morning, and sit tight amidst weapons and work, dazed and deputized in a cold office, and you can't help but feel the darkness thinning towards grimy day, where everything will show plain and truth-ridden for hours. At least I can feel it. Like an old recurring betrayal or an exceptionally private curse.

Behind me stretched the first two weeks of February like a dim prelude to this dreadful now. I watched my comrades-in-arms buzzing around the coffee machine, and closed my eyes for a minute, overwhelmed with the unending limits my life had been reduced to. My only knowledge of Jade, since no one had contacted me, was the publicity surrounding Elise's suicide, along with all the increasingly frequent media speculations and rumors about all the mysterious goings-on in Black Dog's camp, speculations that were fueled by the band's seeming refusal to speak to the press. Nick was smart on that score. Why risk another problem when the media was generating all kinds of interest in the new CD without Black Dog's help? The field office was wearing me down so much that all I got from fire gazing was an extended reflection of my own thoughts. My heart was too tired to dream. All I could hold onto was that as long as Jade stayed close to Nick, as long as he kept himself a willing prisoner of the Mob and stayed away from me, that someday we might have our private games and songs again. That is, if I could sabotage "Project Black Dog." That was the new name for Crensch's mob investigation.

Crensch had briefly returned from Toronto to accept all the congratulations for his "success" with the Hopner case. He "secreted" himself around the field office for a day or two, bouncing on his heels and rubbing his nose and winking and blinking and keeping his distance from us peons and only speaking to Fearless and the press, as behooved an important investigator like himself. Although he did generously invite Piekarski to meet with him to discuss SAYNO's prospective role in his ongoing project. Only reason I knew I was being snubbed was that Piekarski refused to meet with him and then complained to me at length about Crensch's "attitude." As if I could do anything about it.

But Crensch left the field office again, hightailing it down to Washington for a command photo op with Dad before returning to Toronto to hang out with Hugh McCrae and wait for SAYNO to come to his rescue once it had won the war with Providence. I didn't think Crensch was doing much actual investigating, because Fearless hadn't been giving me any tapes or reports to rewrite. He also hadn't invited me to any more off-the-record discussions of Crensch's progress, which probably meant that everyone who mattered was happy with Crensch's new golden boy image. I know that whenever I mentioned the subject of SAYNO's upcoming involvement with "Project Black Dog," Fearless suddenly got busy with other matters and waved me away saying he'd be talking to me soon.

So my only reason for sitting here in the thinning darkness and preparing to fight a war I didn't believe in was the uncertain possibility of having some influence in SAYNO's next project and thereby doing what I could to protect Jade. I was dying for my love. I was killing for him. I was trapped by what I wanted.

Piekarski won the idiocy competition with the BATF guy, which meant that now we could all shove off with Fearless's blessing. I kept wondering what the hell we would do if Lamar Toon peacefully honored the warrant and let us search the compound without resistance. If that happened, it would be pretty hard to justify the full-blown militarized attack Piekarski had pumped everybody up for. In fact, with all the weapons we were lugging down we'd really look ridiculous for the press contingent Kanesh had organized if one of Toon's followers timidly opened the door and said, "Come on in." But Piekarski seemed to think the strength of our presence would guarantee against a peaceful resolution. And I had to admit, he was probably right.

We gathered under a deeply graying sky in an empty lot in Providence, like soldiers on the eve of battle have gathered forever. No one knew what to do, and it took a while through radio communication to get the compound properly surrounded, which meant Toon had to know we were there. Kept thinking about the first circle I'd sat outside at Cara's, and how her girlfriends didn't know what to do either, and put the thought away like it was irrelevant. Item. We made a protective circle around an enemy that we had also made.

At one point an intrepidly pushy reporter shoved a microphone in my face and demanded to know "how I felt." I knew no answer, only the gray-lined sky and all the dull buildings some committee had commissioned for dull lives I was supposed to be pretending to protect.

"Lonely," I said absently, although I meant both more and less than this. What I felt was my life becoming so empty that even my shadows would go bone white and decay. A life of empty glaring light. Without end.

"You mean this is a lonely job?" persisted the reporter.

"Any job you care about is a lonely job." I moved away. Didn't want to know what I meant. I was supposed to be spotting Beisweiler, who was supposed to deliver the warrant with a cluster of six heavily armed agents at her back. Piekarski had of course decided that we SAYNO leaders were needed behind the lines, so it was Beisweiler that got drafted as point woman. He was giving her and her entourage directions for the umpteenth time. Every time a new camera swung in his direction it was necessary to repeat everything. Then the circle got tense and quiet. Cast.

Beisweiler led her little force to the compound's door. Traffic sounds got more obvious in the running anticipation. There were cameras on her, full profile, journalists being a braver lot than Piekarski in the face of danger. She knocked. She looked tough. Cop tough. Like the movies. Knocked again. Waited long enough to lose her edge. I could tell from the sudden slight droop of her neck and shoulders that she had dropped her attention. Toon opened the door. Although I couldn't hear him at the time, when they ran the story later I learned that he dismissed her with low-key irritation. "I'm busy. Morning prayers."

Beisweiler interrupted him with a harsh, "Judith Beisweiler, FBI. We have a warrant to search your premises for drugs and weapons."

Toon asked to see the warrant. Beisweiler fumbled around, had to radio Piekarski for it, and someone had to get it from a reporter and run up to the door with it. Meanwhile, Lamar Toon faced the cameras and stated that the feds had trespassed on his property without carrying a warrant, which was true, and then took the paper from the agent who brought it and read the whole thing aloud.

Actually, he *declaimed* the whole thing aloud like a Roman senator, making dramatic hand gestures while the camera panned the document, and filling his speech with dramatic pauses, which greatly annoyed us drug warrior types. Concluded his performance by saying, "Your warrant is improperly filled out. You've got the wrong number for my street address." He pointed to the "17" on the warrant and the "19" on his mailbox. Then he ordered everyone to leave his property, to stop threatening his life, and to cease interfering with his religious freedom. Then he slammed the door.

Although I couldn't hear his speech, I could see from my station that he wasn't cooperating. I could also see Beisweiler and her posse shuffle around and look confused. Beisweiler got on her radio and briefly explained what had just happened. Then she asked Piekarski for instructions. He looked at me. I made sure to say via radio, so the press would put it on record, that under the circumstances we had to call everything off and get a proper warrant. Piekarski swore off the air and stamped his foot. I let my radio pick up the profanity. The BATF commander yelled that he would tell his people to go for it if Piekarski wimped. He didn't get his agents ready for nothing.

Piekarski got back on his radio and ordered Beisweiler to break down the door. The full force of the law would back her up. Search the premises, confiscate the guns and drugs, arrest everybody. Remember the building was surrounded.

Beisweiler backed off with her agents and held a consultation. Half a dozen BATF guys came over with a battering ram. They weren't exactly offering assistance. They were going to show us how to do the job. Some of our people broke away from Beisweiler and grabbed sides of the ram. The rest followed, which meant Beisweiler was now demoted to being behind the thing and the BATF guys were issuing the orders. A window opened on the second floor of the building and an angry man waved a shotgun and told us we were trespassing and to get off the property in the name of Brother Mink and Buddha. Then he fired overhead. "That's your warning shot. Brother says go. We're praying for our family."

Actually, that was our irresistible invitation. Some jerk fired back and shattered the window, and the agents with the ram attacked the door and destroyed it in less than thirty seconds. Raid time.

Once the battering agents were inside with drawn guns and the press was right behind, my group had to follow as back-up. It was utter chaos because the damn reporters were blocking us so effectively that there was very little help we could have offered, and every idiot with a camera or a microphone was shoving us back for a closer look at all the excitement. I led my six agents to the door and managed to just get inside when a loud blast from a semi-automatic rifle sent me instinctively to the floor. Bullet casing nicked my arm enough to draw a little blood. Bullet ripped Beisweiler's face off, and her body jerked down like a slaughtered duck. One of her men got it in the head and also died instantly. A third took a shot to the chest. It was my lucky job to drag him across the floor and outside while a barrage of friendly fire nicked a BATF guy and slaughtered his Holiness Brother Mink. My guy died while I pounded on his chest and gave him mouth-to-mouth resuscitation. The paramedics threw a cover over him and bandaged my bleeding arm. Which was overkill.

Didn't complain, though. It was fine to be out of it. Sounded like a shooting gallery inside, and yet another agent was fatally shot by the time they'd "disarmed" the angry cult members. Ransacked the place to ruin looking for drugs that plainly didn't exist. Confiscated the "illegal weapons" the BATF had created. Piekarski and Kanesh, who had also been safely on the sidelines throughout, strutted about how sorry they were for all the deaths and how clearly violent and anti-social Bit o' Providence was and how they had to conduct this raid to save the children they were now claiming they had believed were inside. Which was a tawdry bit of fiction that contradicted the fact that all the children had been removed, but nobody questioned him. Piekarski embellished the whole story by saying that I had been "seriously wounded," which to my mind meant I ought to be able to go home. But after the battle, as co-leader of SAYNO, I had to immediately report back to Boston and attend to all the paperwork while the reporters hovered around Piekarski and Kanesh.

And all I thought about on the drive back was that, in less time than it took the "state-approved" families of Providence to gulp down breakfast and gulp themselves off to another undistinguished workday, the government had done a fine morning's work destroying a peaceful religious community—an old-fashioned extended *family*, for Christ's sake. All in the name of some good PR and a budget increase. Which

SAYNO would no doubt get. It took me longer to fill out forms than it took Uncle Sam to end several lives and destroy Lamar Toon's quirky little world. Only time the government ever acted that fast was when there was money or lives to steal. Then it was unstoppable.

Managed to tie up my duties at the field office and get home by four p.m. It was all over the news, of course. Local reaction was highly favorable. NDECC members praised our work. And in a bizarre twist of fate, so did Heppelfauf and his new assistant. Hugh McCrae told some fawning reporter who tracked him down for commentary how much he respected SAYNO, and me in particular, despite the fact I once mistakenly put him in the slammer. We were great friends. Loved to see me working for justice. Very sorry to hear I'd nearly gotten killed.

Clicked it off. Lay back on my couch and stared at the ceiling I was too empty to really notice. Too exhausted from hours of wakefulness to feel the disgust I knew should have been there. Even the morning's violence was getting half absent. A man died as I tried to save him today. Isn't that supposed to mean something? Didn't. Didn't care. Do my job. Kill and die. Tired of life. Tired. Out.

Somewhere else. Dreaming. Finally.

That is, after long silence, I'm dreaming that I'm dreaming.

When it begins, I'm saying a long prayer that frames my life like an eastern tale.
Then I'm a voice of pure fiction, rising and falling like a song or a sea wave from
some lonely witch-poet's mouth. But when the sea waves crest and crash, the
sound turns me into myself and I'm only the prayer her voice keeps forming.
Twisting like a hanged man between dancer and dance. No one knows one from
the other so the witch reads me Yeats's poems for comfort and my heart keeps
knowing the folly of being comforted. "Both nuns and mothers worship images,"
runs the voice like blind honey in my eyes. Someone is blessing me into familiarity.

Familiar slide and crash like the mountain of sand another nightmare nearly killed me in, and the desert sun in a black sky is all there is to look at because the landscape is rocky and desolate and won't be seen. But I am dreaming. Finally, for once. I hear some footsteps like light skidding across the desert, soft like the loom of this quaint, old-fashioned dawn. Heat and quiet are here like eternity. I'm lying on smooth red rock, just like my couch, survival camping in the Nevada desert where the sun is my only enemy, and so survival is getting terrible and simple as the desert makes leaps of light across my eyes, glimmering in the ceiling I couldn't recognize before. My ceiling. But I'm dreaming it now. Like a white heaven in flames. Like the limits of my life falling open. Like a tired flower attempting to crash and burn against the sun.

Red candle for Dionysus. Always south. And like a shade in the shining dark, Jade is smiling down at me and offering to change my bandage. My eyes are open. But for a few seconds I'm dreaming I'm happy, believing that we're dreaming together and that here it's forever. Then I woke to the deadly context of our meeting and stared coldly at him. His being there destroyed everything I ever wanted.

"Where's your car?" My voice was a surprise. It almost conveyed subtle delight. Yet, just before I spoke, all I felt was an honest scream of rage.

"Inside. Where it should be."

Of course. The garage door was the slide and crash I heard in my dream. As I sat up, he smiled like he thought he was pleasing me, seemingly unaware that his unprompted caution was also an unprompted admission of danger. He knew he shouldn't be there. I could have killed him for that.

"Why'd you come?" I asked flatly, firmly taking his hands in mine but exerting no warmth in the taking.

"To keep my promise. To save your dreams. Didn't I tell you I'd come back if I found out that your sadistic Uncle Sam was torturing you for his pleasure—"

"—Torturing me for his pleasure," I repeated softly. "And what are you doing?"

He was perplexed by my absolute coldness. Because even though I was clearly awake, there was still no welcome in my voice. "I heard the news, Pete. About an hour ago. Heard you nearly got killed. Route 84's a straight shot. Had to be here."

"Route 84," I echoed dully. "So, where'd you come up from? Hartford?"

"Waterbury."

"Fastest I've ever driven here from Waterbury was an hour and forty minutes."

"So I broke the speed limit. What do you care?"

"You're good at breaking limits." I said this without emotion, as if it were only a matter of fact. I rubbed his hands a little. He gently tried to pull back, but I did not release them. "How did you elude your guards?"

"What guards?" he asked lightly, smiling into my eyes, rubbing my hands in return and trying to cajole away my unfamiliar reserve. I knew he was wondering why I wasn't myself, why I wasn't even in a role he might recognize. He was determined to "save" me anyway, as if he didn't know there was nothing left to save. Which infuriated open the anger. So I knocked him onto the floor and pinned down his limbs with my body. Then I screamed.

"Nick Nariano's fucking strong men! Pauley Campobello and his thugs! Or are we going to pretend you're not on the fucking lam from your self-appointed minders and jailkeepers, and that the only reason you haven't contacted me in six fucking weeks is that you're so busy being a bass god you've forgot—"

"Pete—"

"Shut up." Cracked him one on the side of his face. Kept screaming. "You think I don't know why you haven't been able to call me? The fact that Penny can't even get through on one of her safe lines tells me you're all under twenty-four-hour surveillance. Or do you take me for one of those governmental clowns you think you're going to 'save' me from?" He started to speak again through his hurt, but I shook him and screamed louder, "Give me the fucking *truth*, Jade. I don't care how much it hurts you to deal with reality. Maybe it's time the two of you got acquainted."

"You're pimping for reality now, Pete?" He was trying to disarm me with his pointed humor. I hit him again for an answer.

"How the hell did you get here?" I meant how did he get in my life as well as how did he escape from the Mob. I could tell he knew everything I meant, and it terrified him.

He choked on the hurt, but he managed to say, "I was driving into Waterbury, where we were supposed to be playing tonight, with my 'minder,' as you call it, in the passenger seat. Donny D'Andrea, they call him. Donny punched in a news station on the radio, and right after the story ran he told me to take the next exit, he needed to find a phone and call Nick. So I did. He got out to make his call and I took off. I didn't care. Who the hell's gonna chase me?"

"At the speed you're traveling the fucking gods themselves ain't gonna chase you." Hit him again. "That's for being stupid. Now tell me the rest."

"As to not calling you. Yes, we were all constantly watched, but Cara pretty much closed off any safe line opportunities that might have existed, and Penny wouldn't even try to arrange any contact. She said under the circumstances her first loyalty was to the music," his voice got a little defiant on top of the hurt, "and that if you couldn't 'figure that one out at a distance you wouldn't know it up close.'"

"I know a lot of things up close. I know Nick Nariano suspects you've said a few things to me you shouldn't have, and he's only letting you live because you bring in money and he thinks he can contain future problems by keeping you under guard. And you know it too, unless you're dumber than I thought. But you've blown away that thread of safety by coming here for no good reason. If you listened to the news with the same attention you give to your compositions, you would have known I was all right."

"I didn't hear 'all right.' I heard 'seriously wounded' and 'nearly gotten killed' and 'four agents dead.'"

"Make it five, Jade."

"Don't understand—"

"I'm on the team assigned to investigate your band's financial dealings. Did you know that? Nick'll know that, he'll know that fast, and he'll also know you came here tonight—took off right after you heard the news story with one of his goons to witness your motive, you idiot"—hit him again. "My name's all over your case—"

"Quit the Bureau," he pleaded. "You don't belong there, anyway. They're killing you."

"Quitting the Bureau won't buy me anything except less control over sabotaging the investigation. Is that what you want?"

"Perhaps now's the time to go away together—" he said softly.

"*Now?* Jade—your fucking picture is all over the media in case you haven't noticed. Where the hell are we going to go?"

"You once—"

"At that point we might have gotten away with it. Nick didn't suspect you were talking to me. Your buddy Les hadn't gone public with your mafia associations and named names. You would have been an unexpected financial loss and your bandmates might have suffered his wrath a little but *we* might have stayed obscure and pulled it off. It might have been just us. Jade—if you take off with me now, we're both dead. He'll find us. He'll go to lengths to find us, because now it'll be a matter of honor. And if you go back to him, you're dead the instant your CDs stop selling, Penny and Cara notwithstanding, although I'm not convinced Cara doesn't want it that way, based on the way she taunted the Christians of Fairfax on your behalf. You won't escape again."

He tried to speak, but I wouldn't let him.

"Do you know what tonight is, lover? Tonight is the night you can't go back from and you can't leave. Tonight is a circle, an in-between time between life and destruction. Tonight, my friend, is all we have." Grabbed him and forced him over to the hearth, where the candle he lit was burning. "Tonight is my last night to have a dream."

He struggled to free himself, but I was stronger than him, and the wound in my arm was too superficial to make a difference. Took an herb satchel from my basket, the "protective" kind, and held it over his face while he fought me. Didn't care. Waited impassively until his struggling got less insistent, waited until his body relaxed and slumped, kept holding him and waiting in awful silence until he was semi-conscious. Then I carried him the way a Druid priest might carry a criminal or a war prisoner intended to be a living sacrifice and threw him on my large oak dining room table. He moaned in pain. Held him down and held the rag against his face to make sure he had no strength to get up.

What use is a god that fails to provide? I read once that in the ancient world there was a reciprocity between worshipper and deity that was perilous for either to violate. When a god accepted generous offerings of bread and beer and incense and slaughtered animals but refused to relieve a deadly drought, the people would drag his statue, the receptacle of his power, through the dead earth and smash it with sticks and reeds. If a derelict god merited such ministrations, how much more so does a derelict bard who destroyed his own ability to provide the living poetry his devotee needs for his drought of a life to matter? Jade had destroyed our stories, our private world, by coming here and making himself a mafia mark. His was a cosmic failure of duty. Mine was an unholy backlash of anger and pain.

Got some rope from the bottom of my pantry. His knees were bent over the table's edge, and the herbs dampened his movements so it was easy to bind each ankle tight against a table leg, and then bind each shin for added security. Decided I didn't want him to suffer the tearing muscle pain in his shoulders and arms that would result from tying his hands tightly to the table legs near his head. I wanted to control the pain. So I passed another rope around the center of the table to tightly bind his wrists so he couldn't raise his hands. Bound his forearms in a similar fashion so he couldn't sit up if he recovered any energy.

He watched me but he couldn't move to stop me. I studiously ignored his protests.

"Come on, guy, isn't this against the law?" he murmured.

"I am the law. Get used to it."

Studied him at my leisure. Goddess he was beautiful in the candlelight. The drug was closing his eyes now and his face looked entranced, like it sometimes did during one of his solos. Tenderly stroked his closed eyes and mouth. He was so close to gone. So close he instinctively tried to suck my finger. Not him but his body yielding helplessly to the sensation. Kissed him firmly into unconsciousness. Gazed at his wine-dark hair falling loosely around his captivating face, stroked his hair and throat until he stirred a little. Then I stepped back again into my private viewing. Imagined him like a long, slow, excruciatingly pleasurable, violent pulse of Dionysian energy lashing through slow, empty centuries like a dragon's merciless tongue. I grew hard in the imagining.

Kept imagining. Kept looking.

I saw him performing in every public arena and noble residence and village square and dirty city side street from ancient Greece to late twentieth-century America. He had always been creating visions for the blessed wanting world. I had always been blessed and wanting, watching him from the shadows of my life like I was now. And how I had always wanted him. Been born to want him. With an ancient, inbred ache.

How do you start things that always are?

If I knew I'd be a god. Or a poet. But now I was remembering that once upon a time I was a god. Or something like one.

Once upon a time I was giddily drunk on very bad wine and my fellow warriors were trying to make me a god because I had killed the most men in battle. Our leader had died in the fighting, but today I had won the war and avenged his death. So I was now the leader, and everyone was paying me homage and drinking to my strength and courage. An early Troy was ours. And they were calling me Ares Red-Hands and they were trying to make me a god, saying that I must never die in battle like my predecessor but live to fight eternally.

It was dark and drunk and comfortable in our night camp. There was a fire blazing out of a stone circle in the middle which claimed our makeshift hall for home. And we had pretty girl dancers to sweeten our victory, and poets to entertain us with stories of great battles, and some of them worked our names and characters into their tales to flatter and amuse. And he came and started his epic in the middle, for these things always are, and created a fictional counterpart for me that made my heart blaze like the fire we called home, that made me burn with a terrible desire to be whatever he created.

I made him sing and chant all night. Used my new power to dismiss the rest. By dawn he finished and I gave him my empty cup, studded with jewels and worth a small kingdom. Then I went with him to the edge of my camp, where I stuck my spear in the ground to show he could answer me freely, that I would do him no harm. "I have killed many. Be in my retinue. Sleep with me like a woman. Play to me whenever I need." He laughed and moved on. Every day I woke to imagine him drinking from my cup. Thinking of him in another battle, I died.

Once upon a time I was an Athenian citizen with a dull wife and duller friends and too many children and a dwindling fortune in purple silk from Tyre. One year the City gathered in an amphitheater to celebrate some new god's feast, and he came down from Thessaly with a train of witches to play for the gods and destroy my heart. I offered him gold to stay with me. I offered him slaves to do whatever he wished. He laughed and moved on. I survived many more years to die of want.

And then I was a Roman senator's wife. Third wife of a second husband three years older than my father. Bored, cynical, and twenty-two. No longer young. I go reluctantly to social gatherings, so my husband can show me off and I can help his career by exchanging gossip with other senators' wives. Then I see one of your performances. You are playing with the house slaves at an important banquet. One I had tried like Jupiter to miss.

This time they say you are Athenian, but others say you just arrived from Gaul. Nobody really knows. And nobody knows how eager I am now for invitations to all the social dinners I used to spurn, how zealous I am to help organize other people's parties, how determined I am to throw myself into the thick of the ugly world, just in case you should be there, or the conversation should turn to music and I should hear your name. How I cry too deep for wretched life when I lean upon my cushion and hold my wine goblet while you sing of love and the gods. How I disguise myself to follow you in secret through the worst sections of Rome, willing to risk my empty life just to be near you, or near the places you might have been. You do not even know. I'm sure that nobody notices, because when someone praises your skill, I affect indifference and I make sure your name is never first on my lips. But how I want your voice. How I want you.

Once upon a time it was the afternoon when we high-ranking Roman matrons were to play before the emperor. It was a diversion that some of the women in my newly embraced social circle devised. We were to learn some simple songs by rote. We were to perform them with the help of trained musicians who would play the difficult parts. You see, we were all so bored. And some of us wanted attention. So I tried to learn the lyre because it was your instrument, and I wanted to know what you felt like when you played it, how your hands must move. But I had no more skill than the other ladies. So I was to pluck a single string while a palace slave played behind a screen.

Our emperor loved the arts. So when we came laughing before him to play, he ordered our slave-musicians to leave, saying we must play to him without help. We were so wretched. We lost our places. We stopped, blushing. Started again. Finished badly. Then he ordered us to stay and watch a performance he had arranged, and you came forward from the shadows to play our songs and put us to shame. Our emperor then commented on the impropriety of amateurs taking the stage, on how our publicly displayed lack of skill hurt our dignity as Roman ladies, and how such things were best left to the Greeks. The Greeks aren't good for much, he added, but they know how to amuse. They are born knowing that.

I am so destroyed.

I want your life. I want you. There's nothing else in my life, so I want to be Greek and amuse. And after the private tears and the fasting and the secret midnight offerings to Bacchus, I seek you out. And I say, in Greek, because Greek is a fashionable language in Rome and I am fluent in languages, and if you are Athenian you might be impressed that I know something of your homeland, I say, speaking suddenly, so suddenly I can't feel what I'm saying, "Please come home with me. My husband is visiting his country villa with his favorite prostitute. He is older than my father, and he doesn't care if I amuse myself while he's gone. I want to know you. I want you to teach me your music. I'll give you my body for your pains. Perhaps I'm not so old at twenty-two. I love you." It is the hardest thing I ever said. I am not used to speaking this way. You laugh. You move on.

Later, I learn that another senator's wife was eavesdropping. My husband has you killed.

Once upon a time I'm a not-so-simple peasant. You pass through my village and the rest of my life is wanting. When I plant seeds, I remember your song and the sun is no longer the same. When I harvest, I remember your song and our provincial feast is dust in my mouth. Somewhere you are opening the world. You laugh and move on and do not know that I am over. Then, in another time, I'm the village priest. You pass through again, singing. I want you, so I arrest you for witchcraft just to have you in my power. But the authorities take you away, laughing.

Jade. You are always bringing me dreams, for these things always are, and so on and on my dreams have gone. And will go. Forever you play—for European aristocrats weary of life, who offer you money afterwards just to play again for them in the privacy of their heart's chambers, for lovestruck women in French salons, for wealthy Victorians entertaining guests in their country houses, for American railroad hobos catching the blues as they can before an early death, for lost and lonely teenagers, for bereaved lovers, for dreamers and hermits and outcasts, for anyone who would helplessly pay his heart's best vulnerability to get taken by your voice and words and storm-tossed rhythms.

Rock 'n' roll is the devil's music. Except that there is no devil. There's only a loveliness in a dark cloud to take you for a time and leave you screaming for other shows. And while he's playing with and for you nothing else matters. But after he exits, nothing that matters remains.

But, to paraphrase Nick, now he wasn't going anywhere. Utterly helpless upon my oak altar. Utterly there for the taking and control. I could do anything, have anything I *wanted.* I could make the god speak at my command. Not even Cara ever had that kind of power. Kept gazing. He was reviving a little now, as I expected he would.

"Tell me a story," I ordered roughly, my voice giving him nothing, not even the compliment of expected pleasure from his words.

"No, Pete, I don't have any stories tonight—"

"Liar." Hit him across the face. Drew blood and groans. "That's your first story, and it's not amusing. Give me another one."

"I don't have—"

Hit him again. "Joy is a serious business, poet, get it right." Then I leaned over and whispered softly and seductively in his ear to soothe the pain I had just caused, licking between the words, and holding the herb satchel on his face with one hand and slowly stroking his thigh with my other. "You don't understand, minstrel. Let's get our roles straight for once. I'm in control. You're not. Tonight, you're going to entertain me. Any way I like. You're going to give me poetry and stories I won't forget, to make up for the lifetime of stories you've promised and taken away. You're mine, Jade. Start rocking." Removed the satchel. His body was tilted and relaxed and wanting in spite of his spirit.

"Free me—"

"No, Jade." I ran my hands through his hair and put my lips close to his in a light brief kiss. Then I spoke, keeping my mouth sensuously close against his. "I'm not going to free you. I can't even free myself." Softly stroked his face. Kept petting his cool dark hair. I knew all the terror he held now under the herbal spell I had cast and it satisfied me as much as anything could. Jade tried to speak but it was getting difficult for him again, although he finally managed to say, "Come on, Pete. What are you going to do?"

"I don't know yet what I should do with you, dream-wrecker." Tore off the front of his shirt. He made a soft groan of protest. "You gave me fantasies to live for and you came here to take them away. You love fantasies. What would you do if someone destroyed all *your* stories, poet? What do you think I should do? *Tell me a goddamn story! Answer me!*"

"I don't know, Pete—"

"—You don't know. And I thought you had more imagination than that. Well, Jade Black Dog, son of Dionysus, I might kill you. I might eat crushed diamonds and kill myself. I might just keep you here until Nick's friends show up at the door to kill us both. I might take pictures of this charming interlude to send to your well-wishers in Fairfax. I might even invite our old friend Hugh over to party." Kissed him deeply, for a long time, for minutes. "Would you like that? Would you like to see Hugh?" Caressed his face. "But I'm not going to free you. That's not what we're here for."

Left him. Went into the kitchen. I knew he turned his head to watch me as I slowly took a large carving knife out of my knife holder and returned with it. Began slicing off his tight jeans, carving his slender body out of the restrictive, revealing denim until I could remove the material. Then I removed his sneakers. Wanted him totally nude.

"Much better," I commented. He struggled a little at the ropes, but his struggling didn't do anything except tighten the knots a little more. "It's physically impossible for you to get out of those restraints," I informed him in the impersonal voice I reserve for reading a prisoner his rights. Then I bathed his face in the herb scent again and softly commanded in a low caressing hypnotic voice, "Relax, Jade, relax. It's all right. Calm down. You're not going anywhere."

Realized that using the herb satchel to help control him was not efficient in the present circumstances, because his struggle and terror tended to mitigate the effects, which tended to lessen anyway when I removed the cloth. But once I had him nearly passed out again an idea struck. Went back to the kitchen, boiled some water, and steeped the herb packet in it like a tea bag. Steeped two more, for good measure. When I returned with my herbal brew I stroked Jade's eyes open, and while he was semi-conscious held up his head and forced him to drink all of it.

"There, guy, that'll help."

"What was that?" he asked, gagging a little.

"Something to make you more submissive. Now, I want you to relax again. Let the tea seep through your limbs and close your mind. Sssh. It will make you relax, make you feel a lot calmer. You high strung rock 'n' roll types need to relax once in a while. Must be torture for you to be carrying all that energy around."

I stroked his thighs again, and watched him get hard in spite of himself, felt his body lose the last vestige of resistance, felt even his mind grow drunk and soft. "Good, I love that. Sssh, my love, ssh. You will remain just conscious enough to do whatever I tell you to do." Stroked his penis while a pleasure he couldn't fight moaned through him. Beautiful soft moans, like when he sang sometimes. "Good. I really love that. People pay your promoters good money for that, don't they?" Stopped stroking his penis and started kissing his mouth. "Jade," I whispered, caressing his throat, "you will not speak unless I tell you to. Otherwise, the only thing I want to hear out of you are those sweet little moans. You know how your voice excites me." Rammed my tongue into his mouth. He moaned louder, but I knew that somewhere deep under his moans was a violent howl of protest that the drug and my assumed power effectively silenced.

Decided to show or test my power by antagonizing him, by letting him know that I knew what he wanted to say but that I was deliberately censoring him. "Yes, Jade, mmmm, you know how hard I get when you sing to me like that. That's very good, my little thunderbird." Softly stroked his face. Then I whispered cruelly in his ear, while keeping my hand lightly on his penis, "I know how much you love to obey. Does my heart good to see you taking orders. Obedience to law is liberty. What's that? Huh?"

He was softly moaning. I got the impression that deep in his heart, he wanted to kill me too, but under the spell, his violent feelings could only manifest themselves as pleasure. "I'm listening close, lover, and you say you want more?" I couldn't believe it but with each verbal onslaught he appeared to get even more weak and helpless, as if that was possible. Couldn't fight me. Even his natural struggle was turned against him.

"Of course, songbird. Of course I'll give you more tea." Which was the last thing he wanted. And I did prepare a second cup and give him more, out of cruelty rather than necessity. And he had to drink it. "I know how much you Dionysian types like to drink." Wiped his mouth. "Sssh, sssh, there's always more where that came from. As long as I'm here, all you have to do is relax. Just relax. The more you want to fight me, the more your body will relax. That's part of the spell. And guess what? I can keep you relaxed, just like this, for as long as it amuses me. Forever, if I have to. As long as you seem to enjoy it." I was stroking him all over now, and added mockingly, "And you really do seem to enjoy it."

Another violent kiss. Then I hit him with all my rage and his body shuddered like he was having an orgasm. "Good. I love the way you look when I hurt you. Love it." Licked his ear, sucked on his throat. "I could hurt you for the rest of my life and never get bored."

Then I just gazed at him in the candlelight. We were well into the dead of night now; well past the slow rise of a moon at last quarter. Its light fell through the window into his dark hair, making him look like every myth I had ever loved and lost, like a slain hero out of my childhood's storybooks. "How many women, how many men, would love to see you like this, Jade? What would they sacrifice to see the god disrobed? What would they give up to be able to take as much of their divinity as they need, until there's nothing left to need? Their childhoods? Years of their lives? Which years? Their tawdry sparse illusions of happiness? How many other people's precious fantasies are we enacting right now? Here, in the dark, in our own private theater where no one else but us can ever know about it? Answer me."

Under the spell, he had to answer, but his voice was clumsy and belonged more to the trance than to himself. "I don't know how—"

"—Come on, lover, take a guess—"

"—Legion—"

"Legion. Is that torture for you, for us to create beautiful dreams together while nobody else knows about it? When so many others—legion—would love to know about it—love to be here—love you enough to destroy you for it? I mean, here we are, creating a beautiful dream together, the one about the sacrificial god laid bare before his devoted servant, who has spent his life training for the work of this sacred moment, who has lived to rend his god from limb to limb and redden his hands and mouth with the blood of his deity, so that he might wear the blood of his deity like a bond to Being—the beautiful dream about the seeker after the Grail who finally finds it sparkling at the bottom of a refuse pit and smashes it—of the lonely alchemist conjuring the devil to do his bidding—of the dragon slayer saving the virgins of his kingdom from menace—of the frenzied maenad killing her god upon the tender fields. Ain't this a classic?"

I had been stroking his penis during this little speech, but I wouldn't let him come. His body wanted to. I wanted to hold him in wanting. "No, my lord, you can't have satisfaction," I ordered. "You will come when and if I tell you to. I hold your power, and I'm going to hold you right here on the edge until I get everything I want out of you." He was stiff to the breaking point but he couldn't explode past it. Of course, by this time so was I, and I didn't know how much longer I'd be able to hold out. Walked away to my hearth and meditated on the red candle until the pressure between my legs abated a little.

Returned to the altar, to all my tortured dream of beauty. "Isn't this just like the way it almost was with your music, that without Penny's support no one would know about either, despite your considerable gifts? Tell me, Jade, who would you be if Penny never got your music out? If your dear aunt were out there banging the ancient drum for one of your other semidivine siblings, and you were utterly on your own? Could your story ever work that way, or is public adoration a predestination thing with guys like you? You see, I used to think it wouldn't matter, that you were so thoroughly your precious art, so acutely self-created, that the opinion of the poor, dirty world could never touch you. I used to believe you were as self-fulfilling as a young god. *I used to believe—*" I screamed. "*How the hell did you get here?*"

His body couldn't react, which infuriated me even more, despite knowing I was the cause of his enforced silence.

"Tell me something, Black Dog, because *believe* me, I'll make you speak—if Hugh McCrae was to have won this particular battle after all, if all your compositions were known only to yourself, who would you be and who would I have been fucking? Who would you be if nobody reacted to your art or loved you for it? Ever? If you were capable of enough passion to risk death to save your lover's 'dreams' but you didn't have a lover with dreams worth saving because no one ever knew enough to want your heart's best gifts. If no one else gave a damn?

"Let's play a game, Jadie. I want a story, and you haven't really given me one yet, so I'll start. In this story we'll pretend you're a brilliant, unknown, poet-musician—no, we'll pretend you're a skillful bass player, more competent than most, easily good enough to make a living at it, but then, so are thousands of other folks, some of whom are luckier or better connected than you. You love music. 'Music is the brandy of the damned,' isn't it? 'Hell is full of musical amateurs,' as the great Shaw once wrote. Well, let's say you are a condemned amateur. How darkly seductive and playful could you be as the years pass and your face gets older and your body paunches and other lesser dream-makers get the recognition you deserve? How would you tease and charm and cajole and draw audiences to you like you drew me? Because the monster would always be in the shadows, in people's closed minds and mouths, mocking you in your obscurity, saying with deadly breath, 'Who do you think you are? You're not so-and-so, but you sure as hell act like you think you're a great artist. If you're so playful and wonderful and all in love with music and living just to create beauty and entertain tired souls, why haven't you made it?'

"And so it gets harder and harder for you to seduce and charm anybody, because there would be too many stupid-ass social expectations set against you that are stronger than you are, and you lose your edge—because face it, Jade, for how many years would you, would anyone, create serious art in isolation? For how many years would *you* believe? You have to make a living, don't you? And you have no other skills. So I can—we can imagine the imbeciles you'd have to fill your life with in your work situation alone, but at least you'd have empty nights to play to yourself in. Maybe you'd stay dark, but not in an attractive, storm-ridden way. Maybe you would stay dark in a cynical way. Maybe you would even get as dark and cynical as me. Maybe you would give up music and write quiet books in quiet tombs and hate everybody for it. That happens. But then the books die. Then what? Can you cheerfully accept the failure of your life's energy and creative output to matter to anyone besides yourself, and decide that the ugly world won, that your heart's best dreams were all dust and worthlessness and you were a fool to ever entertain anything else? I mean, if you didn't have Penny helping you, and an audience listening, and fools like me cheering you on, would you be as playful and confident and alluring as you are now or would you end up like your poor disturbed mama swinging from a rope in prison and cursing your gifts?

"Tell me what you might have been, working some factory job ten hours a day to put food in your stomach and trying to play other people's songs at night for beers so you could feel like a musician once in awhile. Going home from your gigs knowing how much better your real work is than that, and how the one thing you're not allowed to do is prove it. How 'darkly creative and mysterious' could you be then? Who the hell would you convince? Who are you really? Tell me that story, Jade. That's the one I want tonight. Tell me now."

He screamed in agony, but my power was great and he had to speak. "Story. In another life I'm a lonely fiction writer. I live in a monk's cell and you feed me coarse bread and education. I write stories for you. The stories take years to write. Nobody else reads them. Nobody else will ever read them. The stories are like our other lives—"

"—So stop the damn introduction and give me the story."

"I'm a madwoman scholar who writes books and plays music."

"I know you are. We both are. That's why we're here in the end of the madwoman's dream. I want fiction, Jade, not your goddamned biography."

"I can't sing—fiction—" he sort of breathlessly sobbed.

I don't know if this was a fictional statement. He might have meant it literally. Or he might have meant that he couldn't "sing" in the sense of revealing something he shouldn't. Or it might have been his last desperate attempt at speaking a fiction to save himself from speaking a truth. But I do know that the story I had constructed for him to tell had stripped him of his power over me. I had forced him into cursing himself, and I no longer wanted him. His sexually aroused body was disgusting. His lovely face was fat and puffy from my blows. I stood there without feeling, knowing I had consummated this destruction with my words, with a fiction I had created but wasn't sure I entirely believed in. I made him believe in damnation, just as he had made me believe.

I also knew that for me, Jade could never again be beautiful, for I had disrobed and plundered the god. I wanted a god in my life, and rather than accept god's death, I had made him merely human, a state from which it's damn hard to return. "All right," I commanded. "Sleep now. You're done." He did. I untied him, but I left him on the table for the moon to watch over. It was no longer my job. Dying is an art. Read that in a poem somewhere, maybe one by Sylvia Plath. Extinguished the candle.

Coda

Not much else to tell. He left with his rags before dawn. I burned the ropes. Burned the rest of the herb packets. Made my house clean.

He did not return to Penny. There were media reports about Black Dog's "troubled leader" being missing. They became part of the preliminary papers I had to prepare for SAYNO's new investigation, since I was the resident expert on missing persons.

Piekarski used the raid's favorable publicity to one-better Crensch. Worked through Fearless to get the IRS to cooperate with SAYNO. IRS agents started pulling all Black Dog CDs off the shelves and off the air to "further our investigation," meaning the strategy was primarily to force a reaction from the Nunzios.

McCrae did his bit. When asked whether he, as Elise's "close companion," had any insight into her missing son's whereabouts, he answered, smiling, "Well, I'll tell ya. I'm praying for him. I know he often visits an FBI agent friend of his, the illustrious Peter Morrow from Boston. My old friend, too. Good man."

Reporters started calling the field office. I told them I was out.

Then I got fired. For real. Showed up to work a few days ago. Fearless was waiting for me in the reception area, looking jumpy and defensive. Escorted me into his office. Told me without making eye contact that it had become apparent to both the Canadian authorities and himself, as well as to "others," that I had been systematically destroying and altering evidence in the Black Dog investigation. He wanted to know why. He also wanted to know what my connection was to Jade McClellan. Told him we used to be lovers. He didn't believe me, but I got fired anyway. Then he told me Crensch was the new co-leader of SAYNO.

Left. There was nothing I cared to take with me.

Out in the empty building, the courier got off the elevator as I got on. He shoved a package from Toronto and a clipboard at me as the doors began to close between us. Signed. For no particular reason, except that it was my last official act.

The package contained one audio tape and one video tape. The former made me feel again, the latter made me cry.

The audio tape was a recording of another mafia meeting at Fendra's. George was there, and Nick, and the rest of the inner circle. Government had done its work well for once, because Nick was hurling fits over the IRS copping his CDs and interfering with his business. The IRS were bastards but the FBI were still bigger bastards. Knew the FBI was in it. Knew "this SAYNO bullshit" was in it, which could only mean "that bastard Morrow" was in it, and "who the hell can't keep himself away from Morrow around here" but that "looney-tune singer we got there, the one with all the problems."

"Jade McClellan," said George helpfully.

"Yeah, right. So then I find out from Donny he's gone, that he takes off after hearing this Morrow bastard's been shot. So what the hell's Donny's problem leaving him alone, I don't know, but then I hear Morrow ain't been shot bad enough and George hears on the TV here from this Hugh McCrae guy that seems to know everybody in church and government that McClellwhistle's probably off visiting his good buddy the fed, like why the hell can't he keep away from him, are they in love or somethin'?"

Nervous laughter.

"So I'm sick of the situation." End laughter. "So what can I do? I work hard for these guys. Do my best to take care of 'em. Here's the gratitude I get. Less stink taking my cut from the Boston fish markets. Less problems."

"Sure, sure. Dionello's a good man."

"So I ain't got no more product to sell, and I got a crazy musician type for a rat taking off for God knows where."

"Kill the rat," said someone.

"Yeah," said Nick. "If we can find him."

"Kill the other rat. The one that went on TV there and sang," said someone else, encouraged by Nick's response.

"Kill 'em all," said a third.

"Wait a minute," said Nick, "ain't gonna kill 'em all. If we're gonna whack, let's do it right. It's their leader's mouth that brought down the business so it's their leader gonna get hit. Ain't gonna let that pass, and a hit there will show his buddy Morrow that he ain't walkin' over us this time like he did with my wife's family. I'm the man now. Got somethin' to prove."

"Yeah, right," said the chorus.

"Besides, I thought up a plan here. Nobody knows where the rat is hiding. So let's say he were to stay 'missing' permanently. Let's say his body were to turn up in a public place, but be unrecognizable, though of course the feds'll know it's their boy the way they always know it when a rat gets whacked, but let's say his body ended up messed up enough to start a media rumor that he's dead and another rumor that there's a chance it ain't him. You know what I'm sayin'? A media rumor for the fans—a story to go with all the other weirdness that keeps comin' out around the band. And let's say his friends there never see a body they can positively identify. So what can they say but—I never saw a body that I recognized as his, hey."

Nick waited for a reaction, but as no one ventured to guess where he was leading, he continued.

"So we ride out this bullshit investigation. Feds are so stupid they've confiscated their own evidence, what they gonna prove? Huh? That they've got some CDs on their hands? So what? There ain't no more Moon Management, ain't no financial records, they've got shit. So we wait. Coupla years, maybe. Create a new Black Dog. Maybe the rest of the boys'll straighten out, get with the program. Maybe not. But we get some music guys we can work with—like Vinny's cousin—get a new band—maybe call it the new Black Dog—songs by Jade McClellan—let everyone think maybe he's still alive writing the songs somewhere—make some money. Three or four years there's a new generation of kids. They won't know nothin' but a rumor anyway. *Salute*."

"*Salute*, boss."

"Now, how do we find him?"

"His girlfriend used to work for me," said George. "Beth Dundas. Start by asking her. She might know."

"All right George, you do that, and then—"

End of tape. The rest was too damaged to play.

Quiet in my house as feeling returned. Just an awful missing quiet surrounding a slow, dull seep of pain, the terrible ancient quiet of knowing that after all I had given up, the monster was going to win. But then, he always did. He was older. Like ooze and insects. And dream as I might, he was always there. Behind everything the gods created was the ugly suck of entropy, the bad drain.

Then rage thrashed my body into a primal scream of defeat. Dionysus was supposed to be torn apart by an adoring mob, his lovers possessed with divine madness and drunk on the blood of his beauty, a death that only a god could earn. He was not supposed to be silenced by a shadow government of mobsters holding an unknown distant alliance to Hugh McCrae. First feeling. I should have loved him enough to kill him.

Then I knew I did love him. Still. And that I did kill him. I killed him by letting him go, when I could have risked escaping with him somewhere, anywhere, perhaps going to the media together or hiding somewhere in India or moving like nomads across the world fighting to defend each stolen minute of our lives. We could have lived and died like the romantic heroes we sometimes pretended to be. We could have created a better death. We had escaped into so many dreams, would it have been so hard to escape into the world? As long as he was here with me, the music would have been here to defend. But now he would die unknown and his music would be worse than forgotten, it would be transformed in the public mind into one or two bumbling mediocrities and then forgotten. Make some of his bandmates happy.

Screamed like madness returning. Smashed the tape to bits, because so much of it made me feel like the fiction I had tortured him with was coming to terrible truth, and my clumsy attempt at magic was responsible for bringing on this horrid reality. The monster had won by speaking the truth. *Truth!* How nasty and right. I stared at the shattered pieces of plastic from the tape I had just smashed, odd-angled and meaningless in the silence around me, like so many dead flowers going back to garbage, and wanted to cry.

But the tears didn't come until I brought myself to watch the video tape.

The tape was one of those grainy black and white surveillance jobs in which nothing shows more clearly than the digital time counter in the corner of the screen. Perspective gets distorted. So do faces. And voices. Voices fade in and out of the microphone's range so words get lost, and the camera angle omits more than it shows. You have to keep watching, and stopping, and rewinding and watching again to transcribe the dialogue and slice out the life so poorly captured.

Beth's room. Empty save for a three-legged table against a back wall and a battered couch to the right. Except for a lit candle and some scattered tarot cards on the table, there's no evidence that Juno and Beulah ever decorated the place. It is entirely Beth's.

She's sitting on the bare floor, cradling a small acoustic guitar, and gingerly trying a few hesitant, awkward-sounding chords. Her back is against a stained wall, her head just under a grimy curtainless window. I suppose she is playing to the shadows on her decaying couch. She reminds me of a sad, neglected stuffed animal, except that the camera suggests a determined cut to her chin and there's an unexpected resentful intensity in her eyes you'd never find on a teddy bear because it would scare away the customers.

It's an intensity I find uncomfortable to watch, like that of a screaming animal about to be slaughtered by someone who blandly reassures you that, "It's only bones and muscles and nerves; it isn't intelligent enough to feel the way we feel." You believe him, but it's not like a real belief because of the animal's screams. You have to work at it. Especially after the slaughter, when that same someone pets his loyal dog and boasts of his love for his pet.

The kind of intensity life reserves for madmen and children.

She thinks she's alone, and in solitude she has to please no one but herself, so I don't really know who I'm watching. I don't even know if Beth knows her. Would she be surprised to see herself at this moment? Would she be angry at our governments for raping her private persona for public display? Is she capable of hating a society that has reduced her moments of self-regard to the level of absolute privacy? Does she feel the way I feel?

She is surprised to hear a knock at the door. Her face returns to what I know as she puts down her instrument and leaves the screen to answer it. Muffled indecipherable greetings. Like happiness. Then she enters the viewing area with Jade, whose face is still bruised from my blows. They are holding hands. He moves more slowly than Beth does, takes her other hand in his in a slower sadness, and then they embrace. She buries her face in his chest. Then she beams up at him like a pale fallen star seeing her first explosion of dawn. Asks him if he'd like some tea.

He smiles wryly. "No thanks."

"It's cinnamon, from downstairs," she presses.

"Had enough tea lately. Come, sit with me on the couch, tell me stories."

"Tell you stories," says Beth in a happy shyness. "You know I'm no good at stories." But she sits with him anyway. "Jade, my god what happened to your face? It's all bruised. You know all the news says no one can find you. Where have you been? Is everything all right?"

"It is now. Went to look for you earlier at Fendra's. George wasn't there, guess he'd just left some big meeting, and one of the other waitresses said you didn't work there anymore."

"Yes, I work downstairs full time now." Then she asks hesitantly, "Jade, did anyone recognize you at Fendra's?"

"Doubt it. The bar was pretty empty. They were closing early."

She studies him. "I suppose with those bruises on your face—I'm not sure anyone would recognize you. Tell me what happened."

"Yeah, well, had an accident. Here to heal."

"Sure." Beth sounds doubtful. "I understand. You can stay here. No one has to know."

"Thanks. Anyway, thought you might know where George is."

"I don't see him anymore. Hey, aren't you supposed to be like under guard or something?"

"Under guard?" He looks surprised. "I don't understand."

"Your friend Pete Morrow told me—"

"When did you talk to Pete?"

"A while ago, I don't know. Before you were missing. He said you were like being guarded by Nick Nariano, and you had to stay close to your promoters or there could be trouble."

"Have you talked to him since?"

"No. He wanted me to spy for him." Beth tells Jade everything we had discussed, and he listens intently until she concludes with, "But I couldn't anymore, Jade. Not for him and not for George. There were things in my mind bothering me. I'm glad you're here. I really am. And you can stay," she adds shyly, cuddling against him, "but I couldn't spy."

He clearly doesn't know how to respond to her revelations, so he holds her for a few seconds before changing the subject. "Is that my old guitar?" Goes over and picks it up. "Used to fool around on this a lot, before I moved on to bass."

"Your mother gave it to me. I—I was taking piano lessons from her to surprise you with—before she died." Beth is embarrassed to bring up the topic, but as Jade seems all right with it, she just continues. "Anyway, she gave me that—so I've been fooling around with it."

He sits on the floor where Beth had been sitting and smoothly plays a simple chord progression, followed by a scale. The notes sound a little sour even under his expert hands. "It's out of tune. Here." He tunes it for her, then he plays the scale again, which sounds better but not pitch perfect. "That will help, but these strings haven't been changed in years. You should really get new ones."

"Oh, I didn't know. I don't even really know about tuning and what it's supposed to sound like."

"Here's a trick. If you're playing by yourself, forget what it's *supposed* to sound like. Just make sure that when you finger the fifth fret of a string, the open string above it matches it in pitch. Here, listen." Beth comes over to watch. "Here's A, the fifth fret on the low E string." He plays a note and she nods. "Here's your open A string." He plays what sounds like the same note, except it rings a little more. "Should be the same pitch. Works up the frets. D on your A string should sound like open D, the string above. But when you get to your G string, it's your fourth fret, B, that should match your open B. Then it's the fifth fret again, E on the B string should match your high E."

"I think I understand," says Beth uncertainly.

"That way, even if your guitar is flat or sharp compared to other instruments, it's still in tune with itself. Which is all that matters for solo work." He sounds warmly respectful, as if he and Beth are colleagues.

Beth looks a little embarrassed at her clumsy exercises being referred to as solo work. "Thanks. I'll try to stay in tune with myself," she says with a quiet deliberateness. "Jade?" His name sounds like a question she is afraid of asking.

"Yes?"

"Sometimes I wonder what it's like to be you. To know all those things about music. You've had so much time to learn. You know, I think while I was waiting tables and working you were practicing and learning."

"I was. So what?"

"I don't know. I mean, it's weird but while I was growing up and going to school, I loved to listen to music but it never occurred to me to try to play any. I don't know why. Maybe because no one in my family had money or time for that. Maybe I just didn't know how to think of myself in that way, or how to think of myself at all. Anyway, I just wish I had started when I was younger. I'd be better now."

"But you are starting now. If you keep at it, you'll get better."

"I don't know." Beth's voice hovers between regret and something darker. "Even when I've been playing as long as you have—I don't know, maybe, if I try. But by then I'll be in my forties. Kind of late at that point to start a musical career. I think if you don't grow up with it, like you did, it's kind of hopeless."

"I didn't know you wanted a musical career." Jade sounds vaguely amused.

"I didn't either, but if I did, it would be too late."

"Does it matter how old you are if you really like to play guitar? What's wrong with playing in your room to yourself? That can be a sweet experience. I've played alone to myself a lot."

"Nothing. But no one who's any good is happy to do that exclusively. I mean, if playing alone were so satisfying you wouldn't be pursuing a career. Nobody would."

"All right, you got me." He smiles. "But when I think about it, I realize that some of my most creative moments have happened when I was alone. And Xander, brilliant as he can be on stage sometimes, does some of his best work by himself."

"If he's by himself, how would you know?"

"He gives me recordings."

"Why?"

"In case we decide to use one of his solos in a song."

"So is he really playing by himself?"

"Touché," says Jade, grinning.

Beth smiles a little victory smile and presses on, her eyes bright and unrevealing as a lunatic moon. "Jade, when you say that it's sweet and inspirational to play alone, it means something different than if I were to say it. Or believe it. I mean here you are, a brilliant, popular, bass god who despite all his great success says he would prefer to be alone. What a regular guy you must be after all, just dragged unwillingly into the spotlight. Makes people like me feel kind of wrong about having ambitions because if someone like you prefers solitude, well who are we to prefer anything else? But, Jade, if me or a hundred other lousy beginners, late beginners, were to say, 'I prefer to be alone—that's where my most creative moments come from' it's not charming, it sounds like a weak excuse for not excelling, or an admission of defeat. No one would believe we have any creative moments, or any ones that matter enough to want to be alone for."

"Why do you care?" he asks gently.

"I don't know. Maybe for the same reasons you do. Maybe. I mean, I think you must care, or you wouldn't be famous. Maybe you could tell me why and I'd understand it better. The thing is, you can get away with saying things nobody else can, and sometimes I wonder what it's like. Because I would like to be as successful as you are and be able to say to someone like me, say it all generous and charming and humble and everything like you do, 'I want to be alone.' I mean I can say those words, but they don't command the same reaction, and I want to command the same reaction. That's why I 'like' guitar. You can't be 'special' waiting tables."

She looks a little afraid of his reaction but he isn't offended. Only thoughtful. "All right, Beth, I'm here to entertain. If that's your vision, that's your vision. What do you want to do?"

"I want to be you."

"You want to be me." He says this ruefully. "What's your second choice?"

"Not to live a life of second choices. I think a lot now, and I think the reason I love you, the real reason, is because I want to be you. Jade," Beth's voice curls into a breathless pounce, "I want to be mysterious and witchy and musical because I love those things in you and I think other people would love them in me in the same way and I want to be loved. Even when you got hurt in Fairfax, they hurt you because they knew you were more beautiful than they are. I think if I were you and got hurt, I would almost take it as a tribute, that the angry crowd believed I was more beautiful than I really am."

"You want me to throw rocks at you?" Jade is laughing.

Beth isn't. "I'm serious. I don't know what stopped me from being you. But I do know we can't just be anyone we want to be, after a certain age, and maybe not even before then. Otherwise, we'd all be running the world to our own taste and no one would pick up the garbage. So we all have to be 'in tune with ourselves.' Which isn't wonderful. It's more like saying that it's OK to be a mediocrity not because it really is OK but because it's easier than facing your own inherent worthlessness—"

"Beth, what makes you think you're worthless?"

"I have no family. My mother doesn't want me."

"Neither did mine."

"But Elise let you have music early on. And you had Penny. So that didn't stop you from being a god. I have no friends."

"Neither do I."

"What about your cousins? Pete? Your bandmates? Me?"

"My cousins are best avoided. My bandmates hardly speak to me outside of work. I don't know if I would call Pete a friend."

"He cares about you a lot. He wanted me to spy."

"He doesn't believe I'm a god," he jokes.

"Poor dragon, so you go away to your dragon cave and cry when someone stops believing."

"I'm not crying. Just away." He is. Beth doesn't realize she has hit him in a vital spot, that we met over a dragon song. "Anyway, Beth, perhaps you are a friend—"

"—of course I am—"

"—but even you find friendship, or love, a poor substitute for actually being me. So what's a friend but someone who hasn't figured out yet that they want what you have?"

Beth sighs. "But it's different. I'm alone." She indicates her room by making an arc through the air with her open palm.

"So am I."

"But your loneliness and lack of friends is different than mine. Yours is the result of success and talent. Mine is the result of having nothing to offer the world. It sounds wonderful and profound for you to make the comparison and say we're both lonely and everything, but not all loneliness is the same. Let's trade." Jade looks away, at the stained wall and grimy window, but does not answer. Beth is winning.

She continues, "I have no career, even though I work as hard as you do. Harder, probably, because I hate my work and you love yours and you still have time to take off from it, like now."

"I have no career, either, Beth. It could end at any moment."

"Music is like that," she agrees. "Unless you teach or something. But even if yours ends, are you saying your time of glory was just as good as the equivalent time in my life waiting tables—again, would you trade a few months of performing to adoring crowds for bringing bills to impatient customers? I mean, if our respective lack of careers is really the same?"

"They're pulling my CDs from the stores."

She stares at him. "Why?"

"IRS. American government is investigating my promoters."

Beth begins to cry. "Oh my god! Pete warned me about that." Then, "Nick's gonna kill you, I know he is, I know he is."

"That's another thing you don't have in your life," says Jade cautiously.

"Sure," says Beth slowly, "but that's because my life isn't worth killing. In a way, it's nothing to proud of. I worked for George, spying for him, as I said. But when I quit spying, he got angry at the inconvenience and fired me and that was it. I wasn't worth enough to him to get killed. It's odd, isn't it? Maybe someone else would argue that it's always better to be alive, but I'm starting to wonder. Doesn't that depend on the kind of life that's still alive? Oh, Jade, to have your life and talent and power and the world's acknowledgement for a few months or my quiet nothingness for seventy, eighty years? Why are seventy empty years better than even one full one? Unless you think simply on instinct, like an animal, to live at all costs no matter how mindless or meaningless because your biological programming says 'fear death.' And then maybe make a religion out of it. Like at your mother's Bible study, when someone said, 'Better a live dog than a dead lion,' which just sounded like an excuse not to be the lion."

He puts down the guitar and goes to hold her close. His expression is inscrutable, almost impassive, but Beth is nestled against his chest, and so she cannot see his face. Nor can she know that her questions mirrored my forcing him to say what his life would be like if nobody recognized his gifts. Nor that my interrogation broke him.

They close their eyes. They sway. They are trying to comfort each other.

Beth speaks first. "Jade, it's odd how I love you but I'm almost jealous of you. Give me your attitude and spirit." She sounds like a mad little Ophelia. "I won't ever know anyone else like you to teach me. You're like my last chance to believe in something."

"Teach you how to be me," he says softly and generously. I imagine he is thinking how to do it, how to leave this legacy to this bewildered devotee, this would-be priestess-disciple.

"Do you have to be born of Dionysus?"

"Maybe it helps. I don't know."

"It must be wonderful not to know. To be so simply and thoroughly yourself, always, all the time, that you don't have to know. Jade—how I'd love to be able to say to someone like me, 'I don't know.'"

"All right," he says, as if taking a cue from her, "Do you believe you have to be born of Dionysus?" He goes back over, takes up the guitar, and sits on the floor at her feet.

"I don't mean it like a game," says Beth. "When the game's over, I'm still a coffee waitress. I mean it like real life. I want to sit like you with a guitar in my hands and people wanting to be me and asking me to teach them. I want to know that my life is to be envied, that who I am is to be wanted. It's awful, but when you want something so bad, pretense is a mockery."

"How badly do you want to be me?" asks Jade softly, putting down the guitar.

"I'd die to be you." Beth means this, recklessly, romantically, and helplessly.

"Even knowing my pain?"

"Yes. Everyone has pain, Jade. Even nobodies like me. But your pain is divine, not easier to bear, but nobler. You suffer because other people are inadequate. I suffer because I am."

"All right, friend, then I will make you an offer."

Beth listens intently.

"I'm on the lam. If Nick or George finds me, they probably will kill me. With my CDs being taken off the market, they'll think I'm somehow responsible for the investigation."

"Then why did you go to Fendra's and why are you looking for George?" Her voice conveys more curiosity than surprise.

"Like I said, to get healed. Beth, my life is now as lonely as yours. As lonely as old, exiled Dionysus, who sacrifices himself to the mob to restore order and protect his secret lovers from its wrath."

What? Was he going to offer himself to George Fendra to save me from the goddamned Nunzios?

"I won't live much longer no matter where I go or what I do. They'll find me. They'll kill me. Do you want to call George? Bring them here? You know his home number. They'll kill us both, and you'll die like me. It's the closest thing I can give you to the reality you seek."

"Die with you? Like lovers?" she asks doubtfully.

"No." He smiles his soft little Jade smile. "Like twins."

"Die with you like twins or live to be an old lady with no worth or purpose, knowing for decades that I will never have the life I want to have?"

"You decide."

Beth looks at the guitar for a long time. "I'll call."

"I love you." He says it like it was the first time he had ever really loved anybody. But I couldn't see his face when he said it because the tape went black before the words did.

Sat with pen to paper. I had been transcribing the dialogue, and had written the words "I love you," and was—I don't know what I was doing—sitting cold—writing—until at some point enough time had passed for my television to go out of VCR mode and back into regular mode.

Public news. Someone found the bodies on the steps of the Parliament Building at dawn. Like sacrifices to the holy place where we once told stories to the night. A woman in her early twenties, so riddled with bullets they had no way of identifying her. A man whose swollen face, bloated in death, made him equally unrecognizable. Although it "was believed" to be Jade McClellan of Black Dog, this was entirely unsubstantiated as no positive ID could be made. The man had been badly beaten before he died.

Turned it off. Been drinking. Been telling tales.

Maybe someday I won't believe it's him. Maybe someday I'll fashion a life out of one plain good fact, the excruciatingly merciful fact that no one will ever know for certain that the body they found is his. Maybe someday I'll be able to forget that I know better and mindlessly follow the public rumor in a Bacchanalian frenzy of wanting. Maybe someday I'll even kill to nurse and cherish that single meagre fact for surviving the rest of my years. The fact-of-life that nobody knows. Item. This is how the monster of reality wins. In the end, you have to admit that he owns what you think.

So I'm drunk.

Jade, my dreaming dragon love, here is my prayer. I will stay here, alone, until I can believe that you are always out there playing on the edge of the night, just beyond finding, but out there. That as long as I don't look for you, or expect you to come and wake me for night games, you're out there. Gods don't die. Maybe they get dark for a while, but they all return. Have to. It's like a rule.

So until I can believe, I'll wait here. Wait patiently. Wait for the wash and pull of an old, eternal, heartless sea.

Acknowledgments

I carried this story for decades. My bandmates in Point of Ares made that easier. Bill, POA's lead guitarist (and my spouse), provided beta reading, tech support, and the gods' own patience with the long revision process. Ryan DesRoches, the other (and by far, the better) half of POA's rhythm section, designed and maintains my website at http://www.karenmichalson.com.

I am grateful to Donald Weise, whose editorial suggestions are always exactly right, and always a joy to work with. Mr. Weise took on the original version of this story, a monster manuscript that exceeded 800 pages, and guided me through the long revision process of shaping it into this more manageable version. Sometimes magic is real.

The 1990s were a magical decade, but unfortunately, many of the magical people I knew at that time are gone. My thoughts go out to "Buddha" (John Pirolli), Billy Barnum, and other assorted real-life characters from the Boston 1990s alternative scene who have now passed over to another world. Buddha unabashedly lived his life as a modern-day wizard, the Daemon Magus. He understood that rock is magic. Thank you, brother, for seeing through to the life of things, and carrying on anyway.

I consulted several books on the FBI, including Sanford J. Ungar's *FBI: An Uncensored Look Behind the Walls.* However, any mistakes in presentation and liberties taken to conform with the semi-mythical world of the novel are entirely my own.

And as to physical research for scene writing, if anyone remembers a person in jeans and a music t-shirt entering the reception area of the Boston field office sometime in the mid-1990s, looking around for a few seconds, and leaving . . . yeah, that was me.

About the Author

Karen Michalson earned a PhD in English from the University of Massachusetts Amherst, focusing her studies on nineteenth-century British literature and history. She later earned a law degree from Western New England University and ran a criminal defense practice. Somewhere between literature and law, she formed a progressive rock band, Point of Ares, in which she writes music, plays bass, and sings. Point of Ares has released four CDs, two of which contain songs based on her first two *Enemy Glory* books, *Enemy Glory* and *Hecate's Glory*.

The *Enemy Glory* trilogy was completed with the publication of her third novel, *The King's Glory*. She describes the trilogy as "literary fiction tripping the dark fantastic." *The Maenad's God* is her fourth novel.

She keeps a blog called Matter Notes where she writes about the war on the humanities, creativity as spirituality, and her observations on culture and society as a self-described New England recluse: http://www.karenmichalson.com

She lives near Worcester, Massachusetts.

CPSIA information can be obtained
at www.ICGtesting.com
Printed in the USA
JSHW080036051122
32630JS00001B/3

9 780985 352264